R. M. Meluch's
Tour of the Merrimack:

THE MYRIAD
WOLF STAR
THE SAGITTARIUS COMMAND
STRENGTH AND HONOR
THE NINTH CIRCLE

TOUR OF THE MERRIMACK

Volume One

THE MYRIAD
WOLF STAR

R. M. MELUCH

DAW BOOKS, INC.

DONALD A. WOLLHEIM, FOUNDER

375 Hudson Street, New York, NY 10014

ELIZABETH R. WOLLHEIM
SHEILA E. GILBERT
PUBLISHERS

www.dawbooks.com

Author's Note

THE ROMAN EMPIRE NEVER fell and we are it. A history professor told me that. He didn't know he was speaking literally.

Rome has not fallen. It has gone underground. It exists as a secret society, keeping its language alive in the fields of law, medicine, scientific taxonomy, and in the Catholic Church. The secret is easily kept. I mean, you think this is fiction, don't you?

Because Latin is a highly inflected language, you can easily smoke out a Roman mole. He habitually leaves off pronouns when the subject of a sentence is obvious.

Coincidentally, so do I.

Imperial Rome will resurface as a breakaway US colony in the Lambda Coronae Australis system, but not until the twenty-fourth century.

I arrived on planet Earth at the dawn of the space age. I learned the names of the satellites. There were only a handful at the time. (Echo was the round one.) The warranty on the thousand-year Reich had only recently crapped out. TV shows in the day were *Combat, Rat Patrol,* and *Twelve O'Clock High.*

I'm a Battle of Britain junkie.

My father fought at Guadalcanal. I command an armchair.

Star Trek came out when I was ten years old. I read Heinlein, Homer, Verne, and Wells. I took astrophysics in college.

I tripped over Alexander while researching my first novel—a way over the top entirely unbelievable character, except that he existed. The man literally changed the face of the planet. Tyre used to be an island.

He's the guy every Caesar wants to be.

Then I got hooked on Patrick O'Brian's Aubrey/Maturin high seas tales.

From all that, along with a great lot of tequila, Captain John Farragut sprang out of my forehead. And I really did put swords on a space battleship.

Because I cannot write a book without a powerful, conflicted, divided soul, my Roman enemy-ally, the patterner Augustus, manifested as a counterweight at the same time. Beneath the buckler swashing adventure run uncertainties of duty versus conscience, choice and inevitability, and the relative nature of time. Sometimes the answer to an either/or question is yes.

If ever two books were meant to be joined at the spine they are *The Myriad* and *Wolf Star*. Each novel is a complete stand-alone work, but each adds a different dimension to the other. I might have called this volume *Parallel Lives*, but my old *frater* Plutarch took that title. We shall have words.

Parting shot: The favored style in genre fiction these days is no style. I have one. It's fast. It's choppy. If the character is disoriented, you're right there with him. And don't get too attached to those pronouns.

Permission to board the *Merrimack*.

RMM

THE MYRIAD

TO JIM.

PART ONE

Uncertainty Principle

1

A NIGHTMARE RUNS over again and again in a loop. As if rerunning it could make it come out differently. It ends the same every time. Cowboy was dead.

Cowboy had been a split-second stupid and a full-second dead. And dead all the seconds after that. The nightmare reruns. Dead again.

Dead still.

He should have known better. But should've, might've, could've, all mean *didn't*. It was done now. Finished. Fixed. Written and could not be rewritten.

Cowboy was dead.

It reruns:

Nothing ever lived inside a globular cluster. Everyone knew that. Globulars were made up of thousands—sometimes millions—of stars, but all them old, population II types, formed back when the galaxy was nothing but primordial hydrogen. All those millions of stars were too metal poor to spawn a single planet. So the crew and the Marine detachment of the battleship *Merrimack* were surprised to trip a signal beacon upon breaching the perimeter of globular cluster IC9870986.

Merrimack was passing near a clutter of anomalous space debris, when something lurking among the asteroids shrieked an electromagnetic alarm.

"Hive!" the watch called.

Prox alarms blared on board in answer, with an all-stop order and call to battle stations.

The big ship spat out Marine Swifts in a torrent.

Slung clear of the launch bay, Flight Sergeant Kerry Blue glanced back at *Merrimack*, saw the battleship's gunports wink open. *Merrimack* made as grand a gun platform as you could ask to take you into action. Kerry would never admit that to a spaceman; the navvies were already way too smug proud of themselves. Guns bristled—missile launchers, beam cannon, projectile barrels, the whole shop for an unknown enemy. Beam weapons were useless at FTL, but the ship's stopping brought those into play, too.

The Swifts deployed wide, targeting systems on, everything working at one hundred percent, with no sign of Hive interference in the electrics. No sign of Hive at all.

In a moment a voice in Kerry's headset spoke her very thought: "Uh, something's missing here."

Then Alpha Leader: "Hello, *Merrimack*. Where's the gorgons?"

The only thing Kerry saw out here was a company of Marine Swifts streaking the vacuum.

Next she heard Cowboy, in that taunting voice he used to call you an idiot without saying the word: "Hello, Tracking. I don't got a burr under my saddle. Why is that?"

Merrimack's tracking officer responded, ever calm: "Keep your zipper up, Cowboy. Do not fire until target acquired."

"What frogging target!"

The sweat began in pinpricks on Kerry's clammy skin within her pressure suit as she sat in the tiny cockpit. Tense. Eyes scanning every direction. Instruments showed her nothing. No gorgons. She hated gorgons. Always sick before she saw 'em. Rather be in the thick of it, snarled in a giant burr ball, severed legs flapping everywhere. Actually having a can opener chewing on her hull was easier to take than this searching.

She craned her neck around. Weird, actually, to be able to *see*. Normally, she depended wholly on the sensor display to show her plots of things in the perfect blackness. But here the combined light of the cluster's millions of stars shed a weird glow over the interstellar gases. Outside was light.

She could actually see the other Swifts flitting like moths—very fast moths—among the glinting asteroids at the cluster's perimeter. Her squadron in flight looked like what she used to imagine it would before she actually got out here and discovered that space was really dark.

The stars themselves showed as a bright wall, a solid, luminous backdrop against which she imagined legs—lots of serrated, thrashing, biting legs.

But really there was only one very primitive space buoy tucked amid the asteroids, screaming its alien signal. A contraption that looked like a dragonfly equipped with flimsy antenna arrays and foil solar collectors. The colonel's voice sounded: "*Merrimack*. This is Wing Leader. Request confirmation of that Hive sign."

"Wing Leader. *Merrimack*. We are checking that."

Great. Kerry groaned. They don't know.

"It's a Roman trap," someone declared.

"Rome's our ally now," someone else countered.

"Oh, yeah, and we all believe that." Cowboy, in that sarcastic voice again.

Kerry had just let her muscles relax when a spike of laughter in her headset made her flinch.

"Joy, joy! Lookee what's shooting at us! Nine by nine by five on the grid!"

Kerry didn't see it. Fumbled for a lock on the coordinates on her sensor display. Located it.

A missile. That silly junk sculpture of a space buoy had launched a missile. At sublight speed.

Kerry heard a nervous yelp of a laugh. Hers.

Others laughed louder. Claimed to be real scared.

"Eyes!" That was Steele. Warning them this could, after all, be a diversion. Gorgons had been known to throw you a bone, make you look.

"Aw, but this is so *cute*." Cowboy again. "It's shootin' at me!"

"And lookee there. ET's got a laser gun!" Carly's voice.

More cackles caromed within Kerry's helmet.

And Cowboy was off with a whoop. "YeeeeeeeeHA!"

You could tell which Swift was Cowboy's. The one that hauled straight up to the missile, head on, and dead reversed at the very last possible tick. He sped away from the missile, backward, staying in its face, nose to nose, howling like a jack fool.

And flew flat back into a mine.

Opened his hull right up. You could hear the kaboom over the com—half of it. The sound shut off like a switch in mid-explosion—or implosion—and you didn't hear the rest of the boom. And you didn't hear Cowboy any more.

"Cowboy!" someone screamed. Kerry Blue. Didn't recognize her own voice.

Then it was Colonel Steele on the com: "Alpha Flight, what is your situation?"

"Up screwed!" Kerry cried. "Man down! Man down!"

As Alpha Leader shouted over her: "Alpha Flight! Form up, shut up, maintain radio discipline!"

Colonel Steele demanded: "Life signs on Cowboy's can?"

"Negs. No life signs," Alpha Leader responded. "His field's flat and he's got a hole in his hull you can throw a yak through."

The hole by itself was nothing. How it got there—the failure of his deflector field—was the ominous part.

"Cowboy, respond!" Colonel Steele's authoritative bark could wake the dead. Cowboy had to answer.

Didn't.

"What *got* him?" Twitch Fuentes cried, as if Cowboy could be nothing but dead, and Kerry just wanted to reach through the com link and smack him for being so stupid. Cowboy was not dead. Could not, not, not be dead.

"An asteroid!" Dak Shepard answered the stupid question. "A frogging space boulder!"

"What could get through his cowcatcher?" Carly. Not like her to sound so scared.

It was a scary thought, that something could get through the stoutest part of their defenses. The Marines all felt invulnerable behind their cowcatchers—what they called the fat part of their energy deflectors, always turned in the direction of travel. Those fat deflectors kept the space litter from Swiss-cheesing your hull at speed.

What hideous alien weapon could get through a forward field?

The explanation was almost worse. Alpha Leader reported guiltily: "Cowboy's cowcatcher was ... facing the wrong way."

Breathed curses on the link. Sounded like Colonel Steele. Then came his brisk order, "Marine Wing, clear the asteroids. And keep your damn deflectors facing the direction you are going!"

Kerry joined the chorus: "Sir!"

Beam sweeps sliced the asteroid field. Innocuous-looking rocks blew up nicely. Too nicely. Not asteroids after all. This was a minefield. A bloody minefield. One of those highly effective, dirt cheap low-tech traps that don't read on your scanners as devices. The mines did not look like anything. Because they *weren't* anything better than chunks of mineral. A mix of minerals, stable in skinny-digit temperatures in a vacuum. In contact with a beam—or the thin part of a Swift's force field—they got spectacularly unstable.

Not enough punch to do damage if Cowboy hadn't *sat* on one. He took a direct hit through the window in his defensive field and right on the power plant.

A stupid, primitive *mine*.

The hell of it was that a nineteenth-century bullet or even a Stone Age spear could still kill a twenty-third-century marine. It shouldn't. It should not be *allowed*. And that was it—it was your sense of superiority that killed you. Colonel Steele had warned them enough times.

Any jarhead who came out here in a ship that carried swords in its armory should never have sat on a mine.

As the Marine Wing tore into the asteroid field, the battleship *Merrimack* opened up all she had. Together, they beamed, bombed, displaced, flamed, and detonated mines. Residual dust spread, glowing like a snowstorm in the cluster's starlight.

Kerry loosed her guns in blind anger, blasting asteroids back to their component elements till her eyes blurred and Lieutenant Colonel Steele's order banged at her ears: "Cease fire! CEASE FIRE! Wing! Battery! Cease fire! Wing, reel it in. *Merrimack,* this is Steele. Permission to reboard."

"*Merrimack* standing by to receive Marine Wing on port and starboard flight decks."

Flight Sergeant Kerry Blue rode her beam through *Merrimack*'s force field and onto her landing spot on the starboard flight deck. Felt heavy again under nominal gravity.

Gear down, clamps locked. She gripped her seat and closed her eyes for the elevator's stomach-lurching drop inboard to the hangar deck and full gravity. At the abrupt, butt-bruising stop, she disconnected hoses, cables. Popped the canopy, climbed out. "A mine! A stupid dirt ball! Where's Cowboy?"

She pushed through the maintenance erks who swarmed around the returning combat vessels like dull yellow ants in their mustard-colored coveralls.

Cowboy's slip remained vacant.

"Where is he?" Kerry roared.

Erks waved her toward the cargo bay where Alpha Leader had come aboard with Cowboy's wreck in tow.

Kerry ran down the ramp tunnel to the cargo bay. Carly called after her, begging, "No, no, no, *chica linda*, no!"

Kerry burst onto the cargo deck, dropped her helmet.

Cowboy's Swift lay canted askew, twisted, its ass torn open like a ragged metal flower. Front didn't look too bad. The canopy was open, Alpha Leader looking inside, turning away.

Kerry grasped at the faint hope: "Is he—?"

Hazard Sewell turned at the sound of her voice. His fair face turned positively white, looking horrified to see her. Jumped down to the deck.

"Oh, Kerry Blue, don't look." He caught her starting forward. "I mean it. *Do not* look. He—he let the vacuum in."

She knew that. Must've been in denial. The lump in her throat grew near to choking her. Eyes burned. *I'm not gonna cry. Mother of God, I am not gonna cry.*

That was one of Cowboy's expressions—to let the vacuum in. He started it. Everyone used it now.

She was gonna cry.

And—oh, no—the Old Man was on deck. Both of 'em. Lieutenant Colonel TR Steele and Captain John Farragut.

"Captain on deck!"

And everyone snapped to, Marines and navvies alike. Captain Farragut entered with a forceful stride. Toe of one of his boots met Kerry's thrown helmet, sent it skidding. Kerry made an ungainly scramble to retrieve it from the deck. Tucked it under her arm where it belonged.

Farragut had a lot of Cowboy's qualities—a quick smile,

magnetic charm. Damn fine-looking man—which was not to say he was a lean, carrot-torsoed god like Cowboy. Farragut was built like a bull. Between Farragut and Cowboy in an alley fight, you had to go with the captain for sheer mass. That and the fact that John Farragut flat-out loved—loved—to fight. Fearless. Energetic. He drew people to him instantly. Blew into a room like a light going on and woke everyone up. Though, next to Cowboy, Farragut was staid and calm. But, of course, that was because the Old Man was old, like Colonel Steele.

Farragut and Steele were in their thirties.

Blue-eyed, both of them. Farragut like the summer sky. Steele, pale arctic ice. You could cut yourself on Colonel Steele's eyes. Captain Farragut looked Steele right in the ice and demanded, "What happened?"

Kerry had an answer to that: Those bloody alien bastards killed our best man! So she was astounded to hear Colonel Steele saying something else entirely—*apologizing*. "We were sloppy, sir. I take full responsibility for the breakdown in discipline."

The captain's curt nod told him: *You bet you do.*

Kerry's mind reeled with silent shrieks. *What? They killed Cowboy!*

"You let me down, TR," Farragut said softly.

Hazard Sewell, standing next to Kerry, physically winced at that one. Captain Farragut knew every man jack and jane on board, even Marines. And he noticed when you did something really right or really wrong. He could make you feel really big or really, really small. His quiet disapproval cut deep. Be easier if he would just yell.

And Steele didn't explain, or even try to. He just took it. "Yes, sir."

The captain and the colonel exited the deck, and everybody else exhaled. Turned somberly to Cowboy's wreck.

Cowboy always said: Live fast and leave a handsome corpse. Cowboy didn't leave a handsome corpse. They had to hose him out of there and sort out the inorganic stuff with a scanner.

And it ends the same every time. All their rollicking tomorrows stretched ahead in hollow darkness. Kerry retreated to her pod, stuffed her pillow around her ears, trying to make no sound.

Stop thinking. Past was past. Done was done. You can't change it. You can't ever change it, so let it go.

And the loop runs through again. . . .

Captain Farragut caught up with Lieutenant Colonel Steele's quick angry strides. Corridors in the flight wings were wider than in the battleship's main fuselage, allowing the two big men to walk side by side in the passage. "What did happen out there?"

Steele stopped. Anger, barely held in check, burst free. Hurled his helmet against the bulk, all his taurine mass behind it. He flushed red under his white-blond buzz-cut hair. Arctic eyes blazed. "Sir. We got caught with our dicks hanging out and looking stupid."

"Anyone out there?" Farragut asked. No blame. No anger.

Steele struggled to bring his temper down for a landing. He wagged his square head no. "Alive? Not that we saw. Did *Merrimack* pick up anything?"

"No. It doesn't smell like Hive. The early warnings are quiet."

"Doesn't smell like anything that makes sense. And *that* smells like Hive to me," said Steele.

The captain demurred. "The Hive is adaptive, but they don't invent. The burrs have never tripped a mine to know what one is, much less learn how to set one."

"We don't know that, Captain. I don't trust the Romans to tell us everything they tried on the burrs before they palmed the war off on us. And we don't know how old the Hive is, where they've been, who they ate, or what they learned from 'em."

Farragut gave a sideways nod, allowing the point. "But *mines?* No one uses mines in outer space. It's too big. How could anyone know we would be right here? Or that your man would fly backward. He wouldn't have died head-on, would he?"

Steele shook his head. "No. He wouldn't. Or if he'd had his cowcatcher turned in the direction of travel."

"Why didn't he turn it?" Every speck of dust was a bullet to a ship traveling FTL. The forward fields that swept all particles aside were called cowcatchers, though few hands on board had ever seen their namesake or stopped to wonder why one would ever need a device to catch a plodding herbivore. *Merrimack* could, and had, plowed through Saturn's rings. (Heard about that one from the Joint Chiefs, but no matter now.) A pilot always turned his screens in the direction he was going. "System failure?"

Steele shook his head. "Arrogance. Cock full of it." Steele's best guess was that Cowboy had intended to reverse direction again and head butt the missile.

"Did you get any sense out there that that missile or this minefield was meant for us, TR?"

"No," said Steele. "We stepped in someone else's trap."

"Bizarre place for a trap. And accidentally stepping in it? Chances have to be a godzillion to one."

Steele had never taken probabilities and statistics, and he wasn't sure if godzillion was a real number, so he just nodded gravely. "So who were the mines meant for? And what are they protecting?"

"And why here?" Farragut added. "Why right here?"

"We gotta be close to something."

"Have to be," Farragut agreed. "Have to be. But what? Clue?"

Steele shook his head.

"I'll have the minefield scanned. Its placement should point us toward what's being guarded. Have someone retrieve that sentinel buoy so we can analyze it for age. This could be very old news and maybe this is a leftover dragon from a long-gone treasure—what?"

Steele's face sank deeper and deeper into chagrin. Farragut prompted again, "What?"

Steele spoke tightly. "The sentinel buoy has been 'secured.' "

Farragut translated, "Your Marines blew it up."

Steele nodded. "And all of the mines."

One hand loosely caging his face, Farragut peered through his fingers. "Shit, TR." Not angry. Resigned to obvious consequences. If you want to preserve evidence, send detectives or scientists, not Marines. "You know, we very likely wiped out a first contact. I'm pretty sure we never met these folk before."

"My Wing was thorough," Steele said dryly.

"I helped," Farragut confessed. Any chance to run the guns. "LEN's gonna pee the carpet when they read this report."

Naval diplomacy was an oxymoron. Farragut would have let himself laugh, had a man not died. "Cowboy. Jaime Carver." He placed the name at last—the late Flight Sergeant Jaime "Cowboy" Carver.

Steele was not surprised that the captain of a battleship carrying a Marine detachment of 720 and crew of 425 should know one of his Marine flight sergeants by full name. Farragut knew everybody.

And everybody knew Cowboy. Though few knew his name was Jaime Carver.

"Popular man, wasn't he?" Farragut asked.

Lips tight, teeth clenched, Steele answered, "Very."

Farragut must have sensed the rage. He asked softly, "Friend, TR?"

"Dumb kid. Cocky. Balls to the wall. Hard not to like him."

Hard not to like him, and Steele hated him. Heard himself go on, "I knew he'd do this to me."

Cowboy was a funny guy, made everyone laugh. Stellar looks. Always quick to get his shirt off. Girl in every port, and one on board every ship no matter how slim the ratios. Insubordinate. Steele sometimes wished him dead. So startled to get his wish, Steele spoke aloud, "I'm asking if there's something I could've done."

Farragut glanced aside at Steele as they walked. "*Was* there?"

"I don't see it." And Steele had looked hard. As much as Steele hated Cowboy, sending one of his own men intentionally, and without his knowledge, to his death was against everything Lieutenant Colonel Steele lived for. Steele was first, last, and always a good soldier. He had soul-searched and exonerated himself. Cowboy had killed Cowboy. "It was fast."

"It's always fast out here," said Farragut.

"Man was a walking game of Russian roulette." Future corpse, the type was called. "Hell, sir, it was inevitable."

Farragut's voice turned quietly stern: "You have any more of those on board my boat, TR, ship 'em home today."

"Sir. Yes, sir."

Prox alarms blared and quickly silenced. Two sets of blue eyes lifted. "What now?" Farragut murmured, launching into a run.

Space was too vast for chance encounters. Someone crossed your path out here, means you were stalked.

"Ladder up!"

Crew quickly scrambled clear of the vertical passages within the sound of Farragut's shout, for Captain Farragut made his entrances like a cannon shell. He clambered up the ladder, spry for a big man, and bounded to the control room.

Two MPs flanked the hatch on either side. Within was a compact space, daylit, bustling. Technicians and specialists worked elbow to elbow at their stations—tactical, com, navigation, targeting—each in direct communication with his attendant department belowdecks. Multiple large display screens above the workstations relayed visuals and ship's status at a glance. "What've we got?" Farragut demanded.

The prox alarm announced someone not given an approach vector was collision close. "Friend or Foe?"

"IFF says Friend," tactical reported dubiously. And no one was convinced of its friendship from looking at the overhead displays.

The U.S. alliance with Palatine was a brittle one. *Merrimack*'s low-band scanner readings, as translated into a visual, displayed the unholy image of a Roman Striker.

Merrimack's tall, impossibly beautiful XO announced coolly, "Captain Farragut, your new IO is here." A wry brittleness infected her whole bearing. Commander Calli Carmel had a knowing respect for Roman might and Roman treachery.

The concerned pinch in her brow was in clear view with her dark hair pulled severely back into a braided tail to her waist.

Farragut regarded the painted Striker on the display. A sharp-edged, wicked little craft, faster than the *Mack*. "Red and black. What *gens* is that?"

"Flavian," said Calli. Calli Carmel had attended the prestigious Imperial Military Institute on Palatine during the brief conciliation between worlds. Made her the resident expert on things Roman. "Not the worst," she interpreted. "But not the conciliatory party either. *Gens* Flavius voted against the surrender. He's requesting permission to come aboard."

"Permission granted." And to her hesitation, "We're expecting him, aren't we?"

Calli lowered her voice, grim. "Not yet. We never sent our location to the repeater. Our operations are classified, but he found us without being given rendezvous coordinates. It appears we have no secrets from this guy."

"Good quality in an IO, you don't think? What's his name?"

"Augustus. They've given him the rank of colonel." Lofty enough. But not a line officer.

"Augustus what?" said Farragut. "What Augustus?"

"Just Augustus."

"I thought only slaves had only one name."

"Augustus is not a slave name," Calli advised.

"Well, he's not the emperor," said Farragut. "Let him aboard." He quit the control room running. "Clear ladder!" He hooked his feet round the rails outside the rungs and slid, fireman style, to the mid-deck. Marched out the starboard dock to greet his new intelligence officer.

He found the deck crowded with the curious, armed with made-up official reasons to be here, anxious for a glimpse of their uneasy ally.

Not just a Roman, this was rumored to be a patterner, one of the Empire's augmented men designed to interface with a computer and make gestalt sense of the random information within its databases. The Roman Empire valued its patterners highly. Patterners were rare, pricey pieces of equipment. Palatine must think *Merrimack* had a real chance of locating the Hive home world to be sending a patterner into U.S. service.

The Roman uncoiled from his Striker. Tall. They were all tall. Romans were evolving bigger by every generation, and not, one suspected, by natural selection. Captain Farragut at six foot one was unaccustomed to looking that far up. The Roman stood easily six foot eight — max height allowed on board an American space vessel — all in proportion. He was going to have to duck through the hatches. Age, perhaps mid-forties, perhaps fifties. Face like granite. Hair black, tightly curled, close-cut. Carried himself with a dangerous dignity. A disdain.

Captain Farragut offered an open right hand. Augustus

THE MYRIAD \ 17

let the hand hang out there in midair. The flight deck stiffened, gripped in a collective breath hold, turning blue.

Captain Farragut cut easily to the point: "I know y'all broke away from Earth a hundred and a half years ago, but you've got to know this is a sign of friendship."

"An open hand shows you hold no weapon," Augustus corrected. "I do. Ergo." Still no hand.

Eyes bulged from the breath holders.

The captain's voice did not vary from its easy Kentucky drawl. "Then let go of it long enough to greet your duly appointed commanding officer."

The Roman's hand opened, lifted—saluted, greeting the office, not the man. Bootheels came together sharply. No one had ever heard an ancient Roman salute, but you had to doubt an ancient Roman ever managed a convincing heel rap like that in sandals.

Farragut's brows lifted. He returned an American salute. And since no pleasantries were to be exchanged, he ordered, "Mr. Juarez, show Colonel Augustus to his quarters."

"An escort is unnecessary," Augustus countered. "Tell me which compartment you've assigned to me. I am familiar with the layout of a U.S. *Merrimack*-class battleship." Unsubtle reminder there, of Palatine's capture of *Merrimack*'s sister ship *Monitor* during the war. The *Monitor* must have impressed the Romans, because they turned around, gave it back, and offered alliance with the United States against Them, the Hive.

Marauding omnivores from outer space had made strange bedfellows of the United States and the planet Palatine.

Captain Farragut chose to pretend the remark was meant to be helpful. "By all means." He ordered the new intelligence officer to report to sick bay after he stowed his gear in his quarters. Granted him permission to go, and he was gone.

A nervous titter escaped the personnel on the flight deck.

"I think that might have gone better," Farragut said.

The tension immediately bled off with a big deck-wide snigger.

One of the ship's dogs, the bloodhound named Nose, had

given the Roman a sniff in passing and immediately sat down—a signal that he smelled something not right about Augustus.

"I'll put a tag on him," Steele said, but Farragut belayed that: "I don't think he'll get lost."

That was not the point. Steele plunged ahead, "But he's—"

"Roman?" Farragut chided mildly.

There were worse things in this galaxy than Romans.

A squad of Marines waited for Colonel Steele in the forecastle on his way to officers' country.

He felt numbingly cold in recognition:

Dak Shepard. Flew as Alpha Two. A grunt with wings. Big ape. A football washout—too slow for offense, too small for defense at a petite one hundred kilos. Nothing left for Dak but to bash heads for Uncle Sam.

Carly Delgado. Alpha Four. A hard case. All rope and bone. Stick girl. Little pyramid breasts and a wide pointy cradle of hip. Wide face, brutally high cheekbones, and a sharp little chin. That squint did her no good. Too tough to cry. Carly was crying.

Twitch Fuentes. Alpha Five. The quiet one. Didn't trust his English.

Little Regina Monroe. Alpha Three. Reg was making those squeaking sobs. Sounded like a mouse.

And hope against hope, she was still there in the back of the knot: Kerry Blue. Alpha Six. Puffy-faced. Eyes rimmed red. Mouth had that fat-lipped look you get from crying hard. Grieving anger knit her brow.

They were all here but Alpha Seven. That asshole.

Steele braced himself in stony dread as Flight Leader Hazard Sewell stepped forward for his squad. The designated mouth. "We're having a memorial for Cowboy. We'd like you to say a few words, Colonel."

Heart stuck in his boot.

They waited, expectant. Never expected Colonel Steele to say no.

These soldiers all loved Cowboy. Steele's throat constricted so tight he didn't think he could talk.

And then he was talking. Almost without himself. "What I will do for Cowboy's memory is neglect to record in my report that he was in direct violation of procedure, which violation caused his death. I will not put in the record that he did not die in defense of his world but in the act of being a cowboy. And I am only giving him that much slack because he didn't take any of you with him!"

Felt the heat in his face. With his fair skin and white-blond buzz-cut hair he may as well have a signal beacon for a head. Knew he was flaming red.

He roared on, louder, "And if any of you do the same, not only will I refuse to say anything at your memorials, I will jettison your carcass out the air lock where your vacuum-bloated remains will drift for all time. DO YOU UNDERSTAND!"

Alpha squad flinched back as a whole in dumb disbelief.

"The rules exist to keep your sorry asses still connected to your thick skulls and your still-beating hearts. You want me to say a few words? Here: Cowboy got what he asked for. Now, someone go sanitize his personal effects before I ship them back to his wife. I have a letter to write!"

As he whirled toward the hatch, someone blurted, "Cowboy had a wife?"

"A pregnant wife," Steele snarled back. God, how do you write a letter like that? Damn him. Damn him. A pregnant widow. He roared in parting, "Take all his girlfriends' stuff and space it!"

Kerry Blue, looking ill, mumbled, "I'll do it."

It would be mostly her stuff.

Normally, a star cluster offered nothing of interest to a military vessel. The cluster was a beautiful curiosity only, until this one had started shooting.

IC9870986 was a class I globular cluster, meaning, on a scale of I to XII, it was very large, extremely rich, and very much compressed at its center—though "compressed" in cosmic terms meant that the core suns still averaged a quarter light-year apart.

The cluster measured 150 light-years in diameter, encompassing three million stars. At light speed it would take *Merrimack* 472 years to orbit the cluster once; at the distortion threshold, six days. The whole of it measured 750,351 solar masses.

"That can't be right," Steele objected, hearing the statistics read off. Couldn't bite back the words fast enough. Caught sideways glances from the Navy techs, who were embarrassed for him. Steele had just stepped in something and didn't know what. Only knew he had revealed some ignorance.

A scanner monitor muttered into his console, "Marines can work division. Wow."

It was the division that was not working. Steele did not see how three million stars equated to seven hundred fifty thousand solar masses.

Farragut murmured aside to his abashed Marine commander, "Underweight stars. Typical in a glob."

"I slept through globs," Steele growled.

"So did everyone," Farragut assured him. That would be just like Farragut not to leave you out there by yourself. "Globs are of no strategic importance."

Globular clusters were among the oldest features in the Milky Way. In comparison to Sol, the typical globular star was poorer in elements any heavier than helium by a factor of ten. And no heavy elements meant no planets, no dirt to stand on, no military bases. Nothing for a gorgon to eat, and *Merrimack* was hunting gorgons.

But somebody was here. Or had been here.

Captain Farragut wondered, passing through the cluster, if he had not been lured in here. But the Hive did not understand humans well enough to know that humans would find this beautiful. Beauty was irrelevant to Hive existence. The Hive did not know beauty. It knew edibility.

In surrounding space, only one in four stars formed singly. Stars in a globular cluster were all singles, unless one considered the whole system of three million as one colossal multiple star system. Though one could not say these stars orbited one another. They milled.

But lying as it did only two degrees off the galactic equator, this cluster had picked up three rider stars not born with the rest of them. Three heavy stars.

"Two M types and an F8," the monitor reported. "Main sequence."

"Planets?" Farragut asked.

"Affirmative. All three of 'em. Planets in their hospitable zones."

"Let's go look. Take us to the F8 system." Captain Farragut pointed to the white star, heaviest of the three rider systems. His voice was uncharacteristically tight.

A habitable planet was the last thing *Merrimack* wanted to find on the path where she was bound. The silence of surrounding space underscored the captain's misgivings. If the minefield had come from one of those three star systems, then where were the communication signals of its makers? Against what enemy had the mines been set? The cluster lay in direct line with the Hive's last known trail.

The navigator plotted a course toward the white star system. Captain Farragut did not request any special haste to get there. Afraid *Merrimack* was flying toward a mass grave.

Space may be silent, but noises carried clearly through the thin bulkheads of *Merrimack*'s confined world. Crashing. Shrieked curses. Tearing. Kerry Blue was trashing Cowboy's sleep pod.

"Kerry! What are you doing?"

Kerry tugged, grunting. Fabric of Cowboy's shirt gave way after two mighty tugs. Ripped. "Colonel said sanitize his effects," she puffed, getting another grip.

"Sanitize, not annihilate!" her squad mate Reg Monroe cried. "They have to send something home!"

"When I'm done, they can send his shit home in an envelope!" Yarn from a sweater unraveled in curly lengths with each yank. Might've been Cowboy's guts. Kerry whipped the shredded ends at anything left standing of Cowboy's belongings. Screamed, "He was married! Son of a bitch! Son of a bitch! Son of a BITCH!"

Things flew and shattered. Marines ducked for cover as Kerry Blue raged.

Till an iron grip surrounded her, pinned her arms to her sides, and pulled her off her feet. She knew who had her—didn't need eyes behind her head, or even in front to see those braided cuffs to figure this one out—though she couldn't believe it. She went rigid against the hard, hard torso at her back. Like being chained to a boulder. Felt Colonel Steele's voice vibrate against her. "Marine, what the hell are you doing!"

"He was married! Sir!"

"Yeah?" Steele's tone said: *So?*

He set her down on her feet so hard it rattled her teeth, and let her go.

An oddly hurt lump rose to her throat. Her eyes welled, nose thickened. First betrayed by her lover, and now the damned colonel hated her, too.

She turned to face him. "No one told me!"

Rather softly, perhaps mocking, Steele said, "I thought you knew."

"What do you think I am?" she cried, shocked.

Steele's answer snapped right back, flat: "Easy."

She blinked matted lashes, hurt. "No shit, sir." Of course she was easy. She sniffled indignantly, straightened her back, and fought the wobble out of her voice. "I am not an adulteress."

Steele's white-blond brows lifted at the quaint, antique word. Steele looked for a moment as if he might laugh. Didn't. "You're just an old-fashioned girl, aren't you, Blue?"

"What is that supposed to mean, sir?"

An ice-blue flick to the side—quick scan over the wreck-age. "You done here?" he asked.

"Yeah. He ain't worth any more of my time."

Steele snarled to the others, signaling that this show was over. "All right. Someone *else* go through Cowboy's effects! And everyone stay sober at the wake. I remind you we are still under a Hive watch!"

2

"CONTACT! Contact! Contact!"

The Officer of the Deck's voice broke the captain's sleep in the middle watch, four days into the cluster.

"What have you got?" Farragut bounded into the control room, still wearing the T-shirt and sweatpants he slept in. Lieutenant Colonel Steele arrived close behind in T-shirt and khakis, but Steele had managed deck boots as well.

Farragut glanced at the monitors. Knew from the lack of alarms and the quiet telltales that the contact was not Hive. He rubbed his eyes to make the images focus. "Where are we?"

"Ninety light-years from the F8 star," the OOD answered, surrendering her station. Lieutenant Glenn Hamilton—Hamster, they called her. The Hamster, a mellow-voiced, auburn-haired young woman, stood five foot one barefoot. She was all professional, way too cute. Married. Subordinate line officer. Captain Farragut kept her on the middle watch where he never had to look at her. Almost never.

"The second planet in the F8 system is pouring out electromagnetic transmissions," Hamster reported. "Radio, television, satellite bounces. Video shows a humanoid population."

Monitor screens lit up with different images broadcast

from the planet. They showed a somewhat Earthlike world in terms of terrain and climate, with green vegetation. Lean, lithe, humanoid beings with red-bronze skin and dark equine manes moved under a star-spangled sky. There were tall, willowy elfin-faced females draped in flowing, floor-length clothing. And distinctly shorter, harder, dog-muscled males, less covered, their manes showing through slash-backed shirts and tunics.

Captain Farragut did not remember ever seeing anything like them in the archives. "Is this a new contact?"

"Yes, sir," said Lieutenant Hamilton. She lifted brown eyes to her captain. "Congratulations, John."

Grins spread all around the control room. "Sir?" The com tech turned from his station. "If we're just hitting radio waves now, ninety light-years out, that ought to indicate they just invented radio ninety years ago. But we're hitting radio, microwave, and television signals all at once."

"Colony," said Farragut. "Has to be."

"With sublight technology, sir?" the tech asked, dubious.

That stopped Farragut short. Could not have heard aright. He gave a quick once over to all the monitors. "All this chatter is sublight?"

"Electromagnetic, all of it. No bouncing bubbles. No res—lucky for them. Nothing in any of the images to suggest they had FTL at the time these signals started. Look. There's what I mean."

He punched up on the monitor an image of an archaic spaceship belching fire in its landing, a small cluster of beings greeting the ship's arrival.

"I guess," Farragut said faintly, a concession. "No one traveled very far in one of those."

"Then those people had to be seeded," Steele pronounced harshly, arms crossed defensively over his broad chest.

"Oh, God, I hate people gardens!" Hamster blurted.

An officer tried to keep an open mind out here, but one could not love a species who grew other intelligent species as food crops. Gave their kind the ironically tender name of "shepherd."

"All right," Farragut acknowledged. Made to give the con back to his lieutenant. "Maintain speed. Record everything. Pipe all this to the xenos. See if they can sift the languages apart. TR, send a recon squadron ahead. Full speed, full stealth. *Full stealth.* I don't even want those Swifts so much as talking to each other."

"Mission objective?" Steele requested.

"I need to know if those beings are still on the planet." *Merrimack*'s current information was ninety years old. A lot could change in ninety years. "And if they're alive, what is their present level of technology. Watch for shepherds. Watch for Hive."

"Watch for mines," Hamster added.

"Damn the mines," said Farragut.

A League of Earth Nations exploration vessel would have stopped to make a detailed collection of the signals encountered—catalog them, study them—before moving on an unknown life-form. And *Merrimack*, a U.S. Navy space battleship, would ordinarily have flown wide and left the unknown civilization alone. But the planet was located on the Hive highway; it was *Merrimack*'s business now. If the world was dead, Farragut had to know. It would mean *Merrimack* was on the right path. If alive, then Farragut had to know why, *how*, when the Hive had passed so close by.

So the battleship pressed on, flying fast forward through ninety years of video/radio history of the planet, reeling the transmissions in for the computer to unwind, sort, and decompress for playback.

The xeno crew on board studied as fast as they could before the LEN could take over the project, as the LEN invariably did. Yet, not to keep the League of Earth Nations unaware, *Merrimack*'s crew dutifully assembled a courier missile to report the discovery. A quick call for mail, and the courier missile was on its way to the Fort Eisenhower Repeater.

Courier missiles, like torpedoes, could push through the distortion threshold and arrive at Fort Ike, with its Repeater and its Shotgun, many times faster than a manned vessel could.

Out here in unexplored space, on silent run, *Merrimack* was on her own, as isolated as a sailing vessel of old. She had no access to her res pulse that could have notified Earth at once. Resonance was instantaneous. It also was, apparently, the Hive's dinner bell.

Hive seemed able to pick up any resonant pulse, no matter the harmonic. Resonant receivers of human design could not pick up a res pulse not coded to its exact harmonic. The Hive not only detected all resonant pulses, but it could home on them, and eat their source.

From the moment Earth discovered resonance and sent its first pulse—"Watson, come here. I need you!"—Hive swarms had turned toward Earth, and kept coming in multitudes.

The Hive's invading swarms had to get past Palatine first. So the blockade was there, in Roman space. Roman and U.S. ships patrolled the same zone, holding off the ravenous spaceborne swarms.

John Farragut never fought a defensive war. His *Merrimack*, in a flanking maneuver, was now headed around the invasion front in search of the Hive's home world, to take the battle back to its source.

As the battleship moved toward the F8 star, the recorded years folded in. And the crew waited for the sickening inevitability of pictures of the local insectoid life rising in plague swarms—the hideous, consistent, first sign of Hive approach.

The insectoid form, one of the most successful and universal of life-forms in the known galaxy, was apparently resonant-sensitive. Insectoids had an uncanny ability to perceive Hive presence. Insectoid panic was often the first warning humans had of Hive proximity.

But the signals from the F8 system persisted peacefully for an agonizingly long time. Farragut caught a xeno in tears, a sweet, pillowy, "mom-ish" woman with a bottle-red cloud of hair. Farragut asked her what she had found that made her cry.

"Nothing." The xeno daubed tears from the bags under her eyes. "I'm falling in love with this culture. And they're dead. They have to be. I don't want to watch them die. Can't we speed up, Captain? Just—just get it over with."

The natives' clothing changed, their cities spread, with no sign of FTL technology other than their sudden presence. It made no sense. There was no pattern.

"I have a patterner on board," Farragut said. "Let's take him for a test drive." He hailed the ship's MO, Mohsen

"Mo" Shah, on the intercom from the control room. "Is my IO fit for duty?"

"He is being *on* duty," said Dr. Shah. "Did he not report?"

Farragut turned to his XO, Calli Carmel. "Did he report to you?"

Calli's beautiful brown eyes went quizzically blank for an instant, then shared a bemused stare with her captain, as if one of the ship's engines were now giving itself orders. "No."

Farragut answered absurdity with absurdity, "I wonder what he assigned himself to."

Dr. Shah's voice sounded again from the intercom. "Captain? May I be having a word with you?" Confidentially, Mo Shah's tone added.

So Farragut strode aft to the medic's compartment. Detecting the concern in the MO's voice over the control room intercom, Colonel Steele came along as well.

Images of aliens lit up all of the medical officer's screens—pictures of innards, things recognizable as lungs, hearts, guts. Dr. Shah followed the captain's alarmed stare, hurried to interpret the images. "Oh. These are not being signs of slaughter. These are being medical communications. Physicians conferring with each other, I am believing."

"Human?"

"Humanoid." Mo clicked off the monitors. Mo was a placid man, a Riverite, with great brown puppy eyes and a calming voice. Mo Shah's forehead extended halfway up his scalp. He folded his hands and faced his captain. "I am wanting to tell you about your Roman."

Augustus had become John Farragut's Roman ever since he had come aboard. No one else wanted him.

"He did not pass the drug scan," Dr. Shah reported.

Farragut pursed his lips. Spoke at last: "What's he doing?"

"The whole pharmacy," Mo answered. "And the R&D lab."

Captain Farragut took a guess, "Does this drug use have to do with his alterations?"

"I asked him that. He asked in return if I were deferring

to Roman medical authority. I said no. So he told me to be making my own diagnosis."

"He has a chip on his shoulder," said Farragut.

Mo shrugged. "If you are wanting to call Gibraltar a chip, it is being a chip. I am thinking he wanted me to bust him."

"Apparently you didn't."

"I considered it. I checked what we are knowing of Roman medicine—which is not being much. Palatine are being very tight-lipped about their patterners. They are not sharing that technology. So I checked Roman law, and there *is* being a specific exemption for patterners regarding use of controlled substances."

"What kind of exemption?"

"Drug use is being entirely at a patterner's own discretion. He may be carrying. He may be using. He may not be selling, and Augustus is not doing so. So I cleared him. But it is being your boat, Captain."

Farragut could still throw Augustus in the brig. "Did he bring drugs aboard?"

The MO nodded. "Quantities consistent with personal use."

"Is he coherent?"

"Much too coherent, I am thinking."

Farragut nodded with a slight snort. At their first meeting, Augustus had communicated his thoughts and feelings with great clarity and brevity.

Mo continued, "Augustus' medical jacket is only going back eight years. In fact, his *whole* jacket is only going back eight years, which could be when he was augmented. He has filaments in his muscle tissue. I am not knowing how the Roman doctors strung it."

"What kind of filaments?"

"Some are being reinforcements, I am thinking. Others are being electrical connections for his plugging into patterner mode."

"Patterner *mode?*" Farragut had assumed a patterner was a patterner; like John Farragut was a captain. It was not a mode that turned off and on.

Mo explained, "He must be making connections to his augmentations, plugging cables between parts of himself, to be enabling his functions as a patterner."

Farragut gave his head a quick shake as if to shake the weird idea out. He was not sure he understood. Asked slowly, "So when Augustus is not 'enabled,' he's like the rest of us?"

"No. In ways I am not at all sure of, he is not being like us. His gunsights—these," Mo Shah lifted a hand to Colonel Steele's gunsights, black bars implanted on either side of the colonel's eyes. "Augustus is having these, too."

Farragut made a motion like a shrug. "So Augustus' sights are camouflaged better."

"Augustus' gunsights are being *inside* his eyes," said Mo. "And he is being stronger."

"How strong?" Colonel Steele crossed his arms. Even in defensive posture, for the size of his arms and breadth of his chest, TR Steele never looked anything but formidable.

"Stronger than any of us," Mo Shah answered.

"How many of us?" Farragut asked, curious now.

"I am having no idea."

"Just tell me, Mo," Steele abandoned subtlety, since he was never good at it. "If I need to take the son of a bitch out, how many Marine guards do I need?"

"I would be suggesting a gun. He is still being human."

"And he's still on our side until further notice," Farragut reminded Steele. "Unless he's psychotic or suicidal. He isn't. *Is* he, Mo?"

Dr. Shah gave a noncommittal shrug. "Bad temper is not necessarily being psychosis. But you cannot be altering a biological organism and not be having side effects. Period. Only God is knowing what got nicked in Augustus' brain when they did whatever they did to make him a patterner."

"Meaning what, exactly?"

"Meaning—" Mo considered a moment. "Be watching your ass, Captain Farragut."

"Captain Farragut and Colonel Steele! Control room." The XO's voice projected an urgent sort of calm over the intercom. "The recon patrol is coming in."

Farragut and Steele glanced to the chronometers to see what they already knew: The recon flight was early.

Steele breathed a vulgarity, met the captain's eyes, about to apologize for his word choice, but Farragut said benignly, "Let's go see how deep it is."

Merrimack's starboard hangar deck was a wide space, fully three decks high—the entire height of the starboard wing. Elevators brought the Swifts inboard from the flight deck. The Swifts' distortion fields kept them from coating over with condensing ice.

The Swifts were scarcely inboard and clamped down when canopies popped and the recon team jumped down to the hangar deck, tucked helmets under their arms, at attention. Erks had standing orders to ignore Captain Farragut unless specifically called to attention, so they crawled over the returned fighter craft, industrious as ants. Hoses hissed. Recorders were pulled, air reloaded, flight times logged, systems checked.

"Echo Flight reporting, sir!" the young flight leader spoke in a shout. "The natives are still alive in the F8 system—and they have company, sir!"

"Hive?" Farragut guessed.

"Shepherds." Steele's guess.

"No, sir. No, sir." The flight leader's face jerked from captain to colonel. "We ran into more signals from two different sources. There are signals coming from the other two rider star systems."

"What kind of signals?" Farragut asked.

"Same kinds, sir. Videos look like the same humanoids, and we have a computer match on the audio. An exact match on some of them."

"Exact?" Farragut felt his brows contract in doubt. "You mean the same words?"

"No, sir. Identical audios. All three planets are rebroadcasting the exact same transmissions."

Farragut believed the young man, but told him what he was struggling with: "Those three solar systems are ten, twenty, and forty-three light-years apart, and they're sharing messages? You found FTL capability?"

"No, sir. Nothing other than the fact that they're *doing* it. Somehow. Sir. We have no clue how those electromagnetic signals are getting planet to planet. We picked up no sign of ships in transit between the stars, and believe me, sir, we looked. They have spaceships, but every one we detected was flying inside one of the solar systems and clocking no better than seventy-nine percent c. We picked up no FTL-capable ships, and no FTL signals."

"Obviously they do have FTL signals," said Farragut.

"Yes, sir. But we can't detect them."

The captain did not argue with the report merely because it was impossible. "Any evidence of how these beings got to these three planets?"

"None, sir. Absolutely none."

Farragut turned to a very young, very dark xeno who had come to the hangar deck in curiosity. "No evidence? No historical stories in those videos about the great journey to the globular cluster?"

The apprentice xenologist shook her head. "No, sir."

"Not even in any of their children's histories?"

"No, sir. Juvenile broadcasting doesn't seem to be part of their culture. All the transmissions have—what looks to us to be—an official look. We can't be sure, since we can't understand a word. Well, we can understand a few words. *Yes*, *no*, and the like."

All the resources at his command and John Farragut could not get an answer to a question as simple as how three planets separated by ten, twenty, and forty-three light-years were communicating. That was unacceptable.

Merrimack had everything. Provisioned like a small carrier, the space battleship had two compact automated fabrication plants—the technology for which had been lifted from Rome—that could repair the ship's formidable armament. Above and beyond her strictly military defensive, offensive, communications, detection, propulsion, and navigational equipment, *Merrimack* housed in its small sick bay all the equipment of a major hospital. The *Mack* carried a hydroponics garden, raw grain in its two dry storage silos, and stores of meat and milk radiated, microbe-free, and vacuum-sealed. In the spirit of redundancy, the *Mack* also carried a small breeding group of pygmy cows, goats, quail, and ducks for fresh milk, meat, and eggs, just in case the food stores became contaminated or personnel become stranded on an alien planet in the Deep. The ship's galley could be programmed to create anything the ship had ingredients for, from full meals to pretzels and popcorn. There were squash courts on board and a running track. The enormous virtual library was updated every time a launch cycled Fleet Marines in and out from their tours of duty. *Merrimack* had everything.

Merrimack had research labs for the ship's many xeno-scientists to analyze the unexpected.

The xenos weren't working hard enough.

Farragut collected Echo Flight's recording bubbles and made straight for the xenolinguist's lab. Burst in, demanding, "Ham, I need a translation of the dominant language of the F8 planet and I need it now."

Dr. Patrick Hamilton did not rise. He plucked a module from his console and tossed it to the captain in answer. "Here." Then, regretting his flippancy, added quickly, "Sir."

"What is this?" Farragut held the module up to the light. To all appearances it was a standard language module, lightweight, about an inch square, with a three-prong interface.

"From your Roman."

"Augustus," Farragut named him.

"That," Ham confirmed in heavy distaste. "That *thing* is inhuman. Inhuman. That's the word for it! Your Roman comes stalking in here like zombie cyborg from the stratosphere, wired and staring as if nobody's home. Plugs into the main port. Dumps *that* out five hours later." Patrick Hamilton jabbed his forefinger at the module in Farragut's hand. "Five bleeding blinking bloody hours." The linguist slumped back in his chair and covered his eyes. His hand was long-fingered and soft-skinned, an academic's hand.

"And what is this?" said Farragut, turning the module over and over, as if he would see what was so remarkable about it.

"Myriadian. The language. Fifty-five thousand words of it with grammar and idioms." Dr. Hamilton sounded about to cry.

Patrick Hamilton was from Mars. Not Mars the colony, Mars the place where odd people come from. A quirky man of science, Dr. Patrick Hamilton hadn't the steel in him of his line-officer wife Glenn—Hamster—Hamilton.

Farragut did not know what Glenn saw in him. Patrick Hamilton was a reasonably attractive man, in a boyish way. Boyish in the sense of puerile. Perhaps because Glenn's career allowed no time or place for a child, she had married one instead.

"Myriadian?" Farragut echoed. "Is that the major language on the planet in the F8 system?"

Patrick Hamilton, PhD, Chief Xenolinguist on board the *Merrimack,* lolled in his swivel chair, leg hooked over one armrest. "That is the *only* language on all three worlds."

Farragut felt his brain knot. "How did you know there were three inhabited worlds?" The captain had only just learned it himself, and Patrick Hamilton had not been on the hangar deck to hear the recon flight's discovery.

"Oh? Did you find the other two?" Patrick gave a most unhappy, useless laugh. "It's in the words. There are three inhabited planets in the Myriad—that's what the locals call this cluster—the Myriad. The planets are called Arra, Rea, and Centro. The three worlds are all one nation. They also talk about a planet called Origin, which is *not* in the Myriad. Origin is someplace far, far, far, far away."

Of course there would have to be an Origin. Three planets with only one language among them could be nothing but colonies. So where was Origin? "Do they have a word for FTL?"

"Captain Farragut, everyone has a word for FTL from the moment they discover one hundred eighty-six thousand, two hundred ninety-one miles per second. Doesn't mean they have FTL. It's dangerous business trying to piece together a culture from its language. Language comes with a lot of antique baggage; tends to be full of anachronisms and fictions. Elves, emperors, perpetual motion. And a royal furball has nothing to do with royalty or fur. Your Roman says the Myriadians are not flying FTL."

Patrick Hamilton grew more morose in his envy. The despair of the obsolete and inadequate. "Five frazzin' hours."

"And this works?" Farragut held up the language module.

"Plug that in, and all these recordings make sense. It's— it's elegant. I could not have made that with seventeen years and a bevy of graduate student slave labor. It's like I'm sitting here with a bow and arrow and *he* comes along with a disrupter and a triangulated sight. Where's the justice?"

Sad to see an educated man whine like that. Sadder still that a man with a strong, pretty, classy wife like Lieutenant Glenn Hamilton should be referring to his graduate students in terms of a bevy. Made the captain want to slap him. Said instead: "Don't sit there crying in the dust, Ham. I need you."

Captain Farragut brought many a man back to life with those three words: I need you.

And Farragut did need his xenos. Cluster IC9870986—the Myriad—was turning into one of those upsetting, wholly baffling discoveries like the Xi artifact—a slab of lead five billion years older than the universe itself—existing just to piss people off.

"Where is Augustus?"

"Oh, he turned white, unplugged, and left a few hours ago."

The quartermaster had billeted Augustus with the spare torpedoes, partly in intentional slight, partly in consideration of Augustus' height—torpedoes were seven feet long, just four inches better than Augustus—and partly to keep the Roman clear of the American officers, who wanted nothing to do with him.

Captain Farragut found his IO lying half in his pod, half out, looking none too well, nursing a headache with a hand over his eyes. The Roman did not look up at the captain's entrance into torpedo rack room number six.

Farragut paused. "You look like you're fighting to hold onto lunch."

Augustus lifted a three-fingered shrug over his eyes. "Lost that battle." He lowered his hand and demanded flatly, "What do you want?"

"I've been listening to the recordings with this." Farragut held up the language module. "This is amazing."

"You are easily amazed."

"How did you do this?"

That made Augustus laugh. The laugh was neither happy nor kind. "Superior Roman technology. And we surrendered to this?"

Farragut either missed the insult or didn't care. "The commander of my Marines wants to know how you found us when we never sent coordinates to Fort Ike."

"When you started blowing up things at the cluster's perimeter, you were visible for parcs on the low band. You looked like a puffer fish."

Gravitational murmurs were instant but of limited detectable range, becoming quickly tenuous at an inverse square ratio to distance.

"Puffer fish do it out of fear," Augustus added.

"I wasn't afraid. I'm trigger happy."

"I hear that about you. Are the Myriadians still alive?"

"Yes!" Farragut said happily.

"I was afraid of that."

Not a sentimental sort, this Roman. And life was not what either of them had come looking for. Where there's life, there is no Hive—unless the Hive was eating the life. *Merrimack* was hunting the Hive.

"You lost the gorgon trail," said Augustus.

"Looks like it." Farragut returned to the language module, eager as a child on Christmas day to try out his new toy. "If I wanted to say 'we mean you no harm,' how would I?"

Augustus stirred his long limbs. "You want to *talk?*"

Language modules at this stage of alien contact were normally used for *listening*.

"What would you like to say to the Myriadians? 'Why aren't you lunch?'"

Farragut ignored him. "I'm pulling up a dozen words for we and two dozen for you. I don't know which to use."

Augustus gave a wry smile of disbelief and amusement. "Do you just dive into a pool when you can't see the bottom, John Farragut?"

"These people talk over distances of light-years without resonance or FTL. I need that technology. Imagine talking over astronomical distances without the Hive picking it up. And I need it before the LEN kicks us off the site."

Augustus conceded the point, sat up, and became abruptly helpful. "Myriadian *you*s and *we*s are very specific. Your choices immediately establish what you are in relation to your addressee."

"If I say *Ila kendi ru nacon di*, will they at least know I'm friendly?"

"The moment you say that, they'll know you're an idiot. *Ila* is juvenile feminine. And your choice of *you*s—intended, no doubt, to be friendly—is insultingly familiar. The road to war is paved with good intentions. And you forgot the significator."

"The what?"

"That initial click you hear at the beginning of every Myriadian phrase. The pitch signals whether the mood is indicative, interrogative, or imperative."

"Ham says you knew there were three inhabited planets in the cluster before the recon flight knew there were three inhabited planets."

"When you understand what they're saying, it becomes obvious."

"So are there any clues in the words as to how these people are traveling between planets?"

"Only implication by omission," said Augustus. "The words suggest that the Myriad is an autocracy, which suggests that things of strategic importance will not be broadcast. Knowledge is power. Power is tightly held in an autocracy. The really good stuff is not floating about for just anyone to pick out of empty space. There is a lot not said about interplanetary travel—except that the Myriadians travel between planets regularly. By spaceship."

"Not the spaceships I've been seeing." Echo Flight's recordings showed only very primitive vessels.

"The very ones," Augustus assured him.

"We're missing something."

"That's obvious."

"How are they sending messages between worlds?"

"Courier ship."

Farragut made a sound of impatience. "Back to those ships again! Isn't there any mention of some—I don't know—extra step that gets the ships from one place to another. Displacement? Boost gate?"

"Of course there must be. But it's phrased in dubious and alien terms."

"What terms?"

"I don't know. You're the one with the language module. You find it."

"But you made this," Farragut gave the language module a shake. "I can't sift through years of broadcasts. You have to know."

"I forget." Augustus lay back down, coiled his long figure, one arm cradling his abdomen, turned his back on his captain, and closed his eyes, leaving Farragut standing in the compartment, as good as alone. Augustus had either gone to sleep or passed out. Outlets for cable connections showed in the base of his skull.

Captain Farragut ordered to his comatose back, so he would not have to bring him up on charges, "Stand down."

Merrimack had on board a distinguished civilian of immense knowledge and experience, *Don* Jose Maria Cordillera, a quietly magnetic presence on the space battleship. He was revered, even loved, by the company and crew for his humanity and for his personal mission, which he shared with the *Mack*: the complete destruction of the Hive.

He rose courteously from his desk as the captain entered his small quarters. A holographic projection had erased the close walls and opened the compartment to vistas of horses running across green-gold pastures, purple mountains on the hazy horizon, and swallows cavorting in the deep blue sky. Chlorophyll scents and a warm zephyr came from unseen vents. Potted plants, real ones, blended the illusion into the reality of Jose Maria's small living space.

"To what do I owe the honor, young Captain?"

Farragut handed Augustus' language module to Jose Maria Cordillera. "Can a man, even a Roman patterner, really have decoded an entire alien language in five hours? Or has Rome already been here and Augustus just brought this aboard with him?"

"Augustus can and did create this," said Jose Maria. Unrejuvenated, he still looked much younger than his fifty-seven years, even with the silver streaks in his long black hair. "I watched him do it. We had to excise parts of this module, actually. Sometimes his mind would digress into interesting patterns until he forced himself back to the translation project."

"That kind of ability—" Farragut started, searched for the right word. "It's inhuman."

"Yes," said Jose Maria. "It is. What must have been done to Augustus to make him so is also inhuman." He handed back the module gravely. "I was just reviewing some of his observations now. I have many questions for him."

"He's asleep."

"I shall not try to wake him."

Farragut doubted he could. Apparently, Augustus slept like a corpse.

A second recon patrol approached within two light-days of the F8 planet, Arra, and immediately spun around and came hying back to *Merrimack* as if in flames. "They know we're here!"

"How can they?" Farragut asked.

"You were seen," Steele accused his Marines.

"Not us, sir. You were. They've seen *Merrimack*."

And the recon flight played back a news broadcast from the planet Arra:

"Alpha Flight, what is your situation?"

"Up screwed! Man down! Man down!"

"That's Colonel Steele and Flight Sergeant Blue." Farragut recognized the voices. "Where did this recording come from?"

"From the planet," said the flight leader of the second recon patrol. "Arra. Every channel, every station, every city. They're playing it over and over like a national disaster. And they've got video."

On the playback, *Merrimack* appeared as a silhouette of menace, backed by the cluster's glow. Her shape vaguely approximated an antique spearhead, from the long angular shaft that was her central fuselage, to her flight decks delta-swept back on either side, and her top and bottom sails, also back swept to aid deflection. She made a majestic, cruel profile, half seen in the dark.

Then the Swifts—angry little hornets—bulleted from her wings to score the surrounding space with red tracers. Mines detonated with fiery sprays on all sides. And *Merrimack* herself opened up and heaved out a broadside. Vapor briefly shrouded her, hissing from her gunports. The halo of it caught the light of her guns, and the battleship seemed to be on fire. Her volleys, like lightning flashes, gave evanescent glimpses of her true dimension. Turrets swiveled like malevolent eyes.

"The natives have seen this?" Farragut asked, aghast. "They've gotta be scared to death."

"They are."

"This is scaring me, and it's my *Merrimack*!"

The transmission went abruptly black. "And right here must be when we took out the space buoy. Camera was in the buoy. The angle fits."

"So these pictures were taken way back there at the Rim. How did this signal cross the one hundred and ten light-years from the buoy to the F8 system?"

"That's a hell of a question, sir. Given that even two light-days from Arra, the best they're sending out is laser and electromag. We don't have a living clue how they received this."

Farragut turned to his XO. "Commander Carmel."

"Captain."

"Time to step it up. Get me to the planet— Planet name, somebody." He snapped his fingers.

"Arra," someone provided.

"Get me to Arra, now."

"Silent, sir?" Calli asked.

"Lordy, no. Light us up like the Jupiter Monument."

Swinging into orbit around the white-veiled, tourmaline world Arra, *Merrimack* was greeted with a salvo of missiles from the planet's surface.

The XO, Calli Carmel, issued orders for evasion.

Arran fighter spacecraft were scrambling aloft with ridiculous slowness.

Farragut arrived in the control room. "What are they bringing to bear?"

"Sublight missiles, sir. Unknown loads."

"Speed?"

Calli's mouth pulled wryly toward one cheek. "Oh, hell, John, I want to get out and help them push."

"Maybe I should spot them twelve runs and give them a pitcher," said Farragut. But not to fall victim to overconfidence, he checked, "Tac, do we have anyone sneaking up on us?"

"Negative," the tac specialist responded. "The only traffic from the planet is moving sublight and that's all running away."

"What about the fighters?"

"Arran fighter craft haven't even cleared the planetary atmosphere."

"How long till they clear?"

"Not for three minutes yet."

"Three—! I could die and be reincarnated twice in three minutes. Current disposition of the missiles?"

"Distance from *Merrimack* two hundred klicks. Velocity nine kps," tac responded, then quickly updated, "Distance two hundred and ten klicks." *Merrimack* was moving faster than the missiles.

"All right. Turn the missiles around."

"Sir?" his XO questioned.

"Flip 'em, Cal. Return to sender."

Before Calli could express horror, the captain added, "But detonate the warheads before they reenter atmosphere."

Calli dropped her voice, but the control room was not built for privacy. "That's not easy to do, Captain."

"I didn't ask if it was easy."

Commander Carmel still hesitated. "The captain is aware we could just keep walkin' away from these missiles."

"I am so aware. The order, XO."

"I don't want to miss one. If I fail to detonate one, I send a nuke into the Arran atmosphere."

"Then hit 'em before they reach atmosphere. We have enough guns."

"Requires precision shooting. We will be shooting toward the planet. If I miss—"

"Don't miss."

"Aye, sir." And from there, Calli issued orders in frosty efficiency to targeting and fire control, her voice sharp with obedient anger.

A reverse tractor pulse gently nudged the missiles about, sending them arcing back down for reentry. Targeting tracked them. Fire control stood by for detonation.

While anyone monitoring the situation from the planet had a view of the business end of their own weapons.

Captain Farragut let the Arrans suffer a minute of blind terror—watching their own monstrous weapons fall back toward their atmosphere—then issued the order for the passover.

"Calli. Be precise."

"Targeting, do we have a lock?"

"Lock achieved, aye."

"Fire control. Detonate Arran warheads."

"Detonating Arran warheads, aye."

Nuclear fire high above the atmosphere would be visible from the ground.

"Missiles secured," Calli reported without expression.

The tactical specialist reported the Arran fighter craft turning around and heading back toward base.

"Mr. Carmel, your ship," Farragut gave way to Calli. "I'm fixin' to go ashore. All departments, let me know everything I need to know. And somebody, figure out how to say: 'Take me to your leader.'"

* * *

Colonel Steele followed the captain from the control room. He had to hurry; John Farragut moved fast. Steele, commander of the ship's two Marine companies, offered privately, "I think we're looking too far away for these aliens' mother world."

Farragut stopped, turning in the narrow passageway. "Your patrols found something, TR? You know where Origin is?"

But Steele suggested flatly, "Ask the guy who speaks their language."

"You mean Augustus?"

"He cracked an alien language in five hours?" Steele asked in heavy suspicion. "Sure he did. These colonies are Roman plants, just like him."

"Wishful thinking, TR?"

So startled, Steele could say nothing more eloquent than, "Huh?"

"You want to shoot him," Farragut said.

A protest rose, died. Steele confessed, "I do."

Farragut smiled, clapped the lieutenant colonel on his broad shoulder. " 's okay, TR. I talked to Jose Maria. He says the translation feat is well within a Roman patterner's range. He also agrees that those boys downstairs are from way out of town. This is not a Roman plant."

Not well educated for his rank, Steele still did not swallow everything the multidegreed civilian experts on board pronounced as truth, trusting instead to his own instincts. But Nobel Laureate Jose Maria Cordillera was not an ordinary xeno. Known on board, reverently, as *Don* Cordillera, the Terra Rican aristocrat was a sophisticated, gentlemanly, Renaissance man. *Don* Cordillera knew everything. Smartest man God ever invented. Even TR Steele would not doubt *Don* Cordillera.

But Steele also knew that nothing good could come from a Roman.

The captain was an idiot.

That stupid, bright smile brightened the hatchway to Augustus' billet among the torpedoes. "Come down to the planet with me?" Farragut invited.

Augustus hesitated. "In person or VR?"

"In the flesh."

Augustus rolled his eyes, as if speaking to Heaven. "Why did I even have to ask? And me a patterner."

"You're not a patterner when you're not plugged in," said Farragut. "I found out you really did forget most of the Myriadian language right after you worked the translation. You wanted me to think you were just being stubborn. But you operate a lot like a computer. Once you unplug, most of the random access memory falls right out of your head." He waited for comment, idiotically proud of his discovery.

Augustus offered nothing in return. He had not been asked a question, and did not feel like being chatty with idiots.

Augustus' enigmatic stare could not deflate that bright-eyed buoyancy. The captain retained that doggy look — eager and full of infinite, idiotic goodwill, unasked for and unwanted.

Augustus noticed that Farragut had put no surveillance on him. No watchers. Augustus had scoured his own tracks for shadows, but the incredible truth was that there were none. Trusting to a fault, Farragut took in his enemy and turned around so fast it left nowhere to stab him but in the back.

And backstabbing was beneath Augustus. He wanted Farragut to get it looking him straight in the eyes.

Augustus supposed he was meant to appreciate this grand display of trust, and to resolve not to let his captain down. But Augustus disliked personality cults, and John Farragut led by force of personality. In a culture as deconstructed as that of the U.S., without a Roman sense of duty, their people were lost. Like ducklings, they imprinted on the first strong influence they met. And here they were, all of them quacking after confident, dynamic John Farragut.

"What did you think of my introduction to the Arrans?"

"You mean your stupid, grandstanding stunt with the Arran missiles?"

That only paused him for a moment. Farragut hadn't thought the stunt stupid. "I thought it would communicate our overwhelming superior force without launching our own weapons against them. I showed them we could destroy them, but that was not why we came. It worked. Monitors say the Arrans are coming out of their shelters to point at the light when we orbit over."

"They might just as easily have concluded that we like toying with our prey before we eat it. You assume the universe thinks like John Farragut, and I know for a fact that it doesn't. You are bold, forthright, cheerful—qualities you count on to bluff and charm your way through strange waters—but those qualities are not universally admired, I assure you. A stranger is as likely to see you as loud, undignified, vulgar, ignorant, inappropriately childish, and neglectful of my customs."

"Your customs? Was that a Freudian slip?"

"No slip. Quite on purpose."

"Did I do something to offend Rome?"

"Do? You did not do. You are. Your people obey you because they respect—not to mention adore—you."

"And you have a problem with that?"

"Romans lead by force of law. It doesn't matter if a Roman loathes his CO. He follows him to hell anyway. A Roman XO does not suggest a better way to deal with the incoming missiles when issued an order."

Augustus had been monitoring the control room during the encounter.

"Calli asked for clarification," Farragut excused his XO's balk.

"Callista Carmel was schooled on Palatine. Mr. Carmel knows that under a Roman captain, she would be in the brig right now. But she also knows she can get away with that yellow snow under John Farragut."

"You think Calli's question was a thinly veiled challenge to my authority?"

"Thinly veiled? It was damn near naked."

"Had more clothes on than your challenges, Augustus."

"And yet I am not in the brig. Why?"

"Because you want so badly to be there. Well, I'm sorry but it's going to take something very un-Roman and dishonorable like direct violation of orders for you to get there."

Augustus fell silent as a stone. Stared. Had not expected that kind of insight from this man. Was surprised to be surprised.

Very well. The captain was a shrewd idiot.

Farragut's smile returned. "So why are you so jolly eager to get into my brig, Augustus?"

"Frankly?"

"I'm pretty sure you can't do anything else. Yes, frankly."

"I believe Earth and Palatine to be natural enemies. Which is to say the U.S. and Palatine are natural enemies, given that the United States is the only military power worth mentioning on Earth. I am sworn to give my life to Rome. And Rome has seen fit to put its neck under the U.S. heel for the duration of the Hive threat. So here I am. I serve. I don't like it. I don't pretend to. I don't question a direct order in your own command center."

"And that grudge is not getting heavy, Augustus?"

"Can *you* shut off a hundred and fifty years of hostility as quickly as turning out a light?" Augustus countered.

"Oh, much faster than that," John said brightly.

Palatine was founded in the late twenty-third century by a private consortium on a planet two hundred light-years away from Earth in the constellation of the Southern Crown under a U.S. flag.

Once Palatine's infrastructure was in place, its land partially terraformed, the planet self-sufficient, and the government subsidy exhausted, the model colony declared its independence. Palatine, which also called itself Rome, summoned all true Romans from Earth.

And they answered. By the millions. Doctors, lawyers, judges, legislators, philosophers, historians, Catholic clergy, all manner of highly educated people for whom most Earth dwellers assumed the knowledge of Latin was merely a professional necessity or historical interest. Millions left Earth, forswore citizenship in their various nations and pledged allegiance to Eternal Rome.

The Roman Empire had never fallen. It had lived on in secret societies for more than two millennia. The very idea had been a laughable conspiracy theory for those two millennia. Until the Romans of Palatine erected their eagles over the capital of their dictatorial republic and the Senate installed a Caesar for life.

The United States, which had to date never tried to keep a colony by force, declared war on Palatine. The two worlds had remained at war, on and off, for the last one hundred fifty years.

Even during hostilities, Rome/Palatine spread its territory, founding other planetary colonies in its own name.

Palatine was not signatory to the League of Earth Nations Convention and did not restrict its colonization only to those planets without sapient natives. Alien civilizations were absorbed into the empire, some even willingly, attracted by Roman order, might, and technology.

Palatine excelled in mechanization and automation, thanks largely to a genius of his age, one Constantine Siculus, whose innovations were so devastating to the balance of power, that the U.S. Central Intelligence considered kidnapping him. Rome killed him first, after he set himself up as King Constantine of one of Palatine's own colonies. Rome cloned him, of course, but Constantine's clones hadn't his inventive genius. The cloners neglected to consider the impact personal experience had on the formation of the human brain; and the clones were simply not the same person.

Still Palatine grew from renegade colony into a rival, then a menace. Roman Legions, both human and robotic, swept across the galactic south of Near space and headed across the Orion Starbridge toward the galaxy's Sagittarian arm, a territory called the Deep. When Rome claimed the whole of the Sagittarian constellation as a Roman province, to the farthest end of the galaxy, no one could dispute them, even though no human had ever been to the far side of the Milky Way, much less to its far Rim. Just traversing the two thousand parsecs to the Deep took the fastest ship three months.

Then, in AD 2389, the U.S. stunned all the nations of Earth and all the known worlds with the unveiling of a colossal displacement conduit, the Fort Roosevelt/Fort Eisenhower Shotgun. Displacement was known technology; the Shotgun was just bigger. Instead of displacing people and goods from orbiting ships to planet surfaces, the Shotgun displaced whole carriers—U.S. battle carriers—instantaneously from Fort Roosevelt in Near space to Fort Eisenhower in the Deep, deeper than the Romans had ever gone.

And planted American flags in Sagittarius.

Human territory still only comprised a fraction of the galaxy. The unknown was far greater.

In early 2436, Romans ran into something horrible. They did not know it at first. At first they knew only that they had lost a ship, the *Sulla*, in the Deep.

Searcher after searcher disappeared. Even when Rome found the monsters behind the path of destruction, the Empire kept silent. Deep end colonies were eaten alive. Hive impulses caused a million Roman killer bots to self-destruct, and Rome maintained its swaggering mask of invincibility.

It was not until Captain John Farragut and the space battleship *Merrimack* met a Hive swarm and lived to tell about it that Rome sued for peace and asked for help.

The U.S.S. *Merrimack* was the only ship ever to survive a Hive swarm once engaged.

The U.S. agreed to assist, but only on the condition that Rome put its military command under U.S. control. It was a measure of the disaster that Caesar Magnus agreed.

So, in 2443, Rome and the U.S. became locked in an unhappy, unholy alliance, united only in their quest to exterminate the monsters at the edge of the map.

And John Farragut and Augustus became the least likely pair of officers ever to serve aboard the same space battleship.

"During the hostilities I was ordered to suicide before letting myself fall into Earth hands," said Augustus. "Now here I am ordered to serve a U.S. commander. Not just a U.S. commander, but John Alexander Farragut." The words said *John Alexander Farragut*, but the tone clearly said *John the flaming idiot Farragut*.

John Farragut had dealt Rome one of its few defeats in a battle for ownership of a planet.

"You're ready to fall on your sword?" Farragut asked lightly. "Take cyanide?"

"That's a big joke to you, isn't it?" Augustus pulled the cap off a back tooth, produced a tiny vial. "There's your joke." He replaced the vial and the cap.

Farragut's brows twisted, one perplexedly higher than the other. "Ever hear the line, 'No son of a bitch ever won a war by dying for his country?' "

Augustus replied in irony, "Of course. That's why there are monuments to the dead at Thermopylae, Masada, the Alamo, and Corindahlor."

"You don't suppose the Romans at Corindahlor Bridge would rather have lived?"

Augustus bridled in personal ownership. "Don't *ever*

presume you know what was in the minds of the Romans at Corindahlor."

Corindahlor was before Farragut's time. "And you do?"

"No. Honestly, I don't." Augustus sat back, murmured to himself, "What could they have been thinking?"

"You would rather commit suicide than take orders from me? I'd have thought orders to live and serve rather than die and serve would be a relief."

"Shows your own self-serving priorities. I was assigned to you because John Farragut is where the Hive is. In wide-open space, it's John Farragut who gets into the furballs. How do you do that?"

Farragut laughed. "I have no idea!"

"I believe that," Augustus said dryly. The man was clueless. "They gave me to you the sooner to eliminate the Hive. Doesn't make us lovers."

"Doesn't it even make us friends? Civil acquaintances?"

"Earth is next in line if the Hive eats its way past Palatine, so I don't overestimate Earth's compassion. And you would be well advised not to overestimate Rome's gratitude."

3

MARINES SNAPPED TO ATTENTION at Colonel Steele's barking entrance into the fighter craft maintenance bay, which doubled as the Marines' parade deck. "Hallahan!"

"Sir!"

"Jaxon!"

"Sir!"

"Li!"

"Yo! Sir!"

"Blue!"

Kerry Blue straightened, tried to look keen, shocked to be called. "Sir!"

Steele's pale blue eyes narrowed at her. "You all here, Blue?"

"Yes, sir!" Kerry shouted, spirits rising. She was done crying over that lying, cheating, gorgeous bastard Cowboy. A tear stole down Kerry's face. She dashed it away. Well, almost done.

The colonel ignored it. Turned away, barking more names.

Nothing like a mission—a big one—to drag you out of yourself. Colonel Steele was taking Kerry Blue down with the captain to meet the aliens. Kerry refrained from gushing thanks.

The names ended. Kerry was peripherally aware of Reg standing at attention next to her, shoulders slightly slumping, not called. Steele was giving orders for the chosen ones to collect weapons from the armory and to kit up in dress whites and dog collars. Steele exited as briskly as he'd come.

He had not ordered exo equipment—Arra had a nitrox atmosphere, hot, heavy, but breathable at sea level—not even sunglasses. It would not be hideously bright down there, even in the starry cluster; it would be nighttime where the Archon's palace stood when the ship's party went down. They were calling the leader of the three-world nation an "Archon."

This was not just a prime mission, a first contact, but Kerry was getting out of the can and breathing real air. And she was *not* one of those poor sods who were sent on recon to the other two inhabited systems. She could not believe her luck.

At Kerry's side, Reg hissed, "Hell, Blue! Who'd you go to bed with to pull this duty?"

Kerry could more easily name soldiers she hadn't slept with, but fraternization with officers never got anyone anywhere but back to Earth with a dishonorable discharge. "Hell if I know. Steele musta drank something that killed the brain cell that knew who I was—and *don't you remind him.*"

"Do you think if I trash Cowboy's pod I can go on a first contact sortie? What'd you lay on Steele anyway?"

"Nothing!" She couldn't even imagine *that.* "That man has never liked me. He thinks I'm a fu."

Carly ganged in from Kerry's other side: "Yeah, that's why you're going planetside. I think he's hot for you, *chica linda.*"

"He's got a hard-on for me, that's for sure," Kerry muttered.

"Wish I were on his shit list," Reg sulked.

"Yeah, yeah, yeah," Kerry conceded anything they wanted to throw at her. "Just tell me how to get beer stains out of dress whites."

A snicker sounded behind them—that big baboon, Dak Shepard. "Right. Blue's gonna try 'n' tell us those are beer stains. Uh-huh."

"Shut up, Dak."

* * *

Wrinkled dress whites flashed down the ladder rails between decks, a crushed cap clenched between teeth. Captain Farragut blinked at the fleeting apparition, trying to identify the glimpse. Guessed: "Kerry Blue?"

"I didn't give her the name, Captain," said Steele, as if it were the name itself that provoked the captain's skepticism.

"Cowboy's Kerry Blue?"

"She does not belong to Cowboy," Steele said.

Farragut knew who Kerry Blue was. "Your reports on her don't exactly glow, TR. Why is she coming ashore? She's not honor guard material."

"She doesn't get nitrogen narcosis." *Rapture of the deep*, divers called it. Nitrogen at pressure could disorient the susceptible. "When the fur flies, there's no she-dog I'd rather have at my back. I know she'll be there. She don't cross t's, and she don't pass inspection. But no combat-ready unit ever passed inspection."

"You expecting combat?"

"Ready for it."

Farragut nodded. "Make her pass inspection."

"Yes, sir." Steele took the captain's dismissal.

Didn't know what he was thinking when he chose Kerry Blue.

Kerry Blue. The tough/pretty girl Marine with the stupid name who had the starring role in all his wet dreams. Likable girl, good looking in a rough and ready sort of way. Better looking since she ran out of eye makeup. Girl-next-door pretty. The next car door. TR Steele had grown up in a trailer park. There was always a Kerry in the back seat of the next car.

Trailer *park*. An idyllic name for a slum where the landless lived in their mobile shelters stacked three high in the unpretty part of town with hard men, slutty women, and mongrel dogs. And when someone else needed the land, you hitched your gypsy home behind your current mode of transportation, be it pony, ox, automobile, or grid transit car, and moved to another park.

Kerry Blue was trailer trash, indestructible, rangy, loose-jointed. Breasts enough that you knew there was a woman under the uniform, small enough for you to know they weren't bought. Wide shoulders, little waist, superb ass. A lot of motion in her walk. Kerry Blue wore her brown hair pulled back rather than buzz it off. It probably brushed the tops of her shoulders when she let it down.

TR Steele spent too much time thinking about what Flight Sergeant Kerry Blue would look like with her hair down.

She was a great little dog soldier, but unfortunately there was no way in any conscience he could ever recommend her for a commission. So he could just forget about ever seeing Kerry Blue with her hair down.

"You're not a lubber, are you?"

Augustus looked up from his headache. His glower through pain-squinted eyelids answered no.

"We have therapy for space sickness," Farragut offered. And with his saying so, the deck gave a burp, setting them on an eight-degree list. John Farragut put a foot to the bulkhead to stay himself until the deck settled.

A battleship did not rest quiet on the vacuum sea. It heaved and bulged and adjusted within its distortion field. *Merrimack* was not a passenger liner. Fine-tuning was not worth the expense and maintenance of achieving it on a military vessel. The distortions—which allowed for shipboard gravity, for FTL travel, and for hard turns without fatal load shifts and crushing inertial drag—were tuned within working tolerances only. A semblance of Earthlike gravity was needed for the crew to maintain bone mass on long voyages; but it didn't have to be pretty.

You could not even say *Merrimack* rocked. Sway, she might, but having done so, she felt no compulsion to fall back and cant the other way. She swayed and she kept going, drew up short against a damper and left one with an unsettled wanting to tip back upright. Space legs needed acquiring. New hands spent much time in the head.

Augustus roused himself up on one elbow. "I am *not* space sick. I have a lot on my *mind.*"

Farragut glanced about the torpedo storage bay, the bunk netting strung kitty-corner. "I'll get you better quarters."

"Don't put yourself out."

"I wasn't going to put myself out. I was going to put the quartermaster out."

Augustus let the issue pass with an indolent wave of his hand.

"I have an audience with the Archon of the Myriad," said Farragut. "Coming down with us? You feel well enough?"

Augustus slowly uncoiled, rose. "The two questions are unrelated. The answers are yes to the first; the second is irrelevant."

At the appointed time, John Farragut, captain of the *Merrimack*; Jose Maria Cordillera, civilian biologist and Nobel Laureate; Lieutenant Colonel TR Steele, commander of the Marine companies; Colonel Augustus, the Intelligence Officer; several of the xenos; and the Marine guard assembled in the ship's displacement bay, each person posted on a transmitter disk, each with a dog collar snapped round his neck. Without the transmitters, receivers, and collars, the margin of error in displacement was far, far too risky for human transport.

The receivers—landing disks—preceded them down. The LDs arrived like an artillery barrage, banging into thick air and clattering and spinning down to rest on the palace's gem-encrusted floor. One disk missed low; embedded itself like a bomb with a resounding crack and spray of semiprecious stones. Augustus wondered if anyone had told the Arrans what to expect.

Captain Farragut yawned, popped his ears, as the displacement chamber gradually pressurized to five Earth atmospheres, to prevent the abrupt transition to Arran sea level from hammering the party's sinuses in.

Augustus, standing with the Marines, muttered aside to Lieutenant Colonel Steele: "It's a pity your uniforms are so utilitarian. The Archon himself is dressed fairly sedately, but his guard has all the ceremonial gold-trimmed gew-gaws that dictators like. Can't your Marines loop some curtain cords round their armpits and wear big furry hats and hang gold mops on their epaulets? At least put on your medals, Steele. Don't you have enough ribbons to fill up your chest yet?"

Steele flushed. Kept his icy blue eyes fixed straight ahead. Hissed, "You are so full of it."

"You make it too easy."

The *Merrimack* vanished around them.

* * *

At the hour of the Archon's command, just after sundown, the beings from outer space thunderclapped into existence on the black disks in the Archon's audience hall.

Heat enfolded Captain Farragut, air so thick you wore it. His first breath was fragrant, lush, heavy with sea air and living scents.

The landing disks, besides ensuring an intact displacement, bristled with sensors, so John Farragut already knew what would meet his eyes. He was not prepared for the vivid immediacy of it, the astonishing beauty. He could only afford a moment to take it in, the touch of breezes, hot and humid, on his skin; the sound of sea waves rushing softly from somewhere.

Lofty skylights let the starlight in. Wide arches opened to a terrace overlooking an expansive reflecting pool upon which the stars scintillated huge as moons in a deep blue heaven. The moons themselves shone like pale numinous wafers occulting the radiant stars.

Farragut marshaled his attention to the humanoids in the lyrically grand chamber.

Male guards, decked in uncomfortable, showy regalia, regarded him warily with dark, almond eyes.

Tall, deer-eyed, sylphlike women, with flowing manes and elfin faces, clustered along one wall, exchanging glances and private signals, their willowy forms draped to the floor in pastel gauze.

The Archon. The only one who did not gasp or shrink back as the visitors flashed and crackled into existence. Even on an alien face, the Archon's look of satisfaction was unmistakable. His black eyes gleamed. A contained air of power. In charge and accustomed to it.

The Archon was short. Stately as a handsome animal. He wore a shirt of loose, crisp white linenlike weave, with wide boxy sleeves, and a v-slash down the back to accommodate his neat short mane. His loose black trousers would look quite in place in an Aikido practice.

Behind him towered a monumental inscription—what looked to be an inscription—carved in rose granite over a massive throne, but no translation came to mind as Captain Farragut tried to read it, and he feared his language module had failed him. This first encounter could be very sticky without an accurate translator.

The Archon took a quick survey of the aliens, seemed to be deciding which to address. He dismissed the rank of Marines out of hand. Regarded the scientists briefly, discarded them, too. Did not even glance at Augustus. Quickly narrowed his choices down to Jose Maria Cordillera and Captain Farragut.

The various colors may have confused him. The xeno, Dr. Ling was golden amber; Flight Sergeant Blue was brown; Flight Sergeant Jaxon blacker than the Arran night standing at attention next to Colonel TR Steele, who was as white as humans came.

We look like a litter of Labrador Retrievers, thought Captain Farragut amid the monochromatic Arrans. Farragut wanted to prompt the Archon, but had been advised to let the Archon speak first. And he got the impression that the Archon did not want to be helped. Black eyes flicked between Farragut and Cordillera, searching for signs of leadership.

Dr. Jose Maria Cordillera's coloring was closest to the Arran red-brown; his bearing that of a diplomat. A striking man in any setting. Slender, cat-muscled. Jose Maria Cordillera made a dignified, aristocratic presence. His long dark hair, cinched with a silver clasp, flowed down his back like a Myriadian's mane. The Archon wanted it to be Dr. Cordillera.

But he turned to the captain and recited in conclusion, "John Farragut, captain of the U.S.S. *Merrimack*."

With a blinding smile, Farragut greeted him in turn: "Archon Donner."

The Archon returned a very human smile, then corrected his visitor, "Archon. Or Donner. Together is insistent or redundant."

"Captain Farragut," Farragut also corrected. "The rest is too long."

The Archon breathed a light gasp, delighted. "You understood me! You speak my language!" Reciting names was one thing. This alien had just spoken an entire Myriadian sentence.

"Not well," Farragut warned.

The Archon took two goblets from a waiting server and offered one to Captain Farragut.

Customs varied as widely as the stars, but one stood

nearly universal among humanoids as a symbol of unity, trust, and friendship—the sharing of food and drink. It sealed most friendships and just about all unions that could be called marriages.

Hesitation would not wear. There was no doubting the offering's safety, and safety was not the concern. Protocol was. Farragut asked, "Does one just drink, or are there words to be said?" He did not want to slug back the drink if there was a proper ritual to be observed.

The Archon instructed, "If you choose to accept, you drink first."

Augustus, his voice a low murmur across the room, like the waves' rush, footnoted in English, ("The implication being: if you choose not to drink, you are enemies.")

Farragut lifted his glass in a toast, Earth fashion. "To your health." And drank.

In deathly silence, the Arrans glared at him. The Archon's smile vanished.

The cold, sparkling drink went down tastelessly. Something wrong here.

Augustus again, in English: ("The crashing you don't hear is the sound of a giant brick dropping.")

("What did I do?") John hissed.

("You 'you'd' the Archon as an equal.")

("I meant to.")

("He doesn't like it.")

Farragut lifted his brows in a kind of shrug.

The Archon declared coldly, "I am not accustomed to being talked to so!" Then, suddenly amicable again, declared, "From you, I shall take it."

Donner had changed his own choice of *you*. He upgraded Farragut to an equal. The Archon's glass lifted in imitation. "To your health." Donner drank, and the room exhaled.

The empty glasses went away so unobtrusively John Farragut did not notice them going. The Archon's servants were well practiced at being unnoticeable.

Donner introduced no one and asked no names of Captain Farragut's delegation. There was only Donner and Captain Farragut. Everyone else in the room was furniture.

Ill-mannered furniture. Two of the xenos were whispering together, taking great interest in the floor—a mosaic of precious and semiprecious stones set in lead. Cracks in it and in the marble pillars suggested an unquiet earth. The xenos were discussing seismology; the Archon only saw them eyeing the jewels.

"You came prospecting!" Donner accused Farragut.

"I don't know how you boys do things on Arra, but where I come from you don't call your guests thieves," said Farragut. This encounter was being recorded. Farragut imagined LEN diplomats having seizures at this point in the replay.

"Then you are not claiming my world?" Donner asked, somewhat mollified.

"Of course not. You got here first."

The whites flared in the Archon's dark eyes. The room stirred.

("The discreet approach, hm, John?")

("I was just imitating the Archon. He's blunt.")

("Dictators can dish it out, but they don't usually take it well.")

And the Archon had had quite enough of the English backchat. He raised his voice, "This is the same as whispering! Thou shalt not whisper in my presence! When you speak, speak to me!"

"I need advice on how to speak to you," Farragut explained. "I'm new at this language. No disrespect intended. (And, oh shit, Augustus, what did I say now? He's glaring at me.)"

("You used the imperial 'I.' ")

But the Archon resumed a magnanimous air and allowed, "You speak my language better than I speak yours."

"Thank you."

Augustus: ("He's not as pissed as he pretends. We're on camera. A lot of this posturing is for show.")

The Archon stalked across the vast expanse of jeweled floor to give Augustus a hard look up and down. At five foot seven, the Archon looked absolutely diminutive before the six-foot-eight Roman. Donner asked dubiously, "This is a female?"

Colonel Steele smirked.

("It's the height, shrimp,") Augustus shot back in English to six-foot Steele, who had never been called "shrimp" in his life. ("Look at the women.")

Farragut answered the Archon, "He is not female. He is tall."

"Where are you from?" the Archon demanded.

"My planet is called Earth. Augustus' planet is called Palatine, but his people came originally from Earth."

The duality surprised Donner. "Where is Earth? Where is Palatine?"

"A long way from here."

"Outside?" Donner circled the air with a forefinger. He had human hands, four fingers per hand, opposable thumbs. "Outside my Myriad?"

"Outside the globular cluster, yes."

"Where? How far?"

("Okay, somebody give me a distance in local units!") Farragut called to all present.

A xeno fed him the Myriadian translation of six thousand, four hundred parsecs.

The Archon looked profoundly impressed by the reply. The females looked quite vacant, as if they could not count that high.

Donner asked in wonderment, "Where is the *kzachin* you came by?"

Farragut glanced to Augustus, as all the xenos tapped at the language modules.

("I'm pulling up 'hollow,' for *kzachin*,") said Farragut, perplexed. ("Is he saying they travel between planets by 'hollows' or did he change the subject again?")

Augustus answered in Myriadian, "Ask the Archon if his people used the *kzachin* to travel to this world from Origin."

Donner reacted as if a chair had spoken. He would not address a minion, so rather than ask Augustus to explain himself, Donner demanded from Farragut, "What do you know of Origin!"

Farragut deferred. "Colonel Augustus, what do we know of Origin?"

Augustus answered immediately, "The sun is orange. The air is thin. The oceans are less than one percent saline. Origin is larger than Arra, but it is sixty percent the density. Native-born *T'Arraiet* have a much higher bone density than natives of Origin. A day on Origin is thirty percent longer than on Arra. The period of revolution around Origin's sun is roughly half a *T'Arra* year. How are we doing?"

Donner looked astonished.

("I sense a direct hit, Mr. Holmes,") Farragut commented to his Roman Intelligence Officer in English.

Donner exclaimed, "You have been to Origin!"

Farragut shook his head, then remembered that the gesture did not translate. Spoke, "No. It's all deduction. From what you are, he can figure back to where you must have come. He is particularly gifted that way."

"May I have him?"

Refusing a request for a gift was always a dicey thing. Farragut demurred, "Actually, he is on loan to me. He is not mine to give."

Donner beckoned the captain closer, advised softly, "Then you should give him back. He bears you no good."

Farragut nodded. Very astute observation from an alien species. But then one would not expect the Archon to be the dimmest star in the cluster.

"Can you tell me, then, where Origin is?" Donner challenged.

Before the captain could answer, a large, collared animal trotted into the chamber. A boxy-headed, muscular dog-thing. It looked up at its adored master, Donner, then veered to the line of Marines along the wall.

The husky dog-thing raised its hackles and growled at Colonel Steele.

The Archon pointed at Steele. "That one bears me ill." The Archon's guards stiffened, and the Marines stiffened in response.

"No," Farragut tried to tell him.

"Oh, he does," Donner insisted, knowing.

"He does," Colonel Steele confirmed for him.

And on second look, Farragut agreed that gentle lies were probably a bad approach here. He explained, "My ship tripped a minefield at the perimeter of your Myriad. Colonel Steele lost a man."

"The minefield was not meant for you," said Donner. "You must not take it as hostility, Captain Farragut." Donner offered no apology to Steele.

"Who were the mines meant for?" Farragut asked.

"Not for you."

His dog-thing growled.

"Oh, *sit* down!" the Archon commanded.

The dog-thing squared itself like a gargoyle opposite Colonel Steele, sat.

The Arran women tittered behind long, graceful hands, an infectious sound, and in a moment the Earth Marines lost the fight to contain their sniggers. Donner scowled at the women, and Farragut stared at his Marines in confusion. ("What *is* it?")

At that, the Marines sputtered, and the Arran women bubbled with giggles.

Flight Sergeant Cole blurted in English, ("They look like bookends, sir!")

Kerry Blue yelped, stifled a laugh with a whimper. The Arran women tittered, not understanding the words, but the pitch of the voices translated well enough.

"Bookends," Augustus translated, and the Arran women squealed. The Arran guards' lips unstiffened, perilously close to cracking their stony faces.

The Archon stalked to the lieutenant colonel, had to look up to study Steele's dour face—his white-blond hair buzzed flat across the top of his squarish head; his eyes of vivid, piercing blue; his brawny shoulders set straight across.

Donner turned then to his growling, blocky, muscular dog-thing. "I see it."

The women's laughter sparkled.

"What happened to him?" Donner asked Farragut.

Farragut puzzled a moment. Donner's question seemed to refer to Colonel Steele. "Nothing. What do you see that you think is wrong with him?"

"His color."

Farragut was a loss of how to explain Steele's fairness. "That is just his color."

"He has hideous eyes. Yours are merely ugly. His eyes are creepy."

"The women don't think so," Augustus said.

The Archon jerked up short. Partly that the furniture was talking again, and partly from what the furniture said. Donner turned sourly to his women, demanded doubtfully, "Is this so?"

The sylphs dissolved into high, musical Geisha giggles.

The Archon turned away, miffed and mystified. "Well.

Blue eyes. Who could have guessed women liked blue eyes?" Donner returned to Colonel Steele, pointed to the black bars bracketing the outer corners of Steele's eye sockets. "What are those?"

Farragut hesitated, answered, "Cameras."

"And what more?"

The hesitation had not escaped notice. Donner heard the missing "and." Surprising, the nuances that the alien could detect.

Bluntness was apparently the wisest course. "And gun sights," Farragut let the other shoe drop.

"Ah. Is this a gun?" The Archon reached, but Steele's hand clapped over his side arm first.

The Archon's guards bridled, but Donner backed them down, and Steele barked his Marines into line.

Farragut maintained a calm, friendly manner. "Yes, those are guns. Colonel Steele, indulge our host."

Steele briskly unsnapped the flap, unholstered the side arm, and flipped it around, butt end out.

The Archon fit his small hand around the fat grip. "How does this work?"

"It doesn't," said Farragut. "It is coded to its issuant. In your hand, it's a lump of metal."

Of course, the Archon would have to try it. Testing the truth as much as the weapon, the Archon pointed the weapon at Steele, pulled the trigger.

Nothing happened.

Donner smiled. Steele had not blinked.

"What an excellent idea. You must tell me how it is done." He was speaking to Farragut. He relinquished the weapon to Colonel Steele. Donner then pointed to Captain Farragut's sword. "Ceremonial?"

"Actually not. We use them."

The Archon gave a disbelieving cough. Then guessed, "So that you do not poke holes in your spaceship?"

"Oh, I have put holes in my ship," Farragut admitted merrily. "The force field keeps the vacuum out. I am more worried about hitting one of my own guys on the other side of the bulk. This is a useful antique, like Morse code."

"Like . . . ?" *Morse code* did not translate.

"Don't ever throw out your old technology, Donner." Farragut probably ought not advise a new contact, but he had made an instant primitive connection with this alien leader. "Swords are useful." That and John Farragut liked 'em.

Kerry Blue, standing at attention, lost track of the conversation, distracted by a tickle on the back of her neck. She knew there was a white ledge lined with plants high behind her head. The tickle felt like a leaf from a hanging vine touching her neck hairs. She edged discreetly forward. The touch returned, grazed her cap.

Finally she cranked her head back and up to look at the plants.

The plants looked at her.

Under thick coats of iguana green, nictitating membranes flicked over saurian eyes. A very long sticky tongue flicked experimentally to Kerry's cheek.

With wooden slowness, Kerry returned to face forward, adamantly ignoring the lizard plants.

The Archon and the Arran women were chuckling at something the captain had just said.

The Archon explained that no one had used that expression in at least ten years. Augustus had made these language modules when the ship was still ten light-years from Arra, so the slang was a little stale.

A plant stepped down and perched on Kerry's shoulder. Kerry straightened, rigid. Hissed between her teeth: ("*Colonel!*")

The tongue flicked into her ear. She shut her eyes. ("*Colonel Steele!*")

The Marine nearest Steele nudged the colonel and cocked a head sideways to direct the CO's attention Kerryward.

The plant hunkered down on Kerry's shoulder and crooned.

Steele strode out of line, pulled the plant from Kerry's shoulder, and tossed it back up to its ledge.

("Thank you, sir,") Kerry whispered.

The Archon broke off his conversation with the captain and looked quite cross. Kerry assumed that the side chatter had offended him. But Donner's onyx glare was not for the visitors.

"Why are my plants walking?" The soft anger in the Archon's voice promised someone would catch hell later.

Cowed servants scurried to fill shallow white bowls on

the ledges with water. There followed the soft lapping of froglike tongues.

The contented plants hunched down into their places and turned their green leaves to the starlight. The servants vanished.

And Kerry's pet dropped back down to her shoulder. Put a webby foot on her cheek. Crooned.

The Archon broke off again and stalked toward her.

The plant squeaked and dived down the back of Kerry's impeccable white uniform.

The Archon's jewel-black eyes bored into hers. Kerry scoured her language module for words. "I—I got a plant down my back. Sir."

The Archon looked her up and down hard. The fugitive plant, huddling against Kerry's back, pulled her jacket tight across her chest. The Archon's gaze paused at the suggestion of breasts beneath the dress whites.

Donner turned back to Captain Farragut, hesitated, as if fearing he was about to say something incredibly ignorant, "Is this . . . is this a *female?*"

"Yes, Flight Sergeant Blue is female."

"She is pregnant," Donner surmised.

Kerry blurted earnestly to Steele, to Farragut, (*"No*, sirs! I'm not!")

The willowy Arran females looked to be rather flat chested, from what one could see of their figures under all that drapery. Perhaps they only developed breasts when they were pregnant.

Donner looked amazed. "May I have her?"

"No," said Colonel Steele.

Donner darted Steele a nettled glare. "Captain Farragut, is this one permitted to speak for you?"

"Colonel Steele may answer for his Marines," said Farragut.

The Archon puzzled over this lack of absolute authority, when suddenly, the soldier nearest to the soaring arches clutched his weapon to the ready, dropped into a crouch facing the terrace, and yelled: ("Hive! Hive! Hive! Hive!")

All the Marines drew and turned. The Archon's guards also drew their weapons but did not know which way to point. They saw the aliens brandishing weapons out toward their peaceful lake garden.

Kerry's plant must have sensed her alarm as she dashed out to take a position on the terrace, because it wrapped its tendrils around her waist and flattened itself to her back, quivering.

Captain Farragut touched his dog collar, spoke into the link, ("Hive sign planetside. Report, *Merrimack*. Calli, what do you have?")

Sensors in the planetside landing disks showed the exec aboard *Merrimack* not just a full view of the Archon's reception hall, but also the temperature, atmospheric content, and composition of the furnishings. But apparently no view outside, because Calli answered, ("*Merrimack*, aye. What do you see, John? Tell me where to look. We're quiet up here. Shipboard telltales are not, repeat NOT, showing Hive sign.")

("We've got a swarm of insects.")

("Do you want me to shoot the flare? Come back.")

("Negative. Do not resonate. Do NOT resonate. Stand by.")

("*Merrimack* standing by.")

The Arrans milled about, mildly perplexed, slightly alarmed but only by the aliens' behavior. The Arran females giggled tentatively.

Farragut turned to the Archon. "Donner, is that swarming normal behavior for those—" Farragut could not locate the Myriadian word, finished in English, ("Butterflies?")

The Archon said dubiously, "You are afraid of a swarm of *iffretiet*?" Donner gestured out toward the fluttering swarm across the lake.

"Do they usually swarm like that?" Farragut asked.

"Yes. Is it not well?"

Farragut touched his collar. ("*Merrimack*. Farragut. False alarm. Mr. Carmel, pretend it's not. We have native species mimicking Hive sign. Run it down anyway. Assume the Hive has found a way to fox our shipboard early warning.")

("Aye, sir.")

Captain Farragut turned to the Archon. "We will return to our ship now."

"Because of a cloud of, how did you say it, 'butterflies'?"

"Before we make ourselves look any more ridiculous."

The Archon paused, absorbing the words, then laughed out loud, surprised. Still, a guarded look lingered in his alien eyes, as he reflected how strong one needed to be to admit such weakness. "I shall address my people. You must stand with me and give your message of peace."

Augustus warned in a murmur, ("If you appear on camera with him, you validate his authority.")

Farragut sidestepped the Archon's demand without a direct refusal. "We will talk again."

Donner was about to insist they stay, then seemed to catch sight of the pit into which his authority was about to fall. The Archon could not afford to insist and be refused. He stopped, smiled, *commanded* his visitors to go. "Your ship needs you. You shall go quickly. You shall come back."

Captain Farragut nodded, then remembered to interpret his nod for the aliens, "Yes." And to his party: ("Fall in. Disks all. Blue, lose the plant.")

Donner pointed to Kerry Blue. "I want her to stay."

Objection blazed in Colonel Steele's icy-blue eyes. But *I want* from the Archon had the force of an imperative. Refusal was hazardous.

Captain Farragut answered, "Flight Sergeant Blue is on duty. She may accept an invitation when she gets off duty. She is allowed to refuse and I cannot make her go. That is our way."

Donner's eyes rounded. No telling whether the concept of *asking* a female or the captain's inability to contravene her answer was the more shocking.

("The plant, Blue.")

("Tryin', sir.") The lizard plant wriggled within Kerry's jacket. This after she and Reg and Twitch had put so much effort into making her uniform look honor-guard crisp, too. ("Whoa, darlin'. That really tickles. Help!")

Jose Maria Cordillera came to her rescue, fishing out the plant with a clinical grope. It emerged keening, leaves bristling, bulgy eyes soulful, wide-splayed toes reaching for Kerry.

The eyes, the pitiable sounds melted Kerry's heart. ("Can I keep it?")

Cordillera frowned kindly. ("Kerry, look at the light here. And this is what they call *dark*. It will not like the ship. Let us put your friend back with his mates, shall we?")

("Is it a boy?")

Cordillera hoisted the leafy tail for a quick look. ("I have not the foggiest clue.") Tail down. ("Come on. Send him home.") He bundled the plant into her hands.

Kerry had been crying for days. She thought she was done with that, but a tear stole down her cheek. A froggy tongue licked her face.

She gently replaced the creature up on its ledge. It hurt, putting away something that liked her. Kerry Blue felt in sore need of *liking*.

She took her place on her LD. She just knew Colonel Steele was never going to let her out of the can again.

At the captain's signal to the ship, the starry, starry sky, the soaring white columns, the reflecting pool, the bright swarming butterflies vanished around her. She did not hear her own parting thunderclap.

4

MERRIMACK'S COMPRESSION CHAMBER formed around the landing party. Chill. Dry.

No sooner had they arrived, and the captain was pulling off his dog collar. "Right. Anyone tell me what I drank down there?" He flipped his landing disk up with his foot, caught it.

"Ever consider to be thinking of asking that question before you are swallowing the alien substance?" Dr. Shah asked through the chamber's com. "More circumspection concerning what you are ingesting is being in order, I am thinking."

"'Excuse me while I see if your gift is any good' doesn't make for fast friends. Anyway, what can it hurt, Mo? Arran germs are all right-handed. And Donner's an interstellar colonist, so he knows that, too."

Earth's basic genetic code was not universal. The pre-Star Age fear of alien infection had been much ado about nothing. The molecular structure of the Myriadian proteins did not even share an orientation—a handedness—with human proteins, much less a base code.

"Arsenic has no hands," said Mo Shah.

"You told me these boys were lightweights, Mo. I can hold anything they can. Anyway, I didn't taste anything bitter. I tasted alcohol." Robust even among humans, John

Farragut ought to be able to drink any Myriadian under the table.

"I am only using arsenic as an example," said Dr. Shah through the com. "You are assuming your drink was being the same as the Archon's drink. The Myriadians are being expert poisoners."

Xenobiologist Dr. Weng added over the intercom, "The Myriadians have some nasty inorganic poisons. Particularly something they call yellow gas. It's yellow—"

A muttered growl from Dr. Sidowski sounded in the background: "Gee, I wonder why they call it yellow gas."

As Weng continued: "—and the smell, well, no one knows what it smells like. If you smell it, it's too late. It enters through the mucus membranes and does serious nerve damage—"

Ski, talking over Weng: "A total brain fry."

Weng: "—just like that."

Ski, with an audible finger snap: "Just like that."

Weng: "Yellow gas is lethal in parts per trillion."

John Farragut cut the xenos off equably, "I was rather counting on Donner wanting me alive and friendly." He turned to his IO in the decompression chamber with him. "Augustus, what was that remark you made about my validating the Archon's authority? Is his authority in question?"

"Opposition must exist," said Augustus.

Dr. Patrick Hamilton was outside the compression chamber, but you could sense him bristling against the Roman's all-knowing attitude as he announced with great authority over the com, "We have detected absolutely no evidence of any political dissension, or anything like an opposition party, any civil discontent whatsoever in Myriadian society."

"Which in itself argues my point," said Augustus, unruffled, rather bored. "As a true dictator, Donner controls all the media and all the dissemination of information. Given that he has suppressed any breath of criticism, the likelihood of discontent festering appears all the more certain. Totalitarianism may go over smoothly with those compliant muffins who pass for women in this species, but there must be a male somewhere on these three worlds who wants Donner's job. The Archon has a *lot* of guards."

"He does," Farragut agreed.

Dr. Hamilton fell silent, and the other xenos set to re-considering in a mutter-fest.

Augustus continued, "Just because you cannot see dissent does not mean dissent is not there. In this case, the complete absence suggests presence."

Shown ridiculous, Pat Hamilton turned angry. "Leave it to a Roman to know about hidden, antagonistic subcultures working their machinations within an oblivious society!"

"I don't believe the Archon is oblivious," Augustus said evenly. "And I don't believe it's the subculture who is maintaining *T'Arra* secrecy in this case."

"You used that word before, Augustus," said Farragut. "*T'Arra. T'Arraiet.* What is all that?"

"The proper way to say *Arran* and *Arrans*. Just adding your own endings to words is typical American butchery of a foreign language."

"Do what?"

"The *T'* prefix indicates belonging in the same way an *n* ending does in English: Terran, Roman, American. The *iet* is a common plural. If you call yourself a Terran down there, they'll think you're from a place called Erran."

"I don't usually call myself Terran anyway," Steele muttered. The Marine had a distaste for all things Roman, especially the Latin language. *Terran* was too Roman of a word for TR Steele. "*Earthling* is good enough for me."

"Then call yourself a *T'Earth* if you want them to understand you," said Augustus. And to Farragut, "Or a *T'Kentucky.* To attempt saying *T'Terra* does leave oneself prone to spitting."

"So we are *T'Americaiet*," Farragut said, to prove he got it.

"Speak for yourself," said the Roman.

Farragut smacked the wall of the compression chamber with a flat palm. "Hey, Mo, get me out of here! I got things to do!"

"Be breathing deeply, Captain Farragut. It will be going faster."

Even in a quick decompression environment, the nitrogen had to bleed out of the blood before Dr. Shah could release any of the shore party into the ship's atmosphere of fifteen pounds per square inch.

"I got a better idea, Mo. Reverse the decompression.

Squeeze the whole ship up to Arran sea level." Then, with a side glance to Augustus, amended, "*T'Arra* sea level."

"If that is what you are wanting, sir," said Mohsen Shah.

"I do. And patch me through to the control room."

Calli's voice responded in a moment. "Control Room, aye."

"Calli, have Survey find some deserted real estate where we can put down a baseball diamond." The population of the entire planet Arra was a mere thirty million. Next to Earth's trillion, that was no population at all. "Some place the Arrans won't even know we're there. I want to get some dirt under our feet."

"Aye, sir."

"And a beach?" Steele suggested in a murmur at the captain's side. "My dogs like water."

"Mr. Carmel. A beach. And, what the hell, a ski run."

"Aye, sir."

The captain clicked off. "Okay, TR, walk your dogs. But when they aren't playing, they're flying extra patrols. Something is not right with all this and I won't be caught flat-footed."

"Yes, sir."

The captain could trust TR Steele not to trust aliens.

And to the xeno team: "Gents. The *T'Arraiet.* I want to know where these boys are from—and what in Creation is a *kzachin*?" Back into the com. "Mr. Carmel!"

"Control Room, aye."

"Pipe the Archon's address to the nation into my quarters."

"Aye, sir."

Com off, Farragut turned around, "Flight Sergeant Blue."

"Sir!" Kerry snapped to startled attention.

"At ease. It seems you may be in a position to gather some information for us."

The xenos in the decompression chamber started altogether, aghast.

The captain gave a near shrug, answering their protest, "Donner asked for Flight Sergeant Blue."

"He did not *ask*," Jose Maria Cordillera revised.

"I noticed that."

"Pretty uppity for a being whose empire comprises a population less than Spain."

Ignoring Augustus, Farragut continued, "Flight Sergeant Blue, you can refuse this order if you don't feel comfortable with it."

Colonel Steele interrupted, "*Respectfully,* sir. I object to using my soldier—"

Kerry mumbled, "I'll go."

"—as some sort of Mata Hari. Flight Sergeant Blue is not a diplomat. You have no right—"

"I'll go."

"—to put her in jeopardy without advance recon. We know nothing about these beings, what they'll do to her, what they want her for—"

"I'll go."

"Blue?" Steele looked down, as if just now realizing she was there.

"I'll go, sir."

Steele felt his mouth open. Mouth shut. Ice-blue eyes turned back to Farragut. "Permission to speak."

"You're already speaking, TR."

"Sir." The broad shoulders squared off properly. Abashed.

"So keep talking."

With a soft chime, the panel lights turned green, the air within and without the compression chamber equalized at five atmospheres. Farragut turned his attention aside momentarily. "Open the hatch, Mo!"

The seals parted with a sucking sound. The hatch swung open, and Farragut ducked through first. "Flight Sergeant Blue. Go get some rest. TR, you were saying."

Steele followed the captain through the corridor, a half-pace behind, for they were both big men and *Merrimack*'s passages were not generous. "I was saying, this is a very bad idea, Captain. Flight Sergeant Blue has a ninth-grade education."

"Only two less than Lieutenant Colonel Steele," Augustus noted, behind them.

Steele shot a sharp glare over his taurine shoulder. With forced calm, he said, "That's not true."

It had been true at one time. True longer than it should have been. TR Steele had belatedly earned a GED instead of a high school diploma. It had then taken him eight years after that to earn a two-year associate degree. The armed services liked their officers degreed.

"Not exactly a Cambridge man, are you?" said Augustus. He knew a sore spot when he had his heel in one.

"Your point?" Steele snarled.

"Let the soldier do her job."

Captain Farragut stopped, turned full round. "Augustus. You're agreeing with me. Doesn't that concern you? I thought you'd be sneering at my idea."

"No. It's a time-honored tactic. Use of a female operative actually has a high probability of success against an otherwise guarded male. In any sexual species, males become spectacularly unguarded around a female. They fly into your windowpane, run in front of your car, sing to your cat, bring your daughter home drunk. Donner's vast intellectual superiority over females of his own species may leave him especially vulnerable to spilling information to Kerry Blue. I have to recommend for the operation."

"And I recommend against," said Colonel Steele. "Kerry Blue knows nothing of first contact protocol, diplomatic protocol, or any protocol. She's not qualified."

"She's qualified recon, isn't she?"

Steele bit on that one hard. Spoke thickly, "*Not* the kind of training we give our soldiers in recon. For the record, I want to lodge a formal objection."

"So noted."

"And off the record, *sir*, be sure to buy her a red dress for her efforts!"

The captain stared after the Marine's stormy exit, baffled at the vehemence. Steele's scalp showed visibly red through his white-blond hair. Farragut cast an appealing glance toward Augustus, and then to Jose Maria Cordillera, who had been following, cat-quiet, after the three of them. "Is he—? Are they—?" he stop-started. "What the hell was that?"

"On or off the record?" said *Don* Cordillera.

"Either. Both."

The learned man observed, "On the record, there is nothing to suggest the lieutenant colonel's objection is not logical, well-considered, for the good of the corps and for the Marine in question."

"Off the record."

"Off the record, what I just said lies in steaming piles in the pasture."

Augustus gave a slight nod with the lifting of his forefinger, as if accepting a bid from the auctioneer. He bought Cordillera's second assessment.

Farragut frowned, troubled. "Is Kerry going to be all right? What do we know of Arran customs?"

Augustus scolded with a harsh laugh, "You're a Boy Scout, John Farragut. Customs?"

"All right. What do we know about Arran *sex*?" he asked the real question.

"It is not violent," said Jose Maria Cordillera. "Kerry is a seasoned veteran on that front, you must know."

Kerry Blue. They called her the morale officer. They called her lots of things—oddly mean things, considering how much they all liked her. A good eighth of the Marine company and part of the *Merrimack*'s crew had liked Kerry Blue.

"I don't mean that as an insult," said Jose Maria Cordillera. "She is a coarse, loose, ill-educated young woman. I am personally fond of her. She has great heart. You are scowling, young captain."

"That red-dress comment torqued me off." Farragut cast a glower back the way Steele had stalked off.

"It was meant to."

Still the captain fretted. "Is the Archon going to recognize the word 'No' if he hears it?"

"Not to worry," said Augustus. "From all reports, I don't think Kerry Blue knows that one."

The Archon, in his address to the denizens of the Myriad, put his own spin on the encounter with the visitors from outer space. Not to miss the obvious chance for self-glorification, Donner painted the Earthlings in ferocious colors, swaggering marauders tamed by the Archon's wisdom, his firmness, his fairness.

Captain Farragut watched the address on a monitor in his quarters as he changed clothes and oiled his baseball glove. Some of Donner's assurances to his people revealed what the Myriadians feared most: Prospectors. As if Arra were the only heavy world in the galaxy, and beings traveled light-years just to come steal their mineral wealth. Donner let the Arrans know that he put a stop to any alien prospecting.

Donner also felt compelled to assure his people that the Earthlings were not agents from Origin. Apparently all was not serene between mother world and colony.

Farragut noticed a glaring lack of reference to any other starfaring race who might have brought the Original colonists to the Myriad. From the speech it was clear that the Earthlings were the first FTL power this species had ever met. Donner assured his people that *Merrimack* was not a shipload of Arran natives returning to claim their home world. That had apparently been the colonists' biggest fear—that they had colonized someone else's home. Someone with big ships and big guns.

Donner declared that the Arra and the whole Myriad belonged to the Myriadians, and by heaven, Donner had made sure all comers knew that. Donner the hero, the defender, the fearless.

All in all, a very human speech.

As eager as Dr. Watson to match his conclusions with Mr. Holmes, Captain Farragut sought out his patterner.

Farragut slid down the ladder to the storage level, tapped on Augustus' hatch, let himself in.

The Roman was stretched out in his pod among the torpedoes, apparently sleeping. At Farragut's entrance, Augustus rose swiftly to his full height. It was a long way up, and the motion made Farragut flinch—little more than the turn of an eyelash, but a flinch nonetheless. His eyes flicked down on reflex.

The Roman's voice was cold, "I am going to take a piss. Did you think I was happy to see you?"

Augustus returned from the head to find John Farragut sitting on a torpedo. "What the hell do you want?"

"I like it when my crew says, 'What the hell do you want, *sir*,'" said Farragut.

"Then dislike me."

The captain ignored the insubordination. His position of power was such that he could afford to ignore petty battles. If the antagonism escalated, if Augustus harmed so much as the lint on the captain's braided cuff, there was a boatload of navvies and another two full companies of Marines on board willing—eager—to beat the altered Roman back into his component parts and send him back to Palatine in sorted pieces. Regulations made Captain Farragut sacred. Beyond that, John Farragut was beloved.

Farragut let the barb hang. "What do you make of Donner? It's just so damned strange that he's not stranger. I've had less comprehensible conversations with the French!"

"Yes, I imagine the French would find you incomprehensible."

"But these are *aliens*. They ought to be stranger."

"You would rather they buzz and clack mandibles at you?"

"No, I appreciate Donner's not clacking. But he's so *human*."

"Will you be making some point here?" said Augustus.

"The whole thing contradicts chaos."

"Do I look like a believer in chaos?" Augustus touched the gold pendant at his throat, a Da Vinci intaglio of the Human Body, the famous image of a man described within a circle.

Farragut had noticed the pendant before. "I thought that meant everything circles around your dick."

Augustus nodded aside, allowing that. "Point of fact, it does. That aside, this is the shape of the intelligent, land-dwelling universe. The base unit is chordate. A trunk. A head with some sort of CPU in it. Symmetrical to the left and right but not up and down or front and back. Two arms, two legs. Dick/no dick, depending. Life comes in infinite, chaotic variety, but this is sovereign intelligence. Insectoids and exoskeletals rule by sheer numbers, but without thought, without creativity. The Hive is your sole agent of chaos, but its crude intelligence is adaptive, not initiative. So no, I do not find it surprising in the least that an intelligence should look like us, think like us, communicate like us, breathe like us, in short, be fashioned in our own image."

"You're an anthropist," said Farragut with some surprise. The anthropic principle was not a very popular view in the scientific community. Not popular with anyone outside of Creationists. The anthropic cosmological principle held that life—intelligent life—was inevitable. That the universe was created for Man. "God, Augustus?" Farragut asked, surprised.

"I don't know God. I know inevitability. Things that must be."

"Must? Why must? By fiat? Let it be done?"

"*Must,* because it *is.* We are here. Therefore we must be here. Don't try to speak Latin, John Farragut."

"Well, the Hive exists, too. And I'm sure the Hive acts as if the universe exists only for it."

"The Hive is wrong. We must destroy it."

"No argument there," said Farragut, though he could get one from a cult back on Earth which believed the Hive was the door to Heaven. *And spake the Host: Eat of my flesh. Become one with me, for whom the universe was made.*

Augustus continued with his own theory. "The parameters for the existence of life are so small, the universe as we know it so bloody unlikely, that the only rational conclusion is that life exists because it must. I must. And for some unfathomable reason, you must. Things happen the way they are meant to happen. Just as the Roman Empire rose again. It did so because it was inevitable. The time when was uncertain—and much later than anyone anticipated—but the rise was inevitable. The Empire is meant to be."

"Means you expect it to rise one more time," said Farragut. "When all this is over."

"Inevitably," said Augustus.

"Not if I have anything to say about it," said Farragut confidently. "So what makes it inevitable?"

"Destiny."

"You're implying God again."

"And I told you, I don't know God. I do know that I am conscious. Why suppose the force that brought us into being is not likewise conscious?"

"Couldn't be accidental?"

"I have no problem believing you are an accident, John Farragut, but me? No. I was intentional. Was there something else you wanted?" Augustus asked, dismissal in his tone, though Augustus could not exactly dismiss the captain.

"Mo tells me you've been in the personnel medical files."

"And?"

"Stay out," Farragut ordered.

"Oh, I don't care for the trivialities of your crew's little lives. I went straight for *your* jacket."

And the captain's quills laid back. He was happy enough

to draw fire to himself and away from his own. He became cheerful and easy again. "Am I interesting?"

"You have a titanium jaw."

Farragut hesitated. His face lost animation. His answer expressionless, "I lost a fight."

"You lost two fights."

Farragut's brow creased slightly. He answered, nettled, "If you knew, why are you asking?"

"To see how you would answer the question."

Farragut answered with only a slight edge of defensiveness in his voice. "I can't say there weren't nights I didn't wake up kicking, but I'm not going to beat myself up for losing a fight sixteen to one. Which was about twelve too many."

Most men had a severe allergic reaction to the mere mention of such incidents. This man was merely annoyed at having his nose rubbed in it. He had dealt with it, got over it, and set a forward course, full speed ahead. He could look back if he must without hanging his head. Did not like to. Did not go back again and again, picking the scab to see how the wound was healing.

"What'd you do to piss them off?" said Augustus.

"What'd I do to piss you off?"

Augustus gave a crocodilian smile. So Farragut recognized this as a third fight. Remembered what the deck tasted like. But Farragut's anger remained mild, more irritation. Unthreatened. Augustus had not yet cut to the core of his being.

So John Farragut was not a control addict. He did not need to be master of every moment. That explained how he could be so buoyant. No one is ever happy who craves control, because it is not possible in this universe. John Farragut could let go and roll.

Interesting quality in a man in charge of a battleship with planetary siege capability; plus two Space Patrol Torpedo Boats; two companies of Marines with thirty-six Swifts and a battery of thirty-six multipurpose guns; a formidable arsenal of distortion bombs, torpedoes, and missiles, including Space Darts, Space Slugs, Star Sparrows, and a Continental Knife.

So if control is not what drives you, what are you doing out here, Captain? In a position very like a god.

How did a man get to be this powerful if he did not crave control?

Augustus had misread him again. Hard to interpret what Augustus had never seen. "Your children are not yours."

Got him! Saw that shot lodge under Farragut's skin and detonate like a splinter shot. Augustus watched the captain absorb the hit.

Farragut bridled, voice rigid, "Well, Augustus, given that they are two and three years old and I haven't been home in seven, I don't think there's anyone who *hasn't* figured that pattern out."

Farragut could shrug off his physical defeats, when he had fought the good fight and lost. This was bigger than he was. Augustus found the wound that defined the man. All the instincts of a father; but not a father. "Why'd you stay away seven years?"

"I was on my way home when we got the call to the Battle of Eta Cassiopeia."

"And you decided to become a hero instead."

Farragut ignored the comment. Heroism wasn't his goal. It was simply an unconscious quality of his being. "She didn't understand. Wouldn't, I guess. She had to know what I was doing out here. By the time I was clear to go home . . . I found out I was going to be a father, so to say. I . . . couldn't go. I took my leave on Alpha Centauri instead. I was going to make another try at healing whatever had gone wrong there. The second child tore it. I really tried to think of them as adopted. That wouldn't go down. Stuck right here." He put a fist to his chest. "Ever swallow a bone?"

"Try chewing, John."

"Right." Farragut inhaled deeply. Had been holding his breath. "She didn't want a divorce. I couldn't stay married to her."

Apparently couldn't even speak her name. It was Laura.

"I told her either sue me for abandonment, keep my name, the house, whatever the court wanted to give to a woman with two children; or else I'd sue her for adultery, cut her off, disown her kids. She sued. I've never met John and Lacey Farragut."

"John Alexander Farragut, Jr.," said Augustus more precisely.

"Isn't that just the damnedest kick in the teeth?" Blue eyes lifted, terribly liquid.

"So why did you give her the choice?"

"Because I was afraid if I got into a fight with her, I'd kill her. And hurt two innocent civilians who didn't ask to be born or named Farragut." His arms were crossed. "Found what you're looking for yet, Augustus? 'Cause I'm getting tired of this conversation. I can have Mo perform something invasive without an anesthetic if I want this." Farragut headed for the hatch.

"Want to know who are the fathers of your children?"

Farragut ran into the hatch without opening it. Leaned there, forehead to fist. It was the plural that did it. Augustus saw that Farragut hadn't known that part of it. Farragut had assumed a single lover.

Augustus saw the war waging behind the blue eyes. Saw himself reflected in them, the devil in the desert. Farragut did not want to ask. The question was sordid. A carving knife in the heart. He stalled, asked back, "How did you get that information?"

"It was just there. The patterns are there."

Farragut shook his head, lost. "Augustus, I don't know what it is you actually *do*."

"I see patterns in data. The children were DNA-printed when they started school. That's in the FBI files, which are on board *Merrimack*'s database. One father was mapped when he took a position requiring a security clearance. The other was mapped when he was a schoolboy himself. The data is all in there. I saw the matches."

"Lordy, Augustus. I can look at a game of solitaire and miss a play. You could plug me in to the collective wisdom of the known universe, and I still wouldn't see to put that red ten on that black jack."

"I am a patterner."

"But I thought the information didn't stay in your head once you unplugged."

"I retain what interests me."

"Don't you need a program to read a database? What about incompatible file formats?"

"All electronic information is, at its most basic, *on* or *off*. The patterns are binary. The human mind, properly enabled, can read *on* and *off*. The patterns of the data explain themselves. An operating system is just another program. A program is just another pattern. Want the names?"

"No," John croaked. Then he caved. "Yes."

"Sure?"

Wouldn't look at him. Like a surrender: "Tell me."

Augustus spoke two names.

No change registered on Farragut's face at first, except perhaps a slackening, a blankness, confusion. Blue eyes blinked. Still blank. No connections. No recognition.

Then he reared up, a smile washing his face clean.

Augustus tilted his head curiously. "You're going to have them killed?"

Breathing freely, Farragut smiled. "No."

"Then why did you want their names?"

"So I don't suspect my friends." His smile broadened, became positively giddy. "They're no one I know!" The knives dissolved from his back. He muttered a joyful babble, "Small of me ever to think a friend of mine could ever do that to me! Lordy, John, you're an ass."

A truly relieved, enormously happy ass. Sneaking faceless parasites invading his home in his absence were a fact of existence. They could not wound him. Just so long as it wasn't a friend. Farragut had no armor to his stern.

"Yes, to your original question," said Augustus.

Farragut had forgotten by then that he'd asked one. "What question was that?"

"You are interesting, John Farragut."

5

FLIGHT SERGEANT BLUE STOOD at the sentry post outside Sensor Compartment 3. The sign on the hatch at her back read: REDUNDANCY IS GOOD. REDUNDANCY IS GOOD. RE-DUNDANCY IS GOOD.

Colonel Steele had stationed her under the bottom of the ship, deep in the lower sail with the machines. Wasn't really sentry duty. It was a stupid waste of time. No one ever came down here.

Footsteps clanging down the ladder made her power up her side arm.

The Navy had issued her a splinter gun. The two-stage weapon was designed for shipboard use. Not powerful enough to penetrate a bulk, it fired a thin dart designed to lodge deep in human flesh. If it hit your intended target, then you could detonate it, or threaten to. The second-stage trigger sent the signal to splinter the dart into lethal shards. The threat was usually enough to stop the sane.

No one was due. And no one *ever* came down here between watches for any good reason. Kerry took aim up at the hatch.

From the hatchway in the overhead emerged a pair of man-sized deck boots clanging down the ladder rungs, long muscular legs, a long lean torso, long arms, a handsomely shaped Roman head. Face like a granite carving not quite free of the stone.

The Intelligence Officer, Augustus. Kerry wondered if she ought to challenge him. Palatine was an ally now, and this was a full bird colonel. Still, you never knew about Romans. She took aim, inhaled to say halt. Her mouth had gone absolutely dry.

Augustus ignored the weapon pointed at his head. He jerked a thumb over his shoulder in a "let's go" gesture. "You're on, Blue."

Kerry pushed the splinter gun into its holster at her thigh. "Donner called?" Kerry guessed, astonished. Men never called after they said they would. The Archon was truly alien after all.

Augustus turned around in the small space. There was scarcely room enough to do that. He seemed to find it strange. "Why are you here? I thought you were supposed to be resting."

"Colonel put me under the ship for punching out Dak Shepard." It wasn't as if she'd hurt him. Dak was fully twice her size and he'd deserved it. He wouldn't shut up. Colonel Steele had it in for her, was all. Always had.

That was of no concern to Augustus. Augustus gestured up the ladder. "Move it out, soldier."

"The captain said I could only go if I wasn't on duty," said Kerry. "I'm on duty."

"That was smoke," said Augustus. "And point of fact, you're not on duty."

"Says who?"

"I."

Kerry hesitated. "Can you do that?"

She was a little vague on chain of command when it included Romans. Steele was only a light colonel.

"Farragut can," said Augustus.

"Oh." Nothing vague there. These orders came from God. "Oh Gawd. Colonel Steele is gonna do a *burn*."

"Aside from the amusement value, I do not care." Augustus tilted his head toward the ladder for her to fall in.

Captain Farragut put an arm around Kerry Blue's shoulders. It was a brotherly arm. John Farragut was the eldest of a litter of twenty-one; he tucked Kerry under his wing like number twenty-two. Kerry could always tell when a man was interested in her. Despite the captain's warmth, he was not.

He told her she did not have to do this. He briefed her on what he wanted her to get out of the Archon:

What was a *kzachin*?

What was the Arrans' mode of FTL travel and communication?

Where was Origin?

Who was the minefield intended for?

Had another alien species brought the Myriadians to the Myriad?

Did she have any questions?

"Does he have a tail?" asked Kerry.

She had been able to see under the billowy linen shirt a strong back, a sensual curve to Donner's spine under that short-clipped mane. Where his loose trousers had tugged against his legs, she'd seen the impression of a hard-corded thigh. His bared arms were hard, bronze, human enough. Pretty sexy, really. But she didn't know if she could deal with a tail.

There was a bit of eye rolling at her question.

"No tail. Any *other* questions?"

"What does *he* want?" Kerry asked.

The captain and the IO exchanged glances, surprised that she could actually ask something substantive.

The captain confessed, "You know what, Kerry? I honest-to-God don't know."

Augustus spoke past Kerry to the captain, "He may just want to talk."

Kerry mumbled, "Then we're in trouble. I'm not smart."

"Next to the local females, she's a bloody Einstein," Augustus said to the captain.

"Hey!" Kerry protested. Then added, "Sir."

Augustus continued talking past her, "If you're concerned for her tact, remember the Myriadian females are dumb as hamsters. The Archon may well overlook anything she says wrong."

The xenos had reported that the females' brains were physically smaller than the males. It was the land of stupid, complacent women—Troglodyte heaven. Maybe the chief Troglodyte wanted more.

"Kerry called Donner by the wrong 'you' back there," Augustus said. "Did you notice?"

The captain nodded. "Same 'you' that upset him when I used it. He didn't mind when Flight Sergeant Blue said it."

"Donner seemed to think it was cute. He may just want to hear what she has to say."

That would be a first, thought Kerry, as the officers talked over her head.

"And if he wants something else, don't worry about him using force," Augustus said—to the captain, though Kerry thought she just might be real interested in that comment. "Rape seems to be a creep crime in the Myriad—much like child molestation in our cultures. And Donner is not a creep. And we know he won't eat her for dinner. He can't digest her."

"Oh. Thank you, Colonel Augustus," Kerry had to speak. "I feel so much safer now."

That bit of insubordination lifted eyebrows, but neither officer called her on it. Farragut spoke—to Kerry—as if trying to convince himself, "You'll be okay."

Kerry tried to ask, "So what if he . . . ? Should I . . . ?" She could not finish. Never used those kinds of words to officers.

The captain, who always struck her as a bit naive in some respects, did not understand the question. Augustus answered her, "When in Rome."

Kerry understood, nodded. "When in Rome, show 'em how we do it downtown."

"Try to keep it in the suburbs," said Farragut, catching up with the intent. "Don't shock him. Keep your dog collar on. If you get into trouble, bag yourself to an LD, call for displacement and we'll have you out of there right now."

"I can take him," said Kerry.

"I don't want an interstellar incident, Flight Sergeant."

"I can take him." She didn't say *fight* him.

Lieutenant Colonel Steele made an uncomfortable presence in sick bay. Steele never came here of his own power unless carrying someone else. The big Marine asked gentle, older Dr. Shah in near mumbles if the doctor had given Flight Sergeant Blue anything in the way of protection.

Mohsen Shah gave a gentle laugh. "Colonel Steele, a shoe fetishist is having a better chance of impregnating the object of his desire than the Archon is having with an Earth woman. Leather is at least having the same genetic base code."

The lieutenant colonel's fair face turned flaming scarlet. He growled, "I meant protection against disease."

"It is being the same question. Kerry Blue is being—how would you be saying?—bulletproof."

"Are you sure?" Steele shifted in place, recrossed his thick arms. "Viruses mutate."

A Marine with a little knowledge was an annoying thing. Mo Shah sighed. "Ah. I am seeing—you are not understanding the reason why." The colonel was one of those people for whom biology was voodoo. Dr. Shah tried to answer him in terms TR Steele might understand. "Have you ever been trying to mount a Centauran wheel on your Harley?"

"That's a shooting offense where I come from," Steele growled.

"Yes, yes, of course, it is being so." Mo Shah smiled indulgently. "But could some godless Centauran be doing it?"

"Hell, no. The Centauran wheel takes only four lug nuts."

"And they are being metric," Dr. Shah added.

"*And* they're in that *dumb* metric scale," Steele confirmed, punching the air with his forefinger.

"So! Even if you could be adjusting the size of the bolts, there is no use drilling out a fifth bore because the other four holes are not going to be lining up. And you cannot exactly be *pushing* the holes around to be making them space evenly. Are you following me?"

"Follow so far. Hell if I know where you're going with it."

Shah explained, "In very much the same way, an alien virus cannot be readjusting its genetic code to be matching up with ours. It will not be happening. It cannot be happening. The Myriadian viruses are being metric with four bores—and their bolts are being threaded the wrong way. Their genetic code is having an opposite orientation to ours. The Myriadian viruses you are fearing will not even be knowing where they are."

Steele grunted something like thanks, turned red again, and marched stiffly out. Trying not to think about where the Myriadian viruses might be going.

Kerry Blue's arrival split the air with a loud crack. The displacement tech had put her down on the palace terrace. She stepped off her LD and moved to the white railing. Its marble glowed with numinous beauty under the starlight. She leaned on the cool stone and looked out over the lake, the water bedizened with star reflections. Overhead, the heavens blazed with twinkling lights in indigo velvet. She took off her cap and her hairband. Moist breezes ruffled her hair. She inhaled green-and-blue smells.

Sensing someone behind her, she turned around.

Donner. Without his guards. Hands behind his back. "Do Earth people give gifts?"

"Of course."

"Here." He brought from behind his back—wiggling— the lizard plant that had crawled down her uniform at their first meeting.

A startled cooing cry escaped her. Then, suddenly, tears. She cuddled the leafy creature into her arms. Its webby feet clung to her.

"I do not understand this reaction," said Donner, distressed.

"I'm happy," she gushed tearfully.

"This does not appear happy."

"Oh, yeah, it confuses our guys, too." Men hated crying women. And they really hated crying Marines. She sniffled. The plant took up a perch on her shoulder. "But I was told these things can't eat our insects. The molecules are left-handed."

"And is your sunlight left-handed? This creature is a plant."

She smiled brightly. "You mean it's okay?"

"I do not give gifts that die."

She reached for Donner's head. The motion startled him, but he held his ground, as she took his face in her hands and kissed his cheek. His skin felt warm to her lips.

He came away flustered. Recovered his composure. "You were listening to my ocean."

"Oh. Yes. Just now. I was," she said. "That's because it sings."

A smile of pure delight lit Donner's entire face. "It does. I stopped noticing a long time ago. It is pretty, is it not?" He touched her face, his fingers dry, warm, his touch light. "How came you by this color?"

"I was born with it."

"It is better than the others."

The plant moved up to sit on her head. She moved a webby foot off her eyelid.

"What do the colors mean?" Donner asked.

"Mean? What? You mean like rank? They don't mean nothing. It's a big planet. This is just the way we are. I got a white grandfather. I mean really white."

"The grotesque one," Donner began, "with hair like bleachweed and eyes like holes in the day sky—he is your white grandfather?"

A snigger moved up the back of her nose. "No. Not nearly. That's Colonel Steele."

"He owns you?" Donner guessed.

"No. Yes. Sort of. He says die, I die. But he wouldn't say that unless something big was on the line. He doesn't spend us like loose change. He's a lead-from-the-front kind of guy. You're laughing."

"The words. The words are . . . oddly chosen. I do not understand what you said. Captain Farragut is not your Archon?"

"Farragut is everybody's Archon."

The answer seemed to satisfy Donner.

Kerry giggled, touched the lizard plant on her head. "He's humming!"

"You have music on Earth?"

"Oh, lots. Doesn't everybody? They used to think music would be the universal language. But one person's music is another person's cat on fire. Anyone thinks music is universal has never been in our forecastle. Men have been beaten shitless over tunes. And me, I'll Kay-Bar a whistler. Sometimes we sing chanteys—you don't mind the noise so much if it's coming out of your own mouth. And if the guy next to you can't sing—and if it's Twitch Fuentes, he can't—you just sing louder and drown him out. Then Commander Carmel, she's got this operatic screaming fat chick shit she listens to. Splits my head open. And Cowboy has—Cowboy *had* country western bubbles. Music to throw up by. Lying cheating rat bastard music."

Donner was laughing.

"Do you understand what I said?"

Enchanted, beaming, Donner confessed, "No."

A bead of sweat threaded down Kerry's neck. She almost asked if she could take her jacket off, but then realized Donner wouldn't know her request was out of order. He might, in fact, be wondering why she was wearing so many clothes in this weather. Donner was lightly dressed, though the females had been covered and draped into shapelessness, neck to bare feet.

Kerry unfastened her uniform jacket—a chore, with its twenty-two chances to say no—and peeled it off. The lizard plant rearranged itself on her shoulder. The breezes felt soft on her wet skin, cool through her T-shirt. Donner's black eyes went straight for her breasts.

Ha. We're not so alien as the xenos said, Kerry thought. She sighed aloud to be free of the extra layer of fabric, "That's better."

Donner's onyx eyes agreed. Kerry slung her jacket over the marble railing, spread her arms to the sky, and inhaled. "It's great to get out of the can. This—*this* is amazing. It's so beautiful." She could fall right into that deep dazzling sky. Diamonds in velvet. Not that Kerry Blue had ever really seen diamonds in velvet.

"My world is new in your eyes," said Donner, gazing at her, rapt.

"Our sky is dark at night. I mean *dark*. Stars in our sky are little pinholes compared to this." She waved her hand across the glory overhead. "And you don't see the *colors* in them. And you don't see any stars at all in the day. Just a big yellow sun."

"This sounds like Origin," said Donner.

Origin. Origin! *Origin!* Kerry's heart sped up like it did before an FTL jump. Origin! She had just tripped over her mission objective without even trying. She was supposed to find out about Origin. *Damn, I'm righteous fine!*

And without her even coaxing, Donner continued, "The night sky is dark on Origin. One sun illuminates the day. The sun is not yellow. It is orange. We can see two stars in the day sky, depending on the season and where you are in the world. The day stars are not bright because they are close like these are here. The day stars are distant and we only see them because they are supernovae."

Kerry tried not to show how excited she was, but her lizard plant changed tune with her drumming heartbeat. Origin was in a galaxy that had two supernovae in it—which was to say not the Milky Way. Her mates were gonna go hyper. She had a real future as an intelligence operative.

"Have you ever been there?" she asked. "To Origin?"

"I was born there. Before the schism, I returned several times."

Her plant chirped vibrantly.

If Kerry understood him, Donner was saying he had tripped out of this galaxy and back again in a single lifetime. But how long was that? "Long trip?"

"Depends on how you look at it."

Not informative. Kerry needed a time scale. She asked, "How old are you?" She could ask him anything. She was just a silly female.

"Thirty-five years. *T'Arra* years."

She could not remember how Arran years measured against Earth years, but thirty-five was not a huge number of anybody's years. This meant Donner was traveling faster than *Merrimack* could even think about.

"How far is Origin from here?"

"I have no idea."

"Could you take me to see it?"

But Donner had tired of her questions. He reached for the language nodule behind her ear. "Does this come off?"

"Whoa. I need that to talk to you."

His fingers threaded through her hair as he withdrew his hand. "Speak to me in your own way."

"But you won't be able to understand—oh." She switched into English, her voice husky smooth. ("Yeah, okay. I'm pretty sure where this is going. I can be had on the first date, in case you're wondering. You can ignore Colonel Steele. He was just being pissy. I am not cheap; I'm free. But I won't be put in a harem. And, yeah, I think you're a fox.")

A voice sounded in Kerry's ear receiver: ("Oh, by the way, Blue. You've got a monitor on you.")

She jerked. ("Shit!") Her plant jumped, grabbed a hunk of hair and held on tight.

Even Donner flinched a little, thinking it was something he had done. "What is it?"

"Uh. Feedback." She turned her com off, smoothed down the lizard's leaves. "All better now."

The breeze off the lake billowed Donner's crisp shirt, giving Kerry a look at his hard shoulder, his skin an even lustrous bronze. He was a pretty man. Short. But that was his only flaw in Kerry's eyes. The vee slash down the back of his shirt freed his mane, an arrow of short-clipped hair that traced nearly down to his waist. Kerry's fingers strayed to the short curls fluttering in the wind. His hair felt softer than it looked, slid like silk between her fingers.

Donner turned quickly, fixed her with a weird expression that made her reel her fingers back in. Made her know she touched something she shouldn't have. "What'd I do?"

He faltered, trying to explain. Blundered into a mumbling logjam.

Kerry smiled, pointed. "Made you blush."

He went from bronze to red. His teeth looked even whiter within the darkness of that blush, as he smiled—shocked, hopeful, lit-up, dazed—just like an Earthman when he realizes he's going to hit one home.

She could not figure why he was so delighted. She had been told that all the females of this species were easy. The most powerful man in the world, the Archon could just choose any one of those stupid females he wanted.

And maybe that was it. He sensed here an active mind and full-blown personality inside this female body. One that could judge him, could say no. That added an element of personal danger.

She could hurt him. That vast three-planet pride was on the line.

Kerry Blue never hurt anyone who asked nice.

Donner gazed at her, spoke words, incomprehensible words. She tapped at her module, muttered in English, only to herself, because her com was off, ("Damn, Augustus, this thing don't work.")

Donner captured her hand to stop her tapping. He explained, "I switched languages."

"The xenos told me you only had one language."

"I spoke to you in an ancient tongue," said Donner. "We only use it in poetry anymore. It seemed to suit the situation."

"But I don't understand the words."

"You do. Just listen. You will know."

She didn't. The words were beautiful noise in his low, distinctly male voice. She heard an ardent wistful yearning, and maybe that was what he asked her to hear.

He switched back to Arran. "Will you come to my home with me? Not this palace. My home." And at her hesitation he asked, "Or must I ask the male with the creepy eyes?"

"Colonel Steele? He's my CO. He doesn't own me."

"He does not touch you?"

"Steele? No. Oh, no. No." A bluster of laughter came tumbling out. "No. Oh, boy. No. There are regulations against that kind of thing. It's called fraternization. Did I say that right?" She never got embarrassed talking sex. But this was Colonel Steele, for the love of God. The lizard plant licked her crimson hot ear.

"If he wanted?"

"He doesn't. Believe me. He doesn't. And not even. Doesn't happen. No."

"Then I am to ask you?" It seemed to strike him peculiar, asking a female for anything.

"Yes. It's my decision."

"And what do you say?" His eyes were velvet black. Starlight glowed on his hair.

Kerry was accustomed to human soldiers, common men, not an alien commander of worlds. Still, males were males. The night was warm and he wanted her.

"I say yes."

"Blue! We're losing surveillance!" the technician yelled, smacked the transmitter to force his voice through the dead circuit. "Stay near the LDs! We can't see you if you don't have a sight line to a landing disk. Shit." He swiveled away from the console, yanked off his headset. "Sir, I don't think she's receiving."

"What's wrong with her com?" Steele demanded, hovering at the tech's shoulder.

"Nothing, sir," the tech faltered.

"Nothing and she's not receiving?" Steele's impatient anger could stop a man's heart.

"Yes, sir. I mean no, sir. I think she turned it, well, off."

"Are you sure *she* did it?" Steele snarled, reversing the LDs' recordings to watch the encounter again from all angles.

"Pretty sure, sir. We saw her pull the receiver from her ear. Right there." The tech pointed at the playback. Then to the live output from the last disk as Kerry Blue left its range. "And there she goes." She left the palace.

"We don't have a security scan of anything outside the palace," said Steele, turned an accusatory glare to Captain Farragut. "We can't exactly *sneak* a landing disk down."

Farragut nodded. The Archon would probably notice the displacing *kaboom* that accompanied an LD's arrival. He suggested, "Send someone after her?"

"Oh, yeah, like Blue couldn't shake a chaperone by the time she was twelve years old." A muttered comment from an MP on deck, too loud.

"I heard that, Marine."

"Sorry, sirs."

"No," Steele declined the apology, and admitted to Farragut. "He's right."

The tech: "We're losing her. We're losing her. We lost her."

A new voice picked up: "I have her."

Steele, Farragut, and the tech turned as Augustus stepped through the hatchway.

The Roman expanded a flat screen—a typically Roman sort of monitor, incorporating bounce technology. The kind of toy a Roman would have. Even though the surveillance cameras must be fixed on Kerry Blue, the image they transmitted was of Kerry, as if taken from a distance of twelve paces. Augustus must have fixed the bounce transceivers in the gun sights on either side of her eyes, to get this angle of her.

The flat screen showed Kerry Blue climbing into a wheeled vehicle with Donner.

"You put a bug on her." Steele sounded surprised and offended. He should not have been.

"Want to watch?" said Augusutus.

Steele stood like stone. Augustus left the monitor on the console, an apple tree in the middle of the garden.

*   *   *

Flight Sergeant Reg Monroe heard her own teeth grind, forced herself to relax her jaw.

She lined her Swift up behind Dak Shepard's and activated her targeting system. Lock and tone.

And soon enough, Dak's voice sounded inside her helmet, queasy: "Uh, Reg? What are you doing?"

And then the flight leader was on the com: "Yes, Alpha Three, what are you doing?"

"Havin' a wet dream, Mr. Sewell." Reg had no real intention of shooting Dak in the ass. Felt like it, though.

"Turn off your targeting, Alpha Three," Hazard ordered, not amused.

"Yes, sir. But you have to tell Alpha Two to shut up, sir."

Dak Shepard had kept up a lewd, coarse, obnoxious, pointless stream of ship-to-ship comments spewing into her helmet com ever since the flight left Arra.

"Maintain com discipline, Alpha Two," Hazard ordered.

"What? What'd I do?" said Dak. So innocent.

Reg bristled. "What'd you—? Oooh, you bust my balls, Dak Shepard!"

Dak answered sweetly, "You don't have balls, Regi girl."

" 'Cause you busted 'em, you stupid *boon!* Hazard, make him *shut up!*"

Alpha Leader ordered them both to com silence. It didn't last. Dak was at it again in no time, on a tight beam, ship-to-ship, where Hazard Sewell couldn't hear.

Reg ground her teeth.

Back on Arra, under starry, starry skies, Marines were trouncing the navvies eleven to five on a brand-new ball diamond. Marines were splashing in turquoise waters off a white-sand beach; Kerry Blue was on a date with the lord of three planets in his palace with the jewel-studded floor; while Reg, well, Regina Monroe was wedged in this little bitty cockpit, stuck out here on the Rim of the Myriad, on patrol with the king of baboons. Knew she'd had worse days. Couldn't remember one offhand. Combat was better than this.

Dak didn't even shut up as they approached target area. No reverence for the scene of Cowboy's death.

The minefield was gone—*Merrimack* had exploded all of the mines. The space was a big empty now, and Reg didn't know what the hell she was supposed to be looking for.

Hive. Her skin felt clammy and crawled at the thought. She uncovered the portable terrarium of insects installed in her console. She knew the Hive was involved in this somehow, but the ants in the jar said otherwise. The creepy crawling things were behaving themselves. Trying to get out. Crawling. Humping. She covered them up again.

"Screw this," she muttered.

Dak's voice in her helmet offered to assist. What did she want screwed?

"You, Dak! You! Do it yourself, and *shut up!*"

She followed Alpha Leader, circled tight around the former location of the space buoy that had fired the missile with which Cowboy played his last game of tag. Reg moaned, "I could be playing shortstop right now."

She waited for Dak's return comment. It was too long in coming.

Her navigational indicators fell flat. Galactic horizon. Galactic compass. Attitude. All her digitals black. She glanced up from the control panel. "Dak?"

Silence.

"Dak?"

Dak was gone.

"Alpha Leader? I've got a problem, Alpha Leader. I lost coordinates. And—I don't know if this is a problem, really, but I can't hear Dak."

Hazard Sewell did not answer.

"Hazard! Alpha Leader, are you there?"

Alpha Leader was gone.

"Hazard, don't do this to me. Oh, jeez."

She smacked her readouts. Shut down her nav system and powered up the backup. Muttered, "Redundancy is good. Redundancy is good."

But the monitors remained flat. Blank. She requested a systems check. The ship's computer reported all systems functioning.

"Red Four? Red Five?"

Silence.

Twitch and Carly were gone.

The silence was too perfect.

"Dak—oh, God, I can't believe I'm saying this— Say something, Dak!"

The perfect silence remained.

She opened her viewport.
The stars were gone. The Myriad was gone.
"Oh, God," Reg spoke aloud. "*I'm* gone."

Swarms of little mothy things rose from fragrant, dew-damp ground. The grasses were coarse, blue-green, and spongy underfoot. All those stars in the soft, deep blue sky made it like playing under the lights. The light came from everywhere, making the colors liquid and shadows few, blended, without edges.

The captain bounded out to the newly packed pitcher's mound. He dried his hand in the dirt, lifted his cap from his sweaty hair, snugged it back on. Sounds came to him quickly. Deceptively. He panted in the heavy air. It took him several practice pitches to find the plate.

Some men and women came down not to play ball, not to do anything much, just to get out of the ship, to feel hot breezes on their skin and firm ground under their feet. To sit under the weird light, listen to the crack of the bat and ritual shout: Play ball! As if nothing were wrong in the world.

The Archon was shy. It was cute. Here he had a sure thing, and still he tried to impress her. He showed Kerry Blue his house, which was bright and cool. He played music for her. Rather bland and lightweight sounds; she didn't like it much, but it was a sweet gesture. An Earthman would have got straight to business.

When the room darkened to perfect blackness, she supposed, ah ha, this is it. A little disappointed, because when it came down to yab-yum, Kerry liked to see what she was doing.

Then, gradually, the stars came out, little pinpoints of light dotting the room's darkness.

Donner's voice came to her from somewhere in the dark: "What do you think?"

She wondered if he could see her. "I don't know," she spoke toward the voice. "What is it?"

"This is my sky. This is the sky over Origin."

Her heart hied into double time. Ships navigated by the stars. If this recording was accurate, then finding Origin ought to be easy as roll me over.

Her voice vibrated. She hoped he thought her moved by the incredible beauty of it. "This is wonderful. It's just like home." As if a black sky full of stars wasn't something she saw every day, day in, day out. "Can I have this?"

The stars dimmed away as the lights came back up. The room returned around her. Donner smiled at her. He pulled the crystal from the player and pressed it into her hand. "If you want it, I should be very happy to give it."

"Thank you," she whispered. The boffins ought to be able to jury-rig something to play this thing back.

Wait till Colonel Steele saw this. Steele thought she was a screwup. She would show him. She made one bitch of a spy.

She tucked the crystal into her bra. Let Donner watch her do it.

Finally—finally—he brought her to the bedchamber. She did not recognize it as such at first. It was big, with an ornamental fishpond sunk in the middle of the floor. The bed was built level with the floor, so she overlooked it on first glance over. Guess she didn't have to worry about falling out of it.

Donner closed the door.

He touched some switches. Nothing happened. A clearly vexed look crossed his face. Something was not happening that ought to be—probably opening the windows. The air was stuffy in this room. He pressed the switch with more force.

Kerry moved toward the fishpond. Males never liked females watching them when they were experiencing any kind of technical difficulty.

She waved her hand over the water. Jewel-colored fish (well, they looked like fish) rose to the surface and gaped.

Kerry saw her reflection on the water, her lizard plant peering over her shoulder, her own smile flashing back at her with the sudden sense of the fantastical. When she signed on to the corps, she had been told to expect the un-expected. They got that right. Who could have ever pre-dicted she would be here, now?

Cowboy. Lordy, but he seemed a million years ago. Someone from her past life. She wished she could take all her tears back. Wished Cowboy were alive, but only so that lyin' cheatin' bastard son of a dead skunk could see her now. Wouldn't he just die?

She heard a sudden rushing. Air in vents. Guessed Donner got the air conditioner working.

A squeal and a splash made her jerk back with a reflexive yelp, not quite realizing what had happened until the water surface cleared and she saw her plant swimming to the bottom of the pond.

She reached for it—

Her feet left the floor. Her back slammed against the wall, hard. She stood pinned by Donner's hand clamped over her mouth and nose. His face before her was unrecognizable. His own mouth was shut in a tight line. And with his free hand he held his own nose. His onyx eyes beetled with dire warning: *Do not breathe!*

She stopped struggling, and he guided her hands to make her hold her own nose and mouth shut, not trusting her to the strongest of living instincts, to inhale.

Then he ran from door to window, finding them all locked. Something yellow breathed from the vents.

Poison.

Kerry hefted a rock out of the fishpond and hurled it at the window.

It bounced. Of course, a head of state would have bulletproof windows.

She was going to have to inhale. Blood pounded in her temples. Head hot. Lungs burned.

She reached for her dog collar. Tried to remember the evac code.

Hell, there were no LDs from which to be picked up!

She met Donner's stricken eyes.

He strode to her, purposefully, seized her, dragged her to the fishpond and pushed her head under water.

Icy coldness enveloped her, trickled into her ears. Something slimy and finned batted her cheek.

She had to breathe. She fought him.

Like fighting a tree.

Did he have gills that he thought she could breathe down here? She thrashed. Screamed in her throat. Urgently tapped at his arms, as if to signal a sparring partner to let go. Panic crowded in on her. She could not last another second. Writhed wildly.

Inhaled.

Convulsed, gagged. Coughed, and drew in more water. Iciness filled her chest. Floundered. Slapped the water. Her body gave two last spasms of protest, then quieted into a peaceful tingling calm.

Head cottony. Limbs floating away. She settled into darkness and weird serenity. She didn't even feel cold anymore.

And well, glory be, there was the infamous light.

6

Augustus' voice intruded in Steele's earphone without signal or preamble: "Your girl's in deep sushi."

Steele's throw went sailing wild over first base. He nearly collided with the base runner as he sprinted to the nearest landing disk and bellowed for evac.

Because Augustus had reacted the instant his surveillance detected the first miasma of yellow issuing from the vents in the Archon's locked room, Colonel Steele displaced aboard *Merrimack* in time to see the Archon on the monitor, shoving Kerry Blue into the fishpond.

The image blurred, refracted through water and bubbles, as Kerry's head went under.

John Farragut arrived in the displacement bay immediately behind Steele, found the lieutenant colonel parked on a disk and roaring to be displaced down so he could kill Donner.

"Belay that," Augustus told the displacement specialist.

Colonel Steele barked, "Belay *that*. Send me now!"

The D-spec offered by way of apology to Steele, "Sir, we don't have an LD down yet."

Displacement required the most precise measurements, which required three synchronized readings—one from the sender, one from the receiver, and one from the traveler's collar. Displacement without an LD was only eighty percent accurate. The only thing you ever displaced without an LD was an LD.

"I'll take my chances," Steele growled.

"You shall do no such thing, Lieutenant Colonel," said Augustus in maddening calm. *Lieutenant Colonel.* Augustus pushed Steele's short rank up in his face with that one.

Steele turned to John Farragut, just arrived on the displacement deck, "Sir!" But Farragut silently confirmed Augustus' order with a slight shake of his head. Didn't want to cross his Marine out loud, but his frown said, *No way, TR.*

Augustus continued, indicating the haze on the monitor, "*That* is poison gas, and you are going to wait."

"The yellow." Farragut saw it. "The infamous yellow gas?"

Augustus gave a brisk affirmative with a single nod, while, on the monitor, the image cleared enough for him to make out Kerry Blue's face, floating, slack, under the water. Her eyelids hovered, corpselike, at half-mast.

Steele roared, "Then get me an exo-suit! What the hell—?"

There was a splash on the monitor. Swirling water. A glimpse of a second face under the water. Donner's. Contorted, drowning.

"Who got *him?*" the D-spec cried.

"Donner did," said Augustus.

Incredibly, the Archon had dived into the pond of his own accord.

Augustus did not seem the least surprised. "He's buying some breathing room, so to say. No doubt he hit an alarm to summon his security guards. All dictators have them. But he cannot afford to breathe during the time it will take for the cavalry to arrive to rescue him. Even in concentrations measured in parts per billion, yellow gas causes brain damage. And no, our differences in physiology will *not* protect us. Yellow gas is inorganic."

"Get me a breather, then!" Steele ordered. "Why aren't you doing anything!"

"I am," said Augustus, his voice never changing. "I have ordered you a full suit. Ah, here it comes now. Yellow gas can be absorbed through the eyes or through cuts. You are going to secure all your seals before you go down." The Roman was giving orders now.

Steele already had two legs into the suit. Kept glancing at the seconds flying off the chronometer.

"I've got a read, sirs," the D-spec announced, trying to imitate the Roman's dead calm. Failing. The young specialist was nearly jumping out of his seat. "Ready to send a landing disk."

Farragut signaled affirmative with a closing of his eyes, and Augustus ordered, "Go displacement."

The disk vanished from the chamber with a clap.

"God *bless!*" The specialist hissed.

"What?" Steele demanded, testing his seals.

"It's a miss. It's a miss." The D-spec looked up from his console. His upper lip blossomed wet beads. "LD's buried in the floor. No good."

"Again," Augustus ordered without emotion as Steele swore and yelled, "Get it right, you mechanical Roman spy! You're supposed to be a patterner!"

Augustus spoke dispassionately: "Chaos happens." And to the feverish young specialist, "Again. When you are ready."

"Recalibrated," the D-spec reported.

"Check for jammers," said Augustus.

"Checking, aye. And . . . negative jammers."

"Go."

"And . . . sending."

The second LD vanished with a hammering rap of converging air.

Dire seconds tripped away. On the monitor Kerry Blue's image drifted at the bottom of the pond, her brown hair floating around a deathly bluish face.

The specialist: "We are down. And . . ."

"And?" Steele bellowed.

"We were five centimeters high, sir. We are spinning, and . . . we're . . . we're down and . . . we're right side up and. . . . we are functional." The young specialist's eyes were glassy bright. "All green."

Steele closed his eyes, stiffened, motionless on the sending disk, gripping the equipment pack. He felt an extra dog collar bulging in there. He was meant to save the Archon, too.

Heard the trailing end of his booming arrival onto the planet's surface.

Steele jumped off his LD, hefted it up and tucked it under his arm as he pulled a dog collar out of his pack. He turned full around in the yellow haze. Sighted the ornamental pond sunk in the floor.

Rushed to slide the LD under Kerry Blue's floating body. Felt/heard his sleeve snag on something, a rock, a twig.

He held his breath, but did not stop to check his suit's integrity. He swept silken waves of Kerry's hair aside and snapped the dog collar around her cold, rubbery neck, steadied her limp form over the LD.

"She's in place. Do you have a read?" Steele's voice bellowed back at him within the confines of his bubble head helmet. Realized how loud he'd been shouting. "Evac Blue! Evac Blue!"

He glimpsed the flicker of green lights on her collar and in the LD beneath her just before the water smacked in on itself with her vanishing.

Only then did Steele check his sleeve to see if he was about to die.

His suit was still intact.

He attended to the Archon with less urgency, taking great care what his sleeves contacted. He made sure his gloves were clear of the dog collar as he snapped it shut. May have got some of Donner's skin. Too bad.

As he readied to signal the ship, he spied a familiar set of saurian eyes peering up at him from under a clump of pondweed. Steele grabbed the lizard plant, closed Donner's arms around it, and ordered the second evac.

Water slapped into the sudden vacuum and sloshed back over the edges of the pond in the recoil.

Steele touched the switch at his collar to transmit. "How's Blue?"

"Calling geese," Augustus reported.

Steele could hear Kerry coughing in the background— big, honking coughs, gargled curses. Swearing like a stevedore. That was his girl.

"Your MO says we got her in time," said Augustus.

Anger dizzied Steele. Fear. More than he could feel for any other of his Marines. And for what? Kerry Blue was just a slut.

A pretty, funny, sexy slut. What Steele tried to pretend

was scorn—those black feelings that choked him when he saw her draped on a crewmate—wasn't scorn. It was jealousy.

Everything about that woman called to him. Rough and ready. That easy smile. Her live-for-the-moment courage. Her crude honesty. Made him hurt. Made him want her for himself.

Made him crazy.

He took big breaths, as if he were the one drowning. Trying to breathe out the anger. *She's okay. She's okay.* Listened to her cough.

A voice in his helmet—the young displacement specialist: "We are ready to bring you up, sir. Take a position on the LD, please."

"No. I'm staying."

"Not advisable." The voice unmistakably Augustus'. "One tear in your suit and your brain is fried. Not that one would notice given that yours is all meat, but I would suggest you evacuate."

Steele made no move toward the LD. "Just somebody tell me if this yellow shit degrades into something harmless and how long does it take?"

Something this rare and lethal could not be stable.

A moment's pause for consultation, then Dr. Shah confirmed, sounding some distance from the com, probably kneeling on the deck, tending Kerry: "This is being true, Colonel Steele. Yellow gas is taking forty-five minutes to be degrading."

Augustus: "What's on your muscle-bound brain, Lieutenant Colonel?"

"Whoever booby-trapped this room thinks he's killed the Archon. They're going to wait till it's safe, then send someone in here to collect the body. I want to greet whoever comes through that door and beat the living crap out of them."

"Better idea," Augustus countered. "Plant a force field down there and cage the perps when they come in, and hand them over to the Archon. He's breathing up here. He can doubtless do something vastly more cruel and unusual than you are allowed even to think about."

Dr. Shah looked up from where he knelt on the floor tending to Kerry Blue. Cried, "God, the Roman mind!"

But Steele transmitted: "Wait a minute, Mo. I *like* that idea."

There fell another pause. That kind of silence waited on John Farragut to weigh in.

Farragut said, "It's cruel and sadistic."

"And?" Augustus prompted.

Steele waited. Heard Kerry's lung-wrenching coughs over the com.

The captain spoke at last: "And I don't have a problem with it."

"Cut your own line of communication and walked into an ambush, didn't you, Marine."

Oh, he was all heart, Steele was. Stood there like a marble block at her bedside in sick bay. Kerry had been stupid, and the Old Man was here to tell her about it.

The other patients in sick bay seemed to be all victims of nitrogen narcosis, from when the captain squeezed the ship to five atmospheres. Mo had those all breathing heli-ox in a static-free chamber.

Colonel Augustus ducked through the hatchway behind Steele. "You got a visitor, Blue." And the tall Roman curtly dropped her lizard plant onto her cot. It scuttled to huddle under her chin, wrapping its tail round her upper arm.

She burst into tears. Not in front of Steele, you idiot. Not in front of Steele. Oh, hell.

She stroked her pet's leaves, and sniffled. Tried to talk. Her voice croaked out rawly, "Captain Farragut tells me I got you three guys to thank for my life." Mohsen Shah, the Medical Officer for reviving her, Augustus for keeping an eye on her and sending up the balloon, and Steele for getting her out of there.

"Four guys," Mo Shah corrected her. "Donner. Without Donner, we would have lost you. He kept you from breathing the gas. And the cold of the water bought us seconds we were really not having. I am seeing how he came to being master of his universe."

Steele snarled, "Seems to me Donner is who got her *into* the situation."

"And I was rather more interested in saving the Archon," Augustus excused himself. "A grateful dictator is never a bad thing to have."

"Oh, you gots to know I know a crock when I hear it, sir." Kerry sat up, dragged Augustus down to her level by his collar, and bussed the Roman's cheek. "Where's Donner?"

Donner had already displaced back down to Arra, as soon as he was awake, still coughing, in a tearing haste to punish his would-be assassins and his incompetent guards. When Farragut asked him if Donner knew who his assailants were, Donner had replied tersely, "Criminals. Not your concern."

"He gave me something," said Kerry, hands to her chest searching for the crystal.

The crystal was gone. Someone had undressed her and left her in a hospital shift. "It was a recording. Crystal thing. Big as a lipstick. I stuck it in my bra. It's a recording. Did you get the recording? Can you make it play back?"

"We got it," said Augustus.

"Is it good? Is it useful? Can you find Origin from it?" she asked, eager for praise. Kerry Blue could go for parsecs on an atta girl.

Augustus' reply was neutral. "It is in analysis."

Steele's reply was a snort.

Kerry slumped back into her cot. She pouted, petting her lizard. Lotta brass here. None of her flight mates had come to see how she was doing. That stung. "Where's Reg?"

Colonel Steele left abruptly, so she could not see his face.

Captain Farragut waylaid Steele on his exit from sick bay. Beckoned Colonel Steele in close with a jerk of his head.

Here it comes.

It was brief, calm, private. "It's getting obvious, TR. Handle it."

And that was all.

The first flash of anger and denial quickly rose and quickly burned out. Steele swallowed the lump of resentment in time to appreciate the lack of sermon or any meddling suggestions of how to fix it. When a bone tumbles out of your closet, Farragut toes it back for you to make it go away.

Steele acknowledged thickly, "Sir."

Steele stalked to his station. Had his distraction surrounding Kerry Blue caused him to overlook something he should have seen? Cause him to lose track of an *entire flight of Swifts*? Something that would have let him answer that question: Where's Reg?

Where *was* Reg Monroe? Where was Dakota Shepard? Hazard Sewell? Carly Delgado? Twitch Fuentes?

Alpha Flight had gone from late to officially missing.

Steele stared at all the majestic stars on the monitor.

God, if you're out there, where are my people?

No beginning. No end.

Flight Sergeant Reg Monroe had gone to sleep twice in hopes of waking up from this nightmare. Twice she awoke to utter nothingness beyond the confines of her Swift. A space without form. No light. No stars. No air. No readings. No gravity. No burps in her inertia field, as if there were no inertia here. No motion. Felt as if she were parked.

And where was the rest of Alpha Flight? Reg had been flying right behind Dak. *Right* behind him. Where was he? Where was Twitch? Where was Carly? They had to be here.

Where was here?

She tried to turn around and go back. Could not find which direction was 180.

No up. No down.

She punched up intership radio, bouncing bubble, tight beam, broadcast, any and every means she had to contact her flight, to contact anyone.

Except the res. The res switch wore a red lockout on her console. Res pulse was instant contact. Res pulse would bring the Hive.

Activating her resonant pulse would get her cashiered. It would get the Myriad eaten alive.

Though she was not sure she was even *in* the Myriad anymore.

Her Swift would not even tell her how fast she was going. It would tell her what kind of power she was putting out, but it would not clock a velocity for her. There were no referents.

Time. There was time. The chronometer worked. Gauges of internal functions worked. Told her at what rate she was using up her oxygen and her water.

A Swift's distortion field was not nearly as tight as *Merrimack*'s. You lost air in these little ships. The air scrubber was not the best either. This wasn't a pleasure boat. You fought or you did your patrol and you returned to the ship. That's what you did in a Swift.

You did *not* get lost.

Time to get methodical about this. She pulled up the diagnostic screen on her computer. Damn thing tried to tell her all systems were functioning. She pulled up the debug screen.

Reg had enlisted in the Fleet Marines to go to college on Uncle Sam's card. Maybe Kerry Blue was content having no better schooling than the average toaster oven, but Reg did not plan to stay dumb forever. She had not been able to get into the Navy. No spaceman aboard Farragut's boat didn't have an associate degree or better. Mostly better.

There'd been no such requirement to get into the Corps. You had to be stupid to take this job (so said the navvies). But the Corps taught her things. Taught her to fly. Taught her how machines worked. And when her tour was up, the Corps was going to pay for *her* degree. Better than an associate degree. Reg Monroe was going to be an engineer someday, in the Navy, with braid on her sleeve, and she was going to sit at the table with the likes of John Farragut and Calli Carmel and His Fine Self Jose Maria Cordillera.

Reg wanted to marry someone like *Don* Cordillera. Didn't see herself bunking forever with belching nematodes like Dak Shepard. *This* elegant hag was moving up and out, so help her God, and if she had to kill someone to get there, then bring on the gorgons, bring on the Romans. Bring on anything but this.

What *was* this? She had not signed on for this.

This had to end some time.

Heard the whisper before she knew she was doing it. "Let me out."

Tried to concentrate on the screen. Assembly language. Might as well be Chinese.

"Let me out."

She rocked back and forth in her seat. "Let me out. Let me out."

Screaming soon. Bouncing off the sides of the cockpit. "Let me out! Let me out let me out let me out!"

Didn't even try to quiet herself.

There was no one around to hear.

*   *   *

Alpha Flight was still missing as Delta and Echo Flights returned from recon missions of the other two inhabited planets of the Myriad, Centro and Rea.

The flights confirmed that Centro and Rea had both already received the Archon's address to the nation—faster than any Myriadian spaceship could travel, faster than light, faster than even flights of Swifts traveling many times the speed of light had crossed the distance.

"How the blue blazes are they doing that?" Farragut asked anyone within earshot.

No one could answer.

Echo Flight reported Centro to be a struggling little outpost of 900,000 beings, who looked just like Arrans. They were settled in the narrow hospitable zone of an arid world of high winds and a ruddy sun half as luminous as Sol. Most Centrans lived around the spaceport. The heavy elements used in the spaceport's construction had come from elsewhere, probably Arra, because, as Pilot Officer Jan Karowicz put it: "Molybdenum don't grow wild on Centro."

Echo Flight had sighted a Myriadian spaceship in flight in the Centro system, poking along at eighty percent c. The Myriadian ship did not come into Centro's spaceport. "I didn't think it could have seen us, but it must have because it just flew on by," said Pilot Officer Karowicz. "We withdrew from the system so it might feel safe to come home, because it was just running off to nowhere."

Delta Flight reported the other planet, Rea, to be much the same, a small world, lacking in heavy elements and orbiting close to an M8V sun. There were three million inhabitants on Rea, living on the seacoasts. The oceans were bigger than Centro's, rotation slower, same ruddy sky. "Didn't look like any prize, but the Reans seem to like it," said Delta Leader.

If Augustus' description of Origin was accurate, then maybe Rea looked like home sweet home.

"Deck three."

Steele jumped. He had his com open to monitor the control room, waiting for this. *Jesus, God, there they are.*

He took the rungs by twos up the ladder to the control

room deck. Found the Officer of the Watch, little Glenn Hamilton, hovering over the sensor station with an air of guarded alertness.

Steele read the faces on the command platform. His spirits sagged. "It's not my flight?"

"No, sir," Lieutenant Hamilton answered. "Big return." And she snapped impatiently to the tac specialist, "Give me an F, Jeffrey. Which is it?" Friend or Foe?

"Foe," the specialist, Jeffrey reported, finally resolving the signal. The fresh-scrubbed, big-eared college boy looked up from his readouts. "We got ourselves an effing LEN golf ball."

"F 'em back." Hamster crossed her arms. Shortest man jack or jane on board *Merrimack*, Glenn Hamilton looked like a doll dressed up in a lieutenant's uniform. "Confirm that ID."

"Aye, sir."

The bloody gorgons were preternaturally adaptable. It was only a matter of time before they learned to fox an IFF response.

And Hive swarms traveled tightly bunched into giant spheres, giving them the same big round profile as a peaceful League of Earth Nations exploratory vessel.

And though they were expected, the LEN were not expected *yet*. *Merrimack* had sent the notice scant days ago. The LEN were not expected in the Myriad for weeks or months.

"ID confirmed," said Jeffrey.

Lieutenant Hamilton glanced to the chronometer, murmured, "They didn't waste any time."

The LEN had to have been on the frontier already to get here so fast. Just luck.

Bad luck from *Merrimack*'s end of it.

"Recheck ID."

"ID confirmed."

Hamster's auburn brows drew together. "If I didn't know better, I'd say they were stalking us."

"You know better?"

Hamster turned to find the Roman IO on deck. "No. Actually, I don't. Do you, Colonel Augustus?"

"They lost you at the Sagittan Nebula," said Augustus. "*I* did not."

"But," Hamster shook her head. "Why would the LEN be on our tail?"

"Digging for conspiracies, dirty military dealings, secret abominations. Things the U.S. Navy are known for."

"We are not."

"To paranoid defenders of nature, you are."

Hamster turned to the tac specialist. "Jeff, what ship is that?"

"Woodland Serenity."

Steele grunted. When the League of Earth Nations had learned that an American military vessel had tripped over a Class Nine ETI, they would have sped here on fire. "They're afraid we'll uf the contact."

"Wouldn't want to disappoint them," Hamster said faintly.

Courtesies were cursory. League of Earth Nations representatives all but stormed through the long flexuous temporary corridor which connected *Woodland Serenity* and the battleship *Merrimack* the moment soft dock was achieved. They demanded with undiplomatic haste and candor, "You haven't contaminated the site, have you?"

When the LEN learned the full extent of the "contamination," they went hyperbolic, appalled near to rapture at the list of naval transgressions:

Obliterating native defenses (the minefield).

Terrorizing the populace (turning the Arran missiles around on Arra).

Sending a female soldier down for a Mati Hari-style spy mission (Flight Sergeant Blue's recon).

Displacing a sapient life-form aboard *Merrimack* without its consent (the rescue of Donner).

Interfering with an alien nation's internal power struggle (the rescue of Donner).

"I shouldn't have saved the Archon?" Farragut asked.

"No," Ambassador Aghani confirmed. "It was an internal matter. You had no right."

"I had a duty. I'm here to defend the U.S., Earth, and her protectorates and allies. My next duty is to my crew and company. The Myriadian opposition party isn't on that list. I saved the guy who saved my Marine. Local political complications aren't my concern."

"I'm sorry if this is too complicated for you, Captain Farragut," said Ambassador Aghani. "But you're right: it's not your concern." And Aghani ordered *Merrimack* out of the Myriad immediately.

"We're gone," Farragut declared without argument. But Steele advised in a murmur, "Captain, I still have a flight out."

"—*Just* as soon as my patrol gets back," Farragut amended.

"When is your patrol due?" Aghani demanded.

"I am not required to divulge that information," Farragut answered. He had absolutely no idea.

"We are all allies here, Captain," Aghani reminded him.

"Information on Naval operations is available on a need-to-know basis. Why do you need to know?"

"We can give your boats hangar."

Gasps and stifled laughter burst from the Naval personnel on deck; gagging and bristling from the Marines. No one could quite believe the nerve of the LEN suggestion: Just leave. The LEN would pick up the stranded flight.

Farragut answered lightly, "I think not."

Chagrined at their own overstep, the LEN personnel withdrew to their ship. Farragut turned to Lieutenant Colonel Steele. "So when are your Swifts due back?"

"Two hours ago."

Farragut frowned. "They didn't bubble you?"

"No, sir."

"Bubble them?"

"Can't see them."

The captain understood the import. Said anyway: "We'll wait for them."

Steele exhaled, grateful. "Yes, sir."

"Find them, TR."

The captain had a way of giving an order that made it seem not just possible but expected. John Farragut had faith enough to float a battleship. "Yes, sir!" Steele answered, heartened—while knowing full well when people disappear in outer space they stay gone.

Relations with the LEN regrouped into an edgy, adversarial cordiality, the kind of brittle intercourse once reserved for encounters between Earth and Palatine.

Though the United States was a League nation, LEN assistance in U.S. attempts to retain its colony had never gone beyond harsh words. The LEN, over the objection of one of its members, had long since recognized Palatine as an independent nation.

The LEN representatives were now solicitous of Augustus as a member of a conquered people held under the American heel. Their goodwill oozed with the slime of moral superiority. They invited the Roman to add to the LEN's list of complaints against Captain Farragut.

Guillame Kapila asked in flawless Latin, "Are you being equitably treated?"

Augustus might have told Kapila that the Navy had billeted him with the spare torpedoes. Instead he gave the LEN representative stone silence, as if Kapila had addressed a robot.

"Colonel Augustus?" Kapila prompted.

Augustus stared elsewhere.

Kapila glanced to the captain. "Why does he not answer?"

"I don't know. Augustus, why don't you answer?"

"I was not addressed by a recognized entity," Augustus told the captain.

"Recognize him and answer him," said Farragut.

Augustus turned to Kapila and answered frostily, in English, "I am not here to chat with civilians." And back to Farragut: "Permission to leave the deck."

The request sounded wholly alien coming from Augustus. Amazed to be the target of Augustus' courtesy, Farragut let him go.

Augustus loathed people who apologized for their own kind.

And Augustus was not the only one who would not answer the LEN. When Farragut tried to pass the banner to the LEN, Donner would not come to the radio.

The LEN could not get past layer upon layer of intermediaries, secretaries, and toadies that came between them and the Archon, encountering each time lower- and lower-ranking individuals, until the only beings on Arra whom the Earthlings could get to come to the com were juvenile females who recited songs for them.

The League representatives demanded that Captain Farragut assist in making contact, but Donner would not even come to the com for Farragut anymore.

Donner was most displeased to discover that John Farragut was not the Archon of Earth. Donner did not talk to minions.

The LEN, in turn, was convinced that this refusal to communicate was at the Navy's instigation. After all, all rational beings desired communication.

"You didn't want us to make contact," Farragut countered the LEN accusations. "Now you want introductions?"

"The indigenous beings have only heard Earth speak through its belligerents," said Ambassador Aghani. "Now that the damage is done, they must also hear from the peaceful Earth. You will lift this barrier to understanding. Do you understand me, Captain?"

Since Donner would not come to the com, Farragut, Augustus, and the LEN embassy burst down into the Archon's presence in the Archon's own garden.

Donner had been crouched at the lakeside with a little male child, showing him how to skip grains across the water to make winged, scarlet fish leap out and catch them before brilliant azure swallow-tailed birds could swoop down and snap up the grains first.

At the first firecracker arrival of a landing disk, the child ran, keening. The birds scattered, shrieking and flapping. Guards ran to the terrace railing, weapons ready.

Donner rose in annoyance at the Earthlings' thunderous arrival. He tossed his handful of grain into the water to a thrashing turbulence of fins.

Donner looked only at Farragut. "Because you saved my life, I shall not have you shot. I will speak to your Archon. Now."

Farragut muttered aside in English, ("I need a pronoun here, Augustus.") He needed she-supreme.

("Doesn't exist.") No such entity in the Myriad. No such pronoun.

Captain Farragut answered the Archon in Myriadian. "The President of the United States is female. It would take the better part of your year for anyone to get here from Earth. Marisa Johnson's calendar is always full, but I'll relay your request on the next courier. It will take a good sixty days to get an answer."

The alien face assumed the rounded lines of unmistakable shock.

Farragut dropped back into English for a quick consultation. ("Augustus, he's been using a different 'you' to me here. What's he calling me?")

("You have been demoted to a subordinate.")

("How do I 'you' him back?")

("What sort of 'you' would you like? You-servant? You-dog? You-child?")

("Child. That's a good one. Give me you-child.")

Guillame Kapila broke in with grave reservations. ("Captain Farragut, this is not the sort of course I would pursue.")

("That's why I didn't ask you. Augustus?")

("*Inti*," Augustus supplied the pronoun.)

("Thank you.") Farragut turned back to the Archon. "And *inti*, Donner, *you* may address your questions to me in President Johnson's absence, or to the duly designated representatives of the League of Earth Nations."

Donner's bronze face purpled in mounting rage. The League ambassadors hastily searched their language modules, trying to compose words with which to break into this debacle and smooth over Farragut's blundering arrogant insults, when suddenly the Archon broke into laughter, and Farragut grinned.

"*You*," Donner pointed to Farragut, restoring him to equal status. "Walk with me. Not them." He waved the LEN behind. "Only you."

Donner tolerated Augustus trailing behind, perhaps recognizing the effeminately tall Roman's usefulness.

The LEN balked, tried to follow also, but Donner's guards blocked their way.

Farragut could hear the LEN representatives calling, ("Don't think we don't see what you're doing here, Captain Farragut! This shall be reported.")

Augustus caught Farragut's eye and murmured skeptically, ("Those are Earth's ambassadors?")

Farragut shrugged. ("Well.")

It was fast becoming apparent that these LEN representatives were not the sort of ambassadors that one sends between nations. Not at all like Jose Maria Cordillera, who was a former Terra Rican ambassador to the United States.

These were conservationists on a mission to save alien cultures from Earth interference. Edenists. Put simply (and the problem was very simple to them): Man degrades everything he touches. Everything in nature is natural except humankind. Made for less than diplomatic diplomats. The LEN representatives carried the courtesy title "ambassador" to facilitate their contact with alien species.

Could hear them shouting from behind the cordon of the Archon's guards, ("This is *exactly* what we sought to avoid, Captain Farragut! Do you see what you have done!")

Farther up the colonnade, the protests diminished. Farragut heard only alien creatures singing.

The unreal beauty of the star-bright Arran night could make a man forget why he was here.

Up ahead, under the colonnade, servants swept walking-sticks off the cool-shadowed ceiling with an air of evening ritual, shooing the creatures back into the garden.

At the Archon's approach, the menials gathered up their tools and discreetly vanished between glistening white marble columns.

"Your President," said Donner, hands clasped behind his back as they strolled. "A figurehead?"

"No."

Donner coughed, a deep cough like Kerry Blue's. "You pledged yourself to serve a female?"

"I pledged myself to the Constitution of the United States," said Farragut.

Donner puzzled over this. Asked, "This President sends you orders?"

"I left with a mission objective, but orders? No. Not at this distance. Circumstances prohibit use of our instant communications system. So I'm on my own out here."

"Do you mean to say your instant communication system does not work this far away?"

"No. It does work. We don't dare use it here. There is something else out here that uses resonant pulse, and it can track a signal back to its transmitter. We must not resonate. We're on silent run."

Donner gazed up at the blazing host of stars in the indigo sky. Gave a human scowl. The more answers he got, the more questions he had. "And these LEN. What are they?"

"Representatives of the League of Earth Nations.

They're scientists and ambassadors. They mean no harm. In fact, they are here to protect you."

"They don't like you."

"They don't like my interfering in your world."

Donner considered this. Liked the recognition that it was *his* world. Cast a satisfied gaze about his grounds.

Colonies of ambiguous plant/animal things lined the walkway. The xenos called them euglenoids; the Marines called them "land coral." Fans and antlers and ledges and domes and honeycombs of them in all the colors of a tropical sea lay about in reefs in the garden. Feathery fronds unfolded from tough shells under the gentle light.

Donner's world.

Then the rest of the implication caught up with him. "You 'interfered' with my world." The only thing Donner knew that Farragut had done was to save Donner's life. "They would have let me die?"

"You will have to ask them that," Farragut dodged.

"They can give you orders? They have that power?"

"If I stay here, yes. Unless your worlds come under attack from space, they can do that. In a military situation, I *am* the archon. In peacetime, they have jurisdiction over any Earth presence in a sovereign system."

"You must explain your command structure. I do not understand who is in charge. How can it change moment to moment?"

Probably ought not to try to explain about Presidential elections. Farragut said, "The ultimate authority we all answer to is the law. The law doesn't change. The individual in power does."

"These LEN. Are they a faction?"

Captain Farragut could see the route the Archon's mind had taken, filtering information to fit his own situation. The *Merrimack* had taken Donner's side against a rebellious faction. Donner would consider doing the same for John Farragut.

"No. We don't have a world government. The League of Earth Nations is a . . . league." Farragut could not shave the meaning of the alien words close enough to explain himself.

"There is no one supreme power?"

"No. But you must be familiar with this. Your home planet Origin must have more than one nation."

"It used to," said Donner. "It could not remain so."

"Ours did."

"How inefficient."

"Very," Augustus footnoted from behind them.

Donner cocked his head. Had forgotten Augustus was back there. Asked Farragut, "You let him talk like that? Is he not your subordinate?"

"At the moment he is supposed to be. Augustus' people are imperial. They have a single government on his world. But my country controls his world right now."

Donner stopped, turned to face both of them. "You and you are not from one world?" He used you-equal and you-subordinate for Farragut and Augustus.

"Palatine is a breakaway colony," said Augustus.

"And we are enemies," Farragut pointed between himself and Augustus.

Augustus made a *T'Arra* motion of agreement.

Now Donner was completely confused. "But this one is your adviser. He takes orders from you."

"Palatine came under U.S. protection," Farragut explained.

"U.S. That is your nation. Palatine came under you how?"

"They begged," said Farragut.

"We asked," said Augustus.

"A common enemy," said Farragut.

"An enemy not like you and you are enemies," Donner surmised, pointing from Farragut to Augustus.

"No," Farragut agreed. "Ours was a cold war."

"That did not translate. I do not understand 'cold war.' "

"Cold war means we are not shooting at each other," said Farragut.

"At the moment," said Augustus.

"At the moment," said Farragut.

"In a rational universe, we are shooting at each other," said Augustus.

Donner waited for Farragut to counter that. When he did not, Donner asked him, "The universe is not rational?"

Farragut shook his head. "Not since our common enemy showed up."

Donner's dark eyes flicked back and forth, weighing the sides. "What kind of enemy is this that drew you together?"

Farragut hesitated. How to explain the Hive? "Monsters," he said at last. "They eat. That is all you really need to know about them."

"Which protein structure do they eat?" Donner asked. "Left-handed or right-handed?"

Donner's own proteins had a different structure than Arran native life. He would be aware of the difference, and the incompatibility of the two. Wanted to know if he were on the menu.

"Both. All. The Hive is a universal omnivore."

"You think these monsters are here?"

"No. We know they are not." Farragut had come here on the gorgons' trail. Lost them somewhere. Couldn't figure out how.

"And now you will both take orders from those—" Donner made a face of distate, "—those LEN?"

"No. We're leaving."

Without the cameras on him, Donner could admit his inferior position; he confessed his own dilemma: "How do I order a being with all those big guns to stay?" Donner very much wanted John Farragut's *Merrimack* on his team.

Farragut smiled. "I need to take my big guns away to hunt monsters."

"Do the LEN have guns?"

"No."

Augustus added, "You may abuse the LEN as much as you wish. They'll enjoy it."

Farragut darted Augustus a glare. ("Belay that.")

("Aye, sir.")

It was the first time Farragut could remember Augustus calling him *sir*. And in English yet; not for show in front of the Archon. Just between Augustus and Farragut. *Sir*.

Donner sulked, "The LEN have a ridiculous-looking ship."

"They do," Farragut had to agree. The spheroid LEN golf ball lacked the belligerent charm of *Merrimack*.

"Your vessel commands respect."

"She's a brute," said Farragut with satisfaction.

Farragut had used the pronoun she-beloved. Intentional. Did not escape Donner's notice.

"You will leave when?"

Farragut demurred. He was not about to tell the alien he had a flight in trouble. Answered only, "Shortly."

Augustus asked Donner, "Have you ever lost a ship traveling between planets?"

The question—or the poser of it—took Donner aback. The Archon answered, sharply, to Captain Farragut. "No."

("He's lying,") said Augustus.

("I know.") Farragut heard it. The answer was too quick, too adamant.

And, seized by a fit of coughing, Donner told Farragut he was done talking. Bade him go now, and take his LEN with him.

Back aboard *Merrimack*, Farragut turned to his IO and demanded, "How are the Myriadians getting between planets?"

"Transportation is one of Donner's high cards. He won't be giving that one away. It's a tightly guarded government secret. It's not stored anywhere I can access it."

"Augustus already has it." That was Lieutenant Colonel Steele, waiting in the displacement bay for his captain's return. "He's just not telling."

Augustus smiled coldly. "Lieutenant Colonel Steele, you're not even an educated man, so what is your grudge? You were never forced to learn Latin for your trade. Unless higher education is required for bashing heads these days?"

Farragut ran interference. "Colonel Steele is concerned that you'll get into Mack's computer and take over my ship."

"I can't do that," said Augustus.

Farragut looked to Steele for a riposte.

"You can't be sure," said Steele.

Farragut's blue eyes returned to Augustus, like following a tennis volley.

"If it's so jolly possible, flattop, then *you* shove your brain in there and make her open fire on Palatine," Augustus suggested.

Eyes back to Steele. "TR?"

Steele had nothing to answer that.

So Farragut returned to the problem of breaking Donner's secrets. "Augustus, if I get you access to one of Donner's military computers, would you be able to find the pattern?"

Augustus frowned. "Those antique computers have no remote access. It would have to be a physical attachment with a cable. And the Myriadian buses are deathly slow. I think it's a 256-bit data bus. Be like trying to suck Lake Superior through a straw. I can't stay awake that long."

"What can you get me?"

"Tac detected a scheduled flight blasting off for the Rea system. The ship is passing the fifth planet of the Arra system as we speak—at a phenomenal seventy-five percent c." Irony there. The Arran ship was crawling. "I could put a tail on it, see how the Myriadians expect to complete that trip in less than fifty-seven years."

"Do it."

"Requires my using one of Steele's Swift flights."

Captain Farragut turned to the commander of the Marines. "TR, lend us some dogs?"

Steele balked. "Last soldier that Roman commandeered ended up breathing in a goldfish pond."

"At least I didn't *lose* her," Augustus returned fire. Drew blood on that one. "I'm pretty sure the Marine I commandeered is the only member of Alpha Flight currently accounted for."

Farragut teed his palms to break off that discussion before it turned to fists. "Any thoughts on the disappearance of Alpha Flight, Augustus?"

"I think Lieutenant Colonel Steele is having trouble keeping hold of his troops."

"Something *useful*, Augustus?"

"All holes in the ground are not trapdoors."

John Farragut blinked, not making the connection. "What does that mean?"

"Means whatever got you wasn't necessarily meant for you."

"It *got* us."

"So did Donner's minefield. The minefield wasn't meant for you either. Your self-absorbed attitude leads you to interpret everything in terms of self. Your flight's disappearance has nothing to do with you."

"It's *my* flight," Steele jerked the Roman's attention back to him.

"But only for another few hours," said Augustus evenly. "I looked into the Swifts' checkout logs. They're carrying supplies for a short patrol. Their oxygen is running out right now. Dakota Shepard is an air sucker. He's already out. The women might last two more hours. After that, they're the sky pilot's flight."

Sprung from sick bay, Kerry Blue reported for duty. Lieutenant Colonel Steele told her to find a streetlight and stand under it.

He must have seen the pride fall right out of her face. Disappointment sogged down her insides. She thought the world of this man, and he said *that* to her? She tried to project her thoughts in case he could read her mind: *How dare you? How frogging dare you?*

And she must've got through somehow, because Steele said next, "For the next five seconds I'm not your CO."

She had heard about these moments—the colonel's brief windows of opportunity. They came once in a blue moon. He did it to level the playing field when he stepped on someone's tail and couldn't take it back.

Cowboy talked often of what he would do given the chance. If Steele ever told him he had two seconds, Cowboy Carver would piss on Steele's leg. Dakota tried to tell him two seconds wasn't enough time to whip out and launch a pee. Kerry remembered saying, "I don't know, Dak, Cowboy's real fast with that thing."

The point would remain forever moot. Colonel Steele never gave Cowboy any magic seconds. These opportunities were rare. And when they come, you better not blink, because they don't wait and they don't come back.

Kerry didn't hesitate. She clopped him hard on the cheek. And with a second to spare, hit him again.

The second one startled him.

The end of five seconds brought Kerry to stiff, decorous attention. "Thank you, sir."

Steele rubbed his square jaw. "I gave you too long."

"Yes, *sir!*" Kerry wanted to jump up and down. Got him! Got him!

Thought she might have spied a hint of humor in the colonel's ice-blue eye as he barked at her, "Dismissed!"

Kerry danced back to the forecastle. Ha! Got him! Got him! Couldn't wait to tell Reg.

No Reg.

"Where's Reg?"

Lots of eyes focused on anything but her. This was bad. This was real bad. "Where's Reg?" Heard the wobble in her voice. Dread squeezed her chest.

She ran to the pod racks. Banged on the men's partition. "Dak? Dak! *Dak!*"

Grabbed the first spaceman to cross her path—physically grabbed him by the front of the tunic and made him face her. "Where is my team!"

And wouldn't you know it, she had a baby-faced cherry in her fist. Didn't look old enough to drink. Held a rate above hers. He cowered as if Flight Sergeant Kerry Blue were a fire-breathing general. "Yes, um, I think I heard something about one of the Marine squadrons being, um, somewhat . . . overdue?"

Alice, when she fell down the rabbit hole, had company. An odd collection of chatty things. There was absolutely nothing here.

No sense of motion. And that was possibly the hardest part. If Reg at least had the feeling of going somewhere, then she might hold out the hope that she might at length *arrive*.

She was going no place but mad.

Crying hysterically had helped a little. Very little. For a time.

Too frightened to sleep, she was now exhausted on top of terrified. Imagining things. At the limit of hope, patience, discipline, all of it. She broke the lockout from the res pulse transmitter. Hesitated over the forbidden button.

She had been told over and over, don't hit the res, no matter what. It will bring hungry gorgons.

She took a big breath and yelled: "Come and get it!" Brought her palm down flat on the button. She hadn't even coded a message. Just shot off a res pulse like a flare.

She would be brought up on charges, if she lived. Leavenworth looked like paradise from here. They couldn't do anything worse to her than this.

She slumped back in her seat, relaxed and relieved enough to try to sleep. Until she glanced over the readouts. Something was desperately wrong.

She wasn't resonating.

She mashed the button again.

It resonated to the bounds of her force field, and not one step beyond. As if the universe ended at her hull.

Nothing out there. No when. No where. This, this nothingness, this did not exist.

Coffined in hopeless horror, too extreme for screaming or tears. Her last resort had failed.

And that answered that.

She was in hell.

7

THE SHIP'S CHRONOMETERS WOUND UP the days, and still *Merrimack* haunted the Myriad. Captain Farragut refused to believe his missing Marines were dead. Believed against all sense or fact that they yet lived somehow, though everyone else, even Lieutenant Colonel Steele, now hoped only to recover the bodies.

He wished he might have used drones instead of live patrols. But without resonance and without human discretion, drones were useless for long-range reconnaissance when the operator could not tell the drones exactly what to look for.

The LEN wanted the U.S. battleship gone from Myriadian space. Wanted them gone yesterday, convinced that Donner would be easier to talk to without *Merrimack* lurking in orbit. Convinced that Farragut was holding a gun to the Archon's head.

Fed up with the stalling, Ambassador Aghani demanded Farragut inform the LEN of his estimated time of departure. Captain Farragut could not confess that he had a problem. Not to these people. A missing flight was military confidential.

And telling the LEN that he had since dispatched a second flight would torque them off pretty good. Farragut did not want to recall Echo Flight from its surveillance of the

Rea-bound Arran ship. He still harbored hopes of uncovering the Myriadian secret of interstellar travel. But he had run out of time.

Aghani repeated the demand. "Captain?"

Farragut inhaled long, a three-second stall in which answers might come to him—and smiled brightly at the end of it.

Captain Farragut invited the LEN diplomats to dinner.

Like Atalanta's golden apples, a social obligation was a thing the LEN dignitaries could not just run past. They must—must—stop and be civilized. Representatives of the League of Earth Nations held hospitality sacred, especially out here where life was so fragile and tenuous. At any rate, they could not afford to be brusque in comparison to the American military.

Aghani accepted.

The last dogwatch arrived with still no sign of Alpha Flight and no report from Echo Flight. Farragut murmured, awaiting his guests' arrival at the soft dock, "I'm running out of ideas here."

"Eat slow," said Augustus.

The officers' mess had been transformed into something approaching elegant. That *Merrimack* was a long-range vessel was no excuse for barbarism. Some thought a formal dinner was high silliness, but John Farragut could play it, could play any situation as it came. Could throw back shooters or savor a Chateau d'Argent with equal ease. Could listen to cellos or harmonicas (though he could, and did, play the harmonica). So he was altogether at home amid the pressed linen, the gold-plated cutlery, the snowy white china edged in gold leaf and navy-blue enamel. Dressed in starched whites and blindingly bright brass, he welcomed the ambassadors to his table.

Augustus was dressed in formal Roman black of sedate design except for the brilliant red flourish across his back—either a wide sash or a narrow cape—draped from left shoulder to right hip. Augustus watched the captain launch his full arsenal of charm, treating the LEN to the full Farragut—greeting each guest in his own language without use of a language module. John Farragut knew bits of many languages, usually massacred the accent, but most people appreciated the effort spent in trying.

The conviviality did not endure past the appetizers. The conversation at the captain's table quickly took on the dimensions of a battlefield.

Though English was the lingua franca of the League, the League members resented it and seized every opportunity to speak *anything* else. Aghani used Augustus' presence as an excuse to commandeer the conversation into Latin.

The language of Earth's sometime enemy never lost its educated cachet. Aghani spoke Latin flawlessly. The U.S. officers fell into step, until Madame Navarro thought to check, in English, "We *do* all know Latin here?"

Eyes flicked round the table, Madame Navarro's quite sincerely concerned. Others searched expectantly for a confession of ignorance from one of the Yanks.

And got it. "No," John Farragut answered quickly.

But since Farragut obviously did know Latin, he obviously covered for someone else. Would not say who. John Farragut, as usual, drew all the fire upon himself. He bluffed, "I've been told I'm really bad at it and I've been ordered not to try." Then proposed cheerily: "English, why don't we?" And smiled at everyone.

TR Steele avoided his gaze, sat like a stone.

Augustus withheld a smirk. Silently toasted the captain's smooth flanking maneuver, protecting the dignity of his poorly educated jarhead.

There was no such thing as a classless society. Certainly not on a military spaceship. Captain Farragut might as well be king here. Might as well be God. And TR Steele was a grunt.

Built like a brick wall, broad-shouldered, thick-jawed, CO of the half-brig of Fleet Marines on board, TR Steele was not a picture of refinement—and this book was true to its cover. Steele had come up through the ranks starting as a private, his education all remedial and done late. Physical courage and horse sense he had, with medals to prove it, but no Latin.

The flattop made a stiff, solemn presence at the captain's table. Would not, even when invited, call Captain Farragut "John." Probably fearless in the face of a gorgon horde,

Steele seemed daunted by the dizzying forest of stemware at his place setting. Fortunately, he need only drink from all those glasses, not know how to fill them appropriately. And there were no kantiku glasses, so he needn't worry about when to throw it.

Now the utensils, those could be entertaining. Augustus could tell Steele had never seen a bariki hook in his life, or the cracker for the Cassiopeian conch, or the Nisarian skewers for the flaming munsrit.

Augustus wondered if he could get Steele to use the bariki hook to retrieve the creamer from across the table.

Probably not. Someone would rescue him. Either Farragut or Jose Maria Cordillera, who was seated to Augustus' right—perhaps placed there purposely to head off just such an endeavor.

Jose Maria Cordillera did belong here. Dr. Jose Maria Rafael Meridia de Cordillera was Terra Rican aristocracy.

Terra Rica, a former colony of Spain, was on cordial terms with its mother country, and at war with no one. Jose Maria Cordillera owned roughly one-twenty-fourth of the dry land of that planet.

Urbane. Soft-spoken. Humanitarian, with a strong sense of noblesse oblige. Jose Maria was strikingly handsome at age fifty-seven. His olive-toned skin was still supple over sharply sculpted bones. A man of medicine, he disapproved of cosmetic surgery except in the case of wounds, and did not always endorse it even then. Jose Maria Cordillera bore a scar on his brow, got it when his firstborn bashed him in the eye with her silver mug. You could not pay Jose Maria to repair that one.

Jose Maria Cordillera kept the common touch. A nice man. A good man. Augustus found it easy to read what made *Don* Cordillera tick. Jose Maria Cordillera carried a Catholic burden of guilt. He had dedicated himself to saving a universe which had been altogether too good to him.

The LEN rolled themselves out for *Don* Cordillera to walk on. It was *such* an honor to meet him. They were only surprised to find a man of his caliber and refinement on, well, on the *Merrimack*, no offense, Captain Farragut.

"Where else should I be?" Jose Maria Cordillera asked.

The ambassadors would not say so at the captain's own table, but military and intelligence were antonyms in their lexicon. And "Department of Defense" was just too disingenuous. The U.S. ought to call it what it was, the Department of War.

"I like to stay on the front line of discovery," Cordillera explained. *Merrimack* operated on the frontier.

"More like the firing line, I would say," Aghani offered.

"Often," Cordillera admitted. "A doctor is a good thing to have in those circumstances, you do not think?"

The LEN were appalled. "A doctor? They need a medic with a patch kit and a vat of penicillin. You ... *you*, Don Cordillera, are a research *legend*."

"A legend. Well." Cordillera smiled into his Riesling.

"Your work with viruses was pivotal," said Madame Navarro. "You have saved millions of lives. And if you count posterity, countless lives."

"And I see the Hive as a disease of galactic proportion," *Don* Cordillera continued on that line. "A parasite. A very bad parasite that kills its host, its host being worlds. I am dedicated to curing it."

Aghani went rigid, chilled. He set his fork down with unsteady care before he should drop it. "You would *cure* an intelligence? Do we not have a duty to communicate with it?"

The smack of the captain's palm on the table made all the guests flinch back from their rattling china and rippling wine.

Farragut glanced round with a sheepish grin. Lifted his hand from the table, a squashed ant flattened to his palm heel. "Sorry. I was ... communicating."

"Ants on a starship!" Faustino Barron exclaimed, eyeing his food with sudden distaste. An excessively prissy man. Probably should not have seated that one next to Colonel Steele.

"Time to let the aardvark out," Farragut noted to the Marine orderly. Wiped his communiqué on the linen napkin in his lap, then waggled his fork. "Didn't mean to interrupt. Carry on."

The window dressing, strategically stationed next to John Farragut, suddenly gushed in breathy admiration, "How ever did you discover three—three—Class Nine worlds!" Her enthusiasm may even have been sincere. Farragut was a fine looking man, especially in uniform. "That *can't* have been luck."

"Of course it was luck!" Farragut laughed. "Blind, stupid, crash-flat-into-it luck. We were looking for the Hive world."

"Oh, but aren't you afraid you'll *find* it?"

"Afraid? Ma'am, that's what we're here for. We're hunting the Hive."

The picturesque one folded her forearms on the edge of the table, and leaned forward to rest her breasts on them. Putting all her cards on the table, apparently. She breathed, "Isn't it . . . terrifying?"

As he composed an answer, Farragut's blue eyes took on a gleam that Augustus had never seen before, a look that made Augustus set aside his own drink and observe. An amazing look, a bright, insane enthusiasm. And it was not directed at the young lady either. (Had to wonder about her. For a people who expressed such disapproval of Kerry Blue's Mata Hari type espionage, this was an interesting choice of guests to send to the captain's right hand. It was safe to assume her esteemed rank was very lately acquired, and very temporary.)

Farragut's bright eyes were not for her. He was envisioning the Hive. And that look was . . . battle crazy. It washed over his face, animated his whole being. Battle was a topic he could get excited about.

And then he reined it in just as quickly. Wrong audience here. These people would not appreciate John Farragut's idea of fun.

The captain forced his enthusiasm back to room temperature, and answered benignly, "I kind of hope the Hive thinks *I'm* a little scary."

Aghani seized on that thought. "The Hive thinks. The Hive *thinks*. You admit the Hive thinks? Are we not then duty bound to make them understand us?"

Don Cordillera came to the captain's rescue. " 'Thinking' is too strong a term. They react. As one-celled beings to light and heat. The components of the Hive have only the most rudimentary interaction with those not of its own kind—or those not of its own self, for we hypothesize that the Hive is a single, titanic, marauding entity composed of many macroscopic cells."

Farragut further interpreted for the LEN, " 'Rudimentary interaction' in Hive-talk means if it's not me, I eat it."

"Not entirely accurate, young Captain," said *Don* Cordillera. "Burrs, gorgons, soldiers—all the Hive cells—have shown cannibalism. So, more precisely: 'If it is not I, I eat it. If it is I, I may go ahead and eat it anyway.'" And to the LEN, earnestly, "These beings—this being—the Hive is wholly without redemption. When I came out here, I assumed all spacefaring life would be inquisitive and benign and eager to talk. And now I find myself committed to nothing less than genocide. If I find the queen of the Hive, or the nerve center of the being, the single being the murder of which would exterminate the whole, would I do it? I ask myself: could I? And I must answer—yes. In a heartbeat."

"Even if they adapt quickly and might eventually be taught to share?" Madame Navarro begged for reason.

"Burrs don't share," said Farragut.

"They learn," said Navarro. "They could learn."

"They learn that engineered metal—though itself inedible—often indicates that edible beings live inside," said Jose Maria. "They learn that inedible metal spacecraft point the way to and from worlds full of edible beings.

"Adapt they can, but only if it lets them eat—and eat *now*. They store nothing. They plant nothing. They eat their dead and wounded. They are an engine of entropy.

"They have no higher conscious purpose. They have not the least concept of planning or investing. You would think something that voracious would learn husbandry, conservation. They have not.

"The Hive kills host after host. If ever it asked a question, it would be: what is left to eat? It uses, it throws away. And would you even *want* to teach gorgons husbandry, so that they might plant people gardens for future harvest?

"Do remember: entropy is a force of nature, too. What is natural need not be benign. The Hive is nothing less than the living, eating incarnation of the Ninth Level of Hell. Your Excellency, you come in peace and I admire that purpose. I am afraid I come to exterminate."

"Deal me in," Lieutenant Colonel Steele spoke for the first time.

Farragut lifted a finger to say he wanted a piece of that game.

Commander Carmel lifted her glass. "Well said, sir." *Sir*'d him even though *Don* Cordillera was a civilian.

"Oh. Well. This *is* unfortunate," said Aghani, grave.

The delicate Mr. Barron, whose head motions brought to mind a chicken, gave a nervous glance up at the sprinklers in the overhead. His eyes flinched downward. Chin pulled in. Gazed upon his plate with loathing. Asked in great trepidation, "Are we dining in a chemical lab?"

"Oh. Those." Farragut nodded up at the sprinklers. "Standard equipment. All decks."

"I've never seen that on a Naval vessel," said Barron, all but calling his host a liar.

"They're standard on *my* boat. We're a Hive hunter. Those sprinklers spray neutralizing solution for that brown caustic goo gorgons melt down into when you kill 'em. Oh, hell." Turned to the Marine orderly, "Tell the galley we might should skip the French onion soup."

"Captain," Madame Navarro cut in on another tack. "Forgive me if I'm wrong or if I give offense for suggesting such a thing, but I've been given the impression that you, how should I say, that you *like* fighting?" And she shrank away from her question as if she had offended herself.

John Farragut bit back the first answer that sprang to mind—probably a cheerful, "Are you nuts?" He said instead, soberly, "Not a good quality in a battleship commander, you don't think?"

"No!" she cried. The emphatic snap of her head set her earrings to swinging madly. "A man with that much destructive power at his command should have the utmost loathing for violence. The *utmost.*"

"Then we differ."

"Oh, *dear,*" Madame mumbled with the utmost dread and disapproval. The utmost.

"It's the American way," the American representative of the LEN commented with heavy irony, an apology for his barbarous kind.

"War does have a purpose," Augustus proposed, his first offering.

"You mean other than expanding the Roman Empire?" Steele asked Augustus.

Someone had thought to space the entire length of the table between the Marine commander and the Roman intelligence officer when making up this seating chart. It didn't stop the cold salvos from soaring end to end.

"Keeps you employed," Augustus returned.

"Colonel Augustus, I beg you to explain." Ambassador Aghani sat forward, clearly troubled. "I find war senseless. Anathema. The final resort of brute impulse. You see some purpose in it?"

"War trained humankind to survive out here," said Augustus. "For centuries *we* were the only formidable enemy *we* had. There was, for a long time, an assumption among us that any race who could reach the stars would need to overcome internal conflict first. Fallacy, of course. Humankind reached the stars very nicely, still fighting one another. Aggression persists even as intelligence progresses."

"It's a throwback," Madame Navarro broke in. "Baby teeth to be spat out. A diaper to be washed, folded up, and put away forever."

Augustus ignored her. "Those millennia of internecine warfare prepared us for truly virulent foes. On first contact with the Hive, the LEN would have walked out to meet them, smiled, shown them your periodic table, and been eaten for your trouble. Aren't you comforted that there persisted those of us belligerents with guns enough to blow each other to kingdom come, guns which, turned in a single direction, might yet stave off this mindless, soulless terror?"

Madame recoiled. "You *don't* mean to imply that Earth's history of horror and bloodshed could be a survival mechanism, the purpose of which was to prepare us to survive a hostile ET contact?"

"I don't mean to imply any such thing," Augustus answered. "I'm pretty sure I came flat out and said just that."

"Oh!" Madame Navarro appealed in the wrong direction, "Captain Farragut! You cannot agree with this hawkish pretext for violence."

"Well . . ." Farragut demurred.

"*No!*" Madame Navarro insisted. "War is absurd!"

"Well, yes, it has its bad moments," Farragut confessed. "But so does the peace."

The League of Earth Nations considered Palatine's conflict with the United States a civil war. Even though the League disapproved of a governmental system that allowed euthanasia, cloning, slavery, and colonization of inhabited worlds, those transgressions had never stopped any nation of the League—other than the U.S.—from recognizing Palatine's government or from carrying on trade with its expanding empire.

From the moment Palatine declared independence, the Romans and the Americans had been locked in a territorial race. When not at open war, the two nations waged a defensive aggression across a quarter of the galaxy. Their zones of influence expanded like rival pancakes, each trying to bubble through or around the other, while spreading ever wider and wider, planet-stabbing all the way—planting their flags in any solid ground, in every dirtball, from Rim to Hub—the object to hoist the colors, hike the leg, piss on every tree and declare "Mine!" and off they go.

While the rest of the civilized world watched in disgust.

"I don't know about y'all, but our worst enemies have been good for us," Farragut told his LEN guests. "After the Romans captured the *Monitor*, right quick we devised all kinds of low-tech and phase-shifting countermeasures to defend *Merrimack* against the Romans. And it's those same measures that saved our asses in our first contact with the Hive. The Roman ship *Sulla* got eaten. We didn't, and I have Rome to thank that I had a sword on me the first time a gorgon oozed through my force field, shut down my targeting system, and chewed through my hull. So God bless the Roman emperor."

The captain had only one taker to that toast.

"You're not drinking, Commander Carmel?" Aghani noted that *Merrimack*'s XO made no motion toward her wineglass to toast Caesar.

"There is a reason I should?" said Calli. Calli was dressed in formal military whites, but she had done something artistic with all that long shining chestnut hair, and she looked positively imperial at the table, and made the breathy young woman with the plunging neckline next to John Farragut look vulgar.

Captain Farragut intervened, "Mr. Carmel attended the Imperial Military Institute on Palatine. Doesn't make her a Roman. It's a good school."

"It is an excellent school," Aghani allowed. "The best by some rankings."

"It was tough," said Calli.

"The educational system on Palatine is the finest among

all the nations and colonies of Earth, bar none," said Aghani.

"We are not a colony," said Augustus.

"Palatine began as a colony," Aghani revised. "I was complimenting your educational system."

"You were stating fact, Mr. Aghani. Compliments are unnecessary."

"Colonel Augustus, where did you attend?" Madame Navarro asked solicitously.

"I don't recall that I did," said Augustus.

"No school? What? Were you programmed?"

Madame Navarro meant it as a jest, but Augustus answered without humor, "I don't recall that either." Offered nothing more.

Another LEN representative, who had had quite enough of his companions' pandering to Rome, and quite too much to drink, set a fist and forearm on the table and launched into a scold at Augustus, "You don't seem to realize the catastrophic brain drain planet Earth suffered under the Roman exodus to Palatine. Our world harbored and nurtured you for centuries. You used our societies—controlled many of them. You *used* our best institutions to perpetuate your language—religion, medicine, law, higher education—and not for the good of the masses. Oh no. All for the elite and for yourselves. Then the whole spiderweb of you packed up your scholars and your scientists and your judges and just *left*."

"Good riddance," said Lieutenant Colonel Steele. "Take 'em. Better they go to Palatine where I can see 'em, than having a secret society sponging off Earth."

"Whoa, Mr. Steele," *Don* Cordillera said with a slight smile. Attempted to drag the talk off in a lighter direction, "I could understand the resentment if you were a doctor, lawyer, or priest, but that's rather harsh coming from someone who never had to suffer through a Latin class for his profession."

"You'll never catch me talking Latin," Steele vowed.

And there it was. The brick that was bound to drop. Augustus lifted his glass in a toast to the other end of the table. "*Semper fi*, flattop." And watched the Marine turn the color of cheap rosé.

"I don't feel the U.S. is in any way inferior to Palatine," said Calli Carmel. "I think I'm in a position to know."

"Thanks for the backup, Mr. Carmel," said Steele.

Madame Navarro's glass came down hard. "*Mister* Carmel. *Mister* Carmel. I *do* not understand this conceit of denying the sexuality of your female officers. As if femininity were not command material! You Americans must unsex your female officers in order to respect them?"

"I am not unsexed," Calli answered for herself without excitement. "The distinction is irrelevant to the position."

"There are no ladies in the Navy," said John Farragut with a wink.

Except on Christmas Eve, he thought, when the women pull those dresses from the bottom of their storage lockers, with those little bitty shoes, and transform themselves into amazing, soft, sweet-smelling, civilian-looking creatures, and it hurt. Last year John Farragut saw Hamster in that strappy little dress and those strappy little shoes, and he'd walked straight into a bulkhead. Hard. Carried away a mouse that lasted for days.

Madame Navarro scolded Calli, "Your sex may be irrelevant to your position, but denying its existence makes *you* irrelevant. Are we no more evolved than we were at the dawn of civilization when Hatshepsut made herself an honorary man, because one must be a man to be Pharaoh? Submerging yourself to a male identity? *Really*, Miss Carmel."

"I am not an honorary man," Calli said. "'One small step for man, one giant leap for mankind' only includes me if I am a man individually as well as collectively. I am a man. Happen to be a female one, but a man in fact, not honorary, not submerged."

"Oh, stuff and apology. The distinction cannot be so glibly brushed off. You are a woman. He is a man. The division is there. It's biology. The U.S. Navy Space Fleet ought to grow up and acknowledge and accept the femininity of its female officers."

"Separate but equal?" Calli suggested faintly.

The ensuing silence lay like a slab.

Until Calli answered herself, "Not in this man's Navy."

In the thick cessation of conversation, the soft music, the thump and hum of the ship, and all the background noises pushed forward.

Through the partition that separated the captain's mess from the xenos' mess, shouts, mounting in volume, indicated that the scientific gathering was no more amiable than this one. It sounded like they were throwing things.

Something flew past the open hatchway and rolled down the corridor.

"What was that?" said Farragut.

The Marine guard at the hatchway turned stiffly, shoulders dead square within his uniform of navy blue, eyes barely visible under his smartly centered white cap. Answered, "Muffin, sir. Blueberry."

"They got muffins?" Farragut lamented, wistful. Sounded like a funner party over there. More sincere at any rate. Still, "I can't endorse muffin throwing."

Sounds of the melee grew louder. Shouted name-calling. A clash of a metal platter hitting the deck and spinning to rest.

Jose Maria Cordillera rose, bid everyone else stay seated. He set his snowy napkin on his chair, and smoothed the creases from his square-shouldered charcoal jacket and wide trousers of coarse black Tussah silk. When he turned from the table, you saw his only jewelry, the simple clasp of hand-wrought silver which held back his long black hair.

He exited the mess at a calm, cat-footed walk, his soft-soled shoes making no sound.

The shattering of glass beyond the partition made Farragut worry belatedly if he ought to have given Jose Maria a Marine escort.

And silence descended behind the partition.

Moments passed with no sound but a few muted voices.

Jose Maria reappeared in the hatchway, quietly composed.

"What did you *say* to them?" Aghani marveled at the doctor's peacemaking prowess.

"I asked if they had any muffins." Jose Maria produced a plate, lifted the linen to reveal a stack of them, still warm.

"*Muffins?* With bariki and munsrit?" Faustino Barron balked at the culinary gaff, and gazed on *Don* Cordillera as if the esteemed doctor had grown tusks.

"Works for me." Augustus accepted a warm muffin from the basket, held it up in admiration. "Ah. Like LEN weapons. Like new. Only thrown down once."

"That was uncalled for," said Guillame Kapila. "The League of Earth Nations has always accommodated Palatine."

Augustus gave a cold smile. "Which is why when the real menace showed itself, we allied with our most *offensive* enemy."

"Why, yes, they are all that," Kapila allowed, the U.S. was offensive.

John Farragut signaled foul. "Now how'd I get a two-front campaign going here? I expect that from *him*." *Him* being Augustus. "But Dr. Kapila, what did I do to piss y'all off? You haven't liked me from your first 'Permission to come aboard.' "

"Sir, I am certain you are well qualified at your profession," said Kapila, making no attempt to hide his distaste for that profession. "But you stumbled into a Class Nine extraterrestrial intelligence with your battleship, blundered down to the planet's surface, and started *talking*. That is not protocol. It is . . . stupidity."

"Worked at Hispaniola," Farragut offered.

Kapila's eyes flared white. "Invoking the image of the earliest act of American imperialism is meant to make us feel better about this botched first contact?"

"It wasn't American imperialism actually," said Farragut. "It was a Spanish-funded Genoese imperialism at the time."

"There were probably Romans aboard," Steele muttered. Meant it to be snide, but Augustus said serenely, "Did you know Christopher Columbus kept his log in Latin?"

Farragut covered his eyes. "Oh, for Jesus."

When all the LEN guests had gone back through the flexible walkway to their spheroid ship, John Farragut opened his stiff, stand-up collar and flung down his napkin into a wet burgundy stain in the tablecloth. "Was that hideous or what?" Pulled out his cuff links.

"No vote for 'or what,' " said Calli Carmel, taking the pins out of her hair.

"TR, where are our *guys?*"

Colonel Steele had already checked with the control room. His square, bulldog head moved slowly from side to side, grim. "Alpha Flight has not reported back. Drones haven't picked up their IFF anywhere in the Myriad."

The Swifts of Alpha Flight were long since out of air. Steele was already figuring who he had to compose letters to.

Dak Shepard had only a mom. This was going to kill her.

Tough, mean Carly Delgado had no one but the Corps to call family. Big loss, that little girl was. Could have used a dozen Carlys.

Twitch Fuentes. Steele never knew much about Twitch. Better find someone who spoke native Spanish to write that letter, because Twitch didn't know too much English beyond lock and load, so Steele guessed his family didn't know even that.

Hazard Sewell. Military family. They'd understand. Didn't mean Steele knew what the hell to say.

"They're not dead," Farragut said.

"All data to the contrary?" said Augustus.

"I *know* they're not dead," said John Farragut.

"Primary process thinking." Augustus dismissed his certainty. Little boys and madmen believed that merely thinking things made them so.

"We stay here until I find my guys. Echo Flight making any progress?"

"Still surveilling the Rea shuttle," Steele reported. "The Rea shuttle is now moving at eighty percent c."

Echo Flight was following a snail.

"And at that rate they'll arrive at Rea in . . . ?" Farragut left the blank to be filled.

"Thirty-four years," Augustus supplied. "Your years."

Farragut's blue eyes roamed the overhead. A muscle bulged on his jaw with the clenching of his teeth, silent obscenities trapped within. "Something's gotta happen."

"Given that Myriadian ships don't carry thirty-four years' worth of air and food, yes, something must. Buy you a drink, John Farragut?"

"Oh, God, yes."

Though wine aplenty had graced the captain's table, John Farragut had stayed keen and painfully sober, drinking only at toasts.

"'Have we not the utmost loathing for violence? The utmost?'" Farragut repeated his favorite quote of the evening. "I need something to wash this down."

Colonel Steele returned to the control room as Farragut

marched down the narrow corridor, followed by Augustus, and unlocked the bar, and quickly made up for lost time. He pulled a tequila from the rack. Held it up, swishing the worm around the bottom of the bottle. "For Faustino Is-this-okay-to-eat Barron? And how about Madame Save-the-Gorgons Navarro with the strawberry-green lip tint. What was *that* about?"

"Must be an Earth fashion. It's not Roman." Augustus pulled down a shot glass and slid it over for a hit.

Farragut wagged his head as he poured. "I know I've been away for a while, but now I'm afraid to go home."

"What did you make of the twins?" Augustus coiled onto a barstool.

"What twins? I didn't see—oh. Her. The blonde."

"She had hair?" said Augustus—and caught a muffin mid-stern. He swiveled his barstool around, hailed his assailant in the hatchway. "Ah. *Miss* Carmel."

She'd brought muffins.

Farragut lifted the bottle in toast to Calli. "My sexless XO!"

"Oh, shut up." Calli pulled up a barstool and rapped down a shot glass, open end up. "The LEN stalking horse was asking for you, O Captain, My Captain."

"The LEN what?"

"The twins."

"Oh, for Jesus."

Command made John Farragut the most attractive man on board. He would have been attractive had he a toad face, which he didn't. But command also made him inaccessible. Subordinates were off limits to an officer, and every man jack and jane on board *Merrimack* was John Farragut's subordinate.

Water water everywhere, but no one to sleep with. The LEN had set a glass of fresh water in front of the very thirsty.

"The sentry reported she was trying to convince him to let her into your quarters," said Calli.

Farragut shrugged, wondered why he was even being told this. "So, why'd he have to check with you? Did he need help staving her off?"

"He got rid of her all by himself. He was just making sure he'd done the right thing." The sentry had done it by the book. And to the captain's lack of comment, Calli said, "Well?"

"Well what?"

"Did he?"

"Calli!"

She shrugged. "Just checking."

Parched, he might be, but John Farragut would not be herded. Would not be led by his dick. He was feeling singularly trapped, and his kind did not mate in captivity. Preferred to stay with Calli and Augustus at the bar.

And soon the three of them set to addressing their empties by the names of the LEN emissaries, propping the shot glasses up, and knocking them over with muffins at ten paces.

The clearing of a baritone throat broke up the shoot. All three turned.

Ambassador Aghani stood, a rigid dark pillar in the hatchway.

The captain and the XO froze like puppies caught chewing the carpet, muffins burning like guilty brands in their hands. Augustus juggled his, unrepentant.

Aghani let the senior commanders stew in their juvenile poses for a long moment, then pronounced gravely, "I came to apologize for our behavior at your table, Captain. But I see the sentiment would be pearls before an unsuitable audience."

Farragut drew himself up. "What can I say to something like that?"

" 'Pass the muffins,' " Calli suggested.

Aghani pronounced soberly, "Sir, I demand, by the authority of the League of Earth Nations and the treaties to which we are bound, that your vessel depart Myriadian space without further delay."

"No, sir," said Captain Farragut. The very last answer Aghani expected.

Aghani knew Farragut to be impulsive, belligerent, stubborn, but never insubordinate. Aghani put the situation into words the naval officer might understand, "Given that I am the lawful authority here, what you just said is tantamount to mutiny."

"Oh, bullshit, sir." Farragut slung his muffin aside, brushed off his hands. "When you were my guest, I couldn't speak to you the way I wanted, but you are aboard now without my permission. I have a flight away and there's no authority in the universe can make me abandon them. Simple disobedience to an illegal order can never be judged mutiny. We stay. Now get off my boat."

Deep wrathful breaths sounded loud through Aghani's wide nostrils. His lips worked. He restarted in the voice of forced conciliation. "Very well. Stay. You will strike your colors and accept the LEN flag."

"No, sir."

"This *is* mutiny now."

"No, it's not. I'm pretty sure I have to take an oath of loyalty before I can violate it."

"Law requires you accept the LEN flag while you operate in LEN jurisdiction."

Had him there. Farragut replied, "Make me."

Aghani blinked. Calli made a noise in her throat. Augustus shook with silent laughter.

"I beg your pardon?" Aghani tilted one ear forward. Could not possibly have heard that aright.

"I don't accept your flag. I'm not leaving. You're going to have to shoot us."

Aghani stared, airless.

"No, wait," Farragut revised. "Y'all have no guns. You guys open a dialogue. Send over your negotiation team. Y'all are so good at peaceful resolutions. And there you are."

Aghani could not speak. He turned, stiffly, mortified, to go. Felt something soft strike him between the shoulder blades, heard it plop softly to the deck.

Did not turn to see who threw it. Walked woodenly away.

Farragut pressed his lips together, nodded. "You know, I might have handled that better."

"That sound you don't hear is John Farragut's career plunging down in flames," said Augustus.

"Oh, and thanks for the help!" Farragut bent down and retrieved Augustus' muffin. Gave it back to him. "Nice shot, by the way."

"Plead the fifth," said Calli.

"You know you can't plead the fifth in a court-martial," Farragut scolded.

"Not that fifth. This fifth." Clanked an empty bottle on the bar. "Or this one. Or this—"

"Oh, *that's* going to make it all right!" Farragut propped himself up between a barstool and the bar.

Calli's hand beeped softly. She took a report from the officer of the deck: a salvo of courier rockets had just been launched from the LEN. Direction of Earth.

Farragut blew out a breath through narrowed lips. "I gotta be gone before the Presidential order gets here, or Calli, you got yourself a big boat."

"Don't want it," said his second-in-command.

"Bull." Farragut knew her better.

"Not like that," said Calli.

"Jesus Christ, where is my flight?" Farragut stared emptily down at the bar, unfocused. " '*Make me?*' I told a LEN ambassador 'Make me?' "

"John, you're drunk."

"Crapulent. Isn't that a fine Latin word for you."

Augustus, who had been matching him drink for drink, managed a perfect vertical on his brief sortie from the bar to unload several rounds.

"You seem to have yourself a Roman," Calli commented in Augustus' absence.

"I noticed." Farragut squinted. "How'd I do that?"

"You're the finest commander I have ever served, John Farragut. For him being a patterner, it took him long enough to figure that out." She clapped him on his broad shoulder on rising. "I'm boiled. Good night. Good morning. Good something. Outta here."

Augustus oozed back onto his barstool in time to catch Calli's long-legged retreat. A lot of motion in her walk. She let her waist-length hair fall free in its chestnut glory. "And *that* is not a bad piece of work."

Farragut turned to regard him in surprise. "Rumor said you were alternating current."

"I'm AC, I'm not *dead.*"

Calli had the kind of looks that dismantled men's knees, emptied their brains, their bank accounts, and yes, it was absurd as hell to call her "Mr." Carmel.

"You and she?" Augustus asked.

"She's my XO!" Farragut cried, in the same tone he

might say, "She's my sister!" Then, "And as odd as it is to say, she's not my type."

Augustus propped a fist under one sharp cheekbone, amused. "And what is Captain Farragut's 'type?' "

"Maryann." Almost a song how he said it. Blue eyes alight and far away, with a smile of memory. "The girl I left behind."

"Your ex-wife's name is Laura." A prompt, that. John would know whom he'd married.

"Maryann is who I should have married."

"And you didn't. Why?"

"One of those moments when I let my common sense get the better of me. Talked my heart out of something unwise. Doesn't work for me. Unwise was the way to go."

"What made it seem wise to let her go?"

"I knew I wouldn't be there for her. She was fragile. Gentle. Victorian hearts and flowers and butterflies, four children and a rose garden kind of woman. I married someone who could get along without me. Sure didn't mean for her to get along quite so damned well." He peered deep into his glass to see what made him say all that. To Augustus of all people. "Who knew the war would go on so long? And now it's the Hive instead of y'all."

"And that is unfortunate."

Farragut's brows lifted. "Unfortunate for us not to be fighting each other?"

"I am a soldier, not an exterminator. It is my duty to defend Palatine against the Hive, but there is no glory in it. What warrior does not long to prove himself against a worthy adversary? Who is Achilles without Hector? You are only as strong as your fiercest foe. And tell me truly, John Farragut, in your unwise heart of hearts, wouldn't you really like to hurl a broadside into a Roman boat? Mine in particular?"

John Farragut seemed to meditate into his glass. At last he lifted liquid-blue eyes to the Roman. "Love to."

Steele waylaid Augustus in the middle decks corridor. Tautly suggested he consider spelling Echo Flight from its tedious, trudging sortie, ghosting the slow-moving Arran vessel.

The suggestion amused the Roman. "Now that would

require sending another flight. You're offering to put a second flight under my command, Lieutenant Colonel?"

"I'm trading you . . . since you haven't lost the first one. My dogs are tired. So are you human or what?"

Augustus did not answer the question, but allowed Steele to summon a relief.

Delta Flight had just reported to the flight deck when the call came in.

"*Merrimack. Merrimack. Merrimack*. This is Echo Two. Echo Leader has vanished! Repeat, Echo Leader has vanished!"

8

FURNITURE NEVER DID MUCH to alter John Farragut's progress. If sitting at a table, he wanted to get to the hatch beyond it, he was not one for sliding the chair back, standing, and walking around the table. That was not his way. Unless there was food on it, the table was in play as much as the deck. And as for the chair, there was no sliding. He just stood up, and the chair was on its own, and John Farragut was up and over the table, sometimes stepping on it, or, as now, vaulting over it, if he had side clearance, and he was out the hatch before anyone else.

He charged into the control room, reeking a bit, jacketless. He leaned over the com, paused over the speaker to ask the technician, "Who have I got here?"

"Echo Two. Flight Sergeant Khamis, sir," the tech supplied.

Farragut flicked on the com. "Abdullah! This is Captain Farragut. Talk to me, son."

Halting, his voice pitched too high, too loud, the Marine pilot Abdullah Khamis reported, "Sir! We are—" Abdullah paused, checking. "—eight light-hours outside the Arran system. Echo Flight was maintaining stealthy pursuit of the target at velocity of eighty percent c, trailing at a distance of five hundred klicks."

The "target" had been the Arran shuttle with the unlikely destination of Rea.

"Target slowed to submach speed, made some course adjustments as if lining up an approach to something, and then—and then the target vanished. Like down a rabbit hole. Gone. Echo Leader ordered us to hold position. He followed the target's path, matched it move for move, speed for speed, proceeded to the target's vanishing point and—vanished. We tried to reestablish communication, but, Captain Farragut, he's *gone*. We tried everything except res. No answer. Can't see him, can't hear him. He is absolutely *not there*. We lost him."

"*I* got him!" The tac monitor on the other side of the control room reported, quite astonished. He stared at his readouts. Verified, with a startled smile, "I got him!" He flipped on another speaker, from which sounded the voice of Echo Leader.

"*Merrimack. Merrimack. Merrimack.* Echo Leader requests permission to dock."

The tac monitor, anticipating the captain's question, checked his console and reported, "IFF confirmed. It's Echo Leader. He's coming in hot on a direct line from the planet Rea!"

Farragut barked into the com. "Echo Leader. Permission granted. Bag your ass to debriefing, now."

"Aye, aye, *sir!*"

Farragut reached over the com tech's shoulder, switched on the other channel and ordered, "Echo Flight, return to *Merrimack*. Farragut out." He turned from the com. "Hamster, have Mo meet me in debriefing."

"You think Echo Leader is hurt, sir?"

"Not for Echo Leader, for *me*. I need more brain cells for this than I got switched on right now."

John Farragut appeared in the wardroom, in a fresh shirt and clean jacket. Squinted from a banging hangover. Wanted an oxygen mask, but pure oxygen at five atmospheres was toxic, so he suffered.

Echo Leader, Pilot Officer Jan Karowicz, sat, breathing hard as if he had run the forty-three light-years from Rea on foot. Slender, lank, scruffy. Smelled bad. His short, blond hair appeared licked five different directions by a mad cow. The beard was unkempt and not regulation. The captain could not recall ever seeing a bearded Marine.

But that was Steele's problem. Farragut said nothing of it.

Young Jan Karowicz held a glass of water in a quaking hand. Pale. Might have been hungover, but that alcohol smell was all from Farragut. This boy merely stank.

Colonel Steele's eyes rounded on seeing his Marine, evidently finding something shocking in the boy's appearance.

One of the medical department's dogs, a soulful-eyed Golden, laid its silky head sympathetically on Karowicz's knee.

Farragut was ready to begin. "Where's Augustus?"

"Plugged into Echo Leader's flight recorder."

Farragut nodded. "Okay. Pilot Officer Karowicz—Jan—let's have it in your words. What happened out there?"

Karowicz trembled quite a lot. His report matched Echo Two's account exactly up to the point where Echo Leader had vanished. In Karowicz's version, everything *else* vanished.

"And you displaced to Rea," Steele filled in.

"*Displaced?*" A hard laugh. Karowicz wagged his head. "*No,* sir."

"You *did* end up in the Rean system," said Steele.

"Well, yes, sir. Eventually." The pilot officer poured himself another glass of water from the pitcher on the table.

Eventually. The word lifted brows all round the chamber.

Eventually, Farragut asked, "Pilot Officer? Just how long do you estimate your journey took?"

"Fifty-four hours, thirty-two minutes. Give or take." The Marine gulped his water. "Sir."

Farragut looked to the maintenance rate, who confirmed, "His Swift's chron confirms that, Captain. He's *real* low on air."

"No shit. Sorry, sirs." Echo Leader's glass rattled against the table as he set it down. He became aware of the consternation around him, having nothing to do with his word choice. He patted the dog at his knee for moral support, and asked guardedly. "How—may I ask, sir—how long do you think I was gone?"

Tight-lipped, bug-eyed glances surrounded him.

Farragut answered faintly—eventually—"Not long."

Steele made the Marine describe his journey. Karowicz could scarcely call it a journey. Motionless. Directionless. No stars, no referents, no communication. Nothingness for fifty-four hours and thirty-two minutes, after which he emerged as abruptly as he'd gone in, nearly ass-ending the Arran shuttle, which magically reappeared before him, but now in Rean space.

"I have no idea how I got there, or where I was in between."

"He was in a *kzachin*," said Augustus, ducking through the hatchway.

Farragut turned full around in his chair. "Translation, Augustus?"

The captain would have known without being told that Augustus had been plugged into something. The tall Roman looked cadaverous. Eyes hollow, cheeks sunken. The IO answered: "A *kzachin* is a hollow of sorts. Something empty into which one falls. But I like 'bridge' better now. Starbridge. Stargate. Pick one. Wormhole. I don't like that one."

"No? What's wrong with 'wormhole?' "

"Sending a mass through a wormhole collapses the wormhole."

"The Arrans are reusing their wormholes," said Farragut. "So what's holding them open?"

"Worms. Hell, I don't know." Augustus squeezed his eyes.

The interrogation soon ended with Farragut sending the bedraggled pilot officer to sick bay, the dog in gentle escort.

The captain conferred alone with his IO. "Why couldn't you translate *kzachin* before?"

"I did. Try to translate 'rabbit hole' into Myriadian. Oh, they'll understand the words reasonably well—a hole for an animal. But they won't know it's what Alice fell down to get to Wonderland."

"How are the Myriadians seeing these *kzachin* when we can't?"

"Actually, we can." Augustus produced a global projector from his pocket, and activated the imager, transforming the wardroom into a starfield on all sides.

"This is the Myriad." Farragut recognized the dense cluster all round him. "Where are the *kzachin*?"

"We've been detecting them all along. But when you're dealing with a ship's sensors, what goes onto your screen is a computer program's interpretation of the data, not the raw data itself. The ship's computer misinterpreted the data."

"What's the computer been doing to the data?"

"The raw input from a *kzachin* mimics certain aspects of a distant black hole. So the program filters pigeonholed the data into that known slot without regard for the extraneous, nonconforming data, and said: It's a black hole. A *kzachin* registers no distance, so the filters interpreted that to mean 'immeasurably distant,' as in 'too far away to clutter up the tactical display with.' And another thing—*kzachin* are two-dimensional. Look at them sideways, they aren't there at all. Could also be why the filters tossed the data. But now that we can recognize the data for what they are, we can plot the locations of the *kzachin*. They're transparent to the human eye, so I've ascribed to them the image of a colored light."

"Show me."

"Hope you like international orange." Augustus activated the locator program on his projector. The Myriad broke out in garish orange dots.

John Farragut turned full circle, looked up, looked down. "Lordy."

The cluster was riddled with *kzachin*. "Where do they all lead?"

"We know definitely that two of them connect. This one, eight hours outside of the Arran system, leads to this one, forty-three light years away, in the Rean system."

"Does it lead back the other way?"

A slight shrug. Augustus didn't know. He did say, "There *is* a Janus element to the word *kzachin*."

"A what?"

"Janus, the god of gates, for gates have two faces. There is an implication of duality within the word *kzachin*. A coming and going. Cross-referencing spaceport flight schedules for Arra, Rea, and Centro ought to fill in some more connections, but I have no interest in doing that."

Farragut nodded. "Right now I just want to know where *that* one goes." His forefinger found the orange blot in the vicinity of Alpha Flight's last known location. "This is what the minefield that killed Cowboy was guarding. This *kzachin*."

"Probable. But the question then follows: was the minefield guarding against a coming or a going?"

Farragut did not like the possibilities that sprang to mind. The unknown beyond the gate.

"I wouldn't send anything after them except a drone," Augustus went on. "And if you do, be advised, it will not be able to transmit any data back to you until and *if* it finds its way out again. And there's one more thing. The *traveler's* time distortion is not the alarming part of this."

"I know," said Farragut. "Ours is. I did the math."

Immediately after Echo Flight reported Echo Leader's disappearance from Arran space, Echo Leader was announcing his return to Arran space after a fourteen-hour flight from Rea.

Augustus summed it up: "Echo Leader got to Rea fourteen hours before he left Arran space."

"Oh, well this *is* unacceptable behavior in a wormhole. Hell, Augustus, maybe the wormholes *are* all shut and we just don't know it yet."

"Maybe they are."

Farragut scowled. "I meant that as a joke."

"I didn't."

The captain turned a troubled gaze to the glowing orange points on the star field. "Space and time are two sides of the same coin. Mass bends space. Why are the bends so severe here? The Myriad is dense, but is it dense enough for this?"

Augustus rubbed his haggard face, shook his head, spoke into his hands, "No."

"The Myriadians don't have FTL capability, so they can't know of the time distortion. And they can't fly fast enough without the *kzachin* to see themselves return before they've left. But we can. Do you know what this means?"

"Yes. It's a disappointing waste of a seismic migraine." Plugging into patterner mode cost Augustus dearly. "I thought I was going to report to the emperor the discovery of quick, easy travel over vast distances. What I've got instead are fixed-point aberrant wormholes. All the termini are confined to this glob of stars somewhere off the Hive highway, *which,* by the way, we've managed to misplace."

That wasn't the implication Farragut meant, but it raised yet another question, surprising and disturbing. "*All* the termini?" said Farragut, unable to believe such an extraordinary phenomenon could be unique to this globular cluster. "Are there no *kzachin* outside the Myriad?"

"Haven't detected any." Augustus rubbed his haggard

face. Spoke through his hands, "Though we know there is at least one more."

"Origin," said Farragut, feeling cold.

"There is a *kzachin* at Origin," Augustus confirmed. "Your Alpha Flight could have fallen down a very long, furry rabbit hole."

"Do we have any idea yet where Origin is?"

"We know where it is not."

"Where isn't it?"

"The Milky Way."

"Good God Almighty. Are you serious? Doesn't Kerry Blue's recording of Origin's night sky line up to *any*where we can identify?"

"Kerry's star map doesn't line up at all."

"Well, then, is her map necessarily accurate? Maybe it's just a bunch of pretty lights Donner gave to Kerry, and it doesn't indicate anything."

"No. Donner gave Kerry a very fine recording. Fine enough to pull the spectra off the stars and do some distance/brightness calculations. Distance to the recorder, of course. Even if some of the readings are contaminated— and they are—the relative brightnesses and distances are good enough to draw a rough map."

"So what's to say Origin is not on the far side of the galactic hub? Our maps of the far side are suspect."

"Because Kerry's recording was not made inside a spiral galaxy."

Farragut stared at the stars dotting his feet, absorbing that one. Glanced up. "You're sure?"

Met certain silence.

Farragut exhaled. "That's a long, furry rabbit hole, Alice."

"Donner's sky exists inside an irregular galaxy," Augustus told him. "Matter rich, metal poor, full of hot, bright stars. Very young. Very active. Very far from here."

"One of the Magellenic Clouds?" Farragut suggested, trying to keep it in the neighborhood.

"Not sure. What we see of the Magellenic Clouds is one hundred seventy thousand years old, so our information on that place is a little stale. There are no less than two supernovae in Origin's sky, but supernovae are so short-lived, there's no matching them up at this distance. The Large

Magellenic Cloud shows the beginnings of barred spiral arms and there's no hint of that in what I have to work with, so I'm inclined to dismiss the Large Cloud as a possibility. As to the Small Cloud, it's like trying to recognize a man from his baby picture."

"Could you?" Farragut asked his patterner.

"With a better baby picture, maybe. But to what purpose? You can't get there in real time. We can't even travel to the other side of *this* galaxy in reasonable time, let alone voyage to another one."

Farragut brooded so solemnly that Augustus added, "And if you have any idea about flying this boat through a *kzachin*, you let me out first. I am *not* leaving the galaxy."

Farragut paced the small confines of the wardroom. "I need to find my Marines before a LEN rocket comes back and hands me my commission in a shoebox."

"Your Marines are dead, John Farragut."

"My Swifts have homing instructions. If my people are dead, their Swifts will find their way back, and I'll bury my dead."

Augustus gazed round at the vast sea of projected stars, trillions of years deep. "Presupposes they are anywhere they can find their way back from."

Flight Sergeant Reg Monroe watched her air reservoir dwindle to the point of no return. Swifts did not have air scrubbers like *Merrimack*'s. Swifts were short-range vessels. Even if Reg could figure out which way was back so she could turn that way and go there, she would run out of breathable air before she could reach the *Merrimack*.

Reg had, on sleepless nights, already gone over what she would do if ever stranded in space. She thought she was out of tears, but they welled up one last time as she faced the fact that it was time to do it.

She disconnected her environmental alarm, and poked a hole in her heat exchanger, disconnected her carbon monoxide monitor and the control overrides.

She'd always heard carbon monoxide was odorless, but still she sniffed, expecting to smell *something*.

Did not think this was working. She felt vaguely sickish, her throat sore, probably from all that screaming.

Could not keep her eyes open. There was nothing to take

a last look at anyway, she thought, drifting from final consciousness.

Scarcely even heard the proximity alarms blaring imminent collision.

Dak Shepard jinked hard to avoid Alpha Three come bulleting up his tail. "Hey! Reg! Wake up!"

How had Dak known she was sleeping? Dak?

Dak!

Reg forced her eyes open, stuffed an oxygen mask over her face and inhaled huge gulps. Wrapped her hand round the hole in her heat exchanger and fumbled for duct tape.

"Reg, where the hell are you going?"

Crying just to be anywhere, Reg choked. Her viewport was full of stars. Not nearly enough of them, but there were stars and there was Dak.

She taped up the hole in her heat exchanger. Breathed. Breathed. Flushed her cabin of carbon monoxide. Halted her Swift's wild course and steered back toward the others.

"Dak! You magnificent *baboon*! I have never been so happy to hear anyone's voice in my life!"

And the other voices filled her headset with beautiful noise. Twitch. Carly. They were all here. Her headphone clamored with relieved chatter and exclamations. And Hazard Sewell barking, "Alpha Flight! Form up! Call in, by the numbers! Alpha Two!"

"Alpha Two, aye."

"Alpha Three!"

"Alpha Three. I'm gonna throw up. I mean aye." Breathing. Trying to clear her head.

Heard the rest of them call in. All here. All amazed to have arrived together, when each told of losing direction and going different speeds. Carly Delgado had red-walled her thrusters. Twitch Fuentes had come to a dead stop for several hours. Yet here they all were in a bunch, spat from the maw of the same beast.

They were all here. Here. A place where none of the stars matched anything in their spectral catalog. Their catalog contained billions of star prints. Twitch: "Anybody got a star match yet?"

"Not a one. Where *are* we?"

"Not in Kansas, sir."

An orange star lay thirty-nine astronomical units off. They set their bearings by that. Called it North, for the lack of any other referent.

Reg, who really needed to restock her air, did a quick survey. "Hazard, we're inside the solar system of this orange star here. From the planetary spread, I think there could be a planet in the hospitable zone on the far side of it."

"I'm not wasting time planet hunting," Hazard sent back. "Alpha Flight, plot a course back to the precise coordinates where you first reentered real space. What are you reading at that point?"

"Nothing. I got serious nothing," said Reg.

"I got a black hole way in the background," said Carly. "Nothing at that point."

"That's not a black hole in the background," Hazard cried in sudden realizaton. "That's the hole we came through and it's right *there*."

"I see it, Hazard," Carly sent back. "I think you're right. That *is* the hole. It's closer—a *lot* closer—than the sensors say it is."

"What the hell are all you looking at?" Dak squawked over the com. "That? That's a—that's not there."

"Alpha Flight, form up. We are going back."

"*We* are *not!*" Reg shrieked. Her brain shut off. Primal terror controlled this vessel.

"Suck it up, Flight Sergeant Monroe. Fall in."

Hazard ordered his Flight to lock all their Swifts' force fields together into a single shell. They had each noticed in transit that reality ended at the perimeter of their force fields. If they joined within a single field, they might not have to go through the return voyage alone.

"Might? *Might?* You don't know! I *know* I can't go back there! You don't know how much I can't go back in there! You don't even know if that thing has a *back* to go to!"

"*Chica, chica,*" Carly said, in the voice she used to calm snarling dogs.

Hazard reasoned, "There used to be a minefield guarding the other side of the trapdoor we fell down. That means this thing has to go two ways."

"It does NOT!" Reg shrieked. "It doesn't have to ANYTHING! *You* go back, Hazard Sewell! *I* am *not* going in there!"

"Flight Sergeant!"

"What! *What?* What you got, Hazard! You got nothing to scare me with! Court-martial? Sounds like heaven, sir! But it ain't gonna happen 'cause I ain't going in there. You gonna shoot me? Then shoot me. Just you do it *this* side of that fucking *hole* 'cause this elegant hag AIN'T GOING IN! Do you read me, SIR?"

That struck him dumb. Hazard felt he was holding on by his fingernails, lost like no one had ever been lost, and now he'd lost control of his flight. Never could deal with an upset female. Damn whoever let women in the U.S. Fleet Marine Corps.

"Mr. Monroe—"

"No!"

"I got her, sir." That was Dak. "It's okay, Hazard, I got her. Reg, honey, come here and dock with me. Get in here. I ain't doin' so good myself." No innuendoes in the invitation. Just fear. "Don't make me go in there by myself, babe. *Semper fi.* I ain't gonna make it without you."

Human need vibrated in his warm muddy voice.

Crying so hard she couldn't talk, Reg docked with Dak's Swift, crawled through the emergency coupler and squeezed into the one-man cockpit with Dak—the smelly, clammy, sweet, scared ape. She held onto him tight.

With force fields interlocked, Alpha Flight jumped back into nowhere.

Donner granted Captain Farragut's request for an audience, but kept him waiting in his audience hall long enough to make it clear who needed whom.

Captain Farragut and Colonel Augustus displaced into the dark. A storm wind blew rain through the palace's wide, white archways to puddle on the jeweled floor. Outside, rubbery trees tossed wildly, bowing all the way to the ground. The coral plants shrank into hard shells and became spiny brown rocks. Waves in stone-gray rollers crashed at the foot of the terrace walls. Lightning in great purpled trees of fire lanced the furious sky.

Within the Archon's gloomy audience hall, frosted globes faded up to a soft glow. Farragut had wondered at the globes earlier, wondered what they could be. They looked like lamps, but he'd wondered what possible use the

Myriadians would have for artificial lighting in a globular cluster. But of course there were clouds, and probably basements, and he knew there were mines.

The lizard plants strayed off their shelves and huddled over rain puddles blown onto the mosaic floor. They lapped water off the beryl and sapphires, tourmaline and emeralds.

Augustus bided the time studying the walls in the lamplight. "Did you notice this?" He nodded up at the monumental inscription over the Archon's grand throne.

"I saw it," said Farragut. "I can't read it. You didn't include that script in the language module."

"Because it's not Myriadian. It's Original."

"Can you translate it?"

"No. I don't have enough samples of Original."

"So what pattern do you see?"

"The script is boustrophedon."

"That's Greek to me, Augustus."

"It's Greek to everyone else, too. Boustrophedon is a Greek word."

"Then speak English."

"There is no equivalent English word," said Augustus. "Boustrophedon means back and forth, as an ox hitched to a plow treads the rows, this way, then that way. The Myriadians have engraved these lines sinistrorsum, then they turned around and wrote back dextrorsum."

Sinistrorsum? Dextrorsum? "Are you speaking Greek again, Augustus?"

"Latin. Left to right. Right to left."

Wind howled through the colonnade, ruffled all the lights. Rain fell in splattered sheets across the precious stones.

Farragut stopped his agitated pacing (sinistrorsum and dextrorsum) to scan the engraved symbols above the Archon's throne. "I see it." Certain symbols appeared backward when they appeared in contiguous rows. "What's it got to do with anything?"

"We were looking for a language match for these folk."

"Augustus, you expect to find a known language match when we have evidence that these people come from another *galaxy*?"

"I didn't expect to find it," said Augustus. "I just found it."

A lightning flash froze the moment. The air sizzled, left

an ozone tang in Farragut's nostrils. Thunder crashed. The boom rolled out in a rumbling that reached up from the floor and shook his throat.

The Archon chose this moment to make his entrance without greeting. The lizard plants shrank back into their beds.

"What did you bring me?" Donner demanded.

"The *kzachin*," Farragut countered.

"I already control them," said the Archon.

"Then tell me where the *kzachin* at the edge of the Myriad leads," said Farragut.

Donner chose to be coy. Turned his maned back toward his visitors, looking more like a handsome animal than a man from this angle. Still an authoritative figure. "There are so many *kzachin*. I do not know where they all go."

Farragut glanced aside. Augustus' slow blink confirmed: Lie.

("I'm not getting anywhere here, Augustus. Assistance.")

Augustus produced pen and paper, drew a set of symbols—boustrophedon—and gave it to the captain. ("Ask your buddy what this says.")

Farragut offered the paper to Donner. "Do you know what this says?"

Donner would not take it from Farragut's hand. Farragut set the paper down on a polished granite ledge and stepped away from it.

The Archon took his time strolling over to glance at it. Surprise made him pick up the paper and carry it closer to a lamp. His dark eyes flickered back and forth across the symbols, then up to Farragut. "You are missing several lines. And these are cut off."

"But you can read it," said Augustus.

"Of course I can read it," Donner told Farragut, as if Farragut, not Augustus, had asked the question. "This is my name."

Donner's forefinger traced a circle around three symbols:

$$\curlywedge \equiv \zeta$$

He gave the paper back to Farragut. "I hope you did not touch the actual engraving."

"Why?"

"It is radioactive."

"It is inscribed in lead," said Augustus.

"Then you saw a copy," said Donner. "What you have there is the inscription from the inner back plate of a reliquary. The plate is solid thorium. The whole reliquary was made of heavy and rare elements. I suspected they would take it apart." The last part was spoken in an agitated mutter, more to himself, in bitterness.

"They?"

"I sent the reliquary to Origin. A gift. Apparently, they do not hold my gifts in as much regard as they hold the box."

"What was in it?"

"Things with meaning. The box, the box is merely priceless. There is no thorium on Origin. As your man said, Origin has virtually no elements heavier than iron."

"You sent the reliquary to Origin," said Augustus, using a polite *you* spoken to a superior. "Did it get there?"

Donner glanced angrily, one alien to the other. Asked Farragut, indignant, "Does your man mean to tell me the reliquary was stolen?"

"Not stolen. Lost in transit," said Augustus. "Does everything you send into the *kzachin* come out of the *kzachin*?"

Donner paused, seemed about to lie again, then admitted crossly, a dismissal, "As you said, it is a long, long way from here."

Donner's bare feet whispered a brisk retreat across the jeweled floor with his leaving.

Captain Farragut displaced back to *Merrimack* with his IO in defeat. Donner was not going to give away his transportation secrets any more than John Farragut would give Donner guns.

"Well, Augustus, did you get anything from that? Does that wormhole go to Origin?"

"It may," Augustus allowed. "But it may have branches or other hazards. We already know that *kzachin* can distort time. And now I know that some of them may distort it severely. Catastrophically, in fact."

"Based on what? Where did you get that pattern?"

"From this." He held up the paper, between forefinger and impudent digit.

Farragut snatched it from him and regarded the alien inscription. Upside down. "What is this? Where did this text come from?"

"From your own computer's data bank."

"We have this?" Farragut kept staring at the alien signs as if staring would make sense fall into them. "And it matches Original? Then why didn't it come up during our language search?"

"Why?" Augustus picked up a book someone had left in the wardroom, a picture book of fairy tales. It was a popular book on *Merrimack*. The crew made video recordings of themselves reading from it to send home to their children. Augustus opened the book to a drawing. "Here. Search this. Where's Little Red Riding Hood."

Farragut pointed her out right away, asking, "Where is this taking me, Augustus?"

"Child's play, isn't it? But without this specific picture inputted along with a precise set of instructions, your most powerful computer could not have found her if you gave it all year to search. First you would have to instruct the machine that these two-dimensional lines represent storybook characters and that Lil Red is a storybook character. Then there's the matter of color. This picture is black and white, so how can there be a Little Red Riding Hood in there? But you knew the color of her cloak because there's a wolf in the bed wearing Granny's cap and glasses, and the little girl carries a basket of goodies. You didn't need to sift through all these images, checking for parameters, and I don't need color to find Little Red Riding Hood."

"So where is she?"

"Grandma's house." Augustus righted the inscription in the captain's hands. "Planet Xi."

Farragut blinked, all the connections gone blank behind his blue eyes.

Augustus continued, "Your computer checked the Myriadian languages against all known living languages. This is a dead one."

"Oh, no, don't tell me it's Latin."

"Deader than that." Latin had, in fact, been thoroughly resuscitated. "You are holding the inscription from the Xi Tablet."

"The Xi Tablet. The Xi Tablet," Farragut murmured. "I know what that is. I . . . used to know what the Xi Tablet is. What's the Xi Tablet?"

"Oldest known artifact anywhere. It's a twenty-billion-year-old hunk of lead in a fifteen-billion-year-old universe. And it has an inscription on it."

"Why didn't the computer match the symbols?"

"Because the symbols they have in common appear dextrorsum on the Xi Tablet and sinistrorsum on Donner's wall. I told you, the Myriadians write their monumental inscriptions back and forth. The computer did not recognize the inversion. I did."

"If it's got Donner's name on it, then that tablet can't be twenty billion years old."

"Oh, but it is," said Augustus, something like malice, something like enjoyment glinting in his eye.

"Donner's reliquary was solid thorium," Farragut reminded him. "The Xi Tablet is lead."

"Lead 208 to be precise," Augustus confirmed. "With traces of radium 224 and radon 220. Garden-variety lead is lead 206, which is the end product of uranium 238. Lead 207 is the end product of uranium 235. When you find lead 206 or 207, you know you have very old uranium. You know by the isotope of lead what element it used to be."

"And lead 208 is the end product of . . . ?"

"Thorium 232."

"The Xi Tablet is old thorium," said Farragut.

"Very, very old thorium," said Augustus. "Older than the planet it was found on. The Xi system coalesced about five billion years after the Big Bang, at the same time you and I were hydrogen and helium atoms inside stars that no longer exist."

"We are stardust, we are golden."

"We are so lost. So here is a lump of very old lead that has no business being on that planet, or anywhere else in this universe. The assumption has been that the Xi Tablet was on Xi a long time, given that it was buried quite deep. But the Xi Tablet has Donner's name on it, and Donner is not that old, so we may have to rethink that conclusion. Donner sent his reliquary to Origin—through a *kzachin*. We know that *kzachin* can bend time. Echo Leader came out the other end of his *kzachin* aged five days more than the rest of us. Perhaps there's one other rabbit hole you don't ever want to fall down, Alice."

Farragut's eyes widened. "Donner's reliquary stumbled through the wrong wormhole and came out aged *twenty billion years?*"

"Best theory I've got at the moment," said Augustus. "Watch that last step."

Farragut hushed in horror. "Alpha Flight," he breathed.

Augustus nodded. "They may already be back. If they aged twenty billion years, would we even know what they were if we saw them?"

PART TWO

Functions of Chaos

9

JOHN FARRAGUT BARRELED THROUGH the causeway that joined his ship to the LEN vessel, the impact of his footfalls making the flexible connection undulate. The deck bowed up, nearly tripping him. Ambassador Aghani cut him off at the soft dock's end and launched a tirade before Farragut could begin to warn him of the Myriad's wormholes.

"Captain Farragut, you have gone behind the League's back to contact the Arran despite our explicit orders to cease all contact. Must I explain chain of command to you? Furthermore, I don't believe you have a squadron out. That is a deliberate fiction to subvert League authority. I demand—"

"Captain Farragut!" Calli's voice sounded loud from the com on Farragut's hand, overriding the mute.

"Not now," Farragut growled into the back of his fist.

"Now, sir," Calli's voice was quietly insistent.

"What is it?" Farragut asked. His XO had an infallible sense of priority.

"Deck there."

Aghani smiled coldly. "That will be the courier from Earth, conveying your dismissal from your President."

That was not possible—though the bounds of possibility had become extremely spongy of late. No courier could arrive from Earth so quickly.

"IFF?" Farragut asked Calli.

"Friendly! It's Alpha Flight!"

John Farragut rocked up on the balls of his feet and smiled back at Aghani, too happy for his smile to be anything less than purely joyful. "There's my flight," he said innocently, as if his fighters had been out for a little jaunt. He started away, at a brisk march at first, then running through the madly undulating causeway, back to *Merrimack*, roaring as he came. "Get this *hose* off my boat. Seal the lock. Calli! Take us out to meet Alpha Flight. Get those Swifts on board *now!* Go! Go! Go!"

Hatches banged shut and sealed behind the Captain's bulleting return from the LEN vessel. The soft dock retracted, link severed. The breach in *Merrimack*'s force field healed over.

John Farragut paused a moment, knuckle to teeth, eyes tight shut, alone in the corridor. *Sir? Thy will be done. But if it's not too much trouble, will them still alive, okay?*

Merrimack's six engines gave a low subliminal growl, and he felt his ship's power bunch under him like a tiger's muscles preparing for a spring.

Farragut opened his eyes, shouted into his com, "Calli! Do you have radio contact with Alpha Flight?"

"Yes, sir."

"Voice or auto?"

"*Voice,* sir. They're alive!"

Eyes up. *Thank you.*

Merrimack sped out to meet the long-missing Swifts. Her tractors guided the little ships to the flight deck. You could hear the banging through the hull as the Swifts touched down, then locked down; the whir and clank of the elevators hauling them inboard to the hangar deck.

Farragut ran to the access corridor that led to the starboard hangar deck. Crewmen dived out of his path as he charged down tight passageways and ducked through the hatchways. He slid down the ladder rails to the hangar deck.

Someone with the same imperative came sliding down from the top deck after him, fast, skimmed Farragut's hands off the rails, landing him on his back, her on top of him, on the hangar deck in a sprawl. Not too weighty. Kerry Blue.

Flat on his back with an armful of gyrene green on him,

Farragut asked, "Am I not moving fast enough for you, Flight Sergeant?"

"Oh, shit!" She scrambled to get off of him. Too fast for comfort. Kerry Blue had way too many elbows.

The OOD barked, "Captain on deck!"

Heels cracked to attention all over the hangar deck. Still on his ass, Farragut took their salutes. "As you were." And, pulling himself off the deck, "Why aren't those Swifts open yet?"

Forbidding red lights answered from the deck monitors. "Still pressurizing, Cap'n," the chief said. "They're running their Swifts thin. Cutting their oxygen consumption is my guess. We open 'em now, we'd hammer their ears in. No telling what kind of shape they're in."

Mo Shah arrived on deck with his medic team.

Kerry Blue hovered, sobbing. A voice at her back snarled, "What have *you* got to blubber about, Marine?"

Steele, of course.

He shouldered past her to join the medics clustered around the Swifts. "Stay out of the way."

Deck monitors turned green with a soft tone.

"Are we there?" Steele demanded.

"Close enough," the chief answered and ordered his erks: "Pop 'em!"

Cockpits hissed open. Steele tore the canopy off the nearest ship, reached in, and lifted out the ashen, limp figure of little Regina Monroe. He set her down on the deck. She teetered on her feet like something just born. Looked just as wet.

Steele reached back into the cockpit, clasped arms with Dak Shepard and hauled the big guy out of the same little ship.

Other shaken, stinking Marines oozed from their vessels to form up at less-than-rigid attention before Captain Farragut.

Farragut asked, "Colonel Steele, who do we have?"

Steele barked names, "Lieutenant Hazard Sewell!"

"Sir!"

"Flight Sergeant Monroe!"

"Sir!"

"Flight Sergeant Shepard!"

"Sir!"

"Flight Sergeant Fuentes!"

"Here. Oh, God, sir. I'm here. Sir!"

"Flight Sergeant Delgado!"

"Sir!"

Steele turned smartly, his face flushed ruddy, breath drawn deep, voice husky. "Alpha Flight present and accounted for, sir."

"Thank you, Colonel Steele." Farragut's eyes beamed. He strolled to the flight leader. "Rough trip, Mr. Sewell?"

"You cannot imagine, sir."

Farragut clasped Alpha Leader's shoulder. The Marine swayed under his hand. "Could be worse," Farragut said warmly. "By our clocks, you guys died last week."

Hazard Sewell tilted his head, made a speculative moue. "May have done, sir."

"Chief! I want the brains sucked out of these Swifts' black boxes. I want to know where they've been." And to Hazard Sewell, " 'Cause I'm pretty sure y'all don't know.''

"No, sir," Hazard verified, relieved. He had been wondering how he would ever explain what he'd been through. Had to love the captain for already knowing. Should've expected it. "Thank you, sir."

Farragut turned to the medical officer. "Mo. Your flight."

"Aye, sir." Mo Shah took the weary Marines in hand.

Farragut bounded back up to his control room, his steps springing, spirit flying. "We're whole. We're done here. We're out of here. Calli! Make us go away!"

The battleship *Merrimack* backtracked out of the Myriad the way she had come, until the cluster's dazzling millions of suns dwindled to a single light.

Somewhere back here Captain Farragut had lost the trail of the Hive. He needed Jose Maria Cordillera and Colonel Augustus to help him pick up the hunt again.

He found the two together in Augustus' makeshift quarters in the torpedo storage bay. Cordillera, being a civilian, nodded at the captain's entrance but did not stand, so as not to interrupt Augustus.

Augustus, being Augustus, ignored the captain entirely, intent on playing Jose Maria's guitar—Augustus' guitar now, for Jose Maria had given it to him.

"Because he can play it," Jose Maria Cordillera explained the gift.

Jose Maria Cordillera could play, but not like this. Augustus drew amazing sounds from the acoustic guitar—plaintive chords and rills of passionate sadness that found expression nowhere else in the caustic, detached Roman's stony being. No one guessed Augustus had it in him.

"Where've you been hiding *that?*" said Farragut at song's end, marveling. Music tamed the obnoxious beast.

"I don't remember learning," said Augustus.

Augustus had moved some of his belongings from his Striker, altering the torpedo storage bay into an aristocratic Roman chamber—furnished now with rich tapestries of somber hues, a few small pieces of distinctly Roman furniture, climbing plants springing from heavy Grecian urns, a statue, being a copy of the Winged Victory from the Louvre, and a hammock, stretched diagonally between torpedo racks.

"Picked a hell of a time to redecorate, Augustus," said Farragut. "I hope to need these torpedoes soon."

"We are back in the hunt?"

"Tryin' to be. I need you to get me there. Stop that." Augustus had started to play again, and John Farragut was finding it difficult to stay aggressive with those lovely Spanish strains haunting the air.

The pretty melody ceased. From the background, the pounding bass of the young Marines' raucous music pushed itself into notice. Augustus lifted his head to listen. "I think I used to like that in my past life." He tilted his head to listen, as if trying to find the part of himself that responded to the raw noise. Shook his head. "It's gone now."

"How can I help you, young Captain?" Jose Maria Cordillera asked.

"The Hive," said Farragut. "We were on its trail until we stumbled into the Myriad. If *we* ran into the Myriad, why didn't the Hive run through it? Hive swarms travel in straight lines."

"The Hive did not come this way," Jose Maria Cordillera concluded.

"But a swarm came close. And it didn't go in. What could cause the Myriad to get passed over?"

"A mezuzah on the door," said Augustus, loosening the strings of his guitar.

"And what would constitute a mezuzah to the Hive?" Farragut wondered aloud. "Can you think like a gorgon?"

"I can think like a machine, which the Hive does. And Dr. Cordillera can think like a virus, which the Hive does."

Farragut glanced from Augustus to Jose Maria. He opened both empty palms. "So? Why aren't there gorgons here?"

"Something made the swarm turn," said Cordillera. "All things being equal, the Hive moves according to inertia. Something here made the swarm turn. They would have had reason. But I do not see it."

"Augustus?" Farragut prompted a second opinion.

"What do you know about the types of planets found in globular clusters?" Augustus answered with a quiz, as he replaced his guitar in its case.

"There usually aren't any," Farragut answered.

"And there you are," said Augustus.

Jose Maria Cordillera nodded. Of course, why had he not seen that?

Farragut shook his head, still not seeing it. "Where am I?"

"A globular cluster normally has no planets," said Augustus. "Which means no food. Its mass makes it a gravity well. A Hive swarm would steer wide of the gravitational drag. The Hive does not like to expend energy unless it's running to the dinner table."

"But the table is *set*," said Farragut. "There are three living solar systems inside the Myriad. That's a lot to eat."

"Think flat, John Farragut," said Augustus. "Stay *in* the box. Globular clusters have no planets. The Hive won't look for exceptions to a long-established pattern."

Jose Maria nodded agreement.

Farragut shook his head. "How can they be so stupid?"

"How can you be so human? You are an intuitive creature, John Farragut. For the flat mind, data gets sifted through logic gates and Boolean choke points. Things either are or they are not. 'Sort of' is a powerful concept. The Hive doesn't have it."

"So the swarm turned before it got here. Which way did they go? Or should I ask: from which way did they come?"

"I have not figured that part yet," said Augustus.

"Do it. I don't care how you do it, gentlemen, find me a target."

Farragut left Jose Maria Cordillera and Augustus to their task, while he joined Colonel Steele in the wardroom for the debriefing of Alpha Flight.

Steele came to attention before the captain, then glanced guardedly past him. "I hope you haven't brought that thing with you. I won't have a Roman grilling my Marines."

"I have Augustus gorgon tracking," said Farragut.

"Should be easy for him. Birds of a feather."

Farragut waved off the comment. He surveyed the somewhat guilty-looking pilots of Alpha Flight. "Where have your boys and girls been, TR?"

Steele frowned. The frown became a scowl. He hated being asked questions he could not answer. Made him look stupid. TR Steele hated looking stupid. The Roman, Augustus, had made a campaign of making Steele look stupid, and Steele had had enough of it.

But Steele's Marines were only able to tell of nothingness, a spaceless space responsive to nothing, in which there was no speed, no acceleration, no direction. No communication.

Out of the void they had, each and all, emerged together, no matter what each had tried to do in transit, in a place not on any map. They returned the way they came, a vastly shorter journey than the going, with scarcely a breath left to breathe.

"That matches what Echo Leader reported on his voyage to Rea," Farragut said.

"Not quite," said Steele. He stepped aside to let his Marines confess to the captain for themselves.

And the reason for the guilty looks came out.

The Marines of Alpha Flight had resonated.

Farragut ducked his head in a double take. "On our harmonic? You resonated on our harmonic? And we didn't receive it? That's not possible."

The Swifts' black boxes confirmed it. Alpha Leader and Alpha Three had each shot the flare.

"Severe breach of discipline, sir. I'll take care of it," Steele assured him.

It was the worst breach. *Merrimack* was on silent run.

Resonance summoned the Hive.

"There's another real alarming part of this, TR."

"Yes, sir."

"*Both* their resonators failed," said Farragut. "We've got a serious equipment problem with our Swifts."

"*No,* sir," Steele said. Felt clunky. Farragut wasn't getting it. Easy to see why he wasn't getting it. "Both resonators *worked.* The black boxes of both Swifts say *they resonated.*"

"How can that be?" said Farragut.

Resonance had no frequency, no speed, it just *was.* The signature harmonic to which it resonated existed within the receiver. Without the receiver, the resonance was not there. Resonance did not travel like starlight or sound. It existed everywhere at the moment of resonance, then ceased.

And to Steele's confounded silence, Farragut guessed, "*Merrimack*'s receivers aren't functional?" Still trying to stay within the realm of the possible.

"Mack's res chambers are functional. All of them."

"Then?" Farragut waited for answers. None came. Steele's iceberg eyes bulged with impossibility. Farragut argued at him, "But we didn't receive their res pulses!"

"Sir. The Swifts didn't even receive *each other* as long as they were in the ... that place. They *weren't* anywhere. Wherever they were between here and where they went, they did not exist."

Farragut was a moment absorbing that one. Murmured at last: "So where did they *go?*"

MEMORANDUM
To: J.A. Farragut
From: C.H. Wells / Astrogation
Re: Preliminary Summary
Recorders from all five Swifts are functionally normal.
Recordings from all five Swifts are consistent with one another.
Recordings are remarkable for their lack of data.
Of the transit zone, provisionally called "wormhole," the Swifts' recorders register nothing. Data recorders registered only the internal functions of the individual craft. There is no other direct data to be had on the nature of the "wormhole." Of indirect data, it is significant that the Swifts' power output varied

widely, yet all five Swifts arrived at the same destination at the same time.

Journey to destination (elapsed time by Swifts' chronometers): 61 hours 18 minutes.

Return journey (Swifts' chronometers): 64 minutes.

Total time elapsed on Swifts' chronometers: 71 hr 22 m.

Total elapsed time R/T (*Merrimack* chronometer): 149 hours.

Of the destination at the far side of the "wormhole," the location cannot be placed. The destination is, without a doubt, extragalactic. The recordings describe an irregular galaxy which has no match in astrogation files. It is a young galaxy, possibly so young and so far away that no light from it has had time to reach the Milky Way. This theory does great violence to our current understanding of the formation of the universe. Astrogation Department requests a drone be sent through the wormhole to gather more data. [Denied. JF]

Merrimack's data bank contains a partial match for the Swifts' destination. Flight Sergeant Kerry Blue acquired a stellar recording from the planet Arra, purported to be a recording of the night sky of a planet outside the Myriad. Allowing for the Arran recording's inferior quality, it presents a 94% match with the Swifts' recordings taken at the far side of the wormhole.

The Swifts' recordings of destination are noisy. Background radiation is remarkably elevated beyond ambient 2.7 degrees Kelvin. Source of background radiation still under investigation. (See Technical Report, attached).

The foreground star is population I, one of the few such stars in the recordings. K type, singly formed, with planets in regular orbit.

Preliminary identification of destination: Origin.

Farragut passed the memo to his XO. "Send the full report to the Joint Chiefs." Then, with a resigned sigh: "Copy the LEN at Arra. Warn them to stay off the *kzachin*."

"Copy to Palatine?" Calli asked.

"I don't report to Rome."

"Yes, sir."

"Calli," Farragut said after a moment, prelude to a question just thought of.

"Sir." Calli waited.

"Augustus' Striker wears Flavian colors. Why isn't he called Augustus Flavius or Flavius Augustus, whichever?"

"I asked him that," said Calli thoughtfully. She parked her gracefully-shaped rear end on the edge of a console and crossed one very long leg over the other. When she cocked her head, her long braid fell forward over her shoulder. Her brow was creased, perplexed. "Augustus said . . . he was Flavian once removed."

Farragut pulled his chin back. "What does *that* mean?"

Calli was the expert in things Roman.

Her braid swayed with the shaking of her head. "John, I haven't an Earthly clue."

Captain Farragut got rowdy that evening, in the first watch. You could hear him singing—roaring really—from the officers' mess. The Marines took their cue from that and started drumming. And soon they were all trying to rock the ship within its inertial field.

Kerry Blue stood watch in the depths of the lower sail. First watch was the only time the whole ship was awake at one time. Parties, when they happened, happened in the first watch.

The rest of Alpha Flight partied as if returned from the dead. Kerry recognized Dak's lag beat clanging against the bulkhead. Uffing baboon could *not* keep a tempo.

She beat on the bulkhead with the butt of her splinter gun, yelling up, "Step it up, you *boon*!" But no one could hear her.

Kerry was not sure what she had done to deserve separation and exile from her mates. The laughter rolled down here to the bowels of the ship. Anger leaked out her eyes.

When she was spelled at middle watch, she took the ladder rungs at a ringing stomp. Stalked to Steele's quarters, requested permission to enter, stormed in before he could answer.

She demanded to know the reason for this reprimand, and don't pretend it's not a rep. *She* hadn't hit the res sender.

Why was *she* stationed under the ship while someone else who shall go unnamed is partying her brains out? Demanded she be restored to rotation with her flight mates, or you can just damn well show cause, *sir*.

TR Steele turned to her quite slowly, ominously. Eyes narrowed at her. Had not been sleeping, but was undressed, ready for the rack. Barefoot, in boxers and tank top. A dauntingly big man. Boulder-muscled. Looked like something tossed up from a volcano and still smoldering.

His voice, always a bark, came out disturbingly soft. "Flight Sergeant, I don't need my orders questioned by the company joyride."

Aborted words stuck in her throat. Her fists closed, opened, arms searching for somewhere to be. "And just *how* do you get off calling me that?"

"Flight Sergeant, where are you and what time is it?"

"It's the middle of bloody middle watch— Don't I know it! I'm awake and fragging nobody else is!"

She didn't get it.

He felt absolutely naked. Just the two of them in the dim light of his cabin. Would feel more naked still grabbing for clothes. It was nothing she hadn't seen in the gym. Didn't bother her. Bothered him.

And her carrying on like an idiot down damnation road. Her small breasts lifting with each angry breath.

"So what did I do to deserve the Hamster watch with the screwups?"

Glenn Hamilton commanded the ship in the quiet hours.

"Hamster is not a screwup," said Steele. That was beside any point, but he didn't have a good reason for the exile. He simply could not bear to be near her anymore. Afraid of touching her hair in an unguarded moment, or smiling at the sound of her laughter, or gazing at her too long.

And he didn't want her loose at first watch to party and fall into the rack with any target of opportunity who caught her drunken eye. He wished her stray-cat ways would disgust him. It only made him ache not to be the one.

"Yeah, but Hamster's only got the graveyard watch because Farragut's sweet on her and he's keeping her out of his sight. Everybody knows that."

"Oh, *really*?" blistering irony. Might have laughed at her, but he was too terrified that she was about to connect the dots. Hamster is on night watch because Farragut likes her too much. And Kerry Blue is on night watch *why?*

Felt himself turning color. Steele blushed like a flare. Hoped the lights were too dim for her to see it.

"I will not be thrown *under* the ship just because you think you're too good for me."

"If that's what you think, Blue, you're a box of rocks." She was yelling at a man in his skivvies in his cabin. Did it ever cross her randy little mind that he was even male? She was talking to him like he was her father or a gelding.

And—oh, hell—it sure wasn't dim enough for her not to see *that*.

Never more afraid than he was in this moment. She was going to notice. Laughter or horror. Either would hollow him right out.

But she was oblivious. Completely.

"Sir, can I go on the record—"

"No." He cut her off. "Because none of this is being recorded."

His big hand closed round the back of her neck, drew her in. His other arm crushed her to him, and he covered her mouth with his, kissed her, rude, deep, and out of control.

Then, just as suddenly, he wrenched her away from him so she stood on her own two feet, swaying, one hand floundering to catch the bulk as if the deck were pitching. It wasn't. He thrust her at the hatch. "You have four seconds to go if you're going."

She hesitated, and he grabbed her back on the count of two. Made the mistake last time of giving her too much time. Needed her—hot, hard, and now.

She squeaked against his teeth. His tongue bludgeoned its way into her mouth. Her next squeak came muffled. This could not feel like love from her end. His either. Felt like drowning.

Then, miraculously, the rigid tree in his arms transformed into a woman. Her stiff muscles relaxed, body softened to him. Her arms draped round his shoulders, and she yielded to everything.

Women could forgive a lot if you needed them. Kerry Blue had forgiven a lot of men. He felt a primitive need to replace them all.

He pulled the band out of her hair and let it tumble.

Kerry Blue with her hair down.

* * *

Sleepy voice mumbled against his chest in the dark hours, as slender fingers toyed at the damp, springy hairs there, "Been in space a long time, soldier?"

He growled. "I have been in space longer than this— younger—and have *never* mauled a girl like you just got." He stopped short of an apology, because he was not truly sorry. He was not even done.

Kerry slunk back to her pod, a scant stroke before eight bells. The usual graffiti defacing her place in the rack: 0010 0101

She didn't know binary, but she thought those ones and zeros said 69 somehow. Boffin humor.

She climbed unsteadily onto the rack, snapped up the netting. Stupid reg, that. Made you feel like a baby in a crib. But any grunt injured on account of falling out of the rack would be brought up on charges. Destruction of government property.

Secured, she curled into her pod. From below came a hiss. Reg: "Where have you *been*? Are you okay?"

Kerry nodded on her pillow, even though Reg couldn't see. Kerry sniffled. Whispered back, "Had it out with the colonel for reassigning me." That was close to true.

"Prick."

"Well. Yeah."

Kerry snugged her covers around her, her body singing aftershocks. Sorted a torrent of thoughts.

His name. She didn't know his name! Ran through the possibilities of TR. Better not be Theodore Roosevelt. Theodore? Gak. Teddy? Toooo cute. She would laugh. Thomas? Tom? Terrence? Terry? Oh, Kerry and Terry. Oh, no, no, no, no. Trent? Gag. Tiberius? Utter retching. Travis?

Beginning to panic. Did *not* want to know. Had to know. Whispered, "Reg?"

"Yo, babe."

"What's the colonel's name?"

"TR."

Opened the netting to flap her pillow over the side. Hissed, "What's it *stand* for?"

"Tyrannosaurus Rex?"

Reg was no help.

"Fits."

Kerry remembered all the times she had caught him scowling at her. Hot, black looks. She had to go back and rethink those glares. And there had been a holy lot of them. She had assumed he thought her an uf.

Oh, yeah, that's what he'd been thinking. How wrong could a woman be?

She rolled over, hugging her pillow, reliving moments too hot to think on. Flinched at a remembered touch. Sensations and *emotions* too intense. Sex which was not a game. That was new. The sense of a soul breaking over her, pouring out naked. He had touched her. *Touched* her.

"Yows, Blue, your weed is singing up a blue streak!"

Kerry became guiltily aware that her lizard plant, perched at the end of her pod, was humming to the tune of her madly gyrating emotions.

"Uh. Maybe it needs some light," Kerry mumbled. She scooped up her pet and gently hustled it out of the forecastle.

Barefoot, in her skivvies, she padded to hydroponics, there to deposit her jubilantly singing weed with the lettuce under the lights.

She crept back to the rack in the half-light of middle watch. The ship was quiet, as quiet as it ever got. There were always the rhythmic footfalls of joggers circling the outer belt. And the thwapping of a squash ball at any hour. Tough to get court time, and it was a popular sport, to practice wielding a hard object in close quarters without cracking your partner—before you had to do it in anger with a honed edge.

She returned to the rack, reality setting in. This was a career ender. And it would be *her* career, for sure. Him, they would frown at indulgently, slap his broad wrists with a secret wink and a nudge, and out she goes.

Damn you, Colonel. Damn you.

But she found her anger slippery. Couldn't hold it. He'd come to her like a dam breaking. A big, blundering, wounded moose. Love like a train wreck. That kind of passion was a force of its own. An endearing need one must love in return.

Reg's whisper from below made her jump. "Do you think the colonel is cute?"

Kerry clutched her pillow, holding in panic. Why was Reg asking her that? Did she know?

No. This was slumber-party chat. Just talking. Kerry dodged the question, "You know blonds aren't my first choice."

A yawn. Sound of stretching. A sigh. "You don't think he's cute?"

Overwhelming. Magnificent. Breathtaking. *Cute?* "No!"

From the other side of the partition: "I'm cute."

"Shut up, Dak."

Steele put a foot on the first ladder rung, felt the vibration of someone climbing up. He looked down, primed to challenge some space swabbie for right of way. Instead his jaw clenched as he recognized the close-cropped, tight, dark curls on the top of the ascending head. He stepped aside to give way to Colonel Augustus. Hated getting close to him. Could never get past him without comment.

This time it was an arch smile. "Ah. Flattop. Here." Augustus offered him a record bubble.

Steele eyed it suspiciously. He did not want anything Augustus had to offer. Still, the undercurrent of smug, malicious glee put him on guard. "What is it?"

"There are no copies, so you can erase it if you want." Augustus was blithe. "But I wouldn't. It's really impressive."

A horrible prickle stung Steele's mouth at the sound of Augustus' diabolical chuckle. And in case there was any doubt:

"The part where you told her this is not being recorded was not accurate."

White-blonds could not contain a blush. Steele knew he was flaming red. Ears on fire. "You are spying on me!"

Augustus was serene, almost congenial. "You knew I had a rover on Flight Sergeant Blue."

The color drained right out. He had known. He forgot. Or just assumed the recorder had been removed after Kerry's rescue from the poison gas.

Augustus held the bubble in the flat of his palm. "You owe me."

Steele snatched the recording. "You are such a dick."

"You're welcome."

*　　*　　*

Middle watch took forever coming round again. Kerry waited for the corridors to clear, then furtively scampered up the ladder to the officers' deck, let herself into Steele's cabin, heart in her throat. Never felt like this. Afraid she was in love with the moose.

Came in as he was dragging on a shirt, his back toward her. Brawny shoulders flexed, great power in the motion. Her mouth opened, but words clogged, choked. She blurted, "Your name better be Thomas."

He turned, a smile on his lips. Then his brow furled and he stalked the two steps toward her, scowling darkly. He took her face in his hands, tilted her face this way and that to study her side bars.

Satisfied the recorders were gone, he relaxed. The smile returned. "It is. Why?"

"Oh, thank God. I was sure it was Theodore. Is it Tom or Thomas?"

"My friends call me TR."

"I'm not your friends. And when it gets down to the short strokes, 'Oh, TR! Oh, TR!' ain't gonna fly. And 'Oh, Colonel!' is just too queer."

"Thomas, then. No one who ever mattered ever called me Tom. And you better be whispering." He rapped a big fist against the paper-thin bulk.

"That's gonna be tough. I'm a natural screamer."

"I know," he said, grim. Had heard many a name cried in ecstasy from the lower deck, like a stab in the gut.

"Thomas," she tried out the sound. Whispering. "I'm just Kerry."

"I know, Marine."

"Oh." Disappointed. "You're one of those guys who never calls a girl by name so you don't call the old girl-friend's name by mistake?"

"So I don't call *yours* by mistake, unless you mean to quit the Corps, which I wouldn't mind. But that's your choice."

"Oh." Very considerate. She wasn't used to consideration. "You're the oldest man I've ever been with."

"Screw you."

Why had she said that? You're an idiot, Blue. But he knows that. "Any time. What I meant was, you know how they say men are horniest when they're seventeen? I mean, how come you didn't *kill* someone when you were seventeen?"

"Did I hurt you?"

There was that consideration thing again. Not an acquired taste. She liked it immediately. "No. But you gots to know I'm not Snow White."

"That was to make you forget everyone who knows you're not Snow White."

"You're jealous."

"Shit." That was a yes.

"So, um, where do we go from here? I mean, is there ... ?" This meant too much and she was getting scared to finish the question. Afraid to assume. She'd assumed a lot with Cowboy. What in hell had she ever seen in that *boy?* "Are we going somewhere? I mean, if that was it, that's okay, but—"

"That was *not* IT."

She could see through his snarls now. Felt a big smile sprawl all over her face. "So where does that ... go?"

"Hell, Marine. I am so far out of bounds I can't *see* the bounds. I have no authority in this situation. You got an idea, I'll listen to it."

Steele never ever asked for suggestions. But they were in never ever land, so why not. "When can I see you again?"

"That's my girl. All tactical. No strategy."

"I'm waiting for you to kiss me. Now works for me."

She was not used to his smiles. Looked kind of sappy, kind of boyish on his face. Made her twinge inside. Felt the heat between them as he took her face in his hands again.

The hatch lock at her back scraped with a soft, experimental turn. She whirled, grabbed the handle, and fought the bar's stealthy turn. Steele's tree limb of an arm reached over her shoulder to add his strength to hers. She craned around to look up at him wide-eyed, mouthed the words: Who is that?

His head shook, unknowing.

The intruder fought the stiffness, gave the handle a yank, then knocked. "Sir?" Young voice. Male.

"What?" Steele roared.

"You awake, sir?"

"I am now. What is it?"

"Mr. Carmel's compliments, sir."

Kerry muttered. "I can take her. I'll take that beauty queen right out."

The voice went on, "Captain's on the bridge, sir."

"Thank you. Beat it."

"Sir."

Footsteps retreated.

Steele's arms enclosed Kerry, kissed her neck.

And let her go. When she turned around, he had turned back into the granite man she had long known, that dour battle mask engraved into his face. She demanded, "What? What happened?"

He reached for his combat uniform. "Hit the rack, Marine. Sleep in your acid fatigues."

Acid-resistant fatigues were for fighting the Hive.

Gorgons.

But the telltales were still. She didn't understand. "What's happening?"

He said only: "Farragut."

Captain Farragut made an unexpected appearance on the command deck. One of his quieter entrances, in part because he was barefoot, and in part in consequence of the cup of coffee from the muscular end of the pot he nursed. He was supposed to be asleep, and part of him still was. Still in the olive drab T-shirt and sweatpants that he customarily wore to bed.

And Hamster, accustomed to having the bridge to herself in middle watch, inhaled to announce him, but his open hand signaled her to ignore him.

The lieutenant settled guardedly back into the captain's chair. Farragut prowled to the sensor monitors. Ran a hand through his tousled hair. Sharp smell from the cup in his other hand burned the air in his wake.

Hamster sat rigid, as if at attention. She sent a discreet message to the XO's quarters. "Captain's on the bridge." And in no time, Calli Carmel appeared, in uniform. Her long hair, tied back, was still wet from an interrupted shower.

The whole ship quietly stirred.

Hands clasped behind her, Calli stood at the captain's side. "What've you got, John?"

"We're close."

Calli sniffed his cup, wrinkled her nose. "Are you sure you're not smelling *that?*"

"They're out here," he murmured. Lifted his cup to his lips. Made the mistake of looking into it. Looked like a melted burr. He lowered the cup.

Augustus was next on the bridge. Roman chemical-resistant fatigues were black, not the fetching mustard yellow of U.S. issue. Someone must have told him what it meant when John Farragut went sleepwalking to the bridge in middle watch. All of *Merrimack* tiptoed around him.

Augustus placed no credence in prescience in the mystic sense; and the expectancy, which Augustus would pass off in another man, in John Farragut was something else. He trusted it as an elemental perception. Perception of exactly what, he could not name. Chaos, perhaps. John Farragut had a fine sense of chaos. Like the dog that barks before the earthquake, howling at he knows not what. A natural creature-sense for something not yet measured. John Farragut was on the bridge.

So Augustus was not the least surprised to hear the lookout chime: "Occultation at thirty-five by nine on a ninety-degree line."

Hamster: "Stationary or moving?"

"Boogying, sir. Two hundred c."

"Dog it." Hamster's last command as she surrendered command.

"Kill the running lights and fall in behind the bogey," Calli relayed the order as John Farragut slid into his chair.

The captain seemed to increase in stature. The man could probably look commanding bare-ass naked, but he ordered anyway, "Somebody bring me some pants. And a sword."

10

AUGUSTUS TOOK UP A POSITION at the captain's shoulder. "Hell, you're a patterner, John Farragut."

Blue eyes glanced up. "You think?"

Lord of illogic. He was pulling a pattern out of the ether. Augustus muttered. "I wish I could get inside your head and see what you're taking your cues from."

"You can't," Farragut said, confident that a patterner was not a mind reader. Then, less sure, "Can you?"

"If I could, I would not be wishing."

"Not big on asking permission, are you?"

"From you? Pfff." A derisive breath sounded through his lips.

Farragut consulted his monitors. "What are the telltales saying?"

"Silent, sir."

"Tell me about our bogey."

"Maintaining constant velocity," said the tactical monitor. "No energy output. It's coasting."

"It's not an asteroid." An obvious comment.

"Not at two hundred and fifty times the speed of light. No, sir."

"What's our time of intercept?"

"We can head it off in three minutes."

"No. Don't get in front of it. Close the gunports. Shut us up tight."

Merrimack's guns leaked air and heat where they projected through the force field's shell.

"Bring us in easy on the flank."

"Aye, sir."

"We could plant a bomb in its path, sir," Colonel Steele suggested.

"Not without a positive ID." He might take out an innocent ETI. And a frontal attack on an intact swarm was seldom effective anyway. Though a man could easily chop the legs off an individual burr, a united swarm was nearly invincible from the front. No one knew how they did it, but a solid swarm generated a cowcatcher much like *Merrimack*'s.

Closer in, the tac monitor reported, "Getting a reading. It's an infrared source. Leaving a heat trail. If you can call one hundred fifty degrees Kelvin heat. Profile is—" Paused in dread. Made certain. "It's round, sir."

An intake of breath chorused the command deck.

"Sphere?" Farragut asked.

"Yes, sir."

Farragut spilled his coffee into the trash. "Wake up the boat."

Alarms blared, with Calli calling battle stations.

Little of *Merrimack* was, in fact, left asleep. Most personnel had shuffled to battle stations and dozed in their gear by their guns, or sat up polishing their face shields.

From here they knew the drill; they ran it once a week. Disconnected all implants—their personal gunsights, their language modules, anything vulnerable to Hive interference. They isolated and detached all electronic detonators, detached power packs from computerized hovercarts, pulled the cables off the lifts. You never realized how much of the ship was computer driven until you prepared to meet a swarm. But *Merrimack* ran cleaner than most ships, so this was not a major operation.

"You clear your things out of the torpedo bay, Augustus?" Farragut asked.

"I had assistance."

Farragut could picture his Marines dumping all of Augustus' things into that gold-threaded Roman carpet, rolling it up and hauling it to the Striker. "They break anything?"

"Probably. Didn't look."

The captain's pants and the rest of his uniform arrived on the command platform. He dragged on his boots, eyes on the monitors.

Merrimack closed to within passive sensor range. There was no "seeing" while you were running faster than light. But the sensor interpreters could conjure up a visual image on a monitor. They showed a solid ball of ice, a kilometer in diameter, of preternatural roundness.

A dead swarm, it was called, though the company and crew knew by now these were seldom dead, except for the outer layer. This ball would have been traveling for years, maybe centuries. Even as voracious as they were, it was damned hard to starve a gorgon.

The round shape offered the smallest surface area for its volume, for the conservation of heat. Not that you could freeze a gorgon either.

Calli ordered the ship cautiously nearer. A ship the size of *Merrimack* produced a gravitational effect—infinitesimal in astronomical terms or even in macroscopic terms, but there was no telling the sensitivity of a swarm. If *Merrimack* put a perceptible drag on the ball, it could wake up.

The officers on deck stared at the inert frozen sphere. Nothing crawling but the hair up the backs of their necks.

Calli turned to Farragut, "How do you *do* that?"

He shook his head. He could not say how he found his enemy. Even the telltales were quiet.

"Uh-oh." From a tech.

"Talk to me, Uh-oh," Farragut demanded evenly, belting his hanger.

"Uh, sir. Sorry. I just plotted the swarm's trajectory."

Augustus was already ahead of him: "It's headed to Palatine."

"Yes, sir. It'll be there in one hundred years."

"Oh, no, it won't." Farragut.

Hamster squinted at the bleak, ice-encrusted image. "Is it dead?"

"It will be," said Farragut. Turned to his Roman. "Well, Augustus. Here's what you came for."

"You do not disappoint."

Augustus gazed upon his nemesis. At matched speed, the swarm sphere hung in the center of the screen in ugly dead menace.

"Are you *sure* it's not dead?" the tech asked.

"There's a trickle charge in there," said Farragut. To Augustus. "Here's my problem. Every time you cross a gorgon, you teach the Hive."

Augustus nodded. "Like playing chess with a computer."

"Just so. And the Hive would be very predictable if we only knew who else was teaching it. Unfortunately, space is vast and who knows who else it's been chewing on. What I *don't* want happening here is it getting *any* new knowledge before it dies. I want to kill this swarm in its sleep. One shot. Lights out. I don't want them to even know they're dying. I don't want the Hive Overmind to know we're here, only that it lost a swarm here."

Augustus nodded to all that. "I like it."

Hamster offered, "Do you think there's a chance it knows we're here, and the gorgons are having this same conversation in there?"

"Trap? Never known 'em to lie doggo. Anyway, if they were talking, the telltales would show it."

Hive resonance either irritated or frightened insect life. Made bugs a good, cheap early warning of Hive presence. Only dormant gorgons did not resonate.

"That's the other thing," Farragut told Augustus. "As soon as they wake up, they split into hundreds of quick, hungry targets."

"Can you estimate the number in this swarm?"

"Not really. Depends on type. If those are burrs, there's a couple hundred thousand in there. Soldiers are bigger, so there would be less of them, but soldier balls are usually huge. This is a small ball. And gluies—I've never seen dormant gluies, doesn't mean this isn't a glue ball. And we can't tell how deep the dead layer is without an active scan. You scan, you wake 'em up. And round we go. I want to take 'em all out without exploding any of the individuals clear. Can we implode that?"

"That would require ramming a charge inside the mass before detonation."

"That would wake them up."

"Has that effect, yes. And without knowing the internal architecture, it may not work."

"Damn."

"I seem to recall you had mixed results with molten magnesium. There's a certain symmetry in using a weapon that eats."

"Works great on burrs, but it takes too long to eat a soldier. And if they get through your force field, you've got flaming guts stuck to your hull."

"Then I would suggest nukes are still your best bet for a flash fry. Impact trigger. Passive sighting. No guidance system."

The technicians nodded at their stations despite their loathing for the source of the suggestion. A nuclear projectile was the only option.

Energy weapons were useless at FTL for everything except a shot straight backward. If *Merrimack* moved into the swarm's path to line up such a shot, the swarm would detect her heat trail and wake up.

Sighting on passive input was no one's first choice, but a tag would wake the swarm. Anyway, with matched speed, both moving in a straight line, it should be easy enough to calculate the angle off to dispatch a dumb missile.

Using no tracking system would leave nothing for the Hive to skew or bounce back to its source. An impact trigger offered nothing the Hive could deactivate

"Mr. Carmel?" Farragut looked to his XO.

"That would be my choice, sir," Calli confirmed.

The techs were already at work calculating and recalculating the angle off. At two hundred times the speed of light, it was spitting into the wind.

"Do it. Three warheads."

As Calli called for three torpedoes, Augustus frowned ever so slightly. "Overkill, don't you think?"

"I like overkill," said Farragut. "Redundancy is good. Redundancy is good." And while he was being redundant, he ordered the Marine Battery to stand by the guns, but do *not* open the ports.

"Loads, sir?" Steele requested.

"Keep it simple. Exploding shells. No use showing them our whole bag of tricks if it comes to that."

Calli Carmel assumed a mechanical, square-shouldered calm. Might have been an android speaking orders:

"Match speed and vector. Keep us rock steady, Chief."

"Speed and vector, one hundred percent, aye."

"Fire Control."

"Fire Control, aye."

"Acquire target."

"Target acquired. Aye."

"Firing solution."

"Solution acquired and loaded, aye. We have tone."

"Captain?" Calli waited.

"Kill them all."

"Open torpedo bays and fire."

"Shit!" That was Fire Control.

"Fire Control, report!"

The tone changed pitch. And now a shivering sound rattled throughout the ship. Cicada songs.

The telltales had awakened.

"Hive sign!"

"Oh, for Jesus."

"Command. Fire Control. We lost tone."

"Then what's that sound?"

"Res pulse on our harmonic!" Communications cried. The tone had *not* changed pitch. It had *stopped* immediately as the resonance started. "Somebody pinged us!"

Farragut pointed to the resonance sounder. "Turn that thing off. Where'd the swarm go?"

"All stop," Calli ordered, then answered the captain, "It didn't go anywhere, sir. We did. It stopped. We overshot."

A united swarm could do things with physics a battleship could not dream of.

"Get us back, Mr. Carmel."

"Aye, aye, sir." Already doing so. Could feel the engines buck and whine.

With nothing on the screen but stars, Calli prodded, "Chief, why aren't we there?"

"You want me to answer that, Mr. Carmel?"

At two hundred times the speed of light, *Merrimack* had overshot big. The ship kicked in sudden reverse. Engines rumbled in the race to reacquire the target.

A sensor technician reported with professional calm. "Target sighted. Ball's gone hairy."

He restored the gruesome image to the screen. The giant sphere's surface pitted and cracked, the ice pocked. Legs, flailing like cilia, breached the crust, legs by the hundred, the thousand—gorgons eating their way out through a layer of their own dead.

"Fire those missiles."

"Command. Fire Control. We've lost our lock. Gorgons have put up a wobble."

The target was rapidly disintegrating, opening to a writhing mass of maggoty tentacles, the crawling, flailing nightmare, peeling off in clotted mats, and breaking into individuals like baby spiders.

"Burrs. We have burrs."

Clear of the dead layer, some ate each other, still wiggling. Drifting out of the solidity of the swarm, they ballooned in the vacuum, wriggling, astonishingly fluid in the cold, colder than hell. A mystery how they did that. One of the things that made them come to you in nightmares.

"Get a lock. Light 'em up! We are out of time, gentlemen."

And the target exploded on its own, like a pustule bursting, dispersing gorgons in all directions. Thousands of small creatures, bloating in the vacuum swell, flocked toward *Merrimack*.

Fire Control cursed. Apologized.

"Mr. Carmel, drop our bricks."

Merrimack carried solid oxygen along with her, outboard, in the deep freeze of space. Before entering any firefight, it was customary to jettison the oxygen bricks and retrieve them later. Not being edible, the Hive ignored them.

"Mark and drop. Bricks away."

"Open the gunports. Mr. Steele, at your discretion. Fire Control, fire at will. Blast 'em to kingdom come," Farragut barked his own orders. Then turned to his tactical monitors. "What dickhead pinged us?"

"Palatine." That was a guess, but Steele was sure of it.

All eyes on the bridge turned to the Roman who said, "Not I."

And the com tech confirmed, not Palatine. "It's a LEN signature. It's an SOS."

The ship's guns boomed. Her decks shuddered underfoot.

The ship hummed and lurched with the deep repetitive clunk of manual loads firing from the big guns. The engines changed tone in charging up the beam guns and changing phase to avoid takeover by the closing Hive mind. Shouts of Marines echoed through the corridors on all decks. Every monitor, each showing a different angle from *Merrimack*, clouded over with black round bodies flexing their legs, each leg terminating in a mouth.

"Come on, greta! You hungry, ain't ya? Come and get it! Eat *this!*" Dak Shepard pulled the firing lever in gun bay twenty-four. Alpha Flight, serving as gun crew, ducked from the sparks and noise of the great barrel's heave and recoil. Sonic filters dampened the thunder in their ears.

Outside, the shell fragmented into a million shards, cutting the legs off gorgons. Still the gorgons came in limitless hordes.

Immediately, the gun crew straightened to cap and retract the barrel, slide open the breech, and ratchet in another shell.

"Adjust range," Flight Leader Hazard Sewell ordered. "They're getting closer."

"Keep 'em off! Keep 'em off! I *hate* those things."

"Ain't in love with 'em myself," said Dak. "Load!"

The shell dropped into the chamber.

"Close and lock."

"I'm locked," said Carly, stepping away.

A nervous rookie—Cowboy's replacement—watched the black clouds on the monitor. "They can get *in?*" Had heard that they could. Wanted someone to laugh at him for believing that one.

Dak grunted, cranking the firing mechanism. "You bet your favorite body part they can. Ready! Gimme a range! Gimme a range!"

Regi adjusted the mechanical dial for the shifting swarm. Fed out a measured length of chemical fuse. "Consider this a tone," she said. "FRAG 'EM!"

"Clear gun! Come and get it, greta!" Dak pulled the lever as everyone jumped clear. The barrel bucked, sent the fragmentation shell on its way with a roar.

Reg rose cautiously. "Listen."

The six Marines in gun bay twenty-four listened to a tonal change in the force field's hum.

"Gretas." Dak pronounced grimly.

"Wh—who?" the rookie demanded from the knowing

looks of the rest of the gun crew, who listened to the sound and nodded at the name.

"They're on us," said Carly.

Fresh off the last reinforcement boat, the rookie had never trained for this. He was a flier, not a gunner. But when the Battery was forced to manual loads and the Wing was grounded by Hive interference, everyone became a gunner. This was warfare according to John Farragut.

"How can they get through the force field?" the rookie's voice shot up to a girlish range.

"Dak! Gimme a shell here, you baboon," Carly demanded.

Dak complied, cranking the lever that hefted the giant shell to the breech while he answered the rookie, "It's called—" grunt "'insinuation.'" The shell dropped in place. He patted the barrel with a gloved hand. "You got it, bitch."

"Shouldn't we oughta clean this barrel?" Kerry Blue spat on the fat, black barrel. The glob sizzled away clean.

"On a roll here, babe," Reg said quickly. "Come on, come on, we only got time for one more, I think."

The rookie helped Dak ratchet the barrel back. "What's insinuation?"

"Gretas *wiggle*," Dak grunted. "Lock and load! Reg, take it! Range!"

"Range is *can't miss*." Reg cranked the mechanism as close as it would go. "They're *here!* Fire!" She dived out of the way.

"Everybody *clear!* GRETAAAAAA!"

The gun leaped. The force field sizzled with shrapnel and gorgon parts.

The force field hum was erratic now. Gorgons caked the battleship's energy shell.

Came the expected call: Secure the guns. Wing report to the Swifts—except Alpha Flight.

"*What!*"

"Whoa, Regi! Watch the pitch!" Dak shook a finger in the ear that received Reg's shriek. "Help me, here. The barrel's stuck."

Reg leaned on the lever with Dak, trying to haul the extended barrel back inboard. She grunted, a high-pitched girly grunt, "Why everybody but Alpha Flight? Why not us? What's wrong with us?"

"Why you asking me? Push! Put your weight in it. Aw, nuts. Can I get somebody fat on here?"

Carly, not fat, jumped on the canted lever; then Twitch, then Kerry.

The lever gave way suddenly with a tumbled pile of Marines.

With all the ship's barrels locked inboard, the ship's force field smoothed over and intensified against the gorgons' assault.

There were fewer of them now—the gorgons—and it was safe to launch small ships to gun down the remains.

The Marines of Alpha Flight sat useless as the rest of Red Squadron and the whole of Blue Squadron stampeded for the port and starboard flight decks to take the battle outside.

To add insult to injury, Colonel Augustus was receiving clearance to launch his Roman Striker into the fray.

Hazard Sewell took in all the doleful eyes around him, his grounded, insulted flight looking to their leader for help. "Come on," Hazard said, and his flight followed him to the command platform.

Flight Leader Hazard Sewell halted just outside the open hatch, at attention. He waited some moments, ignored. Inside, the control room operated like a living machine, Naval officers and specialists attentive to their stations, conferring in quick, cool efficiency.

Hazard cleared his throat in the hatchway.

At last, Lieutenant Colonel Steele turned.

"Sir," Flight Leader Hazard Sewell spoke for the rest of his flight. "With respect, sir. Why not us?"

Kerry Blue's eyes silently added exploding shells to that question. Glared at Thomas Ryder Steele. Her lips trembled. She thought the moose was protecting her. Pissed her off. She was a United States Fleet Marine, for God's sake.

Steele spoke lightly, too indulgently, eyes on Kerry. "Alpha Flight, report to your Swifts."

And they did, running, only to find their fighters in pieces all over the starboard maintenance deck.

The boffins had dragged out any part of the Swifts that might give a clue about Alpha Flight's journey through the *kzachin* to nowhere. Even Kerry Blue's Swift was disassembled. She recognized her pieces, all coded 0045—hexidecimal for sixty-nine. More boffin humor. "Why *my* crate!" Kerry cried. "*I* didn't go into the frogging wormhole!"

"Yours is the control specimen," Reg told her glumly. "They take a normal one to compare the weird ones against. Cinderella, we ain't going to the ball."

The monitor screens gave the control room a view of what was happening outside. Displayed the unlikely picture of Fleet Marine Swifts firing upon *Merrimack*. They scorched the gorgons off the force field shell with flaming gas before the wriggling monsters could insinuate their way through the ship's distortion field.

More eerie still was the sight of a Roman Striker among the Marines, blazoned in Flavian red and black, picking off burrs with surgical precision.

"Captain, you have to see this."

Everyone who could see it gawked. The Striker spat pulse pellets, ten rounds per second, one gorgon per round. He did not miss. He did not touch the force field.

"Sir, he's not even grazing our shell."

Neither did Augustus hit the Swifts that strayed into his firing path. Missed them by literal hair's breadths.

The tac specialist could not close his mouth. "This is impossible."

Farragut gazed in amazement. "I'm glad he's on our side."

"For now," said Calli.

"For now," said Farragut.

The little fighters quickly scoured *Merrimack*'s hide free of burrs. Then the sortie turned into a game, with Swifts vying with each other to bag the strays, but Farragut sent the recall. "We have an SOS to answer."

The stray gorgons were too few to form up into a viable ball to survive an interstellar voyage. Gorgons needed to swarm in order to achieve FTL. Solo, they were thousands of years from anywhere. These lost monsters would eat each other or disintegrate before they ever made planetfall.

The LEN's resonant message had been a brief one, instructing *Merrimack* where to pick up a courier rocket, which would carry the full message of dire import. The LEN at least had the sense not to resonate from within the Myriad, but this decoy was a bald one.

"The Hive will figure this one out," Jose Maria Cordillera said. "A swarm will follow the rocket trail. Or it will go to the nearest yellow star. And that is Arra."

Nine hundred light-years must have seemed like a safe distance from the true source of the message. But it was only six times the diameter of the Myriad. The Hive would figure it out.

On top of that, there was every indication that the Hive would recognize the sender from the harmonic. There were infinite discreet harmonics. The Hive would know from this particular harmonic who was out here.

Farragut marveled. "For a bunch of learned people, the LEN can be hanged stupid. This had better be important. If Donner's taken hostages, I'm going to let him keep them."

As soon as *Merrimack* gathered all her own aboard, Farragut gave the order to pick up their coal cars—the oxygen bricks— and proceed on an intercept course with the courier rocket, flank.

Calli advised, "Captain, the telltale is still active. We have Hive sign."

"Run. Random vector."

"Running sir. Eight hundred c. Still singing."

"Bad words. Foul language." Farragut slapped the arm of his chair, rising. "We got a clinger."

One of the aliens must have insinuated through the force field and now rode along between the force field and the hull.

"Get it out."

But the systems tech reported, "Negative burrs on the hull. Repeat, we have no burrs."

The com tech reported, "Well, it's somewhere close enough to bother the telltales. And it's got to be pinging up a bloody storm." The tech put the telltales on audio, a chittering scream of crickets and cicadas. You couldn't hear the gorgon itself, but you could almost put words to it, shrieking to swarms far and wide: I got the *Merrimack*! It's here! It's here!

"Turn that off." Farragut turned to Calli. "When you've looked everywhere and can't find it—"

"It's *in* you," Calli finished for him.

Farragut spoke to anyone within earshot: "Somebody find that squealing maggot and squish it."

"Aye, aye, sir!" Calli opened the loud com to broadcast: "All hands, all hands, we have an intruder on board. Look for a gorgon. Systems, clear the vents. Battery, blow the guns clear."

"What's happening?" the rookie asked as Alpha Flight returned to gun bay twenty-four.

"Bug up our nose," said Dak, ratcheting down another shell, big as his chest, and Dak was a big man. "Force field is thinnest over the guns. You gonna open that thing, Reg, or do I gotta talk dirty to it first?"

Reg pulled at the breech lever, muttering. "Piece of frogging fripping low bid crap is stuck."

Dak joined her on the lever, grunting.

The rookie hung back, scowling. "Why do you guys talk so prissy? Why can't any of you just speak Anglo Saxon?"

"Hazard don't like it," said Kerry Blue, trying to push at the lever with her foot.

"So what's that got to do with it?"

"Two stripes on his sleeve says we frogging do as he says. You gonna help here?"

"What are we doing?" The rookie was accustomed to auto loads. He had never seen anything like *Merrimack*'s manual loading system.

"Wasting energy— Cheese and rice, Reg, what'd you do to this thing?" Dak dropped off the lever, sweating.

"Ick, Dak, stop dripping on me." Reg wiped her arm. She stopped on a sudden thought. "Force field goes away at the barrel. Barrel's an air lock. You *can't open the breech* if the barrel is *uncapped*."

"We capped it," said Dak dully, sweating like a shower wall.

"*Did* we?" said Carly.

Dak looked at Kerry. Kerry looked at Reg. No one could remember doing it.

"I bet you didn't." Reg turned the crank. Came a muffled thunk of a tampon snugging home. "You didn't, you baboon!" Reg slapped the barrel. "Try the breech now!"

Dak turned to the rookie as if this had all been an instructional show. "Like that, you see? The barrel sticks out through the force field, so the easiest way for anything to get into the ship is through the barrel."

"Provided no one fires the gun," the rookie filled in.

"Which is just what we're gonna do," said Dak, pulling open the breech. "*Fuck!*"

Dak's jump knocked Reg backward onto the deck. She crab-skittered away as lashing tentacles, wide and black as bullwhips, blossomed from the breech.

Terminal sucker mouths latched onto Dakota Shepard's cheek, tore at his uniform.

More legs sprouted from the breech as a fat alien struggled to squeeze its blobby body through the barrel.

Dak screamed in pain. And Kerry Blue was there with a sword, hacking off ravenous stalks. The severed pieces fell, thrashing, stumps spurting caustic brown dry/wet sludge from the cut ends, mouth end still grasping. Kerry danced over the biting pieces, shrieked at the stinging acid seeping through her uniform. She kept slashing till Dak staggered free, and Reg hit the sprinkler. The compartment rained neutralizing solution, slicking the deck.

The full gorgon emerged like a balloon, its bulbous, space-black body filling out and rounding, freeing more tentacles.

Quick. They were more than quick. But you didn't have to chase them. Gorgons came to you.

Reg stood still, shut her eyes, and whipped her sword in a lemniscate in front of her and let the burr reach for her. She felt the resistance of impact, the squirt of caustic blood, the flapping of severed ends at her ankles. She slashed harder.

Face shields, all polished and ready, hung within reach if only Reg could afford the two seconds to put one on.

Reg cried, "Don't you be flapping all them sucky mouthy legs in my face, you frag bag. Suck my steel, space squid!"

Dak seized a face shield, skated on the slick wet deck to the stumpy side of the wounded alien to stab at its bloated body. "Die, greta, die!" For they were all gretas to Dak Shepard.

Brown acid spurted. Dak twisted his blade in the wound. Gretas self-sealed a simple puncture wound. The thoroughly ruptured alien emitted a grosteque noise, like a balloon sputtering air.

And it died. Dissolving into a brown puddle of neutralized sludge. The heat shut your eyes. The stink stopped your breath.

Carly yapped, "Catch that! Catch that!" chasing a severed tentacle thrashing across the deck.

The xenos had yet to get a gorgon part into stasis to study it intact.

Twitch hurried to fetch a container to collect Carly's prize.

"Oh, you know it's just gonna die," said Kerry, not moving to help, even as the tentacle dissolved in Carly's hands. "See?"

Carly screeched at the melted crap in her hands. "Oh, *futon*!"

There was money in it, a viable gorgon biopsy. Even though no one was even sure gorgons qualified as a *bio*.

Dak turned his face up at the sprinklers, letting the soothing solution pour over his face. When he blinked his eyes clear, he screwed up his face at Reg. "'Suck my steel, space squid?'"

The rookie stood in the pool of brown slime. "Is—is it dead?"

"Does it *look* dead?" Carly said, hands under the sprinklers.

Kerry Blue rubbed stinging brown slime off the back of her hand to reach her caller. "Commander Carmel. Gun crew twenty-four. We got the singer. Waxed it."

The XO acknowledged.

"Lab, are we quiet?"

The telltale cicadas had stopped their shivering.

"Ants are going back into the sand. Looks like we're clear, sir."

Farragut nodded. "Let's go pick up the LEN's rocket." And, under his breath, "Dumb shits."

"Their message was spectacularly ill-advised," Jose Maria Cordillera rephrased.

Hazard Sewell asked Team Alpha, "How'd the new guy do?"

"Who? The frozen pizza?" Carly shot back, daubing Dak's facial burns with salve.

"Oh, no," Hazard moaned. "The new guy froze?"

"He . . ." Twitch had a tough time saying anything bad

about anybody. Had a tough time saying anything. "Did a fine job of staying out of the way."

"Oh," said Hazard.

Said Kerry Blue: "He's no Cowboy."

The day's journey to intercept the message rocket gave Augustus time to sleep off the ordeal of plugging in to patterner mode. By that time John Farragut had worked up a fine anger at the LEN.

"They thought that just sending a courier rocket out of the Myriad would keep the Hive from tracing that res pulse's origin back to Arra? The LEN have badly underestimated our vermin!"

Intercept and retrieval landed two messages from the LEN. One message, for John Farragut, ordered the immediate return of *Merrimack* to the Myriad.

"Can they do that?" Calli asked doubtfully. She knew the LEN had jurisdiction over Earth business in the Myriad, but she did not think their arms were long enough to haul *Merrimack* back on just their say so.

"They think so," said Farragut.

The second message was for *Don* Jose Maria Cordillera. It contained a lot of data quite outside Cordillera's fields of expertise. He passed it on to the appropriate xenos.

The xenos were not long in formulating a report.

"So where's the fire?" Farragut asked the xenos, assembled in one of the labs. The looks on the scientists' faces did seem to indicate a genuine emergency.

Dr. Linley, head of the astrogation team, stammered a bit. "The *kzachin*—the wormholes. They're multiplying."

"And?" Farragut prompted.

Dr. Linley stammered himself into incoherence.

"And the Myriad is shrinking," Augustus answered for Linley.

"And it's bloody shrinking!" The xeno gripped a console to stop his hands from shaking.

The laws of physics said the globular cluster must degenerate, grow diffuse, torn apart by tidal forces. Instead, the Myriad was contracting, minutely, definitely. At an accelerating rate.

The astrogator lit up the image brought by the courier. It was of the Myriad. Then he overlaid the image with glowing lines that mapped all the connections between the *kzachin* inside the Myriad. Collectively, the lines curved toward the center, making the cluster look like a string bag. One need only pull a string to close the whole thing.

And according to Linley's calculations, the aberration must have started nearly ninety years ago—coinciding with the arrival of the first colonists from Origin to the Myriad. It was then that the globular cluster's natural expansion began to slow, then stop, then slowly, minutely, eventually reverse into contraction.

"The Myriad is not fixing to collapse in our lifetime at that rate," said Farragut. "This was worth betraying *Merrimack*'s position to the Hive?"

"It's the acceleration, sir," the xeno's voice shook. "It's geometric."

In geometric progressions, minuscule effects could get rapidly out of hand.

Farragut glanced across all his xenos' frantic faces. "What's causing it?"

"No idea. No idea with any hard science behind it. Except everyone on the team hypothesizes it ties in with the *kzachin*—because of the curvature of the connections." Linley fluttered a quaking hand at the string bag image. "And because it began when the Myriadians started using the *kzachin*."

Of all the *kzachin,* only the *kzachin* through which Alpha Flight took its journey had no connecting point. That wormhole, the one everyone now called the Rim gate, showed as a solitary dot at the outer perimeter of the cluster.

"Well, hell, there it is," said Augustus.

"There is what?" said Farragut.

Augustus pointed at the dot. "I've found Origin."

"You mean the gateway to Origin," said Farragut. "We already suspected that."

"No," said Augustus. "I found Origin."

"Where is it?" Farragut saw only an empty point in space.

"It's ten billion years away."

"*Ten billion light-years?*"

"John Farragut, I speaka ze English better than that. I said years, not light-years."

Farragut was still lost. "Something you chose not to communicate earlier, Colonel?"

"I said nothing, because I didn't believe it. Still don't. As Arthur Conan Doyle said via Sherlock Holmes: when you eliminate the impossible, what's left, however improbable, must be the truth. So I reconsidered. But there's nothing left except the impossible. So I reconsidered again. Dismissing any idea as obviously impossible is certainly bad science."

A buzzing, shiver, and chirp inside the lab made all the xenos inhale.

A dropped glass crashed, shattered.

One of the xenos sobbed.

The flutter of moths, the scrape of cicada wings. The desperate plop of insect bodies beating against glass confines.

Farragut turned slowly to one of the lab's terraria.

Ants poured from their tunnels.

Hive sign.

"Augustus, I'm going to make you explain whatever it is you just said— *Hold* that thought," said Farragut, and into his caller: "Calli. We have Hive sign."

"Yes, sir."

"Find it. Get it off."

"It's not a gorgon hanging on this time. The last one must have ratted us out. Long-range res scan shows two swarms converging on us."

"Anything headed toward Arra?"

"Negative. They seem intent on the *Mack*."

"Good. Got a type on those swarms?"

"They're soldiers."

"Soldier" was the old name for the Hive type which the xenos now called "antibodies." The crew of *Merrimack* still called them soldiers, tanks, or can openers.

"Hive's sending a hit squad?"

"I think so, John."

"Size?"

"Magnitude five and six."

"What in blazes is a six?"

The Navy's scale of swarm strengths had no upper limit. Magnitude five was the biggest anyone had ever seen.

Calli came back, wry: "Bigger than a five, sir."

Farragut guessed he had that one coming.

"They're getting bigger, John. Did you notice that? The closer we get to the Hub."

"Let's run 'em, Cal. Launch wild geese."

"Wild geese, aye."

Two Naval Space Patrol Torpedo boats, SPT boats—"Spit boats" to the crew—readied on the hangar deck to lead off the voracious swarms. Marine Swifts were too short-winded to give a convincing chase. Wild geese had to fly for days.

Calli sent the SPT boats out, resonating on an off harmonic, with orders to rendezvous at the planet Arra after they had lost the swarms.

"Don't lose them too soon," Farragut added last orders. "If the Hive finds out they overlooked three whole edible planets in this neighborhood, I don't want to see what kind of sleeping dogs wake up."

The wild geese took off, honking.

Farragut watched them go till their running lights vanished into the star field. He turned off his screen and summoned Augustus into a wardroom. "Talk to me."

"Origin is ten billion years distant," said Augustus.

"You been withholding information or you just figured this out?"

"Based on new information. When I hooked into *Merrimack*'s system during the Hive battle, I found the flight recordings from Alpha Flight's sortie in the ship's database. The missing pieces were there." Augustus pulled a projector from his pocket, and filled the wardroom with stars. Not the Myriad this time. This was darker space. Bluer, whiter stars. "This is where Alpha Flight went."

"The xenos say Alpha Flight's readings match Kerry Blue's recording," said Farragut. "You already had these pictures."

"Oh, but Alpha's recordings are far and away more sophisticated and informative than Kerry's. Alpha's recordings picked up the background radio noise. Kerry's picture didn't. And that's the smoking gun."

"The xenos said the neighborhood was hot," Farragut recalled. "Is that significant?"

"A background residual temperature way over three degrees Kelvin is significant."

"So it means there's a big event in the region that put out a lot of energy."

"It does. And so there is. There's a quasar in Origin's backyard."

"What are you calling the backyard?"

"Five hundred million light-years."

"Close as I ever want to get to a quasar. If Origin is that close to a quasar, that means Origin is at the very edge of the universe."

"It means no such thing, John Farragut. You are assuming that because all the quasars we can see are three billion light-years away or better, that all quasars are far away."

Farragut had so assumed. "It doesn't mean that?"

"Did you pass astrophysics, John Farragut?"

"I thought I did."

"The fact that we can see the light from no quasar younger than three billion years means that all the quasars are gone. Long gone. What we see is three-billion-year-old light from an entity that no longer exists. Yet here in Alpha Flight's recordings is a quasar billions of years younger than any quasar has a right to be. And then there is the redshift of all the stars in this recording. These stars are moving at astonishing speeds."

"The recording is fubared?" Farragut suggested. "GIGO. This is full of G?"

"Too internally consistent. Too patterned. This redshift is real. These stars were recently—astronomically speaking—shot out of a cannon. The Big one."

"Big Bang."

Augustus nodded. "These recordings have all the markings of a very, very, very young picture of the universe. This is a young galaxy with a young irregular shape, young quasars nearby, young stellar spectra, young speed, young background temperature, and a youthful dearth of heavy elements."

"If this galaxy is that young and that far away, then it's younger than it is distant," said Farragut. "Its light is not here yet and we can't see it at all."

"No, John Farragut. We are looking right at it. This galaxy isn't far, far away. It's long, long ago. This is the Milky Way."

And to John Farragut's silence Augustus added, "Which is why Alpha Flight's res pulse did not reach us, though resonance exists everywhere at once. It was not that Alpha Flight was nowhere to be found; it was no *when*."

"No. Wait," Farragut could not accept this. "If this mess of stars is the Milky Way, why didn't you recognize it before? You're a patterner."

"No one can predict with any precision what an irregular galaxy will grow up to look like. I could give you possibilities, but there are too many dynamics, too many variables, too much data that I don't have to make an accurate prediction. I can, however, look at the beginning point and the end point and tell you if they connect. And these do. This is our galaxy."

Farragut stared disbelievingly at the projection of Origin's stellar neighborhood. "Where is Earth in this picture?"

"It's not born yet. Neither is Palatine. Sol's formation is still five or six billion years off. But you know this place." He pointed at the bright blot of a globular cluster. "The oldest extant features in any mature galaxy are its globular clusters. This is the Myriad."

"This is a much brighter, denser cluster than the Myriad," Farragut argued. "Look at all these blue stars."

Augustus was condescending. "Of course it is. This is the baby picture."

"Where's Arra in here?"

"Arra's star is not a cluster star. It's a population I star that got stuck in here. It's not born yet either at the time of this recording."

Farragut turned to the star burning large and orange in the foreground of Alpha Flight's recording. Origin's star. "Does this star still exist?" he asked, throat gone dry.

"Origin? Thought you'd never ask. Yes, it does. Orange stars are slow burners. They last damn near forever."

Farragut sucked in a breath, trying to inhale patience. Augustus was making him ask for every single thing he needed to know. "Do you know where this star is now?" He stuck his finger on the large orange image.

Augustus nodded.

"What star is this? Does it have a name in any of our catalogs?"

"Oh, John Farragut, can't you connect the dots yet?" said Augustus. "It's Xi."

11

"OH, FOR JESUS," John Farragut murmured. Disorienting, the concept that the impossibly distant Arran home world, Origin, could be the same planet as a local, long-known, long-dead world, on which no trace of life or civilization remained beyond a lump of lead.

Augustus explained his own delayed recognition. "You see, I uffed the logic gates. It is not that Donner's thorium-lined reliquary failed to reach Origin and landed on Xi instead. It reached Origin *and* landed on Xi. The two are not mutually exclusive. Donner's thorium did not age billions of years in the time distortion of the wormhole. It aged all those billions of years in real time. And *that* is how you get a twenty-billion-year-old hunk of spent thorium in a fifteen-billion-year-old universe. The Xi tablet did the last ten twice."

"You said that with a perfectly straight face."

"When you have eliminated the possible, whatever is left, even if it's *im*possible, means you failed to grasp the situation. The Myriad is sitting on a paradox."

"Does this have anything to do with the cluster's shrinking?"

"How could I know? I can't find patterns if cause and effect can play *backward*. We're not just down the rabbit hole, Alice. This is the wrong side of the looking glass."

Farragut recited what everyone knew and never questioned: "The arrow of time flies in one direction and one direction only."

Augustus nodded. "And if nature abhors a vacuum, nature loathes, abominates, and despises a paradox, and I haven't much stomach for them myself. Paradoxes are self-healing."

"We should stop the Myriadians from sending anything more through the *kzachin,*" said Farragut. "Now."

"Yesterday," said Augustus.

Dak Shepard started it. The rest of Team Alpha picked it up right away and soon all of Red Squadron was calling him Peetz, and the infection spread to Blue Squadron.

Afraid to ask anyone in the company, because it seemed to be something a dog soldier ought to know, the rookie Cole Darby furtively approached one of the less snottified spacers.

"Uhm . . ."

The Naval com specialist waited in quizzical irony while Cole Darby struggled to properly couch his question. The com spec's open fresh face showed a near smirk now. Might have underestimated this navy bean's snottifaction. No turning back now. Cole Darby forced the question out. "Um, is, uh, what's *peetz*? Is that like *putz*?"

"No." The com spec grinned. Didn't look so friendly now. Looked predatory. "So you're a peetz, hm." The navvy's red brows bobbed up and down.

"No! No. No. Not me. It's, uh, someone else. I was curious is all. My squadron calls this guy Peetz. But his name isn't Peter."

"Don't bulsh me, Peetz," the com spec said easily. "You're the only toad in Red Squadron."

First peetz, now toad? Worse and worse. "What the hell is a toad?" Cole Darby cried.

"The green guy! Who else is going to turn into a frozen pizza in a furball? The rest of your squadron is blooded and gutted. It has to be you."

"I—" Cole started, realized he had nothing to follow that.

The spacer clapped him on the shoulder, gave him a jostle, friendly-like. "Work it off next furball, Peetz. It's easy:

you get scared, you just figure out who you'd rather have eat you alive—the Hive or your squadron."

Captain Farragut prowled side to side of the control room, goaded by the urgency of the LEN's message, maddened by his inability to answer it.

Merrimack could not go near the Myriad so long as the Hive Overmind knew where the battleship was. *Merrimack* had been biding its time in pointless circles, waiting for the wild geese to lead off the two huge swarms and silence the infernal buzzing and humming that was Hive sign. Once it stopped, *Merrimack* would be clear to travel.

Only it wasn't stopping.

"Calli. Are you *sure* we don't have a clinger on us?"

Burrs could hook onto the ship's force field and drag a full klick behind her.

"I'm sure, Captain. And that's not coming from a singer. It's a sounding. Those two soldier swarms are pinging us."

"Shut down our res chamber."

"Already done."

The lookout sang abruptly, "Wild geese coming in hot and light." Hot and light meant fast with all ammo spent. "Requesting permission to dock."

John Farragut grabbed up the caller, hailed the wild goose leader. "Shooey! What are you doing to me?"

"Captain! Sir! Sorry, sir. They're not buying it."

"Get in here and talk to me."

"Aye, aye, sir."

Captain Farragut met the wild geese on the hangar deck. Lieutenant Schumacher—Shooey—sweating like a fevered pig, pulled his helmet, dripping, from his head, dragged a sleeve across his wet, plump face, squinted. "Sorry, Cap'n. They wouldn't chase."

Farragut cocked his head in surprise. "This is new." He found Jose Maria Cordillera on the deck with him. Asked, "Is this new? Why didn't they take the bait?"

Jose Maria Cordillera shook his head. "I have never seen this behavior. It may have to do with cell specialization. The kind of swarm members which we call 'gorgons' exist to eat. What we call 'soldiers' tend to pursue hard targets. These two swarms may be purposely sent to destroy *Merrimack*. This is all guesswork, based on a statistical field of one."

Jose Maria followed Farragut, who paced a slow circuit around the Swifts in the hangar. The captain touched the empty hardpoints. Shooey answered the motion, "We shot the whole load, sir."

Farragut brushed off his fingers. "What were you packing?"

"Frags and nukes. All ordnance found the target, sir."

That stopped Farragut's pacing. "Did they *eat* the nukes?"

"A chunk of the soldiers detached from the main swarm and snagged our field. We spaced them. After our nukes were spent, the main swarm came at us. We kept ahead of it for a while. Then it broke pursuit and resumed its original course."

Captain Farragut glanced to Jose Maria Cordillera. "They don't do that. Gorgons never walk away from food."

"If they have no hope of catching it, apparently they can," Jose Maria observed. "We may have taught the Hive the real meaning of a wild goose chase."

"Not good. Shooey, what then?"

"We poked 'em. Achieved no critical damage. When the burrs are all balled together big like that, their field is too tight. It's a *big* swarm. They just ate their dead and stayed on course. We got ahead of them and veered away. They didn't pursue us. They didn't even wobble. We shot everything we had." Shooey shrugged empty, soaked arms.

"They're looking for our base." Farragut spoke that as a certainty. "Planets can't run."

Once the Hive located an edible planet, combat was no longer a battle. It was a siege. And Earth's defenses were already stretched too thin to assist out here on the distant frontier.

The Hive must not locate Arra.

John Farragut was better suited to an offensive fight. He was not about to add another fixed target to *his* war.

He summoned his senior lieutenant.

"Hamster. See to the Spit boats. Refuel, restock, rearm. Then pick a team. I have an urgent message to go to the Myriad. Invite Jose Maria to go with you. Take both boats. Depart within the hour."

Upon the captain's return to the control room, Calli rose, clasped her hands behind her back. Assumed, "We're going to lead off the swarms with the *Mack*?"

"I'll take care of them," said Captain Farragut.

Jose Maria Cordillera stood at the wide viewport, watching the SPT boats launch. There was a brute elegance in the snub, blocky vehicles. They wore their armament outboard on racks.

The civilian, Jose Maria, was always a striking figure, trim and elegant against the siege of years. His home on Terra Rica was not a democracy, and Jose Maria did not dress like a democrat. His bolero jacket and gray trousers were of expensive cloth. He stood like a brooding stallion.

The voice intruded at his shoulder. "Not joining the rats, *Don* Cordillera?"

Jose Maria Cordillera turned to the Roman, Augustus. "Rats? I do not understand 'rats.' "

Augustus' gaze remained fixed, over Cordillera's head, on the departing vessels. "*Rata.* The ones leaving the ship."

Lieutenant Glenn Hamilton's SPT boats cleared *Merrimack*'s field, arced away, and vanished on a quick line to the star cluster Myriad.

"That would imply that *Merrimack* is sinking," said Jose Maria Cordillera.

"And are we not going to our deaths?"

Cordillera hesitated, dropped his voice quite low, lest someone overhear this conversation. "Why would you say so?"

"And you the expert on things Hive," Augustus chided. "Level-five and -six soldier swarms. Biggest swarm ever seen and one bigger still? We are overmatched."

Cordillera turned away from the viewport.

Augustus prodded his silence. "I thought suicide was against your religion. You are traditional Catholic?"

Catholics did not call themselves "Roman Catholics" anymore. Not since the exodus.

Jose Maria would only say, "You have cold statistics, Colonel Augustus. I have hope and faith."

"Your God takes a laissez-faire approach to human emergency. In your battle against human disease and misery, Doctor, you must have noticed the innocent and faithful die as quickly and needlessly as the rest of us."

"I have to believe not."

And on second consideration, Augustus noted the doctor had not specified his hope and faith in *whom*.

"Even the god of *Merrimack* has lost hope in this one,"

said Augustus. "Our gallant captain is sending the pretty Mrs. Hamilton out of harm's way and offered you a place in her lifeboat. I know your Captain Farragut. He's not taking *Merrimack* to lead off the swarms. We're going into battle. Hopeless battle. Please don't pretend you don't see that pattern."

"Very well," said Jose Maria. "We are overmatched. We are going to die. Why are *you* still aboard, Colonel?"

"This is what I came for. Living or dying has little or nothing to do with it. I didn't come for anything involving me. I came to fight the Hive. And live. Or die. I have to be there."

"And so," said Jose Maria Cordillera, "have I."

The crew and company of the *Merrimack* prepped for battle, cleaning and loading weapons, polishing face shields to perfect slickness. Deck crews locked down the Marine Swifts in their hangar bays. Computerized controls were disconnected and stowed.

Jose Maria's long glossy black hair was braided and bound up tight so that he looked for all the world like a matador. Though Jose Maria only ever killed to save lives.

The Naval engineers reconfigured the containment fields around the ship's six engines. Not that the Hive could interfere with such a basic reaction as matter/antimatter annihilation, but the mix controls to the containment fields themselves could be vulnerable.

Merrimack's six engines functioned within six discrete containment fields, protected by the most complex phase-shifting security codes on board, constantly changing at quick, random intervals, which prevented the Hive mind from deactivating the force field.

It did not stop the cells from physically insinuating themselves through the field.

Should a Hive cell breach an engine's containment field, *Merrimack*'s own power plant would become a bomb in enemy hands; and Hive cells did not fear suicide.

Augustus presented himself on the bridge in his flight suit, helmet under arm. "Permission to launch Striker."

"Denied," Farragut dismissed him.

Augustus quirked a small smile. "You don't trust me, John?"

"We don't launch small ships around a level-five soldier swarm. The swarms emit a hell of an interference field. All they have to do is fox your IFF and then I'm explaining to your emperor why I shot you. My Swifts don't go; you don't go."

"You're telling me the Hive swarm doesn't fox *your* systems?"

"They can. But Rome was always partial to sending false signals to our equipment, so we got lots of fail-safes."

"I know," said Augustus. "What about *your* systems?"

"Mine? I don't understand."

Augustus pointed between Farragut's eyes. "That's an electrical system in there."

"Bioelectrics are tougher for them."

"But not impervious."

"No. These big swarms can muddle your concentration, make you sleepy, make you think you can't breathe. So far they haven't shut us down."

Oh, great. Colonel Steele popped an inspection right here at battle stations. If one of those leering MP sidekicks of his flicked honey on your face shield, it damn well better slide right off. Kerry Blue didn't fancy licking honey off the deck. Fancied less not being able to see through a smear of burr guts. Her face shield passed inspection.

Then came the weapons inspection. If you got caught with a sanctioned weapon—like something that could shoot through bulkheads—it was a blot on your whole team. This part of the inspection was a waste of time, big bore. As if anyone one would be stupid enough to smuggle a secured weapon from the armory and take it to station.

"Peetz!" Reg cried in anger, as an MP discovered an armor-piercing projectile launcher holstered in the rookie's boot.

Carly cried: "Frogging hell!" Looked like she was about to knife Cole Darby.

You could hear Hazard Sewell's teeth grind as he accepted the blot on Team Alpha.

The inspectors moved on without Colonel Steele once looking at Kerry Blue. She understood the icy snub now. Had to smile.

Small woofing noises escaped from the peetz, Cole

Darby, as elbows accidentally connected with his rib cage. Hard.

A last briefing came over the loud com, explaining the game plan. It was simple: take the swarms out one at a time. *Merrimack* was running out at a fast intercept with the closer of the swarms before the two could combine forces or wake up more reinforcements.

"Why don't *we* get reinforcements?"

Everyone glared at the peetz, and he knew he'd said something stupid again.

Carly Delgado crouched over her short-range blaster, polishing, polishing. Answered flatly, "This is our job."

"Opa!" Dak sang out. "Here comes the Old Man."

"Which?"

"Which," Kerry's mocking echo. "That one."

You could hear Farragut coming, bellowing a pirate song.

"Oh, Gawd," Carly growled. But smiling. You had to.

They said you could tell how bad the battle would be by the exuberance of Captain Farragut's mood.

"Oh, hell," said Reg. "We're gonna die."

Farragut strutted through the ranks, spreading his own brand of buoyant courage, leaving a wide swathe of devastating enthusiasm in his wake. The mood on board turned festive. There wasn't another commander in the fleet who could pull it off. When Farragut got done with you, the tense dread vanished and you couldn't wait for battle. The navvies were singing pirate shanties. The Marine Wing was barking, the Battery hissing and meowing.

Fear, there was no fear. It wasn't a brush with death coming, it was a title shot. If you wanted stoic, grim readiness, you looked to the XO or to Colonel Steele. Captain Farragut was Christmas morning.

He stuck a one-ounce golden eagle to the mizzenmast for first ooze on Farragut's deck. He probably ought to have stabbed it there with a dagger, but he stuck it up with chewing gum. Brandished his sword at it. "Look alive, maties, I mean to win that back myself."

His crew howled at him, told him he was dreaming. Each man jack and jane on board meant to have that eagle for himself.

And the carnival mood did not break until the prox

alarm blared. Revved and ready, everyone snapped to the task at hand.

They were left waiting for no longer than racehorses in the gate. Immediately after the order to drop oxygen bricks, the first swarm hove into view, a speck, looming in a split-second into a colossus, into a mountain, into a world.

"Almighty God."

The enormity staggered. Dirty ice, pocked and clawed, filled the screens.

"God bless it, Captain Farragut! He's *ramming!*" Reg screamed and ducked, bracing for impact. An utterly absurd gesture. Should the inertial fields fail, there would be no shelter, no bracing that would keep any of them whole.

Farragut hadn't told them this part of the plan.

Merrimack, shaped like a cruel and ancient spearhead, plunged into the writhing mountain, a solid mass of armored bodies and grasping claws. Metallic screeching raked the force field—a raw, hideous tearing sheet-metal cacophony that sounded like the ship breaking up. Through the din came Calli Carmel's steady bark at the naval battery to fire nukes.

The ship bulleted out the other side of the packed swarm, and the unearthly scraping abruptly silenced. In *Merrimack*'s wake, flailing chunks of swarm spewed in all directions.

Merrimack spun around, racing back to meet her own nuclear flashes, the blinding brightness dimmed in her viewports. The ship resounded with the drumfire of her guns hammering at the splintered swarm, which was re-forming with *Merrimack* at its heart.

The swarm was everywhere, biblical in its vastness. Each grotesque member a hellish abomination. Monsters formed without gravity or atmospheric pressure, their shapes flowed without logic, a mouth over here, three legs over there, shell plates shifting over amorphous bodies.

Soon, the alien soldiers blotted out the stars, coated the force field inside the range of the naval guns.

The Marine Battery took over from the ship's guns, firing as fast as they could reload, fragmentation shells at close range. Hive soldiers massed thick on the force field. The energy barrier sounded a sickening weird groan as the Hive cells wheedled, clawed, and *insinuated* themselves through it.

Merrimack joggled within its force field to the beat of its pounding guns and Dak's yelling. "Come on, greta! Come on! YeeeeHA! Frag 'em, bag 'em, and tag 'em! You're mine, greta! You're mine! Yeah! *Crap!*"

A muffled whomp bluntly snagged his rhythm.

"Can opener in the barrel," Reg interpreted the blunt sound as Dak beat his impatience against the firing mechanism.

"Not again," Kerry moaned.

"It happened 'cause you're so slow reloading me."

"Oh, frog you, Dak."

You could hear the thing in there, armor plates and razor claws scuffling inside the barrel.

"Are we capped?" Hazard asked.

"Yes, sir."

"Gimme a harpoon." Hazard flipped his face shield down into place.

Dak seized a long shaft, equipped with an evilly pronged head, from the rack. Slapped the stout black grip into Hazard's hand. "Wild Turkey," said Dak.

Hazard looped the sling round his wrist.

"Beer," said Kerry Blue fixing the gauntlets on her gloves.

"Canadian beer," said Reg.

"J 'n' B straight up," said Twitch.

"Jose Cuervo," said Carly.

"I'll do it," Cole Darby offered to take the harpoon. Thought he was being brave and helpful. To his surprise, the rest of the team sputtered scorn and caustic laughter.

"Oh, fat chance, Peetz! Stand aside."

The dawn came slowly, as Hazard Sewell lined up his harpoon on the gun breech. This was first ooze. The golden eagle went to the man who spilled the first gorgon blood on John Farragut's deck. The team had put in their drink orders, because Hazard Sewell would be buying the next round.

Cole supposed it was too late to order vodka.

A clack before Cole's face startled him—Kerry Blue slapping his face shield down for him. A soft hiss between her lips might've been calling him by one of his body parts, but he did not really hear her. He mumbled thanks.

"Ready breech!" Hazard reared back with his harpoon.

"Ready!" Twitch and Carly crouched at the cords.

"Let me have it!"

A yell. Dak flipped the safety. Twitch and Carly yanked for all they were worth. The rear plate flew wide. Hazard's harpoon stabbed straight and deep down the barrel.

With a sickening crunching sound, brown sludge jetted back at Hazard, spilled down his glassy face shield and splattered his deck boots.

"Mark time! I got the son of a pimp!" Hazard crowed, rammed a few more times. Twisted. He pulled out severed bits of claw and armor plating on the wicked tines. Shiny obsidian-black pieces dissolved as Hazard shook them off the harpoon. The heat radiated up. You felt it under your face shield.

Hazard gave another stab, another turn, to be sure the thing was dead. Pulled out the alien gore. "Purge barrel."

The team reloaded. Shut the breech. Uncapped, and blasted the barrel clean.

Peetz poised with his sword to stab at something. He hovered over a claw, but it had already stopped wiggling and had begun to dissolve.

Felt the sword whisked out of his grip from behind.

Cole turned. Kerry Blue had his sword. She pushed another handle into his empty hand. A mop.

"Swab up this crap," she said. And before he could protest, she was cranking up a reload for the gun, and Dak was yelling, "Die, greta, die!" and all the guns were pounding again.

The gravitational backwash bucked the deck. Brown sludge that lately was a gorgon slithered back and forth at Cole's feet. His stomach roller-coastered with it.

He paused over his mop. So would he be an idiot to obey Kerry Blue? Or should he reclaim his sword?

She could hurt him.

Sounds altered. Louder even than the tonal moans of the force field, an unholy scritching, like metal-on-metal, filled the ship.

"What's that?" Cole heard his own voice gone flat. He tried to wipe his upper lip. Hand hit against his face shield.

"Gorgons on the hull," said Reg.

"You mean on the force field," Cole corrected her. Along with the scritchings came a clatter like hail.

"No," Reg corrected back. "They're through the force field. They're on the hull now."

Sudden pressure flux opened Cole's ears. The air stirred. Kerry Blue's ponytail fluttered. Dak brushed his hand over his shaved scalp at the breeze.

"I stand corrected," said Reg. "They're *through* the hull."

It was the force field, not the hull, that kept the vacuum out, so the effect of a hole in the hull was not severe—a slight depressurization as air from the ship escaped to fill the near vacuum layer that normally existed between the hull and the force field. The hole in the hull was not the problem. The *meaning* was horrific.

An alarm clanged, all decks, and Captain Farragut's voice over the loud com: "Swords, all hands. We have boarders."

"Oh, you love this part, John Farragut."

The captain turned from the com. Looked up at Augustus. Admitted with a sheepish smile. "I do, you know."

Augustus withdrew from the control room.

Farragut pulled on chemical-resistant gloves. Opened and closed his fists. Tested the slide of his sword in its hanger. Grabbed a face shield. "Mr. Carmel, your boat."

"Aye, aye, sir."

And Captain Farragut quit the control room to join the fighting at the breach.

The sudden snapping and crunching directly *behind* her iced Reg's blood, made her stomach flutter and her mouth sting. She spun, rearing, her sword lifted.

And lowered. Heaved out the name with a lot of wind and little voice: *"Dak!"*

Dak answered, wide-eyed, cheeks bulging, voice muffled. *"What?"*

Kerry turned toward her chomping teammate. *"Dak!"* Dak Shepard looked like a giant chipmunk.

Dak shrugged his big shoulders, clutched his bag of pretzels. "What! I'm hungry!" Then suddenly commanded silence with a spray of salt crumbs: *"Shhhh!"*

Came the unmistakable clack clack clack from the corridor. Only hear it once, and the sound is branded on your nerves forever.

Reg stole a glance through the hatch, danced back inside behind her sword. "It's a ripe one! Swing hard!"

Soldiers tended to shrink once inside a pressurized atmosphere and they kept shrinking. From their amorphous vacuum-dwelling state they compressed and solidified into misshapen hideousness. Their parts migrated across their bodies, adapting to upness and downness of gravity, trying to get all their legs under them, all their mouth parts into a position to feed.

The smaller and more agile the soldier, the shinier, the blacker, the longer it had been aboard, the harder and denser its shell, the harder to kill.

Well-hardened mandibles clacked in the hatchway. Twitch Fuentes hollered bloody murder, hammered down a mighty stroke on the neckish thing behind the mandibles.

His sword bounced off. Twitch roared. Reg bounced a second stroke off a twisted, serrate leg that sprouted from the thing's back. "God *bless!*"

Dak ditched his bag of pretzels—stuffing it into the nearest opening, which happened to be the torpedo tube—gave his hand a quick rub on his trousers, the better to grip his sword for a huge swing—

But the compact soldier skittered into the torpedo tube.

Reg and Kerry exchanged only the briefest of startled glances before they were ratcheting a torpedo into the tube. Slammed the breach shut. "Fire!"

"Fire!"

The torpedo exited the ship with a boom.

"I'll be damned," said Dak, staring, astonished. "Gretas like carbos better'n raw meat."

"Who doesn't?" Reg wrinkled up her nose. "Got any more pretzels?"

The peetz nudged Kerry. "How do you kill those things?"

"Any way you can."

"I mean—you cut off their arms, they keep wiggling. Swords bounce. What kills them?"

"They die when the Overmind says they're dead."

"How do you know when they're really dead?"

"You know it's dead when you're wading in it."

Commander Carmel's voice on the loud com relayed more locations of Hive penetrations. "Breach, deck five. Boarders in hydroponics."

Kerry sheathed her sword and dashed for the hatch. "We gotta go to hydroponics!"

"That's not our deck!" Reg yelled after her. Running. The rest of Team Alpha stampeding after Kerry Blue.

A bulbous soldier waited at the head of the ladder.

"Blue! Look out!"

Kerry paused on the fifth rung to flip down her face shield and draw her sword. "Fresh one! Mine!" She stabbed up at gaping mandibles.

Twitch, below her, cursed at the brown acid rain on his head. Kerry Blue had disappeared, up and over the top to deck five.

Cole Darby stabbed at a still snapping claw as it hit deck four.

"Yeah, you sure showed that one," Carly snarled and bolted up the ladder.

Cole brought up the rear. Slashed into hydroponics with his team. Found aliens, maybe twenty of them, big as Dak, in all their weird shapes, still coalescing under pressure. Bloated brown bags with legs migrating across their formless forms. Mist beading on their still hardening shells. Pincers tore vegetables from their reservoirs, stuffed them into as many mouths as the monsters had.

No time for thought. No time for cowardice. Cole Darby just hacked them out of his face, away from his feet until hydroponics was secured. The humid compartment was still again.

Reg let her sword drag on the wet deck, pushed back her face shield. "Blue! Bitch babe, you are crazed!"

Kerry shrugged. A saurian eye peered over the edge of her collar. Webby feet hugged her ponytail.

Carly pointed at the lizard plant on Kerry's back, cried, "That's what this was about! We rescued a *salad?*"

Dak hooted, big, knee-slapping laughter. Kerry pushed past him, out of hydroponics as the misters started to rain on them again. "Shut up, Dak."

Calli reported multiple entry points, multiple decks.

At the deck where John Farragut and his naval gunners hacked against an inrush of gorgons from a gaping rent in the hull, Augustus joined the melee, wired and armored, as alien as anything clawing through the hull. A tall, weird fig-

ure in black, his eye movements too rapid in an expressionless face, his blinks deliberate. His footfalls rang with metal
clanks, his deck boots bladed like an old-time street fighter's. His motions were not exactly robotic—too smooth—
but not human either—too efficient.

Cables ran from the base of his skull to the base of his
neck, and from arm to weapon, the hand cannon fit to his
forearm. He pumped projectiles into target after target with
inhuman accuracy, minimal motion, no passion. Farragut
felt one projectile whiz past his ear (hoped that was accuracy) to stab into the gorgon before him, and immediately
detonate. The gorgon erupted from within, splattering Farragut's face shield.

On every side, gorgons exploded, disintegrating in death.
Naval swordsmen gurgled oaths, astonished to be unhurt
amid the close carnage.

No involuntary blinks from Augustus as the gore hit his
face shield. The head would tilt in reaction to the trajectory
of a splash of blood, calculated to catch the glob on his visor
instead of his cheek; but the eyes never left his targets. It
was that, the independent motion of body parts which normally moved in concert that was so . . . disconcerting.

He riddled the grasping aliens with projectile charges,
detonating them in firecracker strings.

"What if you shoot clean through one?" Farragut asked
the question that was on everyone's mind. Anything that
could pierce a soldier's shell could pierce a bulkhead—that
was why no one else was firing projectile weapons.

"I set the depth," Augustus announced, voice flat, disconnected. He launched another salvo toward the breach,
past ears and necks of cursing naval personnel, who felt the
shots breeze near. Detonated the shots as they stabbed
home. The gorgons died, boarding. Their disintegrating bodies clogged the breach.

"What if you have bad depth perception?"

Augustus pivoted. Shot a gorgon rising between himself
and one of *Merrimack*'s Marines. The explosive round bit
no deeper than the target's body. Detonated. The man on
the far side was hit with nothing but gore.

"Well, then you're pretty well screwed, aren't you," said
Augustus mechanically. "Don't talk to me."

Augustus tore off another nine rounds with the speed of

thought, machine accurate with human discretion. Blasted clear a path for a patch unit to get through to the rent in the hull.

Farragut's party advanced to another hot spot.

Met with a closed hatch whose handle would not turn. Farragut rapped with his pommel. "Who closed this hatch?" And into the com, "Calli! What's going on in the galley?"

"Boarders in the galley at last report," the XO answered. "Team Echo answered the breach. Team Echo is not reporting."

Farragut roared back for his patch crew; ordered his troops to gang way to let the mechanics through to the jammed hatch. "Drill it!"

The hatch fell in, edges glowing molten, stench boiling from within, and already Farragut was springing through the opening.

Augustus grabbed him by the scruff of the uniform with one arm, arresting one hundred and ninety pounds of springing Farragut in mid-flight, hauled him back and tossed him behind him, as a soldier's pincers dropped from the overhead, slicing shut on empty air where the captain's neck would have been.

Augustus snarled at the captain for an idiot and shot a path clear to the galley.

The stench within was human vomit and human excrement. Gorgons feasted on human entrails, cotton clothing, and shoe leather. John Farragut wielded an angry sword, slashing at the aliens' serrate mouths, kicking a chair into their ungainly legs, hammering open their shells with his pommel. Projectiles rifled either side of his ears, and gorgons bulged in the detonation. Always maniacal in battle, now with Augustus behind him, Farragut was berserk, invincible.

After an immeasurable time, Farragut paused, chest heaving, mouth twitching, sweat pouring down his face, tears from his wild eyes. He pushed back his spattered face shield, searched for another monster to kill in the dank, smoke-filled galley.

Battle craze ebbed with each panting breath. Upended chairs and disintegrating claws piled in a jagged, unreal tangle in the dimness.

"On your left," a technician announced his own presence as he came up on Farragut's flank. "Galley secured."

"This is Team Echo?" asked Farragut, gingerly moving his foot off of a bone. Could be Abdullah's. Could be Jan Karowicz.

"We'll ID 'em all, sir," the technician assured him, the best he could offer.

The lights flickered, went out.

Someone in the dark: "There go the lights."

Someone else: "No shit."

It was the first time the Hive mind had infiltrated the light controls.

The emergency lights came up soon enough, casting a dim, lurid illumination over the massacre.

You could hear Augustus clicking and whirring, moving with deep metal tread about the carnage.

"Whatever the hell *he* is, can we order about twelve of those?" the tech muttered appreciatively.

Sorry as soon as he said it.

The heavy *chunk* of Augustus' footsteps had halted. Augustus had stiffened, pivoted mechanically, his dark eyes wholly vacant.

His hand cannon leveled at John Farragut's head.

12

A MARINE'S SWORD LIFTED, cocked back to take off Augustus' cannon at the elbow.

"Nev, don't do it!" Farragut barked on the upswing, his hand out to stay the downstroke, eyes maintaining a steady gaze over the barrel of Augustus' hand cannon to the blank eyes behind it.

"Captain!" the Marine urged between clenched teeth. "They've *got* him. Kill him!" His sword quivered, ready.

"No friendly hacking on my boat," the captain said firmly, his sword at his side.

"That's not Augustus!" the Marine said between a snarl and a cry, begging for permission to strike. Could the captain not see that that hollow-eyed thing was not the Roman they all knew and loathed? That thing was going to shoot the captain. Nev could not disobey an order to save his own life. To save the captain, however—

Right hand still leveling the cannon at Captain Farragut, Augustus' left hand lifted, dreamlike.

Nev inhaled, tightened his grip, held his breath.

Augustus reached behind his own head and pulled the cables out of his neck.

Nev froze.

By blinks, expression returned to Augustus' face with a grimace of pain.

"Gorgons in the corridor!" a Marine outside the hatch reported.

"Go get 'em!" Farragut waved his party of Marines out of the galley to meet the enemy. And to Augustus, who was slow moving, waking from a standing sleep, he said, "They got you."

"I—" Augustus pulled off a glove, squeezed his eyes as if pushing his brains back in. "Suppose."

The deck heaved and rocked. Augustus caught his balance with a stagger step. Augustus never staggered.

"You all right?"

"Hell, yeah." Augustus returned to full consciousness with an angry sniff. Anger beyond his normal ill-tempered disdain. Hot anger.

"I thought a swarm couldn't penetrate bioelectrics," said Farragut.

"The *bio* part is functioning just fine, thank you. The add-ons are uffed." Augustus unstrapped his big cannon from his forearm, tossed it aside as worthless. "What else ya got?"

"Ever use a sword?"

"There's always a first time."

Farragut snapped to the single Marine left in the galley, who was guarding the captain's rear at the hatchway. "A sword for the colonel." Then into his hand com: "I need a triage unit in the galley!"

"No, you don't," Augustus commented. "These folks aren't going anywhere."

"I will not have them *eaten*," Farragut snapped back. "Calli, where's the action? Point me toward something to kill."

"Gorgons chewing through the sail. Breach topside."

"Farragut responding."

The captain gathered his cadre and led the way up the ladders to the sail. Farragut called back over his shoulder to Augustus, "Ever notice gorgons always go for the sail as if it were important? Do you think they think it's a head?"

"Gorgons don't have heads," said Augustus.

"A lot of their dinners do!" Farragut vaulted up to the sail, slashing.

No sooner there, than alarms blared to the accompaniment of a drastic sound shift from the *Merrimack*'s force field.

Into his hand com: "Calli, are they uffing our alarms?"

The XO's voice crackled in and out in response. The swarm was fouling intraship communications now. "No, Captain. That's real. Containment Field Engine Three is compromised." And next, her voice was sounding over the loud com, all decks, "All possible force to Engine Compartment Three. Isolate Engine Three for ejection."

Farragut was back on the com, point to point, privately, "Calli, why are we fixing to pop an engine?"

"There are gorgons *in* the engine compartment."

"Understood." And off the com, "Oh, for Jesus." He signaled a retreat from the sail, held the hatch open as he hied his men downside, "Go, go, go!" and jumped down the ladder in the rear. The men sealed the inner hatch, abandoning the sail to the Hive.

"Augustus, if your average soldier cell is—say—fifty kilograms, what kind of blast would a gorgon in the antimatter cause?"

"I'm not wired."

"You can't figure the size of the blast without plugging in to patterner mode?"

"Precisely? No."

"Roughly."

"E equals we'll die."

"That *was* the real question," said Farragut.

Stress fractures sounded through the XO's normal ice calm: "Why isn't that compartment isolated?"

"Access air lock is still unsecured," the tech reported.

"Secure it."

The tech hit all the controls for her to see, all to a red light and no go. The tech explained, "The ship won't let both hatches secure while an animate entity is inside the air lock."

"We are going to blow to kingdom come because the *ship* won't hurt a gorgon?"

"That's about the size of it, sir."

The tech minding the internal systems monitors reported in a shrill hiccup, "Containment field is fluctu—" Broke off and ducked as the containment field reading all but vanished from the board.

Calli darted the systems tech an evil glare.

He recovered immediately, finished, "—fluctuating. It could go any moment."

Calli got on the loud com again. "All units near Engine Compartment Three, I cannot overstate the need for haste. Clear and secure the compartment for ejection now."

John Farragut, en route, on the tight link again: "Calli, what's the holdup?"

When she explained the problem with the air lock, he suggested, "Since each engine compartment is already surrounded in its own discrete field, why can't we just chunk the son of a bitch out as is?"

"*Your* ship, John, won't *let* me. And even if we could, without the second field, the antimatter would detonate the instant it was out of our control."

"Can anyone tell us if we can withstand an engine explosion at close range?"

"Without a complete force field? It has been suggested that when it goes, one should hold on to the body part dearest to you."

"Understood."

He had come to where the corridors were thick with crew and Marines trying to assist. Men squeezed to make way for the captain.

He could see the air lock up ahead. It was a short one, no more than a meter-and-a-half hatch to hatch, pincers and claws holding both hatches open.

All Hive cells were vulnerable to heat, but this was an engine accessway, a place you don't dare bring welding torches or grenades or anything certain to dislodge a gorgon. The hacking was all by hand here.

The gorgon soldier bodies shone black and glossy, hardening the longer they stayed under pressure. They had wedged themselves in and clung to the air lock like warriors holding some narrow pass in an ancient war.

Farragut felt a push—a domino effect of shoving from the rear—someone in the back yelling, "Gang way! Gang way!"

"Captain here!" someone scolded the pushing Marine.

"Gang way, *sir!*" the Marine continued shoving. And, as the man seemed on a mission, Farragut ganged way.

The big Marine barreled at the hatches, slinging a bag,

"Heyaaa, gretaaaaaa!" The bag broke open in flight, scattering its contents into the engine room—pretzels.

The gorgons blocking both hatches turned to follow the motion. And, all together, abandoned their hard-held posts to scrabble after the pretzels.

Marines dived into the air lock, heaved the inner hatch to. "Secure hatch!" their lieutenant ordered.

"Hatch secured!" one cried, slamming the locking bolt in place, and the team lunged back out through the shipside hatchway, shouting to their comrades: "Shut it! Shut it!"

The hatch thunked neatly shut.

The lieutenant barked: "Secure hatch!"

An impotent clanking.

The lieutenant, insistent: "Lock it! Lock it!"

A vulgarity, near screamed.

"Lock it!" the lieutenant raged, hauling the man out of the way for someone else to do the job.

The next men did no better. "*Can't!* The buggers *bent* it!"

Farragut hailed the control room: "Commander Carmel! Both hatches are closed. Can we eject?"

"Negative. We are showing red on the shipside seal. What's wrong, boys?"

"Override."

"Can't, sir. Your ship—"

Marines made way for Captain Farragut. He rammed the bent mechanism. It was his ship; it ought obey him.

It didn't.

"Let's get some equipment up here!" Farragut shouted.

Augustus advanced, shouldered Farragut aside, took the torqued bolt in his hands and, tendons bulging from his temples and neck, bent the bolt back into shape. Palm-heeled it home with a loud clang. "Secured," said Augustus.

Farragut shouted into the back of his hand: "Clear! Control Room, this is Farragut. We are clear to eject!"

Green lights showed on the systems monitors in the control room.

Calli sent the order: "Engineering. Eject Engine Three."

As the systems tech reported: "Engine containment fluctuating—"

"Control Room. This is Engineering. Ejecting Engine Three, aye."

Calli: "Helm! Spin our bow toward the ejection. Now!"

"Redirecting attitude—" the helmsman acknowledged, wagging the coordinates, to spin the stoutest part of the force field at the blast.

Systems tech: "Engine containment flatlined."

The Noise.

A roaring, rending screech of an earthquake, like boulders crashing and metal cracking and sheering. "Jesus, Mary, and Joseph!" Could scarcely hear whoever said that as the lights died. Crew hunched in the dark, an instinctive motion that could not save them from the roar.

"We're tearing apart!"

Even as the man said it, the lights returned, the raking din diminishing fast.

Shaking, absorbing the surprise of being whole, the helmsman laughed. "No. That sound's not us. It's the gorgons!" He stood up. He had been crouched under the console. "That was the gorgons tearing off the force field!"

A moment of disbelief held the control room. It was true. All that grinding shrieking was the thick layer of gorgons tearing away from *Merrimack*'s force field under the engine's annihilating blast, the raking of gorgon against gorgon, bodies igniting from the friction. The gorgons insinuating through the field conducted the sound.

"I'll be damned," said Calli.

The noise died away. In its place, throughout the ship came the first cackles of irony, a smattering of cheers.

"Interesting tactic," Augustus commented to Farragut. "And you still have five more engines."

"Not habit-forming." John Farragut cleared sweat from his eyes with the sweaty back of his wrist. Blinked against the salt sting. He regarded Augustus standing at the secured air lock to the now extinct Engine Three. Sized him up the long expanse from head to foot. "They augmented more than your brain."

Augustus did not deign to comment.

Farragut gave the shipside hatch's bolt a pat, feeling its unyielding solidity.

Marines and crewmen in the corridor eyed the Roman patterner diffidently, assessing. Superman? Cyborg? Satan?

Augustus said only, casting about, "I dropped a sword somewhere around here."

The sword was quickly retrieved, respectfully produced,

hilt first, and the crowd of Marines parted for the captain and his tame Roman monster to pass.

As they walked, Augustus put the sword through an experimental range of motion with a swivel of his wrist.

"Pretty good for a beginner," said Farragut, bald understatement.

Like a duck to water, Augustus with a sword. Augustus had mowed down gorgons and slashed off pincers with the ease of an old hand. "I must have done this in my past life," he said seriously, as if he'd actually had one.

The operation was all mop-up now. Calli ordered a search for remaining Hive cells. Due diligence that, as stranded gorgons tended to dissolve of their own accord. With too few of them remaining to form a swarm, Calli gave clearance to reactivate computer controls, enable sensors, maintenance robots, and lifts.

Farragut hailed the control room. "Calli, where's the second swarm?"

"Fifty light-hours on an intercept course, traveling three hundred c. They'll be here in ten minutes."

"I didn't think swarms could travel that fast."

"It does rewrite the upper limit on swarm speed. It's a big swarm, John. Permission to evade."

"Run it," Farragut allowed. "I want twenty-four hours before we engage again."

"Aye, sir."

"You mean to battle the second swarm?" Augustus asked.

"Why not?"

"Because, statistically you should not have won the first round."

"Shows you how much statistics know." The shakes of dehydration quivered his cooling muscles. Farragut patted the bulk. "My *Merrimack*. She's been used harshly." He kissed his palm and pressed it to the bulkhead. "Nobody can say the *Mack* can't take some *hits*."

He continued down the corridor to the dark outer deck, where the chief stood scowling at the weird ragged gaps in the hull, open to black space and starlight twinkle, only the force field in between.

He turned at Farragut's approach, crossed his beefy arms, becoming the image of an irate father-in-law, who ought to pound that no-good bum who ruined his darling little girl. "Well, sir. I hope you're proud of yourself. I am, sir," the chief said, his sweat-soaked sleeves rolled up. An anchor tattoo expanded on his flexing bicep.

"Patch her up, Chief. We're in it again in twenty-four."

The chief stalked away, muttering.

"I have never heard some of those words," Augustus said, impressed.

"I think he makes 'em up. I'm fixin' to walk a dog. Come with?"

Augustus assented quizzically. He thought Farragut had given all, but after downing a liter of water and a bag of cookies, he was spry enough to tuck a small shepherd dog under his arm and slide down a ladder to downbelow levels.

The captain's walk involved prowling through the remote compartments of the ship where the dog sniffed for the wounded and incapacitated man and the fugitive gorgon. Paused along the way to greet his crew and Marines by name, ask if all their mates were accounted for, praise them, listen to their bragging, their observations, their battle stories.

Apparently the Marines of Team Alpha had a new secret weapon in the form of pretzels. . . .

Colonel Steele walked a waking nightmare through *Merrimack*'s battle-scored corridors. He had lost a team. An entire team. And though he loved all his Marines with a soldier's passion, still the guilty "Thank God!" stole into his thoughts when he learned it hadn't been Team Alpha who had been eaten alive in the galley. And still he didn't know if she was all right.

She. The only she. The center of his universe.

Like being eaten alive by a gorgon from the inside out, needing to know and not being able to ask. *Where is she?*

Needed to know. Needed as hard as he needed to breathe.

And then, as if needing could produce her, there she was.

Knew her by her walk, the loose, easy set of her shoulders, that free-jointed, rough and ready way of moving. The coarse fabric of her fatigues, soaked and patched with gorgon guts and neutralizing solution, adhered to her hips, her ass, making her walk a thing of wonder that brought him to full attention.

A bunch of iguana-green leaves huddled in the crook of her arm—her strange Arran pet. And she dragged her sword carelessly at her side, its tip bumping over the deck grates.

Steele's voice, coarse and dry—what came out at all—could scarcely form one word. "Marine."

She turned. Pushed back a loose lock of wet hair with a cheery, weary smile. "Hi." She lowered her lizard plant to the deck. There was no one else in the corridor.

Her sword clattered to the deck as he grabbed her.

Cold fabric quickly warmed between their bodies. He tore himself from her lips only to see her face, her eyes, her smile.

"You're a gorilla, Thomas."

It jarred him, his name on her lips. He liked it. Liked it a lot. He held her face in his big, callused hand. It wasn't right a soldier should have such soft skin.

She laughed under his mesmerized gaze. "I look like hell."

"No, you don't," he rasped. Swallowed her breath. Hands all over her, assuring himself she was whole and real and here. She was astonishingly, achingly real, and soft in all the womanly places.

Too late, he heard the footsteps. Almost upon them. There was no springing apart fast enough, so he held tight. If he must be caught, he would not be caught skulking.

The gallumphing footsteps rounded the corner with Reg Monroe's jaunty, "Yo ho *HO!*-ly Mary Mother of God!" Clapped a hand over her eyes.

Kerry went from cat-tense to relaxed in the span of a quick heartbeat. "Oh, sheeps. That's just Reg. She don't see nothing."

Reg parted two fingers to peer through her hand at her commanding officer. "Code thirty-three, Mid-deck."

Code thirty-three. Fire code. Steele knew without her saying so that his fair face had gone flaming red. What idiot ever let women in the Fleet Marine anyway?

He let go of Kerry, squared his powerful shoulders, cleared his throat. Damn tough to look forbidding wearing your career dropped round your ankles. Struggled for an appropriate command.

Reg sounded a retreat on her own. "I gotta go get a bucket of vacuum." She scooted away down the corridor.

Steele stood rooted, volcanic breaths loud in his chest.

"Reg isn't a problem." Kerry's feminine voice was light. Thawed him. And he wanted her too badly to worry about his career's dive.

"We should move this out of the corridor," Steele grumbled.

"You got a private shower, don't ya?" Kerry gave a foxy wrinkle to her nose.

Dumb idea. Splendid idea. "You're going to be the death of me, Marine."

"We need a shower, don't we?"

There were worse ways to die.

A very clean Kerry Blue blithely hooked up decking grates, clearing the way for maintenance bots to scour the subflooring of blood and neutralizing solution and dissolved gorgons. Her lizard plant crooned jubilantly from its perch on her shoulder.

A belligerent *clank!* signaled the arrival of Reg, letting her patch kit drop. Fists posed on hips and she put on that snottified attitude, that little foot just pattering away against the deck. Reg wasn't tall enough to make that look at all scary. "You said you didn't like Colonel Steele. Lie to me, bitch babe?"

"I said he wasn't cute," said Kerry. "He's not cute."

"Well, how *is* he? Give, sister. How many times?"

"Ssst!" Kerry hissed Reg silent. Someone was coming.

Dak. Whistling. Dumb and happy as a baboon, dragging the refuse wagon behind him. Come to unload the maintenance bots' reservoirs.

"So, Blue!" he popped a hose into place. "I guess your boyfriend looks pretty good for a ten-billion-year-old man."

"What? What boyfriend?" Kerry blustered, guiltily quick, face on fire.

"Donner," said Dak. "The Archon. I hear talk he's *really* old."

"Oh. *Oh.*" Kerry's panic subsided. False alarm. Dak was talking about Donner. Ancient history. Forgot there had ever been anyone before Thomas Ryder Steele. "Oh, him. Yeah. I heard that about him," Kerry babbled.

"Kerry Blue's decided she *likes* those older men," Reg snickered.

"Reg, shut *up!*"

"I didn't say nothing. Dak, did I say nothing?"

Dak was lost in space. "What did you say?"

"See there?" Reg threw a triumphant grin Kerry's way. Then under her breath, "Give me a number, bitch babe, and I'll shut up."

Kerry hissed, "I lost count."

Reg squealed into her hands.

Dak, accustomed to conversations going wide or over his head, turned his attention to the deep cargo pockets of his fatigues. Fished out a fistful of pretzels.

"Whoa, babes," Kerry stopped him. "You allowed to eat our new secret weapon?"

Dak crunched, offered Kerry a pretzel. "*Don* Cordillera says they're nothing special. The 'composition' isn't special. Thinks it's the shape that's tripping the Hive's jump jets. Thinks the gorgons are mistaking them for something else shaped like this. Move it, mutt." Dak kneed aside a dog that had parked itself in the middle of the corridor where Dak wanted to park his refuse wagon next.

The dog, a standard poodle named Pooh, barked an objection, moved to the side, and sat back down.

Dak dragged his refuse wagon along, glanced up. "Yo ho ho. Lookit here." He hooked the overhead latch and pulled down the grate to reveal a glassy black dome clinging like a giant obsidian barnacle between decks.

"It's a—oh, crap." Dak dropped the hook, gave Pooh a pretzel. "Good dog." Pushed the rest of the pretzels into his pocket to free both his hands. "Tell the captain we got a—a thing."

Kerry dashed to the nearest intercom. "Control Room! Flight Sergeant Blue reporting. We got a—oh, hell. Dak, what *is* it?"

Dak stood on top of a squat, square maintenance bot to get a closer squint at *it*.

Spoke through a mouthful of pretzel. "A gorgon egg. A gorgon turd. Something gorgony."

Kerry relayed into the com, "—a gorgon thing attached to the overhead, mid-deck, Section Nine A."

The OOD acknowledged, said she was alerting the xenos and sending a security team.

Dak turned around on his bot to scowl toward the intercom. "Security team? And what are we? The garbage detail?"

"Shhh!" Reg raised forefinger to lips, catching the edge of a sound shivering somewhere down the passageway. "Hear that?"

A scraping of cicada wings.

Hive sign.

The dog barked.

As behind Dak's head, the solid mass moved, developed features. Pincers sprouted from the shiny black mass. Circled round Dak's neck. And closed.

"Dak!" Reg's scream pierced the ship end to end.

Kerry seized the welding torch from Reg's patch kit, flamed the gorgon. It let Dak's body tumble as it melted.

Reg scrambled on hands and knees to catch the rolling head, tried to push it back onto the gushing neck, keening, *"Medic!* Medic! Medic! Man down! Man down!"

Augustus stood at the tableside, an attentive statue, until they zipped up the body bag. He only spoke when prompted, *"What?"* by a vexed medic under the Roman's oppressive gaze.

"On a Roman ship, he would have lived," said Augustus.

"I didn't see you helping put that man's head back on, Roman," the medic bristled, pulling off bloody gloves.

"I have never done it. I only know that it is done." Augustus quit the sick bay.

The dead Marine's mates gathered round the bag, Reg's high squeaky sobs the only sound for a long time.

Cole Darby frowned, feeling very old. The other Marines had stopped calling him Peetz halfway through the melee. They called him Darb now. He put an arm round the sobbing little Reg, and she did not shake him off. Cole Darby was in. Hell of a way to get there. Asked, "Dak married?"

"No," said Reg, sniffling.

"Was," said Carly.

"Ten billion years ago," said Reg.

"To a gorgon," Carly added.

"Her name Greta?" Darb asked.

Reg blinked drowning eyes up at him in amazement. "Now how did you know that, Darb?"

Cole Darby rolled his eyes sadly. "Oh, I'm just frogging psychic."

Twenty-four hours counted quickly down, in which time the holes in the ship's hull were sealed, normal pressure restored, gun bays restocked, barrels cleaned and capped, decks swabbed and dried, swords sharpened, personnel either rested or boosted, and computer controls taken back off-line in preparation to meet the second swarm.

Once upon a time, spaceships would tow their morgue behind them with the oxygen bricks. Now that was dragging bait. *Merrimack* carried her dead inboard.

Captain Farragut praised his company and crew on their victory, and stirred them up to do it again. We lost some men and women to the bad guys. Here was a chance to make the monsters pay. He told you he wanted a dozen gorgons each to die with the name of one of the fallen on your lips. And he named them, every one. It was a long list.

When he was done, you were mad. You were ready.

Team Alpha beat on the hull, chanting, "Dak! Dak! Dak! Dak! Dak!" as *Merrimack* heeled round to meet the second swarm.

Laws of tactics held that if it works once, do it twice. If it fails once, don't try it again. If it works twice, don't try it three times. Ramming a swarm had worked once. It had shattered the first swarm, killing many of its members, and breaking it down to a survivable battle.

There was little doubt of what tactic *Merrimack* would use this time. The crew hunkered down for impact, irrational, but difficult not to when two faster-than-light objects were set to collide.

"Force to the fore," Calli ordered.

The tac specialist reported, "Impact in five, four—"

You saw it on three. The dead ice ball seemingly hanging in space on the monitor.

"Two—"

It loomed in enormity, in menace. Icy, cratered, black, frigid death.

Merrimack hurtled to the countdown's end. The swarm ballooned to fill the screen, infinite, all-consuming.

Plunged into that hideous grinding roar. The sound shredded the nerves, overloaded the dampers. Resounded in the hollow corridors. Sounds of solids tearing, of absolute zero igniting under searing friction.

Gunners crouched at their weapons, ready to blast the gorgons the moment *Merrimack* broke back into starlight on the other side of hell.

And then the noise stopped, but no star field returned to the monitors.

Gunners hesitated. Where was the target?

And then the realization. They were inside the target.

Merrimack had not come out the other side of the swarm. She was still moving, but so was the target, on the same trajectory.

Merrimack sped onward, embedded in the heart of the swarm, her crew entombed alive, miles of solid hunger pushing in on all sides.

13

LIEUTENANT COMMANDER Glenn Hamilton recognized the power play as soon as she walked into it. The LEN had summoned her urgently from her Spit boat immediately upon her arrival in the Myriad, only to let her wait in an empty chamber, gloomily lit. At last the LEN filed in, taking all the chairs, leaving her standing before a line of them seated behind an imposing slab of judicial desk. A single hot light came on in her face, so she could no longer see theirs.

Then, without greeting, the demand.

"Where is John Farragut! Where is the *Merrimack*!"

Glenn Hamilton did not answer immediately. Waited for them to give away some dominance by insisting. And so they did.

"We specifically ordered *Merrimack*'s return! *You* are not Farragut. Those two little missile-toting shuttles you brought are not *Merrimack*. Why is *Merrimack* not here?"

Glenn Hamilton—the Hamster—took her time composing her answer. Her petite size and doll-like looks had forced her to practice a calm, professional manner for a long time now. Her voice was pleasant, feminine, authoritative.

"You ordered *Merrimack* away," Hamster stated. "We went. *Merrimack* is out of LEN jurisdiction now. Captain

Farragut does not take orders from the LEN in open space. As I recall, you sent to the Pentagon before we left. Have you received the Joint Chiefs' response? May I please see our orders?" She put out an expectant hand.

Expecting what she got. Nothing.

She pressed the LEN noses into the power shift: "In the name of the *Merrimack*, I respectfully demand to see our orders from the Joint Chiefs."

That brought one out of his seat, all but pounding on the desk. "Young lady, you do not grasp the seriousness of what you have done!"

Hamster consciously kept her own torpedo tubes capped, and answered calmly, "No, sir. *You* do not recognize the seriousness of what you have done, and I remind the ambassador—" She shaded her eyes against the light. "That *is* the ambassador back there?—that my rank is Lieutenant Commander, not 'young lady.'"

She still could not see him well. He became the single bushy eyebrow that loomed over his deep eyes.

"This inquiry will not devolve into the trivial. Where is *Merrimack!*"

An inquiry now, was it? "*Merrimack* is engaged in defusing the threat caused by the LEN when you emitted a resonant pulse in this stellar neighborhood. By resonating, you have jeopardized not just our mission but the safety of the three inhabited worlds of this star system. This cry of wolf may summon the wolf. The Hive is very good at tracking—"

"Hive, Hive, Hive. All that exists with you military types is your enemy, no thought to the innocents on the battle-ground. You will undo what you have done!"

"Can you be more specific?" Hamster requested.

"*Don't* play coy with the world government!"

Could always count on the LEN to wave that about as if the world government had enforcement authority.

She tried to answer. "*Merrimack* made contact with the Myriadians. I cannot erase their memory of that. We gave them no technology. As for what you want undone, I am at a loss, sir."

"I think you may actually believe what you say, Mrs. Hamilton. Farragut *would* send in a stooge to lie for him in all ignorance. Which is why we demand John Farragut himself. Not you."

"I assure you this stooge has full authority to speak for Captain Farragut."

"Authority. Yes, yes, Mrs. Hamilton," he tut-tutted her. "But not the knowledge. This is a waste of time."

"I would agree. But I still have my orders to execute—"

"You will not."

"I am under orders to give you a message, and you shall get it one way or another. It's a warning—"

"Indeed. A little late in the day, Mrs. Hamilton."

"You may call me Lieutenant Commander." Mistake. Heard it coming out of her mouth. Playing their game now.

"Yes, Mrs. Hamilton," said the Eyebrow. "Do please, give us your warning."

"You are to stay off the transportation phenomenon which the locals call *kzachin.*"

"The traps," he retranslated the word more to LEN satisfaction. "And what will we find inside them? Which trap holds the hidden answers to this plot?"

"The *kzachin* are not *hiding* anything. Not in the conspiratorial sense. There is no 'plot.' The *kzachin* are dangerous."

A huff behind the light. A chorus of huffs, actually. Something—perhaps a pen—dropped to the desk in disgust. A new voice, possibly female, breathed like a curse, "You people." Then, out loud, "What has the U.S. military done here!"

"I beg your pardon?"

"Pardon not granted. Unforgivable."

"That was just an expression."

"It always is coming from your kind. What kind of weapon or experiment or *trap* have you inflicted on these innocent beings in your monomaniacal genocidal vendetta against the life-form called Hive?"

Oh. Our monomaniacal genocidal vendetta. Why didn't you say that in the first place?

Glenn Hamilton decided to steer the narrowest of courses to get out her message. "Use of the *kzachin* appears to be linked with the contraction of the star cluster Myriad. The *kzachin* also exhibit a lack of symmetrical performance. We are concerned that the apparent time distortion observed in travel back and forth on a *kzachin* may be an *actual* time distortion. I warn you, strenuously, of the danger of causal violation."

"Causal violation is impossible."

"Well, damn, I hope so," said Glenn Hamilton. Winced inwardly. Hoped they hadn't recorded that. "Our xeno team has identified the Myriadian home planet of Origin. It's Xi. Run the data yourselves." She surrendered the data bubble she had been charged to deliver, eager to have done with it and wash her hands of these people.

The LEN inquisitors made no move to play back the bubble. She heard it rolling loose on the desk. The low female voice pronounced: "That conclusion is not just wrong, it's ridiculous."

"This is just like the U.S. military." The Eyebrow again. "To piss mines everywhere. And when we are in danger of tripping them, do you clean them up? No. You tell us: Don't go there. I don't know what sort of smoke and mirrors you are using to create this apparent time anomaly on these traps of yours—these wormholes—but the constriction of this system is real. Your interference with the stellar environment threatens the orbital stability of three fragile worlds—"

"We did not make the *kzachin* and don't call them wormholes. Wormholes collapse under the energy of using them."

"*Precisely* how we know the traps are not naturally occurring phenomena! You tell us to stay out of your traps? No! I tell you: *You* take them away!"

Glenn Hamilton foundered, at a loss for a response. An adult one, anyway. Knew this would never happen to John Farragut.

Okay, so what would John Farragut do?

Could almost hear him: *Choose your battleground, kid.*

Lieutenant Glenn Hamilton snugged her officer's cap on her head, turned briskly as on a parade ground, and walked out.

The balance of power shifted again, right there in the hatchway with their shouts at her back to get back in here. And she would have smiled were she not so angry, were the situation not so perilous. But their impotent outrage had a nice burn to it like strong liquor going down.

She took her warning straight to the Archon.

Donner was not happy about it. He showed her his maned back as he pronounced imperiously, "Lieutenant Commander Glenn Hamilton, I do not deal with subordinates. I do not give audiences to thirds-in-command. I do not speak to stand-ins. And I do not come when summoned. I do, however, answer females who ask for help." That last explained this private audience, without guards or servants or cameras. "Though you are not what we think of as female."

At five foot one, Glenn Hamilton must look quite mannish to the Myriadian.

Donner turned to face her as he continued, "I am quit of your LEN. You may tell them so. They are unctuous, overly curious, and wholly useless. They ask questions; they answer nothing. And they seem physically incapable of using the word *no,* when all those roundabout words they stuff in its place *mean* no. Your language has such a word as *no.* Captain Farragut figured out how to say it."

"The LEN fear offending you," Glenn Hamilton explained. "I can say no."

"You do not fear offending me?" He used the you-subordinate.

Glenn answered with the I-subordinate. "I fear it, but I will do it if I have to."

"Yet the LEN offend me and you do not. If they fear offending me, why do they not give me what I want?"

"The LEN is a league of democracies," Glenn tried to explain. "They cannot make major decisions quickly even if they want to."

"Ah." Understanding and disapproval in the *Ah.*

She could see him trying to cut through their layers and layers of red tape, when he had scant experience with red tape, and probably no word for it. It was nothing dictators ever had to deal with. Donner reacted with dictatorial impatience.

The Archon had got a glimpse of Earth's incredible technological wealth and immediately wanted it. Nothing could be more natural. Glenn Hamilton understood that.

The LEN understood that, too, which was one reason they were so furious at Farragut for giving Donner the glimpse.

We show Donner the candy box, then the LEN comes along and slams the lid.

Donner thinks I have candy to give.

The floor tremored under Glenn's feet. So accustomed she was to the deck's burbles that she didn't think to take alarm right away. Then she did. Earthquake.

Briskly, but without fear, Donner took her arm and guided her to a structural archway between stout marble pillars, still talking, explaining his unhappiness with the LEN representatives. A groan rose from the ground. The chamber shook. Plaster clattered to the jeweled floor.

Donner glanced up to the ceiling as the tremors subsided, white holes showing in the elaborate mural. He gave an inward sigh. "I liked that picture." And to Glenn, "I do not like your LEN."

."Archon, you are going to like me even less."

"You offend me," he warned.

"A soldier does what a soldier must."

"Speak, then. If you must."

He listened without interruption as she told him that Origin had been found.

That it was here, in the Milky Way Galaxy.

That it was dead, an airless, waterless rock with no remains of civilization except the twenty billion-year-old back of the reliquary with Donner's name on it.

That Donner's only means of interstellar transportation, the *kzachin,* defied the laws of physics.

That the *kzachin* distorted time. That use of the *kzachin* most likely was causing the constriction of the Myriad.

That the threat of paradox was real.

That Donner's ships should stay off the *kzachin* and especially not go to Origin, so as not to spread the threat of paradox.

When Donner broke the hideous silence that stretched long after Glenn had finished, it was to ask, "Where did my people go?"

The question startled her. What should be the uppermost thing on the dictator's mind. Not his transportation system, not his immediate danger, not the erosion of his power. "Sir?" She fell in love with him on the spot.

Donner's voice trembled like the ground. "Origin is a world of one billion people."

Glenn Hamilton's answer burned her mouth. She felt like the LEN, spewing poisoned gentleness. "That place you know is ten billion years in the past. Those people are dead now, of course."

The side step did not get past him. Might as well have called him stupid. Donner answered brittlely, "I know that." And he called her stupid back: "Where are their descendants?"

One billion beings breed billions of offspring. And over billions of years, trillions of billions.

Where were they?

Hamster contrived the nicest guess she could. "They may have migrated before your planet lost its angular momentum and drifted out of the habitable zone. Your people had time to see it coming. Stellar decay takes millions of years."

Donner's voice smoldered. "Origin has not the elements for that kind of migration. And if heavy elements could be found or created, where did my people go?"

"Anywhere. Ten billion years blurs a trail."

"Ten billion 'years' balloons a population, if it lives at all. Someone should be left somewhere. Someone ten billion 'years' more advanced than *you!*"

"They could be so advanced they don't recognize you as kin anymore."

"They *died*." Donner answered his own question, since she would not speak it. "Simple answers are often the true ones."

Glenn Hamilton caught herself about to lie to spare his feelings. Said instead: "True."

"Then I shall bring my people here. I must have done so. This is the only place they could have gone."

"But I thought you didn't want them here," she countered. "The sentinel buoy, the minefield *Merrimack* tripped at the Rim gate at the edge of the Myriad—that was set for *them!*" Realization came even as she said it. "The mines were a border guard! You set that minefield by the *kzachin* to keep the people of Origin from coming here!"

"I did not want them here," Donner confessed. Past tense. She caught that. "I *do* not want them to die out even to their children's children."

Difficult to argue with someone you've fallen in love with, when he had every right to his stand. She tried. "In theory bringing people forward in time is not dangerous. But going back is terribly dangerous. Even if it's just the knowledge of this time. Prescience can be catastrophic."

"In theory," Donner qualified.

"Can we at least proceed carefully?" she begged. "Please don't launch a ship to Origin telling them what you know now. Not without a plan for containment. You could erase us all."

"I do not give promises."

He's going to bring them here. Fast as he can. She knew it. He had seen the past and found it unacceptable. The people of his home world were all dead, and this must not be. Donner forbade it.

The wrong ship formed around Glenn Hamilton as she displaced shipboard from the planet. Disoriented, she knew at once that this was not her SPT 1. This had to be the LEN vessel *Woodland Serenity*.

Doubly disturbing, in that she had requested retrieval to her own vessel, and she really did not trust the LEN's French-built displacement chambers to transport snot.

To the first face she met, Lieutenant Commander Hamilton demanded, "Why am I here? Is my boat all right?"

The Eyebrow stormed into the displacement bay, a swarthy man wearing green fatigues as if he were military personnel. Deep brown eyes glowered from under that single bushy brow. "Mrs. Hamilton. Mrs. Hamilton," he scolded her with her name. "This is criminal."

"Yes, this is kidnapping. You had no right to intercept me." She gingerly jumped off the displacement disk lest they opt to send her elsewhere in that frogified death trap. "You will dock with my SPT boat and restore me to my intended destination immediately."

"This way, Mrs. Hamilton."

"We are docked with my SPT boat?" she asked, somewhat mollified.

"This way, please."

She strode briskly after the Eyebrow, her heels clicking a light angry cadence. Her thoughts raced and tumbled. She had made a mess of this. She had not succeeded in warning Donner off the *kzachin*. No, in fact, she was pretty sure she had just spurred him in quite the opposite direction.

Damage control, then. How to contain the consequences? Minimize the damage. Needed to devise a course of action.

Her escort stepped aside, gentlemanly, making way for her to proceed ahead of him through a hatchway to a long corridor. "Mrs. Hamilton."

She tried not to wince. Not that she did not love Dr. Patrick Hamilton, she did. But first thing she did once this was all over was going to be changing her name back to Glenn Hull.

She marched briskly ahead—

Toe hit. Not enough warning to put on the brakes. She slammed full face into a bulk. Nose, brow, chin.

The holographic corridor vanished around her. Now she saw the bulk through teary eyes. Nose swelled.

Language unbecoming an officer.

She spun to face the hatch as it slammed shut, caging her in this small compartment. She announced with level authority, using her command voice: "This is piracy."

She received no response. She paced—carefully—the cell's true dimensions that were visible now. Two meters by two meters by two and a half meters. Slow fear threatened to close in on her. She pushed it away. It was not useful.

Neither was self-blame, though she had a great stockpile of that to face later. She had let herself—and probably her two SPT boats—fall into unauthorized hands. She could not sit here and await rescue. John Farragut would go extragalactic if he saw this.

She did not know how far Captain Farragut intended to run those two swarms, but she could not let him return to this. He would take a baseball bat to the Eyebrow.

Entertaining as that might be, it would not advance her career.

She was shaking. She had lost control of her independent command.

She steeled herself, forced the quaking down. She would just have to regain control.

And when the *Merrimack* returned, *she* would crack the Eyebrow with John's baseball bat.

Her eyes roamed the blank walls. This would never happen to John Farragut.

John, where are you?

Merrimack hurtled onward, shrouded in weird quiet. No scritching. No off-tune hum of insinuation. Everything touching *Merrimack*'s field was dead.

The normal wobble and pitch of the deck was gone. The ship ran rock steady. You could not know from within her that she even moved. The ship felt still as the grave.

With a sudden muffled explosion, the ship lurched severely. Captain Farragut lost his footing. In catching himself, his hand mashed into a control board. Calli fell into him. A technician pitched forward, nose into the console. Came up with a bloody mouth.

Shouts erupted from below. A rumbling shuddered underfoot. Acrid smell of burning plastic laced the air.

"That was *inside*," said Calli. She crawled to the central com and demanded a report.

The answer came: "We have fire, mid-deck, gun bay twenty."

As Calli received the report, Farragut consulted a systems technician, "Did we take the fire-fighting system offline?"

They had taken most systems off line in preparation to meet the swarm.

"Yes, sir."

"Put it back on-line, please." Farragut tended to sound casual in a disaster.

The report from mid-deck was unclear. They *thought* the gun crew had tried to fire an exploding projectile from bay twenty. Best guess was the shell had not made it clear of the barrel. The barrel ruptured on board, leaving a holy holocaust down below.

Smoke roiled too thick for anyone to withstand. They could not extinguish the blaze by isolating the section and opening it to the deep airless freeze of space. They could not even vent the smoke. The ship was buried deep in a solidity of compressed gorgons. There was no way out.

Calli commanded over the loud com, "Battery, hold your fire! No one fire! All units, do not fire. Triage to gun bay twenty. Fire containment crew report to mid-deck." She turned off the com to murmur, "God almighty."

"Why don't I hear the engines?" Farragut asked.

"The engines shut themselves down to nominal," Systems reported. "All vents are blocked. We are overheating."

The engines cooled by cycling coolant past the near zero of surrounding space.

Farragut turned to Tactical: "Are we moving?"

"Yes, sir."

"How fast and which way?"

"Sublight. The collision dropped us out of FTL. We are on the same vector as before contact. The swarm came with us."

"They learn quick."

The navigation specialist with the bloody lip muttered at his console, "Sublight. At least someone will be able to find our dead hull."

"Belay that. Can we steer?"

"We can steer, sir. But we'll lose speed."

To which Systems added, "We can't accelerate without cooking ourselves."

Farragut looked to Calli. His XO concluded, "The battleground is right here."

"We aren't the only ones hurt," said Farragut. "Get me a sounding. How bad off are *they?*"

At the very least *Merrimack* had incinerated a thick layer around her force field and left at a minimum a fifty-meter-diameter path of destruction directly behind her.

"They are dead to a thickness of nine meters all sides except to the stern, which is dead straight back to the surface."

That gave *Merrimack* a few moments in which to think while the enemy ate its way through its dead. But, "We're going to burn up if we don't get some of them off us quick."

"Take the force field down to nominal until the live ones close in," Farragut ordered. The force field was the single biggest draw on the engines. "Are any of the guns functional?"

"Not the projectiles, sir. The pressure on the force field is off the scale. We're buried alive. The dead mass has pushed in through the gun barrels."

"Can we *displace* anything into the mass?"

"Negative!" Systems was quick with the answer. "The displacement unit is tricky at the best of times. It uffs itself without Hive help. If we turn on the chamber, the Hive's likely to displace gorgons aboard."

Farragut nodded. "If the Hive learns how to displace, this war is over." He took in a breath, chest tight. Exhaled hard to expel excess carbon dioxide. Could not seem to get enough air. "Status atmospherics."

"All green," said Calli. She had already checked atmospherics. Twice. "I feel it, too."

"Swarm," Farragut murmured. Uffing their senses.

"Yes, sir," Systems confirmed. "We're not really suffocating. Yet."

"Belay that."

"Aye, sir."

"Stand by to bring the beam cannons back on-line."

"They'll expect that," said Calli.

"No, Mr. Carmel. *You* expect that. We haven't used beams against the Hive in a long, long time."

"Because the Hive always overloads the controls."

"And for all they know, we have learned our lesson and quit using beams."

"You don't think they're waiting for this move?"

"No. I don't think they have it in them to anticipate our moves in a new situation. They learn by precedent, like computers. Computers count patterns back through the most recent choices. We haven't used beams in a long time. They won't expect us to restart now. To react, they'll have to see the threat, evaluate the threat, then neutralize the threat. And I have to hope the time between steps one, two, and three takes more time than it does us to drill a vent to the surface." He turned to Augustus for comment. "That's Plan A."

"I like it," said the intelligence officer. "Given that I don't see a Plan B. Be quick."

"Fire Control, how long will it take to burn through to the surface?"

The weapons specialist pulled his lips tight across his teeth. "More time than we'll have. These are can openers out there. Not soft bodies. They're armored and they're dense."

"How about shooting through the dead?"

"Why would we shoot the dead?"

"I need vents for the engines. Everything behind us is dead. We came in that way. It's got to be pretty soft back there. Can we cut a tunnel back out the back?"

The specialist heaved a useless breath. "It's our best and only shot."

"Line 'em up. Straight shot out the back. Drill me a vent."

"How many cannons are we bringing on-line?"

"All of 'em. Aim anything out the back that can be aimed out the back. For the rest, rake, drill, blast, shoot until we redline."

"And if we redline before we break through to the surface in the back?" Calli asked quietly.

"Then push the line. There is no choice here. We do this or we die here. So we do this."

"Yes, sir."

Captain Farragut picked up the loud caller to brief the ship. Heard himself talking, but no echo of his voice through the corridors. "And God *bless*, there goes the loud com." He tossed the caller over his shoulder. "I'm going to tell the crew in person. Set it up, Calli. Wait till the gorgons eat through to our force field, then give it all we've got."

"You want to wait that long, Captain?"

"I don't want to waste a single erg shooting dead gorgons I don't have to."

Augustus followed him off the bridge. "Don't shoot until you see the blacks of their pincers?"

"Don't swing at the first pitch," said Farragut.

He bounded through his ship, informing his people of the situation and the plan. Arrived on mid-deck, where smoke still rolled in a thick gray cloud from the ruptured hatch of gun bay twenty, its fire wall bowed in, gore spattered on the corridor's inner bulk.

Farragut waved through the smoke to peer through the hatchway to the carnage within. A blasted rent in the hull left a clear view to dead gorgons mashed against the force field's invisible barrier.

"Holy God."

Farragut knelt to pick up a button still sewn to a shred of fabric. He held the button between his palms as he might hold the hand of the dying. Spoke with deep tremolo, "Who is this?"

Augustus watched the fire-suited Marines around him. All in John Farragut's hands. That button might have been—might still be—any one of them. The captain held them in his hands, asked their names. John Farragut owned these people.

A flap-eared youth asked, "We gonna buy it, Captain?"

"Hell no," Farragut answered in a big voice, with a smile and a wink. "It's a piss-poor day to die!"

The Farragut magic that Augustus so loathed infused hope and heart into those despairing faces, when he knew even John Farragut could not get them out of this one.

The captain made his rounds, spreading his idiotic hope through his doomed ship, until the familiar sick hum of gorgons trying to insinuate through the force field surrounded them. He raced back to the bridge. "Stand by!"

"Standing by."

"Do it, Mr. Carmel."

"Fire Control!"

"Fire Control, aye."

"Bring beam cannons on-line."

"Cannons on-line. Aye."

The lights dimmed. The beam chargers cycled to full power.

"And we are charged and green, sir."

Calli gave the order: "Fire. Fire all banks."

"Firing, aye."

The lights dipped again. Sound razored in the confines, a raking sizzle and burn with a closing wall of heat. A ghastly unhealthy warble permeated the beleaguered force field.

Calli and the systems tech looked to Farragut. "More power to the force field?" Calli asked.

"Negative."

"Aye, sir." They needed everything for the guns. If the guns did not cut through, then the force field would only prolong the dying.

An alarm sounded. A red light flashed on the console. Systems reported: "We're cooking. Guns turning to auto-shutdown."

"Override that," Calli ordered.

"Aye, sir." The tech switched to manual.

"Someone give me a depth," Farragut demanded.

"Nine meters to the surface."

"We're getting power spikes!" said Systems.

The swarm interference had reached the beam controls. The firing system fluctuated between shut off and overload.

"Shut down all but the rear-firing cannons," Farragut ordered. "Maintain fire to the stern."

"Maintaining stern fire, aye. Five meters to surface."

Beam chargers whined high revs, then drooped, then screamed.

"Engines redlined! Engines shutting down!"

"Override!"

"Override. Aye, sir."

"One meter to surface. And clear! We are clear to vacuum!"

"Shut down beam cannons! Shut down! Shut down! Take 'em off-line!"

Sounds wound down, the singed smell already clearing with a sudden influx of vacuum-cooled air.

Farragut had thought the vent would stay open only briefly, but the swarm did not collapse in on the burned tunnel, perhaps by virtue of its deadly heat, or perhaps the beams had cauterized the dead into a hard pipe.

The sense of relief was short-lived. The ship could breathe. Now what? You could hear the gorgons wheedling through the force field.

"How many did we kill?" Farragut demanded.

"Thousands." But before anyone could cheer, the tech reported, "We are still badly outnumbered."

Augustus specified, "From one thousand to one, we stand now a much improved five hundred to one—counting our dead, and I don't believe those are up to the task. We'll end up looking like the *Sulla*."

"Stow that, Augustus. Can we still steer?"

"Yes, Captain," Calli answered. "But we still can't achieve FTL. By the time we get anywhere, we *will* be the *Sulla*."

"Can we push another engine out?"

"If you can push a pig through a pitot tube."

What Augustus' answer lacked in respect, it made up for in clarity.

"I see."

A replay of gun bay twenty on a nuclear scale.

"If we try that, the swarm will be dead, but so will we," said Calli. "Has it come to suicide?"

"No, it has not. Nobody die till I say so. And *not* today. That is an order!"

Augustus saw the MP at the hatch roll his eyes, could read the skewed eyebrows: *Right, sir. Whatever you say, sir.* But also saw the men grow heartened in spite of themselves.

Farragut prowled his control room like a bear wanting a back-scratch and not a tree in sight. "I just want to scrape them off. And there's nothing out here. What's out here?"

"Nearest solar system is four light-years off," said Tactical. "We don't have that long. No comets of any size on the scan."

The force field groaned. Five hundred to one.

"I don't want to be eaten alive, John," said Calli quietly, statement of fact.

"How about our engine?" Farragut directed the question to Tactical, not to Systems.

"We can't get one out," Tactical reported, confused. He thought they'd already made that clear. "We'll die, too. And that's against my orders today, sir."

"I mean Engine Three."

"It blew up," said Tactical, feeling peculiar in stating the obvious.

But Augustus saw where this was going. "The antimatter."

Farragut nodded. "The antimatter from Engine Three can't have achieved one hundred percent annihilation. The containment chamber would have blown *something* clear."

Calli snapped fingers toward Tactical. "Res scan. Antimatter. Look for it in the area where we jettisoned Engine Three." Then turned to the captain. "You're right. There must be something left. But it will be only particles and they're flying every which way, fast."

"Particles will do," said Farragut. "Particles are all we want. We get too much antimatter, we'll blow ourselves up."

Tactical located the antimatter ejected from the explosion of Engine Three. A tenuous, expanding bubble of it.

And *Merrimack*, cocooned within its ravenous living asteroid, executed a lumbering turn into the path of the nearest, largest cluster of it.

*   *   *

Reg Monroe gripped and regripped her sword hilt like a batter waiting for the pitch. Watched the dead layer visible through the tear in the hull over the galley, a brown mass smashed against the force field.

The dead began to move.

Carly breathed, "There they are."

Mandibles appeared first, moving, sucking up the remains of their own kind. The force field shimmered and whined as the living monsters began to ooze through the distortion barrier.

Mesmerizing, grotesque, gorgons contorted themselves, flattened, elongated, slithered. And then the first pointed black claw pierced clear to atmosphere. A long serrated leg pushed free, stretched, then another, the thing laboring to pull its body out of the force field, as from thick mud. It expanded as it emerged, forming a shape, organizing a mouth, till it dangled by a single claw, spiderlike, seven meters above the deck, weightless in the limbo zone between the force field and ship's gravity well. Legs waved, searching for purchase, trying to acquire *up* and *down*; the body reshaping, shell hardening.

Cole Darby hissed, "Can't we shoot it?"

"Don't you dare," said Reg. "Hive mind's got the computerized sights fubared. And even if you gots a dead eye, you see where's he's at? He's outside the gravity. That's worse than shooting into water. Refracts your shot. And you miss and you hit the force field? One of us be eating your shot. Got it?"

Cole Darby bowed his head. "Got it."

The ship's loud com clicked. The boffins must've got the calibration recoded. The XO announced shipwide to ready swords, prepare for boarders, and stand by for impact, *Merrimack* was about to ram antimatter.

Reg glared back at the loud com. "We are ramming *what?* We are ramming *what?* What did that woman just say?"

"Eyes up, Marine."

"I *gots* my eyeballs on your boarders, Mister Hazard Sewell." Reg regripped her sword. "I see them crawly things hanging up there like the eensty weensty big ass spider. You just tell me: we are ramming *what?*"

*　　*　　*

Merrimack lost speed in the turn that put her in the path of the antimatter.

"Just as long as we make contact," said Farragut.

"We'll make contact, sir," the navigator assured him.

"How much antimatter are we facing, all told?"

The sensor technicians conferred over the readings. "Between a centigram and a decagram."

"What kind of explosion can we expect from that?"

"You want to know if we can survive it, sir? I don't know."

The ship's engines fed antimatter into the annihilation chamber in precise amounts, measured down to the atom. This mixture would not be precise.

"We're in for somewhere between a twenty- to a two-hundred-megaton blast."

The captain exchanged glances with his XO. Said, "Choose your poison. Fire or chewing."

"I'll take fire," said Calli.

"Fire, it is."

"Fifteen seconds to intercept with the antimatter," Tactical reported. "Thirteen. Twelve."

An abrupt change in the ship's ambient sounds silenced his countdown. The moan of fluctuating energy fields now overlayed with a physical metallic scratch and scrape of hard claws on hull. "They're through the outer perimeter."

And a report from below: "They have gorgons in the galley. Requesting permission to use flamethrowers."

"Negative," said Farragut. "We are low on oxygen. I want to be able to breathe when this is over."

Augustus lifted his brows, said nothing. Optimistic order, that.

"Five seconds to impact. Four."

The specialists tensed. You had to resist the instinct to brace yourself against something. Grabbing hold of something only makes you look silly if you live through it, or sends you to your Maker cringing if you don't.

A glance to the commanders showed Calli Carmel, tall, trim, picturesque, masked in cool dignity, standing in easy posture. Her hands, clasped behind her back were white fists.

John Farragut, alert, bright-eyed, ready to spring into his next action upon impact. Expecting to live.

The Roman colonel, Augustus, behind him, laconic, expecting to die. Going to do it with his eyes open.

"Two, One. Contact."

And nothing. Nothing more than the continued sickening moan of insinuation, and the escalating scritching on the hull.

A curse from the helm.

John Farragut turned, looking like the boy in the Kentucky field when his M-100 didn't go off. "What happened? Did we miss?"

"Force field, sir," Tactical groaned. "Theirs."

A coherent swarm—and this one was entirely too coherent—maintained a weak forward screen against particles in its path.

"We're not going fast enough," Tactical issued the postmortem. "The antimatter particles didn't pierce the swarm's force field."

The clashing of sword-on-pincer carried from below. Calli reported quietly, "They're in."

Five hundred to one.

14

SOMEONE SPOKE AN EPITAPH: "That's it."

Farragut thundered, "No, that is *not* it! Where is that antimatter? Did it bounce?"

"No, sir. We *have* it." Tactical struggled to explain quickly, "A swarm's force field follows the contours of the swarm shape. So there are pits and pockets in it. We caught the antimatter in those pockets. It's coming with us. It's just not contacting any matter."

"Good. There has to be some matter out there," said Farragut. "We push the antimatter into the matter—" He gave a loud clap to explain the finish. "We don't have to be going fast. We just have to touch it."

"Particles, Captain," Tactical reported somberly. "There are *particles* of matter out there. We are light-years from anything substantial. Annihilating two particles at a time isn't going to produce force enough to pierce the swarm field and kill a significant number of gorgons—assuming we can even line up our approach to collide one matter particle into one antimatter particle. It's going to be like throwing one grain of sand into a beach and targeting one specific grain of sand—while moving at near light speed."

"Makes hitting a hundred-and-three-mile-per-hour Kyle Norton fastball look easy," Farragut offered.

"You got it, Captain."

"Need a bigger bat," Calli muttered.

"I need a brick," said John Farragut.

"The oxygen!" Couldn't be sure who all in the control room shouted that.

Merrimack had dropped her oxygen reserves before battle. Bricks of matter as big as coal cars.

"Res scan," Calli barked.

"Oxygen bricks located," Tactical reported. Fed the co-ordinates to the navigator.

"Calli, can you steer us—and our antimatter—on a collision course with our oxygen bricks?"

"I'll make it happen, John." Looked to the helm who nodded, "Happening, sirs."

"Just how low are we on oxygen?" Farragut thought to ask.

"We'll pull it out of our water if we have to," said the XO. "If I get eaten alive, I'm not going to feel much like breathing."

"My thoughts." Farragut nodded. "Somebody give me an estimated time of impact?"

Calli deferred to the helm, who answered, "Ten minutes, sir. Maybe nine if I can squeeze some acceleration without cooking us."

"Calli, your boat. I'm going below." Farragut exited the control room, sword drawn.

"He loves this part," said Augustus, and followed him.

The gorgons had chewed a flanking route around Team Alpha where they were holding the galley breach. Kerry Blue sliced gorgon limbs off as fast as they emerged from the ductwork into the corridor outside the galley, while her team held off the main onslaught within. She grunted a song to herself:

> *Five hundred bundles of legs on the wall*
> *Five hundred bundles of legs.*
> *You take one down*
> *And hack it around*
> *Four hundred ninety-nine bundles of legs on the wall.*

Her sword dragged heavily as if pulling from a gravity sink. Her arms became elastic bands that had lost their snap. She should never have started counting bundles of legs on the wall. Zero was so very far away.

She was hacking number four hundred and eighty-nine

when a crashing and peripheral motion told her a gorgon had dropped from the overhead behind her. And she could not afford to turn.

She sliced mandibles out of her face, the muscles in her back tensing into a knot of primal terror, awaiting the pain, any moment expecting the jaws to pierce her spine. She whirled—

To a splat of gorgon innards hitting her face shield.

The offal slid off to reveal John Farragut cutting down the flanker.

"Ho! Shitska! The high-priced talent is on deck!" Kerry blurted.

The Roman, Augustus, darted past both of them in two long strides to cut down number four hundred eighty-eight coming out of the wall.

Captain Farragut nodded to Kerry. "As you were. Hold out, Flight Sergeant. We're almost out of this."

Sweat streamed through her scalp, soaked her sides. Her muscles quivered. Eyes burned. "Really, sir?"

"Yes. Really."

It was so easy to believe him that she didn't. But a nod from the Roman told her it was really so. She could trust Augustus to put a rosy outlook on nothing.

He didn't tell her that getting out of this might involve sudden death. But they were almost out of this one way or the other.

Came a sound like an ocean roar in a hurricane, like a thunder roll on a mountain, as loud a noise as *Merrimack*'s dampers allowed to sound.

The end-of-the-world roar shook the ship. Kerry crouched to the shuddering deck.

John Farragut winked and was on his way down the corridor, quick as Santa Claus.

"God provides for drunks, fools, and John Farragut. Or did I just repeat myself?" Augustus followed him.

Kerry scarcely heard him for the din. She pulled herself up from the quaking deck, holding onto the bulk. "This is good?" Her words were swallowed up by the roar. She shouted, "Is this good?"

But the officers were gone. And so were the gorgons, which had been clawing out of the duct. Number four hundred eighty-seven never came.

Kerry staggered to the galley hatch. She clutched at the frame and hung onto it with sudden vertigo upon the sight of the gorgons, pressing against the force field over the galley, suddenly tearing away in a blur of living, writhing sludge. They scraped across the energy barrier, shredding, with a noise between a scream and an avalanche. A pelting river of them raked across the energy field.

And abruptly cleared to a light as bright as *Merrimack* permitted to shine through its screen. It shut the eyes.

When the stabbing brightness gave way to cool darkness against her lids, Kerry opened her eyes to beautiful midnight. Green clouds of afterimage floated on her retinae, as she blinked at the peaceful stars showing through the rent in the hull.

She inhaled deeply, able to breathe again with the death shroud's lifting. As if the swarm had been pressing on her chest.

The air stank.

The roaring subsided, and Reg's screech pierced her eardrums, calling God by very familiar names.

Twitch and Carly were doing an elaborate gloat ritual, part flamenco, part chicken dance. "Now you see 'em, now they're frogging *spaced!*" Cowboy used to be very good at that dance.

Hazard Sewell muttered to his God.

Kerry pointed up with her sword to the very peculiar sight of some remaining gorgons caught in the act of insinuation. The few, the squashed, hung within the force field like insects preserved in invisible amber.

And preserved they were. Still alive, the monsters pressed inward, relentlessly, toward food.

"So which one's gonna drop first? I got a dime on that one." Kerry wagged her sword. "Squiggy there."

"I got the runt," said Cole Darby. "The one with the fire in his eye."

"That's not an eye," said Carly. "I think that's an asshole. I got Gimpy there." She picked out a gorgon, which was oozing through the field, leaving one of its legs behind.

"I think mine's dead," said Darb. "I want a new one."

"Cost you."

They fell to arguing about it, till the Navy gunners showed up to relieve them. "Orders from Lieutenant Colonel Steele. Team Alpha report to the hangar deck. Get some space under your butts, Marines."

Flight Leader Hazard Sewell put up his sword, barking. "Come on, dogs, let's go walk ourselves!"

Renewed, awake, alive, Kerry jumped at the chance to fly again. She gave her sword over to a navvy. "Here, spaceman." She yelled back to him as she ran: "Just let me know which one of those buggers drops out of the overhead first! There's money on it!"

Jose Maria Cordillera appeared at the captain's table, impeccably groomed. His long hair was clean, glossy, neatly parted and held back with a silver clasp. Only the slightest bulge of an elbow wrap under one brushed sleeve hinted that he had been in a fight for his life or suffered any strain from it. That and when he seated himself slowly, as if he might break, his back aristocratically straight, "I am too old for this."

John Farragut poured a stiff one for his friend. Alcohol flowed freely throughout the ship with the captain's blessing in the wake of desperate battle, to reward the living and mourn the dead.

"Mo tells me you got a reading on a dissolving gorgon," Farragut prompted.

"I did," Jose Maria confirmed. "Our valiant young Marines endeavored to corral one into my scanning chamber, where it promptly expired for the recorders." He did not sound happy. "I do not know what to make of it. I should like Augustus to review it." His dark eyes found the empty place at the table.

"He's dead asleep," Farragut answered the absence.

Augustus, who had been chemically jacked awake for forty-eight hours, had fallen asleep, hard, directly after the second battle was won.

Jose Maria lamented, "I am not even sure our patterner can help. I just want a second opinion."

"You have a theory?"

"I have a weak hypothesis based upon an unrecognizable agglomeration of molecules. Their form? It is like trying to reverse engineer a human being from a pool of sixty-five percent oxygen, eighteen percent carbon, ten percent hydrogen, three percent nitrogen, two percent calcium, one percent phosphorus, and two percent sixty-odd other elements.

Even in my snapshot of its living form, what is missing is apparent cohesion. What holds this being together? The normal molecular bonds—they are not here. I cannot make sense of its digestive process. A Hive cell eats left- and right-handed proteins alike, though I could not isolate a single protein in its own makeup. It converts organics to energy, but can this process be more akin to combustion than digestion? I should like to hear Augustus laugh at me for that one."

"They convert organics to what kind of energy?"

"I fear Augustus shall laugh. I fear more that he will not."

Farragut pressed, "What kind of energy, Jose Maria?"

"Resonance."

"You can't be serious."

"In an insane way, it makes perfect sense. What else could give them fluidity and cohesion in vacuum at temperatures at near absolute zero? It must be resonance." Jose Maria took a long, fortifying drink, set down his glass. "And I shall venture further out on this most precarious limb and postulate that resonance *is* Hive."

Farragut gave his head a quick shake as if he had water in his ears. "Resonance is a by-product of Hive existence?"

Jose Maria shook his head slowly, eyes on the amber dregs in his glass. "Resonance *is* Hive existence. The Hive and all its swarms and all its cells—what we call gorgons— are a titanic resonant being, and we the parasites within it."

"Oh. So we kill the enemy, we cut our own line of communication."

Cordillera had to smile. The captain had no awe for the vastness of such a being, no compunction at the prospect of being a parasite within it. Only keep his lines of communication intact, and that was all right with Captain Farragut. "If I am right, there is that risk."

"How weak is this hypothesis of yours?" asked Farragut, not liking the sound of this.

"Feeble enough. Here." Jose Maria Cordillera refilled their glasses to propose a toast. "To Augustus laughing."

Augustus woke in a depleted torpedo storage bay, his mouth cotton and dust, his eyelids stuck together. Faint scent of wood spice in his nostrils. He spoke to the scented air. "I heard Spanish music." And he rolled his head, cracked an eye to see who was with him.

Jose Maria Cordillera, sitting on one of the few remaining torpedoes, lifted a finger from the guitar to claim responsibility.

"How long have you been here?"

"A while." Jose Maria produced a computer bubble. "Can you sort this?"

Augustus held the bubble up, squinted at it. Tossed it to the deck, where it rolled through the grating to the metal. "No." He covered his eyes.

"Shall I leave?"

"No. Play. Order coffee."

Augustus did not stir again until the hatch thumped open and shut and the smell of coffee filled the torpedo bay. He smirked at the bearer. "You've been busted down to orderly?"

Captain Farragut set down the coffee service. "I want in on this discussion."

"No, you are running away from your recorder," Augustus saw through him. "You don't want to record any more of those letters."

"There's that," Farragut admitted.

He had lost a lot of crew. Made for a lot of anguishing letters home to Mom, Dad, spouse, sweetheart, and—God forbid—child.

Jose Maria set aside the guitar to pour the coffee.

"Don't give Farragut the guitar, whatever you do. He'll play that country western caterwauling."

"It's bluegrass caterwauling," Farragut corrected, stung.

Augustus rolled over the edge of his pod and, whether at the prospect of bluegrass music or from the pounding within his head, retched. He had little to bring up.

"Is that from wiring up into patterner mode or from . . ." considered what to call his encounter with the Hive mind. "The interference."

"How would I know?" Augustus sat up, reached for the coffee. A tic moved his gaunt cheek.

"They scared you," Farragut guessed.

Augustus replied tersely in scatological Latin.

"They got to him," Farragut told Jose Maria.

"I . . . am so pissed I can't see straight," Augustus breathed in strong emotion he had not felt in this lifetime.

"Did you touch the Overmind?" Jose Maria asked.

"If you can call it that."

"Does it—do they—think of itself as singular or plural?"

"The questions assumes a fact not in evidence."

"Which fact is . . . ?"

"That it thinks. It doesn't *think*. It's all gut instinct. In fact, that's it: it's a gut. Your alimentary canal can function without a brain, and so does it. When I was connected to the Hive, I had no knowledge of the whole, any more than one lung would know the existence of another. I got only impulse, not thought."

"So what 'impulse' did it send to you?"

Augustus scowled in thought, trying to recall, or to interpret, what he had received when the Hive had taken over his connections. Farragut and Cordillera waited.

At last. "This is filtered through my interpretation, mind you. I . . ." Augustus started over in robotic monotone: "Destroy anomalous entity."

"Me?" John Farragut asked. "'Anomalous entity.' Was that me?"

Augustus gave a hard, thin smile. "You didn't look like the rest of us."

For a moment Augustus had been one with all those crawling ravenous things. Anger twitched again under his eye.

"How close did you come?" asked Farragut. "To shooting me?"

"Not." Augustus turned his attention to his coffee, held the cup in both hands, let the steam thread up his nostrils. "I have my own fail-safe."

Of course he would. To keep him from being turned against Palatine.

"I forgot," said Farragut. "You're programmed to self-terminate."

Augustus snorted. "I am not programmed. I am not a cyborg. The organism governs here. *I* am in control." A little too insistent there. "And anyway, who could shoot those blue eyes."

The blue eyes blinked. "*You* could."

"Well, yes. But not because some *thing* told me to. What's your body count?"

Farragut demurred, not liking to reduce his losses to a number. They numbered eighty-one. "It's what we call a Pyrrhic victory."

"Pyrrhic is good. Statistically, you should not have won at all."

"Told you, I don't do statistics."

"I know. Here is the statistical curve," Augustus drew the curve in the air. "And way out here is John Farragut, one of those outliers we throw out of the calculation."

"That's why you're on my boat."

"That's why I am where John Farragut is," Augustus admitted. He took Jose Maria's hand, turned it over to check his chronometer, an antique Jose Maria wore on his wrist. August 5th. "Is this right?"

"Some hangover you had, Augustus," said Farragut. The patterner had slept the clock round twice.

"You throw a hell of a party, John Farragut. Where are we?"

"Twenty parcs out of the Myriad."

Augustus lifted his brows. *Merrimack* was a lot closer to the Myriad than when Augustus had passed out. "The reason for this incautious haste?"

"A 'singular' haste, Colonel Augustus," said Jose Maria. "Donner threatens to change history. We must stop him."

"Or maybe I want to do it myself," said Farragut. And to *Don* Cordillera's appalled expression said, "It's a thought."

"A much-thought thought, Captain Farragut," Jose Maria said sternly. "A dangerous thought. The old question comes to mind: If you could go back to 1938 and kill Hitler, would you? Let us say you do. Let us say in doing so you also escape the classic paradox of erasing your own birth, which would, of course, mean there would be no you to go back and kill Hitler. Let us leave that loop alone *arguendo*. Let us say you go back. You kill Hitler. You save the lives of six million Jews and you prevent World War II.

"Without their Axis allies, Japan fails to bomb Pearl Harbor. You save Hiroshima and Nagasaki. So then all those farm boys and coal miners who left the plow and the pick to enlist on Monday morning, December 8, 1941, never left your country. They never married their French and English and Italian brides. They never attended university on your GI Bill. All the encounters that led to your end-of-the-millennium Baby Boom never happen. The children and grandchildren of those uncreated people are never born.

"In short, you have just erased the lives of millions of people who would otherwise be alive today. How do you justify it? Because your motives were pure? Because the six million lived? Because Hiroshima and Nagasaki lived? How do you trade lives?"

"I am not going back to kill Hitler," said Farragut. "I'm thinking about going back ten billion years and sixty-odd klarcs away to try to mess up the *Hive*'s history."

Never one to let things just happen, if he believed history could be altered, as John Farragut did, then he was all for taking the offensive. "There's a time portal. What's to stop us from going back and trying to exterminate the Hive before it can be born?"

"We do not know when the Hive came into being. Ten billion years is a long time in which to hold onto a plan."

"So we don't wait. If we can identify the Hive home world, then go back and identify the plasma and dust that will coalesce into the Hive home star, blast the holy peaches out of it and interfere with its formation . . . ?" He trailed off, inquiringly.

"Assume it is possible," said Cordillera. "Assume you try. What if you get it wrong? Multibody dynamics are complex. In erasing the Hive we could erase humanity."

"Thousands of light-years across the galaxy?" said Farragut, dubious.

"Ten billion years is a long time in which stars may move. It may be that we and the Hive sprang from the same dust from the same supernova. We destroy them, we destroy us. Or perhaps the Hive ate some other invader who otherwise would make landfall in 1099," Jose Maria pulled the date out of the air. "Some time before we could defend Earth. Or perhaps in your meddling you redirect the comet that brings the first amino acids to Earth. There are too many variables. Too much time. The moment of intersection is critical—that instant when events you change intersect the history of Earth, no matter how minutely. Everything after that moment is in peril."

"And you really think events sixty klarcs and ten billion years away can affect Earth? I mean realistically, not wild long shot."

"They have done," said Jose Maria. "They do. The Hive is upon us now. The Hive crossed humanity's path eight years ago. So let us imagine you succeed in your quest. You erase the Hive from Earth history—take away that intersection—then anyone born after it, will not be."

"Will not be what?"

"Born. Events are interdependent. History is a tower of cards. Remove one card, and this particular structure ceases to exist. The smallest change will have vast consequences. How much does it take to alter the path of one sperm? A missed transport? A second beer? Roll left instead of right? A mote of dust? A sneeze? You take away humanity's intersection with the Hive eight years ago, then everything from the wreck of the *Sulla* forward is vulnerable to change, beginning with the children. After that? Who knows. Perhaps we are subjects of the Roman Empire. The possibilities are myriad, so to say."

Farragut looked quite deflated.

"I do hope I have discouraged you," said Jose Maria.

Farragut nodded, conceding, reluctantly, the point. He spoke a lingering regret, "I took an oath to defend the United States."

"And I took an oath to do no harm. The past is Pandora's box. It behooves us to keep what is in there *in*."

"Then Donner is in a very dangerous position."

"Very. We have taught him that faster-than-light travel is possible. We have told him his home world, Origin, is doomed to die. Donner has the ability to transport that knowledge back to a time when such things cannot exist. If he preserves Origin from its disaster, then those beings of ten billion years ago will expand across the stars, changing worlds—"

"Killing Hitler."

"So to say."

"Then we have to stop Donner from telling Origin about us. Augustus?" Farragut turned to his Intelligence Officer for his take on it.

While John Farragut and Jose Maria were talking, Augustus had lain back down and closed his eyes. He looked dead. His gray lips moved: "Let him go."

"Let him *go?*" Not the answer Farragut expected. "Donner could erase us all."

One eye opened a crack. Augustus spoke condescendingly, "We are here, are we not? Which means he didn't, now doesn't it? This is basic. This is entropy. The arrow of time flies one way. You know this stuff. You sound like a pair of self-important college students having a weighty dorm chat—which doesn't surprise me coming out of you, but *you, Don* Cordillera, I mistook for a grown-up. The ability to alter the past remains what it has always been, a silly romantic notion and beneath you."

Jose Maria spoke earnestly, hand over heart, "I am Spanish."

"Makes you a silly romantic?"

"Romance is never silly." Jose Maria picked up the guitar again.

"You are disappointing." And to Farragut, "You are at least predictable. Before you get too power drunk on this most urgent and desperate mission of yours to save human history and planet Earth, do remember that compliance with physical law is not optional. It's self-enforced. Your philosophizing is nothing but warmed-over sophomoric hash. That you are sitting here in my torpedo bay, talking, means you were created and no one went back and changed what is. God won't allow it. Creation won't stand for it."

Jose Maria fumbled on the guitar strings, stopped playing. "Augustus, you surprise me. Are you being facetious or do you believe in God?"

"For me to suppose myself the pinnacle of intelligence in existence would be a bit parochial, not to mention arrogant."

"But you *are* arrogant," said Farragut.

"I am also *here.* I have faith that Donner will fail to change the history of the universe."

"Because he must?"

"Because he did. You are more arrogant than I, John Farragut. You just wear it well."

"You're awfully sure of yourself when we're talking about things for which there is no pattern."

"Of course there is a pattern. It's called the universe."

"And there is a twenty-billion-year-old piece of lead 208 that says there is a hole in the big pattern," Farragut countered. "Donner is importing into the past elements that don't yet exist."

"He *is,* John? You mean he *did.* It's done. Whatever damage he will do is done—done ten billion years ago."

"Done once implies it can be done again. Your course of

action appears to entail closing our eyes, crossing our fingers and hoping. Never an option I was comfortable with."

"I am not here to give you comfort." Augustus closed his eye.

"You said Donner was courting a paradox and must be stopped."

Augustus spoke to the insides of his eyelids, "I believe I overreacted. The danger is all to the Myriad. The Myriad is collapsing, nothing more. The Myriad is not a Roman province; so I do not care. The LEN claimed jurisdiction; let the LEN save it. For Donner's courtship with paradox, what *is* the effect of paradox? Ever seen one? I shall file paradoxes away with purple cows and not give them another thought." And he was soon snoring.

Upon leaving the torpedo bay, Farragut conferred alone with *Don* Cordillera. "What do you think?"

"He's wrong."

"A patterner? Wrong?"

If anyone could tell a patterner he was mistaken, it would be Jose Maria Cordillera.

"I *know*. In my heart. And so do you, young captain. His argument that he has never seen a paradox, therefore they do not exist, is feeble. Unawareness is not an argument. The dead are unaware. Though it is the knowing that is the danger."

"You lost me."

"Do you know the tale of Adam and Eve in the Garden?"

People of the Book were become less and less common. But Farragut answered, "My dad still brings a Bible into his courtroom. And uses a Colt forty-five for a gavel."

"Then you know this story. It is the knowing, the knowing that changes everything. From the moment you know, return to the Garden is impossible."

"And you're still losing me."

"Once you become aware of the light, you move toward it. Knowing that FTL is possible, the beings on Origin will try to achieve it. Nothing will stop them. The knowing of the possibility makes the achieving imperative. They cannot do as they would have done in ignorance. If Donner tells them of us, we will have thrown an apple back ten billion years. I believe we must get back to the Myriad. No time to spare."

"I'm with you." And into his com, "Calli, best speed."

"Already at it, Captain."

"Then make it better."

And then the captain fell uncharacteristically silent, introspective. Not the ground-down sadness of all the deaths. Rather a wistfulness. "Captain Farragut, I sense you are no longer with me. You are perhaps traveling down the road not taken?"

Farragut smiled. Direct hit. Looked a little embarrassed. "It gets the mind running that way, doesn't it?"

"It is not like you to second-guess yourself. The captain's sights are forever forward. You do not spend your life looking back."

"For her, I do."

"Ah. A woman. I begin to see." The older man smiled indulgently. "All rules disappear."

"Ever think, God, if I could only do it again, I'd do things different?"

Jose Maria shook his head. "Do not we all? Tell me what you would do that you did not."

"In an alternate life, I married Maryann."

Jose Maria's smile was bright white in his olive-bronze face. "Maryann. You should hear how that common name becomes so rare and exotic and precious in your voice. How it sings. Maryann."

"My first love. My only love, really."

"And so why did you not marry Maryann the first time around?"

"She's a fragile soul. I knew I wouldn't be there for her. I married a tougher gal, who could do without me. And she did." His mouth tightened into a chagrined line. "Maryann was sweet. Pretty. Gentle. Funny."

"Did she marry another?"

"Not last I looked. I try not to look."

"What are you afraid of?"

"That she found someone. That she didn't. I'm still not in any position to do anything about it. Do you know how long it's been since I've seen Earth?"

"That is a choice, young Captain. I think you could find your way home again for a pretty, gentle, sweet, funny wife."

"Afraid she still loves me. We get married. I go back to war and get eaten by a gorgon. And where does that leave Maryann?"

"Alone. As you left her the first time. Except this time, she knows she was loved."

Blue eyes turned up to the overhead. "Ah, shit, Jose Maria. Next chance. As soon as we get out of this one. I'm going home and stealing that gal away from whoever's got her."

Kerry toyed with the short springy hairs of Steele's chest. Trapped a few golden coils between her fingers. "I'm coming back as a blonde in my next life," she said.

The blond meadow heaved under her hand with Steele's snort. He didn't open his eyes. "Just don't do it in this life. I like your hair."

Kerry grinned, parked her chin on his chest, peered across the meadow to his face. He looked younger with his eyes shut, all his facial muscles relaxed.

The two lay in a pleasantly tired tangle, enjoying the press of damp skin. Steele's heart thudded slowly under her chin. Sounds from the rest of the ship were noisily peaceful, engines, voices, the whap of balls on the squash court—probably Farragut because there was a whole lot of spectator noise. Men hooting like a baboon troop. There were always plenty of side bets when the captain was on the court, lots of money on the table, lucky pieces changing hands, someone drinking out of a shoe. Voices rose expectantly, fell away laughing. All was right aboard *Merrimack*.

Except that Flight Sergeant Blue was sleeping with her CO. And that seemed right, too, at the moment.

The ship's spirits had bounced after the memorial service for the dead. John Farragut had been amazing. Could keep his dignity in tears. He sent their comrades on their way with words of glory, words for each by name. The service took four hours. You didn't notice the time passing. He had you laughing and crying. And at the end of it, *Merrimack* felt whole.

"Everybody's talking about what they'd do differently. You know, if we can go back in time and change what we did."

Steele's eyes stayed shut. Voice sleepy. Not so much interested in what was being said as the simple act of talking to her. "So what are you thinking of changing, Marine? And it better not be your hair."

"I'd tell Dak not to turn his back on that gorgon. I'd tell

Cowboy not to be such a dick and just fly his Swift forward."

That opened his eyes. "You would bring *him* back to life?"

"Yeah. So I could kick his balls inboard. I'll never get to do that now. That lying, cheating, rat bastard. How 'bout you?"

"How 'bout me what?" He was not going to wish Cowboy back for any reason. Liked Cowboy fine as he was. Dead.

"What would you do different?"

He grunted, didn't answer.

Kerry changed topic, quick as a butterfly changing flowers. "Did that count as one furball or two?"

"Did what count? Those two swarms we just hit? That was two. Why?"

Kerry gave a merry wiggle against him. "I just ticked over lucky thirteen."

Thirteen. The magic number of hand-to-hand encounters with the Hive, after which your survival rate takes an enormous leap.

Steele snugged her closer to him. "Good. Don't get careless."

"Yes, sir." Kissed him. "How many have you been in?"

"How many what?"

"Furballs."

"Thirty. Forty. I don't know."

"Well, hell, Thomas! You're gonna live forever."

"Workin' on it."

She suddenly remembered, and for the first time understood, one of the xenos trying to explain mockingbirds to her. That the boy mockingbird with the most stolen songs gets the girl. Because if he can sing the song of a hawk, it means he's met the hawk and lived to tell about it.

She loved Thomas Ryder Steele for all his hawk songs.

Then he was asking her, "Got any interest in propulsion systems?"

"Me?"

"You see anybody else here?"

"I'm too dumb. Why?"

"You're not dumb, Kerry Blue. Navvies lost most of their propulsion department."

Marines were pretty much interchangeable. They all had

the same basic head-bashing, straight-shooting skill sets. They'd all been trained in twenty-one different scenarios, and were making up more all the time. On top of that, Kerry was a Swift pilot. But if she pranged, they'd just bring another up from the Battery.

Navvies, on the other hand, navvies were smart. They were all excessively educated specialists. They held lofty-sounding ranks, but most of 'em were outside the chain of command. Civilians in uniform—that's what they were. But they knew things. They were engineers.

Merrimack was a long way from home, and there were no replacement engineers to be taken out of a box somewhere on board. If they wanted a trained engineer, they had to haul all the way back to Fort Ike and put in a request, or else they had to educate one right here.

"Sounds like what Reg wants," said Kerry. Reg Monroe had only ever enlisted so she could go to college.

"I already got Monroe." The bodies hadn't been cold when Colonel Steele was surrendering Reg to the navvies. "I'm talking about you here."

She gushed a giggle. "You see me as a navvy?"

No. He didn't. But, "Like to get you out of my chain of command. Think you could be interested in engineering?"

"I'm a Marine. Why don't *you* do it?"

"Too dumb," said Steele.

"Then I guess we're screwed." Kerry laid her cheek to his chest.

He closed his eyes again, ran his hand down her smooth back. "Yeah."

Shrieks cheered from somewhere in the ship. A resounding *hoo ra!* together with a falling groan. Taunts and laughter. Steele guessed the squash game was over.

Kerry lifted her head at the sounds. "Hey. We beat Farragut."

The chant took form: "Serge! Serge! Serge!" Serge Olivero. Big ox of a gunner from the Battery. Any time the Fleet Marines beat Navy was cause for celebration. And winning against Captain Farragut, well that was cause for a near riot.

After a while Kerry asked again, "What would you do different. If you could go back in time?"

"Nothing," Steele said.

"No, really," she coaxed. "Would you . . ." she broke off, afraid to finish. Touched his face as if fearing it would vanish. "Us. Would you . . . not . . . if you had it to do again?"

He dropped his chin to his chest, the better to glare at her.

Her hand retreated. "I just get the idea you don't think this is the brightest idea you ever had."

He coiled her hair around his big hand, imprisoning her head in his grip. Growled at her. "You think I'd have come this way if I had a choice? You're with me, Marine, no matter where this goes. So just get used to it."

She nipped his scowling lips. "Yes, sir."

As *Merrimack* approached the Arran system within the Myriad, the ship's low band sensors picked up the LEN's giant spherical ship in orbit around the planet, with *Merrimack*'s two space patrol torpedo boats near it at the Trojan points.

The LEN sent a message demanding John Farragut's presence aboard *Woodland Serenity* immediately.

"Captain!" the tac specialist started in alarm. "The SPT boats are transmitting the wrong IFF!"

His report silenced all chatter in the control room and brought Farragut to the tactical station. "So what are they sending?"

"There's an embedded code within the normal recognition signals. It's—" Jeffrey paused, double-checking, nodded, finished, "Yeah. It's code beta twelve."

Farragut looked to his control room officers. "What's beta twelve?" Emergency code, he knew that much. But beta twelve was not one he had ever used in his seventeen-year career.

"Hostage situation, sir."

"Oh, for Jesus," Farragut breathed. "*Mister* Carmel!"

Calli took up the loud com: "Battle stations."

15

Lights flashed. The klaxon blared. Colonel Steele reported to the control room. Squeaky clean and flush red. His Marines were at their stations, the Battery at their gun blisters; the Wing sitting in their cockpits in the drop decks.

"What's the LEN ship transmitting?" Farragut demanded.

"Normal IFF. The LEN doesn't seem to see the problem."

"Strongly suggests that they *are* the problem," said Farragut. Looked to his officers for confirmation. "Anyone?"

"That would be my take on it, Captain," Calli concurred.

"Mr. Steele?"

"I agree, sir. Never trusted 'em."

And the LEN wanted Farragut aboard their ship immediately.

"TR, let's see how clean your dogs got their gun barrels. Open all ports. Uncap all guns. Load torpedo tubes. Mr. Carmel, bring us in angry."

Steele saw to the running out of the guns, as Calli barked orders to the helm and the engine room.

When *Merrimack* closed within one light-minute, Farragut moved to the com tech's station to hail his SPT boats on a tight beam. "SPT 1, SPT 1, SPT 1. *Merrimack*. Glenn, this is John Farragut. Respond."

Listened to dead air. Repeated the hail. More dead air. Then, finally, a voice. Not Glenn's, on SPT 1's tight beam: "This is Ambassador Aghani, LEN envoy. You are showing guns, *Merrimack*. May I assist you, Captain Farragut?"

Farragut clicked off the caller, demanded of the com tech, "Where's that signal coming from?"

"SPT 1, sir."

"Aghani's on my Spit boat?"

"Affirmative, sir."

Anger coalesced in John Farragut's face. You heard it in his breathing. He began to get an idea of the nature of this hostage situation.

Farragut clicked the caller on. "Aghani, this is a military channel. Put Captain Hamilton on the caller."

Until the lieutenant commander was back aboard *Merrimack*, Glenn Hamilton was captain of her Spit boat.

"Mrs. Hamilton is not available. May I help you, Captain Farragut?"

Farragut did not ask anything more. Shut the caller off. Too white hot angry even to sound angry, he ordered softly, "Mr. Carmel. Start shooting."

"Fire Control. Wake up five starsparrows," Calli ordered. "Plot some near misses around the LEN vessel *Woodland Serenity*."

"Fire Control here. How 'near' a miss, sir?"

Calli glanced to Farragut who answered, "Near enough they can *hear* the birds. And slow enough for them to see them coming."

"Loads, sir?"

"Shipkillers."

"Shipkillers, aye. Firing solution plotted. Fire Control standing by."

The XO looked to the captain. At his nod, Calli ordered, "Fire shipkillers."

"Fire Control, aye. Shipkillers away."

Farragut hailed *Woodland Serenity* again. "Mr. Aghani, put Captain Hamilton on the caller."

"Captain Farragut," Aghani began condescendingly, broke off in a squawk, "*What are you doing!*"

Shipkillers ringed the LEN ship. The LEN sphere hung

trapped into stillness like a knife thrower's assistant, death brushing all sides.

"I am attempting to establish contact with my officer. You must believe I will do so, no matter your cost." Farragut shut off the caller. To his XO: "Status."

"Star Sparrows clear of *Woodland Serenity*. Not quite a clean miss, sir. We ticked a solar vane. Warheads still live."

"Bring 'em back for another pass."

"Fire Control."

"Fire Control, aye."

"Bring the Star Sparrows about, Davy. Do it again."

"Fire Control, aye."

As the missiles turned a one-eighty, the com tech reported, "Sir, it's *Woodland Serenity*. They are speaking in tongues. Demanding to talk to you."

The missiles headed back for another ringing pass around *Woodland Serenity*.

The com tech yanked off his headset. Reported: "Sir. They are screaming."

Farragut turned to the tactical specialist. "Is *Woodland Serenity* showing arms?"

"No, sir."

"I hope they don't think I'm bluffing."

Colonel Steele assured him, "The *Mack* does *not* look like she's bluffing. They know they can't take us."

"They don't have much to bring to bear, Captain," said Tactical. "Couple asteroid sweepers."

"Are they showing?"

"No, sir."

Fire control reported the Star Sparrows clear of *Woodland Serenity*.

Calli turned to Farragut. "Sir?" Awaited direction.

Farragut took up the caller. "SPT 1. SPT 1. SPT 1. This is *Merrimack*. Captain Hamilton, respond."

Aghani's voice again, indignant. "If *Woodland Serenity*'s auto avoidance had reacted to one of those missiles and twitched it into the path of another, you would have the murder of five hundred civilian lives to answer for!"

"They're not dead, though, are they?" Farragut replied.

"More's the pity." A murmur from behind.

"Not now, Augustus."

The tac specialist reported sharply, "Sir! Both Spit boats

have left Trojan points and are moving *toward* the LEN ship!"

"Aghani, cease the progress of my boats toward *Woodland Serenity* or I will space *Woodland Serenity*."

Calli's brows flew high, but she did not protest the threat.

"Calli. Line it up."

Calli opened the com link. "Fire control. Target *Woodland Serenity* and stand by shipkillers to go hot."

"Fire Control. Targeting, aye. Standing by."

Farragut looked to the com tech. "Any acknowledgment from the LEN?"

"The captain of *Woodland Serenity* is calling you a terrorist. That's an acknowledgment, I guess, sir."

"Calli, are we close enough to hook our Spit boats with our force field?"

Calli relayed the question to Tactical. Received the answer, "Momentarily."

Calli put Engineering on standby.

Tactical reported, "Sir, both SPT boats have stopped progress toward the LEN vessel *Woodland Serenity*."

"Don't care. Calli."

"Range," Calli demanded of Tactical.

"One boat, aye. Now both. Aye."

A glance to Farragut.

"Hook 'em."

Calli: "Engineering. Engage force field hook."

"Engineering, aye. Hook engaging."

Merrimack's distortion field extended like a pseudopod to enclose SPTs 1 and 2.

"Command. Engineering here. Targets acquired. We got 'em, sir."

The com tech reported, "Sir, the LEN captain says our force field is preventing them from displacing their people off our spit boats."

"Well, glory be. How 'bout that?" Farragut breathed, as if the thought never occurred to him before. "Advise *Woodland Serenity* that I will restore their people to their ship as soon as all of my people are restored to *Merrimack*."

The whole command deck could hear the LEN captain's voice through the com tech's headset as he pulled it away from his ears: "This is piracy!"

Farragut took up the caller. "I am towing U.S. boats aboard a U.S. ship. What is the basis of your charge?"

"There are LEN personnel on board those spacecraft!"

"Why, yes, there are. They did not ask my permission to board my boats, but there they are. I shall have to ask them why they're there."

"You will return my people *now*."

"You will be free to collect your personnel pending a head count of *my* personnel aboard my boats."

And listened to dead space again.

Import descended in a horrid chill. *They can't deliver*. The LEN could not comply, because *someone is missing*.

Merrimack reeled in her extended force field to bring the patrol boats back to the flight decks, where they were captured, clamped, and hauled inboard to the hangar deck.

When the deck pressurized, the SPT boat hatches opened to a gunpoint welcome by a Marine detachment armed with splinter weapons.

First to disembark down the ramps were the LEN personnel. Stiff. Trying to show umbrage, but could not disguise their fear in the face of all the guns and the determined, angry faces glaring squint-eyed down the barrels. "There has been a misunderstanding."

"Someone for sure misunderstood something," a Marine muttered, cheek mashed to his splinter gun's stock, keeping a bead on the speaker's forehead. Kept the visitors pinned for the captain's arrival.

The MPs sent a cadre of dogs aboard the returned SPT boats to sniff for booby traps. Dogs had an uncanny sense for rooting out wrongness.

The captain arrived on deck. Said immediately, "Where is Glenn Hamilton?"

Met silence from the LEN, from his own recovered personnel, who stood at embarrassed, blank-faced attention.

Surprising how a face so open and friendly could turn so frightening so fast. The LEN got a gorgon's eye view of John Farragut, the ferocity, the deadly energy. He became someone who threw lightning bolts. He roared into the silence: *"Where is she?"*

Everyone recoiled from the force of it, even his own Marines.

Ambassador Aghani took a breath as if he might speak.

But his eyes only searched for somewhere to look other than at the captain's face. Found only guns and growling dogs.

Glenn Hamilton's second-in-command, Ensign Kenyon Kent, whom everyone called "Ken Ken," filled in at last: "We think she escaped, sir."

Aghani abruptly found his voice. "It's not like that."

"Shut up. Brig 'em." The captain waved an arm at the lot of them.

"Yes, sir," Colonel Steele acknowledged. "With pleasure."

As Marines ringed the LEN boarders, Aghani protested, "We are free citizens of Earth!"

"When Glenn Hamilton is free, you're free. Till then, you're in my brig. And if that's the rest of your natural life, then you know where you're going to die."

And the deep terror in their eyes struck John Farragut with a fear he did not know he could feel.

They can't free her. She's dead.

"You," Farragut barked at his rescued crew, none too gently. "Proceed to ops and await debriefing."

He detained Ken Ken out of the unhappy group. "Talk to me. Where's Glenn?"

"Not sure, Captain," said Ensign Kent. "When Hamster went planetside to deliver your message to Donner, the LEN came in and took over both boats."

"How? How did they get aboard?"

Kenyon's baby smooth cheeks blotched ruddy. "We let 'em aboard. Bagging us was like hunting cows. Come this way? Yeah, sure. Hatch locks. There we are. We were stupid, sir."

"I see that. What about Glenn?"

"We were locked up, but you know these bulks." He rapped a thin partition with a bottom-fist. "We overheard them receive Captain Hamilton's request for displacement back to SPT 1. They signaled *Woodland Serenity* to yank her up there."

"They displaced her to the LEN ship?"

"I *thought* they did, sir. But later—hours later—more LEN came storming aboard SPT 2, ransacked every centimeter, pulled on our faces to make sure we were real. We guessed that meant she got away. And since she's not here, she's either doing a really good job of hiding on board the LEN golf ball, or she's planetside. But, sir, I'm pretty sure *they* don't have her."

"Who turned on the beta twelve code?"

"I did, sir."

"Then you don't walk the plank."

"Thank you, sir."

"Calli!" Farragut called into his com while climbing up the ladder.

"Captain."

"Scan the planet for Hamster's com signature."

"Scan initiated, aye."

"And have Mo do a full physical workup on our guests. Look for contaminants. Any possible physiological cause for paranoia and delusion. Tell him to make it uncomfortable. And if he finds something, make sure *we* don't have it."

"Understood, sir."

Farragut arrived in the control room to receive Calli's report on the search for Hamster. "Her com is not reading. She may have turned off her link to avoid LEN detection."

But there were other ways to track a crewman. "Locate all displacement collars."

Calli signaled the supply officer to punch up the inventory. He reported one collar unaccounted for, logged out to the Hamster.

"Where is the collar now?" Farragut demanded.

"It's . . . not functioning," Calli reported guardedly.

"You mean she's not wearing it?"

"No." That would be a void reading. "We have no reading on it."

It went without saying that you can't turn a collar off. To destroy a displacement collar's locator was to destroy the collar.

"Run the history," Farragut ordered, pale.

"Running it," said Calli.

Given that the collars never turned off, the ship's sensor log would have a continuous record of the activity of all collars at every moment. It did not take long to isolate the moment that Hamster's collar ceased to function.

"Last successful displacement logged on collar P240H was from the LEN ship *Woodland Serenity* to the planet surface forty-two hours ago."

So Ken Ken had guessed right. Lieutenant Commander Hamilton had managed to escape LEN captivity.

"Last intact location of the collar was on the Arran surface."

"When did it flat line?"

"Forty-one hours ago." Calli sounded quite hollow. "In transit."

Farragut grabbed the signal log to read for himself. The signal for the final abortive displacement had originated from *Woodland Serenity*. The LEN had tried to retrieve the escapee using only the signal from her collar. They had initiated displacement *without* a corresponding signal from an LD.

You never, ever displaced a human being without three matching signal sets. The LEN tried to displace Hamster with only two.

"Was Hamster in the collar at the time?" Farragut spoke so quietly Calli scarcely heard him.

"Can't know, John. Not without the LD confirmation." Except that no one ever took his collar off while on a planetside mission. It violated procedure.

The LEN had attempted retrieval knowing they had a very poor chance of transporting a human completely intact. And they had failed.

It was a hideous image. Did not help that it had probably been painless.

"Realign Star Sparrows. Arm shipkillers."

"Positioning missiles, aye."

"Tag *Woodland Serenity*."

Calli relayed the order to fire control. The tags would give *Merrimack*'s missiles a homing signal. No matter how the target attempted evasion, the missiles would follow the tags. And there was no outrunning Star Sparrows. Star Sparrows were faster than any manned ship and good for light-years.

"Tags away."

Tactical announced, "*Woodland Serenity* opening gunports."

What *Woodland Serenity* showed was a total of four of the most basic low-bid lances, useful for clearing debris from its path. The LEN had been better shielded in defenselessness. Nothing could save it, should *Merrimack* fire in anger.

Closed gunports would at least have insured a murder conviction when it was done.

"Target acquired. We have tag lock."

The com tech: "Sir. The LEN is demanding to know our intentions."

"Transmit tag signature to Star Sparrows."

"Fire Control, load firing solution."

"Firing solution loaded. Fire Control standing by."

All the officers in the control room looked to Captain Farragut, as the civilian vessel of five hundred souls sat under *Merrimack*'s guns. Only Calli dared speak.

"Sir? What *are* our intentions?"

The captain's blue eyes were white all round, his thoughts loud enough to hear. He raised his hand—like wielding a gavel—and the officers on deck feared what order would come down when the hand should drop.

A nervous pronouncement from the com tech: "I have a com sig." And to the captain's white-hot glare, he clarified, "Com signature from planetside."

Farragut's voice came out strangled, "Glenn's?"

The tech answered carefully, "It's Lieutenant Commander Hamilton's *com. Someone* just switched it on."

And immediately followed a hail on the captain's direct link. Farragut yelled into the back of his hand, "Glenn!"

For a moment the world stood still. Waiting for whom he would hear on the other end of this link.

Glenn Hamilton's clear soprano, "Captain! Lieutenant Commander Hamilton. Beta twelve. Repeat, beta twelve." Hostage code.

"Beta twelve secured here. I have both Spits," Farragut assured her quickly, still shouting. "Do *you* have beta twelve?" *Are you a hostage?*

"No, sir. Not me. The Spit boats are beta twelve."

"We've secured them. Are you in danger?"

"No, sir. I'm fine, sir. *Hungry.* I can't eat the food."

At last Farragut remembered to breathe. "Is there an LD near you?"

"Yes. I'm in Donner's shack." The Archon's palace. "But I don't have a collar. I took mine off so the LEN couldn't trace me. Now I can't find it anywhere. . . ."

*   *   *

The Star Sparrows were recalled, the tags extinguished.

John Farragut logged out a displacement collar for himself and one with which to retrieve Glenn Hamilton from the planet surface. He issued orders for his LEN detainees to be restored to *Woodland Serenity* without standing trial for piracy, though he still insisted on a full physical examination, unable to believe that such insanity could be naturally occurring.

He gave orders to the chief to resupply *Merrimack*'s oxygen from the planet's atmosphere, and to bring the ship's pressure back up to Arran sea level.

As he collected food from the ruins of the galley, the blue-white planet Arra hung overhead in the starry space that showed through the chewed-out hull. The bright image twinkled through the force field.

And to his shadow, Augustus, Farragut asked, "Why aren't you debriefing my Spit crews with Colonel Steele?"

Augustus snapped a displacement collar around his own neck. "I will review the flattop's inquiry when he is done."

The patterner could plug into the data bank and take in the whole session in the blink of an eye. "Sitting through a Q and A in real time is like sucking a frozen milkshake through a coffee stirrer. And it was vastly more interesting watching you skewer your dignity over another man's wife."

No pretending not to understand. The captain looked chagrined. His big shoulders hunched a bit. "Wouldn't be the first man to do that."

"First one to threaten to blow up a civilian vessel with five hundred live bodies on board."

Farragut offered no comment.

"A question for the captain."

As if refusal would shut Augustus up. Farragut waved him to go ahead.

"Were you bluffing?"

"You tell me, Augustus."

"Either you are a much better poker player than I ever imagined, or else you're psychotic."

When Augustus did not continue that thought to a final conclusion, Farragut demanded, *"Well?"*

"I don't want to play poker with you," said Augustus.

Farragut frowned. Confessed, "I wanted them dead."

Augustus dismissed that lightly. "Of course you did. But fantasy is fantasy and reality is reality. You would not have killed five hundred people to avenge one. You won't even break honor and orders to sleep with your girlfriend."

"She's not my girlfriend."

"But it was embarrassingly obvious to all hands in the control room that *that* detail had nothing to do with the wanting of it."

Till now, John Farragut naively thought he had kept that card close to his chest.

Once upon a time he had talked to Glenn a lot. Back when she was a lieutenant on his watch. She and he had bounced ideas off each other, argued, laughed. Hamster had a sneaky sense of humor and she could rope you in before you knew you'd been had. Because little Glenn Hamilton was married, Captain Farragut had not felt that primitive need to impress her, and she was not his type anyway. She was just a guy.

Then one day he'd been out here in the Deep End too long and he had to remind himself that she was just a guy. A really pretty, good-smelling guy.

And that day Hamster came into command of the middle watch.

"You did manage to make a complete idiot of yourself over a married woman," said Augustus. "A subordinate, no less. A Mrs. Hamilton, no less."

Farragut gave a kind of pout. Lifted blue eyes in appeal, "A *complete* idiot?"

"Absolute."

The grin was boyish. "No use doing anything halfway, hey?"

They were in the displacement chamber by now. They took places over two disks. The tech coordinated signals among collar and displacement disk and landing disk. Green lights.

Farragut gave the nod to the technician. "Let's do this." And the ship vanished before his eyes.

A wilted Hamster greeted her captain with a smart salute, giving way to a wilted smile when he bid her stand down and presented her with two fragrant bags of food.

"Mo said you should eat this." The first bag held a carton

of nutrient broth with harmless crackers on the side. "*I* brought you this."

Hamster melted around the smell of the second warm bag. Trembling hands unwrapped a big sloppy burger. "Marry me," said Glenn and bit into the burger. Groaned in ecstacy.

"Um . . . aren't you married?"

"Actually, here, I'm not." She talked with her mouth full. "I learned a couple of Myriadian customs. I am 'committed' but not 'married' because I haven't consummated the pairing."

"This is probably not information I ought to have," said Farragut.

Hamster covered her mouth and laughed. "It's not a consummated Myriadian marriage without offspring."

"Ah."

They were outside, under the clouded stars, in a parklike area planted with flowering trees and laced with flat stone walkways that meandered around ornamental ponds and little oases of stone carvings—votives or gravestones or art, who could tell?

Though they need not fear Myriadian surveillance—the Myriadians did not know English—Augustus made a quick sweep of the garden for LEN devices.

When he pronounced the area clear, Hamster lost her smile. "I'm sorry, John. I lost it. I never saw it coming. I— Break me." She pulled off her lieutanant commander's pips and offered them.

Farragut would not take her insignia. "Save it till after the inquiry. I don't think anyone will sanction you for being taken in by insane allies. Just tell me—if I hadn't showed up when I did, what were you going to do?"

She shrugged. "I was putting one foot in front of the other. I only got as far as step one—escape. I *was* going to be back in control of the Spit boats by the time you returned. And it was going to be brilliant. Really."

"Should I go away and come back?"

Glenn gave an abashed smile, "If you don't mind."

"How *did* you escape?" Farragut asked.

Glenn started, stopped, a conspiratorial gleam in her eyes. She asked, "John, do you know how to get a ferret into a bag?"

"Is this a joke?"

"It's kind of funny, but no, it's God's truth."

"Okay. How do you get a ferret into a bag."

"You open the bag and the ferret climbs right in."

"And that works?"

"Ninety-nine times out of ninety-nine," said Glenn, hand over her heart.

"You opened a bag and the LEN walked in?" Farragut asked, not quite following.

"Just about. And it's pretty much how they caught me first, actually. They had a cell rigged with hologram projectors so the cell looked like a corridor. They opened the hatch for me, and I walked right in. Hit the wall. They turned off the projectors and locked me in.

"But here's the ferret-brained part. They left the projectors in there. I rerouted the power from the overhead light to the projectors and turned them back on."

"And the hologram corridor was narrower than the real cell," Farragut guessed.

"Yes it was. About this much narrower." Glenn set down her burger to hold one palm flat against her back, the other palm flat across her breasts. "Now, John," she quickly retrieved her food. "If you were holding someone prisoner and you opened her cell and saw an empty holographic corridor instead of a cell, what would you think?"

"I'd look for a Hamster in the wall."

"And you wouldn't walk right in with a stunner in your thigh holster! Zap. Zap. I'm free. I ran back to the displacement chamber—not locked, not guarded, didn't have to zap anyone else. Displaced here. That's about as far as I got. But I was working on it." She took a big bite.

The ground murmured. The ponds rippled. Fish jumped from the water. Birds took flight.

Farragut started like an alert dog, but Glenn kept eating. "That happens all the time here." She caught tomato juice dripping down her chin. "Most people sleep outdoors."

Even with the tremors, it was pleasant here. Warm. Sitting in the alien grass with a pretty woman under the brilliant, starry sky.

But sense of urgency nagged like a bad tooth. Farragut asked, "What about Donner? Did you deliver my warning about using the *kzachin*?"

"Yes, sir. I did accomplish that much of my mission."

"How did he receive it?"

"Badly." She put down half of her burger. Heaved a sigh, stuffed. "I believe Donner fully understood everything I told him. Too fully, really. He did *not* agree to withhold information from Origin."

"Then he's risking paradox."

"Yes, sir. He is."

"Did you explain that to him? He's a reasonable being."

"How reasonable can anyone be when he learns his home world—the cradle of his kind—is a dead ball of dust and he must never go back to see it alive again? He made all the connections, John. He figured out that a billions-year-old civilization ought to have lots of starfaring descendants by now—especially the way his people breed. And he cares. He's a dictator—he's a good one. How do you tell him he must not change the complete death of his homeland?"

Farragut rose. "*I*'ll tell him. Now. You feeling up to it, Lieutenant Commander?"

"Yes, sir." She cleaned off her hands, stood up. She cautioned, "It's not going to turn him, sir."

"Probably not." He could not ignore the human element in human history—and Donner was human enough. Whether on a personal level or on the species level, everyone wanted to live. Your name, your children, your world, your self, your love. And hates and jealousies and sorrows were all human and all part of history, the drops of water that wear the canyon into the mountain. Human tears counted.

Into his link Farragut sent shore to ship, "Colonel Steele."

Augustus muttered, "We need the flattop for this?"

Farragut paused to answer Augustus. "Say a superrace comes along and tells us we must not use the Fort Ike shotgun ever again, so it's going to take us a year to get back to Earth—or to Palatine—with only FTL normal. What is the proper response to an edict like that?"

"A one-digit salute?" Hamster suggested.

"I would expect something with more lead content," said Farragut. And into his link, "Mr. Steele, a Marine guard if you will."

*   *   *

Dr. Patrick Hamilton had been sedated since the second swarm battle, in which he had been parted from his right foot. A bit of a crybaby, Patrick Hamilton did not want to endure the pain and ick factor involved in reattaching his appendage while conscious.

When finally he rose from his sick bay cot, he was dismayed to learn that, though the ship was in orbit around Arra, he was not permitted to displace to the surface to try out his reconnected foot in the starshine on the green Arran meadows.

Since *Merrimack* was back in the Myriad, Patrick figured that Glenn must be back on board. And since it was mid watch, his wife would be OOD. Dr. Pat would just see who was allowed to go where.

As he made his way to the control room, people looked at him as if he'd grown four eyes—or an extra foot. They whispered behind his back, glanced away when he turned round.

He overhead one furtive exchange: "That's Hamster's husband."

"Oh. Him?"

Patrick Hamilton arrived at the control room to find Commander Calli Carmel on watch. He double-checked his chron. It was definitely the Hamster watch. "Where's Glenn?"

The whole control room turned around to stare. More of those weird looks. Embarrassed. Pained.

Finally someone clued him in: While you were sedated, your wife was kidnapped by the LEN, escaped, was presumed killed in a capture attempt, but turned up alive on the planet Arra.

"Oh, is that all?" Patrick said, customarily flippant. Wondered when someone had intended to wake him up to let him know. "Where is she now?"

"Planetside with Captain Farragut."

Someone hissed the speaker quiet, as if he'd said something he shouldn't. Patrick Hamilton glanced at all the eyes that quickly averted in numbing silence.

Feeling as if he was waking up much later than he had thought, Patrick Hamilton asked, "Is there something else I should know . . . ?"

*   *   *

Donner had a monitor screen illuminated in his audience hall, the screen filled with *Merrimack*'s mauled hulk.

The Archon turned from the horrific image to Captain Farragut. "You found your monsters."

"We did," said Farragut, then told Donner in the most exigent terms he could find in the Myriadian language that Donner must not—must not—go to Origin ever again. Must not even let the beings of Origin learn of the existence of starfaring peoples this side of the *kzachin* or of the possibility of true FTL travel. "You cannot tell them anything about us. It will change history."

"How simply you can say so." Donner's tone was tempered, but his mane stood up along his spine in fighting set. "It is not your world. It is not your history."

"It is my *now* and you must not change it," said Farragut.

"Very well."

The dictator's acquiescence took them all by surprise, left Farragut off balance. He had been braced for a storm. Got instead a quick easy *okay*. Captain Farragut looked to Colonel Augustus and Lieutenant Colonel Steele to make sure he had not mistranslated Donner's answer.

And to their startled stares, Donner insisted, "If I must, I must."

Steele breathed a sudden obscenity. Farragut turned sharply. Found Augustus nodding in agreement with the Marine's comment. Augustus spoke in English, ("Even the musclehead figured that one out.")

Farragut caught on. ("Donner already sent the message.")

("Weeks ago,") Augustus guessed. ("Probably the moment we arrived in the Myriad.")

("Then it's all done,") said Steele. ("It's all over and nothing happened.")

("Maybe not,") said Farragut. Hoped so. But would not bet on it. ("It's not like he could just displace a ship to the Rim gate. It would take an Arran ship a while to travel from Arra to the *kzachin* that leads to Origin.")

("How long of a *while*?") Steele directed that to Augustus.

A hint of a smile lurked in Augustus' dark eyes. Black humor there. ("Weeks.")

Farragut's heart sped. ("Augustus! Assume Donner sent

a messenger ship to Origin when we first appeared— Do we still have time to stop that messenger?")

("I'm not plugged in, so I can't run the numbers, but given that Donner is stalling us with this agreeable bullshit, I would have to say yes.")

All eyes returned to Donner. Though the Archon could not understand their words, he must have guessed what they were saying, because he now held a projectile weapon trained on John Farragut's head.

Farragut's posture deflated a little with an impatient sigh. Never appreciated that view of a firearm. He implored, "Donner, logic dictates—"

"No, Captain Farragut. *I* dictate."

The Archon gave his weapon a small lift to draw attention to it. "Primitive enough by your standards, but it's lethal enough for my purposes."

Of course Donner would not be able to see the energy wall Colonel Steele had activated, LD to LD. Charged with security, Steele had been entirely ready for this reaction. Donner might detect only the slightest refraction in the air between him and his target. The greater giveaway was Farragut's lack of concern at having a weapon pointed at his face.

Farragut's steady gaze met the eyes behind the gun. "What *is* your purpose, Archon?"

"To save my home world. This planet—Xi, you call it. Lieutenant Commander Glenn Hamilton tells me it is Origin and it is dead. Tell me, what killed my world?"

"Any number of natural forces could have done it," said Farragut. "Entropy is a basic condition of the universe. *My* home world will be dead in ten billion years."

Donner spoke thickly, deeply felt. "But your descendants will not be dead. Your people travel far. I know my people did not go elsewhere. They have not the means. And if I sent them heavy elements with which to build thousands of ships, then you would find something of them still on this planet Xi, even after ten billion 'years.' Something left besides the back of a reliquary . . ." He broke off with a quaver in the voice, a glistening in the coal-black eyes.

Myriadians cry. Human tears.

Donner snarled, "It means I did not help them. I did not help them *yet.* I see there is a God, and God sent you to show me my error. I am destined to save them. I will change my history."

Farragut suppressed a groan.

The heavy air shimmered with sound. A chorus of cricking, the fluttering of myriad wings, the scraping of serrate legs. The bluster of swarms of insectoid life.

Farragut shivered in the Arran heat, his hair pricking up like Donner's mane at the sound, the sound that stirred only the most elemental dread.

And saw everywhere—from the sponge bushes, from the lake, from the vine trees and coral gardens, from the water and the rock faces—insects rising.

"Hive sign!"

16

DONNER FROWNED, perplexed. Not accustomed to losing the attention of those he held at gunpoint. Might as well be holding a toy for all the regard it won him.

Captain Farragut yelled into the back of his hand, ("Calli. We have Hive sign. What've you got?")

("Nothing. Negative Hive sign. We are quiet. Are you sure it's not another mimic?")

"Dead sure. This planet is being pinged."

The Hive often sent scouts ahead, which always betrayed their presence this way. The scouts' signals back to the Overmind set the local insectoid life to panic. With a being as unified as the Hive, in which the Overmind had instantaneous knowledge of every one of its cells, the concept of stealth was so alien to the Hive as never to occur to it. There were no sneak attacks.

Even Donner, who had never witnessed Hive sign, was instinctively disturbed by the sight of Arran creatures swarming and flapping and creeping out of the ground.

("They haven't found the ship yet. We're all quiet here,") Calli sent. ("Do you want some bugs down there for confirmation?")

("Do it.")

In moments, a terrarium of telltales blasted into existence on an LD. Immediately ants poured out of their tunnels and pawed at their glass confines.

("Hive sign confirmed,") Farragut reported.

Donner stared at the shiny black bodies beetling out of the sand. Listened to the eerie noise all around them. Spoke to Farragut, "Your monsters. They are here."

"They're not here quite yet," said Farragut. "That's the point singer—*somewhere* on planet. He's calling the monsters to dinner. (Calli! Break res silence. Gimme a res scan. Get an idea who this creep is singing to. Any swarms in the immediate neighborhood?")

("Initiating scan.") And, quickly, ("Got 'em. Two hundred light-years out.")

("ETA?")

("Five—whoa. Stand by. We have another sighting, closer.")

("Where?")

("Stand by. We've got another hit. Another. They are waking up on all sides. This stellar neighborhood is lousy with dormant swarms. They're not dormant anymore.") She read off multiple plots, converging on the Myriad. ("Nearest swarm so far is one month out.")

The Overmind woke its dormant swarms in proportion to the size of the bait.

"You will drive away these monsters you have summoned," Donner commanded.

Eyes of alien blue told Donner he couldn't. If John Farragut wanted to, if it were Earth itself, he could not. One month was not enough time for *Merrimack* to reach Fort Eisenhower for a refit, reload, reman. With five engines, dwindling projectiles, nine-tenths of a crew, and great holes in her physical hull, the *Mack* could not do battle again.

"Donner, you cannot bring your people here from Origin. You'll all be eaten alive."

"It's too late. I told them to come."

("Oh, for Jesus. Calli, get us out of here. Displace now.")

The look of betrayal on Donner's face branded his memory as he vanished from Arra. He honestly believed he would never forget it.

John Farragut hit the deck barking. Ordered a res message be sent to Earth. Update the Joint Chiefs of our—oh, for Jesus—our status.

Ordered a res message to Fort Ike. Tell 'em we're coming in hot. Give 'em our laundry list.

Ordered displacement of the LEN detainees back to *Woodland Serenity*. Advised the LEN they would have a rescue operation on their hands in one month.

Ordered a computation: Given the transit times between *kzachin*, what was the best time a vessel dispatched from Arra could arrive at the Rim gate at the Myriad's perimeter?

"Best time?" young Jeffrey, manning the tactical station, said. "Best time is through a connecting *kzachin* in the Centro system. If the Arran messenger left Arran space the moment that *Merrimack*'s first image was seen on Arra and didn't stop at Centro, Donner's messenger ship could be closing on the Rim gate now."

"Ping the Rim gate."

The sensor technician executed a resonant sounding of the vicinity surrounding the Rim gate and its connecting *kzachin*. Reported: "No vessels in transit between the *kzachin* connecting Arra to the Rim and the *kzachin* that leads to Origin."

Which was not to say a messenger ship could not pop out of the connecting *kzachin* at any moment, because there was no way of knowing anything about a ship inside a *kzachin*.

Farragut leaned over the stellar plot. "So if the Arran messenger were to come out of that *kzachin* right now," he pointed at the *kzachin* that connected Centro to the edge of Myriad. "How long would it take him to get from there to the Rim gate—the *kzachin* that goes to Origin?"

"That would depend on how fast he's traveling, sir. We haven't seen Myriadian ships do much better than eighty percent c. Eighty percent c gives him a minimum transit time of two hours."

"Then get us to the Rim right now. We're going to head him off."

"We're a day and a half from the Rim, best speed," Calli reminded him. "Unless it took Donner a day and a half to figure out what he was going to say and launch that messenger, or the messenger stopped off at Centro, he'll be coming out of that connecting *kzachin* any time now. We've already lost this race."

"The messenger has *not* reached the Rim gate," Farragut said, like a command. "Get me there first."

* * *

Racing toward the edge of the Myriad took Merrimack within five light-years of the planet Centro. In passing, *Merrimack* launched an SPT boat and a squadron of Swifts in a flying drop. The Marines had orders to proceed to the planet in silent mode and discover whether Centro was showing Hive sign or if the world lay still hidden from the Hive's ravenous eye. The Marines were also charged with repulsing any space traffic which might try to make the local connection to the Rim gate. Though most of the company suspected that Echo Flight had already seen the messenger during early recon sortie.

Steele suggested in parting that if the planet Centro lay dark, it could yet serve in the coming siege. Steele would look for a suitable base while there. But Farragut told him, "One battle at a time, TR. We lose this one, the rest of them won't matter."

"Augustus—" Farragut blew into the torpedo storage bay. "I have to ask you to plug in. I'm going to need precise calculations coming up here, and I can't afford to overlook any variables."

Augustus turned slowly, lowered, and lifted his lids slowly. "If that is a request, the answer is no. How bad do you want it?"

"It's an order," Farragut rephrased. He looked at Augustus, really looked at him only now, taking in his tired, sour expression, the whole of his makeshift quarters—the sword propped, hilt-down, point angled up at midriff height. Farragut's glance shifted uneasily from sword, to Roman, and back. "You look like you're fixing to fall on that."

"Not now. Eventually. However—" Augustus plucked up the sword in disgust. "This is *not* the tool for the job." Tossed it aside. "It ought to be longer and straighter. This is a gorgon slicer."

Farragut became quite troubled. His voice came out more plaintive than he wanted. "But why will the job need doing? Eventually. At all?"

Suicide, the very idea of it, was alien to John Farragut. He could see himself dying by throwing himself between harm and a beloved, but never an act wherein the whole point of the endeavor was to die.

"Later," Augustus dismissed the question, and before Farragut could press it, the captain's link crackled to life on the back of his hand. It was Calli: "Captain! Res-read! We have the Arran messenger. Just appeared from the connecting *kzachin*. Heading toward the Rim gate at seventy percent c."

"ETA?"

"At present rate, the Arran will reach the Rim gate in three hours."

"And *our* ETA?"

"Nine hours."

"If we can't catch it, then shoot it down. Arm a Star Sparrow."

"Aye, sir. Load, sir?"

"A *fast* one."

An Arran courier vessel would not require much punch. A simple collision might take it out. But a Star Sparrow at that speed might just poke a neat hole in the flimsy ship without detonating.

"Can a Star Sparrow make intercept?"

The specialists had been conferring over just that question. "Negative. Even at optimum launch time, which will be coming up in about one hour—we're coming up short."

"Arm the bird. I'm coming up," Farragut sent, clicked off, turned to Augustus. "Here's where I need a patterner. Get me the precise optimum launch time for a T five forty one Star Sparrow. You'll find the exact specs in the data bank."

Augustus would need to factor in the speed of the *Merrimack*, fuel consumption and acceleration of the Star Sparrow, and the gravitational drag of the Myriad's stars. *Merrimack* was passing through the thickest part of the cluster now.

"You can't catch the Arran," Augustus could tell him without plugging in.

"Get the ordnance there in the best possible time. Can you do that?"

"I will give you the optimum launch time, but it won't do the job, so why are you hurrying to an intercept you cannot make?"

"Because if you give up running out a bad hit and the shortstop just happens to overthrow base, and you get tagged out because you didn't hustle, your own mama will boo you out of the park."

"Ever happen to you?"

"Not to *me!*" said Farragut with some pride. "You run on what you hit. You may get tagged out, but you don't ever quit. Unless it's to the enemy, never say die." And, confiscating Augustus' sword, "And that's not what *this* is for either. You don't quit."

"You have no idea what this is about."

"You got that right. So tell me."

"Later."

"It's always *later* with you. But later never comes."

Augustus plugged cables into his neck. His eyes extinguished. His face slackened and his voice went hollow. "Don't talk to me."

Clambering up the ladder to the command deck level, Farragut caught himself playing the *ifs*, looking for every turn he might have played differently, each second he had squandered, all the moments he might have saved so as not to be running against a time deficit toward an impossible intercept.

If he had not paused to return the LEN pirates to their ship.

If he had simply ordered Hamster to blockade the Rim gate rather than have her try to talk to Donner.

If he hadn't paused to restock his oxygen. Could have done that afterward. Now there might not be an afterward.

If. If. Not a question he normally asked. But faced with a real possibility of everything he knew coming to an end, the ifs came in a barrage.

How much of his life would vanish because of any of those wasted moments? All of his own history? His world. His nation. His self. *Was I killed at EtaCas?*

It wasn't his life that flashed before his eyes—it was the people in it. From his too beautiful, slender and stately, Roman-educated XO, Callista Carmel, to his surly chief, who kept the *Mack* a ship to make you proud, to that obnoxious Roman IO who somehow made himself indispensable, to the unattainable Glenn Hamilton, to that big-eared kid Jeffrey at the tac station, to his civilian Nobel Laureate passenger Jose Maria Cordillera who had become more like a father to him than his own father.

All the people on board. He knew them all. Wanted to keep them.

They were his. He would not let them go.

He could not control what was already done, so he threw off the ifs and charged straight ahead.

He exploded into the control room. "Augustus, feed your numbers to fire control."

The tactical specialist reviewed the firing solution. Shook his head. "Best isn't good enough. The Arran ship will be at the Rim gate in one hundred twenty-one minutes. Star Sparrow will get there in one hundred thirty-five minutes. We can't make intercept." He craned round in his seat to add, "Unless you mean to shoot through the *kzachin* and catch him on the other side."

"No. Under no circumstances send anything through the *kzachin.*"

All evidence suggested that no object could overtake any other object inside a *kzachin*, and energy weapons did not exist at all inside the *kzachin.* Once on the far side of the *kzachin*, the race was over.

"Why?" Jeffrey asked. "We still have nineteen minutes on the far side of the gate to make intercept. The *kzachin* spits you out on the other side of the sun and nineteen light-minutes from Origin."

"Don't forget, as soon as that messenger ship is through the gate, it will be transmitting its little heart out. We can't corral electromagnetic waves. Once that messenger gets through the gate, the genie is out of the bottle. And there's no way I'm sending a Star Sparrow back ten billion years to become the instrument of our own destruction. We catch him on *this* side of the gate or — we catch him on this side of the gate."

"Can't, sir."

Not a word to use to John Farragut. He turned to Augustus. "Why aren't we launching the Star Sparrow yet? It accelerates a hell of a lot faster than the *Mack.*"

Augustus remained withdrawn into his data storm, not hearing, or more likely, ignoring the ignorant question.

The tactical specialist responded for him. "These look like real good numbers Colonel Augustus gave us, Captain. The *Mack* is passing through the core of the Myriad. If we launch now, the Star Sparrow would spend all its energy fighting tidal drag and making course corrections. Course corrections will rob its forward capability in a big way, probably crack it up. Sparrow's kind of speed needs a straight-line path. Optimum launch really is in fifty-nine minutes. We're going to be close." Heard how feeble that last part sounded as it came out of his mouth. Wanted that one back.

"Don't give me close. I need it to be there."

The captain paced, paced huge, as if long steps would speed up his thought process. And the idea came: If optimum launch was fifty-nine minutes off, then why not move the launch platform to the optimum launch point faster? "Redline us."

Calli, "We're already redlined, sir."

"Push."

"Pushing, aye . . . and we have a balk." Expected.

The ship would not obey a fatal instruction without asking verification first. *Merrimack* had accelerated to the distortion threshold.

Farragut nodded. "Did we pick up any time at all?"

"Some," said Jeffrey. Augustus had already recalculated the missile launch and fed the numbers to fire control. "Optimum launch in fifty-five minutes. Deficit to intercept, ten minutes."

"Load launch sequence," Farragut ordered. At these speeds, waiting for human orders and acknowledgments to pull the trigger would eat up split seconds that made differences of millions of miles.

"Load launch sequence," Calli relayed. Then aside, for only Farragut to hear, "The target is a manned ship, John."

"I know." And aloud, "Fire Control, confirm that missile course will take the missile *past* the gate and not *into* the gate in case of a failed intercept."

"Fire Control, aye. Bypass confirmed."

Augustus gave a vacant nod, seconding that. His eyes flickered slightly, quickly, as if reading inward lists.

"Launch sequence loaded. Sequence engaged. We're on auto countdown."

The minutes passed in quiet murmurs, updates, requests, and confirmations.

In fifty-five minutes, the missile whined in its launch tube. The ship's energy coiled.

The Star Sparrow sprang with a scathing shriek. The deck heaved. The ship rang behind it.

"Missile away."

Farragut heard a murmured benediction from Jose Maria. Hadn't known he was on the deck. Farragut demanded, "Tracking."

"Tracking, aye. We are on course. Accelerating well. Perfect launch, sir."

Perfect. Ten minutes too late to achieve intercept. "Take us down from redline."

Calli relayed orders to back off *Merrimack*'s tearing speed. She brought the ship about on a course toward Centro to retrieve Steele's Marine detachment from their sortie.

All attention remained on the speeding Star Sparrow. No one on the command deck spoke above a murmur, constantly updating velocities, accelerations, the deficit to intercept. All indicated the attempt to stop the message from reaching Origin was going to fail.

Farragut tried to convince himself that he was wrong, that failure was good. Augustus was right; there was no changing the past. Those innocent beings on board the Arran messenger ship would get away alive. That was the way it would happen. Augustus was never wrong.

Tried to inhale calm.

Augustus was always right.

And still the desperate need to run as if his world depended on it.

Low, professional voices read off dispassionate progress reports of the Star Sparrow, the Arran messenger, the Hive swarms.

Captain Farragut watched the chronometer. Watched the plots creep across the tactical map. The Star Sparrow was dead on with its estimates, accelerating precisely as calculated.

The variable was the target.

"You're making a race of it, John," said Calli. "The Arran messenger has not kept a constant speed."

"What's our deficit now?"

"Six minutes."

"Augustus, coordinate a firing sequence with fire control." At thousands of times the speed of light, the moment of contact would be brief in the idiotic extreme. He could not risk the explosion occurring a million miles after impact. Detonation by resonant command may be instantaneous, but the decision and execution was not.

Augustus nodded vacantly.

Farragut requested an update. Waited for the inevitable deficit.

"Target is twenty minutes from the gate. Missile twenty—Whoa."

Farragut's head snapped to the side. "Explain 'whoa.' "

"Target is decelerating! Five-minute deficit. Four! Three!"

"Control Room! Fire Control here. At this rate of closure we may overshoot."

"I've got you, John," Augustus assured him from the depths of his altered thoughts. "I'm not slowing this bird till we're there. We aren't there yet."

"*Nineteen-second deficit*! Target still decelerating. Eighteen!" Tactical lost his professional monotone. "Arran messenger turning to line up its approach to the *kzachin. Ten-second deficit.* Five seconds. Four."

And a long pause.

"Status," Farragut barked at the long quiet.

"Deficit holding at four seconds. No."

"No, what?"

Tactical made a fist. Opened it. "Five second deficit. Six. Target is reaccelerating." Dashed beaded sweat from under his nose. "We're losing it, sir."

Calli demanded coolly, "ETA of target to the gate?"

"Five minutes."

At two minutes, Farragut asked again, "Deficit to intercept?"

"Ten seconds," Jeffrey reported gloomily.

Farragut hesitated, ordered, "Push the missile."

The resonant control signal went out to the Star Sparrow's guidance system. "Balk," Fire control reported.

"Override balk."

"Overriding, aye— Distortion! Missile flame out! Star Sparrow is running dead."

There would be no more acceleration from the Star Sparrow, no course correction. The missile sped on inertia.

"Deficit at fifteen seconds. Sixteen. Climbing." The young specialist turned his eyes up. "We're not going to make it, sir."

This is it.

Barring miracles, it was all over. Done is done. Farragut

could only watch and wait out the final minute. Wait—for what?

Hopefully, for nothing. John Farragut inhaled deeply. Chest felt full of heavy air, as if a gorgon swarm were sitting on it.

Told himself it would be okay. In fifty-four seconds Augustus would be laughing at him and asking him to explain why he opened fire on an unarmed, manned vessel, and John Farragut would be feeling ridiculous. He never imagined wanting so badly to be ridiculous.

Searched for Jose Maria on deck. Wanted to say to him: Here's to Augustus laughing.

Felt a presence immediately behind him. A touch, a breath on his hair. A kiss on his neck.

And he was angry. A line crossed and never expected. Farragut's hair prickled, face burned. Did not appreciate the gesture, and the timing stunk. Pissed him enough to snap around from the face of the imminent Judgment, and demand, "What was *that?*"

Augustus elled his thumb and forefinger against his opposing palm, flipped a quick word in American Sign: *Later.*

John Farragut felt himself go wide-eyed. Tough to scare, he was suddenly profoundly terrified. *Later never comes.*

He stared into bottomless eyes. Crushing the tremor out of his voice, he commanded quietly, "Now, I think."

Because he sensed Augustus had no intention of *ever* explaining that. For all Augustus' talk of the immutability of time, Farragut got the feeling Augustus did not expect one or both of them to be here thirty seconds from now, and *that* had been an end-of-the-world stunt Augustus need not live with for more than thirty seconds.

His eyes were suddenly not blank at all. Always, when plugged in, Augustus' eyes became vacant hollows, the thoughts racing deep inside. This time they looked back, aware, omniscient. The patterner had taken in all, synthesized all the minutiae, and saw what he had not seen before this moment.

Farragut stared at him. *You just recanted!*

Saw the answer in his eyes.

MUNDI TERMINUM ADPROPINQUANTE. *Now that we are approaching the end of the world, John Farragut.*

Your individual existence is a statistical miracle. We are, each and every one of us, highly improbable, a one-in-a-million event at conception. History turns on a space big enough for angels to dance on. I do stand by inevitability. But inevitability works on a macroscopic scale. Macroscopic events are inevitable. The blizzard will come. But the when, the where, and the unique shape of each snowflake is a function of chaos. One breath out of place, and that one singular snowflake never forms. I mistook us for macroscopic. Intuition is subconscious knowledge, and while logic says changing history is impossible, intuition says there are things beyond my ken; and you are a patterner, John Farragut. You know. You know. And you're right. You are chaos. I won't explain later, because there is no later. There is no earlier. There is no time at all. Simply put, it was miraculous knowing you, and that was good-bye.

So said the eyes. Aloud, Augustus answered with an ironic near smile, "I still think you're an idiot."

But Farragut understood him as clearly as if he'd spoken all of it.

I'm right!

The floor of the world kicked out from under him. This was the end of the world he knew.

Did not want to be right.

He faced forward, terrified now. The countdown fell on cotton ears.

"Arran messenger ten seconds from the gate. Nine. Eight."

There is no later.

"He's accelerating again." The count sped up. "We have four seconds. Three. Two. Messenger at the gate —"

Closed his eyes.

O God, it's done. If it happens, it will be this instant. I won't even know. Either I'm here or I'm not, and I never was.

Breathed.

PART THREE

A Rational Universe

17

B REATHED. "Arran ship is off the screen."
   Still here. Still breathing. Breathing as if he'd been
running. *Slow it down, John.*

Fire Control was requesting instruction regarding the
Star Sparrow. Now bereft of a target, the missile barreled
off hotfoot to nowhere.

Captain Farragut opened his eyes. "Detonate that damn
thing."

"Detonating, aye." Fire Control sent the res signal. "Detonation achieved."

We're still here, thought Farragut, calming down. Feeling
ridiculous, embarrassed by his fear. Time to face his all-
seeing, all-knowing intelligence officer and collect the inevitable told-you-so. He knew those smug black eyes and
superior expression waited behind him. He turned around
to take it.

"Well, Lu. You were right."

Colonel Oh's amygdaloid eyes flickered, annoyed, her
little bird voice brittle. "Told you so."

Lu Oh was a grating, unlovely presence. With her wide,
wide brow, and tiny, pointed chin, her reedy body far too
delicate for that outsized head, her enormous, black, slanted
eyes, Colonel Oh looked like a twentieth-century caricature
of an alien. And John Farragut did believe she would kid-

nap Kentucky farm boys and do diabolical tests upon them. Though the colonel wore the uniform of a Naval Intelligence officer, John Farragut knew in his heart of hearts that Lu Oh was CIA.

Of all the things he had hoped and feared would change when the Arran crossed the *kzachin*, Lu Oh had fallen solidly in the "hope to disappear" list.

But nothing had changed.

Things happen once. They cannot happen any other way. Everything was the same and where he should have felt relief sat instead a soggy sense of disappointment. Everything was the same.

Earth was still at war with Palatine. The Romans were as imperialistic as ever, still claiming the whole of the constellation Sagittarius as their sovereign space.

Marisa Johnson was still President. Farragut had kinda hoped that might have changed. He had not voted for her either time.

John Farragut's sweet wife, Maryann was still dead. His wife's suicide still weighed on him after seven years. *God in heaven, couldn't you have made that change, Sir?*

Unchanged also were the Roman Legions closing implacably on the Myriad to challenge *Merrimack* for the right to flag the three inhabited worlds in the Sagittarian globular cluster.

Merrimack could not flag any of the three planets in the name of the United States, because the sapient beings who had come through that *kzachin* from the distant past had already claimed them. *Merrimack* had claimed them as LEN protectorates.

The messenger's journey through the *kzachin* back ten billion years to tell the people of Origin of aliens and FTL travel had changed absolutely nothing.

I could have used some help here, Farragut silently suggested to God.

Rome wanted the planets. Rome wanted the *kzachin*. And only the *Merrimack* stood in Rome's way. Great as *Merrimack* was, she was no match for two Legions.

Merrimack. His constant. *Merrimack* was still his, unchanged. Farragut was grateful for that.

Also unchanged was his exec, a diamond in a brilliant cut, Calli Carmel.

Calli was demanding of a technician, "Why aren't those two sensor monitors on-line?"

The screen that ought to be showing the plot of all the *kzachin* in the Myriad was vacant of orange plots; and the low-band monitor, which was meant to register gravitational disturbances, showed only blank white.

"Both monitors are functioning normally," the baby-faced tech attending the sensors protested.

"Then where is the Rim gate?" said Calli. "Where are all the rest of the *kzachin*?" She was pretty sure *kzachin* was what the locals called the wormholes that riddled the stellar cluster. "And what the hell is that?"

That was the blank white low-band monitor.

Impatient with young Mr. Emerson's attempts at fine-tuning the instruments, Captain Farragut stalked to the errant monitor, and tuned the low-band screen his way, with the heel of his hand. Didn't fix it.

"Please, sir, don't hit the equipment. It's not broken. The low band is working," the tech labored to explain, making ineffectual efforts to place himself between these ham-handed command officers and his defenseless instruments. "The low band is registering overload. Happened when the messenger ship went through the *kzachin*. These readings are off the scale. That's why the screen is full. There's something big out there."

"Then lower the sensitivity," said Calli. "And get the *kzachin* map back on here."

The tech's ears were red as portside lights. A man that young could not bear for a woman that beautiful to think him inept. "Uhm . . . They're not there. The *kzachin*. The wormholes. The gates. Whatever you call them. I can't get them on the map because they're not—"

A sudden surge overloaded the force field's damper settings. The deck heaved, pitched the command deck over twenty-two degrees, rocking the specialists at their stations, throwing Calli Carmel into the monitors and knocking the little IO, Lu Oh, to the deck.

The inertial dampers quickly restored balance. Captain Farragut took Colonel Lu Oh's tiny hands and helped her to her feet.

"Are you okay, Lu?" Farragut steadied the IO on her frail-looking legs, and guided a long, straight strand of black hair from her praying mantis face. To everyone else he barked: "What was that? I need a report. Mr. Carmel, what's happening to my boat?"

Calli came up blank. Blank didn't look right on her.

"Gentlemen," Lu Oh announced, readjusting the low-band monitor for the technician. "We have a singularity."

With the monitor's sensitivity crushed down to utter numbness, the low band showed distortion lines running through the points where all the *kzachin* used to be. Farragut had seen such an image before, the Myriad looking like a string bag. Only now someone had pulled the strings.

The core of the Myriad was collapsing—almost fast enough to see. The stars smeared inward on the screen.

"Told you the *kzachin* were wormholes," said Lu. "Sending a mass through a wormhole collapses the wormhole. Now whether there's a threshold mass to these wormholes, or reality finally caught up with them with that last transit, there they go."

"What's happening?" said Farragut. "What am I looking at?"

Lu Oh loved being the One with all the answers. But, in her fashion, she fed out only clues, "If nature abhors a vacuum, it loathes, abominates, and despises a naked singularity. This one is clothing itself."

Clothed singularity. John Farragut had heard that term before. Remembered the more popular term. "Black hole."

"As you see, the universe heals itself," said Lu Oh. "Paradoxes are not allowed. And *that* is what happens when someone tries to go back ten billion years and change history. I told you nothing could change—historically speaking. This, of course, is new." She nodded at the forming black hole.

Farragut stared at the stars' blurry streaks. "Are we safe at this distance?"

"We are safe at any distance outside of the event horizon. Actually, the *Merrimack*'s force field might even protect us *inside* the event horizon, but we would be in there forever. Not where I care to retire."

"Not exactly accurate," *Merrimack*'s chief engineer, Kit Kittering, had entered the control room as Lu Oh was speaking. "*Mack*'s engines would have nowhere to vent if we got stuck in a black hole. We'd overheat in no time trying to maintain a distortion field against that. Colonel Oh's retirement would be pretty brief."

And maybe *Merrimack* could withstand the force inside a black hole — briefly — but her smaller craft definitely could not.

SPT 1 was still outboard.

"Centro!" Farragut cried.

"Is doomed," Lu Oh finished for him.

Centro. That arid little outpost closest to the heart of the collapsing Myriad, where 900,000 alien beings lived. Where Captain Farragut had sent Colonel Steele, SPT 1, and a full squadron of Marines on recon.

Farragut shouted into the ship's res com, "Colonel Steele! This is *Merrimack*! Get the hell out of the Centro system. Get all boats back inboard *Merrimack*, and do it *yesterday!*"

Steele acknowledged receiving the order. Reported that he still had Swifts on the planet's surface.

"Evac, TR. The planet is slipping into a black hole."

"Understood. How long have I got?"

Centro's system pulled perilously toward the stellar cluster's dying core. Uncertain, the captain looked to Lu Oh. "How long does he have?"

Lu Oh's hairless brows lifted, dubious. "On the planet's surface? Outside of a distortion field? Not long at all."

"Won't he have nine minutes after the sun dies at least? The light distance of Centro from its sun?"

"Oh," the IO gave a nasty little smile as if the captain had just said something naive, "Light is not the issue. Gravity is. Gravity was once thought to be a force, but it's not. It's a fundamental property of space-time. The tides are stretching the planet and everyone on it apart even now. The tide will tear them apart before they know the light has died."

Calli was on the com before Lu finished her explanation, "Colonel Steele, get your Swifts spaceborne. Evac. Evac. You are out of time."

Steele acknowledged, and *Merrimack* heeled round to make all possible speed to the planet Centro for dust off.

The Swifts of Red Squadron lifted from the planet surface to dock with the orbiting SPT 1, covering it like an infestation of ticks. One dock remained free. Missing was Alpha Three.

Steele snarled over the link, "Flight Sergeant Blue, where the hell are you?"

"Too frogging far from my frogging Swift, sir! But I got an LD here. Get me the frogs out of here."

Steele swore. Growled at the Marine nearest the displacement controls, "Get her."

In the long, long silence in which the Marine struggled to acquire a green line on the displacement chamber and the world continued to crumble below them, Kerry Blue transmitted again, "I'm three klicks from my Swift, okay? I'll *pay* for the frogging Swift! Take it out of my lunch money! Can't you displace me?"

Steele snapped around to the young stud fumbling at the displacement console. "Flight Sergeant Carver, you got a problem there?"

Cowboy Carver beat on the controls. "Something's wrong. The sun's uffed and I can't get a green light on this fubared piece of Ganchar meat." Cowboy kicked the console with his nonregulation snakeskin boot.

Little Reg Monroe, who fancied herself an engineer, elbowed herself in for a look at the displacement readouts. "What's not happening for you, Cowboy?"

"The LD and the collar won't jibe. I can get receiver confirmation on one or the other, but not both at the same frickin' time, and the displacer won't go without three reads!"

"It's the tidal distortion," said Reg. "This ain't normal space. Kerry's head's too far from her feet here to get correspondence."

Cowboy called over the link, "Hey, Blue, crouch!"

But *Merrimack* must have been monitoring the link, because Calli Carmel transmitted: "Do not displace. *Do not* attempt displacement of a human being."

Colonel Steele swore purple maggots.

"We can't leave Kerry behind!" Cowboy declared.

Steele stabbed him with a icy glare. *Only because you say so, jack piss.* Hated that man.

Colonel Steele ordered his squadron back into their Swifts. Once the Marines were secure in their cockpits, Steele dropped the Spit boat's force field and ordered the

Swifts, "Get off me. Return to *Merrimack* best speed, and don't look back."

The Swifts disconnected and shot away.

Merrimack raced to meet them. Received the spent fighters on her flight decks, and hauled them inboard. The fighters had used up all the antimatter in their reservoirs just to drag themselves out of the gravity well.

But the returned squadron was one Swift light. And where was the Spit boat? The com tech could not raise SPT 1 on the com.

"TR?" Captain Farragut tried. "Are you out there?" And to the com tech, "Is he out there?"

"Can't tell, Captain."

Marcander Vincent, at Tactical, answered for him, "Found him, sir. SPT 1 has descended into Centro's atmosphere."

"Oh, hell, he can't," Farragut breathed, reached over the com tech's shoulder to transmit, "Steele, get out of there. Can he hear me? Is he flying that thing, or falling?"

"Flying, sir," said Tactical. "Spit boats glide like rocks. SPT 1 is moving like it's making descent using its distortion field."

Farragut yelled into the caller, "TR, you answer me now or I will have you at my mast when you do get back here!"

The com link opened with a sound like static. There was no such thing as resonant static. The noise was the clattering of debris against SPT 1's force field. "I'm here, Captain."

"Where are you going, TR?"

"Retrieving a soldier separated from her ship."

"The boffins are telling me you have to wear off right now—right now—if you are going to achieve escape velocity. And in case you forgot, we have a Roman Legion moving in here and due within the hour. Wear off. Acknowledge!"

Received nothing but clatter from the com.

"You are receiving me, TR! Get up here now." Farragut slapped off the com and stalked away with a loud oath.

Colonel Oh presented the navigator with an optimum course to get *Merrimack* clear of the rapidly forming accretion disk and to use the black hole to cloak the battleship's movement from the approaching Legion.

But instead of ordering *Merrimack* out of the Myriad, Farragut told his exec: "Take us to Centro."

Calli relayed orders to navigation. Lu Oh squawked as the helm steered them straight toward a force that could suck *Merrimack* through the eye of a number six needle.

Kerry Blue ran for her Swift. Three klicks away. She could do that. Piece of cake. She could run three klicks carrying a twenty-five-kaygee field pack.

But she felt as if she were wearing fifty-kaygee shoes, and someone was pulling her head up on a noose. The sky—the sky was not. A lurid dark bruise of a storm sky. Purple light lanced off coagulated clouds. The ground poked up and hit her. Her head banged from within. She wanted to pull her own skin off, open her skull, and let her brain out.

She ran on, swearing. *They left me. They left me.* She was going to reach her Swift, by hell, make it back to the *Mack* and piss on Colonel Steele for leaving her here. Had to stay angry, else she would cry.

Semper fi. Oh, yeah, sure, *semper* frogging *fi.* That must be for somebody else. Nobody was *fi* to Kerry Blue. Why wouldn't Steele displace her? She wasn't the first Marine to lose a Swift.

Okay, so he was making her run to her Swift. She would run to her Swift. And just you see where I park it, *sir!*

It had to be just over the next hill. Hill? She didn't remember a hill. She mounted the crest on all fours, clawing at the spongy weeds to pull herself up, gasping, throat raw. Squinted through the gritty wind, water spray, and tears. Heart dropped through the bedrock.

She had taken a wrong turn.

She was sure she had been running toward her Swift, but here she had ended up on the waterfront somehow. *Shit.* She swayed on the thundering ground, shaking. Savage voice within ordered: *Get up.*

Never say die. That's what Captain Farragut always said. Unless it's to the enemy, never say die. *Get up and get to your damned Swift, Marine!*

Which way was her Swift? She thought she'd left it at the end of this road. Wrong road. But there were no other roads.

Did not know where the hell she could be.

A long lightning flash. Froze a picture of hard blue clarity. The cracked road led into the jagged water. And in a trough between frozen gray waves: the peak of a silver fin blazoned red, white, and blue.

Her Swift. Washing away.

"No!" she tried to scream. Got out only a squeak.

The sky roared. A tearing sand wind pulled up the ground. A shadow fell across her with heat, thunder, and noise. She thought a house was falling on her.

The blocky structure fell hard, close, a scant five-meter miss. A hiss of air. A slash of light in the outline of a hatchway.

SPT 1 was here.

A gangway slapped down with a thunder crack.

Kerry pulled herself up, stagger-ran up the ramp, dove through the circle of light.

"Cowboy!" she cried, rolling on the deck under cool lights. He had come for her. She should have known Cowboy would come back for her. Steele would have his hide on the bulkhead for this.

The hatch's shutting cuffed her eardrums. The activation of the ship's distortion field brought instant relief, took the rack from her limbs, the bomb from her skull. Rejoined body to soul. She blinked gritty tears from her eyes to find her savior in the pilot's seat.

Not Cowboy.

"Get your ass off the deck, and man the overrides, Marine."

"Sir!"

Would it *kill* that man ever to use a normal tone of voice to her? It was always a snarl or a bark like she was a galactic fu. So she wondered bitterly why Steele wanted the likes of oh-so-stupid *her* at his right, then realized it was because there was absolutely no one else aboard.

Everyone else had gone ahead. It was she and Steele and no one else.

Kerry scrambled for the copilot's chair. Couldn't see anything out the front viewport but storming mud. The monitors looked worse.

The singularity. You couldn't see *it* exactly. You saw what it consumed—whirling gases catching fire as they rushed and collided at speeds of millions of klicks per hour, all swirling into the vast void.

Kerry wrenched her attention away from the screens to her flight controls. Her instruments were telling that the power to achieve escape velocity from this little berg of a planetoid was a magnitude normally reserved for an FTL jump. Couldn't be right.

She stole a glance to the man at her side. Colonel Steele breathed like a bull in a fight, his square jaw clenched.

The engine whined. The Spit boat waddled aloft. Climbed like a slug. A view out the port showed Kerry the buck and wallow that the force field would not let her feel. Heard a quiet grunt at her side. Stole another look.

The muscles in Steele's arms stood out, tensed hard as stone, as if he were physically pulling the boat up.

"Are we going to make it, sir?"

"They tell me no." Steele slapped the monitors off to conserve power, brought the life systems down to nominal, channeling all available power to the distortion field and the thrusters.

The blocky spacecraft tore clear of the atmosphere—or else the atmosphere ripped away from the Spit boat. Down below, the planet fell away; up above, the stars soared away. Kerry shut her eyes against the conflicting images. Opened her eyes to focus on the instruments. Always trust your instruments.

Her instruments said the Spit boat was not climbing. The spacecraft peaked, stalled. Hung on a breath—

Steele's face was inexpressive as granite, those ice-chip eyes determinedly cold, his big hands steady. But a sweat sheen broke on his white skin. Kerry was not sure what that meant. She never could tell what that man was thinking or feeling.

Red lines striped Kerry's board; the Spit boat's force field had maxed. Velocity showed negative. They were slipping back toward the singularity.

"Punch overrides," Steele commanded, and Kerry batted down the switches.

"Balk," she reported, reading the red lights. The Spit boat would not let her push the engines without compromising the distortion field.

The engine screamed. Distortion field status monitor flickered red. One or the other had to give. "Kill thrusters!" Steele shouted.

Kerry obeyed, quickly, unquestioningly. Would have jumped off a cliff if he told her to. Probably just had.

With the thrusters shut down, engine readings fell briefly

back to safe levels, but soon recommenced a climb toward the redlines.

The river of fire about them darkened, thickened, carrying the Spit boat along with it into a well of infinite depth and unimaginable density. The crash and scrape and searing rain grew loud as the distortion field monitors all flickered red. Kerry looked to the colonel. "What now?"

Those pale blue eyes met hers. She couldn't remember him ever looking into her eyes. He always glared straight over her head, as if there was nothing in her face worth looking at. He had really amazing eyes. But she found no rescue there. All he had to offer was not to let her die alone.

He answered, *"Semper fi."*

"SPT 1 sighted," Tactical reported. "He's spaceborne!"

"Yippee yo kay yay! Punch it, Kemo Sabe!" That was Cowboy. You could hear him yell from two levels down.

But SPT 1 had not achieved escape velocity so much as the planet Centro had been torn from under it.

The event horizon seemed to grow and approach, though truth was space was shrinking and the SPT boat was going into the singularity, *Merrimack* not far behind it.

Captain Farragut beheld the maelstrom through the viewports and the images on the monitors of an all consuming blackness, blotting out space and time. It looked like the end of the world.

God, who created such an unholy holocaust? It eats. It eats everything.

"He's not going to make it," Calli advised. "His field is losing integrity."

Farragut turned to the sensor technician. "Do we have a res fix on him?"

"Sure do, sir. Not precise enough to displace him."

"Then *hook* him!"

Calli barked orders to engineering. *Merrimack* heaved out a distortion field extension in the shape of a frog tongue to snag and surround the failing craft.

"Hook away," Tactical reported. "And . . . Got him!"

As the event horizon swallowed SPT 1.

Captain Farragut had long since become accustomed to not *seeing* anything in normal space; still, he counted on having a visual image provided by the sensors. The monitors did not show the Spit boat. They showed a monstrous wall of oblivion, a titanic cascade of flaming gases falling into it and vanishing. *Merrimack*'s own distortion field showed on the screen like a vitreous thread in the inferno, extending for kilometers, breaking off at the maw of the bottomless pit.

"Engineering! Control Room. Status! Do we have him?"

"Got him, Mr. Carmel!" Engineering reported over the com. "Hook holding."

To the sensor tech, "Can you get a reading beyond the event horizon?"

"Not exactly, sir. We can read inside our own distortion field. We can tell the Spit boat's in there. Problem is we can't use our exterior sensor array to read within our own field. But we got him. Can't tell you too much else about him, but we got him."

"Then get us the hell out of here," said Farragut.

His XO, the navigator, tactical, chief engineer, and the helm were already conferring over escape coordinates. Conferring too long.

"Mr. Carmel, why aren't we moving?"

Calli's brown eyes lifted in a brief, dire glance, then back to the helm's console, muttering over the readouts.

Merrimack maintained its distance from the event horizon, but that meager distance was not increasing. The thing out there was feeding, sucking in dust, with a horrific hiss and flash. And under it all, *Merrimack*'s six engines bellowed, the great ship straining at the edge of all her strength.

It fell to Calli to report, "Can't, sir. We can maintain the integrity of our force field and our hook, and that's a max. We cannot escape. We've got nothing else to give."

Farragut turned to the viewport, astonished. Insulted.

That? That is going to defeat me?

He could not accept it. Said to his XO, "A black hole by definition is where escape velocity exceeds the speed of light. We regularly travel a thousand times that. What is the holdup?"

"It's not the velocity, John. It's the acceleration that's always been the trick to FTL. We travel faster than light, but we never actually travel *at* light speed. Moving a mass at light speed takes infinite force, and that is exactly what it's going to take to drag the Spit boat through the event horizon."

"Break the hook off now," said Colonel Oh. Might've been advice, but it came out a command. "Break off, or we'll be sucked in with it."

Merrimack maintained, steadfast within the torrent of matter raging into the abyss. The atomized debris spilling round the ship might have been the planet Centro with its 900,000 lives. Dead long before they went in, but Lord Almighty, 900,000 of them.

"Did you hear me, Captain?" Lu cried over the swelling din. "Break off!"

"Not without my men."

"You've already lost them! They're inside the singularity!"

Farragut consulted the specialists at the tactical station. "Can Steele possibly be alive in there?"

"Not exactly charted territory, sir," Mr. Vincent answered apologetically. Oldest man on deck. Forty-two. Unflinching. "Theory says the laws of physics break down inside a singularity, but the colonel is not exactly in the singularity. He's inside the *Mack's* distortion field."

"But it's going to take infinite power to pull him *out* of it," said Colonel Oh. "So here you sit like the boy with his fist stuck in the candy jar. The little idiot can't figure out that the only way to get his hand out of the jar is to let go of the candy. Let go of the candy, sir, or we'll die in this jar!"

"We're not talking about candy, Mr. Oh," said Captain Farragut.

"No. No, we're not. We're talking about a corpse! Let go!"

Merrimack's six engines groaned. Farragut addressed the personnel on his command deck, "Someone—someone besides Colonel Oh—plot me the shape of this monstrosity."

The suns at the core of the Myriad had been rotating when they collapsed into the singularity, dragging bent space-time around them, spinning. The event horizon had to describe a moving torus.

"Compute any point that might be more vulnerable to escape than any other point. Black holes give off X rays. Get us out the way the X rays are getting out."

"Aye, *sir!*" Calli responded for everyone, her vehemence directed toward the spindly CIA spook.

"Your Marines are dead," said Lu.

Farragut faced her. Made her look him right in the eyes. "Do you *know* that, Colonel, or is that an opinion?"

"It is obvious," said Lu, staring back, unwavering.

"Not to me," said Farragut.

Mr. Vincent at the tactical station sang out. "We have company. Roman point is on the grid."

Farragut moved to the tactical station, looked over Vincent's shoulder to survey the monitors. "What is he?"

"Striker," Mr. Vincent answered. Small craft. Wickedly fast. Toting some heavy weaponry. "Approaching on the eights at threshold velocity."

Lu Oh vibrated reedy indignation. "This is an inappropriate risk to take to recover a pair of corpses, Captain Farragut. The singularity is as good a grave as any. Let go."

"Striker in range," said Mr. Vincent.

Calli called Fire Control. "Icky, what can you give me?"

"Nothing, sir. We have no weapons. We can't breach the distortion field without breaking up. Gunports are capped fast and barrels secured inboard. We keep sealed or we are *string.*"

"Do we have beam weapons?"

"Not really, sir. Moment they leave the barrels, they'll torque round the event horizon. Might even shoot ourselves in the foot."

Tactical: "Roman showing gunports."

Com: "Roman signaling. Says he's ready to accept our surrender."

"Tell him to call back later," Farragut told the com. "Tell him I'm busy."

"Those words, sir?"

"Sure. Fine."

Lu cried, "Cut hook and hit him!"

None of the command deck officers moved without a word from the captain or the exec, so John Farragut did not bother to countermand Colonel Oh.

"Sir!" Lu insisted—and crouched down at the sound of the Roman Striker rushing past. You could actually hear him, so close he came, so thick were the gases surrounding the ship.

The Striker shot by on a near tangent, swirling the dying gases behind it.

An explosion, muffled, reverberated low through the decks.

"Report!" Farragut demanded. "What was that?"

"Distortion bomb," said Mr. Vincent.

"Penetrate our field?"

"Apparently not."

Without calibrating the distortion precisely to *Merrimack*'s ever-shifting phases, penetration was a trillion-to-one chance. But that shot was not meant to penetrate. "Target finder," Vincent clarified. "He took a sounding. He's got a map of our field now. Depth. Orientation. Right now he's studying it to find if we're open to a fatal blow."

"Are we?"

"Yes, sir," Mr. Vincent said, as Mr. Emerson at the sensors nodded emphatic agreement. "Singularity has pulled us thin fore and aft. A hit anywhere in the stern takes us right out."

"Then figure out how to reel in my Spit boat before this Striker shoots me in the ass."

"Let go of SPT 1," Lu answered.

"Not an option."

"I remind the captain it is not just your ass about to be shot. It's our collective ass."

Below the rising crash and thunder, the helm could be heard muttering into his board, "Thank you, Colonel. I am sure he forgot that."

Farragut spoke over him, "Did someone pull the colors off that Striker?"

"Red and black," Emerson consulted the sensors. "And his sail is peppered with kill badges."

"Red and black. What gens is that?"

Before Emerson could look it up, Calli answered directly, "Flavian."

Tactical: "Roman turning wide."

"Flavian," Farragut echoed. "Is that Republican or Imperialist? Where do the Flavians stand on the Peace?"

"Imperial," said Calli. "Right, honor, and the glory of Rome. Hawk to the bone."

"Good," said Farragut.

"Oh, hell," said Lu.

Tactical: "Striker lining up a kill run." Mr. Vincent turned from his board, earnest. "Sir. We can take this guy. Awaiting your orders."

"You have my orders."

Vincent turned back to his console, scarlet flush creeping back to his distant hairline.

"Steele is dead!" Lu shouted, fists clenched.

Again: "Do you *know* this, Lu?" Farragut asked quietly, right in the enormous eyes, not an argument, a solemn question.

"Yes!"

At the same time, the com tech sang out, "Res message on our harmonic." And he put it on the speaker:

"Merrimack. Merrimack. Merrimack. This is SPT 1. Do you read?"

Calli stepped out of the way of the captain's lunge for the res caller. "TR! *Status!*"

"SPT 1 here. We are intact and shouldn't be. I can't tell what's holding us together. I think we're inside the black hole. Instruments read garbage."

Unmanned probes sent into black holes gave back the same result. The old saying remained true—black holes have no hair.

"I shut down the thrusters," Steele continued. "I have power enough now to bring the thrusters back on-line, but I don't know which way to fly. Advise."

"I've got you, TR. Do NOT activate your thrusters. You are inside *Merrimack*'s field."

"And sucking us down with you."

"Colonel Oh, shut up," Calli ordered.

Colonel Oh ignored her. "Captain, the Roman *has* us! We are sitting ducks!"

"Not much sport in it, is there?" Farragut murmured.

Lu wailed heavenward. "Oh, God. We are acting according to John Farragut's sense of fair play against a goddamn Roman point man with a high score and an easy shot—"

Tactical: "Here he comes."

Calli advised, very low and personal, "John, if you're counting on the Roman's sense of honor not to shoot you in the back, I should tell you that honor regularly only extends to other Romans. It's dangerous to second-guess the Wolf Star."

Farragut nodded. Murmured back, "I know that wolves kill what runs."

"Yes, sir." Calli assumed a posture of cool readiness, hands clasped behind her back, head imperially high.

Tactical: "Striker charging up his disrupters!"

Exec: "Thank you, Mr. Vincent."

Flashes from the Striker's ports drew red, severely arcing lines through the storming gases around *Merrimack,* bounced off her field.

Tactical: "Tracers! Dead on."

Lu shrieking: "*Let go of the Spit!*"

Tactical: "Roman firing."

18

D ID NOT HEAR the shot. Disrupters were point specific. Whether they hit or missed, you never heard the shot.

Did feel the deck heave.

He missed!

The Striker's shot must have hit the singularity, because the black hole's tidal warp dipped and undulated. And, in the trough in the event horizon, SPT 1 appeared—

And instantly catapulted free to tumble end over end with *Merrimack* like a lopsided bolo, with a force that might have jumped them FTL were they in normal space.

"We're loose!"

The stars showed through the viewport as solid lines as the ship whirled round and round, the kind of spin that would splatter all hands through the bulks if not for *Merrimack*'s force field.

"Stabilize ship," Calli ordered.

Helm: "Stabilizing, aye."

Tactical: "Striker tracking us."

"Open fire on Striker," said Farragut. "Shoot from the hip."

"Without acquiring target?" Lu was appalled. "The singularity will foul any attempt—"

Calli: "Fire Control. Full broadside at the Striker. Fire. Fire now."

The ship's power coiled. You felt it coming up through the deck. The battleship unleashed a storm like a solar flare in the vague direction of the Roman point.

Tactical: "Clean miss."

"Line up another round," Farragut ordered.

"Striker wearing off."

Lu Oh scoffed. "You don't get a second shot! You weren't even close! Like he's going to wait around with *Merrimack* at full strength! What an e-jack!"

"Colonel Oh, remove yourself from the control room," Captain Farragut said evenly.

"Fine." Colonel Oh jerked off her headset. "Next time you feel the need to play chicken with a Roman, let me out of the car."

Farragut murmured after her, "You break the jar."

Calli cocked her head the better to hear. "Sir?"

"Talkin' to myself."

A crew of erks locked down SPT 1 upon the boat's docking in *Merrimack*'s port wing.

Cowboy's whoop rang off the metal bulks, his bootfalls clanging on the deck grates with his charge to greet the Spit's return.

Kerry Blue tottered down the ramp like a fragile drunk.

"Ho! Doll!" Cowboy bowled her off her feet into his arms. "Sheeps, I thought you bought the bowling alley back there!" Cowboy stuck a yard of tongue down her throat, then broke off to crow, "You should have *seen* your rescue! Captain did *balls* with the Roman point! He's a wild man! And you!" over Kerry's head to the spit boat's hatchway. "Old Man! And they call *me* cowboy! You are crazed! Fly right into a black hole! You're the Man of Steel for sure!" Winked at Kerry, "At least part of him is!" He grabbed his own part in case anyone missed the reference.

Steele spoke with arctic reserve. "Flight Sergeant Carver. Last I was aware, we had a Roman Legion converging on this position. Has that situation changed?"

"No, sir. They're coming."

"*Then get back to your station.*"

Cowboy gave Kerry a wink and pinch on the ass in parting.

"Captain on deck!"

Steele snapped to along with everyone else.

Farragut waved down the salutes. The maintenance crew returned to their work on the Spit boat. Kerry Blue slumped from attention.

"Welcome aboard, Flight Sergeant Blue," said Farragut with some irony, but mostly it was a real welcome.

"Thank you, sir," Kerry said, breathless.

"And you." The captain gave Steele an unconvincing scowl. He did not finish. The rest could be said later.

"Situation?" Steele requested.

"We're about to get lousy with Romans. I set your Wing to back up the Battery. I'm not launching anybody with *that* out there."

"Yes, sir." Steele was in no mood to take on the black hole ever again.

"You two get your butts to sick bay," Farragut dismissed Steele and Blue.

"Sir," Steele stiffened, at attention. "Permission to obey that order after we take care of the Romans."

Farragut looked at both of them critically. Looked pretty good for having been crushed by infinite gravity. "If you know you're up to it, I can use you."

Steele immediately sent Kerry Blue to join the gunners. Then he said to the captain, "Thank you, sir. How are we going to play this?"

Farragut shook his head. "Let's see what the Romans throw at us before we swing."

"Hey, *chica linda*, I saved a place for you." Carly patted the seat next to her as Kerry ducked into her gun turret. "What's it like inside a black hole?"

Kerry hunkered down next to her gun. "For something that's supposed to have no hair, it was hairy."

"Glad you could join us," Reg muttered. Not like Reg to gush, but she sounded actually angry. "You got *any* idea what went on in this barge to get you back?"

"Not really," Kerry said uneasily. She was getting terrible inklings.

Carly and Reg told her.

"Shit." No wonder Reg was mad. Nobody risked that much for a girl they called the welcome mat. Farragut must have done it for Colonel Steele.

But then, who had Colonel Steele put it all on the line for?

"I feel like Lois Lane," Kerry said shakily.

And funny, now that she thought of it, the man who had come flying to her rescue, flouting orders, had not been Cowboy.

Man of Steel, Cowboy had called him. Colonel Steele as her Superman. Right.

"You are lobster red, soldier girl. You okay?"

"Yeah." Let go of thoughts so insanely unbelievable they pushed themselves away. "Yeah." Kerry shoved nonexistent bangs from her brow. "I need a target. Where's the frogging Romans?"

Orders came over the loud com for all hands to stand down from battle stations. Target was withdrawing from the system.

Kerry slapped her gun, rising. "Aw nuts!" She was in the mood to shoot something. "Frogging Romans."

"Hey, if you want frogging, I'm here for you, Kerry."

Kerry shrugged off the heavy ape arm that draped across her shoulders. "Shut up, Dak."

Merrimack remained on low alert, monitoring both of the Roman Legions' retreat, in case it turned out to be a ruse.

But the battleground had changed. There was nothing here anymore that Palatine wanted, and a lot that it didn't. Farragut did not expect the Romans to challenge him for the Myriad again. This earth was pretty well scorched.

"Captain!" the com tech reported, startled. "There's a sleeper message in your cache."

"From who?"

"It's a res message—untraceable. And it's not signed. But it's in Latin."

All hands in the control room paused at their stations and fell silent.

Farragut said at last, "Well, let's have it."

"It's in Latin," the tech repeated, unable to comply and rather proud of it. He printed off the message and surrendered it to the captain.

"So what's this say—whose Latin is better than mine." Farragut passed the printout to Calli.

Calli translated aloud, "'Next time, when I have a clear

shot at something other than your back, prepare to yield to Rome as my prize of honor, or else die for the glory of the Roman Empire.' " She handed the printout back. " Standard Imperial bullshit."

"That's from the Striker!" someone whispered.

And Farragut shouted as if he could make himself heard through the hull across the lengthening light-years that lay between his ship and the Striker. "I'll be waiting for you, asshole!" He turned sheepishly to Calli, with a shrug of his big shoulders. "Standard U.S. bullshit. He let us go."

The crew on the command deck bridled at that suggestion, except for Calli, who said, "No, sir. He let *you* go. That message is talking to a singular you. There's a difference in Latin."

"Sirs?" the young sensor tech broke in, mystified. "Wasn't that a *miss?*"

"He didn't miss," said Farragut. "He was perfect."

And Calli countered the tech's question with another question, "What are the odds of a miss that close accidentally being at the precise angle, depth, and strength to disturb the event horizon at the exact location which would free our SPT boat?"

"It was a million-to-one shot—" Mr. Emerson started, broke off as he heard what he was saying. Asked incredulously, "He can do that on purpose?"

Calli turned back to the captain. "That was a patterner, John."

"A what?"

"An augmented man. I've never actually seen one, and Rome swears they don't exist. A patterner is a kind of Frankenstein monster/secret weapon/cyborg kind of man. Admitting the existence of patterners would be admitting that Rome is playing with brain experiments on live subjects."

"Violates the Cygnus Convention," said Farragut. "Not to mention any Earthly sense of decency."

Calli gave a sideways nod, allowing the truth of what he said. "Palatine denies it here to hell, but patterners have to exist because that had to be one. It was an inhuman shot. It was too perfect to be accident and too complicated and unique a task to ask of a targeting computer without preprogramming for these bizarre conditions."

Farragut gazed out the port as if he could see which way

the Striker had gone. "I wonder how he's going to explain this back at Palatine. Letting a battleship go. Not just letting us go—he *sprang* the *Merri*-Mother-of-God-*Mack* from a black hole. I hope they don't crucify him."

"Don't worry about him," said Calli. "The record shows he fired on *Merrimack*, and *Merrimack* returned fire. Even if Imperial Command sees through that charade, they'll reprimand him for failure to deliver a victory and that will be the end of it. The Empire understands standard bullshit. It's a Roman invention."

Merrimack returned to the F8 system within the Myriad. The doomed planet Arra hung in a tranquil sea of stars, its clouds reflecting brilliant white into space. To look at the starry, starry sky you would have no idea what had just happened. How to tell the Arrans their world would be dead in less than ten years? The distorted orbit would kill most of the planet's life before the neutrino barrage arrived to blast whatever survived the wintry hell.

The stars looked the same in the Arran sky. Captain Farragut did not know how to make the Arrans understand that quite of few of those stars were gone.

He supposed the Arrans would get an inkling once messages from Rea and Centro stopped coming, and when their interplanetary shuttles discovered the *kzachin* entirely missing. But they might just as easily conclude *Merrimack* was responsible for that breakdown.

"If only we could communicate better," Farragut mourned. "If we had had time to decode their language. Maybe we could have made the Arran leader understand he must not go through the Rim gate. I could have stopped him. Damn the language barrier."

And because of it, 900,000 intelligent beings and an entire ecosphere was gone. Just like that. Thousands of unique life-forms native to the planet Centro, extinct.

Nine hundred thousand dead. A number too big to absorb. Beings he had never met. Without faces, without names, they became a blank, hideous statistic, with numbing power. The mind's defensive inability to take in numbers that large when spoken in the same breath as "dead" kept him from wrapping his mind around it. Captain Farragut could scarcely get his arms round his own eighty-one dead.

"I could have done something. If I could have talked to the Arrans, this would all be different."

No need to communicate the danger to the Romans. A long-range res scan confirmed all Roman vessels exiting the Myriad, in a tearing hurry to cede the poisoned ground to Earth. In abandoning the field, Palatine had just saddled *Merrimack* with thirty million refugees. The planet Arra would need evacuating. And perhaps in more dire need, three million Reans—their colony remote, cut off from their government, from supplies, from communication—the Reans faced shortages, famine, anarchy.

Evacuation was further hampered in that the xenos were having trouble identifying whom to contact on Arra and Rea to organize such an operation.

"I thought you said the whole Myriad had one autocrat," Farragut confronted Dr. Patrick Hamilton, who had managed what communication they had with the inhabitants of the Myriad.

Dr. Hamilton explained with much mumbling and throat-clearing, "Well, Captain, they may have had. But actually, it seems the Arrans have broken down into a sort of, well, civil war."

"Oh, for—!" Farragut rounded on the commander of his half brigade of Marines. "Finish it for them, TR!"

Captain Farragut stalked down the corridor, slapped a bulkhead. Felt its reliable solidity under his palm. Thumped it again, fondly.

"I should have been able to do something."

He'd thought he was alone, thought he'd been talking to himself, but received an unwelcome answer behind him.

"I shouldn't worry about it," the little bird woman, Lu Oh, sauntered softly up the corridor. "So beings who should have been dead ten billion years ago manage to implode their future colonies. If we fail to save them from self-destruction, then whose fault is that? And since they destroyed the wormholes, we can be thankful that they kept that secret from falling into Roman hands."

Farragut gave a weak, unhappy smile. "Well, Colonel Oh, that's one way to look at it."

All those life-forms, and a wealth of knowledge, lost, perhaps eradicated entirely. Gone as if they'd never been.

The link to an ancient world—perhaps the first sentient world in the universe, gone. Farragut could not even imagine what had been lost here.

And Lu, brave and strong when she was in a soft place, was quite happy with the loss as long as Rome lost it, too.

Lu had strolled to a viewport, open to the spangled heavens. "Craps," she said. "Thought we found a secret mode of FTL travel and got instead just another globular cluster with a black hole in the middle of it."

"Another?" Farragut did a double take. "There are *others?*"

"Yes. Globular cluster M 15 has a black hole at its heart. NGC 6624 has one. NGC 6441 has one—"

Farragut broke off her catalog of imploding globular clusters: "How many?"

"Twelve," said Lu. "The Myriad makes twelve."

"Really?" He joined her at the viewport to gaze at the stars. "What caused the other eleven?"

Kerry Blue's patrol displaced up from planetside after a double watch of peacekeeping duty. Double shifts beat the holy hell out of being poked, prodded, and studied by xenos for aftereffects from being inside a black hole. Would have been triple shifts, but Colonel Steele wasn't letting his people sleep on Arra for fear of hostage-taking, so for eight hours Kerry got to return to a civilized, climate-controlled place, where people understood her when she told them to stick it. She went in search of Cowboy.

She found him with a cigar clenched between his teeth, passing out boxes of more. With the lifting of res silence there had been a mail call. Seems Cowboy had received some news.

Someone shoved one of the brown, smelly rolls of weed at Kerry Blue. "It's a boy."

"Him?" she pointed the cigar at Cowboy. "By who?"

Kerry and Cowboy hadn't been together but a few months, and Kerry didn't waste jealousy on yesterday's news. Had to be some past-tense bimbo on the squadron's last R&R on Earth. Kerry bit off the end of the cigar, spat. "So who is the little mother?"

"His wife."

The voice went on talking at her, vital statistics, pounds,

inches, name—he'd named him Cowboy—as Kerry turned to ash.

Colonel Steele, still wearing the mud and soot from the field, gave his report to Captain Farragut. The populace had been burning the capital, with no idea they were scrapping over carrion. And Steele was ready to leave them to it.

"I'm not," said Farragut.

Steele admitted soberly, "Neither am I." He hated police actions. Preferred killing the enemy to trying to quell unruly civilians. Was no good at it. He hated giving the captain a bad report. Hated failing him—and right after disobeying his direct order.

Farragut hadn't spoken again of a captain's mast. Steele felt it hanging in the room, unspoken, unseen, but definitely there, like his own reek.

"Permission to ask a question, Captain."

"TR, you don't have to ask permission to ask me anything."

Yes, he did. TR Steele used to be a boot. He would never lose his respect for authority. Would never, no matter how many times invited, ever call the captain John.

Steele spoke stiffly. "I heard what you and the *Mack* went through to get us out of the black hole. I'm not saying I'm not grateful to be alive, Captain—I *am*—but, was I worth it?"

"Didn't do it for you, TR."

"I'm glad to hear it." Steele did not want that burden of debt on him. The ship, all its officers, his two companies of Marines—they had all been on the line. He never wanted his Marines to die on his account. The reverse was acceptable, but those boys and girls weren't here to defend TR Steele.

"It was for Rome," said Farragut.

"*Rome?*" Steele spat that word out of his mouth like it was shit.

"They think we're weak. If we can't stare down the Romans and not blink when the stakes are big, we'll never get 'em to the bargaining table. I had to show Palatine this is how we do it in the U.S.A.—" He broke off, squinted up at the vent. "Who is *howling*?"

* * *

Kerry Blue shredded Cowboy's pod, the sheets, the pillow, his clothes, his pictures, screaming with every tear.

Cowboy arrived on the scene at a swagger, shirt open to the dimple of his navel in his flat, hard abdomen.

His cigar dropped from between his teeth. "Ho! Blue!"

Kerry spun on him. "You lying, cheating, rat *bastard!*"

She might have shredded him, too, but suddenly she was suspended off her feet, flailing at air.

She stopped struggling when she realized who had her. The braid on the cuff, the breadth of the arms, the hardness of the torso at her back froze her.

"Cheese and rice, Kerry Blue! Are you *insane?*" Cowboy stalked toward her.

"Back off, soldier!" Steele's thunder battered Kerry's eardrum, and he dropped her, hard.

Steele's blue-eyed glare swept over the wreckage and returned to Kerry Blue. "Explain yourself, Flight Sergeant."

"Yeah, explain yourself, dick breath!"

"Shut up, Carver!" Steele roared. And again: "Flight Sergeant Blue."

Kerry shrieked, tears in her eyes, her nose thick. She'd been crying for a while. "He's *married!*"

And today is Tuesday. What was her point? She didn't know Cowboy was married? She *cared?* "And that means something to you?" Steele argued, baffled.

"What do you think I *am?*" she keened.

"Easy," Steele shot back.

"No shit, sir," Kerry admitted. Declared, "I am *not* an adulteress."

Tough to keep from laughing. The little tramp had morals. Steele's spirits lifted, stupidly.

"You're just an old-fashioned girl, aren't you, Blue?"

He saw hurt surprise in her eyes. That little lower lip quivered anger. Steele had to get her the hell off this deck before he saluted her.

With the blackest of scowls Colonel Steele posted Kerry Blue down to the underbelly of the ship to stand guard over serious nothing. He dispersed the gaggle of Marines come to gawk at the remains of Cowboy's spacely belongings.

And to Cowboy, "This pod is a sty, Marine. Clean up your mess." Then blotted Cowboy's record for protesting the order. Felt good doing that. TR Steele could not remember ever despising anyone more in his life, and might have considered murdering Cowboy Carver, if Steele were not so sure the jack stud was going to die young. Not that Steele believed in clairvoyance. He simply knew it was going to happen.

Some things were just inevitable.

WOLF STAR

To Jim, of course.

PART ONE

Scorpion Sting

1

"OCCULTATION, NINE BY TWENTY-FIVE by eighty-eight,"
the tech at the sensor station sang out. "Vector
twelve. Velocity five c."

Which brought the command deck to a coffee-spilling
scramble at stations for confirmation. A bogey. An FTL bogey.

Lieutenant Glenn Hamilton was Officer of the Watch
for the middle watch. She instantly ordered, "Go dark."

Dark mode locked down the battleship's gunports, took
the force field to complete opacity, and adjusted the deflectors round the engines to mask the ship's hot stern from the
bogey.

In moments came the report from the systems specialist,
"We are dark, sir."

Glenn Hamilton gave a single small nod, to herself more
than anyone, and ordered, "Sound general quarters, dark
mode." Then she opened her direct com. Before she could
speak his name, Captain Farragut's voice sounded from the
open com, "Hamster, what are you doing to my boat?"

"Captain, we have company," Glenn answered. "FTL
bogey at fifty-nine light-seconds. Looks like we saw him
first."

Them! the tactical specialist loud-whispered a correction at her. "It's a *them*!"

"Them," Hamster amended her report to the captain. "We have multiple bogeys."

"I'm coming up," said Farragut. Sounded pleased.

Glenn clicked off. She turned to the specialist at the tactical station, Marcander Vincent, a man really too old to be there. Most of the specialists and techs on board *Merrimack* were baby-faced youths paying off their college educations. "Who have we got scheduled out here, Mr. Vincent? Any authorized traffic?"

"None, sir. Target is in the no-fly corridor."

That could not be an accident. No one meets anyone out here by accident. Even when ships were actively hunting, chances of finding were long. Astronomically long.

The battleship *Merrimack* had been patrolling deep Scorpion space to the galactic west of Fort Ike for weeks now, scouring the vastness between stars for just such a bogey—a needle of uncertain existence in this most vast of haystacks. Actually tripping over it took the hunters by surprise.

The only thing not unexpected was that it happened during the middle of ship's night. It was a saying on board *Merrimack*: if something was going to happen, it would happen on the Hamster watch.

"Sir, shall I request IFF?" the com tech asked.

"Negative," said Lieutenant Glenn Hamilton as she passed the log to the XO, just arrived on the command deck with a silent signal for Glenn to carry on. "Maintain dark. Move us into shadow vector."

"Shadow vector, aye," the helm acknowledged.

Captain Farragut arrived on deck like a weather front, all bright crackling bluster, still buttoning his sky-blue uniform jacket. Waved down the call to attention. "Thanks, Hamster," he acknowledged little Glenn Hamilton. The captain stood a full foot taller than his lieutenant.

He moved to the tactical station and landed a hand on the shoulder of the man seated there. "Mr. Vincent, what am I looking at?"

"Multiple-body FTL bogey, Captain. Conga line of them. Quick and dark."

John Farragut's blue eyes flickered back and forth across the readings on the tactical display. He could only see what the sensors interpreted for him. At FTL no one *saw* anything. Farragut glanced to his tall, striking XO, Commander Calli Carmel. "Stalker?"

Calli, who had not been on deck long enough to know, deferred to the Officer of the Watch.

Lieutenant Glenn Hamilton hesitated on a twinge of doubt. "I like to think *we're* the stalker, Captain. Commander. We picked them up on the skew. *We* are shadowing *them*."

The tac spec had all parts of the bogey plotted now. The plots appeared on the display strung out like beads on a necklace, spaced two light-minutes apart.

"Look up here." Calli's long forefinger landed on a plot far ahead of the rest.

"That would be the point man," said the tac spec.

John Farragut nodded. "Has that look."

The look of ships sneaking through space they ought not be in.

Farragut tapped the screen. "Can we get any better picture than this without bouncing something off 'em?"

"Negative," Mr. Vincent reported. "They're buttoned up real tight. Not much in the way of emissions. Unless we get closer, this is as good as it gets."

"Did we get a res scan?"

Mr. Vincent nodded. "Not helping."

Resonance had no location, existing everywhere at once. Even narrowed to a finite target, a resonant sounding came back like a Picasso, and sorting the returns was an art.

Nothing could hide from a res ping. But you could muddy the return. "How bad is the reading?"

"Sir, if this is what we think it is and they peed in the pool, this is what it would look like."

"Okay. Let's tiptoe in." Farragut checked with his officers, "Are we dark?"

"Yes, sir."

"Take us closer," said Farragut.

Calli issued the orders that would edge the battleship into a position at the rear of the dark train. From behind was the only way to get a good passive read on an FTL target. To move in between the plots would put *Merrimack*'s own ass on show to the next plot in line. The command crew had to assume from the way the plots were deployed—presenting the smallest possible profile to their most vulnerable angle—that they did not want to be seen.

Merrimack's slow, incremental progress gave the ship's exec moments to read the log summary of the last hours, and to get her very long chestnut hair brushed and tied back out of the way.

Though the XO did look like she had been summoned here in the middle of the night, she still looked spectacular. Calli Carmel was an extraordinary beauty, which she never pretended not to know. Just never seemed to much care.

At last, *Merrimack* slid into the tail position, where the ship's sensors could pick up the target's infrared print. At FTL, the signals came at you in a Lowrentz splat. It took a computer program to pull the readings apart into a recognizable picture.

Recognizable and familiar.

The sensor tech gave a low whistle, and Marcander Vincent at the tactical station sat back with his arms crossed. "Well, glory be and surprise surprise, we got ourselves a Roman convoy."

"I'll be damned," Captain Farragut murmured.

Exactly what they were looking for.

Earth still used the old geocentric mapping system by which space was defined in relation to Earth, in named wedges fanning out along boundaries of constellations as seen in the Earth sky.

Palatine maintained the same convention despite the Roman home world's off-center location in the constellation of the Southern Crown—because the Roman Empire still recognized Earth as their true home world. Terra, the Romans called it.

A home world to be reclaimed.

Both Earth and Palatine used the same names for the galactic spiral arms: Perseus for the outer arm, Sagittarius for the inner one, with the Orion Starbridge connecting the two.

Earth's solar system was located near the inner edge of the Orion Starbridge. And though traveling the Starbridge would eventually take you to the Sagittarian arm, it did so on a wide sweeping diagonal in relation to the galactic center. A direct route from either Earth or Palatine toward the galactic hub led across two kiloparsecs of thinly starred space popularly called the Abyss.

Two kiloparsecs made for a very long shortcut.

Palatine's solar system lay to the galactic south of Earth, and closer to the hub. The Romans claimed everything beyond Palatine—including the galactic center—as the property of the Roman Empire.

Both sides knew that was all wind. No one truly recognized anyone's claim to any planet which the claimant had not physically flagged. That set Palatine and all the nations of Earth on a planet-stabbing race to all promising star systems in all directions.

Palatine had the early jump along the Orion Starbridge toward the Sagittarian arm of the galaxy. Rome's colonies effectively blocked Earth expansion along that course. And toward Sagittarius was the favored direction.

Being older and denser than Orion space, the Sag arm promised the discovery of older civilizations and the possibility of contact with more advanced technologies. The U.S. was not about to cede that frontier to the Romans simply because a great region of settled and defended Roman Empire barred its path.

For a long time the only alternative to trespassing in Roman space, if one wanted to reach the Sagittarian arm—and the U.S. very much did—required U.S. ships to slog across the Abyss between galactic arms—an unprofitable dark voyage of three months at threshold velocity. So it had seemed the technological prizes of the Sagittarian arm were destined to belong to the Roman Empire.

The balance abruptly shifted fifty years ago when the U.S. pulled off a colossal coup in their successful activation of the Fort Roosevelt/ Fort Eisenhower Shotgun.

A ten-year project of staggering concept and undisclosed cost, the Shotgun could displace entire spaceships—crew, cargo, all—from Fort Ted in Near space to Fort Ike in the Sagittarian arm—thus leapfrogging the two-klarc gap between galactic arms and reducing the three-month voyage to an instant.

Fort Ike lay well in the Deep End, on the far side of the Roman frontier. Fort Ike cut off Roman expansion eastward in the Sagittarian arm.

But from that moment fifty years ago when the U.S.

proved displacement on a gargantuan scale was possible, the danger became that Palatine would build its own Shotgun and box U.S. settlements in the Deep End between Roman zones.

The U.S. had mandated such a thing would not be. The U.S. unilaterally forbade Palatine to construct its own Shotgun—a demand as absurd as Palatine's claim to the galactic hub and just as likely to be respected.

Of course the Romans would try. They must. Word on the wind spoke of a project named *Catapulta*, catapult, a term too akin to "shotgun" for comfort—the concept of hurtling something over a great distance.

Such a project would require two stations: one in Near space and one somewhere out here in the Deep End—which two hypothetical Roman installations the U.S. called the Near Cat and the Far Cat.

The Near Cat would be too close to Palatine and its home guard Legions to make an assault practicable. No one beat Rome in its home field.

As for the Far Cat—Intelligence said the Far Cat would be under construction out here in Scorpion space where the galactic Via Romana of the Orion Starbridge spilled into the Sagittarian arm.

And, lo and behold, here was a Roman convoy—one battleship, two Strigidae, and five Accipitridae riding herd on a long train of heavy cargo cars moving stealthily through a declared no-fly corridor.

Intel got it right.

"What are the odds?"

"Battle stations."

2

MERRIMACK REMAINED DARK, a malignant shadow to the unwary Roman convoy. Of what the *Mack* would do, there was no question. Strike without warning.

Rome had already been warned.

The Roman battleship was not quite peer to *Merrimack*, but the two somewhat smaller Strigidae presented a problem. Each Strix carried a bludgeoning lance. Strigidae were built for one purpose—to hit hard. And the five Accipitridae were quick, nasty; you could see these were packing morning star warheads outboard.

Scuttling the cargo carriers then running seemed the logical course of action here for *Merrimack*. That would be the best way to derail the Roman mission. And, as Tactical put it, "That's real snotty escort."

But Farragut told his exec, "I need a timed strike. We deploy our fighters dark, one flight per Accipiter, and a squadron per Strix if we can. The *Mack* takes a position behind the battleship— Who is this? *Trajan*?"

"The *Valerius*, sir," Tactical supplied. "Captain at last report was Diomede Silva."

"Okay. When *Merrimack* is behind the *Valerius* and all our fighters are lined up behind a Strix or an Accipiter, we deliver one blast right up their engines, everyone on the mark. Then get out. Parting shots at the cargo carriers. Calli, get the numbers and make this happen yesterday. TR, get your wing in their fighters. Brief 'em in their cockpits. We have *no* time."

Navigation calculated the course. The pilot was already maneuvering the *Merrimack* toward the front of the Roman convoy. Tactical timed out the intervals for a silent deployment.

It was a touchy operation. *Merrimack* was to breach her force field and push out flights and squadrons of Swifts at timed intervals. The little fighter ships would glide into position on inertia only, and without IFF.

The IFF *sync-up* was resonant and so undetectable without a precisely tuned harmonic chamber. But an IFF— Identify Friend or Foe—*signal* itself was, by necessity, traceable. With an IFF signal on, the Romans would detect the Swifts' presence. The problem with turning the signal off was that, without IFF, the fighter pilots would be as alone and dark as a human could be. And vulnerable to their own mother ship's fire if something went wrong before everyone was in place.

At the end of the countdown, each fighter would have drifted into the Roman line, directly behind a heavy Strix or a quick Accipiter. Only then would *Merrimack* turn the IFF signal on at the same time as all ships fired hard ordnance into whichever Roman engine was directly in front of them.

They could only use hard ordnance. Beam weapons were no good firing forward at FTL. And firing anything backward into the next ship in line was probably a wasted shot. Any ship normally kept the strongest part of its inertial field presented in the direction of travel.

"All hell breaks loose here," Flight Sergeant Reg Monroe read from the briefing.

Got Kerry Blue's attention. Flight Sergeant Kerry Blue had been dozing, strapped into her cockpit, waiting in the queue with the other Swifts on the flight deck, half listening to Reg Monroe, Alpha Three, reading their orders over the com.

Kerry clicked on: "It *says* that?"

"Baby doll, you know I don't make this stuff up," Reg sent back, her little voice going awfully high.

A deeper, more proper voice next: "I suggest you read

the mission briefing yourself, Flight Sergeant Blue." Flight Leader Sewell there. "You can read, can't you?" Hazard Sewell could be a real hard-ass sometimes. "This is not a milk run."

"Oh, yeah?" Kerry transmitted to everyone in her flight *but* Hazard Sewell. "So far sounds like we're sitting on our hands."

Alpha Two offered: "Hey, Kerry, you can sit on *my* hands."

"Shut up, Dak."

Instructions flew about *Merrimack*'s narrow corridors, all without going through the intelligence officer. The little IO stalked onto the command deck. "You are hitting the *escort?*"

Colonel Oh had not addressed anyone, but she was glaring at the captain. It was the XO who answered, "Colonel Oh, thank you for the extraordinary intercept. Now stand aside and let us do our job."

The IO spoke past her, "Captain, I should be consulted on how best to proceed here."

Captain Farragut kept his eyes on the tactical display. "Colonel Oh, that probably works real well back in Washington, but every second we sit here analyzing options is a second the wolves could spot us and blast our best options to holy hell."

"You are giving away our best option!" Colonel Oh scolded. *Scolded*. "You *must* hit the cargo carriers! They're the whole reason we're out here! They're carrying the heavy equipment to build the Roman Catapult. The cargo cars *must* be the primary!"

"The cargo carriers aren't powered up," Farragut said, information, not argument. He might explain himself to Lu Oh but he could never be said to argue with her. "They're coasting. We'll get a second shot at them. But at the first scent of our presence, those gunships will twitch and we'll have *no* shots at anyone."

Twitches at these speeds put megaklicks between you and your target before your thoughts could travel across a single synapse.

And they had reached the point of no return. Commander Carmel was already requesting go/no go. Captain Farragut said go.

"We are crossing the Rubicon."

Chrons started. T minus 500 seconds. *Merrimack* retracted her force field under her starboard wing for first drop. More of a push, really. The battleship flung the Swifts of Alpha Flight on a trajectory that would bring the fighters into the Roman convoy directly behind the lead Accipiter in 498 seconds.

Merrimack fell back, letting the cargo cars move past. Wholly black, the cargo carriers appeared on the monitors as ghostly renegade skyscrapers. Carrying equipment for building the forbidden Roman Shotgun, *Catapulta*.

Not for long. Only for another 440 seconds.

T minus 440 brought the second drop. Green Squadron was thrown out on a course calculated to insert the fighters into the Roman line behind a stout, brutish Strix.

The edgy watch dragged. Seconds ticked. Seconds grew long when one held one's breath.

The Roman convoy's silent glide processed. Any moment now the Roman lookouts would detect *Merrimack*'s presence and run. Or detect the Swifts in their midst and extinguish them.

T minus 300. Drop Baker Flight behind another small, fast Accipiter.

Odds against this operation climbed. The more ships out there, the more chances for the enemy to detect an occultation.

Tactical counted down the seconds to the next drop. The com tech suddenly cried, "*Radio breach!* From one of our Swifts!"

An eruption of curses on deck, and Commander Carmel demanding: "Who did that!"

Colonel Steele, CO of the Fleet Marine Wing growled, "I'll kill him." He stalked to tactical's station to look over the tech's shoulder.

The com tech held his breath at his station, as if his added quiet could make up for the escaped noise.

"Reaction from the convoy!" Farragut demanded of Tactical.

"No change. No change," Mr. Vincent reported, breathing too hard, unsteady relief in his voice. "No change. They didn't pick it up." Vincent turned from his tactical display to look the captain in the eye, "We got lucky, sir."

Farragut cocked his head. So much for the vaunted Roman vigilance. He wondered if he were not so much in awe of Roman might and technology that he had overestimated them.

He had got away with a mistake he should not have got away with. One he should not ever have allowed to be made.

Tactical uncertainly continued his drop countdown, "Six, five, four—" glancing all the while to the command officers for an abort order. Got none. A rolling signal from the captain said *Keep going*. "Three, two. Drop shields. Drop Charlie."

Charlie Flight away. Safely.

Merrimack's force field resealed.

The countdown continued softly—a long count to let the next Accipiter pass, the Marine Wing lacking fighters to cover them all as thoroughly as Captain Farragut wanted.

Commander Carmel returned to the matter of the radio breach. "Do we have a mole?" One hundred fifty years after the exodus, Roman spies still burrowed deep in U.S. society.

"No," Steele answered, glowering at the tactical display. At the source of the errant transmission. Alpha Seven. "We have a cowboy."

Alpha Seven. Flight Sergeant Jaime "Cowboy" Carver. Shining star of his own universe. Loose cannon. Big mouth on the com.

Calli demanded, "Who did he signal?"

"Tight beam, ship to ship within his own flight," the com tech answered. "It was a very small leak."

"*We* saw it," said Calli.

And Farragut, "Who is Carver talking to?"

"Alpha Six. That would be—" the com tech checked his manifest.

"Flight Sergeant Kerry Blue." Steele filled in the gap quicker than the com could look it up, then demanded flatly, "She answer him?"

"No, sir. She didn't."

A grunt. Might have been approval. Clamped his jaw tight as the last Accipiter glided by, and tactical counted down to Delta Flight's launch.

Seconds stretched.

Voices sound as if at a distance. "Drop shields. Drop Delta."

Delta Flight away.

Could hear his own pulse in his ears as the count ran down for the last drop.

Dropped Delta Flight. All the fighters of TR Steele's Marine Wing were out there now. Small, lightly shielded craft. The Swifts would be easy pickings if the Romans spotted them before the attack clock ran down.

It was *Merrimack*'s turn now, maneuvering into place on elephantine tiptoe. She measured four hundred feet across the wings, and four hundred feet topsail to bottom sail. Her fuselage measured eighty-four feet on the beam and five hundred seventy feet bow to the leading edge of her six massive engines, which added another ninety feet to her stern.

Mr. Vincent had come to the final countdown: "T minus eight, seven, six—"

The engine lights of the Roman colossus hove into actual view.

"Five, four, three—"

Everything could change in the heartbeats between counted seconds.

"Two—"

And on top of *one,* Calli ordered, "IFF on! Fire Control: Away all missiles! Fire! Fire!"

Merrimack discharged her weapons and immediately broke away to avoid getting hit with the wreckage.

Wreckage that did not come.

Couldn't see them. Hell, no one can see snot out here. Bloody space was some kind of hell dark and Kerry Blue was bolting through it faster than her own neurons. Couldn't see what light there was out here. Had to rely on the monitor to paint her a picture she could understand.

She understood it. She just didn't believe it.

"Kerry! You hit anything?" That was Carly on the com.

"Gots! I hit gots!"

Missiles that could not possibly miss, missed. The Accipiter was still dead ahead in Kerry's sights, but her missiles had hied off to deep space like deserters.

Could hear Cowboy on the com. He'd spewed all the words he knew and now he was just making them up.

"Cowboy! You hit anything?"

"Vacuum! Lots and lots of fig pucking vacuum!"

"Roger that!" Carly had come up empty, too. "Boffins must've uffed the missile tracking system. *Frazzit!*" She jinked hard. She had become a target. "Let's get the fork out of here!" Carly swerved back toward the *Mack*.

Kerry's breath got big in her chest. She had to heave it in and out like water. No. *No.* She was not going back to tell Lieutenant Colonel Steele and that pinched-up little Intelligence Officer Colonel Oh that she'd got *this* close to a Roman Accipiter and *missed*. Not acceptable. Cannot *be*.

She circled back.

Of course it wasn't really a circle—so the techs kept trying to tell her. But it felt like a circle. Looked like a circle on her readouts. Drove like a circle as she cranked the stick around. Circling was not what was really happening.

Nothing was intuitive at FTL. You don't circle at FTL. How many times had they tried to tell her? Once your forward momentum drops, you are no longer traveling FTL.

But the Swift's instruments integrated the pilot's intuitive dogfighting motions into the intended result. They built Swifts easy, "So even a Marine can drive one."

Carly's voice came worried over the com: *"Chica linda, a donde vas?"*

"I am going down*town*!" Kerry drove her Swift head-on at a big fat Strix. Too mad to be scared.

Probably only lived because the Strix was busy targeting the *Mack* as Kerry came flying in chicken-wise, running straight up the Strix's nostrils. She barely heard Flight Leader Hazard Sewell screaming in her headset, "Kerry! Break! *Break! BREAK!*"

She drowned him out with her own shouts, "Gotcha Gotcha Gotcha, you rucking—" Squeezing the trigger, *"Dammit!"* Her Swift slid up—felt like up—and over the Strix.

The cannon of Kerry's Swift still carried a full load. She had fired nothing. "*Mack! Mack! Mack!* Alpha Six coming in. My crate is uffed! It thinks the Roman Strix is a *friendly*!"

But it wasn't just Kerry Blue's crate. It was all the Swifts who were failing to fire.

Cowboy on the com: "Something's wrong! *Merrimack*, we're getting our noses blown out here!"

"Tactical, what is our status?"

"We're getting pounded, Captain."

"I can hear that." The Roman shots hammered and hissed against *Merrimack*'s defensive field. Farragut had to shout over the noise. "What's our score? What percentage hits?"

"Zero."

"Say again."

"Nada," said Mr. Vincent. "Nil. Zilch. Ninguno. No strikes, sir."

Farragut moved in, caged the man in his station, one hand on his chairback, one on the console, and hovered over his shoulder to see for himself. "We were *this* close. How could we miss?"

Mr. Vincent pointed to a screen showing a replay of their attack run, slowed down to something the human eye could follow. Farragut watched *Merrimack*'s shots slither past the Roman ships.

"Looks like Palatine's got some kind of new deflectors. Look at that." Vincent's fingertip traced the arcing path of a missile swimming purposefully *around* its target.

"Doesn't explain the guns balking," said Farragut.

"No, it doesn't," Vincent agreed. Had to rethink this.

A voice from the battery shouted over the intercom: "A hit! I got a hit!"

Tactical tilted his head in interest at his readouts, footnoted for the captain: "Sir, that was a dumb shot that got through."

It was strictly against standard practice to use dumb shots in a crowded firefight. It was too easy for a dumb shot to hit a friendly. Dumb shots did not respect IFF.

Calli caught the meaning in a moment. *Dumb shots don't respect*—"Rome has our IFF!"

Colonel Steele bellowed, "Change the IFF signal!"

Wasn't Steele's order to give, and Calli ignored him. The IFF *was* changing. Constantly. Which was why no one could quite believe Rome was sending the same signal. The signal altered at machine random—which was not truly random. Machine random was a coded sequence, calculated from an initial seed signal.

"They have our program," Mr. Vincent concluded.

Captain Farragut nodded. "Rome knows the song. Let's make 'em lose their place in the hymnal. Signals!" He spun round to the signals tech. Young kid. Big ears. "Stand by to reseed the IFF program on my mark."

"Signals, standing by."

Colonel Steele turned purple wondering why they were not reseeding *now*. Right now.

"TR, stand by to give the 'all stop' on Mr. Carmel's mark."

Steele opened his com link to his fighter wing. Waited for the signal.

"Helm, stand by to stop, on Mr. Carmel's mark."

"Helm standing by, aye."

"Mr. Carmel. Mr. Steele. Drop us out of this party."

Calli gave the word. *Merrimack* reversed thrust, as Colonel Steele barked to his Marine pilots: All stop.

A momentary quiet fell as the pounding of Roman ordnance against *Merrimack*'s inertial field ceased.

The stars reappeared. The Swifts reappeared.

And in a moment, the Romans reappeared and the pounding redoubled. At sublight speeds, beam weapons were back in play. They sizzled against *Merrimack*'s field.

The enemy craft, visible now, had become cocky, fearless, feinting rams, veering away at distances of mere meters. Acted as if they were bulletproof. The Romans did not seem to notice anything suspicious in *Merrimack*'s drop from faster-than-light travel.

"All stations, here is the sequence: The instant—and I mean the *instant*—that we reseed the IFF signal, the Roman craft will no longer be identified as friendly, and *Merrimack* will feed every torpedo, missile, beam, cannon she's got up the *Valerius'* stern."

Calli acknowledged, satisfied, grim, and Colonel Steele gave a ferocious, "Aye, aye, *sir*!"

"Stations, report. Signals!"

"Signals ready. Standing by to reseed IFF."

"Fire Control."

"Fire Control ready, aye."

The gunners of the Marine Battery reported in, ready. "Oh yeah, ready. Aye."

Farragut propped his fists on his hips, with a broad smile, angry: "Send seed. Fire!"

"All stations: Execute!"

You heard the gun crews shouting, "Fire! Fire!"

And braced for the sensation of the ship's coil and discharge, for the torpedoes' hiss and cannon boom, for the victorious cries from the ship's gunners and Marine Battery and from the fighter ships over the com.

Heard instead from Fire Control: "Balk! We have a balk all banks!"

An oath.

The balk was confirmed on all banks. The battleship's guns and the Marine Battery's cannon alike refused to fire on the designated targets.

Steele was bellowing into his com to his fighters, "Wing! Report!"

"We got gots! Negs! Negs! No hits!"

Too stunned even to demand *say again?* Steele breathed, "Damn. God damn."

Calli turned to the signals tech. "Did the change of seed transmit?"

"*Yes,* sir." The kid's big ears were crimson. "The Roman ships changed IFF the instant we did."

"The *instant*?" said Calli.

"*Any* lag time?" said Farragut.

"None, sirs."

And Tactical confirmed, "Enemy is singing in tune. Right on the beat."

Calli and Farragut met gazes. Instant understanding passed between them.

"Then it's not a mimic," said Calli. "It's a direct feed. Off of *us*."

The same signal that sent the new seed to the Swifts also fed it to the Roman gunships.

"Can't be," the signals tech said. "The signal we sent was resonant. For Rome to pick that signal up would mean—"

"It means *they're on our harmonic*!" Farragut roared.

The command crew were trying to absorb the magnitude of the disaster when a voice on the com, Flight Sergeant Cowboy Carver's, crowed: "A hit! I got a hit! Blew that frigging cargo car to fragging bits!"

And so he had. Because the cargo carrier was empty.

All the cargo carriers were.

And the situation became altogether clear, hideous.

Merrimack had not just happened upon a cargo train carrying equipment to build a Catapult. *Merrimack* had been led to find a train of empty boxes under a heavy escort.

Farragut surveyed the battle that had gone to hell. *No one ever meets by accident out here.* "I was so busy feeling lucky I forgot to feel stupid! It wasn't luck. It was *bait*!"

And he had bit the hook.

3

CALLI WATCHED THE captain's face smooth in amazement, his eyes wide with surprise, and something else. Admiration? Like a brawler in a fistfight knocked over double might give a breathless gasp: *good hit*. Staggered but not down. Never down. The day John Farragut didn't get up would be the day *Merrimack* gave him a U.S. flag blanket.

An easy man to fight for.

The signals tech mumbled, stunned, at his station. "How can this be happening?"

John Farragut took up that question to the res operator without the despair. "How *can* this be happening?"

Resonance exists outside of four dimensions. It does not follow spatial limits and so is impervious to time. A resonant pulse exists in the instant, the now, and then does not. It has no echo, no persistence. Unless your res chamber was tuned to that unique harmonic and waiting for a signal, the pulse may as well not exist in your universe.

Rome had *Merrimack*'s harmonic.

"There are infinite res harmonics," Farragut spoke what everyone knew, then what everyone wondered, "How could they get *ours*?"

"Espionage," Colonel Lu Oh answered before anyone else could. Calli heard the accusation in it. Did not have to look to know which way Colonel Oh was facing when she said that.

Calli's education at Palatine's prestigious Imperial Military Institute had been equal parts help and hindrance throughout her career. Her training there had made her an exceptional officer, but it left her loyalty forever suspect.

Colonel Oh was not the first CIA skakker leech to set her hooks into Calli Carmel's back.

Calli kept her voice soft, hard. "I suggest you turn those eyes elsewhere, Mr. Oh."

John Farragut turned to the signals tech, "*No* signal lag? None at all?"

"None, sir," the signals tech confirmed, woeful.

IFF itself was not resonant. Could not be. Resonance had no location, and an IFF signal source must be locatable in order for friendly ordnance to avoid it. However, resonance was the only way to synchronize signals between ships light-seconds apart. *Merrimack* had sent the seed to the fighter craft via resonance, so all ships would receive it at the same instant.

"In that case it's not just our harmonic," said Calli. "They've got our IFF code *sequence*. We only fed a seed change to the Swifts." The seed started the program at a common point. From there the IFF signal changed according to the "random" program.

And the Roman IFF changed along with it.

"Captain, they've got our master code," said Calli, the only possible conclusion.

Blue eyes rolled as if heaven were still the direction opposite artificial gravity's pull. "Oh, for—" Farragut interrupted himself. "Note to file: the moment we get out of this we warn *Monitor*."

Monitor shared much with her sister ship, including codes. One gets cut, the other could bleed, too. "Aye, sir." Calli gave a sharp nod.

Marine pilots screaming on the com in their Swifts were audible across the command platform. Orders, warnings, curses, sometimes a cry that abruptly ceased.

Colonel Steele, white and rigid as a block of ice, died every time one of his Marine's plots blinked off the tactical screen. "Shut off the IFF!" came out of his mouth like an order.

"Belay that!" Farragut's counterorder brought him an ice-blue glare of utter betrayal.

Before Steele could say something else ill-advised, Farragut grabbed hold of Steele's sleeve, and said in a whisper, "TR, we *can't.* The Romans are right up in our faces spitting. What is more predictable than for us to power off our IFF? I've bit this hook, I'm not fixin' to swallow it."

A thick muscle bulged at Steele's square jaw with the clenching of his teeth. He could not argue. Farragut was right. Why the man was the captain.

"It's such an obvious thing for us to do," Farragut said softly. "They have to be ready for it."

Calli picked up the logic trail from there. "So if we were to cut out IFF, what would be the Roman countermove?"

"Don't know. Don't care. We're not playing their game. What *we're* going to do is send the recall. Make the Romans think we're fixin' to tuck and run."

"Are we?" Calli asked.

"Thinking about it. And while I'm thinking—God *damn*!" Broke off at the sight through a porthole. A Roman ship so close he could see it. *See* it. See its interior lights winking through its torpedo tubes.

Merrimack's recall signal brought the Swifts swarming back toward the battleship's docks on either wing.

But the Swifts could not get close.

The battleship *Valerius* belched forth fighters of its own to intercept them, while *Valerius,* the two Strigidae and the five Accipitridae continued to hammer the *Merrimack.*

Merrimack's field groaned and rasped with every strike. The battleship's violent jinking to deflect the Roman salvos from her engines also kept the Swifts from lining up any kind of safe approach.

"This is a loss, Captain," Intelligence Officer Lu Oh, advised. "Do not hand the enemy its objective."

She was telling him to run.

Colonel Steele's white face, his bulging muscles, his blanched fists were as loud as a shout: *No!*

Captain Farragut nodded. "We *should* run. I hope the Romans don't wonder why we're not doing that."

"Are we done thinking about it?" Oh prompted. "Do we have a plan now?"

"We do—"

The artificial gravity gave a burp that brought stomachs to throats, rising on a wave and not settling back down. Lights browned down, brightened up.

The systems monitor reported a flux in Engine Three. Contained. Stabilized.

Farragut kept speaking through it with no change in voice, "—If we can switch on the IFF transponder in that Wren we liberated back at the Abyss." And to his XO's uncomprehending stare he filled in, "That little Roman spy-ship we commandeered last month. Wearing French colors."

"*That* one," said Calli, lights going on.

"That one. Where did we put it?"

"The boffins are dissecting it in the maintenance hangar. Starboard wing."

Lu Oh spoke skeptically, "You're suggesting we send the Wren's signal to the Swifts instead of our own IFF?"

"Not *instead* of ours," said Farragut. "*With* ours."

The signals tech had to speak. "Sorry, sir. I don't get it. What will that accomplish? The Romans will just pick it up and mimic it. Apparently, whatever we feed to the Swifts' IFF sounders, we feed to the Romans' IFF sounders."

"That's why we're not going to feed the Wren's signal into the Swifts' IFF sounder. We're going to feed it into the Swift's *emergency* sounders."

A distress call, like an IFF signal, was meant to be heard, and be traceable to its source.

"A false SOS is against all conventions of war," Calli advised, very softly.

"We're not sending an SOS. We're just using the emergency equipment. All my ships will be sending two discrete signals. And the instant we activate the Wren's signal, our guns are going to target *Merrimack*'s IFF signal."

Calli's neatly shaped eyebrows lifted. She motioned to one of the techs.

Already poised on the seat edge, the young man flew from the command platform. His boots clanged on the deck grates all the way to the starboard maintenance hangar.

Steele, a brave man but not a scientific one, missed the connection that everyone else on deck seemed to be making. "What keeps *Merrimack* from shooting my Marines?"

Or were his pilots forfeit here?

Farragut answered him. "We code a NOT operand into

our targeting system and direct all ordnance to hit *Mack*'s IFF but NOT the Wren IFF."

Steele was unconvinced. "What keeps a missile from carrying out the 'hit our IFF' command before it gets to the 'don't hit the Wren IFF' command?"

Farragut caught his balance against a deck tilt, and answered his doubting Marine commander. "If I remember right, the NOT operand has precedence in computer decisions. In machine language NOT means absolutely NOT, while in human talk it's usually negotiable." He looked to the signals tech and targeting specialist who were coordinating the program over the com with the tech in the maintenance hangar. Lifted his brows for confirmation.

"Uh, yes, sir," the signals tech hesitated. "It does. NOT has precedence. Within its own statement it does."

Targeting added, "If you get your NOT outside the right statement, it'll negotiate like hell."

"Then let's get it in the right statement and get it there quick. I don't want the Romans to think we've got anything left in the bull pen."

The ship's field hiccupped. Pressure quit. Boxed the ears with its sudden return.

Tactical mumbled assurance, "We don't look like we got skat." He yawned wide to pop his ears.

Colonel Steele paced a trench into John Farragut's narrow command deck. Screams over the com bludgeoned the big man's stony nerves. The fighters, trying to return to the battleship, could not possibly dock with a bucking target.

"TR, send a verbal recall. Insist your pilots get back here right now."

Merrimack's pilot, intent on letting nothing line up anything on *Merrimack,* heard that. "Do you want me to let them approach, sir?"

"Hell, no."

And to Colonel Steele, who looked like he'd been stabbed in the gut after dutifully relaying the impossible order to his desperate Marines, Farragut said, "I'm just feeding their arrogance."

"You're feeding them my Marines." Steele whispered that, so as not to be heard arguing with the captain on his own command deck.

"Rome doesn't want to erase your dogs, TR. Those Accipiters could have mopped them all up by now. They want the *Mack*."

Steele paled in realization. "Hostages."

Farragut nodded. "The Romans won't kill all of our Swifts. They baited us. Made us come to them with our boats out. Gave us something to lose. Rome wants us to stay and try to rescue our fighters—because Rome can't afford to get into a footrace with the *Mack*. That big battle heap of theirs can't accelerate fast enough to catch us if we run."

"The Accipiters can," Tactical advised.

"Those Accipiters don't want to catch the *Mack*." Without their heavy hitting comrades, the light Accipitridae were no match for *Merrimack*.

"We aren't running without my Marines!" Steele hadn't meant to say that aloud to his captain. Waited for a rep.

But Farragut said firmly, "No, TR. We are not. Targeting! Status!"

"We are loading code to target *Merrimack*'s IFF, and waiting for the Wren code to load the NOT command before transport to the active library."

Farragut clicked on the intercom. "Maintenance hangar! This is Farragut. Get that code NOTted and up here *yesterday*."

The ship shuddered around them. Beyond the hatch, a crewman spilled into view, half falling from an upper deck. He dangled from a ladder rung, flailing for his footing. Recovered and scrambled back above deck.

A crewman in a space suit.

The XO had not ordered the crew to suits. To wear one without orders won you a rep at least, hard time more likely. Wearing a suit meant you saw a high chance of dying.

Wearing a suit against orders meant you knew you were as good as dead already.

Calli snapped to the nearest MP. "Brig that man."

Farragut was on the intercom again: "Maintenance hangar! Farragut. Tell me something."

"Maintenance here! Wren code ready to load, sir!"

"Targeting!"

Targeting picked up the cue. "Loading code, aye."

"Com, what is your status?"

"Com has the Wren IFF ready to send into all ships' emergency sounders. Com standing by."

Calli turned to the captain. "Priority of targets, sir?"

Captain Farragut answered at once, "The battleship's engines. Any open gunport. Get the *Valerius*. Ignore the little skat."

Calli had to shout instructions over the thunder roll of a heavy salvo hitting *Merrimack*'s field.

"Targeting! Status!"

"Targeting ready, sir."

"Fire Control, stand by!"

"Fire Control, ready and standing by, aye."

"Signals, stand by!"

"Signals standing by, aye."

"Com, stand by to feed Wren signal into the Swifts' emergency sounders."

"Com standing by, aye."

Farragut met his exec's gaze. "Ready, Cal?"

"On your word, John."

They waited. Calli nodded at the sensor display, at the Roman battleship looming, all its gunports gaping. "Here he comes."

Desperate sounds filled the waiting. A Swift on approach cracked against *Merrimack*'s field. Over the com, his flight mates shouted after him. A flight leader cried out, forlorn, betrayed—why won't *Merrimack* let them dock?

"Oh, for Jesus." Farragut signaled Calli, "Call it."

Calli ordered: "Com, send Wren IFF."

"Sending Wren IFF, aye."

All U.S. ships' emergency sounders began chirping with the Wren's IFF signal.

And immediately after, "Fire!"

Merrimack opened up everything. Techs braced themselves against the nothingness of another balk, another failure.

Blessedly, they felt the ship's power bunch and deliver. Heard, felt, the screech of ordnance leaving *Merrimack*'s barrels. The angry smell filled the corridors.

Merrimack's force field opaqued with overload of sudden luminosity.

The tactical display reimaged in a moment, showed the Roman battleship *Valerius* heave. *"Got him!"*

Voices on the com—several of the fighter pilots at once—crowed, "Yeah!"

The command deck erupted with jubilant cries, all the techs on their feet, shouting.

Farragut ordered, jubilant, "TR, cancel the recall. Have your dogs beat the blue peaches out of 'em!" Though he scarcely needed to; the Swifts were already raking up the Roman fighter craft in a shredded cloud.

"Aye, *sir*!"

Celebration quickly subsided as the scene on the monitors rolled out. Watched in a kind of horror as the Roman battleship convulsed, twice, from within. Had the look of internal explosions.

The shimmering aura of *Valerius'* force field flickered, snuffed out. Another heave. Smoke belched from her gunports. And the great ship went silent and dark.

4

"THEY'RE HURT." Farragut lunged forward, gripped the console, wide-eyed. "Oh, for Jesus. We *hurt* 'em."

Out came the white flags, stiff and unfluttering in the vacuum, on the Roman ships.

Over the com from a Marine Swift: "Delta Leader here. This skigspawn Strix is showing white! Do I have permission to shoot his ass!"

"Stand by," Farragut sent.

"Stand by?" Cowboy Carver from Alpha Flight there. "Stand *by*?"

Colonel Steele got on the com. "Stand fragging by, Marine!"

Farragut again: "Marine Wing. This is Captain Farragut. Collect the bricks."

Oxygen in solid form was often towed outboard of long-range vessels rather than waste habitable space on board. And because hydrogen could be acquired anywhere, a ship's oxygen bricks were also its water supply.

"You may acquire your targets, but do not fire unless fired upon." Farragut clicked off, murmured to the white-flagged battleship on his monitor. "Your turn."

Valerius appeared to be listing, as if it had lost its orientation in space.

And came the hail from the Roman commodore. He announced himself as Decurion Diomede Julius Silva of the Imperial ship *Valerius*. He already knew his foe's name. "Captain Farragut, your assistance, if you please."

Farragut returned: "Commodore, strike your colors and show me your sincerity."

The Roman eagles reeled inboard from the *Valerius*. The escort Strigidae and Accipitridae followed suit, but their force fields stayed lit.

The Swifts buzzed round them like suspicious hornets.

"Captain Farragut, will you back off your fighters?"

"No, sir," said Farragut.

In the delay, the Swifts requested permission to fire. The small Roman fighters had all gone inert. Perhaps because they had been under remote control, but perhaps not. The Roman fighters were not showing white, so Farragut gave the Marine Wing permission to take them out.

At length, the force fields of the Strigs and the Accipiters winked out. The Romans were completely at *Merrimack*'s mercy.

Now John Farragut leaned over the com on straight arm and asked, "What do you need, Commodore?"

Coughing and a blaring alarm sounded behind the Roman's stoic voice. "I request evac and decontamination."

"You got it," Farragut sent. And to his XO, "Bring 'em over and tank 'em."

Farragut expected no treachery from his prisoners. Surrender in space was, by necessity, cordial. Vacuum was merciless. To run up a white flag in deceit was unconscionable. Only pirates—stupid ones—and terrorists tried it. God help everyone if space warfare ever degraded to that. Combatants of civilized nations were always aware that next time it could be you or your brothers in arms under that flag.

The rules were strict. Between each other, Palatine and the United States abided by all conventions, written and unwritten, of ships in distress and ships in surrender.

The Strigs and Accipiters, though intact, did not attempt to turn the situation. Nor did they run. As suspected, those ships were running lean, little more than gun platforms with engines. Without their mother ship or their oxygen bricks this deep in Scorpion space, they could only run as far as their cold, slow deaths.

The Roman commodore transmitted helpfully, "To facilitate evacuation I should tell you, Captain Farragut, we do have U.S. LDs and collars on board."

"Oh, *really*?" Now there was an unhappy surprise. Landing disks and displacement collars were not equipment the armed forces left lying around for the taking.

"They are correctly coded to your displacement chamber," the decurion added.

"I don't doubt that," Farragut said, less than pleased.

"We had intended to board you, sir. Though not like this."

In ten minutes the displacement engineers reported having received thirty-five Roman crew in space suits.

This was going too slowly. The *Valerius* was going toxic. "Bring over the rest of them," Farragut urged haste.

"I'm advised that is all of them," the displacement tech reported.

Farragut hailed the Roman commodore. "You running a light crew over there?"

The decurion's tight silence told Farragut he had not been running the *Valerius* light. Silva spoke at last, "If you could scan for survivors, I would be personally obliged. I am told you are a compassionate man when not being ferocious."

Hell, when he wasn't shooting at you, John Farragut was the Easter Bunny.

"I can do that. Get on your disk, Commodore."

The decurion allowed himself to be displaced from his crippled ship to the enemy battleship *Merrimack*.

The thundercrack brought to *Merrimack*'s displacement chamber a broad man, weary, older. Silva had twenty years on Farragut. He wore a sidearm so he would have something to hand over to his adversary.

A Colt .45. Antique weapons were often used for ceremony. Farragut turned it over appraisingly. "My Daddy has one of these."

Marines escorted the captives to *Merrimack*'s detention compartments. Honor dictated they not attempt escape until they made landfall, but it would not do to tempt them.

There were terribly few of them from *Valerius*. *Valerius* was built like a chambered nautilus, its chambers locked and segregated in battle to save the crew from total annihilation in case of a breach. As it was, the annihilation was *only* eighty-five percent.

Com open, Farragut overheard his decontamination team's exchanges as they surveyed the interior, searching for trapped survivors. A specialist breathed in his suit, "Good God, we gutted her."

TR Steele stayed clear of the prisoners. He was a bad winner and a bad loser. To TR Steele's mind, the good Romans were back in the *Valerius*.

Steele proceeded down to the hangars to receive his returning fighter pilots, those who had survived this debacle.

He was descending the ladder as Cowboy Carver jumped down from the cockpit of Alpha Seven and slung his helmet at the little intelligence officer who waited there. "Hey! Oh! Why didn't Intelligence have a clue here?"

Colonel Oh caught the helmet. Let it drop. "You will report to Ops for debriefing, soldier."

Still on the ladder, Steele shouted, pointing at Cowboy way on the other side of the hangar deck. "I get that man first!" Steele jumped down the last rungs of the ladder and started across the deck with great strides.

But another Marine pilot got to Cowboy first. Kerry Blue. Cowboy, seeing her coming at him, opened his arms for her, tilted his pelvis forward, and gave a bedroom grin. "Hey, you, beautiful bitch babe, come to your hot dog!"

Kerry folded him on the deck with a hard kick in the balls. She spun away and blundered straight into Colonel Steele. She backed her face off the wall of Steele's chest, looked up at his marble frown. She anticipated his next orders and acknowledged, "I'm walking the down decks for two weeks. Yes, sir. Aye, sir."

Steele's pale blue eyes flicked toward the groaning figure on the deck, back to Kerry Blue. With a very quiet growl he said, "One week if you do it again."

Not one to question orders, Kerry immediately stomped on Cowboy. Then lifted a salute to Colonel Steele. "Thank you, sir."

"Get out of here."

"Debriefing, soldier!" Colonel Oh barked. In Oh's reedy grating voice, the bark was closer to a yap.

"Not her!" Steele bellowed, more forcefully than he meant to.

Lu Oh, not terribly observant for an intelligence officer, didn't seem to notice anything odd about it. Must have thought Steele was merely giving his punishment order precedence over Intelligence's interrogation.

And, if challenged, Steele would be hard pressed to explain to himself why he was shielding Kerry Blue. He didn't have a good reason. He just didn't want that spider woman near his Kerry Blue.

Once she was safely out of sight, Steele caught himself shaking. Shaking.

What Antarean grughole ever let women serve on a battleship anyway?

Captain Farragut invited Commodore Silva to dine with him.

A detached sort of man, Silva. The true enormity of his loss seemed to have bounced off his weathered hull.

Typical Roman, he hadn't the same notion of the sanctity of human life as most Americans. The planet Palatine had no state religion. Not that the practice of religion was forbidden, but most Romans prided themselves on their rationality. The saying went, "Adam was a Roman." Meaning that Rome, like Adam, had chosen the apple of knowledge, science, law, and order over blind obedience to a shepherd god long ago.

"They told me you were brave, Captain Farragut," said Silva, sampling the captain's Kentucky bourbon after dinner, before returning to confinement. "They did not tell me you were especially cagey."

Farragut agreed he was not very sneaky.

"Then why did you not turn off your IFF?" Silva asked.

Farragut gave a sideways nod. Could not exactly say why. "Got the feeling you wanted me to."

"I did," said Silva. "Quite counting on it, I was. You were tipped off?"

"No, sir," Farragut chuckled a bit at how wrong that guess was. "*No,* sir."

"How many moves ahead do you play the game, Captain Farragut?"

John Farragut creased his brow, not sure. "Depends on your batting order."

"Chess, captain. I was speaking of chess."

"I don't play chess."

"You don't say." Silva set aside his glass. Surprised, interested. "I had taken it for granted that expertise in chess was a prerequisite of the strategist."

"Baseball. I play baseball. You were expecting heat. I got you to swing at a change up. You going to tell me how you got our recognition codes?"

"Are you being coy with me, sir?"

"No," said Farragut, perplexed. As if he had just asked the Roman something obvious. He had discovered the hard way that Rome *had* his codes. He certainly did not know how Rome got them. "I told you I'm not sneaky."

Hidden things smoothed Silva's haggard features. He indicated the MPs, "I think I shall have these young men show me back to my quarters now."

There was still another play left in the game.

A message from the Joint Chiefs sat on top in the com queue, coded within codes. It said Palatine was calling for pickup of prisoners of war; can you respond?

The time of the message predated *Merrimack*'s battle with *Valerius'* flotilla, so John Farragut was puzzled. "They wouldn't even have known we have prisoners to exchange."

"The Roman message is not an exchange offer," the com spec said. "It's just a 'Here they are. Come get 'em.' "

Farragut read the message for himself. Palatine had given the Pentagon coordinates of a space buoy, which purportedly contained a small number of U.S. prisoners. The buoy was equipped with life support for five days beginning yesterday. The message said, in effect: Come get them or let them die.

"Is this addressed to the *Mack*?" Farragut scanned the header.

"No, sir. Palatine sent it to the Pentagon. The JC relayed it on the common band to any U.S. ship. We're in the neighborhood."

"I don't like it," said Farragut.

"It's a bad neighborhood," his exec agreed.

"Can this be a false message?" Farragut asked the com tech. "We know Rome has our harmonic and our IFF sequence. Do they have our encryption codes, too?"

"I guess that's always possible, Captain. But it squares

with all the cross-checks, and the message doesn't ask for us. Anyone could respond," said the tech. Then, "It still smells like bait."

"Given that we're one of the few ships in the neighborhood, yeah." Farragut checked the chron. Four days. The prisoners—if there really were prisoners—had four days. "But you can't bait with a Red Cross. Calli, respond to the JC on the LRS Marine harmonic."

The Long-Range Shuttle had brought relief soldiers to the *Merrimack*. Its recognition system operated on its own discrete harmonic. "Accept the mission on behalf of Lieutenant Popovich." Popovich was an accepted code name when you had reason not to identify yourself.

"You're going to walk into another trap?" said Colonel Oh, more accusation than question.

"No," said Farragut. "I'm going to send the LRS into the trap."

"And whom are you sending on the shuttle?" Oh's voice made it clear it would not be her.

"I'll go," Hamster volunteered. Lieutenant Glenn Hamilton was a young officer eager to make her bones with something dramatic and maybe shake off that too-cute nickname.

"Not you," said Farragut, not even considering it. And to Lieutenant Colonel Steele, who had lifted a hand as if making a bid, "TR. You're in."

Lu Oh, dumbfounded at the eagerness of these fish to snap at another hook, did not even try to speak again.

Prisoners. Where had Rome taken prisoners *from* out here? Farragut reread the message for clues. "Wonder who they've *got*."

Call-ins were infrequent. The *Merrimack* was isolated in her secrecy. The crew was never sure what was happening across the stars. The Long-Range Shuttle had just made the difficult rendezvous to bring replacements, but even the replacements' news was two months old.

The LRS wore U.S. Marines colors. Nothing about the shuttle connected it to the *Mack*. It was a generic transport, the kind that regularly ferried troops between Earth and the Deep End. It would serve perfectly for this mission.

And Lieutenant Colonel Steele was the perfect man for the job. Trust TR Steele not to trust a Roman. He would make sure to have the prisoners deloused of any Roman motes and other surveillance devices before delivering them to the *Mack*.

But it was going to kill TR Steele to obey the rules of exchange. Steele hated wearing a Red Cross almost as much as he hated wearing League of Earth Nations' green. Under either flag he was obliged to take no offensive action. The directions to the space buoy were specific. Variation from the approach route would not be tolerated.

Steele kept his fists clenched as if physical bonds were biting into his stout wrists. Yet he would not have sent any of his Marines on this mission without going himself.

His LRS obediently entered Roman space on the specified vector. The shuttle's scanners picked up the Roman spotter ships hanging back at a lawful distance. The Romans could not buzz an invited rescue craft. Steele could tell they wanted to. As much as he wanted to lob a few rounds at them.

Against all natural impulse, Steele stayed on the beacon. Ready for any trick. Ready for any treachery. Ready for anything.

Anything but this.

The nature of the trap became clear as soon as the air lock opened between the buoy and the LRS, and Steele saw the prisoners.

The gift itself was the trap. It was a strike at U.S. morale.

His Marines' morale went straight to their toes and kept on going to down decks.

"Oh, Jesus. Jesus God. Oh, Jesus."

"Shut up."

"Sir."

Steele raised a wooden, mortified salute to the ranking prisoner of the three.

The man seized Colonel Steele's sleeve, the insignia on it. "Marines," he croaked at the mastiff badge of the 89th Battalion. Meant Steele would be attached to the Third Fleet. The officer asked in horror, *"What ship?"*

Steele, already very fair, turned stark white. He could not answer the man. He motioned toward the shuttle's hatch. "This way, sir."

The displacement tech on board *Merrimack* who was logging in the displacement collars and LDs confiscated from the *Valerius* discovered that the equipment was not of Roman make. This equipment was U.S. issue. No wonder it worked so perfectly with *Merrimack*'s displacement chamber.

"So who were you stolen from," the tech murmured to a collar, checking its serial number. "Who's your mama?"

Serial number began with P29ZG. The tech did not need to read any further. He dropped the collar and ran to find Captain Farragut. Findings this explosive had to be reported in person.

The captain was on the port hangar deck awaiting the arrival of the LRS which carried the freed POWs. The displacement tech hesitated, afraid to approach him. Too many people on deck. The shuttle was already on its way down the elevator from the landing dock.

The information burned sour in the displacement tech's throat. He held back, shifting foot to foot, mentally willing the LRS to hurry.

Clamped down, the shuttle opened its hatch. Colonel Steele was first down the ramp. He threw up a salute without meeting the captain's eyes. Then stepped aside to make way for the three rescued POWs.

Gasps sounded all around the hangar.

The displacement tech withdrew. Captain Farragut just found out where the stolen collars and LDs came from.

The men filing down the ramp were well known here. Captain Matthew Forshaw, Commander Napoleon Bright, and Lieutenant Commander Jorge Medina.

Command staff of a battleship.

There was no one on deck who did not want that deck to open up and swallow them.

"God Almighty, Rome has the *Monitor*!"

PART TWO

Turnabout

5

GAVE THEM BACK. Just gave them back. High officers, thrown out like space bilge. The tactic was outrageous, insulting.

And in arrogance beyond arrogance, they had given Captain Forshaw a medal—the crimson-and-cobalt Caesar Cross, for great service to the Empire. As if Matthew Forshaw had willingly handed the *Monitor* over to Palatine.

The medal remained where the Romans had pinned it to Matthew Forshaw's uniform. It hung like an albatross he could not take off. For even if he physically removed it, it would still be there. It would never ever be gone.

It took a whole lot to make Captain Farragut angry. He was spitting mad. He grabbed the damned thing, tore it from Matty's tunic, stuffed it in the annihilator, kicked the container shut, and mashed the control button with his fist.

He breathed, terribly softly, "No excuse for that." Straightened up, clasped Captain Forshaw's right hand and hauled him in for a fierce hug and a hearty thump on the back. "Good to see you, Matty. *They* have made a *mistake*!"

Some color returned to the faces on the hangar deck. Good to see John Farragut on the offensive again.

Farragut released Captain Forshaw and grasped the hand of the *Monitor*'s XO, Napoleon Bright—a tall man, standing woodenly, his face all the more pale for the blue-blackness of his hair. "Brighty! How are you?"

"Been a whole lot better, sir."

Farragut's left hand joined their clasped right hands, warmth and strength in his grip. "Get up, Brighty. Get up so we can kick their nuts in."

Brighty nodded. "I'll be there."

Then Farragut welcomed Jorge Medina. The lieutenant commander's normally olive skin was a cadaverous gray.

Farragut looked round for the fourth, who ought to complete this set. "Where's Sophie?" The senior engineer Sophia Soteriadis was not here. "Is she alive?"

Commander Bright said, "They kept her."

John Farragut had some foul words to that.

Rome had kept those who made the battleship run—its techs, its engineers—further negating its commanders to inconsequential.

More pressing than the insult was the danger. Sooner or later, Rome was going to figure out that they could use *Monitor* to operate *Merrimack's* systems by remote.

Farragut turned to his chief, Ogden Bannerman, "Chief, pull the plug on any system that can be accessed by remote command."

The Og grunted, "Aye."

And to his senior engineer, Ariel "Kit" Kittering, "I need a full assessment of our exposure in two hours. Include a report on any messages our captive ships got off when we bagged them."

"Two hours? I can't possibly—"

"One hour."

"Two hours, aye."

Farragut opened his direct link to the command deck. "Calli, prep a courier missile to apprise the JC of our situation. Get it off to Fort Ike best speed. And move us."

"Course, sir?"

"Don't give a rip. Anywhere but here."

"Aye, sir."

Farragut told the quartermaster to find some compartments appropriate for his guests. Then turned to the freed prisoners, "Matty, Brighty, Mr. Medina, y'all free for dinner?"

Waiting for Captain Forshaw in the Mess, John Farragut chatted with Brighty—or rather chatted at Brighty, who was understandably reserved.

Lieutenant Commander Medina showed up at the captain's table, his face and white shirt spattered with red. "I, uh, regret to inform you that Captain Forshaw will not be joining us." He listed a bit as if he would faint.

Napoleon Bright frowned. "Are you okay?"

Medina's eyes were in outer space. "No. I don't think so, sir."

Farragut came round the table. "I don't think so either. Stay here. Don't touch anything explosive or pointy." He grabbed a fistful of curly black hair on the back of Medina's head, as a big animal might grab a cub. "You'll be okay. That's an order."

And ran to meet the medics in Captain Forshaw's quarters.

Calli Carmel, overseeing a refit of the *Merrimack*'s control systems with Kit Kittering, was startled to see Captain Farragut in his dress trousers, jacket abandoned somewhere, his shirtsleeves rolled up, and him hunkered down in a maintenance pit with the techs.

In motion was Captain Farragut's natural state. However, hands-on grunt labor was a little outside the norm.

Calli stood at the edge of the pit. "What happened to dinner?"

"Not hungry," said Farragut doing battle with a stubborn bolt. "Matty went good Roman and Lieutenant Commander Medina is half in the tub."

"Good Roman" meant suicide. Romans used the term because a good Roman would rather die than live in dishonor. Marines used it because, as far as they were concerned, the only good Roman was a dead Roman.

The normal method was to open a vein in a tub of warm water and fade away. There were no tubs on *Merrimack*.

Calli stammered, "Did he— Did Matty—*succeed*?"

Farragut muscled a spanner round. "Oh, yeah." Paused to wipe moisture off his upper lip with the back of his wrist. He sat back on his heels. "I should have known. I should have done something."

Calli's long legs folded into a crouch by the pit, so she could speak softly. "Your brain doesn't work that way, John."

"It should have. God bless it, it should have! I'm the only

one who could have talked him down." He gave the ratchet another snarling turn. Let it dangle. "Hell, Cal." He sat back again on thick haunches, gave a graveyard grin up from the pit. "We got ourselves another fine mess."

Calli was still too incensed to smile. "They took us down, they kicked us, they pissed on us, and, oh, Lord, they know everything there is to know about the *Mack*."

"They will." Farragut tugged on the spanner. "As soon as they finish dissecting *Monitor,* you bet they will."

Calli took off her own jacket, climbed down into the pit to help pull. "John?" she said. Grunted.

"Yeah, Cal?" Grunted back.

Calli let go the spanner. Pushed a long stray hair out of her face. "This is all defensive."

John Farragut was an aggressive fighter. "Them's fightin' words, woman."

She nodded. Asked, speculative, "Where *is* the *Monitor*?"

Farragut saw wheels turning behind Calli's brown eyes. And he was desperate for wheels. He dared a guarded smile. "What's on your mind?"

"You said the Romans will know everything about *Monitor*. You're right. They will. But they probably don't *yet.* They'll need more time to take *Monitor* apart and analyze her."

"And?"

"Let's grab her back before they learn any more."

Farragut let the spanner drop altogether. He propped his elbows back on the edge of the pit. "Oh, yeah. Grab her back. Just grab her back." He tried out the preposterous sound of it. Allowed, "It does have improbability in its favor. What else does it have to say for itself?"

"I'm serious, John. Just do it. Quick. Dirty. Before they can think."

"Before *we* can think."

"While they are still defending a captive ship about which *we* know *everything*! We will never be in a stronger position."

"That's a scary thought right there."

"Why are we even thinking defensively? We are afraid they'll use *Monitor* against *Merrimack*. So let's use *Merrimack* against *Monitor*. We're sitting here figuring out every possible thing they could do to us with what they learn from

Monitor. Let's do it first. While we know the field and they're still reading the playbook."

"I like the attitude, Cal."

A reedy voice intruded from above: "She learned that on Palatine."

The disheveled captain and exec looked up at the intelligence officer standing at the edge of the pit, her little hands neatly folded.

Lu Oh was always neat. She was such a tiny figure that Calli and Farragut had never looked up at her before. From this angle, Lu Oh's narrow nostrils, her slitted, slanted eyes, and her heart-shaped face made her look like a predatory insect.

"Mr. Oh, I could get real tired of that tone," said Farragut. And to Calli, "Mr. Carmel, let's go talk to Brighty."

Commander Bright was not a useful source of information. On questions of where *Monitor* had been operating, on what mission, and the battleship's last known location, he was peculiarly uncooperative.

Farragut was losing his very long patience, when the intelligence officer intervened, "He can't answer you, Captain Farragut. You are asking for classified information."

Farragut felt his eyes grow huge. They had to look like blue-yoked eggs. "He can't tell *me*?"

"Given the nature of what you intend, absolutely not."

"Oh, bullskat. Brighty!" Farragut implored.

Brighty maintained a sullen silence.

"We don't need him, John," said Calli. "We can back figure a rough window of when *Monitor* was captured. It can't have been long, or the JC would have red-balled us by now. Since the Romans dropped Matty, Brighty, and Jorge in the Deep End not too long ago, *Monitor* had to have been captured in the Deep End.

"In the time since *Monitor* was taken, the Romans did enough analysis to get our harmonic and our IFF sequence and our location. That takes more sophisticated equipment than ships carry on board. *Monitor* can't land, so they have to be dissecting her at a space dock.

"Palatine has a limited number of space docks big enough to accommodate a battleship with the right technical resources to do what they had to do. And only one of them is in striking distance of the Deep End. That's Daedalus Station on the galactic Via Romana."

Napoleon Bright registered mute surprise. He would neither confirm nor deny her conclusion, but his expression told it all.

John Farragut considered Calli's line of reasoning. Said at last, "So, tell me, why do I need an IO at all if I have you?"

"Because *I* work for the United States," said Lu Oh. Implied that Calli Carmel didn't.

Farragut ignored Lu, still talking to Calli. "You know this idea is still half-cocked."

"Half-cocked is better than dickless," said Calli.

"The situation could fast become thoroughly cocked," said Lu Oh.

Calli put it to the captain: "Go? No go?"

John Farragut had a dangerous gleam in his eyes. "Go."

Napoleon Bright broke his silence. "What? What are you planning to do here?"

"Get *Monitor*."

"Get—? You are actually considering doing this?"

"No, I'm past considering and well into planning it now."

"Sir. Reconsider. I have recently acquired a real respect for Roman cunning and resourcefulness."

"Calli's had that respect for a long time," Farragut assured him.

"No one is questioning Mr. Carmel's respect for Rome," said Colonel Oh. "Can you be absolutely certain Mr. Carmel is not delivering to Rome the complete matched set of *Monitor* class battleships?"

Calli countered, "Brighty, can you be absolutely certain your ship fell to Roman cunning and not to the blundering of an intelligence officer? Talk to us. Brighty, this is *me*."

Lu Oh pressed, "Captain Farragut. Roman Imperialists hid underground like a festering boil for two millennia. And when they surfaced in the year 2290, there were millions of them. Millions, and no one ever suspected. It is probable to a certainty that there are *still* Roman moles among us, highly situated."

"If there are, you couldn't find them if they were wearing name tags," said Calli.

Farragut tried to make peace. "I can't go around suspecting all my own people, Lu."

"Not all of them, Captain. But as far as I'm concerned, anyone who speaks Latin is suspect."

"I speak Latin," said Farragut.

Lu's voice dropped, witheringly, "Captain Farragut. You don't speak Latin."

To which Calli added in a near mumble, "You don't, John."

"*Et tu,* Calli?"

Calli's eyebrows canted up at the center, apologetic. "You're really bad at it."

And Lu Oh announced abruptly that she wanted out.

Out? John Farragut withheld a smile and asked amiably, "You want to walk, Mr. Oh?"

"I am taking the LRS and our Roman prisoners back to Earth."

Farragut blinked in surprise, unused to people challenging his command. They might question him, but never bypass him. John Farragut was as easily ignored as a freight train.

To Lu's self assignment, he said simply, "No, you're not."

Lu Oh rose from her chair. "Sir, I am."

"Colonel Steele, detain Mr. Oh."

Steele nodded to his MPs posted at the hatchway. They advanced with unholstered sidearms.

"You have no authority over me," Lu Oh declared. As if standing within a force field. "CIA."

So now she runs up her true colors. Farragut had known for quite some time. "Mr. Oh, you are on my ship, wearing the uniform of a Navy Intelligence Colonel. No one of authority has told me you are anything else. As a Naval officer, you are either delusional or mutinous. This is my ship. That's my insignia on your sleeve. You are destined for my brig." He nodded the go ahead to his Marines. "Mr. Steele."

"Aye, aye, *sir*!"

"Less enthusiasm, if you please, TR."

"Sir."

The great squared white-blond boulder that was TR Steele could have picked up the stick figure that was Lu Oh and broken all her little bones. Not entirely without intelligence, Lu Oh offered no physical struggle.

6

THE BOUNDARY BETWEEN U.S.-controlled space and Imperial space was a spongy thing, especially in the Deep End. No one guards a vacuum. And no one recognizes a claim you have not tread on or flagged. The present war had begun when Palatine drew a line in the stars and the U.S. crossed it.

Still Daedalus Station lay in undisputed Roman territory in the Orion Starbridge.

Fortunately, space was unimaginably wide. No one really ever ran into anyone else by accident out here.

Getting to Daedalus Station was not the problem. Getting at Daedalus Station could be suicide. There would be guard ships around Daedalus, and a garrison within.

Lieutenant Commander Jorge Medina, only slightly more cooperative than Napoleon Bright, did manage a nod to that. There were many guards and a garrison at Daedalus. Approach would be impossible.

Calli proposed pulling the numbers off of *Merrimack* and hauling her in under apparent control of the *Valerius* and the Strigs. If detected, she would either look like the *Monitor* in tow, or the newly captured *Merrimack*.

"Well and good," said Farragut. "Unless they know that my *Mack* blew the blue peaches out of *Valerius*. I've got to believe Decurion Silva got off a 'We're going down' message before he surrendered."

"He probably tried, but it didn't go," said Calli. "Kit says *Valerius'* res chamber boiled down at our first strike. There are no such messages in the communication logs of any of the other captive ships. Which makes sense, because it's *Valerius'* place to send that call."

Jorge Medina offered cautiously, "Don't Romans often have—what do they call them—spotter craft? They hang back and watch and run home to give reports. There could have been one at your battle with *Valerius*. Rome will know everything."

Calli conceded, "There's a chance there was a spotter craft we missed, but without confirmation from *Valerius* that signal will be suspect."

Farragut considered this gravely. "I don't like that chance, Cal."

Calli would not be turned, "In the Empire, no one is going to pass on news like that until it's confirmed. Assume the worst case scenario—there was a spotter. He sent the message. To *whom*? Not to Daedalus Station. Daedalus is a maintenance site, not a battle platform. Especially in Rome, dishonor is not news quickly shared. And not with the techs, it's not."

Farragut rephrased what she had just told him, dubious, "We are gambling that the wrong people don't know the outcome of our encounter with *Valerius*. What are the odds of that?"

"Good, actually. Roman security is constructed like a chambered nautilus, just like its ships. Everything is compartmentalized, encased in fire walls. Keeps them from the kind of informational hemorrhage we're suffering now because *Merrimack* and *Monitor* are in sync. Also keeps their left hand from knowing what their right hand is doing." She had graduated from the Imperial Military Institute. No one knew Romans better than Calli Carmel. "It's a good shot, John."

Jorge Medina was shaking his head, his mouth pressed tight shut, looking frightened.

Farragut said, "It's thin, Cal. If they see *Valerius* at Daedalus Station, we won't be the ones doing the grabbing back. I wish I could try it. I think I want it too much. I'm sorry, I can't run this nag."

*   *   *

Throughout the narrow corridors and tight compartments of John Farragut's battleship, technicians reworked control circuits, codes, and frequencies. Captain Farragut arrived at his command platform, glanced to the signals board where the normal IFF indicator was benignly blinking. He ordered, "Turn that off."

"IFF off, aye."

In a moment, Farragut asked the signals tech, "Mr. Remi, why are we still chirping?"

"I—I don't know, sir. It's off. We are not generating this signal."

Farragut bounded down to the signals station to see for himself as Mr. Remi explained, "It's our IFF code, but we're not generating it. It's being relayed through our res chamber from an outside source."

Farragut could not remember ever feeling more shocked. What he had been dreading was already happening.

"Monitor."

He stared at the sounder, seeing now the trap he had *not* stepped in. The near miss. A sensation like a bullet singeing his eyelashes.

During battle, when he had realized that the Roman ships were deflecting *Merrimack*'s ordnance by sending *Merrimack*'s own IFF code, the logical countermove on Farragut's part would have been to shut off *Merrimack*'s IFF.

Rome would have expected that.

And because *Merrimack*'s captain was known as an aggressive fighter, Rome might also have expected Farragut to launch ordnance targeting *Merrimack*'s IFF code at the very moment he shut his ships' IFF down.

The Roman answer to that ploy was here flashing on Mr. Remi's signal board. By remote control from *Monitor*, Rome prevented *Merrimack* shutting off her own IFF.

If this had happened during the battle, Farragut would have shot his own fighters.

But we never cut IFF, so that is not how it happened.

He wondered aloud, "Do they know we know?"

"They'll know that we just now tried to cut our IFF," said Remi. "They are monitoring us, so to say."

Monitor was on *Merrimack*'s resonant harmonic.

They think we're killing ourselves right now.

"Okay, let's die."

"Sir?"

"Disable the res chamber. Take it apart." And he sent an order to the maintenance hangars to pull all of the Swifts' res chambers as well.

An invisible link severed. The IFF sounder went silent.

A sudden sense of deep isolation closed in. Space seemed vast and dark. *Merrimack* was utterly alone.

For several moments no one spoke. As if mourning their own death.

"Hamster, tell my XO we're going to Daedalus Station."

Merrimack moved toward the Orion Starbridge without meeting any resistance. The war had a wide front, and neither side had enough resources to defend all its strategic points.

Napoleon Bright showed up on John Farragut's command platform like a ghost without a castle. "Captain Farragut, I cannot take part in this operation."

"No, Brighty, you can't," said Farragut. "Neither can I. Someone would recognize us."

"And they *won't* recognize Mr. Carmel?" said Brighty.

"She's not as famous as you or me. I just hope Cal doesn't run into anyone from her school days."

Calli was arranging the insignia on her Roman uniform. She said, "We are going to the armpit of the Empire. Graduates from my school don't end up at Daedalus."

"You sound pretty proud of the Imperial Military Institute," said Brighty, a touch of suspicion in that. More than a touch.

"It was very useful," said Calli. "Know your enemy. You should at least try to learn Latin, Brighty."

"I refuse."

Jorge Medina seconded the refusal.

"Jorge!" Calli said in surprise. "You don't speak Latin?"

"I speak Spanish, and I'll thank you not to call that a Latin tongue. I am an American. Here. For your disguise." He produced a Roman campaign badge. "I took it from one of our guests. It looks very impressive. It goes here."

"Latin should be easy for you, Jorge," said Calli, as Jorge pinned the campaign badge under her left pocket. "It's something educated people know."

"No. It's something the bad guys know."

"Romans aren't all bad," said Calli.

"No. Yes. Yes, they are," said Jorge. "They are bad. They were born bad. They are bad. That is why we have to shoot all of them we can before someone can call another truce."

"Amen," said Brighty.

"That's a Latin word," said Calli. And to John Farragut, "How do I look?"

"Screechin'," said Farragut. She looked head to toe a Roman decurion.

A black jumpsuit from *Valerius* had been altered to fit Calli's very slender form. She had liberated a set of Silva's commodore's eagles for her collar. She fastened her hair back with a decorative set of bronze Aldebaran scarab cricket pins borrowed from a deceased Roman crewwoman.

"Those fancy bug pins regulation?" Farragut nodded to the hair ornaments.

"No," said Calli. She knew which rules to bend and which to obey.

"I should like to go with you," said Lieutenant Commander Medina. "I know the ship. They won't recognize me. I will keep my mouth shut."

"*I* know the ship," said Calli. *Monitor* was *Merrimack's* older twin. "You won't know when someone is talking to you, Jorge, and you don't know this is a campaign badge from the Aliquidor siege." She unpinned the badge Jorge had given her. "I was in kindergarten during Aliquidor." She handed the flashy badge back to him. "Thanks anyway, Jorge. Don't worry. I'll get your ship back."

Her handpicked attendants reported to the hangar deck, honor guard sharp, worthy of Arlington duty, only they wore Roman black and marched to a Roman cadence.

"Oh, Gawd," said Farragut with a horrified laugh, impressed. The men looked authentic as hell. "Get out of here before I brig the lot of you."

Calli lifted an Imperial fist to her chest in salute. "*Domni.*" *Sir.*

Merrimack continued onward with *Valerius* in front of her, the Strigidae and Accipitridae surrounding her on all sides, high and low. When their flotilla tripped the Roman perimeter net on slow approach to Daedalus Station, Calli Carmel was on the command deck of the *Valerius* to receive the hail. A bank of floods illuminated the Roman craft and the dark *Merrimack* erased of all insignia.

"What ship?" came the demand.

"What ship?" Calli shot the demand right back in crisp aristocratic Latin. "Get that infernal thing off me, skakker. We are not here. You see nothing."

A very long pause followed, stretched long. Marines, huddled at their guns in *Merrimack*'s battery, got tired holding their breath. One whispered, though there was no point in whispering, "This isn't gonna work. No way this can work. They're checking. They're calling reinforcements."

"No way this would ever ever fly on Earth," said another, ready to shoot his way out of this.

But they were not dealing with Earth. After fifteen minutes the floodlights went off. The Roman guard ships wore away.

Calli Carmel did not join in the expressions of shaky relief breathed by her attendants. That had been the easy part.

The *Merrimack* parked in dead space with the *Valerius,* both Strigs, and four of the Accipiters. Calli, her attendants, and a small Latin-speaking tech crew approached Daedalus Station alone in the fifth Accipiter.

Daedalus Station stood dark as surrounding space. The Accipiter's scanners picked out the familiar silhouette docked there. Like a titanic spearhead. *There she is.*

The *Monitor.*

Calli's pilot guided the Accipiter to a station dock. Her crew secured the lock, ventilated the tube, and opened the ship's hatch.

Calli and her attendants—an appropriately odd number of them, five—marched smartly up the tube, in perfect step for the surveillance monitors. Calli inserted her old Imperial Military Institute ID into the reader at the side of the locked hatch.

And klaxons blared throughout Daedalus Station.

7

C OMMANDER CARMEL'S GUARDS turned pale, cold, but re-sisted breaking into a panicked run as the alarms shrieked. They stayed at disciplined attention, as pictur-esque as a president's pallbearers.

Calli appeared nothing more than annoyed. She inserted her rejected ID again. And again. She hit the reader with her palm heel in a grand show of impatience for the monitors.

The Roman sentries who came to investigate the ir-regularity saw, via the surveillance monitor, a very pretty decurion on the other side of the hatch beating the ID reader and spewing invectives—Latin, Anglo Saxon, vul-gar English. "I—am—so—damn all—tired—of—this—programmer—iggarspit! I'll show you technology that works!" She pulled a Roman disrupter from her thigh hol-ster and took aim at the ID reader.

The hatch hastily opened. "Decurion!"

Good thing they stopped her, because the disrupter would not have fired for her. The weapon was coded to a deceased Roman from *Valerius*.

The ranking sentry saluted, and put out his politely de-manding palm. "May I?"

Calli chucked her ID at him and made to continue on her way past him.

The sentry called after her, "*Domna,* this is an IMI pass." He sounded apologetic.

"You idiot, this is—" She stalked back and seized her pass from him, looked at it angrily, and let her high outrage dissolve into chagrin. She snarled under her breath, "Balls." Threw her Imperial Military Institute ID to the deck. Patted her pockets, produced a Senate ID, and clipped that one to the outside of her breast pocket as if that put everything in order. "Where is the idiot in charge here?"

"This way, *Domna.*"

The praefect was not a self-assured sort. Direct attack by a strong, angry, scenic decurion set him immediately adrift. "I don't understand. You are saying the IFF stratagem did not work?"

"You call that debacle a stratagem? We lost—" Calli interrupted herself, as if catching herself giving away too much. Finished softly, cryptically, "It had *mixed* results. I need to see—" She flipped out a palmscreen, made to consult her notes, and read from it in stilted English, "—the 'pilot override.'"

"The pilot override has nothing to do with IFF. Anyway, we haven't been able to access the pilot override. May I see what you have there?"

"Absolutely not." She flipped her palmscreen shut and pocketed it. "I am not here to answer your questions. I will see the *Monitor* now."

"At once, Decurion." And to the sentries who had brought her, he said, "May I see the decurion's authorization?"

The sentries opened empty hands. They did not have it.

The praefect extended a requesting palm to Calli, "May I?"

Calli spoke arctic steam. "I understood this was already handled."

"I'm sorry, Decurion. I'm sure it should have been, but you know how it goes."

"No. This is *not* how it goes," said Calli, cold menace.

"I—" The praefect didn't know whether to apologize or try to explain, and didn't know how. "This is a secure project, you understand. Is there someone we can contact?"

Calli gave her long chestnut hair a mesmerizing toss with a turn of her graceful neck. Her voice became silken knives.

"Yes. Do. *Immediately*. Numa Pompeii." She dropped that fifty-megaton name with breathy menace, "You check with him *personally*. Tell Numa you are giving me a headache that could last for *nights*."

A threat, sexually charged. Her already tense escort struggled to remain expressionless. That Calli Carmel possessed beauty beyond any measure was simple fact. But none of them had ever known her to *use* it. Danger arced like an ozone burn. The XO was pulling out all the weapons in her arsenal here. They were in deep trouble; Calli Carmel had fallen back on her looks.

The praefect rose.

Daedalus Station was protected in its isolation, and Palatine was light on its internal police in secure places. A Roman was sworn to the Empire, and the Empire in turn trusted its citizens. Its soldiers more so. Betrayal of that trust was repaid with extreme brutality that extended to your children and your spouse. You could trust your fellow Romans to do their duty.

The praefect assumed the decurion loved her family. It did not occur to him for an instant that she might not be Roman. "This way, Decurion."

"If you are going to send a message, use the resonator, not a bloody telegraph!"

Rufus Novo had not realized he had been tapping. He set down the stylus, apologized through the partition, and turned up some white noise for privacy.

He flipped the decurion's discarded IMI pass over and over in his hand. Tapped it.

So all standard procedures and protocols crumble in front of a beautiful angry woman. Just like that. Callista Carmel was not on any list Rufus Novo had seen. This was too irregular.

Inattention to procedure was what got Rufus Novo posted to this bunghole of the Empire in the first place.

Still, it was not for Rufus Novo to question a decurion's word.

He had run a check on the IMI pass. The pass was genuine and valid, if very old, and this Callista Carmel was the coded holder. The card reader had only rejected her access to the station, not her identity or her ownership of the pass.

He cross-checked her identity with Imperial Military Institute records, and found that, yes, Callista Carmel had attended. Graduated. *Cum laude.*

That should have stopped him, but he tried to pull up her subsequent military career history and got nothing. Novo could not find which Legion she belonged to.

Gave him a queasy feeling. She was either not on the roles, or Rufus Novo was treading on some very deeply placed toes here.

Should have stopped right there.

Got it into his head to call Numa Pompeii. (Hadn't she told him to? Immediately? Personally?)

Well, the personally part had been directed at the praefect, but Novo decided someone ought to do it.

He located the general's calling code in the universal log. Local time zone information came up as he logged the code into the com.

Middle of the night, Isis Station.

Should have stopped right there.

It only made sense that a man like Numa Pompeii should have companionship that was the caliber of a woman named Callista. A tall beauty with wide almond eyes and a walk like a gazelle. Novo had to wonder if he were about to step on the big man's dick. And wake him up to do it.

Rufus Novo tapped.

The Numa Pompeii he knew kept his head and his dick in separate quarters.

Rufus Novo initiated the call to Isis Station.

Calli moved about *Monitor* with one eye on her palmscreen, as if she needed a diagram to find her way.

The praefect followed her. He was a gaunt man, more scientist than soldier. His name was Rubius Siculus. He had become keenly attuned to politics and what patrons could do for you or to you. "May I ask, Decurion, the nature of the problem General Pompeii has with us out here at Daedalus?"

"Strategus" was the word Siculus used. General. It was Numa Pompeii's rank. Though most people called Numa Pompeii by his most august title of *Triumphalis.*

Calli answered grudgingly, *"Merrimack* has her protects on. Someone tipped our hand. This is unforgivable."

The praefect saw that Calli knew quite a bit about the

project. More than he, apparently. "That can't be. We detected first phase success. *Merrimack* shut off her IFF at—"

"—At precisely fourteen hundred thirty-one hours and fifty-eight seconds PPMT on the eighth," Calli finished for him.

The engineers of Daedalus Station quickly checked their logs. Looked up again like a lot of bobbleheads. Gave astonished nods to the praefect. She was right.

They wondered how she could know that. No one outside Daedalus knew that.

She had to be Imperial Security. Imperial Security had tentacles no one else could see.

The attitude around her abruptly transformed from guarded suspicion to deferential dread. No one barred her way to *Monitor*'s control box. By now the engineers were only mildly amazed that she opened it so quickly when they had been trying for weeks. They only asked, "How did you do that?"

"How did you not," said Calli. Not a question. Scorn rather.

She made a show of pulling Captain Matthew Forshaw's authorization from the control box.

An engineer dared a defensive grumble, "If I may say so, Decurion, we could work more efficiently out here if those who have information shared it with those with a need to know."

She gave a cold, cold glare as if reading the engineer's ID off his badge and committing it to memory for later treatment. "I will make sure your comments are shared with those who need to know."

A voice, as clear as if originating in the compartment with Novo rather than from two megaparcs away, answered from the com: "Ops. Isis Station."

Rufus Novo tried to imitate the confident brusque menace that had carried the decurion past any challenge, "General Pompeii, at once."

Didn't work. "Who are you?" the querulous voice returned.

Novo quailed. Why did she have to ask that? He wasn't anyone. "Rufus Novo. Daedalus Station."

"Rank!" the dragon at General Pompeii's gate demanded.

"I—I'm a sentry on Daedalus Station. I have been ordered to check something with General Pompeii. Personally."

"You're a *what*? Who is your CO?" The dragon was old guard Roman, with little or no love for Novos—those come-lately Romans, whose kind had not suffered through the Long Silence. "Have you ever heard of chain of command, Novo?"

"I have orders." Sort of. "I am trying to verify an authorization to a secure site."

"The triumphalis is asleep." She hung out Numa Pompeii's augmented title. Not *just* a general. An enormously successful conquering general.

"Wake him up."

A dead pause. Then, "Novo, are you tired of living?"

"Just tell me—Decurion Callista Carmel—does she have authorization to the project at Daedalus Station? Can you find that for me?"

"Hold," the voice ordered.

Novo waited in silence. Except for the sound of his own tapping.

"What are you doing now?"

A Roman engineer tried to peer over Calli's eagled shoulder as she loaded numbers into the resonator, a 160-digit harmonic code (being the birth dates of John Farragut's twenty brothers and sisters in ascending order, except for the twins, placed third and sixteenth).

Calli said only, "You *do* know that one ship can control the other, if you know what you're doing?"

"Yes, *Domna*. That's what we've been trying to do."

"I did say 'if you know what you're doing,' did I not?"

Rufus Novo waited at the res com. Tapped.

He braced himself for what voice would eventually sound over the com. Or would the answer come in the form of Daedalus Station sentries bursting through the hatch, dispatched to arrest whoever was making midnight calls to Numa Pompeii?

The clarity and immediacy of the voice made Novo jump in his seat. A familiar, crumbly, booming baritone he had heard so often on military broadcasts. Joy in it, "You have secured the *Merrimack*!"

Novo choked, his face burning, stammered, "No, Triumphalis."

The sleepiness came through now in the growl, "Then why are you calling me!"

Because I'm a bit of an idiot, Triumphalis. "It's about Decurion Carmel—"

"Callista! Is she asking for me?"

Callista. By any gods left in the world, Novo had gone and done it. *Callista.*

Novo, you just woke up a senator/strategus—a triumphalis—fourth man in the Empire, to challenge his girl-friend.

"No *Domni,* I— Does Decurion Carmel have authority to access *Monitor*'s master codes?"

Very cross, completely mystified by the question, Numa said: "I have no doubt that Callista Carmel has full authority to do whatever the hell she wants on either *Monitor* class ship. What is your question?"

Novo foundered. "That was the question, *Domni.*"

A curse. Dead air. The click of disconnect.

Novo dropped his forehead to the console. More than a bit of an idiot.

Numa Pompeii's bedchamber was a spacious compartment on Isis Station, soaring two decks high and decorated in overwrought senatorial splendor. The heavy tapestries, the muraled overhead, the ornate bronze filigree were not to his taste, but rather expected of his august rank. He settled back into the velvet-and-eiderdown comfort from which he had been roused.

Unsorted thoughts came, as they often did as he drifted toward sleep.

Callista Carmel.

He had not thought of that silly, ridiculously pretty bitch in a long time.

Didn't know who she had smiled at to get into the Institute. The only women General Pompeii trusted in the fighting ranks looked like well-upholstered tanks.

Calli Carmel had called for him. Good. He needed a laugh right now.

The general was a man of duty. He accepted the great responsibility that went with his great power and these gods-awful rich tapestries. The matter of another Kali weighed, crushing, on Numa Pompeii's broad shoulders. That pinheaded Novo had no idea.

He had chuckled when he'd thought Callista Carmel was in captivity and asking for him, as if she thought she could get any special consideration from him.

But the error was his. She had not asked.

So why had her name even come up?

Numa Pompeii had been anticipating for several weeks now a report from Decurion Diomede Silva of the *Valerius* with news of *Merrimack*'s capture. Numa had *not* been expecting a weird question from a no-ranking Novo.

Does she have authority?

Yes, Terran operations were not compartmentalized like the Empire's. Which was why this ploy—using the *Monitor* to control *Merrimack*'s IFF—ought to work. The two ships were too closely linked. Such a danger never presented itself in vessels of the Imperial Legions.

Why was anyone asking after Callista Carmel?

And why call her decurion? A clumsy, inaccurate translation of her Terran rank. Why try to translate it to Latin at all? The Novo was ignorant, but was that the all of it?

The nagging seed grew weeds in his comfort.

And Numa wondered if he had not been speaking at cross-purposes with his midnight caller.

He rolled to his com. "Gemma, get that man back on the com!"

"Who, *domni*?"

"Whoever just called me. Get him back on the com *now*."

Calli dispatched the five members of her escort, one by one, back to the Accipiter on pretext of fetching this or that, until all five were safely off *Monitor*. She muttered, apparently to herself but meant to be overheard, "What the hell is taking them so long?"

There was nothing for them to fetch, and she certainly did not want her attendants to come back. In case something went wrong now, only she would die.

Calli's Accipiter was powered up and ready to run—without her, if need be.

Calli immobilized *Monitor*'s air lock hatches, including

the open hatch where the docking tube connected the *Monitor* to Daedalus Station.

Standard ship design in any modern vessel included a trigger enabling the automatic shutting and sealing of all interior hatches in case of sudden decompression. Calli disabled that feature on *Monitor*. All open hatches were now frozen open.

Personnel aboard Daedalus Station, except for those in the compartment adjacent to the docking tube, would survive a sudden separation. Anyone on board *Monitor* would die.

There was a term for it back on the *Mack*—letting the vacuum in.

"What are you doing now?"

Calli stood up, faced the praefect, Rubius Siculus. "You know what? I can do *nothing* here. Some squidhead trying something very scientific like trial and error triggered all the fail-safes and has locked up everything."

Red in the face, palm out, the praefect ordered, "Decurion, I need to see what you have been working from. I insist you hand over your notes."

Calli surrendered her palmscreen. "Take it to hell." And marched away.

"Triumphalis!"

Numa Pompeii did not have a visual, but he heard Novo salute the com, fist to chest.

Numa gave a weary growl. "Is Callista Carmel trying to meddle with *Monitor*'s controls?"

"Yes, Triumphalis."

"What—" Numa pressed his hand to his forehead, trying to force this inquiry to make sense. He found he could not even phrase a proper question. "What—exactly—is she doing and how?"

"I'm not sure, *domni*. Shall I put her on the com?"

The general's silence was brief, stunned, volcanic.

General Numa Pompeii felt he'd been hit in the face with a hammer.

Put her on the com? She was *there*?

Who knew a woman with looks like that could have such balls on her? He was hard put not to laugh. *Decurion* Carmel. Did laugh. It was horrible.

Numa Pompeii thundered, "Callista Carmel is a U.S. Naval officer, you bubonic squid! Detain her!"

8

CALLI CARMEL TRIED not to look hurried as she hurried through the passageways of *Monitor*. At any tick now, *Merrimack* would summon her sister ship out of soft dock. And Calli's decurion persona, if not Calli herself, would come apart as *Monitor* tore free from Daedalus Station.

The air lock in sight, Calli checked her breathing. She must be the picture of calm crossing into Daedalus Station.

Survival instinct howled at her to run. She maintained her purposeful measured march.

Heard running steps behind her. "Decurion! Decurion!" It was the praefect, Rubius Siculus.

Calli kept walking, face forward, cursing inwardly. She shouted up, so her voice would carry behind her, in her most annoyed voice, "What *is* it, Praefect?"

Her boot sole touched the softer surface of the docking tube. Almost, almost, almost there. But not there. She pictured, very clearly, this tube suddenly flapping like a withering balloon and spitting her into space. She could only imagine that kind of cold. Wondered, chilled, how long she would have to endure it before it killed her.

She was halfway through the soft dock when the tube jerked rigid, straight flat, under her boots. It had started.

Calli caught her balance, swore, broke into an all-out run for her life. Heard Rubius Siculus stumbling after her.

She launched herself into a flying dive at the air lock. Flew through the hatch into Daedalus. She grasped at a handhold as the structural groans shook her throat. Her long hair lifted, fluttering, in the bitter cold. Klaxons blared the decompression warning. Separation was imminent. The tube was tearing. She had to get this hatch shut, now.

The docking tube bucked. The airflow became an outward roar. The praefect was right there. His fingers clawed, white, at the station hatchway.

She might have kicked him back into the tube and shut him out, none the wiser. Instead she whirled, grabbed Rubius Siculus' gray uniform with her free hand, hauled him in with strength she didn't have, and slammed the hatch shut with both of them on this side of it as the soft dock tore away and *Monitor* pulled free.

Calli had fallen to the deck of the small compartment, gasping. Eardrums numb.

Alarms sounded far away and gauze-covered. She touched her wrist to her upper lip. Drew her wrist back bloody. She had blown a sinus.

Calli rasped (sounding alarmed was easy), "Why is that ship moving?"

The praefect pulled himself up to his quaking knees, confused. "I don't know."

Calli lifted her com to her mouth and hailed her Accipiter—in Latin—"What is happening?"

The response, keeping character, came back also in Latin: *"Domna!"* The tech refrained from thanking God Calli was alive. Said instead: *"Monitor* is moving apart from Daedalus Station. Shall we pursue?"

"Wait for me," Calli ordered. She rose precariously to her feet. Tried the inside hatch. It was locked.

All the station hatches between her and her Accipiter would now be sealed. Standard procedure in a Roman emergency. The chambered nautilus in action.

She turned to the praefect, "Rubius, can you open this?"

He seemed about to comply when his com shrieked alive: "Breach! Breach! We have a security breach!"

Rubius Siculus checked the caller's ID on his com. One Rufus Novo. Not sure who that was. The praefect shut him off with a mutter. "Astute bastard." Alarms banged at his eardrums. Breach was damnably obvious.

He turned to Calli, locked a meaningful gaze straight into her eyes. He opened his mouth rather helplessly as if searching for words. Calli was horrified that he might be about to thank her for saving his life.

The praefect's com reactivated. Novo again, overriding the shutoff: *"Callista Carmel is a U.S. agent! Detain her!"*

Rubius Siculus, stunned, answered softly, "Was that an *order*, Novo?"

"The Triumphalis Numa Pompeii told me *himself*! Arrest her! Arrest her!"

Rubius Siculus turned wide, amazed eyes to Calli.

Calli made a droll moue, as if this were all too peculiar for comment.

The praefect clicked the com off, opened another channel. "Security. Brig Rufus Novo." And to Calli he concluded, "This Novo must be in league with those pirates making off with *Monitor*."

She nodded. "That would make sense. Distraction tactics."

The praefect signaled his station defenses, "Contain *Monitor*! The ship is in hostile hands!"

Calli spoke low, with a touch to the praefect's forearm, "Careful, Rubius. They have hostages. Not *all* those men still on board *Monitor* can be enemy agents." It stung her to say so, when she knew that exactly no one aboard *Monitor* was an enemy agent. They were all loyal to Rome, and they were all dead.

The Praefect nodded, accepting the warning.

Calli tugged at the interior hatch. "Can you override this? I need to get to my Accipiter at once."

The praefect complied eagerly. He opened all the doors that stood in her way.

Later, when he realized he had been taken, Rubius Siculus would think she had saved his life just so she would have someone to open the doors.

And that should have been the reason. But that was not why she had done it. She had not been thinking that far ahead at the moment. His was simply a life within her reach.

An enemy life, but *there*.

She had just spaced all the Roman techs left on board *Monitor*. Death was common in war, and she had killed before, but it was always cleaner when you knew your enemy and he was shooting back at you. This made her feel like a thug. She had done it because she must. She would never brag about this one if she lived to tell about it.

Rubius Siculus opened the last door for her, and Calli escaped from Daedalus Station. Her Accipiter immediately joined the Roman pursuit of *Monitor*. Calli hailed the dead ship for show: "Those persons controlling *Monitor,* respond immediately or you will be destroyed."

Her other four stolen Accipitridae, as if answering a call for reinforcements, took up places in the rear of the pursuit group.

The heavy patrol which Calli had bluffed past on her way to Daedalus Station moved now on an intercept course to head off *Monitor*'s flight.

Monitor veered ninety degrees to the port and eighty degrees off the horizon. Showed her heels to the patrol.

"Enemy has powered up sternside weapons," someone in the pursuit group reported.

The Romans had off-loaded all hard ordnance from the U.S. battleship, leaving *Monitor* with energy weapons only. At speeds faster than light, energy weapons were only good straight back. Aft was the only shot *Monitor* had.

Which was well. If *Monitor* had only one shot, no one would wonder at her clumsy aim and, from that, figure out that the fleeing battleship was operating under remote guidance.

As *Monitor*'s rear firing weapons powered up, the chase ships flared to vacate the direct stern position, losing ground as they did.

The patrol commander ordered all chase vessels to acquire *Monitor*.

"They have hostages," Calli warned, trying to keep the chase ships from opening fire.

"Hostages are forfeit."

Calli dutifully signaled her Accipitridae, "Target enemy. Stand by to fire."

"Target acquired," her Accipitridae acknowledged. "Standing by."

The patrol commander, just now discovering that he had Accipitridae in the rear of his posse, transmitted in annoyance: "Accipitridae, are you in this?"

Accipitridae were the second fastest ships Rome had.

Their speed came at the cost of their armor. The commander must have thought Calli's fast ships were cowering back there.

"Message received, *Domni*," Calli acknowledged. "We shall engage the enemy."

"At your *leisure*!" the patrol commander snarled over the com.

Calli signaled her ships: "Accipitridae, fire upon the enemy."

9

MISSILES FROM THE Accipitridae slammed into the Roman sterns.

Accipitridae hadn't much punch—morning star warheads in this case—but their targets' defensive fields were concentrated toward the fore, so the morning stars hit hard. The detonations rattled the ships' systems, and hurled the whole patrol into confusion while the Accipitridae sprinted away as only Accipitridae could and *Monitor* sprang to threshold acceleration.

At the same time Praefect Rubius Siculus at Daedalus Station called for assistance. "All ships! We are under attack!"

The patrol commander, loathe to let go his quarry, demanded, "Identify your attacker, Daedalus!"

"It's the *Monitor*!"

A horrid chill engulfed the Roman patrol. Already flinching from each other, anticipating another shot in the back, now it seemed the enemy held the secret to the unthinkable.

Monitor had been running away from them—fast. For *Monitor* to be pounding now at Daedalus' gates far to the rear could only mean that *Monitor* had displacement capability.

No ship could displace on its own.

Could not be. Must not be.

Was not.

The patrol commander looked at the ominous spearhead image relayed from Daedalus Station's sensors. The signature shape of a U.S. *Monitor* class battleship. All its gunports flashing. He shouted the sudden dawning:

"That's not the *Monitor*. *That's* Merrimack!"

"We need assistance," Daedalus Station called. "We are under heavy attack! They—oh, God. They have *Valerius*. *Valerius* is opening fire on us!"

Valerius was a hollow ship, declawed and down to only one fang. But the Romans did not know that. To those looking up her torpedo tubes, the Roman battleship appeared its redoubtable self.

The patrol commander snapped back, "Lock your damned perimeter, Daedalus! You're impregnable. The enemy is not trying to take the station, you ass. They can't! They're just trying to lure us back so *Monitor* can escape."

The patrol commander was right, but it was already too late. It only took a moment's confusion for a combatant to lose contact with an FTL target in space. You cannot do battle with a faster enemy who won't stay the field. This had become a battle against a scatter of birds. *Monitor* had gained an insurmountable lead. And with that, *Merrimack* and its puppet ship *Valerius* lifted the siege of Daedalus Station and fled in two different directions.

In the Deep Empty at the fringe of extragalactic space, *Monitor* and *Merrimack* met up and traveled side by side. With no backdrop of stars and interstellar matter against which to occult, they were virtually invisible.

Captain Farragut reactivated his ship's resonator long enough to send a two-word message to the Joint Chiefs on her old harmonic: CODES COMPROMISED.

Anything further *Mack* might send on her own harmonic, Rome would detect, too, so it was worse than pointless to say more.

Then he shut the resonators back down. Outer space reverted to its primal vastness, leaving them alone and blind as wooden ships in the middle of a merciless sea.

In the captain's Mess aboard *Merrimack,* while killing a bottle of Kentucky bourbon, talk turned to fighting sails.

"How far could they see, the old ships?" said Calli. "To Earth's horizon. Eighteen miles?"

"A little farther, I think," said Farragut. "If they climbed a mast."

The lower the level of bourbon in the bottle, the stronger gravity got, so they were, both of them, flat on their backs on the deck.

"How far can we see without a res scan?" Calli asked.

"Accurately? No more than a light-second." 186,000 miles.

"Oh, hell, John. We are out here."

"Aye, matey." The glasses were abandoned. They were passing the bottle now. "Ye make a fine pirate, Mr. Carmel. Here's to ye."

"To Numa," Calli countered. "I could not have done it without him."

"If you say so." John Farragut passed the bottle. "How did you know this was Numa's project?"

"Numa Pompous Ass? Had to be. Has his big thumb-prints all over it. Somebody said the word 'arrogant' and I suddenly knew. Returning *Monitor*'s command staff—that was pure Numa."

The familiarity in her voice raised John Farragut's eyebrows. "Cal, you mean to tell me General Numa Pompeii himself taught you at the Imperial Institute?"

"No. He didn't. He was an instructor of several of my classes—the Institute gets the really big guns in peacetime—but I can't say he taught me. I listened to what he taught the others in the class. Me? He looked over my head. Talked around me. Ignored me. I can't say Numa ever instructed me."

"Because you're Terran?"

"That. And." She pressed her full, perfect lips into a hard, perturbed line. "I actually asked him that. I caught him in the hall. I think I had to grab him to make him stop and face me."

Farragut broke in, merrily dubious, "He's pretty big, isn't he?"

"He's very big. I was pissed. I had smoke coming out of my ears. Don't laugh at me, John."

Farragut hid his smile, but crinkles of mirth betrayed him round his blue eyes. "I've never seen you this torqued."

"You've never seen me this drunk. And I *was* mad. The man would not teach me. I finally made him tell me why."

"And Numa said?"

"Numa gave me this slow once-over look, head to ass, and with this pissy smile said, '*You* will never need to know anything.'"

"He has a point."

"*John!*" She smacked him on the arm, calling him traitor with his own name.

"Oh, for Jesus, Cal, do you own a mirror?" He had to stop her from emptying the bottle on his head. "Whoa, that's good bourbon. I never said you weren't the best exec ever to run a battleship. But he's right. You never needed to know how to tie your shoes. Much less how to steal a battleship out of a secure Roman installation in the Deep End."

Calli lay back. The compartment had become blissfully fuzzy. "I only got away with it because Lu Oh was right."

Farragut shook his head, puzzled. Lu Oh? Right? "That you're a Roman spy?"

"That my plan was lunatic. We just caught Daedalus with their trousers round their knees. They should have been better defended."

Farragut agreed. "So where are all their big guns?"

"They're busy elsewhere. On something more important."

They both let the silence gather in. Afraid to think.

What could be more important than defending Daedalus Station?

"Shotgun," said Farragut at last.

Calli nodded. "Rome's building a Catapult. You know they are. Somewhere other than where we were looking for it."

"We've got to get ourselves refit before that project goes operational, or it'll be us caught with our trousers round our knees."

They sobered as they drank, facing the peril of getting home. "The Romans have our codes," said Calli. "They have the schematics for our ships. They've forced us off our regulation harmonic and our IFF. They've got all of *Monitor*'s hard ordnance. And we made them look stupid. It would be a mistake to assume that they *are* stupid. They're going to hunt us down, John. And if they can't catch us alive, they *will* kill us. You know there's got to be a decree out there now that *Monitor* and *Merrimack* shall not see home again."

"Never paid much never mind to Roman decrees," said Farragut. Gave a leonine yawn.

As long as *Monitor* and *Merrimack* stayed out here in open space, they were safe from any hunter. They were also useless.

Their hunters would need a pinch point to make intercept.

"They'll be looking to jump us on approach to Fort Ike," said Farragut.

Fort Eisenhower was the only installation in the Deep End big enough, secure enough, to hold the battleships. The only other suitable installations lay a three-month journey across the Abyss.

Farragut nodded to himself, sure he was right: "They think we'll head for Fort Ike."

"So what we're really going to do is . . . ?" Calli left the blank for Farragut to fill in.

"We're going to Fort Ike."

Their trail split in three.

Monitor would continue on under dead tow of the Marine LRS under command of Calli Carmel. With her went *Monitor*'s two surviving officers—Commander Napoleon Bright and Lieutenant Commander Jorge Medina—and two squads of Marines. Undermanned and feebly armed, *Monitor* would be an easy target if found, but for most of the journey *Monitor* would be running where she would be impossible to find, up here in the extragalactic dark above the disk of the Milky Way. The LRS would drag *Monitor* the long way around, overshooting Fort Ike, to make their approach from the Abyss side of the fortress.

By then, Captain John Farragut with *Merrimack,* carrying all the Roman prisoners, should have reached Fort Ike on a tortuous course. Upon arrival, he would send armed chase ships into the Abyss to meet up with *Monitor* and escort her in to the fortress.

On the third path would travel hollow *Valerius* and all the captured Roman Stigs and Accipiters, unmanned, under control of a computer program. If that flotilla made it to Fort Ike, good. If they were recaptured, then at least they would not take *Merrimack* or *Monitor* down with them.

Badly as Farragut wanted to keep his captured ships, he could not afford to hold them near *Merrimack* or *Monitor* for very long. The Roman ships carried too much enemy equipment, which meant too many chances of singers, homers, snoopers, and remote detonations. Too many ways Rome might turn the situation back around again.

Anything that had been in Roman possession was a liability and must take a separate path.

Boarding *Monitor* was like boarding a mausoleum. The ship was spooky. A giant, frozen, empty *Merrimack*.

This is what we would look like dead, thought Kerry Blue. Her lamp threw hard shadows into all the black hollows. Everything was jarringly familiar, jarringly alien in its abandonment.

Commander Carmel led the way, floating up the hatch into *Monitor*'s lower sail, followed by Commander Bright, then Lieutenant Commander Medina, with Kerry and the dog soldiers in the rear.

Robots had already deloused the ship, making several searches for Roman bugs, traps, and screamers. Automatons had also cleaned out the remains of the Roman techs who had died in the vacuum. Those had been bagged, tagged, and loaded aboard the *Mack* for delivery home to Palatine before the ships split trails.

Still it looked like a place you would expect to meet a corpse. The boarding party's lamps made a poor substitute for ship lights, sickly illumination pushing the blackness back only as far as stark shadows.

The light, the shadows, the crust of frost made what should have been a friendly ship into a haunted place where all intruders should die horribly one by one.

The only sounds Kerry could hear were her own breathing in her suit, and the occasional observation, spoken softly, over the com link in her helmet.

Then herself, saying, "Cheese and rice, it's creepy." Hadn't meant to send that. And to Commander Carmel's turnaround glare, she added, "Sir."

Calli Carmel could dart daggers with those almond eyes. But this time the knives sheathed and the commander's soft murmur sounded in reply, "Yeah."

They floated past Carmel's stateroom. It should have

been Carmel's, but the nameplate read: NAPOLEON BRIGHT. Weird and comforting at once. It didn't look right, but it was like that moment in the nightmare when you realize none of this is real. This was *not* the *Mack*. The *Mack* was whole and light and noisy, full of people and armed to the bloody teeth. This was only *Monitor*.

Napoleon Bright's stateroom stood bare, stripped to the vents. So was Captain Forshaw's, his safe drilled, emptied of all his keys and codebooks, data slips, and manuals.

The Romans had also popped the safes in ops com and in the missile control room. Kerry guessed she sort of knew they would.

The enemy techs had scoured the ship clean of any portable equipment, small arms, splinter guns, stunners. Hydroponics had been harvested to the last pea, to the last root of the last pea plant. Uniforms, boots, space suits, torpedoes, cleaning bots, bedding—the wolves had taken all of it.

And the Swifts. They'd taken the fighter craft. Kerry's chest tightened to see the slot for Alpha Six empty, where her Swift should have stood at clampdown. Hers.

Funny how the anger rose, even when she knew this was not her ship, this was not her fighter slot, and she should have known the wolves would remove the fighters from the battleship. They'd probably done that first.

The lifts were all disabled. *We did that.* But without grav it was easy enough to glide hand over hand up—*Along? Down?*—the ladder the four hundred feet from bottom sail hatch, through eight decks of fuselage and all those equipment compartments in the sails, to topsail hatch. Carmel, Bright, Medina, and *Merrimack*'s chief—the Og—eyeballed everything in between. Scanners were well and good, but most booby traps were still found by those who knew what things ought to look like and what didn't belong.

The Marines were there in case the lookers found something.

As satisfied as she was ever going to get, Commander Carmel finally ordered reestablishment of atmosphere by means of some dumb generators from the *Mack*. *Monitor*, of course, didn't have any.

Found out *Monitor* was not airtight either. Kerry ended up pulling maintenance duty, assigned to plugging little pea holes in *Monitor*'s hull. Damndest things. Neat, perfectly round, and there were a whole bunch of them arrayed in perfect straight lines clean through all of *Monitor*'s bulks and interior partitions. Like someone had taken a laser drill and bored three times through the entire 570-foot length of her fuselage, bypassing the engines.

Kerry pictured Roman techs shooting up the ship for sport. Maybe Rome's answer to Cowboy Carver had done this.

For himself, Cowboy was supposed to be helping patch holes, but he was too busy trying to aim a splinter through one whole row of them with his sidearm.

When *Monitor* was airtight again, Calli Carmel tried again with the atmosphere. It worked this time. And she ordered the LRS rigged to provide minimal grav. Enough to give you a sense of up and down.

Helmets came off. Commander Carmel ordered the dogs in—the real ones, with four feet and cold noses—for yet another inspection: a bloodhound named Nose, and the chief's dog, a big, smart standard poodle named Pooh.

"What the hell is that?" Napoleon Bright's already craggy face went distastefully askew.

Someone had shaved Chief Ogden Bannerman's dog and if the Og ever found the baboon what done it, he'd nail him up by his foreskin, by God.

The baboon had given Pooh a poodle-do, with shaved face, floofed-out chest, and pom-pom ankles. Pooh had enough intelligence to look embarrassed about it. Hung his head as he passed under Commander Bright's scowl.

"That would be a dog, Brighty," Calli said.

Cowboy Carver stood there beaming like an altar boy, and Kerry Blue had a fair idea which baboon's foreskin was on the block. Would have been. But Kerry knew for a fact that Cowboy didn't have one.

The dogs did their sniffing, and at last the space suits came off. Underneath hers, Carmel wore dress-down khakis—the Navy issue color charitably called khaki—a kind of dirty sand or baby shit or dried mud kind of no color color. Didn't matter, because anything looked like a designer creation on Calli Carmel. Captain Farragut was on the real good-looking side, too, but Carmel? Carmel just wasn't fair.

If you had enough money the surgeons could make you

look like Carmel, but they couldn't make you stand like Carmel, move like Carmel, *be* like Carmel.

Commander Carmel hauled on a zippered jacket as well. At the best of times—and this wasn't—atmosphere on a naval vessel was not cruise ship grade. Running on batteries, this one was damned cold, and the burbling grav made it so drafty it moaned like a haunted castle. Unsecured hatches somewhere below decks flapped and clanked like dungeon chains. One slammed shut. Boomed through the ghost ship.

Kerry was grateful for her scratchy black pullover.

Then there was Napoleon Bright—decked out for the White House—overdone in full dress blues with *all* his medals—not just the ribbons—every bauble from every dustup he'd ever been in hanging on his chest. Ten years older than Commander Carmel, Commander Bright had a lot of crap there.

Nobody dressed like that underway. Yeah, it was what he'd been wearing when the Romans threw him back like a dead carp, but Commander Bright had been given normal clothes his size back on the *Mack*. And he'd been wearing 'em. Looked really fruitcakey here in all his geegaws.

The pooch patrol returned for treats, and Carmel pronounced the *Monitor* secure. That's when the wheels came off the mission, and Kerry had to draw her sidearm.

That's when Commander Bright turned to Commander Carmel and said dismissively, "Thank you, Mr. Carmel. I will take it from here."

PART THREE

Firing Squad

10

KERRY HELD HER BREATH. That sure sounded like Brighty had just dismissed Commander Carmel.

No one else around her was breathing either.

Calli Carmel's beautifully tapered eyebrows lifted, surprise. She gave a bemused smile that silently said *What?*

Commander Bright ignored the look. "Lieutenant Commander Medina, begin start-up routine."

It sounded like Commander Bright had dismissed Commander Carmel, because he had dismissed Commander Carmel.

So there was the reason behind all his chest froufrou. The better to look like the master of this ship. Brighty was due for captain's stars. Overdue. He had ten years on Carmel. Nine on Farragut.

Looked like iron. Might have been handsome, but he was too hard. Jaw of iron. Eyes of volcanic rock. His hair was black as outer space. He could be as frightening as one of Kerry's stepdads.

Still, one thing Kerry had learned in her two years with the Fleet Marines: you don't ever want to get on the fang side of Commander Carmel.

Calmer than Kerry Blue would have been, Commander Carmel said, "Belay that, Mr. Medina. Brighty, get serious."

"You are free to disembark my ship, Mr. Carmel."

Oh, hell. Oh, God. Kerry felt herself shift into combat mode. As if she had jumped clear of her skin, and now floated above, watching, hyper aware, moving her body by remote.

A Marine's duty altered according to the demands of the situation. Kerry's Wing had been trained on twenty-odd different scenarios.

This was not one of those scenarios.

Commander Carmel did not so much as change her breathing. She had that luxury.

She has us.

And just in case there was any doubt which side the Marines were on, Flight Leader Hazard Sewell popped his holster strap, and stepped forward with hand on the butt of his sidearm to close ranks with Commander Carmel.

May have just blown the bottom out of his career there. *Nothing like sticking your dick way out there, Hazard.*

But it was decisive. That's what separated the Hazard Sewells from the Kerry Blues. There was nothing like knowing which side you were on when fur this size flies.

"Mr. Carmel, contain your Marine."

But what Carmel told Hazard was, "Carry on, Flight Leader. Patrol, fall in. We are going back to the LRS."

"Dismissed," said Commander Bright.

"Oh, no, you're coming too, Brighty," said Carmel. Like he was still a friend. Like she could pull this skat out of the fire before it ignited. And to the lieutenant commander, "Come on, Jorge."

Commander Bright struck that wide, lord-and-master stance. "Mr. Carmel, you will not give orders to my officers on board my ship."

Officers? He had *an* officer. Used to have. One. Lieutenant Commander Jorge Medina, who froze.

Carmel turned and let Brighty have it. "Commander Bright, you *lost* your ship." Then softer, to his wide eyes, "You made me say that."

"I am XO of the *Monitor,*" said Napoleon Bright flatly. "What is your rank, Carmel?"

Carmel was tired of playing this game. "Mr. Bright. This is not a battleship. It's salvage in tow. We cannot power her up. Anything that has been in enemy hands is suspect, you know that. And for that matter, you're not an active officer; you're a returning POW."

"I never surrendered," said Commander Bright. "I did not relinquish command of this ship simply by being absent from her deck for a period of time."

"Brighty, I have no assurance that you haven't been altered in your captivity."

"Your MO found nothing."

"Absence of evidence—"

"Is no evidence."

"I've got a reasonable suspicion, growing more reasonable as we speak. Anyway, Brighty, I've got my orders. This is my mission. This ship stays dark."

"You may have orders from John Farragut, but John Farragut does not have authority over me or authority to reassign my ship to you or anyone else. Lieutenant Commander Medina, begin start-up procedure *now*."

Carmel countered, "Lieutenant Commander Medina, you have my order."

There was a man with his balls in the pincers.

For herself, Kerry's duty was clear enough. She was a little fuzzy on Naval chain of command, but even if Commander Bright won this pissing match, Kerry could not sink below her nostrils in it by following Hazard Sewell's orders. She was pretty sure her chain of command didn't change just because she was standing on someone else's deck.

Lieutenant Commander Medina was in the hanged-if-you-do shot-if-you-don't seat. At those command ranks, wrong decisions were fatal. Sometimes the right ones got you shot, too.

Jorge Medina hesitated. That narrowed it down to one choice now. Since he was belaying Mr. Bright's order, he damn well better decide to keep belaying. If he decided to execute Bright's order now after a pause that long, no one would ever follow him to the head let alone into battle against a Roman legion. Officers just don't get that long to think.

Lieutenant Commander Medina spoke, "No disrespect, Commander Bright, but it is my understanding that Commander Carmel has command of this mission."

Napoleon Bright's hard lip curled into a grisly smile. "No disrespect, Jorge. I'll have you brought up on charges of mutiny at Fort Ike and have you shot."

"Aye, sir."

Carmel gave Medina a curt, "good man" type nod, then aloud to present company announced, "In the very remote event that Mr. Bright's charges have any merit, I take full responsibility for actions taken here."

"That bullskat absolves no one," Brighty declared. Made eye contact with each and every Marine, "You are sworn to the Constitution to do *your* duty—"

"Just so," Carmel cut him off. "Mr. Sewell, remove Mr. Bright."

The court-martial will be interesting, thought Kerry. *Whoever wins, we get to watch a really big kielbasa go down.*

The Marines stepped forward, hesitant to touch Commander Bright, the uniform, that formidable rack of braidage on his cuffs. To their silent question, Carmel added, "As polite as you need to be."

To be polite meant, in the words of John Farragut, "Beat the blue peaches out of 'im if you have to."

Hazard acknowledged, "Aye, *sir*!"

Dak Shepard and Hazard Sewell took up a position on either side of Commander Bright.

Cloaked in his command invulnerability, Brighty vowed, "You touch me, I'll have you mutineers shot!"

"Take him," said Calli.

Hazard and Dak grabbed the commander's arms and started hauling. That put Brighty in a position you don't ever ever want to be in—with two guys named Twitch and Cowboy at your back with shockers.

"Lieutenant Commander Medina, draw your sidearm!" Brighty roared.

Lieutenant Commander Medina's sidearm remained at his side.

"Lieutenant Commander! You fail to carry out an order of your CO in wartime, the sentence is death!"

"I am aware of my duty to my CO, sir."

Calli accepted Medina's allegiance, and signaled everyone to return to the LRS.

Kerry Blue never ever thought to be walking with her weapon trained on a back of Navy blue. Next to captain's sky, and the red, white, and blue of Old Glory, that was the color of God Almighty.

Brighty did not go as quietly as Colonel Lu Oh had. Brighty was bigger. Fell harder.

The medics on board the LRS put him under. Gave him a transfusion and a blood wash, then put his blood back in him. It didn't sweeten him up any, the blood wash didn't sift out any Roman motes. Brighty woke up just as mad as he went under.

"Put him out for the duration," Carmel ordered.

Suited Kerry fine. She knew sure as squid spit who would pull guard duty if Brighty were put in detention awake.

Carmel turned to Medina, "How are you feeling?"

"Am I being put under, too?"

"I asked how you were feeling."

"Like crap, frankly. But do you mean did the Romans alter us? I don't think so."

"They did something to Matty and Brighty. This isn't like them."

"It's not *un*like them," Medina said, a reluctant confession. "Matt Forshaw was proud and he was tough. But when he lost *Monitor*—he was dead before he pulled the trigger. He died before he ever got to the *Mack*. And the XO is an arrogant dick. I don't mean that in a bad way. That's just the way Brighty is."

"This went beyond arrogance, Jorge. Brighty just drove a class four torpedo through his foot."

"If he shows up at Fort Ike with his ship in somebody else's control, he can forget about ever commanding anything bigger than a supply barge. To a man like Napoleon Bright, that's a fate worse than death. So he had nothing to lose by trying to get his deck under his boots."

"And you, Jorge?"

"I'd like to stay awake and serve. Do you want this?" He offered his sidearm, stock end out.

"No."

Perhaps Medina did not trust himself, or did not expect to need it again, but he gave the splinter gun over to the nearest Marine, Flight Sergeant Kerry Blue, who stowed it in the weapons locker.

They shouldn't be needing weapons. As long as they kept *Monitor* dark and ran silent, the ships were as detectable as a hole in the vacuum. The voyage should be nothing but tedium from here to Fort Ike.

If anything happened underway, it was going to happen to *Merrimack*.

* * *

Something very small, very fast, belted through John Farragut's command center. The crew heard it pierce the hull, zing through and bang out the opposite side all at once. It seared the air with its passing.

"Ho! Skat! What was that?"

Farragut lifted his com. "Systems. Farragut. We just had an incident. What was it?"

The techs on the command deck came out of their stations to inspect the bulkheads. They found a pea-sized hole in the fore partition, and a matching one in the aft. Neat. Perfectly round. It had been too fast to leave any tearing in the metal edges.

Farragut bounded off the platform and into the adjacent compartment to see if there were matching holes there. There were. "Nice hole! Turn on the outside lights."

The ship's outside lights illuminated—and were visible through the lined-up holes.

"Oh, yeah." The tac specialist Marcander Vincent crouched before the pea hole in a one-eyed squint. "We blew it out our arse."

Something had ripped the ship stem to stern. Clean. Without casualties. Fortunately it was not the hull that kept the vacuum out. It was the force field that kept the ship intact, and kept everything outside out.

Kept out everything except whatever this was.

"Engines?"

"Missed all six."

Merrimack's huge power plants occupied most of her stern, so a miss of that proportion was an amazing bit of luck. Or not luck at all.

"All stop."

Acting exec Lieutenant Glenn Hamilton relayed the orders that dropped the battleship out of FTL.

"What was our speed when we took the hit?" Farragut requested.

"Twelve thousand c," Glenn Hamilton answered. "You don't think that was the problem?"

"No. But it can't be helping. Systems! Farragut. What's going on with my cowcatcher!"

"Systems are A-OK. Nothing aberrant with the force field. Integrity one hundred percent."

"We took a bullet, gentlemen. Somebody want to tell me how?"

"Would love to, sir! As soon as we have a bloody clue!" Senior Engineer Kit Kittering had come up to the command platform. She was a well-engineered, wide-shouldered, boy-shaped young woman with a two-dimensional waist and large doll eyes, her hair in an angular wedge cut. She touched a finger to the foremost hole. "It had to be traveling well over threshold velocity. And it cannot be particulate."

"That's not possible, Kit."

"I know that, Captain." And she gave a small woof as another bang and zing ripped through the ship.

Kit looked down, blood flowing from the pea-sized hole in her uniform. "Oh, my." Kit parted her shirt to inspect her abdomen. "Oh, my." Her doll eyes rolled back and she crumpled to the deck.

Farragut ordered the MO to bag his ass to the command deck. Called for battle stations.

Only after Lieutenant Hamilton complied did she question the order in a whisper, "*Battle stations,* Captain?"

"This isn't natural. Somebody is out there. Move this boat! Somebody is shooting at us!"

Glenn Hamilton obeyed. Didn't believe him, but obeyed.

Then Marcander Vincent at tactical reported, "Occultation. We have company."

"I know that." By instinct, John Farragut had known that. "Loc?"

"Just about everywhere, sir. Barrel orbit around the *Mack.* Pacing us move for move."

"Evasion course," Farragut ordered.

"Can't evade any wilder than we are, sir. Inertials are maxed."

Any more velocity, any more severe turns, the forces would overwhelm the dampers and throw everyone through the bulkhead.

"Somebody get that gall-blessed CIA spook up here."

The hostile took another shot. A perfectly straight shot without Coriolis curve or any angle that should have accompanied *Merrimack*'s wild maneuvers. The bullet's impact to the ship's nose and the ship's tail was effectively simultaneous.

"How do we defend against this?" Glenn murmured.

"Defend?" said Farragut. "*Shoot* the bastard!"

Merrimack ran out all guns. "Where is he?"

"Right there," Marcander Vincent said, amazed, staring straight ahead.

On the forward display had appeared a small Roman Striker, in black-and-gold eagles, holding its relative position before *Merrimack*'s bow.

Black and gold. Even John Farragut knew that one. Didn't need Calli Carmel here to tell him this was *gens* kiss-my-ring God's-gift-to-the-Empire Julian.

Once upon an ancient time, a Roman's *gens* was his family. These days, the *gentes* were more like ideological or political factions.

The current Caesar was a Julian.

"Fire," Farragut ordered. "Fire everything."

From Fire Control: "Interrupt! We are not firing."

"A balk?"

"*No,* sir. We're getting an interrupt signal from somewhere."

Somewhere would be from the Roman Striker. *How?*

"He's inside our fire control system!" Fire Control called up.

"How is he getting through our force field?" Systems snarled into his console.

"Close the gunports!" Farragut ordered.

The battleship's field was most tenuous within its gunports. The force field offered only minimal resistance within cannon barrels and torpedo tubes.

Even as he obeyed, the fire control officer warned, "We close ports, we can't shoot him."

"We can't shoot him now."

"Yes, sir."

The inertial field pulled in to a tight seal. They all felt it in their ears.

Fire Control reported, "That did it! Fire controls are responsive. But now we're limited to energy weapons."

Meant that *Merrimack* could not fire forward.

Dwarfed between two MPs, Colonel Lu Oh arrived on deck. Farragut roared, "Lu! What is shooting at us!"

"That is a patterner, Captain."

"Oh, for Jesus."

Farragut had met one of these once before. Should have

recognized the unreal accuracy of the shooting. This was not the same man. That one had been in Flavian colors.

This one would not be in any mood to be gallant.

"Lu, how is he shooting through our field?"

"If he knows our phase pulse programs—and he does—he can predict the pulses through all levels and weave a shot through," said Colonel Oh.

"Even a computer can't do that."

"An altered human mind interfaced with a computer can. Patterners are programmed to detect patterns. They predict things. And they can send their reactions to properly interfaced control systems."

The image of the Striker hung before the battleship's bow in black-and-gold arrogance.

"Is this Kali?" Farragut asked.

Kali, the ultrasecret Roman project with the ominous code name of the destroyer Kali.

But Lu said, "No."

"Then what is Kali?"

"Calli is the name of the mole to whom you gave command of the *Monitor,*" Lu Oh said dryly.

"Kali? Calli? Not likely," said Glenn Hamilton. "A little obvious."

"Of course. That would be arrogant, wouldn't it?" Oh said, sarcasm overthick.

"What is Kali?" Farragut asked again.

"I don't know." And to his dubious glare, Lu Oh said, "Captain, I don't. I *do* know we are in grave danger here. I must not be allowed to be taken."

"Com. Hail the Striker. Ask him what he wants. If it's Lu, he can have her."

The com tech relayed the question.

A machine voice answered with the Roman's demand, "Surrender. Abandon your vessel."

Farragut almost laughed. That itty bitty boat was going to take the *Mack*? He jumped down to the com station, leaned over the tech's console, and answered for himself: "You expect me to unload an intact battleship?"

"That condition can be amended."

Another shot ripped through the *Merrimack,* hit an engine compartment this time. Missed the engine itself with no margin to spare.

"We were lucky," Systems reported.

"I don't think so," said Lu Oh.

"Okay," Farragut sent over the com. "What happens to my people in their life pods?"

"They will be picked up," the mechanical voice returned.

"By who? When? There's no one out here. My people will die."

Captain Farragut was stalling, of course. He had no earthly intention of abandoning ship. He just wanted the Roman to tell him if there were any other Roman ships in the region.

A patterner could probably figure out what Farragut was trying to do.

The Roman response came as a whistle across the top of John Farragut's head. Singed his hair and made him duck. "*Hel*-lo!"

Rising from his crouch, Farragut gingerly touched the top of his head. A few burned brittle strands of dark-blond hair fell away.

He wondered if that had been a miss.

The Roman sent: "Next, I will take out an engine."

Farragut turned off the com. "Ram him. Redline."

Merrimack sprang at the patterner's little Striker at full acceleration—daring him to explode an engine he was about to wear.

The Striker dodged deftly to the side, but by then the momentum of *Merrimack's* large mass carried her megaklicks into the Deep.

The charge forced the Striker to come full about, which meant dropping out of FTL and reaccelerating in the opposite direction from its previous travel.

"Evasive maneuvers, Captain?"

"No." Course deviation became impossible near threshold velocity. "Run us up to the gate."

The contained detonations in all six engines roared, muted through the dampers. Still they shook the ship. Gauges climbed into red zones on all the consoles, and the ship grew warm even with the heaters turned off.

"Where's our friend? Is he doing his electron act?" Farragut drew orbits in the air with his forefinger.

"No, Captain," said Tactical. "He's behind us. Nine hundred thousand klicks. Closing slowly."

Farragut said nothing, seemed to be listening. And all other voices on the command platform stopped. Listened, too. Waiting on the shot.

That did not come.

At last Lieutenant Glenn Hamilton spoke for all of them, "Why isn't he shooting?"

"He can't," said Farragut. "He has to be in front to shoot."

"Now how did you know that?" Lu Oh cried.

"I didn't. I found that out when we blew past him. He didn't fire a flanking shot. Everything he's sent through us has been straight front to back. All we have to do is keep in front of him for the rest of our lives."

"Or six days, which is when he will overtake us at his current rate of acceleration," Tactical reported.

Farragut nodded. He would think of something before then. Because he had to. In the meantime, "Where are we headed?"

"Galactic north northwest."

In other words, nowhere. Fast.

11

THE WELCOMING LIGHTS of Fort Ike shone at a great distance.

The voyage had been long and dark. The destination, now in sight, lay just out of reach.

Where were the trace ships come to run *Monitor* in? John Farragut should have got here first. He was meant to come out and meet her.

It could not be that he could not see her. Dark as *Monitor* and the LRS were, Farragut knew exactly where to look. They had planned for this.

He was not here. Meant that *Monitor* had beat *Merrimack* to Fort Ike. That could not be good.

Calli ordered all stop, and opened visual ports. All hands gazed at the lights, their long journey almost done.

Question was how to take the last step without an escort. There had to be a Roman ambush waiting out here in the dark for *Monitor* to announce her presence.

But if she did not announce her approach, the perimeter guards of Fort Ike would start shooting as soon as they detected her.

Fortress guards could be fairly twitchy about battleships of questionable loyalty closing on the Shotgun.

*   *   *

The Fort Eisenhower/Fort Roosevelt Shotgun was nothing less than a set of long-distance, titanic-scale displacement chambers.

Displacement quickly became impracticable over distance. Synchronization became error bound. And with any displacement, verification necessitated three points of information—the receiver, the sender, and the thing in transit. Time distortion over distances greater than fractions of a light-second limited the use of displacement collars and landing disks for moving people.

For displacing ships, the enormity of the endeavor was beyond all but the most ambitious of imaginations. The imaginations that had conceived this.

The colossal scale still amazed. The Shotgun used resonant verification for synchronization. Two eight-cubic-kilometer regions of perfect vacuum served as its sending and receiving chambers.

The stations lay on either side of the Abyss, Fort Theodore Roosevelt on the Orion Starbridge in Near space, and Fort Eisenhower in the Sagittarian arm—the Deep End—a separation of two full klarcs.

Using the Shotgun, Earth ships jumped clean past the whole of the Roman Empire without ever spending an instant *in* it, besting the fastest courier missile by ninety-four days.

So it followed that Fort Ike and Fort Ted were the most heavily fortified outposts in the known galaxy.

How to approach it when you looked like a hostile?

In the end, Calli was more afraid of the guns of Fort Ike than she was of any Roman lurkers. She decided to betray her existence.

You come into Fort Ike lit or you come in dead.

The code she used to announce herself would probably send up the red flag all by itself: "Fort Ike. Fort Ike. Fort Ike. Commander Callista Carmel with LRS seven eight four and recently liberated United States battleship *Monitor* in possible company of unseen hostiles. Request heavy escort immediately."

The space cav came charging out, bristling. Their Rattlers were brute, brassy, Yankee-designed craft: swift, snub-nosed, and angry. They were beautiful—even if many of their heavy guns were trained on *Monitor*. They were not shooting. Yet.

The voice that answered Calli was terse, suspicious. "Stay *on* the bubble, *Monitor*. Do not deviate."

The laser path appeared for her to follow. "Thank you, Sergeant. We do know the drill."

"Adjust your speed to ten K klips."

"Ten thousand klicks per tick on your vector, aye."

Monitor followed the line. Like flying into a jewel box.

Gases and particulates from all the ships coming and going had strewn the emptiness with a tenuous veil of smog that glowed in exotic, delicate colors, and haloed all the inhabited globes and stations that made up Fort Eisenhower.

The Shotgun itself was a perfect black void, lasered to an immaculate emptiness. But that made it perfectly transparent. You never saw *it*. You saw particles blaze on annihilation as they drifted into the Shotgun's perimeter field. On days of heavy pollution the annihilations described a glittering cell of a honeycomb.

Riding the beam in, Calli wondered why she was picking up no chatter on the secure channel of patrols searching for the Roman lurkers she had reported. Then she realized they had changed the code, and those conversations were now closed to her.

Good. Unsettling, but good.

Monitor's approach shut down traffic in the crowded space lanes for the best part of an hour. Calli could hear the ferrymen complaining on the open channels.

In the absence of any explanation for the delay, the rumors germinated, bouncing about the local channels, that Spacecraft One was headed through the Shotgun.

So Calli approached the fort to the tune of "Hail to the Chief" on the Marine channel.

On Calli's advice, the *Monitor* was led under bomb squad escort to quarantine in a heavily armed sector of the Fortress, far away from the civilian spheres and the Shotgun itself.

Calli and her crew were taken to debriefing under heavy guard, where she established her identity, told her tale, and ordered Commander Bright delivered to the military infirmary.

Hours later, Calli was sitting in a bar at Station Ibex,

unwinding with some old comrades from her *Inca* days (who still called her Crash Carmel) when the MPs came to collect her with sidearms drawn, safeties off.

"Hell, Crash, what'd you do?" said Vittorio Ricci.

"Brighty's awake," Calli concluded. Tossed back her shot, rapped her glass on the bar. Took her leave from her mates, "Gents."

Serious now, her friends made to stand with her, demanding to know the bullshit charge, but Calli motioned them down. "This won't take long." She signaled to the barkeep that the last round was on her, and she went quietly with the MPs. Tolerated the nudge in her back with the gun barrel.

She was thrown into detention and held under the kind of stark and brightly lit security they used for dangerous and suicidal terrorists.

She marveled a bit at the overkill. Brighty had unloaded quite a heavy shovelful to win her this treatment.

Still, the conclusion of the matter seemed obvious and inescapable, so she hadn't the sense yet to be frightened.

She waived legal representation, against strong advisement.

"No need," she said for the ninth time, this time in an interview with the stationmaster, General Paxton S. Pike of the U.S. Fleet Marine Corps. "I don't want to blow this thing out of proportion."

"You have an astonishing sense of proportion, Commander," said General Pike. The man's small eyes crowded the bridge of his nose, leaving too much face on either side of them. "I've heard megalomaniacs do."

Woke her up. Coming from a military judge.

This interview was not an investigation. General Pike had already sided with Brighty.

But there was no sense painting the man into a corner. The stronger the general declared his position, the harder it would be for him to back out of it when he realized that Brighty had taken him for an idiot.

Calli spoke evenly, "I prefer to keep this as informal as possible."

"Informality is not possible at all. Not with a charge of mutiny and treason."

"*Treason?* What hat did Brighty pull *that* from?"

"You wish to lay countercharges?"

"No, sir."

"According to your statement in debriefing, Commander Bright made a bid for command, which you assert you rightfully held. What would that be, if not mutiny?"

"That would be a mistake—which I excused on medical grounds."

"How generous of you."

"I don't think it was generous. It was reasonable."

"You think?" Small eyes gleamed as if Pike were about to play a trump card. Which he did with a folding of hands and leaning across the table, "Commander Bright passed the detox screening."

"Oh." Came out with genuine surprise and dismay. And anger. "Well that *is* unfortunate." It was going to be blessedly difficult for Brighty to get a medical out without a medical excuse. They had taken away his emergency hatch. Damn them. What were they thinking? "Still, at the time, he was under a great deal of mental stress. He'd been captured by the Romans. He'd lost his ship."

"*He* lost *his* ship, Mr. Carmel?" The little eyes were positively ablaze, animated. Paxton Pike was on his feet. One more exchange like this, and he would be across the table. "*His* ship is here. *Where is yours?*"

This line of questioning was getting certifiably ugly.

Calli did not answer immediately. Sat back in her chair to reassess the man.

Rather homely, rather toadish. In an age when anyone of means could look any way he wished, Paxton Pike was defiantly homely. The sort that resented the kind of incredible beauty that never looked his way. He had walked in hating her. No use even talking to him.

"Everything is in my debriefing statement, sir. I would like to know Mr. Bright's version, if I may."

General Pike smiled. Politeness never got an impala out of a hyena's jaws either. "Just what do you think Commander Bright's *version* is?"

"I cannot guess."

"Of course you needn't guess. You were there. You gave the *Monitor* class codes to Palatine, which allowed them to capture *Monitor*. You gave them time to dissect *Monitor*, then made a big show of rescuing it. That was a daring raid, wasn't it? It was dangerous. It was impossible. Wasn't it? Not if you just walk in to Daedalus Station, say hello to your old compadres, and waltz out with the signature ship of the greatest class of United States battleship ever built. Then you arranged for *Merrimack* to fall into Roman hands while you bring this Roman-infested *Monitor* here as a Trojan horse."

"Oh," said Calli. Then, cheerily, absurd, "I needn't have worried. That takes Mr. Bright completely clear of a mutiny charge. He's gone completely crackers."

"Did you or did you not propose a toast to Numa Pompeii. 'Couldn't have done it without him?' "

Afraid she flinched at that one. Had Brighty pressed an ear to the partition when she'd said that to John Farragut? Maybe he even had a recording, edited to her disadvantage. "To Numa Pompous Ass. Yes, I did. If Numa Pompeii weren't such an arrogant ass, I could not have retrieved *Monitor*."

"Yes, yes, you retrieved *Monitor*. Do you have anything to corroborate your weird and self-aggrandizing tale of derring-do?"

None of the men she had with her now had been on the mission to retrieve *Monitor*. "Lieutenant Commander Medina can counter certain of Mr. Bright's claims."

"A codefendant?" General Pike dismissed that suggestion.

"That does make for twice as many people telling my story as Mr. Bright's."

"Someone else?"

"No one here."

"How convenient. Especially if *Merrimack* doesn't show up."

"Jolly *inconvenient,* I'd say," said Calli.

Even *Monitor* herself was no witness. Calli had kept the ship dark and powerless. The battleship had been retrieved by remote control by means of resonant commands. *Monitor* had nothing to say for herself.

"Where is *Monitor*'s black box?" Pike demanded, following the same line of thought.

Calli let some annoyance slip. The *box* was there. It was a big red empty. "Given that the first thing you do when you capture an enemy vessel is pull its flight recorder, I feel confident in saying the recorder is in Roman hands."

"I'm confident of that as well," said Pike. "And since the first thing one does with a captured vessel is pull the flight recorder, where might be the black boxes of those eight—was it eight?—Roman ships you claim to have captured?"

"On *Merrimack*."

"Of course they are."

"My entire crew and Marine squadron can attest to the capture of the battleship *Valerius,* two Strigidae, and five Accipitridae."

Little eyes flickered at the proper Latin plurals. A red-blooded American would have said two Strixes (or Strigs) and five Accipiters. "Which you let go."

"We did not let them go," said Calli. "We programmed them to come here. It's in my report."

"Any of those programmers here? Besides you?"

She might have sighed. "No."

General Pike looked like a horse with its nostrils full of snake stench. She recognized the type. Hard-corps Marine. Conservative. Nationalistic. Loathed all things Roman and all traits associated with Rome—intellectualism, elitism. Calli's education made her one of Them.

"So, Commander Carmel, you programmed the captured ships to come here. They're not here. Where are they?"

"I don't know. The course is computer random."

"Where is *Merrimack*?"

"I don't know. *Merrimack*'s course will be John Farragut random."

"We pinged the *Mack*."

Calli started up straight in her chair. "You—!" Stopped. Settled. On first arrival she had told the debriefing officers—emphatically—do not NOT ping the *Merrimack*.

So it made sense that the first thing this baboon went and did was ping the *Merrimack*. And received no echo.

General Pike went on to report in tones of dire triumph, "We received no return echo on *Merrimack*'s harmonic." An *Ah ha!* in his voice. "If *Merrimack* is still in U.S. control, why is there no echo?"

He meant that to be an unanswerable question. Calli answered, "Because she's running dark." *You dick.*

He heard the *you dick* though she did not actually speak it.

Calli continued, "You have, however, successfully assured the Romans—who *are* monitoring *Mack*'s old harmonic—that *Merrimack* has *not* arrived safely at Fort Ike. *You* just told the Roman searchers that they were still in the hunt. They will appreciate your service."

"You are speaking for Rome?"

"On that, yes," said Calli, standing up to await dismissal. This interview could not get any worse. "I can assure you of that one."

All kinds of civilian traffic came through Fort Ike, from every nation of Earth and from many of the individual League nations' seven hundred and two colonial worlds, and several of the spacefaring alien civilizations within the LEN protectorate zone. All kinds of traffic. Except Roman.

No Roman ships were allowed near the Shotgun, much less through it. The U.S. Navy would fire upon any Roman ship detected within the LEN protectorate, and would impound any Roman trade ship in LEN space, liberate its cargo, and usually return its crew after questioning them as spies. Roman trade was not welcome at Fort Ike.

Which did not mean that Roman goods did not come through the Shotgun, as many League nations still traded with Rome.

The Marines who had accompanied *Monitor,* except for Flight Leader Hazard Sewell, had not been confined upon arrival at Fort Ike. But neither were they issued the customary boarding passes that would allow them free passage from station to station at Fort Ike. Fort Ike was an expensive place. Without the military passes, the Marines were beggars with their noses pressed against the glass of wonderland.

All the civilian delights were closed to them. They could only look out the station portholes at the jewels hanging in the sky—small artificial worlds, casinos, brothels, hotels—with the glittering space liners moving majestically in the colored clouds among them.

The U.S. stations within the Fortress were obvious for their flags. Bigger than everyone else's. No one flew more flags than the Americans. The eighty-two stars and thirteen stripes were everywhere.

You could make out the Australian station immediately—

one of the oldest stations in the Space Fortress—the one oriented upside down from the rest. Always a good time at the Station Down-Under-Way-Out-Here. If only the Marines could get there.

The Marines' obedience to Commander Carmel's and Flight Leader Hazard Sewell's illegal orders had been an error in judgment, said Napoleon Bright. So he let them off with a stern, magnanimous reprimand.

"A rep? A *rep* and we're supposed to be *grateful*? Oh, he can eat—" Carly Delgado dredged her vocabulary for Mr. Bright's menu.

"Hey! Hey! Hazard don't like that kind of talk," Twitch Fuentes backed her off.

"Hazard ain't in charge here, *is* he?" Carly snapped. Wrong thing to say and she regretted it on the spot.

A somber silence fell. Then Carly and the other members of Alpha Flight immediately vowed to clean up their language out of respect for their incarcerated flight leader.

They choked on the words that rose up when they saw Brighty running loose, glad-talking with station officers, *too* jolly, buying tall drinks and telling taller tales.

"Why doesn't Carmel charge that son of a b—eachball?"

They couldn't understand. And could not come to attention for Commander Bright when they crossed paths in a station corridor.

The Navy did not salute indoors, but soldiers of the Fleet Marine normally showed respect to senior Naval officers by coming to attention. Alpha Flight did not.

Brighty's companions looked silently askance at the Marines' lack of regard. Mr. Bright could demand their salutes, and they would have to give them. He daggered them with his gaze as they stood in a sullen, silent, glaring knot. He started to speak, then thought better of it. Moved on.

One of his companions hissed, "What the hell was *that*, Brighty?"

"*Merrimack*'s Marines. Standing by their mutineer."

"You're going to take that?"

"They are only ignorant," said Brighty. "Loyalty is a good quality in Marines and dogs, don't you think? They are a small concern."

The Marines heard that. Cowboy turned around to start

after him. "Small! Why that—" Cowboy grabbed his own dick. "I'll show him small!"

His flight mates wrestled him back.

"Put it away, Cowboy. You don't got anywhere to put it," Kerry said.

Cowboy hollered down the corridor. "Talk big while you can, squidass!" Turned away, muttering, "He won't talk that way when the *Merrimack* gets here!"

Reg Monroe, the nearest thing Alpha Flight had to an intellectual (she had taken a couple of engineering courses) shook her head, troubled. "Doesn't it bother anyone that Brighty's not afraid of that?"

"What's that supposed to mean, Reg?"

Reg held her arms crossed tightly under her breasts. "*Mack* was supposed to be here. Supposed to be here a fine while ago."

"Yeah. So *Mack*'s overdue." They shrugged. *"And?"*

"You mean nobody else gots the idea that Brighty expects the *Mack* to stay overdue for something like *ever*?"

12

"WHERE THE HELL ARE WE?"

"Somewhere in that vicinity, Captain." Navigation gave the unfamiliar coordinates. They didn't sound real.

Running. *Merrimack* had been running for days. The Roman Striker edging closer by the day.

Running out of days.

Apparently the only shot the Striker had with his force-field-piercing bullets was in *Merrimack*'s line of travel.

Merrimack could not afford to let the Striker get in front.

It was down to a footrace now. A race *Merrimack* would lose.

The Striker's smaller mass gave him a minutely higher threshold velocity. So he had been closing at a steady creep for days.

Black and gold. The Striker wore the infernal colors of *gens* Julian.

A Julian was not going to throw a race.

Merrimack needed to pull something out of her hat.

"So let's shed some mass," said Farragut.

"Captain, we can't possibly shed enough mass to make any possible difference."

"Can if we shed it in his face." He left the command platform to consult his engineers. He took the ladders. Farragut had no patience for lifts.

"Can we deploy a robotic arm out far enough to drop a limpet net in the Striker's path?" he proposed to his engineers.

Just dropping a bomb on the Striker would have no effect. Any simple explosive device would deflect upon contacting the nose of the Striker's force field before it had time to detonate. To counteract this effect, the limpet net had been designed to drape completely around the nose cone of an enemy ship's force field. The limpets would detonate against the ship's sides where the force field was maintained at lesser strength than to the fore.

"Captain, we are as good as hurtling down a concrete luge," his senior engineer answered. Kit was back on her feet, her middle still taped. "We can't extend the force field a micron, much less stick a pseudopod as far as we would need to get a net in the Striker's way."

"I don't intend to extend the force field at all. Can we stick a bare arm out the side?"

"Unprotected?"

"Why not? We're not exactly passing through asteroid fields out here."

The engineers consulted at some length. Ran the numbers. Came back, "Don't know."

Earthly instinct made one expect that something hung out the side of a vessel moving very fast would snap off or drag or flap. But this was extragalactic vacuum. There was no air. No drag. What inhibited the *Merrimack* from exceeding threshold velocity was her inertial field. Naked matter hadn't the same limitation.

Question was if poking the proposed mechanical arm through the force field was feasible. If so, dropping the net in the Striker's path should present no problem.

Whether a patterner could avoid the nets or withstand the limpets remained problematic.

"At the end of the day: I don't think we can destroy him that way, Captain," said Kit.

"Destroying him would be nice," Farragut allowed. "But I just need to slow him down. Would it slow him down?"

"If we can get something on him or make him twitch, hell, yeah. But he'll just make up the lost ground in time."

"Then we do it again. We can maintain a dead run longer

than he can. If I can keep him from passing, we can run all year."

Calli Carmel had not been desperately surprised to be in confinement at Fort Eisenhower. Her experience on Palatine made her a natural subject of suspicion. But she had been investigated—exhaustively—several times in the past. Her past was an open book.

The U.S. intelligence community did not like the book.

During most of the last peace, Calli had grown up in the U.S. Embassy on Palatine, where her father had been a Marine guard.

When her parents' marriage was breaking up, Calli's father was reassigned to a place where he could not care for her, and Calli's mother—who only had Calli because she used to be in love with Calli's father—did not want her.

Calli's best friend, the ambassador's daughter, begged her parents to let Calli stay with them. She need not have begged because the Aartens dearly loved young Calli, and she was good company for their Martine.

Years later, when Martine Aarten left to study music in Salzburg, back on Earth, Calli stayed behind. Calli had inherited her mother's maternal drive and her father's pride in the military. She applied to the very elite Roman Imperial Military Institute on Palatine. She had made acquaintance with many influential Romans by then, and with the ambassador's sponsorship, she was accepted.

Her classmates included two of Caesar Magnus' offspring—Claudia and Romulus. Romulus fully expected to be the next emperor of Rome. Calli admired Caesar Magnus, but the nuts had fallen and rolled way out of shouting distance from the tree.

Friends she had many, and lovers a few, but she remained one step outside Roman society. You really weren't anyone in Rome without a *gens*. She had two offers of adoption, but that required renouncing her U.S. citizenship and she declined both.

By the time she graduated, the peace was already crumbling. Calli and her friends understood that their kisses good-bye meant that next time they met could very well be in battle. And understood that neither could expect any hesitation on the guns. Romans understood things like that.

Even some of her old friends thought—hoped—that Calli was a Roman mole. That she was just forbidden to tell them.

They would still have to shoot her if they came against her in battle.

Calli Carmel was pulling chin-ups in her solitary cell in Fort Eisenhower when a guard asked if she would see a visitor.

"As long as it's not General Pike," said Calli without breaking rhythm.

A very tall, very young, long-limbed reed of a man with a distinct starboard list, owing to the weighty satchel hanging from his shoulder, entered Calli's cell. A space lawyer. Good-looking in a scruffy way. Too young.

Calli peered at him from over the bar. "Does your mom know you're here?"

The young man let his satchel flump to the deck, straightened to full height minus an inch or two for sloppy posture. Said cheerfully, "I'll take that as a compliment."

Calli paused on the downstroke to hang from her bar like an ape. "No, I mean it. Are you old enough to drink?"

"I'm actually only a year younger than you are, Commander. I'm your attorney. Rob Roy Buchanan."

Calli let go the bar to accept his outstretched hand. "You *are* a drink. Do you know what the court got you into here?"

"The court didn't appoint me. I volunteered. Campaigned for it is more like it." His smile was genuine, disarming. "Okay, I begged." He needed a shave. The face fur didn't age him any.

"Look, Robby, you're cute as hell, but you better stay in the shallow end for your first case."

"I'm not that young, Commander."

"You said."

Sweat patched a vee down the front of her gray shirt. Rob Roy's opaque brown eyes made a quick foray there, then looked away, somewhere—anywhere—else. Dove into his satchel. "I wish you had let me on the case sooner."

She propped her hands on her hipbones. "There shouldn't *be* a case."

"I could have done something about that if I'd been at the hearing." Rob Roy glanced up from his excavation of his satchel.

"It wasn't a hearing. It was a barbecue."

"I know. I know. General Pike appointed himself case administrator." Rob Roy straightened up with a raft of papers. "Pike was Napoleon Bright's sponsor to VMI."

"Good," said Calli. That solved everything. "Demand he recuse himself." If the judge was biased, bounce him off the case. Simple.

"The time for that was before you ran him up the yardarm," said Rob Roy. "I made the request. He refused."

"The holes in Brighty's 'case' are big enough to shove Uranus through. Paxton's a purblind idiot not to see that."

"That attitude is not helping your case, Commander."

"It's not hurting it either, Robby. That man had the verdict in before he met me."

"So what's your strategy?"

"I don't have one, Robby. I assumed just because I was right, that rightness would be obvious to a purblind idiot."

"It *is* obvious. To me. But innocence is not enough. It seldom is. The hard—really hard—proof isn't here. For witnesses you've got a codefendant, and a bunch of Marines who didn't see anything that we need them to have seen, and a brain-dead *Monitor*."

"Get the charges dismissed because they're based solely on one man's say-so."

Rob Roy winced. "But there is the point of damnation. The one man. Your innocence comes only at the cost of Napoleon Bright's ruin. You are guilty because, in the eyes of Paxton Pike, you *must* be guilty. The alternative is unthinkable to him."

"Then he has to learn to think harder."

Rob Roy brought his hands together before his lips as if praying, thinking. Then countered with a hypothetical, "Commander, if you asked John Farragut to swallow a whale without a shred of evidence to convince him that he should, would he? On your say-so alone?"

"Don't mention John Farragut and Paxton Pike in the same breath, Robby." Of course Farragut would.

"General Pike is suffering from the selective vision of partisanship. The old school in which you back your boy right or wrong. The wrong is apparent, but he's your boy and he's right because he's your boy."

Calli had to accede to his line of logic. She'd seen it before. "That kind of thing is rampant on Palatine."

"Well, it's not unknown here either. Men see what they want to see. What they need to see."

"Leaves Pike with a very flimsy story. It's propped up with spit. It can't hold up in a court-martial."

"Oh, it's pure argle bargle, but it'll make haggis of our defense," said Rob Roy. "We got nothin.'"

"I'm still innocent until proven guilty."

"No, you're not. Because your innocence means Napoleon Bright's guilt. When the verdict is in, either you or Napoleon Bright has to be a treacherous monster. The truth is one or the other. I know which side the truth is standing on, but when push comes to shove, you don't want to be standing by an air lock, Mr. Carmel. As for the other judges, they will come down on either you or Napoleon Bright based on the evidence, however thin."

"Thin? There isn't any."

"Bright's argument is based on missing evidence. He's making the missingness strategic. It'll stand because Pike has to make it stand."

"He's case administrator! *He* shouldn't be in this at all. You sure this isn't your first case, Robby?"

"Arrogance kills. People are arrogant in the Deep End."

She was about to say something else, something about General Pike and his arrogance, then did a double take. Realized, "Me." This child-faced lawyer had just called her arrogant. "You mean me."

"Especially you."

She sat down. "I am not participating in any more kangaroo proceedings until I subpoena witnesses."

He sat down next to her on the spartan cot. Opened a notescreen. "Who do you want?"

"John Farragut."

Rob Roy Buchanan rolled his cute brown eyes. "He'd be my first choice. He's not here."

"I'll wait for him."

"How long?"

"Till doomsday."

"General Pike will let you do that." He eyed the confines of her cell. The best that could be said for the small, stark, unprivate space was that it was clean.

Calli rose, jumped up to grab her chin-up bar. "Then you'd better bring me some books, Robby."

The Striker gained ground by the hour as *Merrimack*'s engineers designed and built the robotic rig by which to hoist the limpet net into the Striker's path.

They ran the numbers over and over, calculating what effect pushing the robot arm out through *Mack*'s inertial field at threshold velocity would do to the ship's integrity. *Attempting* to calculate, more like. The physics of *threshold* were imperfectly understood. Having no hard numbers, the engineers got no hard answer. The proposed procedure had never quite been done before.

With the contraption installed and ready to deploy came the moment of decision: go/no go.

Captain Farragut turned it back on the engineers. "I'll put it to y'all first: Do you want to wait to be executed or do you want to try to escape out a tunnel you dug which might cave in on you?"

Tunnel. They nodded to each other. Yeah. Definitely. Tunnel was good.

Kit nodded before the captain. "Tunnel. I like tunnel. I think."

"Tunnel's got my vote." Farragut winked a bright blue eye, ever cheerful facing a dare. He called it: "It's a go."

Glenn Hamilton summoned the ship to battle stations out of the edgy, monotonous high alert in which they had existed for days. The waiting was over. It was time to live or die.

The robotic arm pushed a counterphase shaft incrementally outward through the field's phase layers. Tonal changes in the field had an ill sound. The engines rolled a low, rocky thunder.

It was in the nature of threshold velocity that it required constant acceleration to maintain it. So the *Merrimack*'s six engines were already running at capacity. Had been so for days. A notice over the intercom from the systems techs warned of an engine spike. The engineers acknowledged. Slowed the deployment of the robotic arm.

The robotic arm with the limpet net approached the outer shell of the force field.

Came a moment in which no one breathed. The robotic

arm, the limpet net, extended through *Merrimack*'s inertial field.

Lights dipped. The deck dropped. Stomachs lifted toward mouths. Ears popped. "Balk!" Systems reported. "We have engine balk! We are on auto shutdown!"

Shit! "Override!"

"Too late!"

The Striker shot past.

Her engines down, *Merrimack* hurtled forward on inertia only—which meant she fell off threshold velocity.

"Striker's in front!" Tactical reported.

"Sound blast alarm. Prepare for impact."

13

TIME PASSES SLOWLY FOR those who wait. What seemed like days to the traveler near to light speed could be years to those at home.

It made no sense for Farragut to travel as slowly as light, for it took extreme energy to do so, but traveling near light speed could be the only reason *Merrimack* was taking forever to get to Fort Ike. While Calli waited.

She had been speaking flippantly when she told Rob Roy to bring her books. But he brought them, and she read them. Interesting choices. He checked in on her often. Was good company, intelligent, cheerful, and easy on the eyes.

On New Year's Eve, he bundled into her cell, bright-eyed, merry, and smelling strongly of Scotch. "I tried to bring you a drink," he said, slumped on her cot, pulling an empty plastic glass from the deep pocket of his long trench coat. "They were searching visitors. So I drank yours, too." He tugged out another empty glass. "Happy New Year."

"Happy New Year, Robby."

"Don't call me Robby."

She nodded, all right. She licked a drop of Scotch out of one of the glasses.

Rob Roy's eyes widened at the motion of her tongue. He floundered to his feet and blundered toward the door. "I gotta go." Called for the guard.

Calli caught his collar before the guard came to let him out. Said low, "Happy New Year, Rob Roy." Feathered a kiss on his scruffy cheek.

In the seconds it took to bring the engines back online, Farragut had time to wonder why he was not dead. He belayed any proposal of evasive maneuvers. Something was wonderfully wrong with this situation.

Senior Engineer Kit Kittering, moving carefully, checked the ship's integrity and cried, "Where's the net?"

Half the robotic arm stuck out there, severed, limpet net gone. It should still be attached. It was not.

"Where did it go?" Kit cried. "It's not as if it could break off in the *wind*!"

"We *got* him?" Farragut dared suggest, incredulous. "I thought a patterner would have seen that coming. We hung that net out right in front him. Where is he?"

"Ahead of us," Marcander Vincent reported from tactical. "Straight-line course. Close parallel to ours. No course deviation. But slower. He's fallen off threshold." The specialist turned round from his console to meet the captain's gaze. "Sir, could he have flamed out, too?"

Farragut gave a baffled shrug. Ordered, "Hell, if he's moving slower, *get us in front of him*!"

His techs scrambled to obey. *Merrimack* edged forward, closing the gap, klick by slow, wary klick.

The Striker gave no signs of aggression, or even of awareness.

Pulling alongside, a scant twelve meters separating them, the *Mack*'s sensors captured a clear image of the enemy. The limpet net encased the Striker's nose, all limpets detonated. But the Striker's force field remained intact.

Merrimack deployed a pair of snuffers to fly up the Striker's exhausts and send its engines into shutdown.

The missiles met no resistance, and the Roman ship's force field vanished.

Merrimack delicately hooked the Striker, without actually bringing it inside her own force field, in case the Striker should be running an auto-destruct routine.

Farragut suited up to join the boarding party, against his acting XO's protest. "Captain, you can't," Glenn Hamilton said, standing in his path, drawing herself up to her full height—fully a foot shorter than the captain. "This is a trap."

"Hamster, you've got to be kidding. This wolf is hosed." And he spoke into the intercom on the back of his hand, "Mo, join us."

"Aye, sir," the medical officer, Mohsen Shah, responded. "I am being there."

The techs established soft dock, and forced the Striker's hatch for the boarding party.

Inside the Striker's air lock, all seemed well. The emergency power was on. Atmospherics read normal.

But sensors did not read the stench. Helmets off, the boarding party knew what the sensors had not told them. The pilot was dead. Dead for a while, from the smell of it. Air scrubbers kept the ammonia levels within tolerances, but it left enough fetor of human waste to wrinkle the nose and the whole face with it. "Oh, for Jesus."

They found the pilot at his station, dead, but not entirely. His body draped over the back of his seat, arched backward, sunken eyes turned up in a dried stare. They might have been blue. His mouth had fallen open. Dried blood caked under his nose. He looked like he might have once been as fair-skinned as TR Steele, but his skin was blue now.

Cables protruded from the back of his neck, his wrists. The cables connected him to the console that was awake and blinking, waiting instruction.

Mo Shah detected the faint pulse of the comatose, but no brain waves.

The medical officer's hands motioned abortive starts round the cables, afraid to unhook the man from the machine. Mo Shah had taken an oath: *Do no harm.* "I am having no idea how to be helping this man."

Farragut read the signs, the blue-black fingernails, asked, "How long do you figure he's been like this?"

"I will be guessing seventy-two to ninety-six ship hours," said Dr. Shah.

"Four days!" Farragut cried. "I have been running from a fried vegetable for a half a week?" And immediately to the corpselike Roman, with a comradely pat on his emaciated shoulder, "Sorry, Lucius. Nothing personal." For all Romans were Lucius in the slang of wartime. Then he murmured, "What *is* your name?" Reeled up the Roman's dog tags. The chain left a beaded black bruise imprinted on his pasty blue skin. "Septimus. Mo, take Septimus here to sick bay."

"What to be doing about . . . ?" Mo Shah trailed off, faced with all the cables. "I could be killing him."

Farragut pulled the plugs from the Roman's neck. "*I* could be killing him." He tossed the cable ends away from him. Cleared for the doctor. "Do what you can for him."

Back aboard his own *Merrimack,* as the battleship slowed for turnaround, John Farragut gazed at the perfect blackness of nowhere.

His acting exec, Lieutenant Hamilton came to his side, spoke faintly the understatement, "We are somewhat behind schedule, sir."

Farragut nodded. "Calli's going to think I stood her up."

"That would be a first for her."

And Farragut challenged Glenn to a game of squash. It was well past the hour for him to be turning in, but John Farragut never slept after battle.

They had not played together in a long time. Used to be they played every day. That was before he noticed how pretty she was.

The score was more even than it would have been had Farragut kept his eye on the ball instead of his opponent. Came down to it, he thought he'd salvaged a win when he hammered a rocket off the front wall, sent it sailing across the length of the court to strike high on the back wall. Then he got to watch little Hamster try to muscle it off the back wall and just hope it had enough to reach the front wall.

The little green ball sailed weakly the length of the court, losing altitude fast. It was not going to make it.

At the last moment, the ship's gravity bobbled. The deck felt like it was sinking. The ball whimpered the last yard to touch the front and drop in a wall-hugging dribble to the deck without giving Farragut the least chance at a return.

Glenn cried out, shock and glee, a lot of yesses.

Farragut howled his betrayal, "*Merri-Merri-Merri-Mack!* How could you do this to me?" He pressed his hands to a wall, talking to his ship.

Glenn winked, with a little swagger. "Hey, *Mack* and me." She crossed her fingers tight. "Like this."

"Are you done?"

"Oh, *no*," Glenn laughed. She jumped up and slapped the front wall. "High five, *Mack*!"

"Hamster, you can't high anything."

"Patrick, are you going to let him insult me like that?"

Farragut turned. Up in the gallery stood her husband. Didn't know how long he'd been there. Dr. Patrick Hamilton.

Good-looking in an artistic way. Women said so, as long as he kept his mouth shut. He had great intelligence, which did not include common sense. Patrick Hamilton was the kind of man who, when single, always got a first date but seldom got a second.

As tall, but half as wide, as the captain, Patrick Hamilton was in no shape to avenge John Farragut's insults to his wife.

Patrick Hamilton spoke to his wife, "Did you ask him?"

Farragut assumed he was "him," and turned to Glenn to receive the question.

Glenn looked a little embarrassed. Tried to put Patrick off, "We've been playing."

"I can see that."

"Ask me what?" said Farragut.

Glenn tried to wave it off. "Later."

"Ask me what?"

Backed into it, Lieutenant Glenn Hamilton drew herself up into as much professional dignity as she could manage in gray sweats, size five sneakers, a damp headband, and frayed ponytail. "Can I keep Calli's job?"

"No."

Glenn gave a resigned nod. Expected that. Sure wished she could have chosen her own moment to ask. It might have gone better. Looked up at Patrick. "He said no."

Patrick asked, "Why?" An edge of demand in it.

"Patrick," Glenn tried to hush him, but Patrick said, "No. I should like to know why."

Glenn masked chagrin well but still looked like she could just die. Patrick Hamilton refused to know how things were done or not done in the U.S. Navy.

Farragut spoke to Glenn, "I'll recommend you for your own command if you want."

Shut Patrick up pretty well. Lieutenants were often given command of their own small ships. The kind of ship that had no use for a xenolinguist.

"Think about it," said Farragut. Not sure whether he was hoping she would go or stay.

He looped a towel round his neck, heading for the showers, when Patrick called down again, not letting go. "She's done a great job as acting exec. She can do the job. Why not let her stay in it?"

Farragut turned blue eyes up. Fought the impulse to ask Glenn what the hell she saw in this guy. Fact was, she saw enough in Patrick Hamilton to marry him, and that was a done deed. Had even let him hang his name on her.

And fact was that Glenn Hamilton hadn't the service years and she knew it. Could not fault her for asking. Humble just didn't get the job done.

Fine officer. Just not ready. She was twenty-six. A strong professional twenty-six, but command of a ship this size wanted a longer perspective and more brutally hard knocks than twenty-six years could give her.

Farragut answered Patrick, "You *do* know that I still have an XO? Calli Carmel is still exec of this ship. Lordy, Ham, wait till the body's cold."

The drums wove into Calli's nightmare. The sound became the death march, drumming in a firing squad. That hideous cadence that had become a staple of horror movies. The sound of impending execution.

She writhed, swimming toward consciousness. She was asleep; she suddenly knew that. This was not real.

Still she heard the drums, and that confused her.

The awful last roll sounded, snapped to silence. She could have sworn she heard the fateful orders. Not the words precisely, but the traditional vocal intonation, distinct and recognizable as the drums: Ready. Aim.

The shot. Bolted her up in her cot. *That was real!*

She was on her feet instantly, yelling at the monitors: "Get me my lawyer!"

Rob Roy Buchanan was there too soon. Meant he was already on his way before Calli had started yelling.

"It's out of control, Commander." Rob Roy dropped his overladen satchel. He looked like he'd slept in his coat. "The wheels of justice have fallen off. It's time to call in markers. Biggest ones you've got. Who do you know?"

"Uh," she pushed back her long loose hair, gathering sleep-fogged wits. "Ambassador Van Aarten. But I can't ask him to—"

"I already called him. He's on his way. Who else?"

"My God." The strangeness, the speed, collided with her nightmare. Left her dizzy. "Rob, they *shot* someone. I heard a firing squad!"

He nodded. "You did. 'Fubar' doesn't describe what's happening here."

"Who?" Calli demanded.

"Who what?" said Rob Roy, not understanding the question.

"Who did they execute!" Calli shouted at him.

"Lieutenant Commander Medina."

"No," she said. She believed him. She just did not accept it. "No. It's insane."

"Good description for it." Rob Roy nodded. "On the side of the angels, they exonerated your Flight Leader Hazard Sewell. He hadn't the rank to be held criminally liable for following orders of a superior officer."

"Mine," said Calli, hollow. "My orders."

Abashed, Rob Roy was forced to confirm, "Yours."

A tremor moved her long fingers. She was astonished to see the motion. Astonished at her own terror. "They killed Jorge." It was unreal. Yet suddenly terribly real. It sank in past all her veils of certainty. She was in the hands of murderous idiots.

Rob Roy gathered himself for the rest of the news. Calli heard the difficulty in the silence. Finally, he spilled it, "They're separating out the charge of treason and moving up your court-martial for mutiny."

"What about my witnesses?"

"Pike decided Farragut's testimony is immaterial to the mutiny charge."

The words that followed sounded odd coming from a pretty woman. As executive officer of a battleship, Calli knew a lot of them.

"I told him that," said Rob Roy. "Verbatim, I think. I have a contempt cite to show for it." Produced it for her.

"How can Farragut's testimony be immaterial!"

"Pike says it doesn't matter whether Farragut gave you command of *Monitor* or not. Pike's reasoning—if you can call what's happening inside Pike's head reasoning—is that Farragut had no authority to give Commander Bright's ship—his words, don't look at me like that—to you, and you should have known it."

"I still have the right to subpoena witnesses."

"Not when they've been pronounced dead."

Calli made her fingers stop their trembling. They extended long, still, and straight. "I have been arrogant."

"Yes, sir."

"John's not dead, you know," she said, quiet, certain.

"I have to believe that," said Rob Roy Buchanan.

She looked up at her baby-faced lawyer, comforted by his presence, grateful. "How did you know to call Ambassador Van Aarten?" Suddenly she wanted badly to see Van Aarten again. He had been a second father to her. Thoughts of him were warm as a blanket by the hearth on a snowy evening.

Rob Roy answered, "He seems to have been your foster father de facto, if not legally."

"He was. But how did you know that? How do you know so much about me?"

"I'm a fan of yours, Commander. I tripped over you while I was studying Farragut's career."

"Why were you studying John? A case?"

"No." Rob Roy stood up regally with a Napoleonic pose, though he was probably close to twice Napoleon's height. "Commander Carmel, you are looking at the greatest military strategist ever to captain an armchair."

"Ah, one of those." She had to smile. If only to keep from tears.

"I'll have to tell you sometime how *I* would have won the battle of Corindahlor Bridge."

"Corindahlor Bridge was a victory for our side," Calli pointed out to him. "Or is your armchair on the Roman side?"

"No. I'm on the American side. But, you see, *I* would've won it without making martyrs of the Roman Tenth. Big mistake that part. Alamo. Masada. Thermopylae. Corindahlor. Did more for the losers than the victors."

"So why did such a brilliant military mind not try a military career for real?"

"I'm in the Navy."

"You're a lawyer."

"Know your strengths. Know your limits. As a soldier, I make a fine lawyer."

"Then win my case," she told him, dead serious.

"I will. I have to. I'm not going to lose you." Stopped, amended quickly. "This one. The case. I meant to say I'm not going to lose this one."

"No, you didn't."

"No. I didn't."

General Pike came out of his seat as if ejected when the report came in that *Merrimack* had been sighted on approach to Fort Eisenhower.

"Destroy her," said Napoleon Bright.

General Pike snapped right round.

"It's a Trojan horse," Commander Bright said to Pike's demanding, startled stare. "We won't get another chance. You know as well as I do, we have to take her out right now."

General Pike regarded his protégé a long moment. The kind of moment as exists near light speed. The moment seemed eternal, though it was only a moment.

14

NEVER SHY OF DRAMATICS, John Farragut kissed the station deck upon safe arrival at Fort Eisenhower, sprang to his feet, clapped the grit from his hands, spat, asked lightly of the first person he saw, "Is Calli still here?"

The wide eyes he met belonged to a dockworker, who dropped his maintenance bot. "Captain Farragut!"

Farragut nodded acknowledgment. Yes, he was Captain Farragut.

"You're dead!"

"Oh? How do I look?" He grinned. Did not expect an answer to that one, so he repeated his first question. "Commander Calli Carmel. Did she get away?"

"Oh, no, sir. She didn't get away. They shot her."

The look on Farragut's face vaporized the nerves of anyone in his path. Did not abate even when he learned the dockworker was mistaken; the guns the man had heard had been for Lieutenant Commander Jorge Medina.

Calli had been released. An order was out for Commander Bright's arrest.

They caught him. But not before Brighty hit John Farragut in the fist with his face.

The stationmaster, one General Pike, ordered John Farragut to his office. Railed at him with a spray that set Farragut to blinking at every *s* and *p* and *t*. Demanded to know: "What did you do with the patterner!"

Farragut blinked. "Sir?"

"The pilot of this ship!" The image of "this ship" showed on all the displays in the general's office — in section, in 3D, at all angles. This ship was the Roman Striker which Farragut had delivered to Fort Eisenhower. The little ship that had nearly taken *Merrimack*. "Where is the pilot!"

"Oh. Him," said Farragut. "I bundled him up and dropped him for Red Cross delivery."

That despite Roman insistence that the man would die if detached from his ship. Perhaps he would, but Farragut had already done the detaching, and had no intention of delivering that ship back into enemy hands.

"I suppose you gave over his dog tags, too," said Pike sourly.

"No." Farragut produced the tags. "I don't think Rome's going to have any difficulty identifying that boy."

The general glanced at the tags before he clamped his hand shut round them in a tight fist. "Septimus," he snarled. "Suggests there's at least six more of those Satan-built things."

"And it's way past time someone told me what Satan built," Farragut suggested.

"We would know *exactly* what a patterner is, if *you* hadn't handed this one back to the enemy!"

"I gave a critically wounded soldier to the Red Cross," said Farragut. "In accordance with conventions of space warfare."

"Yes, yes, yes," Pike waved away the annoying rote. "You gave up covert technology along with him!"

"The components were not exactly removable," said Farragut. "I would not stoop to that."

Pike stiffened. "You suggest I am stooping?"

"Are you, sir?"

Pike was on his feet, vibrating. "I don't know why others think the sun rises and sets on your ass, but mind you, Captain, that opinion is not shared here!" And tore the bark off Farragut's tree for the next five minutes.

At the end, General Pike said stiffly, in dismissal, "You will deliver a copy of your debriefing to my replacement."

Replacement? "You're being promoted?" Farragut asked.

"Are you trying to be funny?"

Farragut's eyes were wide in confusion. "Was I funny?"

"Not in the least."

"I just wanted to know if congratulations were in order."

"Get out."

"General Pike? I have a CIA agent in my brig. Could you arrange for her to be collected—?"

"Out!"

Farragut learned only later—sitting with Calli and her very young lawyer in Mad Bear O's space bar—that General Pike had been promoted below the bottom of the galactic birdcage for his role in Jorge Medina's rushed execution. Only because Pike had realized his mistake in time not to open fire on *Merrimack* was he not drummed out of the Fleet Marine altogether.

There were no nonhumans in Mad Bear O's. Not that they were excluded; they chose not to come. Different species tended to socialize with their own kind when out to relax. Each had its own idea of what constituted fun, relaxation, flirtation, beauty, music, stink, or noise. Where species mixed, you knew business was being conducted.

John Farragut, Calli Carmel, and Rob Roy Buchanan were here to get drunk to the strains of a jazz trio improvising in a chromatic scale.

Calli sang the blues for Napoleon Bright. She had tried to get him considered a med case. But Pike had slapped a certification of perfect health on him. Not the sort of official record you can elbow into the annihilator. Therefore, Brighty was officially sane and fully responsible for everything he did.

Calli rattled the ice cubes in her Scotch. "In the Roman army the sentence for giving false evidence is bludgeoning to death."

Rob Roy shooed a fat little beetbird off the table. "This isn't Rome."

"Yeah." Calli looked away, out the clearports, to the lights of ships coming and going. "That's why we're going to shoot him."

An expectant snare drumroll ended in a brief hesitation and a leaden thump.

Thrrrrrrrrrr *stomp*! Thrrrrrrrrrrr *stomp*!

The sound carried through the hull, through all the decks and bulks of the station. Hideous. Inescapable.

That menacing thrrrrrrrr *stomp*!

The firing squad waited, expressionless. They did not look entirely human, but Fleet law mandated they be human. And provided for one of the weapons to fire blanks so that any of those executioners might hide behind the hope that he had not killed one of his own.

The drummers advanced like windup soldiers. Thrr-rrrrrrr *stomp*! You could not see their eyes under the shiny black brims of their caps.

The witnesses looked unhappily human. Stern. Uncomfortable.

Brighty advanced in cuffs and hobbles. Unrepentant. He showed more anger than fear. He shot a cold black unwavering gaze Calli's way.

She did not flinch.

Her lawyer stood behind her, looking like a boy dressed up for church. General Pike had mandated, if he was going to attend a military execution, Mr. Rob Roy Buchanan had damn well better get a haircut. And a shave.

Rob Roy's uniform was perfectly tailored to his tall lank frame, perfectly clean, creased like new—because he never wore it—but Rob Roy had a boy's knack for squirming within his clothes so as to look perfectly sloppy mere moments after passing inspection.

At Calli's insistence, Rob Roy had made an eleventh-hour bid for a stay of execution on grounds that the prisoner could be under the influence of an unknown Roman contaminant.

A quick med review found nothing. No stay could be granted. But an autopsy was promised.

When the moment came, Brighty refused the blindfold. A sound like a groan or a sigh came from somewhere—from the witnesses, the drummers, or the firing squad, you couldn't tell.

It was a dare: If you are going to shoot me, you're going to have to look me in the eyes.

The drums silenced just long enough for you to feel relief at the cessation of that infernal thrrrrrrrr *stomp*! When the drums started up again, it was with what someone called the death rattle.

A command passed to the sergeant at arms. Came the litany of the end: Ready. Aim.

Brighty stared down the guns, then pivoted his head slightly to fix a lizard gaze on Calli.

If he were looking for her to crack, he would die disappointed. She showed only regal professionalism. Looked him in the eye without faltering.

Had anyone been looking her way they might have seen her hand steal behind her back, palm open, and accept the hand that slid into it—her lawyer's—and squeeze at the final command.

PART FOUR

Wolf Star

15

FORT THEODORE ROOSEVELT WAS huge. Its array of lights made the glitter of Fort Eisenhower seem provincial and dim. The star city that had grown up around Fort Ted sprawled wider than some solar systems, more populous than many colonial worlds.

The space fort lay only eighty light-years from Earth, in the direction of the galactic rim, just north of the galactic equator in the constellation of Auriga.

The Wolf Star—which was not Wolf 359 and not the third closest star to Sol—lay two hundred light-years from Earth in nearly the opposite direction from Fort Ted. You could see the Wolf Star from Earth, south of the galactic equator in the constellation of the Southern Crown.

Only two hundred sixty light-years separated the Wolf Star from Fort Ted. The Wolf Star was close enough to be a menace.

The Wolf Star's inhabited planet was properly called Palatine. It was also known as Rome, as it was the seat of the resurgent Roman Empire. The names were interchangeable. Rome. Palatine. But no one ever called its citizens Palatineans. They were Romans. They were also called wolves, lupes, and countless derogatory terms, but never Palatineans.

The Roman Empire stretched across the galactic southern plane of Near space, as far as the nations of Earth expanded across the northern plane, each trying to outflank the other.

Rome had the edge toward the galactic hub in Near space. Several Earth nations from the Asian Pacific had effectively cut off Roman *and* U.S. expansion toward the rim.

Altogether, humankind had spread over less than one-eighth of the galaxy. Expansion was somewhat self-limiting. The U.S. had not been able to hold a colony at two hundred light-years distance. At fifteen hundred light-years, most nations could consider their colonies temporary holdings. Any people it took you two months to reach were not going to pay your taxes or obey your laws. That was human nature.

The Wolf Star kept a tighter grip on its possessions and had spread its control farther—and thinner—than Earth. Only one hundred fifty years old, the Empire was vast. At first independence, Rome had launched an imperial binge that spread its reign to four hundred planets. Unlike the nations of Earth, Rome would flag any planet it got to first, inhabited or not, and did not hesitate to incorporate alien civilizations into its Empire.

To populate its colonies, Romans bred like guppies, leaving their zygotes in incubators, so that many Romans had only Rome to call their father and their mother.

The soldiers of Rome's mighty Legions numbered in the millions, including aliens, child troops, and automatons. Rome's mechanized fleets, the killer bots, were beyond U.S. counting.

The biggest force ever seen in one place had been at Rome's sesquicentennial, when fifty Legions of foot soldiers marched before the Capitoline—the mountain-sized imperial complex on Palatine—while far overhead, fleets of warships flew in precise formation before Caesar's space-borne residence, a mountainous structure nearly as massive as the Capitoline, called Fortress Aeyrie. The gold work on Fortress Aeyrie was all real. The blue-white fire spouting from the gold griffin acroteri was hologram, as were the eagles soaring in the hologramic clouds around the gleaming fortress. When in orbit, Fortress Aeyrie's lights were visible from the planet's surface even in daylight. The Praetorian Guard, Caesar's formidable elite, kept a highly visible presence around both residences.

The Praetorian Guard traditionally wore Caesar's own colors. Caesar Magnus—born Ulixes Julian Eugenus—was a Julian, so the guard ships shone black and gold.

The show of force had astonished everyone, even the citizens and slaves of Rome.

The Wolf Star's astronomical proximity made the United States' Fort Ted the most heavily fortified place in the known universe. A siege of Fort Theodore Roosevelt would win Rome nothing but the forever quagmire of a war of infinite attrition.

Flight Sergeant Kerry Blue did not see the approach. Knew better than to try to look. You never saw anything on approach to either fort coming through the Shotgun. They shut you down to minimal life support, turned off your lights, enclosed your whole ship in a gargantuan reflective foil, which made you look like a titanic popcorn bag. Then you popped.

They say you felt nothing, because displacement was instantaneous, but Kerry always did. You popped into another giant foil bag of nothing. You didn't even make a thunderclap, the way you did when displacing into an atmosphere. They pulled the foil away from your ship and, glory be, there was Fort Teddy taking your breath away.

Kerry and the Marines had made the trip in a standard transport. The majestic battleships *Merrimack* and *Monitor* had been bagged and dragged through the Shotgun dark as dead carp. Usually the battleships' arrival attracted a lot of attention, but *Merrimack* and *Monitor* had been smuggled in quiet this time. Most denizens did not even know the big ships were here.

The Marine transport ferried Kerry's company through the historic district of Fort Ted, past clusters of antique stations that still revolved, past the gaudy districts of Chinatown and Ecstacy, and the blue ocean jewel sphere of Vwakikikikik, more often called Squidville. The Marines stared through cupped hands pressed to the clearports at grand hotels and casinos of the Starry Starry Way and the transparent-sided Eros Hotel where lovers coupled in the starlight. This was a high accident area among ferryboat traffic.

Cowboy and Dak howled to their own transport pilot: Stop, stop, stop, let me out.

Cackled at their cleverness. As if every bunch of Marines to pass Eros did not yell the same thing.

Passing within visual range of a Vwakikikikik ship, Cowboy planted his full moon in the transport porthole. The transport received an immediate message from the Vwakikikikik ship, and the pilot snarled back at Cowboy as he ran the message through the translator, "You get me written up, Marine, and I'll have you serving with the squid!"

But the Vwakikikikik message only requested the name of the vision of loveliness glimpsed through the U.S. transport's sixth starboard side porthole.

No one ever saw Cowboy look that shocked. He'd been sent up by a squid.

"Squids got humor!"

He was really, really impressed. Tried to get the pilot to send back, "Her name is Dak," but the pilot was not playing.

Finally the transport docked at a hybrid station in the old town, a military core that had sprouted a lot of civilian appendages—shops, service centers, ferry docks.

The cavernous arrival concourse was a milling hive of beings coming and going, or just sitting in the middle of the deck.

Reg Monroe, carrying her few belongings, squinted at the thing parked in her path. "Is he doing what I think he's doing?"

A big hairy musinot had plopped itself in the center of the concourse, just a'strumming on his old banjo.

Cowboy Carver clapped his hand over his eyes as he veered around the musinot. "Oh, *jeez,* bucko, put on some dignity!"

Kerry was staring in a different direction, pointing, "Arrans!"

Hazard Sewell followed her stare. "Glory be, so they are."

Recognized them for their very tall willowy females clad to the eyes in soft robes, and the shorter red-brown males with their upright manes.

Knew them from the Myriad.

A cluster of three million stars in the Deep End where Roman expansion pushed into U.S. space. What a Pandora's box that had been.

Shuddered to remember *Merrimack*'s hopeless stand

against two full Legions and one wicked little Striker. Felt guilty for feeling grateful for the event that spared *Merrimack* and resulted in *this*.

Here was a shuffling train of evacuees. The Arrans were to be relocated to the dead Planet Xi. Arran plants and animals were even now being transplanted to Xi with its newly restored atmosphere. The relocation was an insanely huge undertaking. But the project had a certain romantic logic and the kind of humanitarian idealism that money sticks to, so funding had, for once, not been a problem. There had been an opposition by those who did not want the ancient site disturbed, but the detractors had been out-shouted by the supporters and by the simple fact that thirty million refugees had to go somewhere.

Cowboy ducked and leaned, trying to see if he could make out any sign of breasts on the females. Dared Twitch to go feel one and find out.

Just because Twitch did not talk well did not mean he was stupid. He suggested Cowboy go back and help the musinot.

The Marines stopped at a cross-course, trying to navigate through all the distractions. Cowboy turned full round to follow the progress of a truly spectacular, tall woman with eleven miles of legs and a curtain of shining chestnut hair, in the company of a sloppy, sort-of attractive, very young man. "Hey! Isn't that Mr. Carmel's lawyer?"

Reg Monroe squinted. "Yeah. That's Rob Roy Buchanan." Wondering why he'd made the jump from Fort Ike to Fort Ted.

Dak looked, too. "Yeah. That's Mr. Carmel's lawyer. And look what he caught! That's some hot—holy mother—*that's Mr. Carmel!*"

No one was accustomed to seeing Commander Carmel in mufti. With her hair down and her skirt up, she was nearly unrecognizable.

Cowboy called, "Hey! Mr. Carmel!"

Her head turned. Saw a line of male Marines raising salutes.

You didn't salute indoors, but they were just impressed as all hell.

Carmel just shook her head, a little annoyed, a little amused. Walked on.

She was no sooner out of sight when you'da sworn some-one barked *Eyes right!* for the way all those jarheads snapped round in unison whiplash in the other direction.

What spun 'em round was Hot Trixi Allnight, star of the dreambox. The interactive neuron ticklers activated all the appropriate nerve centers and made long black nights pass-able on deep space runs of months on end. Experiences in the dreambox programs—the expensive ones anyway—were nearly indistinguishable from real encounters. Only "nearly" because a virtual babe never called you a creep and demanded you take her home right now. The Navy pro-vided its deep running battleships with the best.

All these men knew the touch, taste, smell, and weight of Trixi Allnight, the soft buffet of her peppermint breath, the tickle of her blond hair. The timbre of her soprano moans.

And here she was in the flesh.

The male Marines were jumping like crazed rabbits. Cowboy urgled: "It's Trixi! It's *Trixi*! And—" seeing Dak beside him, "—what the *hell* are you doing in my dreambox!"

Dak grinned stupidly. "We ain't hooked into no dream-box, Toto. We are in for real Kansas."

Of course Trixi had never seen any of them before in her life, but she was a consummate professional. She made eye contact, smiled as if delightedly surprised to see them again, and blew kisses. "Oh! Hel*lo*!" as if she knew them. Inti-mately.

She singled out awestruck Twitch Fuentes and gave her kittenish nose a wrinkle. "Oh, and *you*. *You* were *so* good!"

A shining red glow transformed Twitch, as if her saying so made it all real. The others hooted and heckled. Cowboy and Dak pummeled Twitch back to reality.

Carly Delgado and Kerry Blue, whom most of them knew well, really well, stood ignored like a pair of wet muddy boots after a long trek on a dirt world.

Carly curled a hard lip, said to Kerry, "Plastic mama ain't got nothin' on you, *chica linda*."

Kerry appreciated Carly's effort there, but still scoffed, comparing herself to the pale-pink, fluffy-blonde confec-tion, "Oh, yeah. Right."

"Yeah. Right," someone passing behind her corrected firmly, *not* scoffing. Sounded like he meant it.

Kerry turned, but the only man back there was Colonel

Steele, quick striding away, well down the concourse, and it couldn't have been him.

Though he wasn't gawking at Hot Trixi Allnight.

Naval engineers were in a panicked rush to devise a refit that could return *Merrimack* and *Monitor* to service as soon as possible, when Admiral Mishindi announced, "We got a break. Palatine has sued for a truce."

"No!" Calli cried hard on the echoes of John Farragut's roar, "No!"

The admiral regarded the pair indulgently as a hunter might two favored hounds. "And the president and the JC have accepted."

Bringing another loud chorus of language, the kind Hazard Sewell did not like.

Admiral Mishindi weathered their outburst mildly. "I sympathize. But we need this."

"No, we don't!" said Farragut. "Admiral, we *don't*. We just got a hole blown out of our defensive net. They got our codes. They got *my* res sig, they turned two RBSs into boat anchors—"

"RBSs?" Mishindi looked to Calli for translation.

"Really Big Ships," Calli supplied.

"—They've got these cyborg patterner things that can drive pea holes through a full force field. And *they* want a truce? That means they're hurt worse than we are. We have to press the advantage now!"

"With what, Captain Farragut? You haven't the *Merrimack* to fight with. You propose to throw rocks?"

"I'll throw turnips if I have to."

"Oh. That could work."

"Just let me fight! We can't have a truce now! They'll use the time to build their Catapult and make copies of *Monitor*-class battleships to use against us!"

"And they've been caught committing war crimes," Calli added.

The report from the autopsy Calli ordered on Napoleon Bright had come in. The exam had been a Sargasson one, the kind that found things that instruments of human make could miss. The seaweedy alien race had a gift for sensing wrongness, even among beings as altogether different as humans were to them.

The Sargasson had detected cells within Brighty's brain that were "not right." A DNA analysis of the identified cells produced a near match to Brighty's code.

"Near?" Calli had said.

Near was another word for *not*. What the Sargasson found turned out to be cloned matter within Brighty's head. Dead and decaying, the cells' function could not be divined.

Calli had then ordered a Sargasson autopsy of Matthew Forshaw, but the area of Forshaw's brain that corresponded to the area of Brighty's corrupted cells was gone. It was the part of the head which the late captain's suicidal shot had blown away.

And Calli had to wonder if some subconscious part of Matthew Forshaw had known this and moved his hand.

"How did you know?" the human medical examiner had then demanded of Calli.

"Brighty was XO of a *Monitor*-class battleship," said Commander Carmel. "*We* don't snap."

The genetic tampering, the biological warfare, was a crime against humanity and a violation of the conventions of space warfare.

"They can't call a truce," Calli told Admiral Mishindi. "Not when I want to shoot the first one I see."

"That will have to wait, Captain Carmel," Mishindi said. "We'll listen to their talk and rebuild as fast as we can."

"Captain who?" said Calli.

"Oh, don't look shocked, Cal," said Farragut. "It's in the bag."

Promotion. The big one.

Calli had served as captain of ships since she was a lieutenant, but captain in fact—not a field rank—was something else. It was crossing the kind of crevasse that put you up where angels sing.

"No one announced it," said Calli.

"The formal announcement is only waiting on your assignment," said Mishindi. "And since it's now out of the bag, I may as well tell you it's hung between two—*Monitor* and *Wolfhound*. *Monitor* is, of course, the prestigious assignment—would be, if she were in any shape to go anywhere. The old wolf hunter is a bit long of tooth, but she's a tough ship and ready to go now and I want you on board her as soon as you're done here."

"I'm ready to go right now," said Calli. "What do I have left to do here?" She had no business in Fort Roosevelt.

"I'd like you to sit in on the first round of peace talks, Captain Carmel. As someone who knows Romans."

"Here?" Farragut cried. "They're coming *here*? That maxes it. Admiral!" he beseeched, all but on his knees. "Don't agree to this. They have no interest in talking peace!"

"Neither do I, Captain Farragut. It remains—we need the time."

Alarms blared fortress-wide: Roman ships at the perimeter.

Fighters and sentry Rattlers scrambled to intercept, launching with an amazing spray of hot trails that painted fortress space in Fourth-of-July-colored fire.

Fortress sentinels ordered the Roman ships to stop and they had done so.

By the time Farragut careered into fortress Ops, the Roman flagship had identified itself.

There was really no need. There was only one ship of that make.

"Oh, for Jesus, it's the *Gladiator*."

Not dark. Not trying to hide its presence. It was lit to proper menace, a dark lustrous bronze, big as the Colosseum, with the same blocky architectural lines designed to evoke awe. Romans had always a sense of style, which carried to the brute grandeur of their battleships. Even out there on a scale by which we are all puny, it intimidated.

Sentinels warned: *Gladiator* gets no closer, or we burn her.

The Romans objected to the rough treatment when they had come invited with peaceful intent.

"Peaceful intent? In *that*? They brought that here?"

"It's not getting in," Admiral Mishindi said matter-of-factly.

Even gunships of the United States' closest allies could not approach Fort Ted without high-level clearance.

And over the com Mishindi said, "Park the gunboat, Triumphalis. Do not attempt to approach the star city, or you will be destroyed."

You could hear amusement in the imperious voice as the Roman general pointed out that he was, in fact, stopped and waiting instruction.

Numa Pompeii was notified that ferries would bring the Roman diplomats into a secure station within the Fortress.

With that, the Fortress stepped down from full alert. That left a swarm of fighters on patrol around the Roman ships, but sent back to the rack anyone whose sleep cycle was now.

Mishindi allowed himself a relieved slouch in his seat. "No shooting. Thank God."

"Amen," said Farragut. "I'd've hated to miss it if this had turned into a real party."

16

"CAPTAIN CARMEL, HOW do you say *podexes*?"

Calli looked to the Marine who had stepped forward. Others hung back, listening expectantly for the answer.

"It's *podices*," said Calli.

"Told you," one of the hangers-back hissed to another.

Calli caught the look of alarm on Colonel Steele at his Marines' sudden interest in Latin plurals. She told him, "They just want to make sure the Romans understand them when they call them assholes."

Steele grunted, reassured, order restored to his universe. And in a moment, "What was that word again?"

Calli strode up the curving corridor of the old station, conversing with Captain Farragut and Rob Roy. A squad of Marine guards, which Colonel Steele had attached to her, marched behind.

Clearing the bend, she came face-to-face with the great, medaled boulder that was Numa Pompeii.

Everyone stopped, very still, very surprised.

The Roman general's eyes flared with momentary startlement. Narrowed. He advanced on Calli slowly, a fuming bulk, as if he might scare her from her stance. Calli held her ground.

General Pompeii reached across his body, a motion like reaching for a sword hilt at his opposite hip, but with a slight bow as if the sword had stuck.

Abruptly, he straightened up, throwing his arm wide, the weight of his body behind it, backhanding Calli off her feet and into the bulkhead. She slid to the deck, and all guns behind her pointed at Numa Pompeii.

From her sprawl on the deck, Calli lifted a staying hand to her Marines. "I earned that one." She rolled, groggily, to hands and knees, crawled to her feet. "Put the hardware away, boys."

John Farragut passed her a handkerchief. She touched it to her nose. Blood.

Numa Pompeii's heavy breaths in his massive chest exploded into thunderous speech. "*You!* Presumptuous little *bitch*! Don't you ever *think* to use—"

"Hey!" she cut him off with a sharp, light-toned bark. Surprised him to silence. "You get either the slug or the sermon. You don't get both. We are square. You keep talking, mister, I let them shoot."

The Marines' facial muscles ticked. Watched Numa's mouth. Wanted his lips to move so they could shoot him. Please, please, please, let us shoot him.

Farragut murmured aside, "Nose, Cal."

She touched the handkerchief to the drop of blood about to fall from the tip of her nose.

Numa afforded the Marine squad a contemptuous glance. No fear in it. Asked Calli, "Are you laying all of them or just him?" A sideways nod to Farragut.

"Hey!" Farragut this time. "You. Me. *Outside.*"

Outside would be anywhere without military witnesses.

Farragut's bright blue eyes took on an eager gleam. Numa had half again John Farragut's considerable mass, but Farragut was ten years younger. And John Farragut could be crazy.

Then Numa drew back with a near smile and courtly apology—to John Farragut. "I overstepped. I have no off-field quarrel with you, Captain Farragut."

Numa Pompeii stepped around the Marine squad and continued on his way.

Rob Roy, who was quite white, standing flat to the bulkhead, blurted, "What was *that* about!"

"I, uh—" Calli sniffed. Daubed her upper lip to see if the bleeding had stopped. "Took his name in vain."

Her slender, intellectual boyfriend—and all the other males present—were taking measure of themselves against the Roman mountain. Coming up short. Calli overheard the edge of daunted admiration from one of the Marines, "That was one *big*—"

"Hey, Cal, couldn't you have found someone bigger to torque off?"

"Be careful, John," said Calli. "They don't just feed those boys vitamins on Palatine. He would have taken you."

Farragut drew up in insult. "You have so little faith in me?"

"I know Numa."

"I can take him," said Farragut. Had to. John Farragut did not readily hold a grudge, but he had one against Numa Pompeii. Owed him for Matty Forshaw. "Get those Red Crosses and white flags out of here; I'll take him."

Palatine had sent a number of eloquent ambassadors to Fort Theodore Roosevelt for the talks. Some of them sounded as if they earnestly believed they were here to negotiate a lasting peace.

And then there was Numa. A big, brawny, upholstered rock. His voice could be deep, bellowing thunder or a quiet, authoritative baritone. Numa was in every way larger than life, a hard-living, caber-tossing, hammer-throwing man's man, whom Romans loved and Calli loathed. He could be charming as hell. Wielded confidence like a steamroller. Everything out of General Pompeii's mouth was fact. The man had no opinions. This was the voice of God.

Admiral Mishindi passed a rhetorical note to Calli during the proceedings. *What the hell is he doing here?*

Calli felt like a cheating student, sneaking a glance at the com on the back of her hand under the table to read Mishindi's note.

It continued: *I know it's his battleship that brought the ambassadors, but what is a general doing in peace talks? Talking! Any reason he's not muzzled?*

Admiral Mishindi, Captain Farragut, and Captain Carmel were attending as observers and could say nothing. Numa Pompeii had a speaking role.

He's a senator, Calli sent back.

Not for real? Mishindi returned.

Calli answered: *Really.*

A general AND a senator? And that's not a conflict?

Not in Rome.

Above the table, ambassadors searched for "a common dialogue." They dug at the philosophical root of the U.S./ Roman conflict as if, in it, they would find the basis for lasting peace.

One emissary called the war a battle with one's evil clone. He said that part of the dispute was that neither side could agree which was the clone.

"No question there," said Amos Curtius Americanus. "Roma Eterna. We have been a state since 776 BCE."

"That Rome existed first is not in dispute," a U.S. diplomat allowed. "But the fall of the Roman Empire is also a documented fact. The United States of America became the host to that dead empire's parasitic seed. A seed that ate out our hearts and brains, and took, like a cuckoo's chick takes, our strength and our knowledge for its own ends. In the end the Empire stole our property. The planet Palatine is—and remains—a U.S. colony."

"And where do you suppose the United States came from?" said Numa Pompeii. "Accept it or not, your nation was founded by a secret society of Romans to be our government in exile. The United States was founded as a Roman colony. America was, and still is, ours."

Farragut sent under the table: *Don't give a skat who was up to bat first. Just give me the final score.*

Calli did not see Farragut's note. Her gaze was fixed across the wide, wide mahogany table on Numa as he dropped his observations into the proceedings with indolent disdain. Some of his remarks were thinly veiled barbs, the sole purpose of which were to provoke Calli Carmel.

Calli was an observer and had no leave to speak back.

Calli did not want to say anything. She just wanted to lunge across the table, grab Numa's eagles, and beat the smirk off his condescending, self-satisfied, supercilious face. She visualized blood, imagined the sensation of cartilage crunching under her fist. To someone else had already gone the privilege of rearranging his nose, but it could use readjusting. His was not now and probably never had been a handsome face.

Numa finally said one thing too many—something about Rome not decorating its stalking horses with captain's stars in reward for being good bait.

"Oh, that's it!" Calli, brand new stars and all, was on her chair and launching across the table.

But the mahogany top was wide, and John Farragut had seen this coming. He got Calli by the back of her jacket and hauled her back into her seat.

To the staring ambassadors, Farragut said, "What the captain said, I believe, is that it might be a good idea to remove the military presence from these proceedings. Is that an accurate paraphrase, Mr. Carmel?"

"Something like that," Calli muttered, tugging her jacket back into a smooth fit.

They found the door before they could be shown the door.

Out in the corridor, walking very fast to keep up with Calli's furious stride, Farragut asked, "Why are you letting him get under your guard like this?"

Calli stopped, spun on him. "He's . . . he's *you,* John. A swaggering, obnoxious, bullying you. The pack leader. The one men listen to. Men hang on his words. Women lie down for him. He owns the ground. He's *your* evil twin."

Farragut considered this a silent moment. "I'm better looking."

"You're a lot he's not. The point is: he's *the man.*"

"So what?"

"He acts like I'm not even in the war. Like I'm a dance club hostess tripped onto the battlefield."

"His problem. You can't be offended if you don't respect the one judging you."

"I do respect him. I wish to God I didn't, but he's *the man.* Spits farther, pisses farther. Oh, how could you know. The outfield backs up when you step in the batter's box."

"That's because they know I can't bunt."

"*Won't* bunt, John. There could be a man on third and we only need one run to clinch it; John Farragut would still be swinging for the fences. They respect you."

"That kind of respect will kill me. Captain Carmel, you brought the *Monitor* home. And if he don't respect that, well damn, take your base. We both read *Five Rings of Power,* 'If the stratagem works once—'"

"Do it again." Calli finished the text for him. She had used Numa's terrific arrogance once to her advantage at Daedalus. "Problem is, I can't do anything. We're at peace."

"Not for long. You know what's behind this."

She did. "Palatine's building their *Catapulta*, their Shotgun. They're stalling to get it done. But there's something else."

Farragut cocked his head, curious.

"It's been bothering me, John. *Monitor* should have been under much heavier guard. Even considering that the Roman Catapult would demand a heavy guard at two widely separated stations. They shouldn't be spread that thin. Rome doesn't have our population, but the Roman military outnumbers us. Bad."

"You think we were meant to recapture *Monitor*?"

"No. I don't think that. I think—" Hesitated to finish the thought. Did so anyway, "I think someone back-doored them."

A third combatant? Farragut hadn't considered it. *"Kali?"*

"Who knows. I don't know. You know what, John? I don't know what the hell I'm talking about. It's all gut guesswork. Come on. I'll let you buy me a beer."

"I thought your drink was Scotch these days." Meant it as inane banter. Her boyfriend Rob Roy Buchanan always ordered Scotch for her.

Shocked the hell out of him when Calli started to cry. Girl tears.

Farragut guessed he'd better buy her a beer.

17

THE SIGHT OF AMERICA from space expanded the chest and thickened the throat every time. It had been seven years this time, by his mother's chron. Only slightly less by John Farragut's.

On the approach up the long, long drive to the sprawling white plantation house, one of his sister Amanda's mares cantered alongside the split-rail fence in the bright sunshine. Mockingbirds sang in the century oaks. A kingfisher cackled in the weeping willow alongside the creek.

Mama welcomed him as if he had returned from the dead. He was not very surprised, but disappointed, that his father was not here. Justice of the State Supreme Court, the elder John K. Farragut had business in Frankfurt.

Captain John A. Farragut had made the judge wait seven years. It was a measure of power how long you could make others wait for you. Judge Farragut was never on time, and he waited for no one. His Honor was not going to drop everything and run out like one of the family dogs simply because the boy finally decided to pay his old man a call.

The dogs did—assorted coonhounds, bloodhounds, foxhounds, and beagles came running to flog his legs with their tails. There was also an ancient African gray parrot, who remembered him; a collection of uppity cats, who really could care less; and a lustrous, golden Xanthin serpent, who rose up like a cobra in delight.

There were half a dozen underage siblings still in residence at the homestead, and John knew from his mother's messages that sister Lily's marriage busted up last year and she and her seven kids were home again, so you can just forget about getting your old room back, John Farragut.

His other fourteen sisters and brothers flocked home at the eldest's return with a flotilla of their children to take over the coach house.

Congress was in session, so Catherine flew in from D.C. for dinners and jetted back every morning.

There was also in temporary residence a houseguest of His Honor's, a man called Jose Maria many-many-middle-names de Cordillera, a cultured Terra Rican aristocrat, charming, and warm enough to thaw a frozen hell.

Guests were sacred around here, and Mama just collected *Don* Cordillera in with the rest of the brood.

Family dinners had always been warm and lively. With this many Farraguts at the tables, it was a party every evening. The old dinner table only seated thirty-two with the insert, so Mama had another brought in.

On the first evening Mama just had to have an image record taken of the family all together. Sixteen-year-old John John went AWOL for that. Upstairs to his bedroom in a loyal sulk. Family image indeed. Not without his father!

Mama's "Get yourself down here right now John Knox Farragut Junior!" went ignored. As did the: "Don't make me come up there!"

It was Captain John Alexander Farragut who went up there. "Put it aside, John," he advised quietly, leaning in the doorway. "It's just not helpful."

John John glared at his brother—the eldest, the best loved, the captain, the hero. The one who could make Father madder than anyone on the planet. "I don't take orders from you!"

"No one's askin' you to. There's a higher power talkin' here. Honor thy mother." He turned to go. Added: "There's a 'Thou shalt' that goes with that, and it's not comin' from me."

When reason fails, there was always the chain of command to fall back on. Mama got her image.

She sent it to the judge, who displayed it proudly in his chambers. Messaged his wife back that he had a fine brood, and he sure wished the boy had picked a better time to come calling.

Jose Maria de Cordillera accompanied John Farragut outside after dinner one evening to walk off the meal. It insulted Mama if you didn't overeat, and both men had done their duty.

The Terra Rican was trim, wasp-waisted (Mama would take care of *that*), in his late fifties. He wore his glossy black hair long as a horse's tail, held back in a silver clasp.

Farragut noted his Spanish-style riding boots and asked if he would like to see the horses. "My sister Amy's got some decent nags here."

Amanda's Triple Crown champion, a venerable stud now, held court in the upper pasture.

John Farragut and Jose Maria de Cordillera saddled up a pair of the stables' lesser lights and rode in the pinewood, the earth deep beneath them, the sky soaring above. A blanket of brown needles muffled the horses' hooves and gave a softness to the ground, a piquancy to the forest scents—pine resin, humus, horsehide, leather tack. Grackles squawked in the green canopy.

Jose Maria de Cordillera rode a thoroughbred. John Farragut, a big man whom horses thanked to stay off them, sat astride a hulking majestic black Belgian with hooves the size of dinner plates. It put him very high, but fortunately the trees' lower limbs had atrophied in the shade of the canopy; otherwise his head would be in the branches.

"Tell me, Captain Farragut, are you related to David Farragut of the *Saratoga*?"

"No. I'm a direct descendant of Michael Farragut of the *Abraham Lincoln*."

"I hear you are doing interesting things to your battleship, young captain."

Interesting was the subtlest term for it Farragut had heard. "Most people say I'm an idiot."

On how the refit of the *Merrimack* was to be done, John Farragut had some definite ideas. He wanted mechanical and manual backups for everything—for all stages of delivering ordnance—sighting, loading, arming, launching, triggering. He wanted dumb switches and chemical fuses—nothing that could be jammed by outside signals. He wanted backup oxygen canisters with demand regulators.

The Og had asked him, "How you gonna move this boat, Cap'n? You want we should install pedals?"

Senior Engineer Kit Kittering had been interested in the answer to that one as well.

Merrimack's engines were shrouded in six discrete phase-shifting barriers. Any one power plant could muscle the ship home. If all six were compromised, John Farragut would just have to get out and push.

No, he had answered. No pedals. He would trust the engines.

He did, however, want a backup switch to initiate or override the antimatter jettison system.

It was all very *interesting*.

"You think I'm an idiot, Jose Maria?"

Dr. Cordillera had a Nobel Prize to add to his curriculum vitae. His was an opinion worth considering.

"You are a battleship commander," said Jose Maria. "I am a mere microbiologist. I assume there is a method behind the madness."

"There is. I'll tell you. When I was fourteen, the judge dropped me in the middle of Cumberland Forest with nothing but the clothes on my back and said, 'See you in two weeks.' "

Properly, John K. Farragut was a justice rather than a judge. But he had been "the judge" to John A. Farragut since he could remember, so there was no changing now.

"Those two weeks taught me the value of really low tech."

"Your father has a sadistic streak, I think."

The judge was a loud, earthy, opinionated man with a great horselaugh and coarse charm. Had a generous streak as wide as the mean one. He kept a Bible at his bench and had been known to use a Colt .45 for a gavel.

"The judge has his own way of doing things," Captain Farragut allowed.

It was several days before Captain Farragut got around to asking his father's guest, "What brings you to the judge's house?"

"You, Captain Farragut," said Jose Maria. "Your *Merrimack*. I need to get to the Deep End."

"What makes you think *Merrimack*'s fixing to go to the Deep End?"

"You are," said Jose Maria, statement of fact.

"I hate it when civilians know more about my next mission than I do."

"I do not know your next mission. I merely related some of my observations to certain members of your Joint Chiefs, and they suggested I might like to go as an observer aboard *Merrimack* when she sets spaceward again."

Farragut bridled. Did not like being saddled with passengers. Especially unasked.

"Are you going to tell *me* these observations of yours?"

"I shall tell you everything," Jose Maria said, his smile becoming benignly cagey, "When I am in the Deep End aboard *Merrimack*."

Brought Farragut's head right round, eyes big. Jose Maria de Cordillera knew Captain Farragut intended to leave him behind.

John Farragut broke into a grin. Muttered, "Damn civilians. Can't order 'em around. Can't shoot 'em."

Jose Maria's smile remained.

"I don't travel with civilians," said Farragut.

"The Joint Chiefs said it was all right."

"The Joint Chiefs need talking to. If we get boarded and you're not in uniform, the Romans will *sell* you."

"Then I shall buy myself."

Farragut was about to point out the costliness of that proposal, when he took another hard look at the man. A crisp, understated air of extreme wealth dwelled in every detail, in the fiber of his coat, the simple styling of his clothes, the spare elegance of his jewelry. Jose Maria de Cordillera lived in a rarified tax bracket beyond even the Farraguts'.

John Farragut and Jose Maria Cordillera were in the judge's study by now, an Old Boy sort of room done in leather, scented of cigars, brandy, and gunpowder. Handsome portraits of Amanda's racehorses wearing wreaths of roses decorated the walls, along with antique fowling pieces, leather-bound law books, and other manly artifacts.

Jose Maria stood before a rack of swords. He gestured toward a single-edged Chinese blade on the rack. "May I?"

John Farragut gave a sideways nod to say he was his

guest, and kept talking, "The *whole idea* of taking a civilian — a civilian of a neutral planet yet! — on a mission to the — "

The *whole idea* fell to pieces as the sword moved in Jose Maria's hand. The blade became a living extension of the man, disappeared into a flashing blur. The man himself moved like a great lean cat — smooth, fluid, aggressive — his stops so clean, instant, and complete, they defied inertia. He turned with a light, balanced pivot. Brought the sword about in the wink of an eye, as if it had displaced rather than moved through the space in between *there* and *here*.

When Farragut's eyebrows could lift no farther, he found his voice, "Jose Maria, you sure you're not a warrior?"

Terra Rica was a neutral world, and Jose Maria de Cordillera a man of medicine. He was a grandfather sixteen times over, a number rapidly multiplying as happens in devout Catholic families.

"This is not warfare," said Jose Maria, bringing the sword in from a flashing lemniscate to tuck up behind his arm at rest. "It is an art. If you want to kill someone, use a Colt .45. Or a disruptor."

"There are drawbacks to having weapons with that kind of punch and range on board a spaceship." Farragut pulled a pair of dueling sabers from the rack, scooped up a pair of V masks on the blade of one, and invited, "Have a go?"

They withdrew outdoors to stake out places at far sides of a wide, empty corral, synched their V masks, and registered themselves and their swords with the program.

The blind, dusty darkness of the mask was replaced by a large hall, occupied only by the two of them. They adjusted the mask settings until the images of each other stood within sword's length.

"Test. Test."

They extended blades to their counterimages, touched swords. Heard the tinny clank, felt the light pressure of the contact.

"Okay."

"Very good."

"Set," Farragut commanded the program. Touched his hand to Jose Maria's virtual blade. Felt the razor of pain. Felt blood hot and wet in his palm. "Reset."

The pain and blood vanished. He nodded satisfaction. Looked to his opponent. "Ready?"

"Sir." Jose Maria bowed.

Farragut cocked his saber back in both hands for a mighty swing.

Quick, too quick, Jose Maria was *there,* under Farragut's cocked elbows, and opening up his rib cage. The sword actually fell, clattered against a virtual wood floor. Farragut's hands clutched at his gushing chest. Knees hit what felt like wood.

Choked. Ripped off the mask.

Gulped dusty air deeply into his undamaged chest in the aftermath of vanished pain.

Jose Maria's voice sounded above him, solicitous, "Are you well, young Captain?"

"Yes, dammit. Embarrassed." Hauled himself to his feet. Mask jammed back on. "I want a rematch."

The second round was almost a battle, John Farragut's brute strength against Jose Maria's cat-footed finesse. The elder man became the instructor. "Do not watch my eyes, young Captain. My eyes will not cut you."

From anyone else, Farragut might have taken insult, being offered advice during a competition. But the doctor was so genuine, and so skilled, Farragut took it for the help it was meant to be.

Ended up dead again, winded and wiser. He spoke up from the ground, blinking sweat and sunlight from his eyes, "Don Jose Maria de Cordillera, would you mind working for me?"

"In what capacity?" Jose Maria refastened the silver clasp in his long black hair.

"Weapons instructor for my Marines. Or is that against the Neutrality?"

"I cannot see how it could violate neutrality unless you mean to arm your *Merrimack* with swords," Jose Maria said in whimsy.

"I do. You in?"

Jose Maria absorbed bemusement. Said at last, "I can teach martial arts. How you make use of it is your business."

"A little sophistic there, hm, Jose Maria?"

"A lot sophistic. *Mea culpa.* I shall do penance."

Something slipped there, past the man's temperate benevolence. A hostility against Rome.

And it was personal.

18

A T THE NAVAL SPACE FLEET base outside of Lawrence, Kansas, Marines ran through the shoot/don't shoot drills—or in this case, slash/don't slash drills, for they were armed with swords. The program presented friends and foes unexpectedly—colonist, Roman foot soldier, ship's dog, LEN emissary, Roman Centurion, U.S. Marine, cow.

Farragut was damn serious about this part of the sword training. If you don't pass this part of the final screening, you don't serve on board *Mack* when she flies again in anger.

And Flight Sergeant Kerry Blue wanted to serve on *Merrimack*. All the Marines did. Because John Farragut was damn serious about who got slashed and who didn't. She had to get this right.

Fortunately, racquetball had always been a popular sport on the *Mack,* so they were all pretty good at not whacking each other in close quarters.

Squash was also popular. Squash was the captain's game, because the ball was smaller, harder, and the damn thing didn't bounce. You had to smash it like hell to make it go. You give Farragut the wrong shot and he'll smash you back to Philadelphia, rocketing that little green bullet around all four walls of the court. But he'd never nailed anyone with his racquet.

Still left the problem of separating friend from foe. Neither racquetball nor squash was any help with deciding that.

"Do you slash or don't slash the cow?"

Nobody quite knew.

"It's a dumb question. Don't slash the cow," said Cowboy.

"Are you *sure*?" said Kerry.

No. He wasn't quite sure. Was pretty sure.

Not good enough for Kerry Blue, who usually passed tests by the skin of her teeth. "You gotta *know*. And you can take it from me, telling an examiner his question is dumb never *ever* works."

"I'll ask Jose Maria about the cow," Reg Monroe volunteered quickly.

"No, it's my question. I'll ask him," Kerry said.

"I'll ask," said Carly. "I speak Terra Rican."

"Like that man don't know English better than any of us," said Kerry.

Twitch Fuentes turned to the nearest Y chromosome. "Just what *is* it with the girls and the old guy?"

Cowboy shrugged. "They think just 'cause Cordillera's good with a sword that he's good with his sword."

"Could be," said Kerry with a haughty, you-can-be-replaced shift of her shoulders. "I don't think there's a soft spot anywhere on that man's body."

"He's *gorgeous*," said Reg. "He moves gorgeous."

"Oh, yeah, the moves." Carly fanned herself with her hand, suddenly very very warm.

"He's re*fined*," said Reg, in what she thought was a refined voice. "Something you baboons wouldn't understand. He's dynamic. Intelligent. Rich."

"Rich," Carly said.

"Rich." Kerry nodded.

"Old," Cowboy said.

"Which means his kids are grown up," said Carly. "Got that skat over with. Can he be any more perfect?"

Flight Sergeant Shepard weighed in with a mouth full of pretzels and salt crumb spray: "Okay, so what's he supposed to see in you?"

A three-way pause, then, "Shut up, Dak."

John Farragut took to the sword naturally. Disruptors, splinter guns, tag seekers, and contact stunners were really too civilized for his inner barbarian. Although he was a decent, compassionate man, once committed to killing an enemy, he found the true violence of hacking sword to bone held a savage satisfaction he didn't get from modern, sterile exterminations at long range.

He had mastered all the training routines which Jose Maria had left for him while Jose Maria trained Marines in Kansas. By the time Jose Maria came back to Kentucky, Farragut was eager to try out a new program. And Jose Maria had brought one. It was called *Nemo*.

"What's it about?" Farragut asked, loading the program into a V mask.

"You will see," said Jose Maria.

They went outside to an empty corral on the Farragut property, which had become John Farragut's usual place to practice with his sword. The corral gave him a wide space without real obstacles to interfere with his virtual training world. He shut the gates to keep out children and horses.

The new routine's space requirements called for a long, rather narrow fighting area. Farragut pictured a banquet hall, and positioned himself appropriately, away from the fences, which he would not be able to see during the simulation.

He fitted on the mask, plugged in the leads.

The sun's warmth and scents of the corral's horsey dust vanished into the virtual biting cold and wet salt sting of sea spray. Nothing at all like a banquet hall. A metal deck rolled underfoot. The heavy buffet of open air nearly unbalanced him. He saw, by the flicker of lightning, that he was on the heaving deck of an antique submarine on an angry iron gray sea. Waves spilled white foam over his sealskin-booted feet. He gripped the sword in both hands.

Something rose from the spume—dark, blue-black, fantastical—like a giant beanstalk, but with suction disks. A tentacle.

File name *Nemo*. Farragut barked a startled laugh. "It's a giant squid!"

The stalk whipped about, circled Farragut's legs, constricted. And suddenly he was upside down, in midair, high above the deck. Blood rushed to his head. The thing swung him in the howling, bitter wind, dizzily high.

His stomach heaved with the drop.

Prickle of grass stubble bit into his palms. He cursed, because he'd lost his grip on his sword. Blunt solidity of compressed dirt against his back confused him. Couldn't see. His mask had gone black, blank. A horse nickered from somewhere. He must have exited the program. Had not asked to.

He pulled off the mask. Inhaled warm dust. Could not open his eyes for the bright sun stabbing from above.

Quiet crunching of grit under bootsoles neared. A shadow across his face let him open his eyes. Looked up at Jose Maria de Cordillera haloed by the sun.

"What happened?" said Farragut. "The program quit on me."

"You died, young Captain."

"Did not." Then, rather meekly, "Did I?"

"Headfirst onto the deck. Your skull split open." Jose Maria offered down a kid-gloved hand to his fallen pupil. "Death was instantaneous."

"Oh," Farragut said, disappointed. "Well, hell." Then, protesting, nearly a bleat, *"It was a squid!"*

"Yes."

"A *squid.*"

"You did not expect a squid? Well, then, fight within the moment, young Captain. Do not anticipate."

Farragut snugged the V mask back over his head. "I want a rematch!"

"I thought you might." Jose Maria reset the program, stepped out of the corral. "Do not laugh at the squid."

"Right." Farragut tested his grip on his sword, flexed his knees into a mobile, stable stance. This was a matter of pride.

It wasn't like he could expect to be fighting tentacled monsters on board his *Merrimack.*

At the Naval base in Kansas, Cowboy Carver, Dak Shepard, and Twitch Fuentes battled the giant squid in the new *Nemo* program, while the women of Red Squad were still messing with the No Guns program. Kerry Blue, Carly Delgado, and Reg Monroe weren't finished with that asymptote with the bullwhip. Hated—*hated*—that cocky, sneering, leering son of a beagle kicker. Even with the program toned down, the bullwhip hit you like a two by four. The pain seized up your chest, blotted out your vision, while that guy *laughed,* and the bullwhip sizzled the air, and there was the death stroke because suddenly you were pain free and breathing easy in the dark of your mask.

Before they left this program, the women were determined to hack that stupid whip into pieces, then yank out the guy's hose and hack that into pieces, too, before killing him.

Came the day. Bullwhip came at Carly, licking his thin, smarmy lips, and laughing at her brandished sword. Carly wasn't big, and she was bone thin, but most people had the sense to be afraid of her. Bullwhip didn't. "Little stick girl," he taunted. "You are going to take my scalp?"

"Hell, no," Carly said. "I'm taking your ears and your tail."

Literal—machine minds were always stupidly literal— Bullwhip answered, "I don't have a tail."

"The hell you say."

And Kerry and Reg snagged his bullwhip on the backswing as Carly charged in from the front and tackled him low. Kerry and Reg sliced the whip into twelve pieces while Carly choked the guy into the ground, bony forearm across his throat. She held him down while Reg debagged him for Kerry to do the deed.

Kerry froze on the upstroke, shrieked, "He don't have one!"

And everything vanished. The program ab-ended, as programs will when the parameters are exceeded.

Carly and Reg were left holding down air on the parade ground.

Kerry pulled off her V mask, yanked her sweat-matted hair free from its band. She hovered over the empty spot on the ground at her feet where Bullwhip should have been. "Well, *damn.* No wonder he was so mean!"

"So what do you do with the cow?"

"What?"

They were back to slash/don't slash drills.

"The cow," said Reg. "What's the right answer? Slash or don't slash?"

"I don't *know,*" Twitch brushed aside the question, annoyed.

"Well I *gotta* know," Reg dogged him. "I'm not gonna get left dockside for not slashing the cow when the examiner thinks we're having burgers for supper."

Twitch let his shoulders slump. Reg was not going away until he gave her an answer. He asked, "Is it mad?"

"What?" Reg wrinkled up her face.

"Is it a mad cow?"

Reg gave an angry tsk. "Cows don't get mad." Reg Monroe had never seen a live one and had no interest in livestock, but she was pretty sure from the pictures she'd seen that those tranquil stupid creatures couldn't mount a convincing mad.

"Oh, yeah, they do," Twitch assured her. And the issue became terribly funny. Cowboy and Dak started doing mad cow imitations. Devolved into sniggers.

Reg walked away, let her sword drop over her shoulder. "You guys are useless."

"Oh, *sync-up*." Kerry fit her mask on to return to the drill.

Cowboy called from behind her, "Hey, Kerry Blue!"

Kerry spun round, sword in hand. Cowboy was there. Flying at her with a wild maniacal moo.

And ran right up her blade to the hilt. Her sword point jutted red out his back.

Hot sticky splash wet her hands. Cowboy's sagging weight dragged down her sword. "Oh, hell! Reset!" she commanded the program.

Instead of resetting, her mask went dark. The weight, the wetness, the smell remained.

Kerry ripped off her mask with a sticky hand to see what was hanging on her sword.

Howled, *"Medic!"*

Lieutenant Colonel TR Steele stormed into Internal Investigations to yank his Marine out of interrogation.

"Colonel Steele, we are not finished here."

"Yes, you are, *sir*!" Steele told the II officers. "You do *NOT* take up *anything* with my Marines without going through me!"

Yeah. Anyone kick Colonel Steele's dog, it'll be Colonel Steele, thought Kerry, standing expressionless at attention. It was an oddly comforting thought. She would choose, a million times out of a million, her chops-busting CO over these cold, desk-riding ferrets, the dreaded double-Is.

"Colonel Steele, we are not talking mere negligence here," an investigator explained. Full colonels all of them. There were no low-ranking double-Is. "There is compelling evidence that the incident under investigation was not an accident. There exists a computer record from *Merrimack* of the Marine saying quote I want him dead unquote. An incident regarding a married lover. One Jamie 'Cowboy' Carver as a matter of fact."

"I didn't know the fid-squucker was married!" Kerry cried out loud.

One big jutting forefinger and a tight-shut mouth from Colonel Steele told her to slam it.

"Internal Investigations has a duty to find the truth behind the incident," said the investigator.

"*I'll* tell you the truth behind the incident," said Steele.

Truth was Cowboy Carver was an oversexed son of a rabbit who couldn't keep his shirt on or his pants zipped. Truth was Steele wanted him dead. Truth was he was glad Kerry killed him. Truth was Steele only regretted that Cowboy hadn't stayed dead. Damn medics were too damn good. Truth was Kerry hadn't checked the V mask parameters before running the program.

And truth was Colonel Steele proceeded to lie for Kerry Blue. Steele took the fall for not controlling the situation.

Internal Investigations let Kerry go. Slapped Steele with a rep.

"One last question, if you will, Lieutenant Colonel?"

Steele waited. Posed in a silent demand: *Ask, damn you.* Knew, just knew, the double I was going to say: *So, is she any good?*

The investigator twirled a light stylus indolently. "So what *is* the proper answer to that cow thing?"

It was raining when Colonel Steele ordered Kerry Blue to get her ass out on the perimeter for sentry duty.

She'd known this was coming. Well, it beat the hell out of Internal Investigations detention.

She pulled up the hood of her slicker, shouldered her splinter weapon. "Sir?" she asked at Steele's back, the prelude to a question.

He roared, patience at an end. *"What?"*

"Why'd you take the hit for me?"

He thought she was being coy. Turned to bellow at her. But Kerry was looking up at him with honest puzzlement. She didn't know. The little idiot had no clue.

His voice dropped into the gravel, soft with restrained anguish. "Don't ask me that, Marine. Don't ever ask me that."

"Captain Farragut, your crew and Marine contingent have suffered more casualties during *Merrimack*'s refit—at peace, *in dock*—than any five other ships in their most recent battles."

"It's not uncommon for soldiers to suffer casualties Earthside, Admiral Mishindi."

"From car crashes and skiing! Not from sword wounds!"

"Haven't lost anyone," Farragut offered.

"Close. You came very close with that Carver fellow."

Jamie Cowboy Carver. That had been over-the-line back-from-the-dead close. "Yes, sir."

"*And* I've been receiving an ungodly number of med reports of reattaching limbs and closing deep wounds. Your blood requisition is way over budget. What I really mean to ask, John, is: what the hell are you doing?"

"We're shaking out the bugs. It's a new way of fighting for them."

"It's old! It's millennia old! What do you think you're doing making your crew fight each other with swords!"

"They're not fighting each other. They're fighting virtual enemies with swords. But they're in real close proximity to each other. Makes a difference when they can do real damage to each other."

"Yes, yes, it does. The difference is *they do real damage to each other*!" Mishindi bellowed the obvious, the whites of his eyes stark rings between the darkness of his irises and the darkness of his face.

"They're learning not to. They're getting damn good at not hurting each other. Takes time is all."

"And the value of learning to fight with swords *at all* would be? Something I can tell the JC?"

"The value is that there's no on/off switch with a sword. No signal jamming against a sword. No shooting a hole through your bulkhead with a sword. And a sword can get through an exo-suit."

"This is ridiculous. Unnecessary. Wasteful. And—*swords*! It's—it's something I'd expect out of Rome!"

"No. Funny, that," Farragut smiled. "Romans like the newest, best, highest-tech toys. They've always loved new inventions. Hand-to-hand fighting is a lost art in Rome. Of course, they all think they're hand-to-hand experts by birthright. But none of them train on it. They'd sneer at my swords like a German tank brigade would sneer at the Polish cavalry."

"I'm sneering, too."

"Difference is the tanks and the cavalry were on ground that favored the tank. I'm going to fly a Cessna under the Iron Curtain and land it in Red Square."

"Low-tech tricks don't win wars."

"And all this is my last line of defense," Farragut admitted. "This is for when I'm backed against my own bulks by a Roman boarding party carrying jammable two-stage weapons and radiation armor. I can say hello with a one-stage open-up-your-skin weapon with considerable intimidation value." He pulled a Civil War era sword off the admiral's wall and whistled it through the air with all Farragut's sizable mass and strength behind it.

The admiral jerked back on reflex. Recovered, as Farragut had come to a peaceful halt. "Possibly. Do put that back. It's quite valuable."

Farragut did.

"Not saying I approve," said Mishindi. "I don't—but I've never put a leash on you, and I've never been sorry for that. Anyone else, I'd reel you in. But you are who you are, and your alarming casualty rate *is* on a marked down-tick. So I'm going to let you run with this, John. Don't make me sorry."

Farragut saluted, awaited dismissal. The admiral held up a finger to signal pause as his com burred a red chime.

Farragut waited through the yes, yes, I see, and the thank you, to the end of the transmission. Admiral Mishindi returned his attention to Captain Farragut. Asked soberly, "How much faith do you have in your 'backup' system?"

"We're good to go as soon as the primaries are."

"The primaries *aren't*. But I need you now, ready or not."

An expectant inhale. "Rome broke the cease-fire!"

Mishindi shook his head no. Rome did not. "We did. As we speak a U.S. strike force is crossing into Roman space."

Farragut was torn between reactions. It was what he wanted. But, "They couldn't wait for *me*?"

"No. Not for anything." Mishindi folded his hands. His dark face looked rather gray. He gathered in a breath to speak the unspeakable: "Palatine has a working Shotgun."

19

THE ROMANS CALLED IT Catapult instead of Shotgun, but it did the same thing—effected huge-scale displacement across an astronomical distance.

Its first test shot gave it away. Gravitation was a weak force, but a distortion spike of that size rocked the low band across a three hundred light-year radius and woke up the Pentagon.

Sensors on several colonies immediately zeroed in on the epicenter. Pinpointed the location of the Near Cat.

The location of the second Cat was less certain. Gravitational effects dropped off quickly with distance. The low-band monitors could only be certain that the second Cat was a good two klarcs distant in the Deep End.

No matter. The U.S. need only shut down one end of the Catapult to reduce this Roman end run to a one-handed clap.

U.S. warships stormed across the Roman territorial boundary, steering a wide path around Palatine, to the Near Cat with orders to shut the Catapult down. By any and all means. The rules of engagement in this war had changed. Undisputed Roman space was now in bounds, and any Roman ship not flying a Red Cross could be shot without provocation.

It was a reflection of the desperation of the situation that the JC cleared *Merrimack* for battle—and that only because *Merrimack* could run away if she got into trouble. This was a siege on Roman ground. The Romans must stand; Farragut had the option of running away.

"And you *will* call for a tow if your ship controls get overridden," Mishindi ordered in parting. Hoped Farragut would not get a chance to ignore that order.

Captain Farragut stranded his weapons instructor Earthside, and made all speed to the Near Cat.

A space fortress surrounded the Near Cat. Rome called it a Citadel. It was a kicked hive, swarming with angry ships encased in shimmering force fields.

Force fields only shimmer like that when hit. In this beam-laced space everything shimmered with the diffuse brilliance of deflected shots.

The Fortress grid illuminated like a lightning sky. The blasts gave shape to it—a geodesic containment grid engulfing a region of space equal to the volume of the Moon. And within that, rings of armed sentinel stations guarded another grid, which housed the Near Cat itself.

Hardpoints in the outer grid bristled with guns. And those were reinforced by a net of Roman battleships emplaced within the grid, becoming, themselves, hardpoints in it. Each point maintained a section of distortion wall—a modern take on an ancient Roman tortoise. The ships had locked shields, trading mobility for combined force. So long as the ships held position, they were all invulnerable, and the Citadel impregnable.

The Roman ships at the Citadel acted in either of two discrete roles—those emplaced in the grid, and those free harriers who actively engaged the U.S. attackers.

Merrimack's approach to the hot zone met with a belligerent, fear-tinged demand for IFF. U.S. forces were touchy regarding large newcomers approaching from the direction of Palatine—which was also the direction of Earth. The guard ships confirmed *Merrimack*'s sig and let the battleship pass.

In the battle zone, the paths of mobile plots showed on *Merrimack*'s display as a tangled writhing serpents' nest of besiegers and defenders.

Farragut found his former XO already there with her aging wolf hunter, a game, sturdy little ship with a crew of thirty, *Wolfhound*.

After reporting in to the siege commodore, John Farragut sent *Wolfhound* a greeting: "Captain Carmel!"

"Welcome to the show, John. Do you see something wrong here?"

Only just arrived he'd already noticed it. "Where's the rest of them?"

Too few Roman vessels defended the target. Rome had vast firepower. And, for as many ships as swarmed about the titanic space Citadel, there should have been more. Many more. Where were the Legions of Rome if not here? Where were its killer bots?

"End run?" Calli spoke her worst fear.

In an end run scenario, an enormous Roman force would be vaporizing Washington D.C. even now.

The problem with that scenario—from the Roman perspective—was that an attack on U.S. soil would bring the League of Earth Nations into it, and Rome would prefer to let those dogs sleep. In fact, it would serve Rome not to retaliate; this U.S. invasion of Roman space could bring the LEN into the war on the side of Palatine.

Farragut took a different guess. "Maybe there's a hundred Legions fixing to come blasting through the Cat."

In that case it was imperative to shut the Catapult down quickly, *now,* before such a thing could happen. But how?

The Roman force field was impervious to any weapon. Stronger than a solid wall, the field wall consisted of layers within layers of phase-shifting distortion screens that pulsed in erratic time.

Calli asked her engineer, Amina Patel, if her ship *Wolfhound* could weave a path through the grid layers between the pulses.

Amina assented provisionally, not very happy about it. Yes, with a stutter step, pausing, advancing, and back stepping in the correct sequence of intervals, you could possibly get a small ship through. Sideways. But, Amina pointed out, *Wolfhound* would be vulnerable to the harriers while going in, and open to the ships in the adjacent grid points while staggering through the layers.

And once through, there were the Citadel guns. And, because those guns had no one else to shoot at, "We would be the only girl at the dance."

"But the inside gunners have to tag us first," said Calli.

"They can't afford to shoot and miss. Tag shots are the only safe shot they've got."

Amina had to nod. This was true.

"They're shooting in a bottle," said Calli. "A ricochet could hit just about anything in there."

A tag insured delivery of ordnance to its target and only to its target.

"And so they will launch all their tags at us," said Amina.

"What's top speed of a tag?" Captain Carmel asked. "Or more to the point—can we outrun a tag?"

"Ye–es." The two syllables held reservation.

Amina's next question was how the captain intended to get her ship out again. It required the same sideways stutter step to exit the field as it did to enter. "To avoid the tags inside, we would need to be running in circles around the Cat. We stop running to stutter step, we get tagged. And at that distance, we get tagged, we get hit."

"Then we'll burn the tags before they can touch us," said Calli. "Just get us in where we can do real damage."

"Brings us back to how to keep from getting shot while we're stutter stepping in." Amina was not arguing. She simply needed to know.

Calli got back on the com: "John, I need a favor."

Told him she intended to run at the grid and tiptoe through the grid to the inner space.

Farragut did not seem surprised. Asked, "Where do you want to penetrate?"

"Next to the *Gladiator*."

The mammoth Roman warship held an anchor position within the grid.

Senior Engineer Amina Patel politely asked her captain if she were out of her mind. But *Wolfhound*'s XO, Lieutenant Egypt (Gypsy) Dent, was nodding as Farragut replied over the com: "Good choice."

Gypsy spoke aside to Amina, "Didn't you hear the Roman chatter when we first got here?"

Amina had heard the insults. The Romans had called *Wolfhound* "that henhouse," their term for a ship whose captain, exec, and engineer were all women.

That made *Wolfhound* a target beneath notice of the Triumphalis Numa Pompeii and his great battleship *Gladiator*.

"He never pays attention to me," said Calli. "He's too

proud to shoot at us. He'll leave us to the Citadel's inner guns."

Farragut asked, "What are you fixin' to do in there, Cal?"

"Don't dare tell you, John." She didn't quite have that much faith in the security of her com link. "Can you get me in?"

"Yeah, I can pick a fight with Numa."

"He'll cut our flank," said Amina.

"No, he won't," said Calli Carmel. "He's going to watch John Farragut."

"I can get you in," Farragut repeated. "I can't get you out."

"That's all I want, John."

Calli outlined the plan to her crew. And only because it was somewhat suicidal did she ask them if they would have trouble following her orders.

No. They came here to kill Romans. Even Amina said, "Tell us where to punch it." Insulted that the captain supposed they might balk.

Touched at their faith, their willingness to follow, Calli wanted to cry. And Farragut, an expressive man, would have, but she did not.

Merrimack opened up a hammering barrage of solid ordnance at *Gladiator. Gladiator* picked off the projectiles with gamesmanlike ease, as *Wolfhound* began her run at the grid.

Run was too strong a word. Calli with her *Wolfhound* staggered, sidestepped, and lurched through the pulsing layers of the defensive field.

And hoped Numa Pompeii was even half as arrogant as Calli thought he was.

Pompous bastard, don't fail me now.

True to form, *Gladiator,* engaged in its shooting match with *Merrimack,* gave no indication of noticing Calli's ship.

But angry eyes opened in the imperial ship *Trajan,* the ship emplaced next to *Gladiator* in the grid. *Trajan*'s side ports opened, showed guns.

And hesitated.

Perhaps because *Wolfhound* lay in a direct line with *Gladiator.* Or perhaps *Wolfhound*'s very near proximity to *Gladiator* posed the problem.

Or maybe *Trajan* was unsure of the consequences of firing between layers of the force field.

The imperial ship did not fire.

But *Trajan*'s ports were not closing, and Farragut did not like those angry eyes following Calli.

Farragut hailed the U.S. cruiser *Edmonton,* asked a favor. "Norris, punch *Trajan*'s headlights out for me?"

"I can hit him," said Captain Norris, with no questions, even though he saw no apparent point to the exercise. *Edmonton* launched a load of crap at *Trajan*'s face.

Trajan lost interest in its side game. Turned its sights on *Edmonton.* Let the Citadel guns carve up the foolish little wolf hunter passing alongside.

Farragut heard *Trajan*'s commander speaking on an open channel, meant to be overheard: "Target practice for you, Citadel. Don't hit me in the ass."

And *Wolfhound* was through! Leaping instantly to speed.

Wolfhound's visuals were useless, nonexistent, at this speed. The ship's readouts had to translate an FTL propeller blade's view of the battle. The image on the tactical display looked something like a simple model of a hydrogen atom—the computer's interpretation of *Wolfhound*'s whirling path inside the grid, orbiting the Citadel several times a second.

Tags launched from the Citadel's sentinels, clouds of them. Made the sentinels look like milkweed pods bursting open.

A tag's only function was to catch a target, latch on, and give homing ordnance an exact mate against which to detonate. Tags hadn't the *Wolfhound*'s acceleration. And despite the tags' tiny mass, they made wider turns. On an ever-turning course, in which every meter demands a course correction, the tags quickly spent their very small fuel supply, and died.

Wolfhound deployed a flurry of her own tags, targeting the stationary sentinels and the sensor stations that made the Catapult work.

Those tags that touched the vital sensors of the Catapult died on contact. Those tags that nested on the sentinels sang out their bull's-eyes, only briefly. *Wolfhound* launched a salvo of homers after her tags. But her missiles met with intercept, or else lost their way as their tags were erased. Only one of *Wolfound*'s missiles tagged up and detonated—to no effect—against a well-shielded emplacement.

Numa's scorn for Calli's intrusion appeared entirely justified. She could not have supposed taking down the Near Cat could be as simple as squeezing one small ship inside the Roman first line of defense.

In her tight, whirling flight, *Wolfhound* lapped some of the tags that were chasing her. Ran into the rear of a swarm of them. Most bounced off her forward shield. One stuck.

And a Roman missile was *there*, mated with its tag. It detonated on *Wolfhound*'s bow.

From outside the grid, Farragut tried to keep an eye on Calli, though there was nothing he could do for her out here except pound at Numa and keep his own hide free of stickers. He just had to wait and see what Calli thought she could do inside the grid.

It was beginning to look like she'd flown herself into a kill jar.

He watched for Calli's ship to emerge from the blast that landed on her bow.

She should have been able to take that hit, especially taking it straight on the nose like that. But maybe the tightness of her turns had distorted her forward screens, because *Merrimack*'s sensors clearly showed the speeding *Wolfhound* putting out all her lifeboats.

20

LOSING SPEED, WOLFHOUND TRAILED steam and smoke. The tags, which she had been eluding, gained on her stern.

Her lifeboats were not properly boats. They were very basic, very temporary, survival pods; flimsy tissue-foil sacks equipped with minimal air, a rebreather, and an uncomfortable heater.

Calli kept the life pods close to the ship, inside *Wolfhound*'s shield, instead of launching them clear of her ship, until *Wolfhound* bubbled all over with foil blisters, wearing the lot of them outboard like a mama spider carrying its young.

A Citadel gunner sent an inquiry to General Pompeii: "Cease fire?"

"No," Numa returned, emphatic. "If *Mister* Carmel thinks Rome won't take out her life pods, she is sadly mistaken. Until she surrenders, or her ship is destroyed, those pods are targets. If she's going to hide behind her lifeboats, then tag them. Tag them all and shoot them."

On board *Merrimack,* Marcander Vincent reported from his tactical station: "Sir. Roman gunners are launching tags at Captain Carmel's lifeboats. She's losing speed. They'll make contact in another minute."

Farragut nodded. "I think she's counting on it."

The command crew looked to Captain Farragut in surprise.

"Sir?" Lieutenant Glenn Hamilton asked.

"I just hope Numa doesn't see what I'm seeing," said Farragut.

Numa Pompeii refused to know Calli. Still, he must see what she was up to, if he was looking.

"Launch a planet killer at Numa."

Lieutenant Hamilton ordered up the planet killer, then said, "It won't do anything, sir."

The planet killer would create a huge, expensive light show, and momentarily blank out everyone's clearscreens. It would have no effect on the grid.

"It'll make him look," said Farragut. "At me."

Instead of?

Hamster took another look at Calli's fleeing *Wolfhound* wearing its coat of lifeboats.

The life pods were tissue thin, opaque, but so filmy they concealed little. Normally you could make out the shapes of people inside, like larvae in a cocoon. Hamster did not see anything at all pushing at the foil sides.

Where were the elbows? The knees? The hands? The butts?

Calli's life pods were neat sausage balloons.

Someone was going to notice that oddity in a moment and warn Numa.

"Planet killer armed and ready, Captain!" Hamster reported.

"Fire."

"Fire planet killer!"

The planet killer smashed into the grid, lit it up like a white dwarf star. Filled the com channels with curses and Roman scoffing.

Another spume of smoke belched from *Wolfhound*'s stern.

Wolfhound's shields flickered out. The ship lost more speed, and a whole flock of tags caught up and latched on to every available surface.

Because the wolf hunter was entirely encased in life sacks, the tags latched onto the life sacks.

The Roman sentinels launched homing missiles after them.

"They're shooting the lifeboats!" Marcander Vincent reported.

"So they are." Farragut's fingers crossed themselves.

As the homing missiles launched to mate with their tags, *Wolfhound* spun, shedding her coat of foil sacks like a snake its skin.

Because all the tags were stuck to life sacks, *Wolfhound* discarded all the tags along with the sacks.

Sending the homing missiles chasing them.

Toward *Gladiator*'s sternside engine ports.

A Roman missile will not detonate against a Roman ship, but it will detonate against a tag stuck to a U.S. life pod thrown up against a Roman battleship's stern.

Things happen quickly at these speeds. General Pompeii saw the trap as it hurtled up his battleship's engines. Emplaced in the grid, *Gladiator* could not evade. Numa shouted on the open channel: "Deactivate those homers!"

He had noticed the sacks were unmanned, but not empty. Empty, they would have been collapsed flat. These were filled with gas. Probably hydrogen because they sent fireballs exploding up his engines as the homing missiles ripped through the sacks and slammed against *Gladiator*'s stern midway through Numa's warning shout.

The great ship canted, juddered, and rocked. The grid wavered.

Into that fluctuating crack in the Citadel's impenetrable shell, the U.S. ship *Gettysburg* drove three robot seeker-killers.

Trajan, moving to take up the breach, thinned out another point in the grid through which two attack ships penetrated the perimeter. While the crippled *Wolfhound* miraculously reacquired her force field, her speed, and her atmospheric integrity.

Gladiator's guns were turning round. Calli had Numa's attention now.

Farragut saw it coming. Ordered *Merrimack* to line up a saber, "On the big, fat bully."

"Targeting *Gladiator,* aye."

"Fire saber."

Nothing happened.

"This is not a balk!" Fire Control warned sharply. "Someone is in here!" An outside signal had taken over his control systems.

Not ever to be caught staring into the headlights, Farragut did not waste an instant wondering how this was happening or spare a breath to swear. Instantly he ordered computer controls shut down and called for manual overrides. "Anything that can receive remote commands—pull the plug!"

Flight Sergeant Kerry Blue had been waiting in her Swift for orders to launch. Got this instead.

Popped her canopy to squawk: "Manual over—! We are doing this skat for *real*?"

Climbed out of her Swift, still squawking, because the lights had dipped, and something was for sure wrong. She pulled her Swift's remote recovery module from its compartment and tossed it into the pilot's seat to make sure her fighter wasn't going anywhere without her.

Her boots made a running clang up the starboard ramp tunnel. She scampered up the ladders three decks to the battery and shimmied into her team's gun blister, where Reg Monroe was bringing the mechanical junk to bear, jacking up the loader.

Got the shell ratcheted into the cannon.

"Okay, here's the fancy part," said little Reg, resting a moment, flopped over the black barrel nearly a yard in diameter, puffing. "How do we aim?"

"Look out the window," said Carly.

The open clearport was full—full—of bronze-colored Roman hull.

"Who is that!"

"Com chatter's saying it's the *Scipio*," said Hazard Sewell.

Point-blank was an absurd term out here. In the absence of gravity, projectiles don't fall off their trajectories. Still it had become the accepted term for the range at which you cannot possibly miss.

Scipio rode—point-blank—alongside *Merrimack*. Something shimmered between them, hard, like glass. "What is that?"

"Our force fields are touching!" Hazard Sewell relayed from the command deck. "Hold your fire! We can't shoot. The shell will blow back in. Nobody fire!"

"Then they can't shoot us either, right?" said Reg. Hopeful. "Right?"

"I think," said Hazard, not comforted by that. This could not be good.

Kerry Blue pushed Cowboy away from the clearport so she could see. "So what are they *doing*?" Saw nothing but bronze hull.

The sounds were horrific. Electric groans and scraping squeals, sounds like nothing they had heard before.

Of something that had never happened before.

Scipio had matched phase pulses with *Merrimack* and was prying open her force field, like a starfish with a clam in its clutches.

"We're going to get our guts eaten," said Marcander Vincent on the command deck.

Captain Farragut, amazed, turned to his specialists on deck. "Someone want to tell me how the *hell* this is happening?"

Best they could offer him was to report that *Merrimack*'s phases had not been recalibrated during the refit. "They weren't broke, so no one fixed them."

Rome still had *Monitor*'s black box. Apparently no one considered that Rome had had the entire time span of the kangaroo truce in which to study *Monitor*'s workings and pull her phases from that.

"They did tell us the *Mack* wasn't ready," said Hamster.

"Oh, but we are," said Farragut. Called for suits and swords.

Glenn Hamilton's voice came over the loud com shipwide just before it went inoperative: "Prepare to repel boarders."

"I don't believe it," Twitch Fuentes mumbled at the sword in his hand. "I don't fragging believe it." This was for real.

Cowboy swaggered cheerfully, shirt off inside his exo suit, and sporting a red scarf on his head, a gold earring, and an eye patch. He kept repeating, "Arr arr, matey!" until someone told him to learn another letter of the alphabet.

The exo-suits were the same as the Romans wore. Except for the manufacturers' logos on the generators, the suits were identical on either side.

Mainly the suits provided deflector shields against beam fire. All were equipped with breathers in case of gas; sonic filters for the ears in case of sonic grenades; and energy dampers to protect against stunners. You could still get stunned through an exo suit, but your opponent needed to push the rod through the exo's energy layer and touch you with it, delivering the jolt right into you rather than through the exo-layer.

Because slow-moving objects could pass through an exo-suit, and because *Merrimack* carried redundancy to fanaticism, *Merrimack*'s crew wore helmets and kevlar clothing under the suit's energy shields.

The searing screeching of the force field's parting had stopped. The next sound was the clanging of the *corvus,* the Roman grappling hook, banging on *Merrimack*'s hull.

Reg Monroe crouched in place with her squad, cornered. The lights had gone, and no one turned on their headlamps. They listened in advancing horror to sounds of Them.

"Why don't they just kill us?" Reg breathed. "They could just as easy chuck a nuke in and close us up, and that would be that. Why don't they just do it?"

"They want the ship," Kerry murmured. *Thank God they want the ship.*

Hazard hushed them silent. "Listen!"

Thumps against the hull.

Hazard whispered, "Can anyone make out where they're going to force their way in?"

"Me, I'd come in the fighter shafts," Reg muttered.

And so they did—on the starboard wing—prying up the caps on the fighter lifts.

Came the hiss of atmospheric bleed out. Roman ships kept a thinner atmosphere. The breach sucked *Merrimack*'s air in with *Scipio*'s.

"They're in."

21

THE ROMANS OF THE invasion ship *Scipio* entered dark *Merrimack* warily, breathers clenched between their teeth, heads low. They used scanners in the dark hangar rather than illuminating their lamps. Did not like that they hadn't been met at the breach. Roman soldiers preferred fighting in solid ranks. They did not like this guerrilla skat.

Still, they could not expect the Americans to play to Roman strengths. When you reach into a cobra hole, you'd best expect to meet the fanged end.

A whole file boarded unopposed. Others waited for the area to be pronounced secure before committing any more troops to the enemy craft. This hangar, its crouching fighter craft, its silence, smelled more and more of a trap.

But the first troops found no one. Nothing sprang out at them. But they could not go deeper until they were sure flankers were not hiding here.

The cobra wanted them deeper in the hole. But, just as the Romans could not expect the enemy to play to Roman strengths, neither would Rome play into a U.S. trap.

Sensors could not detect the loc of warm bodies within exo-suits, and the sensors were detecting no motion other than their own. Yet the Roman captain knew the dirtlings could not be far.

They were here. They had to be here.

The Roman captain turned his disruptor on the nearest U.S. Marine fighter craft—a Swift with the Arabic numeral 6 emblazoned on its hull—and raked it bow to stern.

Worked. Flushed a dirtling out of the overhead. She dropped, screeching: "That's my crate!"

Someone crying after her, "*Chica linda*, no!"

Kerry Blue, madder than a wet zil, landed both boots on the Roman captain's shoulders, mashed him to the deck. Went down with him, disruptor fire flashing off her exo-suit. Pummeled him bloody.

She straightened up, hauling her sword edge across the advancing chest. The gushing stopped quickly with the heart's stopping. Just like in the simulators.

The hangar was in chaos. Kerry's sonic filters maxed with the din of screaming all around her, the screech of searing metal hit by deflected fire, the scattered crashes of severed equipment falling from the overhead, and triumphant shouts of "Arrrr!"

Captain Farragut, imitating a caged panther on the command deck, demanded again, "Status."

Lieutenant Glenn Hamilton hesitated to report that the battle was going well. It was going too well.

Roman boarders had breached Red and Blue docks, and the cargo hold. But Red dock was already secured, and very red.

Glenn expressed a concern that the Romans might decide to cut their losses, withdraw their bloody stump, and lob a bomb into the *Mack*.

"Then let's lob a bomb into *Scipio* first," said Farragut.

His techs pointed out that *Scipio* was shielded against *Merrimack*'s gunports. The Romans were not so careless as to leave an opening in front of any of *Mack*'s barrels, even though they had deactivated *Merrimack*'s computer controls.

"The mountain came to Mohammed," said Farragut. "Haul a cannon down to Red dock and shoot through the breach."

"*Haul?*" A thousand-kilogram cannon from the battery, three decks down, then all the way out to the starboard wing? "Uh, how, sir? We're on manual. The robot skids are not functional."

And, a sign from God, the antigrav failed.

As Hamster's hair lifted from her shoulders and her feet left the deck, she said, "I know Who loves you, John Farragut." And Colonel Steele bellowed for a Marine detail to bring a cannon to the starboard wing.

"Do *what*?" Cowboy protested, scrambling to action, fleet, agile, and upside down as a cockroach, propelling himself up the ramp tunnel, hand over hand along the overhead pipes. Kerry Blue had long suspected Cowboy had vermin in his ancestry.

Spurning the ladder, Cowboy sprang like Superman up through the hatch to the gun blister. Too hard. Weightless, he bounced himself off the overhead, banged his helmet, caromed back down, only to bowl Twitch Fuentes off the ladder.

Already in the gunroom, Kerry asked Reg, "Shell?" As Reg unhooked and unlatched the cannon moorings.

"Still one in there," said Reg. "We never got one off."

The grunting gorilla, Dak, wrenched the deck bolts loose.

Bolts off, the cannon lifted from its moorings. Kerry pushed the big gun toward the hatch, as Cowboy's head popped out of the hole like a prairie dog. "Ho—!" His head disappeared under the swinging cannon.

Kerry heard a metallic thud. She'd hit something. "Cowboy?" Kerry called down.

A lot of words she didn't know, then, "She's trying to kill me again!"

Kerry tsked, maneuvering the cannon into position to guide it down the hatchway. "Oh, shut it, Cowboy. I did not try to kill you! I *did* kill you, but I was *not* tryin'. And if you hadn't been brain dead, you'da had the sense to stay that way! This isn't gonna fit. Cowboy, Twitch, you're gonna have to take the ladder off!"

"Just push. It'll fit!"

"It will *not*!"

Cowboy pulled and Dak shoved. Between the two of them, they wedged the cannon tight in the hatch. The cannon hung up on the ladder.

"It doesn't fit," said Dak.

Cowboy said, "Kerry, don't push! Now look. You got it stuck. You got a wrench up there? I'm gonna have to take this whole ladder off."

There was a quick exchange of tools through the available gaps in the cannon-clogged hatchway to unbolt the ladder above and below. Kerry yelling, "Come on! Come on! We gotta go *now*!"

Ladder rungs clattered as Cowboy yanked it clear of the hatch. Shouted, "Move it! Move it!"

Kerry gave the cannon the gentlest of pushes. One thousand kilograms smashed into the deck below, bent the grates.

"God *bless* it!" Cowboy cried.

Kerry jumped up, pushed off the overhead and went air-swimming down the hatch headfirst to help dislodge the cannon from the deck.

Cannon mobile again, Cowboy, Dak, Twitch, Kerry, Carly, and Reg shepherded it down decks, like floating an elephant. They could not afford to get a mass that size moving too boisterously in any direction. Slight taps from it hurt, and turns were hard lessons in inertia.

The cannon crushed all the fingers of Twitch's right hand as the corridor turned and the cannon did not. Twitch kept up with the rest of his squad, crying.

Reg pointed up at a different sound. Knew that one. Usually liked it, but not this time. A Roman retreat clarion.

Kerry cried, "Oh, hell, they're going to close the doors! Move it! Move it! Move it!"

The cannon clanged, blundered, clunked, and smashed through the corridors. Made it to the ramp tunnel where it was clear sailing. Had the cannon hurtling toward the Red dock, Cowboy yelling, "Git along, little *doggie*!"

Came time to stop it, but Cowboy, Dak, Twitch, Kerry, Carly and Reg together did not come near to a thousand kilograms, and with a dearth of anything to grab onto as a brace, they skidded along with the careening mass.

Cowboy jumped in front of the cannon, hands out as if commanding it to stop.

It mowed him down—*"Cowboy!"*—and kept going. Bumped at the bottom of the ramp tunnel, bounced, like a slow motion missile, straight at a Swift.

"Not my crate! Not my crate!"

And plowed into the scorched side of Alpha Six.

Hazard Sewell with another squad of Marines—Echo Flight—was already in the hangar fixing braces in the Roman boarding hatch to force it to stay open against the sounding retreat.

Echo Flight helped disengage the cannon from Kerry's Swift, and then set it down, carriage-side to the deck. The Marines maneuvered the cannon to point at the breach; bolted it to the deck grates.

The two flights looked at each other. "We waiting on a command?"

"Com's down," said Reg.

"At will, I think," said Hazard.

Cowboy—bruised but still game—said: "Well, hell. Fire!"

The manual load fired dirty, the boom resounded to the limit of the sonic filters. The recoil ripped up the deck grates and shot the cannon backward into the bulk.

The shell found its mark, blew through *Scipio* and detonated deep within. The Marines could hear, then smell, the fire inside.

Their celebration was cut short with the flash of Roman lights signaling a decompression warning.

"They're gonna pull out without closing up!" Echo Leader motioned everyone up the ramp tunnel. "Get out of here! They're gonna space us! Go! Go! Go!"

"Captain, *Scipio* is preparing to disengage," Kit Kittering reported.

"Oh, no, you don't." Farragut spoke to his enemy, as if Romans were there on deck with him. Farragut was ready for this. During the melee, he had teams of erks weld the Roman grappling hooks in place, and jam at least one of them at the root, so *Scipio* could not just cast off the line. "You finish this dance."

Scipio had its hooks into *Merrimack* and could not get them out.

The communications tech, in some surprise, reported, "Getting a signal from *Scipio*."

"How? Our com's down."

"It's on the radio. Captain Edward Sejanus is demanding *Merrimack*'s surrender."

Farragut laughed aloud in shock. "He said *that*?"

The com tech put Sejanus through to the captain's console so Farragut could tell him for himself, "Are you nuts?"

Sejanus sent a crackling reply, "I could destroy you."

"You're going to have to."

Destroying *Merrimack* would require destroying *Scipio* with it.

"I don't believe you, Captain Farragut. Your profile shows you the furthest thing from suicidal."

"And I'm not threatening suicide. *You're* the one fixin' to pull the trigger, *Capita*. You go do what you think you have to do. I'm working here." Motioned across his throat for the com tech to disconnect.

Captain Farragut left the command platform. "Your boat, Hamster." He had his sword.

Farragut met TR Steele in the corridor on his way to the starboard ramp tunnel. "TR—your big guys and your crazy guys. With me."

Colonel Steele counted himself with the big guys, Serge, Dak, Ski. Gordo. And Delgado—crazy, not big, but then wolverines were only about twenty-three kilos.

Captain Farragut led the charge into smoky *Scipio*. Hacked his way forward, stormed onto the Roman command platform, and demanded Sejanus' surrender.

Sejanus came out of his scarlet-draped command chair, eyes flaring. The word *No!* came out of his mouth. Might have been an expression of horror, but it was the wrong answer to the demand. Farragut's sword stroke sent his head tumbling to the deck. And Captain Farragut accepted the surrender from *Scipio*'s second-in-command.

No ship from either side had interfered in *Merrimack's* and *Scipio*'s single combat, not out of chivalry but because the two had been merged into one force field and neither side could shoot the foe without damaging the friend.

Sensor-blind and occupied with their own survival, no one on *Merrimack* had been aware of what had been happening in the battle for the Citadel. They had just got *Scipio*'s com tuned to the U.S. channel, and *Merrimack*'s techs were just learning how to aim *Scipio*'s guns when the U.S. recall sounded. All ships were ordered to abandon the field.

The U.S. assault force had managed to damage the Catapult, and the fleet was withdrawing.

Captain Farragut requested permission to press the attack. He was told to withdraw; the objective had been achieved.

"No, it's not! The objective has *not* been achieved. Get Mishindi on the com!" Farragut shouted, then begged Admiral Mishindi to let him continue the siege. "Damaged isn't good enough. We have to destroy it. I'm still in this!"

"Captain Farragut, you have your orders."

"We can take out the Cat!"

"Not your call, Captain Farragut."

"Please, sir!"

"Not my call either. With. Draw." Bit out two distinct words.

"Where's Calli?" Farragut asked. "Is Calli still trapped inside the grid?" Nothing would stop him from going back and getting her.

But no. Calli Carmel's *Wolfhound* was in retreat back to Earth with the rest of the assault force. John Farragut had no more excuses. Nothing to do but drag *Merrimack* back to Earth under *Scipio*'s power.

PART FIVE

KALI

22

"**Y**OU BLOODY MINDED APE!**" Admiral Toracelli railed at Captain Farragut. That for show in front of the LEN investigators. In private, with a near grin, he said, "John, you're a wild man."

"Yes, sir."

"*And* you were told to ask for a tow if you got overridden."

"I got a tow," said Farragut.

Toracelli waggled an admonishing finger at him. "Someday. Someday."

"What is the LEN doing here, sir?"

"Demanding a restoration of the cease-fire."

"Bull*skat*!" Farragut was volcanic.

The admiral continued calmly, "We said something to that end. A lot more roundabout and polite. The LEN are bringing the United States up on charges in the World Court for violating the cease-fire and for barbarism. Quite a speedy process, you know."

Speedy as Plutonian mud. Farragut sat. You could fight a whole war before LEN injunctions could go into effect.

"And the LEN are naming you personally for war crimes."

"*Me?*" Didn't believe it. Felt it like a punch in the gut. War crimes. "War crimes?"

"We're standing for you. Not to worry."

Farragut was not worried. He was insulted. And, a feeling man, deeply wounded. *"War crimes!"*

"The swords. All too gruesome."

"I was *boarded.* The lupes didn't ask my permission, and I sure as hell didn't grant it. I hadn't surrendered. I defended my ship."

"You beheaded Commander Sejanus. *Beheaded* him. On his own bridge."

"Was he more dead than if I'd shot him?"

"You do see the point, though?"

"No. No, sir, I do not. It was combat. The LEN is taking off points for neatness?"

"The combat part is the sticking point. Rolls us back to our being the side to break the cease-fire. You see, it wasn't a lawful combat to begin with in the LEN books."

"What do you want me to do, sir?"

"John, we're getting you out of Dodge on the first stagecoach."

"As long as that stage is the *Merrimack,* I'll be happy to go."

"The *Mack* is vulnerable."

"I think I just proved she's not."

"We still don't know how Rome's getting your codes. Carmel *was* a prime suspect."

Farragut's back stiffened. "I trust Cal better'n I trust my own mama."

"She did turn in a superb showing at the Citadel. Carmel, that is, not Mrs. Farragut."

Captain Carmel had not shown the least hesitation to fire on Romans she had known at the Institute. Nor they at her. It was a typically Roman sort of respect.

"Still, it looks like you have a Roman mole," Toracelli went on. "And I'm damned if I can find him. In its current condition, do you honestly trust *Merrimack* with your life?"

"Change her phases, I trust her with all our lives in the Deep."

"Who said you were going Deep?"

"Where else? Shotguns need two stations. We dinged the Near Cat. There has to be a Far Cat. And since a whole bunch of Roman Legions didn't displace through to the Near Cat when we were attacking it, that means there's lots of stranded Romans in the Deep End."

"More than likely," Toracelli acceded.

"Where is the Far Cat?"

"Not precisely sure."

Farragut's eyebrows skied. "Then where precisely am I going?"

The grav disturbance had given a rough plot—a stellar neighborhood. But it could not pinpoint the location, or even narrow it to a reasonable haystack in which to search.

"An adviser will brief you when you clear Fort Ike."

Oh, hell. I'm picking up another spook at Fort Ike, thought Farragut. "Not Colonel Oh," he insisted.

"No. Not Colonel Oh. She's flying a desk. Not even CIA." Toracelli assured him. "One more thing, John. Kali."

"Calli? My Calli?"

"No. K-A-L-I. Indian goddess with fangs, bloody tongue, skull necklace, dead baby earrings, walking over her husband's dead body. That Kali."

"What about her?"

"It's a Roman code word, associated with the Deep End. We had thought it was the Far Cat. But a thing named Kali—" he let the sentence hang.

"They don't build to import avocados," Farragut finished for him.

"Exactly."

Farragut sat forward, forearm across knee. "Vic. You're talking to me here. What aren't you telling me? Where am I going?"

"Honest to God, I don't know." Toracelli laughed at the bizarre sound of that even as he said it. "Our source is not talking."

"We're mole-infested and you trust this source without so much as a—" He broke off with the coming of the dawn. Who could win that kind of trust. "Oh, for Jesus."

Because suddenly he knew who he was picking up at Fort Eisenhower.

"Permission to come aboard—is that the correct way to phrase the request?"

"As if I could stop you. You're a determined man, Jose Maria."

Captain Farragut's civilian adviser boarded *Merrimack* like a houseguest, with a bottle of Spanish wine in hand and a kiss on either cheek.

"I've had easier times digging a tick out of my hide than keeping you off my boat."

"Please," Don Cordillera protested, hand to wounded heart. "The tick is a parasite. I am a symbiote. I know the location of that which you seek, and I need someone to take me there. And so." He spread his arms to say here he was, on board *Merrimack,* bound for the Deep End.

Farragut inspected the label of the bottle in his hands. A fine vintage Rioja. "This has lived way too long. Come on and help me put it out of its misery, and tell me how the hell a Terra Rican neutral civilian happens to know where the Far Cat is."

Kerry Blue. In flagrante.

Her partner jackrabbited away. Couldn't ID him from the white ass that bobbed through the hatch.

Flight Sergeant Blue shrugged her jumpsuit up over her shoulders to free up her arm and hoist a salute. Left her still unsnapped stem to stern, leaving a sliver peek of young strong spare flesh on display.

Colonel Steele, revving up to yell at her. Too mad to think of what to yell. Distracted. Kerry Blue didn't wear underwear. Left a tuft of wayward fur on show. Steele snarled, "You're out of uniform."

Kerry looked uncertain. Her salute wavered. "Uh, yes, sir." Not sure if she'd been given leave to do something about it. And because he looked so red-faced mad, she dropped from attention, snapped up, resumed her salute.

Steele growled, jerked his head in the direction of the hatch through which her partner had made his escape. "Carver?"

"No-oo!" Two or three syllables worth of no. "Not if he was the last—" Met the colonel's ice-blue eyes. Stopped. Said, "No, sir."

Too much protest. Told Steele what he already knew— that she was still stuck on Cowboy Carver.

At least she was making a real effort to try to hate him.

For Steele, hating Cowboy required no effort at all. Of all the men who had used Kerry Blue, Cowboy Carver was the one Steele wanted most dead. Cowboy was the worst. Because Kerry Blue had loved him.

Steele did not demand a name from her. He did not want to know. He paced back and forth in front of her, mad as hell, with nothing acceptable to say. Finally: "Marine, do you want to transfer out?"

Shock on her face. Her answer emphatic, "*No*, sir!"

"You are ruining morale."

Her brown eyes got very wide. Dumbfounded, she blurted, "*Sir?*"

They called Kerry Blue the morale officer. She was no Trixi Allnight, but she was here, she was real, and she was usually to be had. And she gave no reports on her studies of comparative anatomy.

"Discipline," he corrected himself. Glad his face was already a furious red. Ears felt like they could ignite his hair, were his hair long enough to touch them. The only morale Kerry Blue was crushing was his. "You're bad for discipline."

"I didn't think it was that big a deal. What I was doing."

Not to her, it wasn't. It was a big deal. To him.

Tough. Soft. Pretty, in a rode-hard way. A good-hearted tramp. Not stupid. Not smart. Not a real deep thinker. Kerry Blue lived for the moment. Open. Everything that was Kerry Blue was right out there. She would follow him to hell.

"Sir, I want to stay."

Like removing his own rib, Steele told her, "You are going back to Fort Ike on the next LRS."

John Farragut and Jose Maria de Cordillera had euthanized the Rioja as well as a respectable Barca Velha, and were halfway through a bottle of Cassiopeian Barbaresco when Jose Maria got round to answering the question of how he knew the location of the Roman Far Cat.

"My wife, my Mercedes, accepted an irresistible engagement with the Palatine government. In the nature of a terraforming."

Dr. Mercedes Francesca Diego de Seville de Cordillera was a preeminent xenoecologist who had made many practical contributions to human colonization efforts. Her specialty was the successful insertion of Terran life-forms among native species without upsetting the natural balance, thus preserving the alien ecosystem while establishing a co-habiting system capable of sustaining human settlement.

The assignment that Palatine offered to Mercedes had been secret and long term. So secret she did not even know where she was bound until she arrived. She was permitted to record messages to her husband, which were scrutinized and sanitized before delivery to Terra Rica. Even Jose Maria was not to know the planet's—which was to say his wife's—location.

But Mercedes and Jose Maria had a code, the sort of code only a man and a woman deeply in love for thirty years could devise. And this man and this woman had stratospheric IQs so not even a Roman patterner could detect a code within their missives, much less penetrate their meaning. All their secret words were based on referents not contained in any database, things known only to two people in the universe.

So Jose Maria came into possession of the coordinates of a planet in the Deep End called Telecore, which served as the supply base for the construction of the Far Cat.

Which coordinates he gave to John Farragut.

Farragut tentatively accepted the data bubble. He admonished the Terra Rican, "This is a betrayal of neutrality."

Terra Rica was strictly neutral in any conflict between the United States and Palatine. And Jose Maria de Cordillera was a man of no small consequence. A personal violation of neutrality could put his world in a bad position with the Roman Empire.

"Apparently, there is no trust between us for me to betray," said Jose Maria. "I am trying to get to my wife. That is all. If the Romans will not take me, their sorrow if I seek help elsewhere."

"I don't get it, Jose Maria. Why do you need me? If you want to go, why not just go? Take one of your own yachts. You'd be a hell of a lot more comfortable. And you could've been there by now. Terra Ricans are allowed to use the Shotgun, and don't tell me you can't afford the toll."

Jose Maria lifted dark eyes to the low overhead with exposed ductwork. "I can afford luxury. Does not mean I need it. I prefer to go aboard your battleship, young Captain."

Farragut set the data bubble aside carefully. "There is more to this story than you just told me."

"And so there is."

Jose Maria set aside his drink, continued soberly.

Mercedes had been homeward bound on board a Roman ship, the *Sulla,* when her messages ceased, and *Sulla* was never heard from again. The ship came in to no port. Its crew—Jose Maria managed to get the ship's manifest— were not to be found. He contacted relatives of *Sulla*'s crew. They were all steadfastly silent, the way good Romans could be.

If Jose Maria could get to the planet Telecore, he could backtrack *Sulla*'s molecular trail, perhaps pick up a transmission.

"Only if they were transmitting electromagnetic signals," said Farragut, which surely Jose Maria knew. "You can't trace resonance." Then thought to ask, "*Can* you?"

The Nobel Laureate shook his head no. "I cannot. But if *Sulla* met a foul end, as I believe it did, it must have transmitted by all means possible. There would be an SOS."

And any SOS was, by necessity, traceable to its source.

"Wouldn't someone have picked up the SOS by now?"

"I believe there was one. Palatine already answered, shut it off, and whited out the sphere of waves coming toward traveled space."

Opened Farragut's eyes. "*That* is quite a conspiracy theory." Jose Maria did not strike John Farragut as a paranoid man. But, "Death of one's wife will do things to your head. I know."

Jose Maria had not said that word aloud, but he did not argue it. "I am deeply sorry that you know that, young Captain."

Farragut found himself with a mouth full of foot and couldn't spit it out. He apologized, "I sure didn't mean to say your wife was—might be—" hitched on the word. Blundered on, "Dead."

Jose Maria closed his eyes, shook his head with a sad, benign smile. Refused the apology, admitting, "I believe that she is."

"No. I shouldn't ever have said that. I didn't mean it. I don't know that. You can't know that."

Jose Maria lifted bright black eyes as if finding something interesting in the piping. Let the tears drain inward, unshed. "That is the cruelty of it. The false hope. And it is false. Because I *know*."

"That's just worry talking."

"Concretization is the scientific term. But you must believe me. I know. *Sulla* met with more than an accident."

"What? Did you find something in Mercedes' last message?"

"Nothing said. Things unsaid. The silence round *Sulla*'s disappearance runs too deep. It was not long after that we began to hear whispers of Kali."

Farragut said he had heard that whisper.

"Whispers only. Nothing more," said Jose Maria. "A project the size of Catapulta—Shotgun—call it what you will—it does not lend itself to total secrecy. Too many workers. Too many specialists. Too much equipment. Too much money changing accounts. It was secret in the details, but everyone knew Rome was building a Catapult.

"I can find no one who knows or is willing to speak anything of Kali. You can tell those who do know by the dire look that overcomes their visages at the mention of its name. And they do not speak."

"Not a warm puppy sort of a name," said Farragut. "Sounds like a name for a terror weapon."

Jose Maria gave a provisional nod. "Something terrible. Kali is the Destroyer."

"I thought Shiva was the Destroyer," said Farragut.

"Kali is Shiva's consort. Consort of Time and the Destroyer. The goddess Kali was enlisted to kill demons, which she did, and drank their blood. But once there were no demons left to kill, she kept on killing across the cosmos, annihilating all in her path."

"Sounds like a Roman weapon run amok."

"I do not know. It does not do to parse Roman code names too finely. I think it is safe to say this Kali is a destructive thing. And I know in my heart of hearts, by accident or by purpose, it destroyed *Sulla*."

23

A DOZEN OR SO LIGHT-DECADES into the Deep, someone and eight or twenty of his buddies started pounding out Farouq's Percussive Symphony Number 3 on the overhead with swords. It started that way. Had since devolved into a ship-wide 'cuss jam that was loud enough to shake the vacuum.

Someone clacked out a soprano counter line on the kirki sticks. Could be Kerry Blue and Carly Delgado. Someone else pulled an interesting *twok twok twok* out of what sounded like a cannon barrel.

And someone was way off beat. Probably that big lummox Dak, who had always been rhythm-free. Or Serge, bashing away like an orangutan on sprox.

Whoever had sleep cycle during the middle watch was S.O.O.L. because Farragut put up with the noise. Farragut was probably drumming on the hull with his usual exuberance.

TR Steele had taken his dogs aboard lots of ships. Had respected most of their captains, none more than this one. None had surprised him more than this one. Energetic. Fearless. Farragut never shrank from a dustup. And Steele's dogs loved him. Farragut could dive in and be one of them—the front liners—howling like a coyote, drum on the wastewater stack, without losing his command presence.

Something Steele could never do. Could only get a headache from the boisterous 'cussing, and wish he knew how the hell Farragut did that.

Blessed the chime for general quarters that pierced the din, shutting down all the artistes, and had them running for the gun bays.

Merrimack had picked up an SOS.

Jose Maria de Cordillera beat Farragut to the command center, his heartbeat still pounding out Farouq's Third. "What ship?"

"Not *Sulla,*" said the young Officer of the Watch, who knew Don Cordillera's story.

And Jose Maria was disappointed until he saw the ship. "Holy God."

Thanked God it was not *Sulla.* The drifting husk of a ship looked for all hell as if it had been chewed. The SOS was a dormant signal.

"Dormant?" said Marcander Vincent. "Hell, it's dead."

Merrimack illuminated her floods and turned several slow circuits round the wreck, to identify what it had been—Roman make, big, a transport, nominally civilian, but the sort that often served as pack beast to the Legions of Rome.

"Cal—" Farragut started. Stopped.

Not Cal.

His hand landed on his XO's shoulder, and the captain hung his head, apologetic. "Ah, hell, Bast."

He had not slipped like that in weeks. Sense of danger made him fall back on his old faithful. But Calli was not his anymore. Wondered if the admiralty had given her the *Monitor.* He'd been rushed out of town too fast to know.

His XO was Sebastian Gray now. Same height as Cal. Same age. Not as fun to look at. Easy enough to work with. Had not shown what he had under fire on *Merrimack* yet. Deserved respect.

The captain took names seriously. The misspeak was not a minor uf in John Farragut's book. He started over. "*Commander Gray,* what are we looking at?"

A wide scan located the derelict's cargo cars strewn over several milliklicks like dead planets of a dead star. The food cars had been pillaged, the machine carriers and oxygen bricks left intact.

After multiple scans turned up no contagion and only moderate corrosives on board the derelict ship, Farragut ordered Old Glory reeled in and a Red Cross run up the yard.

He sent a medical team with a Marine guard on a skiff to board the wreck. They limpet-docked and entered through an existing hole in the hull.

It was slow work. Flight Sergeant Kerry Blue negotiated the passage gingerly through the tear, mindful of the jaggedness of the metal edges and the flimsiness of her spacesuit. The suit's material was actually rugged but unnervingly thin.

A lock of hair, come loose from her band, floated in Kerry's face. She tossed her head inside her helmet trying to puff the strands out of her mouth, her eyes. Floating ends tickled her nose. She lifted gloved hands to her faceplate on reflex, pawed at the visor.

"Something wrong with your suit, Marine?" That was Flight Leader Hazard Sewell doing a Colonel Steele impersonation.

Kerry spat. Hair stuck to her lips. "No, sir."

Black. Even the stark light of their lamps could not dispel the blackness within the dead ship. The wreckage inside had mostly found a resting equilibrium against the bulkheads. There was not much floating about loose. The ship had been this way for a while.

Torn, corroded holes pocked the corridors as if the ship itself were diseased. The clear signature of Roman beam fire scored the decks. It took some real nutsifaction for the crew to have done that to their own ship. Or maybe banshees had got hold of the weapons and gone on a rampage. Kerry had seen some weird things out in the Deep, but this was a tough read.

They discovered uniforms on most decks, shredded and darkly stained, but no bodies in or near them. No bodies at all.

They did find dog tags. Collected those. Two hundred forty. Two hundred forty-one. Two hundred forty-two. And would the frassing MP turn off his helmet mike or count to himself please?

Nothing remained of the ship's food stores. The ship's weapons were all here. All had been discharged, emplaced guns and sidearms alike. The wreck, her name was *Hermione,* had put up a fight for all she was worth.

The ship's mess was devoid of even coffee beans. Hydroponics had been harvested messily but completely. Holes with dirt trails gaped in the soil of flowerpots in the officers' quarters where houseplants had evidently been yanked out by the roots. The chief's fish tank was frozen to the overhead by its own water, its artificial plants encased in the ice, but not the fish. The fish were MIA.

Computer banks waited, unscathed, for a command. The pattern of mayhem spoke of rage and perhaps hunger, but not of human intelligence. Knowledge was power, and the attacker had left *Hermione*'s knowledge behind like so much junk.

Kerry found pieces of shoes—soles, grommets, and laces, but not the rest. She recognized the Roman military type. The missing parts would have been leather. Also missing was the wool lining of a very nice ylene jacket.

The Romans were keen for woodwork, but Kerry hadn't seen any real wood on board.

A floating milky gleam caught the light of Kerry's headlamp. She gathered in a couple of the pearly beads, stilled them in her gloved fist, then opened her hand for a look.

Yelped. Flung them away.

"Marine?" Hazard's alarmed inquiry sounded in her helmet.

"Teeth!" she screeched. "I got teeth!"

"Fangs?"

"No, you dwit! Somebody's teeth!" She rubbed her gloved hands on the nearest surface as if something were stuck on them that could be wiped off. The teeth had been terribly clean. That didn't matter. There was teethness on her hands. She danced off the bulk, altogether creeped.

Merrimack hailed the med team. The unfamiliar voice that sounded in Kerry Blue's helmet had to belong to Commander Sebastian Gray: "Survivors?"

"Negative." Kerry Blue recognized the answering voice as the MO's. Mo Shah was about five paces away from her, methodically collecting floating teeth. "Personnel are being gone. Probably being dead. They are not being here."

Kerry was not sure which nightmare was more hideous,

that the crew were dead or that they were alive somewhere, in some state, naked and without teeth.

"Then haul on back to *Merrimack*." Captain Farragut's voice this time. "We've just been pinged."

Kerry joined the orderly scramble for the skiff.

A hail of something pelted the skiff. One of the somethings smacked Kerry's shoulder as she towed herself aboard the skiff. "Captain, we've been tagged!"

The Marine behind Kerry pulled the tag off her suit and chucked it out to space.

Merrimack's lookout reported, "Roman signature coming in high and hot on the eights. Single. Looks like a Fury. Closing."

A relief in a way. Anyone would rather face Romans than whatever had done this to *Hermione*.

Farragut's first orders were for the force field tech to scrub the tags. "Any homers on your screen?"

"Negative, sir."

The com tech reported, "I'm receiving the Roman's demand: Move away from the Roman ship *Hermione* or be destroyed."

"We have a Red Cross flying?" Farragut checked.

"Yes, sir."

The Roman Fury came into engagement range. Engagement range was anything within a quarter light-second, the range within which a ship's scanners perceived a target approximately where it actually was. The range was closer than the distance between the Earth and the Moon.

Farragut said, "Inform the Roman we are a rescue ship responding to an SOS."

Still the Fury approached, all weapons ports open. It deployed another flock of homing tags. Its commander called Farragut a murderer. Told him to take down the false flag. He meant *Merrimack*'s Red Cross.

"We *found* your ship in this state," Farragut responded. The Fury had to know that. The threats were all bluster and cover fire. "Stop it with the spitwads." Already *Merrimack*'s outboard lasers seared the second round of tags off *Mack*'s hide. "You can't shoot a rescue ship."

"Get away, you carrion eater."

Carrion? So the Roman knew the ship was dead? How

did the Roman know that? *Did* he know that? Or was this more bellicose talk?

"Get your lice off our property, *Merrimack*." The Roman referred to the U.S. med team. "Do not touch the flight recorder. Touch nothing. You are not a rescue ship."

"Neither are you!" Farragut shot back. "Your boys and girls on *Hermione* are dead and you know it. You're a salvage scow."

A silence. To call a soldier a salvager was the deepest insult. The Roman came back with a spitting, angry, "Strike your Red Cross."

Farragut knew he'd just been dared to step out in the alley and say that. He put the com on mute and asked the Og if the med skiff had made it back aboard. Told yes, Farragut ordered his new XO, "Strike the Red Cross. Get us a firing solution on the Roman Fury and stand by to fire."

Commander Sebastian Gray's brows lifted, but he issued the orders and reported back, "Striking Red Cross, aye."

Targeting had nailed a sounder bull's-eye on the Fury, but held fire. The Roman ship flew no Red Cross, but it was still inside the rescue zone.

Very strict, tacit rules held out here. Everyone was vulnerable out here. When not part of a battle zone, hostiles observed a one light-second no-fire radius around the source of an SOS.

Farragut asked the Roman if he wanted to step outside, then moved *Merrimack* outside the radius.

He was only slightly surprised that the lighter Roman Fury took up the challenge.

Tac reported: "Roman Fury is leaving the radius!"

And because it did so, Farragut ordered, "Stand by to switch control routine."

In the natural order of things, the smaller Fury was no match for the battleship *Merrimack*. This dare was in no way even, unless the Roman was packing spare aces on board.

Merrimack's controls flickered. "There it is," Kit Kittering reported from Engineering. Expected it. "Roman Fury is attempting override."

Merrimack shut down all its code recognitions and activated the backup routine. The battleship's controls stabilized immediately. Plan B was working.

"Your mole doesn't have up-to-date information," Commander Gray commented.

"Doesn't look like it," Farragut murmured, glad to hear his new exec sound impassive. "Let 'em have it."

The XO ordered, "All stations, fire at will."

The Fury had no Plan B. At its failure to sabotage *Merrimack* by mimicking her old command codes, the enemy ship turned tail, squidwise, to retreat at its most defensible angle.

Despite her greater mass, *Merrimack* was a powerful, quick ship. She ran down the Fury, forced it to turn, dropping it out of FTL.

The Fury waddled at sublight speed, angling for an escape vector. *Merrimack* bludgeoned the Fury with broad waves of disrupter spreads—bludgeoned carefully, trying to crack the eggshell but still leave the yolk intact. Great fire sprays struck the Fury's inertial screen.

Realizing there could be no escape, and that the *Merrimack* would likely smash the yolk along with its shell on one of these salvos, the Fury ran out the white flag with the symbolic half roll. The Roman surrendered.

"Anyone get the idea Farragut is just a little disappointed we didn't get boarded?" Cowboy sheathed his sword and stowed it in Kerry Blue's locker with suggestive motions of the blade. "I think he gets off on that swashbuckling skat."

"So do you, you *boon*." Kerry Blue slammed the locker shut on Cowboy's fingers.

Interrogation of the Fury's crew—there were fifty of them—gave little clue as to what had befallen the derelict transport *Hermione*. The prisoners claimed not to know. Their insistence was too adamant. They knew. And they were afraid.

Merrimack circled back to dead *Hermione,* shut off its SOS sounder, took the hulk in tow along with the Fury, and continued on her voyage to the Far Cat.

Roman craft had a certain majesty to them. Where American ships had a belligerent beauty in the clean, brute, utilitarian lines of their equipment, the Romans added stylistic design components. Only details, but telling details. A blunt, rounded end to a metal shaft where a simple square cut-off would have done. Their colors were richer. Their objects looked more substantial. They suggested grandeur, permanence.

Lieutenant Glenn Hamilton sat on the Fury's command deck. Felt as if she were on a stage set. And she was getting into character. Ensconced in a chair like this, she had to be monarch of something or other. She was tempted to try on the cape.

Romans could also go way over the top with flashy, gaudy accoutrements of past glory—oak wreaths, capes, gold cuirasses molded with muscle, shiny greaves, boots, all kinds of boots, embroidered togas, and those leather-flanged armor skirt things a man had to have truly great legs to wear with confidence. Though the Romans' undress uniforms were very dignified, practical, and sharp, their dress uniforms could be Las Vegas flashy.

So there was a deep-scarlet command cape with embossed gold shoulder pins draped over the Fury's command seat, demanding to sit on Glenn Hamilton's shoulders. She refrained. Partly because the thing was awfully shiny—borderline, or maybe over-the-line tacky—but mostly because Lieutenant Glenn Hamilton was five foot one, and the cape would drag on the deck, making her look like a little girl playing dress up instead of a Roman *domna*.

She seldom felt short on board *Merrimack,* unless someone reminded her with the stupid nickname *Hamster*—and thanks a heap for that one, John Farragut. She was accustomed to giving orders to truly big Marines. But the dimensions of this Roman ship were overlarge. Monumental was the word for it.

She assumed an imperial posture.

She was reviewing the ship's log when the Aldebaran scarab crickets, which clung heraldically to the hatchway, let out a chorus of chirping. Startled, Glenn Hamilton checked her chron. No, it was not later than she had thought. It was the scarab crickets that were off.

Some Roman with way too much time on his hands had conditioned the insectoids from the time they were larvae to sound off at intervals precisely coinciding with the changing of the Roman watch.

The Aldebaran scarab crickets were big, at least one foot

long, bronze-colored, metallic-looking, and so seldom moved they might well be fixtures. The Romans used them as architectural decorations. The scarab crickets had that grotesque elegance Romans fancied. Their distinctive lines, a popular motif in Roman jewelry, were familiar to everyone, though Glenn Hamilton had never expected to be sharing decks with live ones.

She had got used to the giant bugs, scarcely knew they were there, till they started singing out of time.

"Who wound up the gargoyles?" said the tech who was trying to decipher the Fury's navigational computer.

Glenn Hamilton turned toward the hatchway and ordered the decorations to shut up.

They obeyed every bit as well as any Terran insect would.

"God bless it!" Glenn rose from her seat, as suddenly one gargoyle detached and swooped across the cabin with a whirring of metallic wings. The deck officers ducked with wordless shouts.

"I didn't know they had wings!" one cried from under a console.

Other giant scarab crickets detached from their posts and set off in bulk-bouncing panic throughout the Fury.

Glenn Hamilton hailed the *Merrimack,* "Captain, I may have a situation here."

And immediately winced at how inept she was going to sound explaining why she was bothering Captain Farragut to report badly timed scarab crickets. No wonder she had only been "acting" exec of the *Merrimack*. Couldn't see Sebastian Gray making a misstep like this. Hoped Farragut didn't have her on the box, and the new XO wasn't listening in on her transmission.

She was rescued by an improbable coincidence. Over the open com, she heard Marcander Vincent on *Merrimack*'s command deck sing out, "Occultation at four by twelve by one twenty!"

They had a situation.

24

"I SEE IT, HAMSTER. Good eye. Join up and go dark."
Lieutenant Glenn Hamilton was not about to tell
Captain Farragut she had *not* sighted the bogey. That her
situation had only to do with an antic scarab cricket.

"Tuck us into *Merrimack*'s force field," she ordered her
skeleton crew. "Take us dark."

Her crew were some moments figuring out how to obey,
unfamiliar with the Fury's controls. They must have hit
something wrong—or else a timer had run down to zero—
because the Roman ship suddenly went darker than they
had wanted.

"*Merrimack*. Hamilton." Glenn opened the com. "We—
uh—blew a fuse." The accepted term for when you accidentally uffed an entire system. "We are flying dead stick."

It was hardly unexpected that the Roman ship would
have system bombs in place in case of capture. Something
had cued the Fury that it was no longer in Roman hands,
and the ship refused to obey any more enemy commands.

"Do you have life support?" Farragut sent.

"Yes, sir. And com, apparently."

"Suit up your crew in case there's a second bomb. We're
going to hook you."

"Aye, sir." Glenn clicked off. "Crew to space suits," she

ordered, then dove out of the way of a swooping scarab cricket. "And contain those gargoyles!"

One of the Aldebaran monsters alighted in her command chair, and jacked itself up on its six legs, buzzing, its eyes—all four of them—staring at Hamster in bugly rage. Or was that horror?

Lieutenant Hamilton lifted an image tablet with which to squash the scarab cricket, but she hesitated too long. Looked at it too long.

The scarab cricket's size, the quantity of whatever was inside it, the prospect of that whatever squirting out all over her magnificent chair, made her think better of the squashing course of action.

She yanked the scarlet cape off the back of the command chair, whisking it over the scarab cricket in one motion. She wrapped up the gargoyle's buzzing fury (or was that fear?), and pushed the whole bundle—scarlet yardage, cricket, all—into a Marine guard's arms. "Shove that out an air lock."

A dreadful pause. "We're dark, sir," the Marine reminded her. Opening an air lock would betray the ship's darkness. Hamster ought to know that. Worst luck in the world to get a stupid order from a commanding officer.

Worse still, Captain Farragut happened to be sweet on this particular officer, though the Hamster was the only man jack or jane on board who didn't seem to know that. And Farragut, who was usually all kinds of smart, thought no one noticed.

I just pointed out stupid to the captain's Hamster. I'm gonna get skinned twice.

But no skinning was forthcoming. Glenn Hamilton shut her eyes, admitted, "You're right. Do something with that, soldier."

The Marine tucked the red bundle under his left arm, very relieved. "Sir."

He marched out. Hamster could own up to a mistake. Captain had good taste.

"What have we got?" Farragut asked Tactical after he had sounded general quarters.

"Sphere, Captain."

A sphere was the most energy-conserving shape—having the smallest possible surface area for the volume, offering the least direct exposure to the deep freeze of space.

"LEN golf ball?"

The League of Earth Nations' round discovery vessels ranged everywhere. Both sides, Roman and U.S., regularly boarded them as suspected spies.

"Too big," said Mr. Vincent. "Vector out of the deep Deep End."

The com tech discreetly hand-signaled for the captain's attention. A request, if the captain chose to notice.

Farragut nodded for the com tech to speak.

"Mo Shah," said the com tech, apparently having the medical officer on hold. "Wants to know if you 'are being exceptionally busy.' "

The captain took the medical officer's hail. "Am I *busy*? Just a *little*, Mo." A little irony there. "What do you need?"

"I am observing a coincidence, perhaps being worth noting," said Dr. Mohsen Shah. "A great agitation among the insectoid life in the lab was preceding the call to general quarters by moments. There is being an appearance of a connection."

The Riverite doctor professed a creed in the connectivity of all life. "Noted," said Farragut. "Thanks, Mo. Out." Clicked off, not about to press the ship's ant farm into service as the new long-range lookout.

It was not possible that the ship's insects detected anything thirty light-minutes distant. The coincidence could be nothing but coincidence.

Farragut regarded the orb on his scanner display. He probably ought to simply report the sighting to the Joint Chiefs and plot a course around it. Leave the first contact to the experts in that sort of thing.

But by now his techs could tell him more about the bogey. It was five klicks in radius, moving at one hundred times the speed of light, and sporting a low-level force field.

It was also moving on direct vector *from* the coordinates identified by Jose Maria as Telecore, the planetary base for the Far Cat.

"Doesn't look Roman, but it sure as hell smells Roman," said Mr. Vincent at Tactical.

"Move us into its path," said Farragut. "Ready to roll out the welcoming mat."

"Ready Roman welcoming mat, aye," said Commander Gray, alerting Fire Control.

"And get us a res scan."

The res scan came back altogether weird. The sphere acted like a vessel but its composition was in no way reflective of a vessel. Dense, solid, dead, and cold.

"Mr. Gray, what do you think?" Captain Farragut asked his new exec.

"I think the Roman is foxing our res scan," said Commander Gray.

"Me, too," said Farragut.

"Sir," Marcander Vincent called out. "The target twitched. Started the moment we scanned it."

He amplified the image on the display to show the sphere close up. Its surface pocked and moved.

Commander Sebastian Gray blinked. "Did you see that?"

"I'll be damned," said Farragut.

It didn't smell Roman anymore. It smelled truly alien.

"Get Hamster's husband on deck," said Farragut. Patrick Hamilton was a xenolinguist. "Have him ask this ETI where it thinks it's going in such an almighty hurry."

"ETI, sir?" said Commander Gray. That the thing was extraterrestrial was beyond question. But intelligent?

"If it's FTL, it's I," said Farragut.

Gray looked blank. "Sir?"

"If it's moving faster than light, there's an intelligence behind it. Res scan it again."

As the tech took the res shot, the sphere moved again. It definitely moved, its structure changing.

"Target is breaking up," said Marcander Vincent.

The sphere's twitches were coincident with *Merrimack*'s resonant scans. But the events could not possibly be connected.

The res scan revealed that the sphere was expanding. It was composed of cells in a honeycomb pattern except for the ice layer that coated the whole, which continued to rupture as the inner layers of cells moved underneath, expanded, dislodging the outer layers, changing.

Farragut ordered another snapshot of the new form. "Scan again."

The sphere became more agitated.

The command crew exchanged glances. What was becoming obvious they still refused to accept. That they could be observing cause and effect here was improbable to the point of impossibility. Harmonics were infinite. Nothing could monitor them all at once. And chances of this sphere just happening to share *Merrimack*'s particular harmonic by accident were nil.

The crew on the command platform watched the displays in amazement.

Sounds of men shouting and banging on the bulks and ductwork pushed to Farragut's attention. A battleship was not a soundproof place, but this noise was excessive even for *Merrimack*. He gave a quick order, "Quiet that unit down."

"Aye, sir."

The sphere was breaking up. Its surface crumbled away to the layer below, became ciliate, flailing like a titanic rotifer. Then cells of the honeycomb broke off. Hexagonal shapes became rounded, then sprouted wreaths of whip-thin tentacles and flew, as if floating in water, each cell roughly a meter in diameter, not counting the cilia, expanding in the vacuum.

Alive. They looked alive.

"Move us out of the sphere's way. Let's see where it's going."

"It's going toward *us*," Marcander Vincent said as soon as the pilot had altered *Merrimack*'s course. "The plot changed course as we did."

Farragut moved to the tactical station to look at Mr. Vincent's tactical array. "How? How did it change? Where's its power plant?"

"It has nothing," said Mr. Vincent. "I think our sensors are uffed."

"Are we sure this isn't Roman?"

"Captain, we are so unsure of anything about this thing that—look at that!"

The detached cells flitted, swarmed together like fish in a nonexistent current in the vacuum sea. They moved toward *Merrimack* in a tenuous cloud followed by the crumbling mass of the sphere.

The cells attached themselves to *Merrimack*'s force field.

That, too, should be impossible. The battleship's inertial screen was frictionless. There was nothing for the things to latch onto.

"Jink," Farragut ordered.

"Jinking, aye." The pilot jerked *Merrimack* on a random jag of a course.

The things—giant spidery, centipede-like things—stuck fast as barnacles. "I think they've hooked our field."

"How the hell—" Farragut stopped, hearing background noise louder than his own voice. "I thought I ordered those men to shut up."

"It's the prisoners, sir," Mr. Gray reported apologetically. Tough to get Romans to obey orders. "They're screaming."

"I can hear that. What's their problem?"

"There's an insect in their compartment."

"And?"

Gray felt silly even reporting this. "There's an insect 'acting erratically' in the prisoners' hold."

"Aldebaran scarab cricket?" Farragut held his palms a foot apart.

"Someone's pet sicalian." Gray held his thumb and forefinger an inch apart. "For some reason that has them all screaming."

Farragut did not need to ask what the prisoners were saying. He could hear some of the words from here, some of them in English: "Run! For the love of God, run!"

Farragut looked to his displays, at the disintegrating sphere, the flailing things attaching to his force field. He asked his XO quietly, "How do the prisoners know there is anything out there to run from? Did someone tell them?"

Gray shook his head. "We made sure they knew as little as possible, sir. All they have to go on is our sound to general quarters and a deranged bug."

"And the chewed-up hull of the *Hermione*," Farragut murmured. "I'm thinking we might oughtta listen to the lupes on this one. Let's get some vacuum between us and Them."

"Aye, sir."

Gray gave orders to the pilot that took *Merrimack* up to high acceleration. The ship sprang at all right angles from its former course, five times faster than the sphere had shown ability to travel.

The sphere and the swarm of detached riders sprang along with *Merrimack,* matching speed and direction.

Mr. Vincent reported, "Looks like we're *dragging* them."

"They have a tractor on us? Unhook 'em."

"No detectable hook. I can't detect their propulsion system. Can't detect their tractor force. Can't detect what's keeping them mobile at two point seven degrees Kelvin. So there it is, Captain. This isn't happening."

Commander Gray shot Marcander Vincent a scowl, but Captain Farragut was accustomed to overlooking comments like that from his overaged tac specialist. "That's it," said Farragut. He'd run out of patience with these aliens. "Planet killer into the heart of that ice ball."

Said that just as Dr. Jose Maria de Cordillera arrived on the command deck. The doctor wore an expression of shock, not at the incredible scene on the sensor display, but at the captain's order to destroy a first contact.

Farragut turned away from Jose Maria's shocked face. Muttered, "Civilians."

Jose Maria Cordillera pulled back his dismayed expression, and kept his criticism, if he harbored any, to himself. He looked at the displays. "They can't get in. Can they?" He gestured at the black, ciliate things collecting on *Merrimack*'s force field.

"They're not *going* to," said Farragut. "Do we have a firing solution on the sphere?"

"Target acquired, sir," said Commander Gray. "Target is losing integrity fast on its own. It's going to break apart before we can blast it open."

"Fire," said Farragut.

Sebastian Gray ordered Fire Control to launch the planet killer.

"Planet killer away. Contact in three seconds, two, one. Contact. Detonation."

"Target destroyed, sir," Marcander Vincent reported.

"Mostly," Farragut said, watching the nearer of the sphere's scattered bits break apart further, sprout legs and swim toward *Merrimack*.

Jose Maria breathed something in Terra Rican in a tone of wonder. Then in English, "They *move*."

Farragut demanded, "How many of Them are there?"

"Minimum fifty thousand discrete entities not counting

the big pieces. Not sure if some of those aren't made of multiple units. Sir, what *are* they?"

The crew tended to ask Captain Farragut impossible questions, as if he knew everything, as if he were God.

Farragut stared at the alien things swimming in literal nothing. He could see them now, without sensors. Could look out a clearport and see their bulbous bodies, their masses of black tentacles clinging to the frictionless energy field. Each of their dozens of tentacles opened and closed at the ends like sucking mouths, serrated at the openings, like teeth.

They had the appearance of living beings, though they had to be machines. Nothing could live out there, motile and mobile in the extreme cold. No natural being could achieve FTL by biological means.

The things were expanding. Free of their sphere, they bloated in the vacuum but did not burst.

A hum, becoming a growl, sounded from all directions at once. It was the force field under siege.

One of the ciliate things looked to have inserted one cilia *into* the force field.

No one bothered to say that was impossible. Mr. Vincent said only, "They're coming in."

25

CAPTAIN FARRAGUT ORDERED COLONEL Steele to launch his fighter wing. "Have your dogs burn those barnacles off my boat."

But the Swifts never even got out of dock. The fighter lifts stalled in their shafts as all ship's controls began to fail.

"Not again!"

"How did the Romans get our new codes!" Steele bellowed.

"I don't think this is Roman," Mr. Gray advised the captain.

"Romans are very good at not looking Roman," said Steele, who trusted Romans only to stab him where he wasn't looking.

"They've outdone themselves this time, TR," Farragut murmured, dubious.

He didn't believe it, because the Roman prisoners were scared. Beyond scared, screaming in a very un-Roman panic.

Someone said, *"Kali!"*

Farragut felt his skin prickle, gone chill.

He barked over the com to the Fury. "Hamster, displace your crew back on board *Mack,* stat!"

On receiving no response from the Fury, he notified the com tech, "Get ahold of her. Get the Fury crew back here *yesterday*."

"Aye, sir."

Farragut took in a deep breath—as if he could not draw enough air. As if there were not enough oxygen in it. A quick check of the meters showed the ship's atmospherics reading at normal levels.

He exhaled hard to rid his lungs of carbon dioxide. Inhaled again. It hadn't helped.

Sebastian Gray, who was inhaling hard, hand to his chest, caught the captain looking at him, asked, "Is it just me?"

"No," said Farragut. He looked to the displays, at the spidery things encasing his ship with their bodies. He felt like a fly being wrapped in silk. "They're doing this."

He ordered his thunderstruck crew: "Prepare to repel boarders."

Boarders? Below decks crew and company traded mystified grimaces. There were no other ships in the area. *Boarders*?

Jose Maria watched the creatures on the force field oozing—*insinuating*—their way in.

Jose Maria murmured with a scientist's fascination. "This is fantastical. I wish my Mercedes could see—"

The sudden silence, the unfinished thought, made John Farragut look aside to see what had happened to Jose Maria.

Jose Maria had turned gravestone white. He resumed, voice dead flat, "She did. She saw this. The last thing she ever saw."

Farragut's gaze snapped back to the squashed looking things in his force field. *This?*

"They can't get in," Sebastian Gray echoed Jose Maria's earlier thought, with little conviction. "Can they?"

The chief, who had just arrived on deck, scoffed, fists on his fleshy flanks, "Without the codes? Impossible. Even God can't crack the *Mack*'s shell."

"Oh, for Jesus, Og, I wish you hadn't put it that way," said Farragut, who had a deep faith in an old-fashioned God, the jealous one.

A metallic scritching sounded from somewhere, everywhere. "What is that?"

"That's your impossibility on the hull, Chief."

"How the hell—" Og let the question hang. A display showed one of the things emerge from the force field and fall under *Merrimack*'s artificial gravity onto the hull.

An alarm sounded. The crew didn't need it. The pressure in their ears told them what happened. Hull breach.

"I *hate* that," Farragut said. Opened his jaws wide with the sudden dip in air pressure.

The ship's air rushed out the hole in the hull to fill the space between the ship's exterior and its force field—a space that varied from five to twenty feet in width. *Merrimack* was a big ship with a lot of surface area, so it was a significant, though not deadly, event.

"They're in," said Mr. Vincent.

From the Romans in their detention hold came screams such as one might imagine from men being eaten alive. But the prisoners were in an interior hold. None of the intruders scratching at the hull could have got to them. At least not yet.

But the prisoners felt the pressure change, and they knew what it meant. This ship was about to turn into the *Hermione*.

Farragut listened for weapons' fire. Hearing none, he signaled the deck where hull breach was located. Tried several times. Then: "Hey down there. Report." The intercom was dead.

Farragut roared for the whole ship to hear: "All hands to swords! Destroy all—" hitched on the word—"monsters!"

Flight Sergeant Kerry Blue was still in her cockpit, waiting on the stalled lift stuck between decks. She heard nothing from outside. Had not felt the pressure drop.

She tried to get a read on the ambient atmosphere to see if the erks had opened the flight deck to let the vacuum in yet. She got no readings at all. Damn. Did not want to go out there in an uffed crate. She let out a string of language, then asked into her com, "Did anybody hear that?"

Her com was dead.

She unbuckled quickly. Had to get out of here before they launched her.

She pulled off her glove and lay a palm to the canopy. It was not cold, so she popped the canopy, using the manual spring. She climbed onto her Swift's fuselage, looked up the shaft.

Having trouble breathing. Damn space suit was uffed, too. She took off her helmet, inhaled. Wasn't any better out here. But now she could hear an awful lot of shouting. Something was wrong, wrong, wrong.

She dropped her helmet into the cockpit, put her gloves back on, and had at the lift cables, feeling like she was back in boot camp. She clambered like a monkey, up the dark shaft, swearing.

A wind from below fluttered her hair. *Oh, skat, they got the lift working again and they're opening the deck to the vacuum!*

Screamed, "Don't open it! Don't open it!"

But the cables to which she clung were not moving down to launch her Swift, and the wind was not the kind of gale that would signal her imminent death by vacuum. This was just a hull tear somewhere making the air circulate oddly.

She leaned her face against the cable, breathed relief, "Oh, frag. Oh, hell."

An odd sound came from below, a clattering scritching, something like dog toenails on metal, but moving vertically. The sound was nearing.

Kerry leaned way back on the cables to look down around her Swift.

A black shape filled the shaft. Lots of whippy legs. Rising fast.

Colonel Steele stalked down the ramp tunnel to the starboard hangar deck to see what had become of his fighters. He met an alien in the corridor. An amazing, nightmare thing in this familiar, orderly place. It had pried up one of the deck grates, and several of its many tentacles fished underneath for something dropped there.

The sight threw him not an instant. Steele drew his standard issue sidearm—the splinter gun, not the sword. The gunsights bracketing his eyes triangulated the direction and read the distance from the constriction of pupils to the focal point of his gaze. Vibration in his hand signaled target acquired.

The splinter gun fired true. The sliver penetrated the black body, which gave a violent jerk as Steele immediately depressed the second stage trigger to explode the sliver inside the target.

The alien ruptured nicely. Its punctured remains deflated to the deck. Seemed to be melting through the grate.

Steele did not stay to observe it. He had to burst open another one he saw clinging to the overhead, and another chewing through the bulk.

He took aim down the ramp tunnel to another thing galloping up from the hangar deck, its tentacles madly slapping. The sliver hit home, but the second stage detonation failed.

Steele fired again.

Detonation failed again, winning Steele only a thrashing mad alien, with two slivers in its belly, rolling up the ramp tunnel.

From elsewhere in the ship, other shouts reported weapons' failure.

The snaky mass left the deck, sprang at Steele. Steele saw it coming at him like a giant jumping spider, but with many mouths at the ends of many tentacles.

And he opened it up with his sword.

The blue-black mess spilled a brown stinging gush as it hit his torso. It shrank to the deck, sloshing its innards out.

Steele hadn't even thought about doing that. Didn't even know how the sword got into his hand. After all the drills, it was reflex now.

As the tentacles stopped their spasms and the thing went still at his feet, Steele vowed he would never, ever, question any dumb idea of Farragut's ever again.

Kerry Blue in a nightmare chase. Climbing for her life in this dark shaft from the most enormous of spiders. Could not move fast enough. Tentacles gained on her up the shaft.

She climbed as fast as she could, hand over hand, on the cables. Tendons straining, muscles burning, her own fierce grunts urging her on.

Near to the top. Almost there.

Glove touched deck as something touched her boot, bit a chunk out of it. She screeched.

With a sudden tightness in her collar, she was rising — fast — without effort, like puppy lifted by its scruff.

Colonel Steele. Hauled her up and threw her aside.

She rolled, pushed her hair out of her face to look up from the deck. Colonel Steele with a sword. Brought a Herculean downstroke to land on the black swarm of tentacled hideousness that emerged from the shaft.

The thing fell back down the hole.

A sharp yelp sounded from below. Inchoate cursing. Cries of more disgust than pain. Something loathsome had fallen on Cowboy's head.

A tentacle, severed from the monster, still lashed on the deck. Steele kicked it down the shaft.

Cowboy's gagging outcry echoed up the shaft.

From farther below, came other voices. "Shoot 'em! Shoot 'em! Shooooot!"

And the scritching of many many legs.

Colonel Steele cupped his hand to the side of his mouth to call down to them. "Splinter guns are inoperative!"

A shout returned up the shaft, "Then we're frogged, sir!"

With someone else crying, "It's over. It's all over!"

And closer, from Cowboy, who had to be climbing the cables, "It ain't over till the Cowboy's dead!"

Colonel Steele flipped his sword in the air a half turn endwise, caught it, so that he now held the blade between fingers and thumb, wary of the sharp edge. He called down the shaft. "Carver! Yo!"

Cowboy wiped brown slime off his face, squinted up. Saw what Steele held. He freed up a hand to receive it. "Ho!"

Steele let the blade drop.

Cowboy caught the sword deftly by the hilt. He swung down the cables to battle the monsters that threatened the rest of his squad.

Kerry sprang up from the deck. "Any more where that came from, sir?"

Kerry Blue had her flaws—lots of them—but indecision in battle was not one of them.

Steele signaled her go. Did not have to tell her where to go or how many swords to come back with as fast as she could. In a fight for your life, you want to be beside Kerry Blue.

26

THEY WERE GETTING HARDER, the gorgons, developing shells, making it tougher to slice through them.

Observations of the enemy passed quickly through the ship by shouts:

They dissolve when they die.

Close your eyes when you open them up. That brown slop that squirts out of them is caustic.

Hacking off their legs does NOT kill them.

Those suckers at the ends of their legs can take a chaw out of you right quick.

They're really ugly.

Thank you, Einstein.

You can't squash them.

So who tried to squash something that can squeeze through a force field?

Same idiot who tried a fire extinguisher on them.

As if something that came in from the vacuum would mind cold or oxygen deprivation.

But the swords still worked, even against the hard ones.

Kerry Blue hacked at flailing mouth-legs until her muscles were laced with fire, and she kept hacking. *I will not be eaten alive.* She was not even afraid anymore. Tired, in pain, angry, her stinging eyes watering. She had no room for fear.

At some point the main lights went back on. The air came in cooler through the vents. Kerry heard a splinter gun detonate. A lift running. Jubilant hoots. "We're back in this!"

They were guessing these gorgons got their strength in numbers. The company and crew had apparently hacked them down to critical unmass, and the monsters couldn't do their jamming tricks anymore.

With that, the bone-weary inner numbness lifted. The prey became the exterminator. *Merrimack*'s crew and company fought with strength they didn't know they had left. It became sport to hunt down and kill these tentacled rats trying to leave the ship.

When she could find nothing left to kill, Kerry dragged herself into a lab, sat on the deck, and pulled the chain for the sprinkler that was there in case of chemical spills. She let the water wash over her face. Carly Delgado crawled in to sit back to back with her under the cool stream. A dog joined them.

Other Marines staggered in, pressed in with Kerry, Carly, and the dog, in a wet knot.

Kerry passed the chain around, too exhausted even to keep it pulled.

A tippy tappy skitter rushed past the lab—a stray gorgon down to a dozen legs, with Cowboy in hot pursuit with raised sword, wailing like Tarzan.

Carly cracked an eye, but Cowboy and the thing were already past. "What the hell was that?"

"Just one damn thing after another," said Kerry.

Colonel Steele found them there. No one stood up, and Steele didn't make them.

Steele stripped to boxers and T-shirt, his uniform sopping with brown slime and shredded from tentacle bites. Kerry and Carly scooted over to make room for him under their sprinkler.

Steele sat heavily, a mess, his white skin blotched with red chemical burns, his eyelids so swollen you couldn't tell his eyes were blue. The water rinsed brown filth from his white-blond crewcut, from the gold thatch on his chest. Blood from a gash on his arm thinned and swirled down the drain.

Kerry leaned against him. "Thanks, Colonel." She meant for saving her life in the lift shaft.

Steele grunted.

In a moment, "Sir?"

Steele snarled, *"What?"*

"Can I stay?"

A whole string of foul words. There was a yes in there among them.

"Hoo ra," said Kerry Blue.

Farragut strode through the corridors, talking to his crew, his Marines, thanking them for a job well done, asking them to account for all their mates, checking all decks for stragglers or wounded.

Returning to the command deck, he looked about for one not here. "Where's Hamster?"

Commander Gray said, "You mean our diminutive, red-headed lieutenant? I have not seen her."

No one had seen her.

And Farragut realized he had not seen *anyone* from the Fury.

He hailed the displacement deck. When he finally got someone on the com, it was a maintenance tech who had to check the displacement log in the computer.

"Negative, Captain. No displacements at all the last three watches."

Farragut had ordered the Fury crew to displace back to *Merrimack* when the gorgons first attacked.

That was about the time the ship's controls started to go down. Displacement required precise readings and confirmation from three discrete sources—the LD, the collar, and the displacement chamber. They must not have acquired a signal lock.

Farragut got on the com. "Fury. Farragut. Respond." And to the com tech. "Did they receive that?"

"I don't know, sir."

"Keep hailing them."

"Aye, sir."

Into the intercom, "Mo! What are your insects doing?"

The ship's medical officer was up to his elbows in wounded. An orderly checked on the captain's question, reported, "They haven't calmed down any."

To Tactical: "Get a scanner on the Fury. Put it on the display."

Farragut prowled the command deck end to end, fretting the thirty seconds it took to get an image of the Fury up. Asked anyone, "Did they take swords aboard the Fury?"

"I don't think so, Captain," said Commander Gray.

The image of the Fury appeared on the tac screen, still riding alongside *Merrimack*.

Riddled with holes chewed through its hull.

The com tech reported before Farragut could demand, "No one is responding."

"Hamster? Hamster!" Farragut called into his wrist com, shouting, as if that would help. *"Glenn!"*

Captain Farragut displaced aboard the Fury with a troop of his least exhausted Marines in space suits, armed with swords.

The Fury's command and control was choked with smoke. Farragut could not see his glove in front of his visor. He switched over to scanner mode, which threw an instrument reading onto his visor, giving him a weird sort of vision.

He left a team of technicians in C and C to try to restore the ship's atmosphere, while he and the Marines set out in search of the crew, wading through brown sludge, which they now knew to be dead gorgons. That was a good sign. Maybe.

If the crew survived whatever had killed the gorgons.

He came to a sealed hatch, locked from this side, hot to the touch. Had to be fire on the other side.

Farragut signaled his techs at C and C. "Dix. Farragut. Do we have fire suppression?"

"Negative, Captain. Controls are operative. And the fire suppression system is *spent*."

"Roger that." Farragut hailed *Merrimack*. "Gray. Can you withdraw the force field at the Fury's midships for a minute?"

"At the hot spot? Yes, sir."

In moments, the smoky air inside the Fury began to stir. Midships had depressurized entirely, while the thick air from the rest of the Fury whistled toward the vacuum in a muddy swirl through many jagged holes in the decks, the partitions, the vents.

It was a long minute before the force field was restored. Farragut could see dimly now by the minimal light of emergency lamps.

He unlocked the hatch—it was still warm—and opened it.

A charred chamber lay utterly black on the other side. There was no smoke, but he could not see because there was no light. Had to watch the display on his visors to keep from falling through the holes. There was very little left of the deck.

Farragut and the Marines passed through several more hatches until they came to one sealed and locked from the far side. Farragut tapped out shave-and-a-haircut with his sword hilt.

The hatch unlocked and opened at once.

A lot of helmets clustered at the opening. Faces behind the visors broke into elated smiles.

One crewman rashly popped his helmet seal. Farragut guessed the Fury's atmospherics had been restored because the man was still breathing, still smiling, without his helmet. "Glory, glory, are we glad to see you, Captain!"

The rescued crewmen told Farragut that they had started the fire.

"Figured whatever wiggles at two point seven degrees Kelvin might have a problem with heat."

And they had been right. Problem was, the amount of heat it took to kill the gorgons was enough to destroy everything else and use up all the available oxygen.

"I thought we'd cooked ourselves," said the crewman. "And when you let the vacuum in, I thought that was hell freezing over." Proudly showed his space suit's air gauge, reading dead empty. "I was down to my last sniff."

Farragut was counting up present company. Counted short. Five short. Throat tight, he asked, "Who did you lose?"

"Ximeno, Faqry, Williams—big Williams, not little Williams—and Brownie. Oh, Brownie bought it ugly."

"Where's Hamster?"

"She's not in here. We led the suckers this way and she stayed out that way to throw in the toaster and lock 'em in."

Here was the engine compartment. The crew had taken refuge behind the thickest bulk in the entire ship.

Farragut took off his helmet. "Did she find a place to hide?"

"She was going down to the magazine to jettison the bombs in case the fire got out of control, so we wouldn't blow up the *Merrimack* with us."

Farragut glanced up at the sound of scratching. "You've still got gorgons alive in here."

The Marines had brought over extra swords, passed them out to the Fury's crew.

Farragut pointed up toward the scraping noise. "Kill all of those." And he ran back the way he'd come toward the ship's munitions store.

He came to a hatch, locked from the far side. He hailed the techs in C and C to override the lock. The lock spun, and Farragut tore the hatch open.

And jumped back as a jet of flame shot from the opening, taking his eyebrows off.

A muffled gasp from behind the flame: "Omigod!" The blowtorch abruptly pointed up and shut off. Hamster's shocked face behind a visor looked to be all eyes. "Captain!"

"Oh, for Jesus, Glenn!" Farragut took off his glove with his teeth, brought his fingers gingerly to his naked brow.

Lieutenant Hamilton yanked off her helmet, her red-brown hair matted against her head. "I'm so sorry. Please say my guys are still alive!"

"Most of them."

She shrank at the sound of scratching from above. "They're still here!"

"Not for long. Dogs are hunting down the last of them. Guns are working again. But *these* work all the time." He brandished his sword. "Lordy, Hamster, I give you a ship and look what you do. Couldn't you have made a bigger mess?"

What might have started as a laugh ended in a sudden scream of pain.

Tentacles from beneath a jump cart had lashed out and taken a bite from Glenn's thigh.

Farragut kicked over the cart. Brought his sword down on the gorgon so hard the blade stuck in the deck between the dying halves.

He caught Glenn to him as she buckled. Held her close, her head tucked under his chin, his ungloved hand holding the back of her head, his lips on her hair.

When she was standing steadier he had to let her go. She wobbled a little, her weight on one leg. A lively stream of blood trickled from her thigh. Her face went very white, a shocky glaze coming over her eyes. "I'm sorry I trashed the ship."

Farragut gathered her up like a bride, carried her back to the LDs.

"Put me down, John, I'm gonna ralf."

He let Glenn get her good leg under her, and lent her balance as she threw up. Then he snapped a displacement collar on her. She felt limp and quaking as he lifted her again and displaced back to *Merrimack*.

He meant to carry her to sick bay himself, but met Dr. Hamilton on the way—looking frantic but whole, healthy, and unblooded. Xenolinguists were not on board for their fighting skills.

Farragut brusquely bundled little Glenn Hamilton into her husband's arms and went about his duties.

After both ships were pronounced secure, the lab ants gone back to their holes, and the crew fed, the relief tactical specialist called Captain Farragut to the command deck to observe a fragment of a gorgon swarm still out there, floundering in space, disintegrating into debris. As if they needed a certain number in their swarm to maintain viability.

Farragut thanked the specialist and went in search of Dr. Cordillera to run that idea past him.

Jose Maria was not in his quarters. He was not in sick bay.

People had seen him. He had been in the thick of the battle. "He was magnificent," an awestruck crewwoman assured him. Jose Maria was picturesque with a sword, and apparently devastating as well, because even the crewmen were impressed.

But no one could tell the captain where *Don* Cordillera was now.

Farragut was beginning to feel something like fear, when suddenly, quietly, he found him, Jose Maria, in a crouch, on the balls of his feet, his back resting against the bulk, his sword on the deck before him, his hands over his face. An image of remorse, but he could not possibly regret killing those marauding parasites.

He had got himself cleaned up. His clothes were immaculate, his black hair neat and glossy as a show horse's tail. An elegant and lonely figure down there.

"Jose Maria."

Still in his crouch, Jose Maria de Cordillera straightened his back flush to the wall, and lifted his wet face to Farragut. "She is gone."

"Mercedes," said Farragut. He leaned against the wall with Jose Maria, but stayed standing. "You don't know that, Jose Maria. There's still hope."

"Oh, I will find ways to deny it, too. But I know she is gone."

"How," Farragut challenged.

"I can tell you the date and the hour. I woke in the night, in sweat and terror. I sat straight up and spoke her name aloud. It was only later that I learned the *Sulla* was missing. There is no scientific explanation for what happened to me, but such things have been reported in old wives' tales for ages. I do not discount the tales of old wives merely because they appear to defy current bounds of reason. The popular record is too strong to ignore. I knew she was gone."

"You're talking clairvoyance," said Farragut, arms crossed, skeptical.

"No. I think I am talking telegnosis. I do not disbelieve what I cannot explain."

Of course not. He couldn't and still be Catholic.

"My Mercedes and I had a connection. Perhaps a resonant harmonic. She lived and I felt her presence with me always. And then, suddenly, I did not. I carry an empty place where she always was," said Jose Maria, hand to his heart. He sighed, deep and sorrowful. "You know. You *know*. And still you hope. The persistence of the human heart." Tears spilled from his black eyes. He reverted to his cradle tongue. "*Dios! Dios!* She was so scared. She died in terror and I was not there."

27

KERRY BLUE SLOPPED THROUGH the remains of the melted gorgons. Stuck her mop in the wringer. Grimaced at what came out. "Ugh."

Dak lifted another deck grate for her to mop up the sludge underneath. The muck pooled deep down here in the lower sail. "Need a hose over here!"

Merrimack carried a lot of things—a full hospital, a partial torpedo fabrication plant—but she did not carry automated cleaning equipment. That was why God invented Marines.

Captain Farragut came through without his normal buoyant cheer. His face looked unusually moody. He stopped to watch his Marines work, and his expression got positively angry. "No," he muttered, to himself it seemed. Then louder, stepping forward. "No." He yanked the mop out of Kerry Blue's hands. "You're not doing this."

Okay by Kerry Blue. Colonel Steele might not like it, but the captain was the captain, and who was she to argue with the captain?

Carly, Reg, and Cowboy looked up from their work to stare at Captain Farragut.

"Stop, stop, stop. All of you."

The Marines foundered, confused. Did the captain want them to come to attention?

"Put that *down,*" Farragut zeroed in on Twitch Fuentes, who was clutching a vacuum hose, unable to believe he could be getting off this crummy detail. And right under Colonel Steele's nose, too.

"Colonel Steele," Farragut barked. "Issue sidearms to your dogs and come with me."

"Sir," Steele acknowledged.

And so off they went to the detention hold.

The hold was weirdly quiet within, and Kerry wondered for a moment if the prisoners weren't all dead. Or preparing a trap.

Captain Farragut made the MPs unlock the hatch. The instant it was open, he charged right through the hatchway, ahead of his armed escort. They scrambled after him in time to see him *roar* at a bunch of Romans standing in rigid ranks: "What the hell was that!"

The prisoners remained at parade perfect attention. They had begun the assault with such a poor showing—all that screaming—that evidently they decided to scrape their *dignitos* together and meet their fate like Romans. In disciplined futility.

Farragut must have been the last thing they expected to come bursting through the hatch.

But here he was, breathing fire. He stalked up to the front line of soldiers and grabbed one by the throat— looked like a lion with a baby zebra—and slammed him up against the bulkhead. *"You knew!"*

Kerry could see the furtive glances pass among the other Romans. Could tell from their perplexed stares that no one had told these men that the monsters were all dead.

They were slowly getting a clue, though, and they were incredulous. Looking at Farragut like a fragging archangel with a flaming sword.

Kerry would swear he had fire jetting out his blue eyes.

Farragut roared again, *"When the hell were you going to tell someone!"* Got no answers out of them other than their imbecilic, stunned stares.

Farragut dropped his baby zebra to round back on Colonel Steele. "TR. Get my boat cleaned up. *Them.*" He thrust a finger at the Roman prisoners. "Make *them* do it. Your dogs do *not* pick up any equipment that doesn't shoot!"

"Aye, *sir*!" Steele acknowledged enthusiastically.

The captain stomped out, smoking hot.

The Marines shepherded the Romans out of detention, armed them with vacuum hoses and mops and rags.

They came along tentatively. Docile. Amazed.

Kerry enjoyed poking in the back anyone who did not move fast enough to please her. She liked this detail much better. She'd been trained in twenty-four scenarios. This was another new one, but far and away the best ever.

One Roman, his hands stinging raw from the caustic slop, looked to Kerry and asked, in English, "What *is* this crud?"

"Dead monsters," said Kerry. "They melt when you kill 'em."

"Where are they? The monsters?"

"Under your stupid feet, you dwit!"

"*All* of them? Where are the rest of them?"

"We killed them. Shut your face bung and use that mop or I'll take it from you and you can use your tongue." Kerry leveled a sighter beam on the Roman's crotch.

Caught Reg, from the corner of her eye, screwing up her brow at her and mouthing silently, *Face bung?* Cowboy sniggering, "I love you, Kerry Blue." And Dak, shoulders shaking silent guffaws, working up to say something. She didn't even let him get his mouth open. "Shut up, Dak."

The prisoners mopped in silence.

Farragut came by again. Looked like God in Navy blue. He supervised a moment in silent, frowning approval, then turned away without speaking.

It was not like Farragut not to say a word or twelve hundred.

To his back someone called, "Captain!"

A Roman.

Farragut turned, blue eyes raking across the prisoners. Kerry could tell that Farragut knew the speaker wasn't one of his own. Farragut knew the voice of every last one of his company and crew down to the lowest grunt. He even knew hers.

As the captain took a step toward them, the Roman prisoners all dropped their cleaning equipment. The Marines took immediate aim with their splinter guns. But the Romans were only coming to attention. Then—unbelievably—saluted.

Farragut turned his back on them and stalked out.

A service for the dead.

At times like this TR Steele was in awe of Captain Farragut. You'd never know the captain was American blue blood. He talked like just folks and could brawl like a street dog, or he could stand up there in front of God and everyone with his tear ducts wide open, and it didn't make him any bit weaker.

Steele would have looked like a sap.

Steele set his jaw hard as a headstone, just glad someone was crying for his boys and girls, because he sure couldn't.

Lieutenant Glenn Hamilton was back on her feet the next day, her leg still encased in a med sheath to restore the chunk of muscle the gorgon had bitten from her thigh.

She retreated to the hangar deck, carrying out a solitary damage assessment. She was off duty this watch, but she did not want to deal with Patrick right now. So she worked.

She hugged a memory she thought she had imagined. On the Fury, when Farragut killed the gorgon that attacked her, when he caught her falling. The feeling of safety in his arms. The way he'd pressed her to him, his hand behind her head. His lips on her hair. She'd felt that. Thought she made it up, but she *felt* that. John Farragut kissed her hair.

Farragut was always hugely affectionate to everyone. But that, *that* had been a little over the line.

John Farragut kissed my hair.

She had never seen him afraid, because Farragut never feared for himself. She had felt him afraid there on the Fury. Heard the catch in his breath, felt the tremor in his hands as he held her close to his thrumming heart. Held her as if she was a precious thing he had almost lost.

She was not even sure it happened the way she remembered it. The way she wanted it to have happened. It had shocked her. Not an unpleasant shock. It was very easy on the pride, coming from the captain of the *Merrimack,* after her own husband—one of the few men on board fortunate enough to be sharing his bed with a flesh-and-blood woman (a damn pretty one at that, Dr. Patrick Hamilton!) on *Mer-*

rimack's long tours—Patrick Hamilton hooked into a Hot Trixi Allnight virtual joyride.

"But she's not *real*," Patrick Hamilton had defended instead of apologized, baffled by her hurt anger.

"*I* am!" Glenn had cried.

He did not get it.

Patrick also had trouble carrying her the rest of the way to sick bay when John had given her over to him after rescuing her from the monsters on board the Roman Fury. Glenn's one hundred pounds got rather heavy between decks, and Patrick had to set her down once to regroup.

Glenn had not married Patrick Hamilton for any brute qualities. Patrick was an intelligent, boyish, slender man, with a dry sense of humor. Companionable. Could be very sweet. Could be very inconsiderate. Hell, Patrick Hamilton could be an ass.

Left her vulnerable to dreams. That big, swashbuckling John Farragut could harbor a secret love for her was too much like a dream she wanted too badly to believe right now. It was too easy on the pride. Too easy on the heart.

She convinced herself she had imagined too much into the encounter on board the Fury.

Convinced herself she had imagined all of it.

Until suddenly she was alone with him again.

She had just made note of a couple of inoperative lamps, when John Farragut dropped out of the lift shaft. He had been doing a visual inspection of the cables—had probably been swinging on the cables, knowing John.

He looked startled to see her here. Then sheepish. Awkward, the way he had never been with her. For an indecisive instant he seemed about to beat a retreat on some pretext.

Then his expression changed. The blush was still there, but he had decided to hold his ground and own up to what he had let show. He glanced about the vacant half-lit hangar. Gave an abashed smile, as he might if caught stark naked. Spoke, embarrassed, ironic, "Hi."

His blue eyes met her gaze and did not look away.

She had imagined nothing.

Suddenly it felt dangerous to be here. Heat welled. Fear. Sexuality.

Glenn should just walk up the ramp tunnel and report the inoperative lamps to the Og.

So why am I not walking? she wondered. Suspended in the moment. Listening to her own heart pound. Watching John Farragut's eyes.

He had shown his hand. Now he was waiting for a move from her.

She ought to go. Why was she stringing this out when she had no intention of going through with—with what?

And realized she had no intention of stopping whatever was about to happen. She felt warm and longing and she was going anywhere this man wanted to lead her.

A light metallic ping of something dropping on the deck made her break her gaze. She heard its clink, plunk through the grate, and roll-spin to a stop.

John Farragut crouched, lifted up a deck grate, retrieved what had fallen beneath. Stood up with her wedding band between his thumb and forefinger. Dropped it into her palm. "Klutz."

The back of his fingers brushed her cheek before he ceded the field.

Two days after the battle with the gorgons, John Farragut came to see Jose Maria in the lab. The ship's medical officer, Mohsen Shah, was with him, puzzling over beakers of sludge. Gorgon remains.

"Machine or biological?" Farragut asked.

The doctors shook their heads. "I am having no idea," said Mo, and Jose Maria had no words at all.

"Animal, vegetable, or mineral?" Farragut tried again.

Again they shook their heads. Jose Maria lifted one of the beakers, gave it a swirl. "Fluidity," he said. "I am—I am entirely at a loss."

"But that's the dead phase," Farragut nodded at the dirty brown stuff. "Can't you reverse engineer it from that?"

"This—this—*soup* consists of common elements and un-exciting compounds," said Jose Maria. "What is missing is the code of its existence. It moves itself. It moves itself at near absolute zero in total vacuum."

"Well there's another axiom out the porthole," said Farragut.

"A lot of traffic through that porthole lately, young

Captain." Jose Maria let himself sit. His stately posture slipped. "We are back to square one, and I do not know where to go."

"You can come to the command deck," said Farragut. "We're approaching your wife's planet."

The planet Telecore—the construction base for the Far Cat. From there, Farragut hoped to find the Far Cat. And Jose Maria had hoped to find his wife.

"We passed through a noise zone, like scramscat transmissions," Farragut explained on the way. A Roman installation would try to mask, diffuse, scramble, and scatter its signals escaping into space to imitate natural radiation and stellar noise. "But we came out into a clear zone. The scramscat stopped."

"That is odd," Jose Maria agreed. Why scramble when you are sending nothing in the first place? "Then might the Romans have seen us coming and have shut off all transmissions?"

"I can't imagine how you could take a whole *planet* dark. I mean someone would microwave their leftovers. Something. Then again, these *are* Romans." Farragut argued with himself.

He took his ship to stealth mode, altered course, sounded general quarters. *Merrimack* approached Telecore from an overshot angle.

Still the scanners detected no transmissions from the planet.

He would have expected someone, even on a small colony, to let something slip. Activate a remote, signal a friend, forget to cancel the automatic feed from a weather satellite.

The planet they approached was dark. Physically dark, shrouded in brown clouds with little albedo.

Jose Maria moved forward, tense. "That is not the planet Mercedes described." *A blue-green jewel wrapped in white lace.* "I fear I have led you into a trap."

He'd been given the wrong coordinates. Jose Maria would have sworn to heaven, and bet all of Terra Rica, that the Romans could not have broken his and Mercedes' code.

And Farragut still believed that. "Damn peculiar sort of trap." He turned to his scan tech. "What's down there?"

"No life, sir."

"I asked what *is* there."

"Yes, sir," the scan tech said quickly, did a quick read of the major features. "There was a settlement here, all right. Ruins. Looks like Roman construction. Dead vegetation. Can't even say it's rotting. There's no bacteria."

Jose Maria jerked in physical startlement. Farragut said, "Now how the hell does *that* happen?"

The scanner looked for it. Found it: "The planet's hot! Radiation, sir! Not naturally occurring!"

Farragut nodded. Had feared, expected that. "Known signature?"

"Yes, sir," the scan tech confirmed. "There's a match in the system. It's *Roman*."

"Did someone blow up Rome's nuclear installations down there?"

"No, sir. Not that kind of radiation signature." The tech turned from his console to look up at his captain, wide-eyed. "Looks for all hell like a Roman Legion took a neutron hose to the whole world."

28

THE PLANET TELECORE SWIRLED under the high muddy winds of nuclear winter. Impact craters and scorched trenches pocked and laced the ground. A Roman sanitation crew had done a thorough job here.

Of Dr. Mercedes de Seville de Cordillera's terraforming artistry, or of anything else living, there was nothing.

"The cleaners were here," said Mr. Vincent.

No wonder *Merrimack* had met no guard ships. There was nothing here to defend.

Mr. Vincent shook his head at the readings. Bitter. Astonished. "So their Catapult goes operational and they just erase the whole base."

Rome had been known to take terrible measures to keep its secrets.

"Where are the people?" asked Jose Maria.

"They killed their workers," Vincent said.

Farragut shook his head. "Unlikely. Romans aren't as stupid, inhuman, and wasteful as they're cracked down to be."

Despite U.S. propaganda, even he knew that Romans were not comic book thugs who disposed of their servants like movie extras. "I have to believe they moved their people out first.

"Something had to turn septic for them to do this. I'm sorry, Jose Maria, we're not going to find anything down there." Farragut clasped Dr. Cordillera behind the neck and gave him an encouraging shake. "But we know your wife wasn't there. Mr. Gray, move us out."

Glenn Hamilton lay in bed, drifting uneasily near sleep, her back to Patrick, the ship on guarded alert moving through space that should be thick with Romans but wasn't.

A buzzing clamor made her jerk and sit straight up, shaking like a shell-shocked soldier.

Patrick mumbled sleepily, "That's just one of the Roman clock bugs. Aldebaran scarab crickets."

"I know what it is," Glenn snapped, shaking.

Patrick rolled over, forced his eyes open. "You okay, babe?"

"I—uh. Pavlov's dogs. I—associated the noise with something else. Sorry I woke you up. It's nothing."

That sound had preceded the gorgons' attack, so the two events had become entwined in Glenn's mind. Unconnected, of course.

Still she did not sleep.

Listened to the scarab cricket ricochet off the corridor walls.

The call to general quarters came while the ship was already on high alert. Up ahead lay a field of interstellar debris, which the scanners identified by silhouette as a fleet of dark ships. A rough count of fifty. Some had the size and aspect of transports. Some were unmistakably Roman ships of war.

Normally ships in a group will orient to a single axis, choosing a collective *up* and *down*. These had assumed a chaotic array. No doubt doing their best imitation of an asteroid field.

"Res scan the lot of them," said Farragut. "Let's see who we have and how they lie."

"And if they suddenly wake up, we'll know Rome's got our new harmonic," Mr. Vincent muttered.

But nothing woke up on being scanned.

The scan synthesis was so long in coming, Farragut demanded of Tactical, "Report."

Mr. Vincent gave an un-Vincentlike, heartfelt croak. "Oh, my God. Oh, my God." Before he went dumb.

He sent the image to the captain's display.

The command crew all moved forward as one, some with hands to mouths, some with mouths gaping uncovered, eyes huge and unblinking, or else blinking very fast against horrified tears.

Fifty dead ships. Knew they were dead and not playing at it for the ragged holes in their hulls. The sensors showed no shimmering halos of inertial shells. Nothing that might hold in the ships' atmospheres.

Farragut heard Jose Maria murmuring in Latin. Alarmed him for a moment, then recognized the words as the Lord's Prayer.

Captain Farragut ordered *Merrimack* to drop out of FTL so he could relay the horrific images to the Joint Chiefs on Earth by res pulse. Res messages at speed got very spotty on the receiving end.

"Are you getting this?" Farragut encapsulated a voice message and transmitted that.

Got a terse, single word acknowledgment back: "Receiving."

Merrimack wove a grim path through the graveyard of ships. Came upon a huddle of smaller ships, unarmed or lightly armed. Passenger types. All knotted together as if enclosed in a kill jar, surrounded by space buoys.

"What are these doing here? What is this group?"

Senior engineer Kit Kittering's voice shook. *"That's the Far Cat."*

This space was the Deep End displacement chamber of the Roman Catapult. They had tried to get out.

"Oh, for Jesus, why didn't they *tell* us?"

The command platform had become deathly quiet. Everyone staring.

Someone murmured into the silence, "There be monsters here."

Merrimack dispatched skiffs to the dead ships. Marine crews boarded the derelicts to pull their black boxes. And collect five thousand, five hundred and three sets of dog tags.

Oxygen bricks were plentiful, littering the area, abandoned. Whoever had attacked these ships had not been short on breathable air reserves. Or did not need air at all.

Merrimack did. The battleship had spilled a lot of air in fighting the gorgons off the Fury.

The Og appropriated a few tons of the solid oxygen, took the bricks under tow, and drew up a due bill payable to Rome. Even at war, *Merrimack* did not steal from the dead.

A stillness held the ship. The *Merrimack,* normally filled with raucous life, sounded like a machine and nothing more. The crew moved through her like ghosts, distracted, stunned or on the verge of tears. Spoke quietly. No one joked. They were preternaturally kind to each other.

Someone had spaced an Aldebaran scarab cricket, which had gone mad and would not shut up. Now everything hushed.

Jose Maria de Cordillera wore black.

"This is the end of the world as we know it," said Jose Maria, standing at a clearport, watching the Marine skiffs move through the graveyard of ships. "We are here thrown back to the twilight of civilization, when existence could end in a moment. When there were monsters on Earth."

"When was that, Jose Maria?" Farragut asked. He had never believed in monsters.

"Many times. The Black Death. The great earthquakes. Or even when men become the monsters. Killing without mind or mercy. When there is nowhere to hide. The death that comes suddenly and ends everything you know.

"We have returned to that elemental time. This universe we have civilized and rewrought in our own image is once again a pitiless place. We see ourselves diminished back to our true tenuous position in it. The unknown horror could strike in the night and obliterate everything we know. Or erase us entirely."

Farragut gave *Merrimack*'s bulkhead the kind of stout thumping pat he gave his dogs. Answered, "Not on my watch."

"Good lord, Dak. Don't lose your head over a little bug." Kerry ducked—from Dak, not the bee. "It's not as if it's got a stinger."

Dak swatted madly about his head, boxing his own ears trying to get at the furiously buzzing bee.

Several of the crew kept hives full of stingless bees. On a

normal watch, the bees were rather cheerful, actually, and the honey wasn't bad as long as you kept them away from Suriya's murkflowers. You didn't usually see them attacking people. And not Dak, who did not smell particularly sweet.

"The bugs!" Dak's huge hands flailed. "What's with the fragging bugs on this ship?"

Concerned over the mood of his ship, Captain Farragut consulted his MO. But he found Dr. Shah as depressed as anyone.

The last thing Farragut expected. Mohsen Shah was a tranquil, philosophical man. A Riverite by creed, which made him slow to anger, and long of patience. Riverites accepted everything—transgressions, misfortunes—as part of life's flow.

"Mo, are you corked?" Farragut asked.

Mohsen lifted deep brown, red-shot eyes to Captain Farragut. Mo's looked like the face on the barroom floor. But he shook his head, no. He was not drunk.

"We of the River are not believing in endings, but I am looking at this." Mo Shah gestured at the hideous images on all the screens in his dispensary. "And I am—" His voice stalled out. Started over, "This is the end."

Abrupt. Stark. So unlike Mo's ever-flowing speech, the statement brought Farragut up short.

And Farragut wouldn't have it. He stalked around the dispensary, clicking off the displays. "Mo, I swear to you—" *Click. Click.* "Look at me, Mo." *Click.* "I swear to you: this is being no such damned thing."

He locked gazes with Mo Shah, and meant to stare him down. Would have, but a whiskermoth dove right into his eye.

Farragut's one eye screwed shut against the oily sting. Mo Shah became animated, now having a patient to attend.

Farragut glanced around the lab with his mothless eye. "Your bugs still acting up here, Mo?"

"Not still. Again. Please be opening your eye."

Farragut forced his lids apart to receive a gentle jet of liquid, washing out the moth and its irritant oil.

Mo continued, "The lab insects were finding peace again, but, as you are seeing—you *are* seeing?—the insects are being antic again."

"When did they stop? When did they start?"

"Do not be rubbing your eye."

"Mo, when did the bugs stop 'being antic' and when did they start again?"

"I am looking and will be telling you when I am finding," Mo said evenly, opening his file to consult his lab notes. Found the notation. "The time of the insects' quietude was coinciding with the destruction of the so-called gorgons. The beginning anew was happening while *Merrimack* was orbiting Telecore. Why is the captain asking?"

"The captain is having improbable thoughts, Mo," Farragut murmured, thinking back on disconnected things—

I res-scanned Telecore.

Nothing can pick up a random res harmonic.

—as he watched the ants clawing at the top of their terrarium in Mo's lab. His skin crawled right along with them.

He lunged across the lab table, slapped on the intercom, "Lookout! This is Farragut!"

"Lookout, aye."

"Watch for—" Farragut floundered for words, "What did we call that alien sphere in the ship's log?"

"Alien sphere," said the Lookout.

Farragut's brow furrowed in disappointed surprise. "We *did*?" Could have come up with a better term than that. "Scan for alien spheres."

"Aye, sir," said the lookout, then, much sooner than expected: "Sighted them, sir. Three. Four. Five. Seven . . ."

"Where?" said Farragut. "What are they doing?"

"Nearest plot at seven hundred megaklicks. Farthest—we're still finding them, sir. What they're doing? They're all moving FTL, coming right at us."

"*Battle stations.*"

29

CAPTAIN FARRAGUT AND HIS SPECIALISTS weighed their options against the oncoming horde. They had the luxury of discussion. The closest sphere was still twenty minutes out at its best speed. And if the specialists needed more time for discussion, *Merrimack* could outpace the aliens.

Tactical ran a comparison of the spheres' vectors. A bit disconcerting, the result. The spheres came from various directions, but all converged on the precise location from where *Merrimack* had sent her last res signal.

"You can't home on a res signal," said Farragut. "Resonance has no location."

"Tell that to *Them*!" Marcander Vincent snapped.

That man was going to ride a console for the rest of his career, if he didn't finish it out in a brig instead. Farragut said only, chiding, "Mr. Vincent."

"Sir." An apology, Vincent-style.

Farragut resumed his briefing. "Since no one told the gorgons they can't home on a res pulse, and since I'm not fixin' to run and hide from those murdering bags of sludge, I need to know the best way to kill them from as far away as possible. We learned the hard way not to let them get close."

Jose Maria, who had been invited to this meeting, asked, "Why did not the Romans learn these things? Why did so many Roman ships die the same way?"

Hamster suggested, "They probably lacked the ammo to take out all the spheres sighted so far. I know we do."

"So I'll shoot us empty, take out as many of the closest ones as I can, then go reload."

"Brings the question again," said Jose Maria. "Why did not the Romans do precisely that?"

"Dammit, Jose Maria—" said Farragut. A slight frustrated smile crept over his face. "That's a damned good question."

His techs tried to look for answers in the flight recorders from the *Hermione,* the Fury, and the Roman ships at the Far Cat, but the recorders were encrypted, impenetrable.

Farragut gathered up the recorders and took them down to the detention hold. He all but *threw* them at the Roman prisoners. "From your dead buddies at the Far Cat. Let me know if you get in the mood to share anything you learn from these."

Turned to storm out.

"Domni!"

The captain paused. Turned. Glowered through the hatchway, waiting.

The Roman spoke, "No one has ever *ever* survived contact with Them."

Merrimack was the unspoken exception.

The Roman's face twitched, wrinkled. His chin quivered. Tears fell. "You just watch the transmissions of soldiers dying, until the signals stop."

"You're alive," said Farragut, an accusation. "How did the Fury survive?"

A guilty sob. "We ran like hell, *Domni.*"

"Are you going to give me the code to unlock these?" He nodded at the black box recorders.

Saw the man struggle between fear of dying and fear of aiding the enemy. In the end, he was more afraid of committing treason. "I can't, *Domni.*"

Farragut left the recorders with the prisoners. "Watch some more dying." He stalked away.

Behind his back he heard Jose Maria speak to the prisoners, in Latin, before the guards could close the hatch. "I have a question."

Farragut spun, glaring at him. Jose Maria met the captain's angry glare. "If I may."

Farragut gave Jose Maria a silent, curt go ahead, wondering what in heaven the neutral Terra Rican civilian could have to say to the Romans.

Jose Maria turned back to the prisoners. "Did you destroy Telecore?"

"We?" The Roman circled with his finger to indicate we, the imprisoned company. "No. We—Rome—had to. Telecore was infested with Them."

Scorched earth was an old tactic. Older than Rome.

Jose Maria asked, "Is—was—Telecore the gorgon home world?" A hopeful edge in his voice. Perhaps the Romans destroyed the monsters' nest.

"No," said the Roman. "They came from—from out there, and started eating everything. Those things cannot have a home. If those things ever had a home, they ate it."

"What became of the people?" Jose Maria asked softly. "Rome had a thriving colony at Telecore."

"Evacuated," said the Roman.

"To where?"

The quivers again. With more breath than voice, the Roman answered, "To the Catapult."

Farragut landed on the command deck. "Let's keep this simple. Here's our strategy. Don't let them get close. We're going to shoot really big skeet. Mr. Gray, do we have a firing solution?"

"Star Sparrows lined up on the nearest eight spheres," Commander Sebastian Gray reported. "Awaiting your order."

"Warheads?"

"Incendiaries and nukes."

Farragut nodded approval. The gorgons could withstand vacuum and near absolute zero cold. They could not withstand high heat.

"Let 'em have it."

Mr. Gray spoke into the com. "Fire Control. Command Deck. You have permission to fire Star Sparrows."

"Firing Star Sparrows, aye." That was Hamster, OOD in fire control. She sent again: "Star Sparrows away."

First impact came in eight minutes. Savage cheers burst on deck as the gorgon sphere blew into burning pieces.

The second impact should have come thirty-two seconds later, but the second sphere *dodged* the Star Sparrow.

Farragut jumped at the display screen, not sure what he'd just seen there. "Targeting. Farragut. Course correct that missile."

"Correcting, aye. Target acquired."

But the sphere twitched again before Targeting was done speaking.

Mr. Gray, got on the com immediately. "Targeting. We have an evading target. Ride the Star Sparrow in."

A difficult task, given the speed discrepancy. The Star Sparrow was moving much faster than *Merrimack*. But, unfazed, a gangly V-jockey named Raytheon—called Wraith—pulled on a visor to take resonant remote control of the missile.

Relativity made for a disorienting picture in the visor. The Star Sparrow's instants were much closer together than those of its pilot back on *Merrimack*. But Wraith loved this stuff. Rode the Star Sparrow like a madman, and plunged the nuke into the gorgon sphere's black frozen heart. *"Yeah!"*

The horde swelled, burning like a nova.

Farragut blew out a breath. Exchanged glances with his XO. "We had to work for that one."

Gray nodded.

The third missile was due for contact by now, but its target had altered course also.

Wraith took over remote control of the third Star Sparrow and redirected the missile toward the target. The Star Sparrow drew nearer and near. Tactical counted down time to impact.

"Six, five, four—"

The gorgon sphere blew apart like a dull Fourth of July rocket, without burning lights, but with a wide, wide spray of black bits. What would have sparkled on the Fourth, here sprouted legs and wriggled.

Farragut lost a step there. An effect without a cause. "Did I blink?" He'd missed three, two, one.

"Mr. Vincent, did you count three, two, one?"

"No, sir."

The Star Sparrow and its warhead still showed intact on the tactical display.

"What did we hit that gorgon ball with?"

Tactical just looked baffled.

Wraith reported up: "Didn't touch it, sir. Unless you count a res sounder."

"The sphere blew up *itself*?"

"Looks that way, sir," said Wraith, and Tactical nodded, concurring.

"They can't have our harmonic," said Senior Engineer Kit Kittering.

"I would say they do," said Tactical.

"Change harmonic," said Farragut. "Synch up Targeting."

With the new harmonic established, Targeting took a res sounding to locate the target.

The target moved the instant the res signal pulsed.

"Oh, for Jesus. Is there anyone in the Milky Way who doesn't have our harmonics!"

"Captain, *we* didn't even have that one," said Mr. Vincent. "I fed in my GRE scores."

"Then we must be sending out our code as we log it into the targeting system." Farragut stalked over, jabbed a bunch of numbers into the res sounder manually, and slapped it home.

Mr. Vincent hesitated. "Sir, we don't know what harmonic you loaded. We can't target on it."

"Good. Scan with that one."

Mr. Vincent did. Of course, no reading appeared on the targeting system. Targeting had no idea what harmonic to monitor.

But when Tactical took yet another sounding with yet another harmonic, it was clear that the sphere had, in fact, changed course in between soundings, apparently in reaction to the resonant scan sent on Farragut's mystery harmonic.

"Jesus, Mary, and Joseph," someone said.

At Hamster's suggestion, the erks turned the *Hermione*'s res sounder back on and gave the hulk an FTL shove on a tangential course as a decoy.

The alien spheres ignored the decoy. As if they recognized *Hermione* as a bone they had already picked clean.

Recognized it how? "Those things can't be the same spheres that ate *Hermione*," said Mr. Vincent. "Their top speed and where we found *Hermione* don't add up. Means these things have to be talking to each other."

"And I'll bet you the Qarfin Bank they're talking in resonance," said Mr. Gray.

"Impossible," said the senior engineer.

"Kit, the weight of evidence has crushed that argument just about flat," said Farragut, and without taking a breath started shouting very fast: "*Cease fire!* Recall remaining Star Sparrows!"

Mr. Gray acknowledged, ordered the recall, then questioned his captain, "Sir?"

"We're not the only ones learning here. We're *teaching* them! That's what happened to Rome! They taught the gorgons all their weapons, all their technology, all their tactics, and *that's* how they got slaughtered."

30

JOSE MARIA LOOKED A BIT startled. Took a moment to shake off a few axioms, then nodded. These giant clots of frozen aliens separated by light-years were learning, sharing knowledge, adapting.

Merrimack's best course of action for the moment was to steer clear until someone could come up with a better one. Rome had not been able to pull back and think, damned by the same weakness that lost them the Near Cat—Rome had stationary targets to defend. A fixed site was death in a space battle.

"Sir, if we stop resonating, can we shake the gorgons off our tail?" Mr. Vincent asked, as if Captain Farragut knew everything about the aliens.

The crew thought the captain knew everything because they needed for him to know everything.

"Well, let's run a little experiment on that," said Farragut. "Mr. Gray, take us dark. Sneak us around *behind* a couple of those alien spheres then ping 'em. If we get a picture of their butts, then, Mr. Vincent, I would say the answer is yes, we can shake them. TR, you don't look real sure about this."

Colonel Steele tended to remain silent in the company of educated men and women, but his frown was speaking loudly. He cleared his throat. Hoped his question wasn't stupid. "If the gorgons home in on res pulses, why aren't there a bunch of gorgon balls headed for Fort Eisenhower right now?"

A squirm-making silence grew long, before Hamster said, "Who says there's not?"

Several sets of eyes grew very big. Commander Gray snapped fingers at Mr. Vincent at tactical, who quickly organized a resonant scan of a two-klarc radius surrounding Fort Ike.

And located the alien spheres. A lot of them. On trajectories originating from the general direction of the galactic hub. At present speed the nearest of the spheres were still six years out. But at the end of those six years, the same thing that destroyed the Far Cat would be at Fort Ike.

"We've got our own fixed site to worry about."

Rome had apparently constructed their Deep End displacement chamber farther into the gorgons' territory. If Rome had obeyed the U.S. sanction against building a Catapult in the Deep End, then it would have been Fort Ike who discovered the monsters.

Or someone else. "Mr. Vincent, scan all U.S. colonies in the Deep End. A hundred-parc radius. Find me who's in trouble out here."

Found what they did not want to find. FTL spheres moving toward every one of Earth's deep colonies. At current speed, the predators were two years out from the planet New California, and a scant six months out from the globular cluster IC9870986 a/k/a the Myriad, where the LEN were conducting an emergency evac of two lightly populated planets. That planetary evacuation's short deadline just got nine years shorter.

"I do *not* want to explain this to the LEN," said Farragut, hand over his face. "And I'd rather eat gorgon guts than tell the Archon of the Myriad. We just have to kill all these things before it comes to that."

A bee banged around the command deck, smacking off the consoles and attacking the techs, its little abdomen pumping the instinctive motion of bee rage in racial memory of a stinger.

"The insects," Farragut said following the bee's manic path. "How do the insects figure into this?"

"There is an appearance of connection," Jose Maria allowed.

"Are they ratting us out?" said Farragut. Did not wait for an answer. "Mr. Gray, space all the ship's insects. Every last cricket, bee, ant, moth, earthworm—no forget the earthworms—insects. Insectoids. All of them. Out the air lock."

"Please." Jose Maria held up a hand.

Commander Gray hesitated, looking to his captain as Jose Maria pleaded quietly, "Stay the bees' execution for a time, young Captain. The insects did grow calm in between our battle with the aliens and our visit to Telecore. It suggests the insects are reacting to the aliens rather than calling to them."

"Reacting to what, Jose Maria? Why are they bouncing around *now*? We don't have any gorgons on board."

"Do we not?" said Jose Maria.

Farragut went momentarily dumb. Would have thought that answer obvious.

Jose Maria went on, "Are the gorgons perhaps an infection that is suppressed below detection but does not quite go away? Or did we pick something up at Telecore that only the insects can sense?"

Farragut didn't like it. Didn't accept it. "I think I'd notice if we had gorgons on board. And I can't take the chance. The bugs are going out."

"There has been enough death."

"They're *insects,* Jose Maria."

"They are innocent lives. Perhaps more than innocents. Might they, in fact, be warning us?"

Farragut loved the man but was about to throw him off the command deck.

Then Lieutenant Glenn Hamilton said, "I think they are, Captain. Warning us."

"Oh, for Jesus." Farragut rolled his blue eyes. *Women and civilians.*

But he ordered a shipwide search for "anything gorgonoid."

Thoughts ran more to homicide than to extermination. Colonel Steele knew he wasn't going to find anything out here. This was an idiotic assignment.

TR Steele had gone hull-walking outside the ship with F/S Cowboy Carver. Searching for gorgons. Felt like he'd been sent to fetch a left-handed baseball.

Artificial gravity was odd out here. Fluctuating. The direction of its attraction roughly inward toward the ship, but unpredictable. The shimmer of the force field some thirty feet above (beside? below?) them made the surrounding blackness surreal.

The atmosphere was feeble out here, so Steele and Cowboy wore space suits. Magnetic boots helped them keep their footing on the hull. Didn't want to lose contact. The force field could be dangerous. You did not want to touch it.

But the boots also made simple walking more like a march through mud.

Cowboy moved with a cowboy swagger. Lean, all muscle even to the brain, Cowboy's body formed a wedge from shoulders to narrow hips. Women thought he was gorgeous. The only woman who mattered, Kerry Blue, still thought Cowboy was gorgeous. She hated him too hard. Meant she still loved him. For that, Cowboy ought to die.

Starlight shone in a red Doppler smear on this side of the ship. Lamplight took a strange bounce from the force field, brightened the gray metal hull.

"Hey, what's this?"

Cowboy kicked at *this*. A thigh-high pile of black, crusted *stuff*, big lumps of it, as if some titan forgot to clean a gigantic grill.

"Clean it up," said Steele.

"Me?" Cowboy squawked. "I didn't do it." And opened a com link, "Hey, Captain. Something odd out here. We got barnacles."

Since when did Cowboy Carver report directly to Farragut?

Farragut responded, but not to Cowboy. "TR, find something?"

"Sir, I—" Dammit. Had not meant to take this to the captain. Could not exactly tell him never mind now that crater-mouth Cowboy had opened the com. "I *think* it's molten debris blown out of the Fury stuck on the hull. It looks like big burned carbon lumps."

Cowboy poked at the pile with his gloved forefinger. It didn't give. "You know, I think this might be Kerry Blue's cookies. I just throw 'em out the airlock. So *this* is where they land."

Kerry Blue made cookies for Cowboy Carver? Steele wanted him so very dead.

Cowboy took his knife to the crusted stuff. The blade did not so much as prick the surface. "Yep. This is Kerry's bakery, all right."

Cowboy crouched down to try to wedge his blade between the black heap and the hull. His helmeted head bent over his work, intent.

Steele blinked in the peculiar light. Might be hallucinating out here. One of the crusted blobs seemed to move.

Did move. Was *opening*.

Disbelief made time stretch. A slow-motion quality to it. The solid heap took on shape, grew a pincered head. Or was that a clawed arm? Turned glossy as a beetle's back. Pincers sharp as razors parted to encircle Cowboy's bent neck.

Blue-white flame leaped from Steele's blowtorch in a hard jet. Cowboy ducked and rolled, swearing. "Gak! What are you trying to—*ho, skatbricks*!" Dodged a fiery, thrashing pincer.

The other globules opened—briefly—under Cowboy's and Steele's blowtorches.

Over the smoldering remains, Cowboy's clap on the back of Steele's shoulder rocked Steele a step forward. "Thanks, Old Man."

Cowboy. Steele had just saved Cowboy's life. Steele snarled. "What was I thinking?"

And Cowboy laughed. Never knew Colonel Steele could make a joke.

"They weren't the same thing," Cowboy said at debriefing.

"They have to be the same thing," Steele told the officers and scientists.

"No," said Cowboy. "Gorgons got whippy bitey leggy things all over a blobby bag body. Those things out there were armed and way bigger. They got jointed legs and pincer things."

Steele rapped down a beaker of sludge on the table between himself and the investigators. "They look the same now."

One of the examiners leaned forward to sniff the beaker. "Which creature is this?"

"Yes," Steele said, sour.

The lab had specimens of melted gorgons and specimens

of the creatures Steele and Cowboy had dispatched on the hull. Without labels on the beakers, no one could tell which was which.

"A red blood cell does not look or act like a white blood cell, neither of which looks or acts like a cell from a muscle or from the brain," Dr. Cordillera offered.

Farragut listening in, leaning back against a wall, got into it here: "Jose Maria, you're saying we're fighting some huge space body's white blood cells?"

"I cannot know. I am throwing out analogies from my own frame of reference for consideration." Jose Maria lifted the beaker from the table. Gave the brown sludge a swirl before his eyes. "They die the same. How is our insect life faring now?"

Farragut had forgot all about them. A quick demand for report revealed that the bees of *Merrimack* had returned to their hives, their buzzing a soft, peaceable hum.

"God Almighty."

The implications were astonishing—the two sets of monsters were the same. Insects could sense them both.

And, more significant still: "We have a warning system."

Farragut signaled the command deck: "Mr. Gray, cancel order to space the insects."

"Aye, sir."

"If I may be so bold, young Captain," said Jose Maria, a preface to advice.

"Go ahead, Jose Maria. Your guess on these things is better than mine."

"I advise disabling the ship's resonance chambers. Res pulse exists everywhere at the same instant, which means there is no effective difference between sending and receiving—one touches the harmonic either way."

"You mean if the JC contacts us—"

"I believe such contact would betray your ship's position to the predator."

The ship's res specialist agreed in theory, though he still didn't know how anyone or anything could pull a location off a res pulse. He excused himself from the debriefing to go disable the ship's resonant chambers.

Merrimack altered course, ran dark until she was in a position calculated to be well behind the gorgon spheres stalking her.

"If we don't come out behind the gorgons, that means they can track us without our resonating," said Farragut. "And it means the insects are going out the air lock."

The only way to know was to resonate.

The scan tech hesitated on the switch, warned, "This could betray our new position."

"If they don't already have it," said Commander Gray. "Execute scan."

Took a resonant scan of the area *Merrimack* had vacated. And glory be, there were the gorgon spheres, roaring blindly away after *Merrimack*'s old position.

A second scan revealed the gorgons turning hard about. Expected that, but still came as a shock "They've reversed course. They *do* locate by res pulse! They're chasing us."

Farragut was about to signal the lab to ask what the insects were doing, when an entire of swarm of bees invaded the command deck with an enraged hum.

Farragut moved carefully, so as not to crush any bees. "Let's see if we can't give the gorgons a wild goose to chase."

He ordered *Merrimack* to turn toward the galactic hub and resonate again to encourage their pursuers. Then go dark and double back, disable all res chambers.

In moments the bees quieted, settled to a placid search for anything edible in Jose Maria's ruby collar tack and in the red-and-yellow console lights before they gathered up and went home.

Steele stood uneasy on the command deck, eyes shifting, as if They were listening. Mumbled near to a whisper, "We *think* they can't see us, but we *know* we can't see them." Didn't put much faith in the testimony of bees.

"I believe we threw them off," said Commander Gray. "But, Captain, the lieutenant colonel is correct. The darkness works both ways. Tough to fight what we can't see."

Actually, Farragut could think of a few options but did not want to use any of them. "I'm not fixing to teach those gorgons one more blessed thing about us."

"That doesn't leave us with much to do out here," said Colonel Steele.

"Orders?" Mr. Gray asked.

"I'm beginning to like the Roman suggestion," said Farragut, and issued the order: "Run like hell."

"Any particular direction, sir?"

There was really no choice but to fall back, regroup, and organize a mass extermination. "Fort Ike."

Commander Gray instructed Navigation to plot a course to Fort Ike, and relayed the order to the helm. "Run like hell."

"Running like hell, aye."

"Occultation nine by fifteen by one forty-eight," the lookout sang.

Farragut had not thought there were any alien plots on this path. "Take us wide of the sphere."

"Not a sphere, I don't think, sir." Positive ID was tough with a passive scan. Then, "Occultation twelve by twenty by one thirty."

"Identify," said Farragut.

"Possibly ships. Possibly human make. Occultation eighteen by three by one ten."

Bogeys. Three of them. Something very deliberate in their placement.

No one runs into anyone by accident out here.

"Occultation eleven by eight by twenty."

"Oh, for—" Farragut pounced on the tactical station, watched the plots appear. On the left. On the right. On the up. On the down. The plots constricting like a snare. Didn't need a fine scan. "That's Roman. Pilot! Ram it to the gate! We're going through!"

As *Merrimack* sprang, the Roman ships opened fire. Their positions were staggered so each had a clear shot at *Merrimack* without danger to their counterparts on the far flank.

Merrimack ran out her guns and charged, blasting through the closing gauntlet. Did not need to take out the ships. Only had to make their field generators dip. There was no stealth in this maneuver. Just punch and speed, which *Merrimack* had. Ran at the force field barrier—

"Yeeee HA!"

—and through.

Merrimack ran full out. You could hear the engines, feel the deck throb, take savage joy in the strength of this ship. The Roman ships turned about to give chase, and you had to laugh at them, because they hadn't a prayer of catching up.

Cowboy Carver shot the moon out a sternside clearport.

The Roman ships could not catch *Merrimack*. You had to wonder why they were still back there, chasing. But they hung in, dogging *Merrimack*'s widening lead through two watches.

Merrimack would enter Fort Eisenhower's fire zone in eight more hours.

"Those ships follow me into the fire zone, I'm keeping one as a souvenir," said Farragut watching the rear display.

Then, from the lookout: "Occultation five by two by thirty."

No! The mind would not accept it.

Those coordinates were in *front*.

"Occultation five by nineteen by forty."

Elation turning to sand.

"Occultation ten by nine by nine."

From the pilot, hope descending: "That's not the space cavalry coming out from Fort Ike, is it?"

Farragut, stoically, "I don't think so, son."

Watched the tactical display, the angry lights blinking on before of them, one by one by one.

Tactical started, "Sir, it's a—"

Farragut nodded. Knew what this was. "It's a Roman Legion."

Dead ahead.

31

Farragut shouted over the intracom: "Og! Redeploy force field. Brace for a hit from any direction." A split-moment before Marcander Vincent sang out from the tactical station, "Javelins headed toward us, from all quadrants. Nineteen of them. Twenty. Impacts in twenty-nine to forty seconds, sir!"

"Battery! This is Farragut. Target incoming javelins."

The pounding of the cannon thundered through the decks with the hiss of the ship's beam weapons discharging. The burn smell snaked through the tight corridors, carried up to the command deck.

Merrimack's force field crackled and groaned, made a sickening light show through the clearports as the ship took hit after hit.

"Colonel Steele," Farragut sent up to the battery. "I just counted fifteen javelin strikes." Five intercepts out of twenty hostile missiles. "Unacceptable, TR."

"Yes, sir," said Lieutenant Colonel Steele.

The Marine gunners' second chance was already on its way—a salvo of thirty javelins. Impact due in eighteen to twenty-three seconds.

Farragut had been in a fistfight like this once. That one had been sixteen to one. Best tactic against multiple attackers was to run. Not sure that card was still in the deck. Surrounded like this, *Merrimack* was caged in an energy field the size of a small solar system.

"Mr. Gray, we're in a bag. Punch us out of here."

"Aye, sir."

In a fistfight the first punch usually gets blocked. So Commander Gray issued instructions for a lunge forward at the oncoming Legion, a zig *down,* a zag toward the rising starboard, and a charge forward again in hopes of carrying the *Merrimack* past the Legion and forcing the largest bar of this Roman cage to reverse direction.

The helm fed the course to the ship's battery so the gunners could adjust their shots accordingly, then executed the escape action.

The Legion was ready for it. They gave little reaction to all the feints, anticipated the end maneuver and went straight to countering that one. The Legion split, with the rear guard executing an immediate full reverse. One of the rear guard caught *Merrimack* a hammerball square on the stern.

Merrimack's force field fluttered. Gravity hesitated, came back hard, buckled the MPs' knees to the deck, cracked the techs' foreheads to their consoles. Farragut dropped into a linebacker crouch. Jose Maria went down like a cat.

Then a torpedo strike concussed the ship, peppered an inner corridor with slivers from the ship's own hull blown inward.

Ears popped open as air rushed out of the ship to fill the gap between the punctured hull and the inertial screen.

An erratic groaning of a force field in distress warbled through the pounding of the ship's guns. "Systems, do we have a containment field going bad on us?" Commander Gray asked.

"*Yes,* sir," the systems tech reported. "Engine Three's containment field is fluctuating. Mr. Kittering is— Go ahead." That last spoken into the tech's headset, to the senior engineer.

"Put her on the box." Farragut waved a come on.

The systems tech clicked his com link onto the speaker, through which Kit's voice became audible, "—need to space Number Three."

"Kit, this is Farragut. Is that engine critical?"

"No, sir. Just keeping a contingency plan in place. This engine is NOT going to reach critical. I won't let it."

"Kit, you might rethink that. When it comes time to jettison an engine, can you—" He paused, reconsidered what he was about to ask, pushed ahead anyway, "*Aim* it?"

Kit's voice went softly icy, as if he had suggested she cut off her arm and throw it out a porthole. Reminded him of the cost of the thing, and reminded him that the engine was *not* critical.

"Yes, I know the cost. It's one-fifth the cost of the surviving engines, which *are* going to fall into Roman hands if I don't do something drastic. Can you aim a jettisoned engine?"

"Sir, I'll—make it happen."

"Mr. Gray, coordinate this."

"Aye, sir. Target, sir?"

Farragut gave a nod at the tactical display, which had identified most of the member ships of the Legion. "Cal's buddy."

The Roman flagship.

"*Gladiator,* sir?"

"*Gladiator.* We take out Numa, or we got nowhere to run."

"May I make a suggestion, sir?" Commander Gray offered.

"I'll take any you got."

Sebastian Gray spoke in a stop-start staccato, attention divided between the com chatter on his headset, and the plots on the tactical display. "We probably won't be able to get a jettisoned engine close to any of the Roman ships, especially *Gladiator*. They'll avoid it or just shoot it. But Mr. Kittering can probably arrange the containment mix so that when the engine blows, it'll hose antimatter everywhere. Now if we can stick some *matter* onto the Roman force fields right before that—"

"Tag 'em!" Farragut roared.

Merrimack launched homer tags at all Roman vessels within range, especially *Gladiator*. Any Roman tags which might be clinging to *Merrimack*'s field were not just deactivated but scoured off. There must be no particle of matter attached to *Merrimack*'s defensive barrier when the antimatter was unleashed.

Kit, reported up: "Engine Three, ready to jettison."

"Jettison Number Three."

"Jettisoning Number Three, aye. Engine away."

Without its containment housing, Number Three's anti-matter collided with its matter. The force of mutual annihilation sprayed the engine's surviving matter and antimatter in a wide, widening bubble, detonating all warheads in its radius.

The sphere of antimatter grew, reached back to *Merrimack*. Washed harmlessly over her force field.

Commander Gray on the com: "Battery! Recommence fire! Tactical! Status of the Romans!"

"All incoming Roman ordnance destroyed." Mr. Vincent reported. "No damage to the Roman ships. Repeat: No damage. Not even any detonations against the Roman shields."

"How can that be?"

"The lupes must have cleaned the tags off their force fields same time we did."

Commander Gray looked cheated. "Now how the hell could they know to remove dead tags? Unless they saw us do it. But still. That is damn fast thinking."

"Don't beat yourself up, Bast. It was a great plan," said Farragut. "Points to Numa."

A ripping blast inside the ship slammed Farragut against the bulk. Split his lip against his teeth. He tasted blood. Heard shouts muffled by the sponginess in his eardrums.

"Systems, what was that?" Commander Gray demanded, crawling up his console from the deck.

"Roman beam shot caught one of our cannon shells leaving the barrel. Looks like the shell detonated half in, half out of the force field. Gun bay twenty-five is a code thirty-three." Fire code.

The Roman shooter was either vastly lucky or impossibly good. Either way, that was a one in a million shot. Impossible really.

Then he did it again. This one caught the shell more in than out of *Merrimack*'s force field. Ripped two gun blisters off the ship, with cannon and crew, and left the hull torn open. Only the heavy blast wall, which backed the gun blisters, kept the ship from more catastrophic damage.

Two in a million.

"Lock down!" Farragut ordered, and the shouts echoed throughout the ship, "Lock down! Close and *seal* all ports!"

Farragut turned to Tactical. "Mr. Vincent, there's a Striker out there. Find it!"

All of *Merrimack*'s guns reeled inboard, the force field solidifying over the ports.

Except one. Gun bay sixteen was stuck open.

The command officers listened to the exchange between Colonel Steele and the gun crew over the intracom, Colonel Steele roaring in some unknown tongue, but everyone understood what he was saying.

Gun bay sixteen reported, "Cannot close the gunport. We have a foreign body in the cannon."

"Can you dislodge?"

"Won't budge in or out. It's big, sir. And it's in here."

"Nature of the foreign body. Something blown back?"

"No, sir. It looks like— Sir, it looks like another gun barrel."

"Oh, for—" Farragut pulled off his headset. "Systems, get me a picture. What is he looking at?"

One of the ship's external monitors picked up the unlikely scene from the outside. "Located your Striker, sir," said Mr. Vincent, putting the image on the display.

A very small Roman ship, carrying under its fuselage a missile launcher nearly as long as the Striker itself, had thrust that launcher's 30-millimeter barrel in through *Merrimack*'s gunport, right up the cannon barrel, so that its maw was inside *Merrimack*. The Striker had managed the maneuver without sustaining any damage to itself. The precision was unreal.

The Striker's colors were not black and gold. This one was not Julian.

Farragut put his headset back on. "Gun bay sixteen. This is Captain Farragut."

"Sir! Gun bay sixteen, aye."

"Serge." Farragut recognized the voice. Big Brazilian ape. Played a mean game of squash. Could remain vertical carrying an awful lot of alcohol. And evidently never ever blinked. "Good man. Serge, can you load a shell and blow this guy out?"

"Can't load, sir. Enemy's barrel is sticking right up through the cannon breech. He is *in* here. I might be able to discharge small arms up his nose, but it might make him sneeze. Please advise."

Farragut responded over the com, "Any chance this guy has fried his brains out like our poor Julian friend Septimus did?"

"Don't think so, sir. We're in direct contact. I'm getting vibrations through the barrel. Like something moving around over there in the Striker."

And in case there was any doubt, came a strange voice, muffled, flat, not Serge's: "I live."

Farragut squeezed the com as if it were Serge's big beefy shoulder. "Get out of there, son." Took off the headset, shook his head at the damning sight on the display.

Commander Gray asked, "Is that a patterner, sir?"

"Oh, yeah."

"*Know* him?"

Farragut nodded.

An angry little ship. Red and black. *Gens* Flavius. First patterner Captain Farragut had ever seen.

Remembered the Myriad. The *Merrimack* in a tug-of-war with an event horizon. Farragut refusing to let go of two crewmen to turn and defend himself.

Rather than take the kill shot in the back, this red-and-black Striker had made an impossible shot that set *Merrimack* free.

The Striker's parting words: *Next time, when I have a clear shot at something other than your back, prepare to yield to Rome as my prize of honor, or else die for the glory of the Roman Empire.*

Commander Gray hadn't been there.

"I owe this one my hide," Farragut told Commander Gray. "And he's come to collect."

The com tech held up a link, "Captain. Numa Pompeii, for you, sir."

The command deck became quiet, a weird oasis of stillness amid shouts of emergency, which rang through the rest of the ship. A stillness as acrid as the smoke. Whites showed full round all the eyes on deck. Everyone knew what this was.

"Let's have him," Farragut nodded to the box.

Waited for the demand.

His gaze strayed to the systems monitor screen. Number Four Engine containment field was fluctuating.

The com tech routed the Roman signal to the speaker and advised the Roman, "Go ahead, sir."

"Captain Farragut," the disembodied baritone voice of Numa Pompeii inquired.

"I'm here," said Farragut. Standing straight up. Gaze level, distant, slightly to the starboard.

"We will not board you, *Merrimack*," said General Pompeii. "Surrender or die."

How quaint that sounded. How weird that he meant it.

Farragut mentally ran through all the possibilities, thoughts racing faster than light. All scenarios came back to those two. Surrender or die.

Still, he tried, without hope, "We are carrying fifty Romans in detention. Do you want to talk to them?"

"They are Romans," said General Pompeii. Meaning Romans were ready to die for Rome. "Your decision, Captain."

A feeling like a knife in the gut. With someone else's voice, Farragut spoke, "Mr. Gray. Strike colors."

Gray nodded to the Marine guard.

With the smallest hesitation, a motion like a sob in her shoulders, the Marine obeyed, laid a reverent hand to the panel that slowly furled Old Glory and reeled the flag inboard. And because it seemed the thing to do, she extinguished the ship's exterior lights that had illuminated the colors for so long through the eternal night.

Numa's voice sounded again through the speaker, "Not enough." And he pressed the demand, "Farragut, your surrender."

"I'm choking here, Numa. Give me a second."

Numa waited.

Farragut lifted his face as if looking for God, took in a breath. He asked, a rather desperate stall, "Terms?"

"You have my terms. Surrender or die. Now."

Farragut opened the shipwide intercom, so all of *Merrimack* would know what was happening. Sounded like someone else speaking. Could not be he, because he could not even breathe. "General Pompeii, this is Captain John Farragut. *Merrimack* surrenders."

PART SIX

In Manus Tuas

32

FARRAGUT RASPED, "FORCE FIELD."

Commander Gray saw to the force fields, brought them down to minimal, presenting only enough barrier to prevent air escaping, and down to nothing around the air locks.

The Roman boarders would have no trouble getting through.

The exec also initiated capture protocol, commencing destruction of sensitive files. Asked Farragut, "Who has the CT?"

Farragut pointed to himself and spoke without voice, "I do." Then he got Lieutenant Hamilton on the com, his words escaping one, two at a time, "Everyone. Cargo hold."

Glenn Hamilton had known him a long time, so she understood him. Captain Farragut wanted his crew and company assembled in the only place big enough to hold them all.

As they congregated in the cargo hold, Farragut detoured to sick bay. Kissed his medics, laid hands on the wounded, pulled covers over the faces of his dead.

Jose Maria had accompanied him to sick bay, and there he stayed when Farragut departed for the cargo hold.

Wondered how he would speak, but he found his voice

in time to talk to his crew and company as the Romans approached.

He named the dead. Thanked the living for their loyalty and courage, and their superhuman fighting spirit. "What faced us here was beyond even us. And it only proves that nothing under God is invincible.

"You know I'm not the giving-up type. But I won't sacrifice your lives to keep this ship out of Roman hands. You are far too valuable. I expect we will be separated. Should this be the last time I talk to you, I need you to know: there is no guilt in stopping your fight now. We did all we could. I have surrendered. Respect my surrender."

A ship's dog trotted in, a big-hearted mutt who sensed he was needed. He climbed up on the cargo crate on which the captain stood and sat at the captain's side.

Farragut interrupted himself, hand on the dog's head. "Reminds me. Og, have your boys leash the dogs—the four-footed ones. I don't want any of these guys getting shot trying to protect us."

He continued to the assembly, "And I need y'all to do something for me. Survive. You will—I promise you will—see your families and your homes again. And none of you dare feel bad about that. You have served your country and your world honorably. Never a better crew, never a better pack of dogs prowled these decks."

A smattering of barking crackled from the Marines, quickly quieting again to listen, for already there intruded the clanking of the Roman *corvus*. The bang of a boarding skiff coming up against the hull.

"And if I could, I would thank each man jack and jane of you face-to-face by name. But Numa's knocking at my door here—"

The deep thump of a hatch opening. Many boots tramping in unison.

"Be proud, as you have made me very, very proud."

The dog snarled, hackles lifted, teeth bared, as Captain Farragut gave over his sword to Numa Pompeii in formal surrender. Normally, the ceremonial antique weapon these days was a revolver.

General Pompeii quirked a half smile at the sword. "A little over the top. But that's you, Captain Farragut." Numa passed the blade to an attendant. "Join me for dinner, Captain?"

"No disrespect to the Triumphalis, but I am the farthest thing from hungry," said Farragut, and before Numa could press the invitation, said, "How the hell did you locate us?"

"That was easy. Once you betrayed your location at the Far Catapult, I drew a straight line from the Catapult to Fort Eisenhower. You would not be far off it. Not that you don't have sinkers and sliders in your arsenal, but you are at heart a fastball pitcher."

Know your enemy.

"Dammit Numa, you know what's out there! And you send a Legion after *me*?"

The Roman nodded. "I know what's out there. The *Merrimack* is fresh meat. And I need fresh meat, because *They* learn."

"The meat is not as fresh as you think," Farragut took mean pleasure in disillusioning General Pompeii. "In fact, it's pretty well tainted. The gorgons figured out how to shut us off."

Numa's eyes masked shock, suspicion, doubt. Rather mockingly he said, "You're trying to tell me your ship was boarded?"

"That's a surprise?" said Farragut. "The gorgons boarded plenty of Roman vessels I've seen."

"You have an intact ship and a live crew and you tell me with a straight face your systems were shut down and you were boarded."

"Here's my straight face, Numa." Farragut turned his face to the side, pointed at a fresh star-shaped scar in front of his ear, precisely describing the outline of a gorgon leg-mouth.

Numa's color darkened, his victorious shine dulled. His mouth set into a sullen line. He spoke flatly to his guard, "Show the captain to his accommodations."

There was a cot, but Jose Maria found John Farragut sitting on the deck in his solitary detention compartment, his back against the bulk.

Farragut looked up at his visitor. Jose Maria was dressed in casual aristocracy—wide black trousers, a light taupe tunic wrapped round his narrow waist, his hair pulled back in its silver clasp.

"They treating you okay, Jose Maria?"

"Very well," said Jose Maria, coming to crouch at near level with Farragut. Balanced on the balls of his feet, shod in soft, expensive galoug-skin slippers.

"Did you have to buy yourself back?"

Jose Maria shook his head. "Rome appears to have turned a blind eye to my less-than-neutral behavior."

"They don't want to get into it with Terra Rica just now."

"That would be my take," Jose Maria agreed. The focus of his black eyes traveled from the captain to the cot back to the captain on the deck. "Penance?"

"Unraveling a bit. How are my crew? Have you seen them?"

"Rebounding better than you," said Jose Maria.

The captain had lost weight, which he could afford, but without the usual fire, he looked hollow. His bloodshot eyes fixed in a barely open squint.

"They quote you often. The shock is wearing off and they are, as you would say, working up a good mad."

Farragut scowled a satisfied scowl. The news seemed to cheer him. "Good. That's good. What ship are they being held in?"

"This one. *Gladiator.*"

Farragut's brows lifted, intrigued. Blue eyes traveled the confines, searching for something conductive to rap on.

"Are you eating?"

"Sometimes."

Farragut made the guard who brought his food taste it first. If delivered by an automaton, he did not touch it.

"General Pompeii is vexed at your refusals of his invitations to his table."

"Oh, good for Numa."

"You should go, young Captain. Romans do not invite losers to the commander's table."

"I don't think I could swallow."

"They say you are not sleeping."

The question struck him as odd. Brows dropped over squinted eyes. His head tilted. "You working for them now, Jose Maria?"

"Paranoia is a symptom of sleep deprivation."

"Answer the question."

Jose Maria touched Farragut's face. "No, young Captain. I am not in league with Rome."

"Sorry." Turned his face away. Breathed into his hands. "I don't dare close my eyes very long. I don't want them putting anything in my head."

"I cannot prevent them from doing as they will," said Jose Maria. "But to the limit of my ability to do so, I will tell you if that happens."

Farragut nodded. "Deal." Then seized the wide sleeve of Jose Maria's tunic, as he might the robes of a father confessor. "This, *this,* Jose Maria, is the end of the world. Not the gorgons. This. Surrender." Tears wet the expensive fabric. "I know how Matty felt."

"You *do*?" Jose Maria said, quietly alarmed. After losing the *Monitor,* Matthew Forshaw had blown his brains out. "Is this a suicide watch, young Captain?"

"No. No. Just—damn, this is tough." Tears flowed freely now. "I want another shot. Reset. Go back. I want a rematch and it's not going to happen." He sat back, sighed. Calmer for the outburst. "And I think—was this what the judge was trying to prepare me for with the choke holds? He used to put a forearm right here and say, 'You gotta know if you can take it.' Was *this* what all that was for? And you know what? That's a load of jaggerskat, Jose Maria. I can choke just fine without all the rehearsals."

"You should sleep."

Farragut closed his eyes and nodded. "I should. Can you stay?"

"I shall. For as long as I can."

"Wake me when you go."

"Deal."

Guilt said he should sleep on the deck. Farragut was not the sort to haul around that kind of load. He followed common sense onto the cot and passed peacefully out.

"I begin to take insult, Captain Farragut." Numa Pompeii showed up in John Farragut's detention compartment in person to voice displeasure at the captain's latest refusal to dine with him.

Numa Pompeii was not missing any meals. The Triumphalis carried a lot of flesh on a very large frame. Farragut was down to his college weight.

"Well, that's a start," said Farragut, not bothering to stand.

"There should be respect between officers, even on opposing sides."

"Yeah, there should be," said Farragut blazing back to life. "Except that you're a swine, Numa."

"I won. You lost. The lack of civility is uncalled for."

"I had a lot of time in here to hear it calling. What you did to prisoners of war is proscribed by all conventions of war, and you're talking to me about civility?"

"I don't know what *you* are talking about, sir."

"Matty Forshaw! Napoleon Bright! What you did to them is a war crime."

Numa looked genuinely puzzled. "I let them go. And I arranged for pickup. It's not as if I stranded them in outer space. It was simple, elegant, legal. Moral. I even gave Mr. Forshaw a medal." Then, to Farragut's homicidal glare, "I admit even I was surprised to learn how hard he took it."

Farragut, stonily ironic: "You were."

"Matthew Forshaw killed Matthew Forshaw. And your people killed Napoleon Bright."

"I'll be damned if I let you do to me what you did to Matty and Brighty."

"Oh, no. You're too big a fish to throw back, Captain Farragut."

"I meant the brain alterations, you smug baboon."

"What alterations?"

"Ingenuousness doesn't look good on you, Numa."

"I am—" the general chose the next word carefully, "ignorant." Could not ever call himself innocent. "What alterations?"

"You had foreign cells inserted into those men's brains."

"No, sir. I did not. I believe that you believe what you say, Captain Farragut. But you are wrong. Do I play mind games? Of course I do. But not like that. If you know your enemy at all, then you know that is not my style of warfare."

"I thought I knew you. But I know for a fact you put something in Matty and Napoleon, you lying sack—"

"DO not shout at me, Captain Farragut. No. I did nothing to Mr. Forshaw and Mr. Bright. Someone is lying to you. Your CIA is not above slandering me to you."

"The CIA had nothing to do with it." Farragut did not tell Numa Pompeii that the autopsy had been at Calli Carmel's order. "And it's not slander. I *saw* the Sargasson autopsy."

Numa took an unconscious step back. Face betrayed little, but the concern that escaped looked real. He resumed, guarded, "Troubling, if true. If true, I had no knowledge of it."

Unlikely. And Farragut did not believe it. Just who could do something like that to Numa Pompeii's prisoners without the Triumphalis' knowledge? There was no way.

And then the thought.

Oh, for Jesus. Could it be that Imperial Intelligence was every bit as honorable and law-abiding as the CIA?

"Snakes?" said Farragut. *Spies.*

"Snakes," Numa Pompeii muttered.

Numa Pompeii had his own Lu Oh? Farragut almost felt sorry for his opponent. Not really. But he stopped trying to figure out how to kill him with his bare hands.

Numa continued, displeased: "Whatever your seaweedy allies found in Mr. Forshaw and Mr. Bright would have been the work of someone with less faith in my simple ploy than I. Someone saw fit to gild my lily."

"Your lily was a piss in the eye."

"Yes, it was," Numa admitted. Had meant it to be. "I trust Mr. Medina was not 'altered.' "

"No," said Farragut before he could wonder at the question.

Numa nodded, seemed satisfied, relieved.

Farragut spoke aloud, realizing only as he was speaking it, "Jorge Medina was a Roman mole."

Numa nodded as if the news were very old news. "For a moment I was afraid whoever gilded my lily might have butchered my own man. I do loathe snafus on that scale."

Numa Pompeii did not notice Farragut's struggle to contain his shock. Jorge Medina. Red, white, and true blue Jorge Medina who wouldn't speak Latin to save his life. Quiet, devoted lieutenant commander of the *Monitor*. It had been Jorge Medina who betrayed *Monitor*'s and *Merrimack*'s codes and harmonics to Rome.

Numa mused aloud, half to Farragut, half to himself, "I'm told that Medina never broke cover, so I'll be damned if I can figure how your CIA smoked him out."

We didn't smoke him. Farragut's mind all but whited out from all the lights going on. *It was all a huge mistake. Lord Almighty, Paxton Pike accidentally executed the right man!* It was hideous. Farragut fought down graveyard laughter, said tenuously, "Sometimes our intelligence staggers even me."

"Why the trumped-up mutiny charge, though? Why did you not simply execute Medina as a spy?"

"I—" Farragut couldn't lie. "—Have no earthly idea what they were thinking when they executed Jorge."

"Useful creatures, moles. I dislike them. I am fortunate not to have been born during the Long Silence. I would have made a very bad mole."

"A very, very *large* mole," said Farragut.

"And you were no Cinderella before you stopped eating." Numa dropped a fresh uniform and a pair of spit-shined dress shoes—size large—on him. "You *will* join me for dinner."

The Triumphalis' table was on a par with that of the White House, decked in Roman splendor. The French doors opening onto a formal garden were perfect in the depth of their illusion, even to the movement of the air, and the scents of greenery and hyacinth. The cutlery was gold and had the heft to be solid throughout.

Farragut struggled through the appetizer. Finally dropped his gold fork and took up his wine goblet. "Oh, fuck it, Numa. Just keep this topped."

The general's deep rumbling chuckle sounded sympathetic. He lifted a wine decanter, but Farragut said, "What else you got back there?"

Numa Pompeii poured him Kentucky bourbon instead.

Farragut approved. "Well, that's better." Felt the burning comfort go down. "Is this my stash?"

Numa nodded. "We liberated it."

Farragut lifted a toast with his bourbon, "Here's to you being in this seat next go round."

"You threw some pretty hard language at me back there, Captain Farragut. War criminal. Lying sack."

"Baboon," Farragut added. "I called you a smug baboon."

"And you have an apology for me now?"

"No."

"You're a sore loser."

"I'm a piss-poor loser, Numa."

"Now tell me truthfully, Captain Farragut, were you actually boarded by Them? What do you call Them?"

"We call them gorgons. Among other things."

"Odd. So do we."

"Not so odd. Earth and Palatine might be Cain and Abel, but underneath it all still brothers."

"And you're honestly telling me the gorgons boarded you?"

Farragut tired of the question. "Ask the crew of the Fury." He had no need to insist to this man.

"You've brainwashed the crew of the Fury."

Farragut gave a little jerk of surprise, then said, "I get it. They never saw a live gorgon. They saw a lot of sewage-looking stuff we claimed was gorgon remains. We made it all up."

"You made them swab your decks, threatened them, ignored their salutes. And they love you."

"*Do* they?"

"*Merrimack* would be the only ship ever to survive boarding."

"I've been told."

"The troubling thing is that the boarding does, as you say, 'taint the meat.' Whatever you did to combat them won't work twice."

"The gorgons that boarded the *Mack* are all dead. Who are they going to tell?"

"They're all connected somehow—which is why we call the gorgons collectively the Hive. They have a colonial intelligence."

"Across parsecs of empty space?"

"It would appear so."

Farragut was not accustomed to sharing intelligence with the enemy, and did not intend to start now. He only fished for confirmation of some of his own suspicions.

He offered a lot of nothing that could be news to the Roman general. Told him that *Merrimack* had not observed a Hive sphere travel faster than two hundred times light speed. That gorgons had no apparent means of propulsion, no apparent means of cohesion. That gorgons fall apart when they die.

Numa asked, "Ever seen an individual gorgon travel FTL without latching onto something else?"

"Haven't seen it," said Farragut. "On shipboard they don't move any quicker than a diamondback."

"Which?"

"Which what?"

Farragut learned then that the monsters came in not two, but three different forms—most common being the bundles of legs, which Farragut had assumed was the only flavor gorgons came in. Another, which must be what Colonel Steele and Cowboy met on the hull, a variety the Romans called soldiers—bigger, harder, fewer legs, viciously barbed, and they traveled in bigger spheres. And a disgusting third form Numa called gluies.

"Gluies. What's that in English?" Farragut asked.

"That *is* English," said Numa. He described white, revolting, sluglike things with nubby little teeth, and a paralytic poison. "Are you going to bring anything useful to this table, Captain?"

"Ask your patterner," Farragut said, feeling uncooperative. Surely the pilot of that infernal little Striker with its barrel stuck inside *Merrimack* could tell Numa Pompeii everything *Merrimack* knew about gorgons.

Numa Pompeii said, "The emperor's patterner is an obnoxious Flavian. I talk to him as little as possible. How do you kill them?"

"I outran one," said Farragut. "He self-destructed."

"How do you kill the *gorgons*," said Numa, irritated. "Not patterners."

"It's like this," said Farragut. "You can develop all kinds of fancy poisons, but in any battle with a cockroach, a shoe always has the last word."

"Gorgons don't squash," Numa argued, a momentary lapse into stupid literalism.

"Numa, you're disappointing me. You don't deserve this." Farragut reached across the table to grab his bottle of bourbon.

The general quickly caught up. "Low tech. Your swords. Your damn swords."

"Which I owe to you and Jorge Medina. Thank you, Numa, for forcing me to arm my crew with swords. I think I will apologize now for everything I called you."

Numa had a lot of words for Farragut's apology.

"And gorgons burn," Farragut offered.

Numa shook his head. "Flash point is too high and they burn dirty. You kill yourself trying to fight them off a ship that way."

A sudden brassy chirruping and a frantic buzz made Farragut's skin roughen and prickle. Aldebaran scarab crickets fled their heraldic perches flanking the archway. They flew away, screeching.

Numa set down his glass, laid his linen napkin on the table. "You'll have to excuse me, Captain."

Numa rose, offering no explanation. Saw that Farragut knew the signs.

Farragut rose without prompting. "Put me in with my crew?" he asked as the guards stepped forward to collect him.

Numa nodded to the guards, granting that.

Bored stiff in captivity—Kerry Blue figuratively, the guys literally. Kerry was randy, too, but yab-yum was not a spectator sport and there was zero privacy in detention except for that curtained area, and Kerry Blue did not do toilets. Showers, yes, but there were no showers in here, and everyone stank.

She had to settle for kicking butt at poker to pass the time. They used banana chips for coin. Had nothing else. For clothes they were down to tanks, T-shirts, sweats, and deck mocs. Anything with buttons, zippers, hooks, or heels had not made it into detention. Not exactly Red Cross-approved quarters either, this meat box.

Then someone—the Hamster—heard bug noises through the partition—Aldebaran scarab crickets—which she claimed meant gorgons were stalking the ship.

Oh, good, what we need. A little panic in here. Kerry took one card. Didn't get the flush.

The hatch opened and Captain Farragut came in like daybreak. It was always good to see him. He looked good slimmed down like that, even though he was way too old for Kerry Blue. And he was the only one in this tank clean, shaved, and in uniform. Maybe thirty-eight wasn't so old.

Kerry tossed down her cards, uncrossed her legs, and jumped up from the deck. "Hey, Captain!"

And suddenly there were a lot of people talking at once. Most asking the captain if there were gorgons. It shocked Kerry when Farragut nodded, "I think we have gorgons on our tail."

Someone asked: "We're running, right?"

"I wasn't told." And the captain went round talking to everyone. Took his time getting to the Hamster, as if she were nothing to him but another officer. How the woman could be that blind to a man's interest was beyond Kerry Blue—but *hel*-lo. This time was different. Somebody woke up Sleeping Beauty. The Hamster was blushing, and doing little eye things, and little almost-smile things.

Kerry moved closer to listen. The captain's and the Hamster's words were all business, but the body language was saying "I want you bad and there are way too many people in here."

"*Gladiator* can easily outrun a gorgon sphere," Glenn Hamilton was telling Farragut. "Numa will run."

"Unless he's been ordered to turn and fight," Farragut said, very softly. "If Caesar orders it, the Romans will stand and die like the three hundred at Corindahlor."

"No. He wouldn't," said Hamster, dropping the flirty bit. Didn't sound like she believed herself. "Romans have never won against the gorgons. He has to run."

A ship within an inertia field gave no sense of its true motion, so Kerry couldn't guess which way *Gladiator* was taking her.

But she could hear the ship's guns erupt.

That was when Captain Farragut slapped the bulk and roared, "Dammit, Numa, run!"

Lots of pounding of outgoing ordnance. Hissing beam fire. *Gladiator* was unloading the whole rock pile on something out there.

Could be our guys coming to the rescue.

Kerry didn't believe herself either.

The lights flickered. Flickered off. Everyone looked ghastly in the yellow-green chemical glow of the emergency lamps, like they were dead already. On the deck overhead, someone's smart snappy Roman march step gave way to running footfalls. The ship's force field mooed like a dying gurzn. Kerry only ever heard a field urgle like that once before.

"We got gorgons on the screens," Kerry said to no one, anyone, in the dark.

Knew now why John Farragut was in here.

Numa Pompeii was allowing the captain of the *Merrimack* to die with his crew.

33

U NGODLY NOISES FROM THE force field told the prisoners
that the gorgons were insinuating their way through
the ship's defensive screen. That metallic scritching had to
be tentacles against the hull. It would not be long now.

Glenn Hamilton cocked her ear to the changing sounds.
"They're in."

"We're going to die in this cage!" someone cried in the
crowded detention hold.

"Belay that," Farragut ordered.

After a slow, agonizing while, sounds of weapons fire diminished within the ship. Did not mean the enemy was on
the run. You still heard enough scritching. Meant the gorgons were overwhelming the computer controls.

The air felt thick in Farragut's lungs.

He waited for the expected miracle. Heard it in the
smallest *snick* amid the shouting and banging uproar that
resounded through the big ship.

The detention hold's locks had failed.

Farragut bellowed, "Open that hatch! Look alive! Those
closest to the hatch, get out and get clear! Do not block the
exit!"

Kerry Blue shuffled with her squadron mates toward the
hatch, inch by inch, stinking bodies pressed together—no

one exactly pushing, but no one leaving any space between himself and the person in front of him.

There was just no herding seven hundred people through one hatch fast enough when your lives depended on it.

Kerry craned her neck round, looking for Farragut. Glimpsed him. Way in the back of the back. Kerry looked up at Colonel Steele, damp skin of her arm stuck to his. "Orders? When we get out of here?"

"We still have our orders from Farragut," Steele growled. "Stay alive."

The Romans made no move to stop the POWs spilling from detention, so even John Farragut, at the tail end of the file, got free of the hold. By then the Romans had switched from beam guns to ceremonial bayonets, antique revolvers, and roundsaws to combat the gorgons. Anything with a blade was in use. *Merrimack*'s crew and company found no useful weapons to be had.

Farragut sprinted to an unattended sensor compartment, and ordered his senior engineer, Kit Kittering, to locate *Merrimack* on the plotter screen. But the screen was dark and stayed dark. *Gladiator*'s sensors were all down. The only thing operative in the room full of unfamiliar equipment was the battery-powered backup lamp.

"That's why no one is in here," said Kit. "Even if *Merrimack* is out there, we won't be able to see her."

"*I* see her," said Farragut, startled, looking out a clearport.

The *Merrimack*. Right there. So close he could not take in any more than a wide stretch of gray hull. Only knew the ship was *Merrimack* because she was his.

Kit's great round doll eyes briefly widened at the featureless gray bulk. "John, that could be any ship."

"No, that's my *Mack*!" He knew her every inch, every flaw (she had none), every dimple. "She's gotta be hard docked and inside *Gladiator*'s force field to be that close. That's her port side and *Gladiator*'s got to be docked to her cargo bay two. The access will be three, maybe four decks down from here and twenty meters that way. Where would I find a vertical access in this hulk? Are you familiar with the layout of a *Gladiator* class battleship, Kit?"

"*Gladiator* is the class," said Kit. Rome had constructed only one. "I don't think the blueprints ever got out. Anyway, John, I don't think they would have the *Merrimack* right—"

Surprised shouts sounded from three, maybe four, decks down, in English: "*Merrimack!* It's *Merrimack*! She's here! She's open! This way!"

Clanging on the vents took on a distinctive Morse rhythm. Reg Monroe started spelling aloud the taps. "That's the captain! *Merrimack* is here!"

Kerry heard it, too. "Where? How do we get there from here?"

Dak came loping up, pointed with a broad, twice-broken finger. "Take this corridor to the T intersection. Go right. Take the ladder. Hard to starboard and down the ramp."

Carly wrinkled up her face at him. "Now how the hell do you know that?"

Dak nodded backward. "I asked a guy back there."

"You asked a *Roman* for directions?" Reg's voice ascended off the register.

"Yeah." Dak's big sloping shoulders shrugged.

None of his mates could believe it. But that *was* the direction all the excited shouting was coming from.

"He said we better hurry. The lupes are gonna push her off."

Reg, Carly, Twitch, Cowboy, Kerry, and Dak looked to Colonel Steele. Steele was about to give the go ahead when Cowboy yelled, "Gorgons! Six o'clock on the real fast!"

Aliens were coming up the corridor behind them—a black mass of ugly.

"Go!" Steele ordered.

As ready for combat as a clutch of rabbits, the Marines of Alpha Flight took off at a barefoot run, the hideous scritching rolling hot after them. At the T intersection the way broke right and left. Cowboy, in the lead of the retreat, broke *up* in an acrobatic leap, swung up on a pipe, kicked an access panel out of the overhead, and hoisted himself up.

Down on the deck were gorgons on all sides—a clot on the left closing in, more on the right barreling off the way the Marines wanted to go, and the mass of gorgons from behind, moving in fast. Cowboy in the overhead, hanging upside down like a trapeze artist, yelled, "Come *on!*"

Steele seized Reg by the waist and threw her upward to Cowboy, who caught Reggie's wrists and hauled her up into the vertical shaft with him.

Kerry next. Too high. Separated her ribs on the downward yank as Cowboy caught her wrists. She went up breathless, stunned with pain. Tried to climb up past Cowboy to where Reg was, higher in the stack. Could not breathe.

Carly, crowding in from below, gave Kerry a push on the ass. "*Chica linda,* some *help, por favor*!"

"Kerry's hurt," said Reg.

"She's okay," said Cowboy. Caught Twitch Fuentes. "Move it up. We're on a real deadline here."

Kerry climbed, grimacing.

Steele, down below, called, "Big load, coming up."

"Hey! Hey! Don't get personal!"

"Shut up, Dak."

Oofs from Steele, like boosting a sleeper sofa. Lots of weird sounds from Cowboy and Twitch, hauling Dak up into the shaft.

Kerry had to stop. Curled around a waste pipe. Looked down. No one left down there to boost the Old Man up. And Colonel Steele was not a small guy.

But stampeding gorgons with snapping tentacles converging on you can make you fly. Big yells, and Colonel Steele was up. Dak caught his wrists and heaved him into the overhead just as the gorgons from the six- and nine-o'clock corridors connected at the T intersection below the shaft. Looked like a snake's nest down there.

The whole snarl of them swarmed to the three o'clock and stampeded onward—the way the Marines wanted to go.

Reg whispered, "They didn't look up. Why didn't they look up?"

Kerry clenched her teeth, wrapped one arm around her rib cage. "Don't really give a squid."

"They want something bad that way," Dak said, filling the vertical access, shouldering his way up the stack.

"*We* want something bad that way," said Carly. "That's the way to *Merrimack.*"

"Lupes must've slathered up the *Mack* real tasty. You think?" said Cowboy.

"Could be," said Carly. "I'd still rather be on *Mack* than here. This boat ain't exactly vermin free."

A glimmer of light returned to the bottom of the stack. The gorgons had passed on by. Steele clambered down, headfirst, for a recce, checking all three corridors.

"Clear?" Cowboy asked.

"*Not* clear." Steele twisted around upright. Sounds of gorgons' skittering toothy feet approached. "Marines, proceed up. We'll try to circle around to the dock from the next level. *Move!* Blue, you can move your ass faster than that!"

Fighting tears, nostrils flaring, Kerry acknowledged through her teeth: "Yes, sir!" Followed Reg up the shaft. Better off mad. Kept her mind off the pain.

The Marines moved like a line of rats, nose to tail, Reg leading. Reg had a sense for how ships were put together, and she brought them out on a catwalk twenty feet above the loading dock where great cargo doors lay open like parted jaws to swallow eager gorgons swarming from *Gladiator* to *Merrimack*.

The gorgons moved with a singular will. Ignored the Marines up above and the few Roman soldiers on other catwalks around the dock. Kerry crouched on the grating, arms round herself, head between her knees. The doors. The doors. Right down there. And no way to get through them.

The alien rush ebbed. There came an exchange of shouts in Latin from the dock and elsewhere, but no more gorgons.

"There's our chance!"

Carly had no sooner whispered when a ratcheting clangor filled the empty space.

The cargo doors were cranking shut.

"No!"

Cowboy leaped down the twenty feet, rolled on the deck, and up to his feet. He charged at one of the Romans at the winch.

The Roman dropped him with an easy crack of the butt of his beam gun across the side of Cowboy's head. The Romans continued cranking at the winch. Got up a rhythm. The cargo doors were clattering together easily, faster.

Dak and Steele vaulted over the catwalk railing, hung from the grate, dropped to the deck, and rolled. Steele roared at Dak, "Help them!" Of the Marines stranded above, while he, Steele, ran at the doors. He had nothing to wedge between them. They boomed shut before his nose.

Colonel Steele had been a drill sergeant once, in the

dawn of his career, and still sounded it. "Open this!" he thundered in a voice that might have made even Romans obey, had they understood English.

Didn't seem to. They exchanged shouts with the upper decks. Acknowledged orders. Gave their weight to reluctant levers that creaked, budged, banged into position.

A clunking sounded from outside the hull. The sound of separation.

"Merrimack *abst!*"

Cowboy pried himself off the deck. Jumped at the doors like a caged kangaroo rat. "No! No!"

Reg stared, stunned, from the catwalk. Met the dark eyes of a Roman soldier at one of the levers. Oddly sympathetic eyes. The Roman spoke to her in English: "No tears now, pretty Yank. You didn't want to catch that ship. We're going to blow it up."

34

Upon boarding his gorgon-infested ship, Farragut had been met by a squad of Marines at the dock, who were passing out swords to all boarders having only two legs. "Compliments of Lieutenant Hamilton, sir. Glad to have you aboard, Captain Farragut."

"The Romans left these?" Farragut felt the satisfying weight of the blade in his grip. It was good to be armed again.

"Yes, sir. We were surprised. They took everything else."

Maybe because the swords had worked once against the aliens, Numa assumed the swords would not be effective twice. Or maybe it was just because Numa disdained swords.

"I do love that man's hubris," said Farragut. Took possession of his ship.

Nothing computer operated worked over here either, the ship smothered by whatever force the alien mass exuded. Air was still tough to draw. Numa had managed to off-load thousands of his gorgons on to *Merrimack*.

But the gorgons here acted differently than the last swarm *Merrimack* had encountered. The gorgons of the last swarm had attacked whatever was closest. These snubbed the easy snack in pursuit of something irresistible.

"The Romans stowed something mighty tasty on board is all I can think," said the Marine who accompanied Captain Farragut through *Merrimack*'s corridors, hacking a path through those few monsters still interested in random prey.

The captain's first order was to run out his flag.

The Romans had taken the Stars and Stripes, so someone quickly made up one and hand-cranked Old Glory out. Not perfect but just as proud and more defiant for its flaws.

"Captain on deck!" a Marine proudly announced Farragut's arrival on the command platform.

The few techs and specialists there leaped to their feet. Farragut took stock of who he had: Ben Mueller, the com tech who normally sat mid watch. Marcander Vincent, *Merrimack*'s junkyard dog of a tac specialist, scabs on his face, both his arms bandaged from a close encounter with a gorgon. Qord Johnson, the cryptotech, young guy, freckled, flat-nosed, with fuzzy rust-brown hair and amber eyes. The second-string pilot, Jul Cortez. They all cheered as if the captain could breathe life into their dead systems just by being here.

Farragut clasped their hands, embraced them, grabbed his little lieutenant behind the head and kissed her on the mouth. Under the circumstances it didn't raise any eyebrows. John Farragut was an expressive man.

A deep, ratcheting clatter made him rear back, alarmed. Sounded like cargo doors shutting, and he shouted to anyone, "Why are those doors closing! We're not all here! I am not abandoning our people on *Gladiator*!"

An anonymous voice shouted back from below: "Ready or not, yes we are, Cap'n! *Gladiator* closed first! They mean to space us!"

The ship heaved, canted. Farragut fell against a control panel.

The voice again. Pretty sure it was the Og: "We didn't do that, Cap'n! We were pushed!"

Ready or not, *Merrimack* was departing with the crew she had.

"Who is here, Hamster? Do I have enough to fly this boat?"

"Maybe half, Captain," said Lieutenant Hamilton. "Maybe."

"Colonel Steele!" he bellowed. "TR! You on board?"

"Don't think he made it, sir."

"Commander Gray?"

No one had seen the XO.

"Hamster, looks like you're acting exec again." Wanted to know if her husband had made it on board, but now was not the time to ask anyone. "Find out who we've got, and fill in the holes. I want this ship operational and all the gorgons dead. Does that uffing Striker still have its barrel stuck inside gun bay sixteen?"

With all systems fouled, he might be able to take over the patterner's demonic little ship. But the report came back from someone who ran all the way up to gun bay sixteen and back, "No, sir."

As *Merrimack* drifted apart from its captor, Farragut got a visual of *Gladiator*—coated with gorgons. Half of Farragut's crew was still on board that ship.

"Kit!" Farragut bellowed at the top of his voice. Knew his senior engineer was on board. She had come over with him. "Kit, can we steer?"

His engineer ran to the command deck to answer, gasping for oxygen. Took her a moment, hands on knees, to catch her breath. "Don't know, sir. We've got a strange mess in the back. A mad heap of gorgons—thousands—tens of thousands—outside Engine Room Six."

"What are they doing?"

Kit straightened, opened empty hands. She had no good answer. "Biting. They're even biting each other. Like there's something in the middle of them they ALL want."

"In Engine Six?"

"No, sir. In the maintenance shed right outside. And every compartment adjacent to it. God knows what's in the maintenance shed. They want it."

Captain Farragut and Lieutenant Hamilton spoke at the same time. "Bait."

Looked at each other.

"Why would the Romans put gorgon bait there?" said Kit Kittering.

"To lure the gorgons off *Gladiator*?" Hamster suggested. Seemed obvious.

"Well, it concentrates them real nice. A lot of them, anyway," said Kit. "Containment systems are functioning. Gorgons can penetrate them, of course, but it takes them time. I could seal off the affected compartments and lob in an incendiary. Take out about nine-tenths of our gorgon problem in one crack."

"No!" said Hamster.

Kit turned arctic. Knew her job better than any mid watch officer. "Just because *you* burned out the Fury, sir, doesn't mean *I* don't know what kind of bomb to use to contain destruction to only the maintenance shed." Told *her*. Captain's sweetheart be damned.

"No," Glenn Hamilton said again. Appealed to Captain Farragut. "I think there's already a bomb in there."

Farragut lifted his eyebrows—thinner eyebrows since they had grown back from his brush with Hamster's blowtorch aboard the Fury. He murmured. "What good's a lure without a hook?" And to Kit. "What do you think?"

Kit had to concede, with a pained nod. The God-blessed Hamster was right. "Got to be a bomb on board." That would explain why the Striker's barrel was absent from *Merrimack*'s gun bay. "And I bet it will take out more than the maintenance shed."

Gladiator had some systems controls back, but the intercom was not one of those, so the crew were shouting orders between decks. It was all in Latin, except for Colonel TR Steele bawling like a bull, "Pompeii! You can't do this!"

Merrimack. The Romans were going to blow up *Merrimack*.

Steele's mission presented itself—the reason God had stranded him on *Gladiator*. While TR Steele breathed, no one was going to blow up the U.S.S. *Merrimack*.

Kerry Blue never ever thought any responsibility so huge would fall into her hands—never when there wasn't some equally expendable grunt next in line to take up where she failed. Never thought she would have anything of value to offer Colonel Steele. But Kerry Blue had had lots of stepdads and had grown up learning bits of lots of languages. Kerry, Carly, and Twitch could piece together some of the Latin the Romans were bellowing for all to hear.

A lot of it was just yelling from soldiers locked in combat with the gorgons. But the voices that mattered were very loud and speaking very clearly to make their orders heard— calling for *Merrimack*'s destruction.

Kerry, Carly, and Twitch isolated three from the din.

An authoritative, high tenor voice, dubiously female, from an officer type addressed as *Domna,* giving orders.

A brassy male voice, grating. Made you hate him instantly, sight unseen. Had to be a tech in fire control, whose name was probably Bellus. He would be the one with his hand on the detonator.

And a third someone who was gauging a safe distance of separation between *Merrimack* and *Gladiator* for detonation. Reporting status updates to *Domna*.

It was going to be a hell of an explosion for distance to matter. The Romans had probably tied the device into the antimatter in *Merrimack*'s engines.

Steele pointed in the direction of the brassy one, Bellus. "That's the guy at the switch?"

"Yes, sir," said Kerry.

"You sure?"

Hated it when he asked her that. The man could make her doubt her own name when he asked her that way. Kerry was sure. She thought.

Carly answered, "Yes, sir."

Steele ordered all of them, "Take that man out."

Trying to find him in this maze was the problem. Sounds banged round the metal bulks, and became more confusing the closer the Marines got to Bellus. They listened and advanced by stops and starts, dodging Romans and gorgons at every turn.

Had to be getting close, but the brassy voice sounded from everywhere now. Right behind that partition. Or was that just an echo cracking back from the opposite direction?

"Oh, skat!" Carly hissed.

Bellus hadn't made a sound. Carly was listening to something else.

"What did you hear, soldier?"

"*Domna*'s asking for confirmation that they've reached safe distance for detonation," said Carly.

All the Marines heard a word in the tech's response to domna: *Confirmo.*

"I think I understood that one."

"Shh!" Carly was trying to listen. "*Domna*'s ordering Bellus to arm the detonator."

They all held their breath, waiting to pounce in the direction of Bellus' acknowledgment.

As soon as the brassy one opened his mouth, the Marines made a stealthy sprint in the direction of his voice.

They jumped through a fire door to another section of corridor.

Now any of three closed hatches might shield Bellus. Or other Romans who would detain them. Or gorgons.

The Marines waited, listening for the voice of brass to bray again.

"Dammit, Bellus, say something!" Cowboy muttered through clenched teeth. "Can't kill him if he don't talk!"

Carly turned to Steele. "Colonel, he ain't gonna talk again till it's too late! It's too late!"

Because *Domna* had begun a sequence anybody but Dak could figure out: *"Novem, octo, septum, sex—"*

"Take a hatch!" Steele ordered out loud. "Cover all of them! Terminate any enemy on the other side. Go!"

Twitch and Carly dashed for the farthest hatch.

Reg and Cowboy took the middle.

Kerry, Dak and Steele stormed the closest one.

"—tria, duo, unum."

Steele tore open the near hatch to empty darkness. "Damn!" Skidding round.

Domna's order shouted from above: *"Fiat!"*

Let it be done.

Cowboy leaped through the middle hatch with Reg, her little hands cocked back in bear claws—

As the hand of the Roman at the console inside the compartment depressed a switch, an indicator light turned green, and the Roman reported in a brassy crow: *"Fit!"*

It is done.

35

Reg's scream pierced the battleship.

"Ho!" Cowboy reeled back, finger in his ear. "Mind the decibelage, girl baby."

The Roman, Bellus, had whirled from his console, brandishing a bayonet. Had he stabbed or poked, Cowboy might have made a grab for the weapon, but Bellus sliced the air between himself and the Marines. Reg and Cowboy stumbled backward out of the compartment. Cowboy slammed the hatch and leaned on it to keep Bellus in.

Carly popped out of her hatchway, "What happened!"

"What the hell do you think happened!" Cowboy yelled. "He pushed the button on *Merrimack*! He got a green!"

Steele bellowed for status.

"Fubared!" Cowboy hollered.

Kerry's mind went into dumb overload. *It's all moment to moment now.* Held her side with one hand. Pulled Dak from his salt-pillar stance with the other to follow Colonel Steele, who signaled the squad to fall back.

Retreated into *Gladiator*'s labyrinth of moody corridors. Following a man who didn't know the way but was decisive about it.

Stopped somewhere. Didn't know where, didn't care. Thirsty. Kerry was hellfire thirsty.

There were a lot of bushes here. An atrium of sorts. The Marines breathing hard as if from a twenty-klick forced march.

Steele gathered his Marines into a huddle.

Kerry was shaking mad, breathing through her teeth, eyes wet.

Carly a dry, hard mean.

That big lummox Dak looked like a motherless child.

Little Reg squeaking, trying not to sob out loud.

Twitch's long-lost tic had come back.

Cowboy was taking off his shirt.

Hazard—they'd lost Hazard Sewell way back at the detention hold. Hoped he hadn't made it to *Merrimack*.

Reg squeaked between sobs. "I don't hear the captain anymore. He'd be talking to us if he were here." She motioned a Morse tapping. "He must have—" Could not speak where Captain Farragut must have gone.

The captain's silence left a pall. Like God had died.

"Later, Monroe," said Steele. "Captain's order still stands—stay alive." Steele was pulling up foliage from the trees and bushes in the atrium, passing them out to his squad like ammo. Kerry wondered for a moment if their leader, their rock, their lifeline had snapped. She accepted a philodendron. Hoped Steele didn't think you could eat these.

"Listen up. Here's your new objective," said Steele. "We're going to find this ship's hangars, and hijack a transport—a fighter craft, a shuttle—anything to get us out of here. We are jumping ship."

A hearty "Yeah!" from Cowboy.

"*Gladiator* won't have deployed its small craft. They're a liability in a battle with gorgons, so all boats should be inboard."

"Sir? If we do get out—won't we be gorgon meat out there?"

"As long as we don't attack the gorgons or resonate, they might not even know we're out there."

Might. Not an encouraging word.

And the idea of not attacking the enemy was alien to the Marines. Stealing away while others fought for their lives felt like desertion. But this was not their ship. These were not their people. *Romans* could not run away from this fight.

But we can.

Getting to the hangars was going to be a problem. Since *Merrimack* detached from *Gladiator*, the remaining gorgons—and there were a lot of them—had scattered into an every-monster-for-itself feeding frenzy, eating the nearest living or once-living thing.

Steele shook a palm frond at his Marines. They were all loaded with vegetation now. "Any gorgon you meet, throw it something to eat, and run."

Clad in nothing but sweatpants, Cowboy muttered, "Hope gorgons don't pass on the salad and come for the meat."

But the tactic worked for a time. As long as the Marines had something to throw to the many many mouths, the gorgons did not feel the need to chase.

The Marines moved at a dodging, furtive run. Felt like mice when the world has gone to cats.

Avoided a contingent of Romans, ducked into a dark compartment. Held their breath.

Became aware of the bigness of the space they were in. Sensed it in the eddies of the air, in the smallness of their breathing when they finally exhaled.

Eyes adjusted from dim to only the most minimal emergency lighting. They were in a stowage area. Or a hangar. Cold. They could see their own breath rise in the eerie lamplight. Hard-edged shapes loomed, still as statues, in the mists of their frosty breath.

The shapes.

The hair pricked on Kerry's scalp. An awe so deep you don't want to move. "Those are Swifts!"

And Reg did her one better: "Those are *ours*!"

Kerry limped in to touch her beloved Six's cold, cold hull. Swifts. Of course, the Marine wing's fighter craft would be here. *Gladiator* would have harvested the useful parts before blowing up *Merrimack*. God bless their vulturous souls.

Kerry's eyes leaked joy.

Leave it to Carly to whisper, "Now how do we get out? I don't think *Gladiator* is going to lower her force field for us."

Reg hissed. She didn't dare shout. Not now, so close to escape. She motioned big. "Colonel! Over here."

Reg turned an emergency lamp on a set of hangar doors.

The lamp's dim glow glinted on a crusting of ice at the seals. The doors themselves looked cold enough to stick your hand to. Reg whispered, afraid to say it, too good to be true: "The force field is down!"

It was true. There were enough gorgons left on *Gladiator* to keep the ship's computer controls suppressed. "We can get out!"

Unfortunately, the system failure extended to the Swifts as well. Cowboy was already in his cockpit trying to start up his machine. The Swifts were nonfunctional except for their most basic systems with a mechanical on/off, and the magnetic antimatter containment systems. Otherwise, they were brain dead.

"You'll have to hand adjust all life support," Steele told them. "Use your backup heaters, and the demand regulator for air."

There were no space suits. It was going to be uncomfortable. And no thrust.

"So how do we get out?"

A scratching at the inner hatch made them all hunker down, go silent.

Reg mouthed a warning: "Gorgons!"

The scratching came again. With a snuffling.

"Gorgons don't sniff," said Carly. "Gorgons don't breathe!"

Dak moved stealthily to the hatch, sword at the ready, to check out the snuffling visitor.

He relaxed, lowered his sword and let in a dog—the Chief's dog, Pooh—happy as hell to see Dak. Always a smart dog, the poodle didn't bark, only padded from Marine to Marine in hand-licking, tail-lashing, frightened-eyed joy.

Kerry expected a reaming from the colonel for wasting time with the mutt, but Steele only whispered loud, "Shut that hatch! Get the deck locks off your fighters! Push the Swifts up against these doors!" Jerked his head toward the ice-encrusted outer doors.

They had to breathe on the chocks to unfreeze them and get the Swifts' gear free. Kerry knew where this was going. *Colonel means to open the doors and let the rush of air sweep us out to space.*

She put a shoulder to her Swift. It wouldn't move. Pain stabbed her separated ribs, and folded her to a crouch. The

Old Man stalked over to shove her crate flush up against the icy doors for her.

Snarled at everyone else to make 'em snug, so the Swifts won't crash on their way out.

Steele always had a sandy voice anyway, it was all gravel now. A comforting, domineering you-got-a-job-to-do-and-here's-how-you're-going-to-do-it rasp. "At some distance from the ship, you should regain systems controls. Do NOT resonate. In fact, pull your chambers out right now."

"Uh, Colonel?" Cowboy raised his hand, like preparing to ask a question of an idiot. "How are we supposed to open the hangar doors?"

Idiot question. Even Kerry knew the answer to that one. There were seven Marines here, six Swifts pushed up against the doors.

Steele ordered Alpha Flight into their cockpits.

Dak stripped off his T-shirt. Offered it to Steele. "Gonna get cold in here, sir."

Steele gave a taut nod. Put the shirt on over his tank top.

Carly and Reg took off their tops, offered them, too. The big man's blond brows screwed up at them, but before he could say something about the size, Carly said, "Mittens. You got to get the doors open wide enough for us to be sucked out before you freeze solid. You ain't dying for nothin', sir."

He accepted their salutes. Wrapped his hands in the women's shirts as Carly and Reg scampered, freezing, to their Swifts.

Dak, looking round in near panic, whispered, "Who's got the dog!"

Twitch's voice, muffled, from his cockpit: *"Yo!"*

Kerry was leaning against her Swift, one hand on the handhold, crying silently because she couldn't even lift herself into her cockpit. Steele stomped over, growling. Hauled her up and deposited her ungently into her fighter. Then strapped her in like a child into a safety seat. Fished out her oxygen mask and her regulator for her. Tugged her straps tight. Treated her like a brat child he had lost patience with.

Old Man really hates me, thought Kerry, taking it.

Hates me, and he's going to die for me.

"Clear your arms, Marine." Steele held the canopy over her.

"No, no. Wait, wait, wait."

Grimacing, like there was a nail in her side, Kerry pulled the red crowbar from her Swift's emergency hatch. Handed it up to Steele. "After you get out of this hangar, you'll need it against the gorgons."

He frowned at the red crowbar in his hand, odd, shifting expressions on his face. And Kerry reached up, grabbed his head, kissed him on the mouth. Felt a sudden warmth down to her groin. Let go.

"In case I never see you again," she said to his ice-blue eyes. "And if you do see me again, you can court-martial me. Give you something to live for."

"Get your arms in the cockpit, Marine."

"Yes, sir. *Semper fi.*"

The canopy closed over her, sealed.

She watched the colonel, a stocky figure, walking away in the dark. Never looked so small. Never looked so big.

Steele stowed the crowbar so it would not fly away, tethered himself tight to a stanchion, and took the red safeties off the windlass.

Kerry gave him a thumbs-up through her icing canopy.

Last saw him muscling the crank round for dear life.

An icy fog rose, debris swirled up, and her crate began to slide.

Ice cracked like thunder. The doors parted. Kerry's Swift tilted. Her hands gave a reflexive clutch as if she could catch herself. Her canopy rapped against the doors, made her yelp. The fighter lifted, scraping.

The outrush was a whirlwind now. Kerry's Swift banged back down, jarred her ribs so hard she couldn't breathe, and the whole crate canted over screw-wise. The canopy struck again, and she rolled.

Up. Sucked against the doors, straining to get through, a hailstorm of things clattering against her fuselage. The doors were parting slowly, slower.

Oh God, Colonel, keep cranking.

A stomach-heaving pitch and roll. Then an all hell cracking and banging. A weightless leap—

Through! And slammed back round with a dizzy swing and an awful crack. Her gear was hung on the door, her Swift flapping in the hurricane wind.

Kerry closed her eyes, teeth chattering. Helpless, cold, and going to die.

Screeching metallic tearing hammered at her ears. Felt it in her chest.

Then the end of sounds. Floating free. The Swift tumbled into the dark. Kerry's damp hair floated off her scalp.

Opened her eyes.

The only lights were those on her gunsights, implanted on either temple. Those lights were powered by her brain, so she was surprised they were still working.

She shivered, cold, the heater throwing only enough to bake her feet. Her muscles quivered in dehydration.

She groped with fluttering hands for the drinking tube. If there wasn't water in here, she was going to flat line.

She sucked on the tube, and, hallelujah, there was the most wonderful stale flat water in the universe filling her mouth.

She relaxed. Might live.

Tried to see out through the canopy. Then focused on the canopy itself.

A crack.

Fear coiled round her gut. That jagged white thread looked like a crack in her canopy.

She tried to lean forward for a better look, but Steele had her strapped in immobile. She loosened the straps, pushed herself forward in her seat.

It was a crack.

Without a force field, only one centimeter of cracked polymer stood between her and forever, hundreds of degrees difference on either side of that thin barrier.

Panic tugged, screaming, at the edges of her consciousness—the depth of space on the other side of that cracked shield. The enormity. The infinity. She was alone with her own breathing in her mask, her primitive heater at her feet.

The crack snaked longer and she flinched back. Scarcely felt the pain jerk her ribs.

She watched the crack, as if staring at it would keep it still. Breathing too hard, too deep. Tried to slow it down. Her breath. The crack.

It grew again, lancing toward the seal.

No. God, make it stop.

A loud beep. Kerry shrieked.

Console lights powered up. The force field came up round the Swift. Pressure and warmth filled the cockpit. The crack in the canopy spread seal to seal and Kerry told it to go to uffing hell.

Her com link gave a gentle buzz of life. She pulled off her regulator and yelled into her com. "This is Alpha Six! Can anyone hear me!"

"Alpha Six! Alpha Three! I am the happiest hag west of Vega!"

"Reg!"

"Chica linda! Donde estas?"

"Carly! *Estoy acqui!*"

"Where the hell is *acqui?*"

"Alpha *cinco, acqui!*"

"Twitch! Oh my God, Twitch." Kerry was laughing now.

Heard a woofing on the com that had to be the dog, Pooh.

"Yeeeeeeeee HA!"

"Cowboy!"

Reg reported that her sensors had picked up a heat trail. Big one. "Gotta be *Gladiator*. Do we follow it?"

"Follow *Gladiator*?" Cowboy squawked. "We just got out of that hole."

"Don't know about you, but I forgot to pack a lunch," Reg shot back.

"Well there won't be any food on *Gladiator* if the gorgons win," said Cowboy.

"If the gorgons win, the rest of the Legion is sure to send a robot back to collect the teeth. It can collect us, too. I'd rather be a prisoner than starve out here."

Carly put an end to the debate. Ordered the flight to form up and follow the heat trail.

Alpha Flight caught up with the heat source while Kerry was on point.

Glory be.

"That's *Merrimack*!"

Cowboy laughed like a hyena. He had seen the Roman, Bellus, on *Gladiator* send the destruct signal, had seen the light turn green on the console.

The destruct signal *went*. But: "How the hell is *Merrimack* going to *receive* the signal with all those gorgons on board uffing the systems? Did those squid-humping gits ever think of *that*?" He howled in gloating triumph.

Carly was sending: "*Merrimack! Merrimack! Merrimack!* This is Alpha Four! You have a bomb on board! Repeat message: You have a bomb on board!"

"They aren't responding," said Reg. "I guess they're not receiving that signal either."

"If they kill enough of the gorgons—and knowing Captain Farragut, they will—and someone don't disarm that bomb, their systems come back on and *Gladiator* can still destroy the Mack with the flip of a switch."

"No!" Kerry cried. *Not in front of my face. Not after all this.*

But how to warn *Merrimack*?

"Captain! I'm picking up a Morse signal!" Marcander Vincent reported, surprised. "Dead ahead. Light beacon. Claims to be Alpha Four. Says we have a bomb on board."

Already figured that out. Still surprised, Farragut moved forward to see the beacon. "We have *people* out there?"

"Alpha Four says *Gladiator* tried to detonate the bomb."

"Using what kind of switch?"

"Can't ask, Captain. Ben can't get a tight beam out of this gorgon nest, and we can't send a light signal forward at this speed."

Farragut was about to order his senior engineer to the command deck, when she appeared on her own. Ariel Kittering had never looked quite real—porcelain skin, China-black hair, baby-doll eyes. She appeared now like a mannequin.

"Did you hear any of that, Kit? Romans have a remote detonator that didn't work."

"Yes, sir. I—" She held an X-ray clutched tight in her fist.

Farragut knew that Kit had commandeered equipment from the dental lab, and apparently managed to shoot some X-rays into the heart of the gorgon swarm, which filled the maintenance shed, to get a better look at what was inside.

"What've you got, Kit?"

She stammered a bit. "Rome took a page from our playbook. Redundancy is good. Redundancy is good. There's a backup destruct mechanism in there—with a timed chemical ignition." She flapped the X-ray uselessly. "And I never seen a gorgon inhibit a chemical reaction, so the clock is . . . running."

"How long do we have?"

Kit checked her chron. "Eleven seconds."

Startled techs grasped at their consoles.

Farragut, very softly, "Kit, are you serious?"

"Nine. Eight. Seven. Six. Five. Four. Three. Two. It has been an honor serving under you, Captain Farragut."

36

"Now Kit, why are you scaring the royal blue peaches out of me? We're still here."

"Honest to God, Captain, I don't know what happened."

"I can tell you what *didn't*," said Farragut.

Kit checked the X-ray. "All I can think is the gorgons *ate* the *fuse*."

Consoles lit up.

Barking resounded through the ship—Marines, turning the gorgon tide. The enemy was on the run.

Farragut asked if anyone had got at the bomb yet to disarm it.

"Not yet, Captain. We haven't got inside the maintenance shed yet."

Ben Mueller at the com reported, "Receiving a tight beam transmission."

"Please say that's not from *Gladiator*."

Gladiator's force field went up. Numa Pompeii congratulated his crew on their victory against an enemy against which all others had fallen. Told them to press the offensive until the ship was rid of every last gorgon.

The communications officer informed the general, "We are picking up English transmissions among unknown vessels and—*Merrimack*!"

"Sad for them they shall receive no answer," said Numa Pompeii, hands clasped behind his back.

"But they *did,* General," said the communications officer.

The Triumphalis' glacial calm rippled, returned. "It's a hoax."

"Quite a good one. That is John Farragut's voice." The communications officer offered General Pompeii an earphone.

Numa turned to his adjutant, deadly polite, "Kindly bring my fire control officer before me."

Portia Arrianus was a squarish woman, a long-time veteran, confident of her work, even before a scowling Numa Pompeii. "We sent the destruct signal," she told him simply. "Systems confirms it. *Apparently* the signal was not received."

"*Merrimack* is receiving signals *now,* isn't she?" Numa Pompeii pointed out.

"Yes, Triumphalis."

"So send the destruct signal again."

Arrianus never questioned orders, but the Triumphalis could not have thought this one through. "If *Merrimack* has overcome its gorgons, is it necessary to blow her up? Wasn't the point of this operation to destroy gorg—?"

"Send the destruct signal."

Arrianus opened her com link to fire control. Spoke stiffly. "Bellus. Are you receving?"

"I am here, *Domna.*"

"Send the destruct signal again."

"*Domna?*"

Like chewing and spitting, "Send the destruct signal again."

"At once, *Domna.* Rearming destruct trigger," Bellus acknowledged. Then, "Ready. At your command, *Domna.*"

Arrianus glanced to Pompeii. There was to be no reprieve. She ordered, "Let it be done."

Waited. Waited too long.

"Bellus? Have we detonation?"

The com link remained inert.

The communications officer reported *Merrimack* was still talking. The unknown vessels *Merrimack* was talking to were apparently U.S. Marine Swifts.

Portia Arrianus saw her career shredding under Pompeii's glare. She barked into the com link: "Fire Control. Why don't we have detonation? Bellus! Acknowledge!"

Got no response.

Pompeii seized the com link, but even Numa Pompeii's roar could not wake the dead—Bellus lying on the deck, a red crowbar in his skull.

Merrimack's Marine company hacked, slashed, and clawed their way through the mass of gorgons in the maintenance shed. The killing went faster once small weapons' controls returned. And soon they were wading in the goo that was all that remained of a gorgon upon dying.

Techs disconnected the Roman explosive device from Engine Number Six and hustled it out an air lock.

With the Roman bomb safely outside the battleship's force field, the techs asked the captain where he wanted it.

Farragut was not really concerned with it once it left his ship. Space was vast. The universe could end before someone tripped over it.

"Kit! Just what the blue peaches was the ultra tasty gorgon bait Numa planted in my maintenance shed?"

"It wasn't blue peaches, Captain. It was a res sounder. We pulled the harmonic out of the chamber, but no one's told me if it's that exact harmonic that jacked the gorgons' interest or if any old res pulse would do it for them."

"Get that data to Jose Maria."

"Already done, Captain."

Glenn Hamilton reported in surprise that *Gladiator* was the only battleship in the region. The rest of the Legion must have kept running. Only *Gladiator* had turned back to repel the gorgon menace.

Merrimack hailed *Gladiator,* but the Roman ship was unwilling or unable to respond.

"Numa, talk to me or I am opening fire."

Glenn Hamilton questioned quietly, "We're attacking *Gladiator*?"

"They've got our people."

"I know," she said thickly. "And something else, John." Glenn moved in close so only he could hear. Made him lean down an ear. "They've got *all* our food."

"Are we in a day's range of anywhere?" he mumbled, glancing round at his techs.

"No, sir."

"Then to hell with him." Didn't wait for Numa to respond or not. "Give Numa back his bomb."

Merrimack slung the bomb at *Gladiator* and detonated it with a beam shot when it got close. The thermonuclear explosion hadn't much punch coming from outside the battleship's force field, but in this case it was the thought that counted.

Cowboy heeled his Swift round at the blast. "*Merrimack*'s opened fire on *Gladiator!* EeeeeeHa!"

"Cowboy, no! Alpha Seven, join up! That's an order!"

Carly might as well be shouting orders to a gorgon.

Didn't know if Cowboy knew *Gladiator* was operational. Alpha Seven ran straight into a beam cannon pulse and broke apart.

The com tech on *Merrimack* yanked his headset off at the piercing scream on the Marine channel. Knew that scream, long and anguished. Kerry Blue. Everyone knew Kerry Blue.

Farragut looked to the com tech. "You okay, Ben?"

The com tech replied laconically, replacing his headset. "Marine Swift down, sir."

"How did that happen?" said Farragut, shocked. How could he have Marine Swifts out there? Apparently there were great gaping holes in his chain of command. "Get those Marines on board! Then beat the tar out of *Gladiator*!"

Hamster advised, "*Gladiator* has run out a Red Cross."

With a string of words Farragut did not normally use, he lunged at the console and shouted into the com, "What's next, Numa? Grab a baby for a shield? Strike the false colors, and fight like a man!"

"Captain Farragut." The voice was of Numa, himself, on the com. "Run out a Red Cross of your own and come with me, please."

John Farragut sent back, "Numa, what's Latin for 'bullshit'?"

"No need to translate. I understand Anglo Saxon well enough."

"I want to make sure I'm communicating. Strike the Red Cross!"

"I can't. I am ... choking here, Captain Farragut."

"Captain!" Marcander Vincent cried at his tactical station. "Roman Legion entering fire zone!"

Ship after ship blinked back in, all sides.

Farragut roared into the com, *"You baited me with a Red Cross?"*

"This flag is not bait, and if it were up to me, I would do as you suggest and step out alone in the alley. But it is not up to me."

Not up to him? Who could force General Numa Pompeii to run out a Red Cross against his will?

Numa said again, pained: "If you please, Captain Farragut. Run out a Red Cross of your own."

Doing so would shield *Merrimack* from Roman fire—if it were an honest Red Cross. If Rome had not abandoned all sense of human law.

"*I* can't!" Farragut sent back. "I am *not* on a mission of mercy."

"Apparently, you are. This way, please."

Gladiator moved out.

Merrimack fell in behind, but acquired a firing solution on *Gladiator*'s stern. "Numa, send food back here or I am shooting your damned flag!"

When the Romans actually dispatched a skiff, Farragut nearly shot it for a Trojan horse. But the skiff brought only food.

Two days' worth.

"Not enough!"

Numa signaled back: "It is enough."

If Farragut had not seen the hecatomb at the Far Cat, he would not even have considered cooperating further in any way. But he had seen, and half his crew was aboard *Gladiator,* so he told Lieutenant Hamilton, "Run out the Red Cross."

Then ordered the helm to follow *Gladiator* on its mission of mercy. Did not know where they were headed. Was afraid of what he would find when they got there. Finally, he thought to ask his navigator, "Where *are* we?"

In the Abyss.

*   *   *

In transit into the Abyss, Captain Farragut collected the names of the missing. He already knew that his new XO Sebastian Gray was not aboard, but no one could say what had become of him.

Alpha Flight had returned to *Merrimack* without Flight Leader Hazard Sewell. No one aboard was sure what had become of Hazard Sewell either. Lieutenant Colonel Steele was reported dead, even though Flight Sergeant Kerry Blue swore—swore a lot—that Steele was still alive. He had to be.

Patrick Hamilton was on the list. Surprised him. Glenn had not let on. Looking back, yes, she had the bearing of someone carrying a heavy burden inside, alone. He had seen her in the ship's chapel. Glenn Hamilton never went to chapel. He asked Mo Shah to look in on her for him.

If she needed an ear, John Farragut's was the wrong one.

The journey lasted less than two days. During that time, the ship's cryptotech, Qord Johnson, tried to re-create some of the ship's information. Immediately upon surrendering to *Gladiator*, *Merrimack* had run an information destruct protocol that had vaporized the contents of Captain Farragut's and Commander Gray's safes and all the red files in the data banks.

Qord Johnson was the only man on board who could reconstruct the codes. He hummed while he worked, happy to be alive.

The captain looked over his shoulder. Qord looked up, met the captain's eyes, gave a shaky grin. "They used to shoot cryptotechs on capture, didn't they?"

Once upon a time there'd been someone on board a Navy ship who was assigned to shoot the CT if the ship fell into enemy hands.

"I heard they used to do that," said Qord.

Farragut nodded. "They still do." And to Qord's open mouth and wide wide eyes, he said, "Carry on." To Tactical: "Got a plot yet on where we're going, Mr. Vincent?"

"Not sure, sir. Possible target dead ahead."

"*Possible* target? Can I get some more information than that, Mr. Vincent?"

"Could be just a nebula. Can't get a fix on it to measure it. It's a bit nebulous, so to say. Vector galactic normal." And, like dropping one shoe: "Could be a nebula."

"Could be a refractor," Farragut supplied the other shoe.

It was a common stealth tactic, to refract electromagnetic emissions around oneself. If the scattered light up ahead was not a nebula, then someone was hiding there.

Farragut got on the com, "Hey, Numa, have you ever known a Hive sphere to refract?"

The return message came from one of the general's adjutants: "That is not a Hive sphere."

The Romans knew what it was. Farragut had to wait and see, since Rome was not telling. Not over the com.

Gladiator led *Merrimack* into the refracting field. The Legion did not follow.

The two battleships came out the other side of the scattered signals to a clear zone.

Farragut recognized the approach, but the sight that coalesced on the sensor display still came as a shock.

"Captain!" Marcander Vincent turned from his console to show the amplified image.

A fortress, built like a mountain towering above its own reflection, hanging in the dark of space. The computer-enhanced image lit it up gold. Its griffin acroteri, normally spouting blue-white fire, stood quiescent.

Glenn Hamilton came forward from her station, breathing an invocation. "That looks like —"

It looked like what it was. "That's Fortress Aeyrie," said John Farragut. Caesar's mobile palace.

Captain Farragut had just been summoned to an audience with the Emperor of Rome.

37

"What would Caesar be doing out here?"

The image on the display was, without a doubt, Fortress Aeyrie, Caesar's mobile residence. But Captain Farragut could not quite believe that Caesar could be in it so far from Palatine.

But then the Empire did have a crisis out here of extraordinary magnitude, so perhaps Farragut should expect the extraordinary of Caesar.

"There's no Praetorian Guard!" Lieutenant Hamilton cried a warning.

Caesar never went anywhere without his Praetorian Guard. This had to be a fraud.

This fortress had no guard ships at all—unless one counted the half Legion that had just escorted *Merrimack* here. Only a force field shell protected this place.

The real Fortress Aeyrie had a legendary force field. If Fortress Aeyrie should ever fall into a black hole, it could remain intact and self-sustaining for a thousand years. It did not really need guards. Still, it always had them. Fortress Aeyrie was never without squadrons of guards and flocks of hangers-on, lackeys, sycophants, and petitioners. You never saw Fortress Aeyrie hanging alone in space.

"But that *is* Fortress Aeyrie. And those *are* Caesar's eagles," Marcander Vincent pointed out the distinctive eagle standards on the display image.

"So where is the Praetorian Guard?" said Glenn Hamilton.

"Glenn, you were right the first time," said Farragut in hollow realization.

There is no Praetorian Guard.

He was just beginning to wonder if anyone were left inside the fortress, when slowly, there appeared a break in the impenetrable field's shell and a beacon to ride in on.

"I'm not docking my *Merrimack* with that," said Farragut and got on the com. "Numa, you give me back one of my LRSs for me to pilot in myself, or I don't go."

It disturbed him that General Numa Pompeii complied.

Farragut snapped sighting brackets on either side of his eyes. Not that he would carry a gun into Fortress Aeyrie. But so that his command crew would be able to see whatever he saw. He left his com link open so the command crew would hear him also, and he could hear them.

He left the command deck. "Hamster, your boat."

Alone in his LRS, on slow approach to the wayward mountain, Farragut was struck by the sheer size of Fortress Aeyrie. Built like an iceberg, the lower mile of it housed all the machinery that served the hundred-meter-tall residence built of rich rose granite inlaid with black marble polished to a glossy brilliance. The fortress summit, normally ablaze with white-and-gold firestones, stood dormant in milky translucence.

Golden hangar doors parted for Farragut's LRS. "Not the servants' entrance," he overheard someone back on *Merrimack* say.

He rode the beam in, set the LRS down, locked down. Golden doors closed him in. The air pressure gauge turned green.

A Roman soldier, arrayed in bronze cuirass and scarlet cape came to the LRS to show Captain Farragut the way through the fortress, up to the immense double sequoia doors of Caesar's audience hall.

It surprised Farragut a little that he was not taken first somewhere to make him presentable. *Merrimack*'s captors had stripped out all of the captain's personal effects, so he was still wearing the dress uniform he had worn to General

Pompeii's table, but torn now and stained with blood, sweat, and gorgon gore. He smelled pretty bad and needed a shave.

He muttered into the com link on the back of his hand, "Hamster, get ready to run. If you don't see Caesar when these doors open, get the hell out of here."

Towering twin gods flanked the giant doors—Diana and Apollo, golden-skinned and armed with bows and arrows, she in a scant shimmersilk tunic, he in less. On a twelve-foot god, the fig leaf presented at eye level, and John Farragut was glad of the foliage.

The twin gods moved to open the massive doors. Farragut locked his eyes forward. First thing he saw had better be Caesar.

Apollo and Diana stepped to either side, admitting him to the Presence.

Farragut recognized the man on the dais, though it was a shock to see him so haggard. The emperor had let himself age authoritatively, with white temples and distinguished lines in his skin, but it was unusual for a man of his wealth and resources to go to jowls like that. Julius Caesar Magnus.

John Farragut had been before kings and presidents many times before. The Presence did not intimidate. It did impress.

The hall was huge. Alabaster columns soared to the distant ceiling, under which the architrave moved in a procession of larger-than-life tribute bearers from all the worlds of the Empire.

Above Caesar's massive throne a pediment niche housed the generously figured goddess Ceres with a pregnant she-wolf at the foot of her throne and a globe in her hand, which Farragut recognized as planet Earth. Three mother images there. An unsettling grouping.

At the right hand of Caesar stood Numa Pompeii. Already a big man, dressed here in ceremonial armor, Numa looked huge.

On Caesar's left stood a lean, very tall man with an opaque gaze, who had to be a patterner, dressed in gray. He was not perfect enough to be an automaton. He had to be human, though cables ran from the back of his neck to an outlet in the shimmering wall like an ancient electrical appliance. His attention seemed entirely inward.

A very long approach bridge of snowy marble stretched from the dais to the entranceway where Farragut stood. On either side of the bridge, the floor appeared to drop off to an eternal expanse of blue sky.

Farragut glanced down on soaring golden eagles and miles of white clouds. Heights never scared him and he was in no mood to admire the beauty. He marched straight up the bridge to the Presence on his raised dais.

The Presence handed Farragut back his sword. "Captain Farragut, thank you for coming."

"I was invited at gunpoint, so I'm not going to pretend to have manners," said Farragut, belting on his sword. Lion-head finials on Caesar's throne watched him with topaz eyes.

It felt good to be armed. Farragut demanded of the great Caesar: "What do you want?"

"A truce," said Caesar.

"We're done here." Farragut turned to go back the way he came.

"Captain Farragut, we took you for a reasonable man."

"Sir," Farragut turned his head to face the emperor, his body only half turned. "I am *reasonably* sure I am holding all the high cards at this table. I've seen your hand, and I am not sitting through a hot air storm while you're holding nothing. You've got yourself a two-front war, haven't you? You want us to put *our* war on hold while you deal with that godzilla you woke up. No. No truce. You want a cease-fire, you surrender. That's my first, last, best, only offer."

Dour silence held the great hall except for the rush of the wind under the bridge and eagle wings.

"Like I said, we're done here," said Farragut. Walked briskly back across the snowy marble bridge.

"Captain Farragut."

Farragut wasn't turning this time. Did not slow his pace.

"Captain Farragut."

The second "Captain Farragut" made him stop. That the emperor had spoken his name—twice—at his back—made his skin crawl right up it. He waited for what was to follow.

Let Caesar say it to his back. "We would like to discuss—"

Started walking again.

He had reached the sequoia doors when he heard a clatter on the marble—a sound exactly like a gilt eagle scepter would make toppling down the steps of a raised dais. Then a rustle of rich fabric—like an old man standing. An abject voice: *"In manus tuas."*

Farragut felt his eyes grow huge in his head.

Into your hands.

Words of ritual. Taken from the last words of Christ. Shorthand for a last surrender: *Into your hands, I commend my spirit.*

Farragut turned round to face his nation's mortal foe.

With slow steps, Caesar descended the dais where his black-and-gold eagles lay on the floor. He opened his empty hands. "Rome surrenders."

Farragut spoke in a near whisper, "What have you got yourselves into?"

"We are a desperate nation."

"I figured that part out, sir. When the hell were you going to tell us?"

"We have no other possible choice. We are being eaten alive. Yours—and now *Gladiator*—are the only vessels to survive an encounter with Them once engaged."

"The only of how many encounters?"

Caesar did not answer. Closed his eyes.

And did he see behind those creased lids the holocaust at the Far Cat?

That vision came to Farragut in the dark.

General Numa Pompeii could not keep quiet any longer. Words exploded out of him without leave: "It is not any great talent or secret they have, Caesar! They use swords and manual controls! His ship has low-tech backup systems. We can do that! We have their great secret. You don't need to—"

Caesar held up his hand to signal silence. *"Stratege,"* he said. "Do we have their numbers?"

Numa did not answer that.

"What hands will lift those swords?" Caesar asked, fatally.

"We have colonies," said Numa. "We have numbers."

"We have willing amateurs. We have Hive fodder. They still have their best."

"What are *we*?" said Numa with a thumping fist to his armored chest.

Caesar beckoned his general in for a murmur. Said

something that first slackened, then hardened Numa's face. The general turned away from the old man's whispered words, chastised.

Numa did not speak again.

Caesar spoke aloud to the patterner stationed on the other side of his throne. "Augustus. Can you show Captain Farragut the map?"

The patterner did not acknowledge the request. Did not move.

But the blue sky and the eagles vanished, and John Farragut was standing on a marble bridge in outer space. A three-dimensional star map surrounded Caesar's throne.

It took Farragut a moment to get his bearings. He was in Fortress Aeyrie in the Abyss. From there he found Palatine, Earth, and Terra Rica, in the Orion Starbridge. What he could not identify were the glowing orange dots cluttering the Abyss like stars. There were not that many stars in the Abyss. And each orange plot was labeled with a vector. The orange plots were moving FTL. Not a stellar motion.

"Hive swarms," Caesar identified the orange plots for him. "Gorgons."

Farragut felt his pulse leap. "Caesar, these spheres are going to home in on this res scan!"

"This is not a live resonant scan," Caesar assured him. "This is a recording made weeks ago, from elsewhere. The gorgons do not know where we are now. A tragedy that planets cannot run and hide so."

Farragut took a moment to assess all the vectors on the map. He saw it now—where many plots converged on a single point. "Well, hell. All roads *still* lead to Rome."

"Do not suppose they have not found you, Terran. There are hundreds of them headed for Fort Eisenhower. As for these," Caesar gestured at the monsters in the dark. "Once they have devoured Palatine, your world is next in line. And they do move in straight lines. Your terms, Captain?"

"Take it up with President Marisa Johnson and Congress," Farragut said curtly.

"I have no intention of sitting through a hot-air storm," Caesar echoed, mild and reasonable how he said it. "You are a decisive man, Captain Farragut, and I will have this done quickly. You have the authority to dictate terms on this side of the Abyss."

"I do?" Farragut blinked, spoke into his com, "Glenn, check the regs." And back to Caesar, "You want to bypass Marisa? Why?"

"President Johnson and your Congress are politicians. You are a soldier. I will surrender to your U.S. Navy. You have power to accept for the Navy and for the United States by extension of that."

Farragut was speaking into the back of his hand again: "Hamster, can I do that?"

There had been a feverish scramble for the Naval Codex back on *Merrimack*'s command deck. They had the reference now and Glenn Hamilton's answer stumbled over the link, "Yes. Yes, sir. Actually, you can. The captain of a commissioned capital ship in the Deep End in wartime, has authority to speak for the United States."

"We're not in the Deep End. We're in the Abyss."

"We checked that, too, sir. Deep End is defined in the regs as the space this side of Fort Theodore Roosevelt."

"Oh, for Jesus," he spoke to the stars. He crossed the bridge back to Caesar, stood over the dropped scepter. "Sir, you're gonna wish you asked President Johnson. Here are my terms. Palatine maintains its internal government, but not a skatload else. All Roman military units will swear allegiance to the U.S. Constitution."

"Obedience," Caesar amended. "Not allegiance. Allegiance is already sworn and cannot be foresworn."

"Fine."

"And not to the U.S. Constitution. To you."

"I'm sworn to the Constitution and I obey the Joint Chiefs, so that still leads y'all back to the Constitution."

"If that is where that road leads," said Caesar, conceding. Then, "What will be our Trade status?"

"You're an Earth colony. Always were."

Farragut saw Caesar and General Pompeii bristle. That term was a bitter one. It threw the mighty Empire back to its colonial beginning. But Caesar did not argue. He asked harshly, "Are you done?"

He was not. "Where were all your killer bots?" Farragut demanded. "I want those under direct U.S. control."

Palatine had robot fleets, hundreds of thousands of unmanned vessels equipped with a wide variation of weaponry.

"We have only those rolling out of the factories now," said Caesar.

"No." Mama Farragut's boy was not so naive. "You've got thousands. Near on millions. Where are they?"

Caesar had just been called a liar. He stared John Farragut in the eyes. His voice was soft, brittle. "Robot ships are equipped with a kill switch. The kill switch does not just deactivate the robot; it causes the robot to self-destruct." He took a deep breath for strength, finished. "The kill switch on a robot ship has a resonant trigger."

"The Hive found your harmonic," Farragut guessed.

Resonance was instantaneous. Caesar nodded. "Destroyed them all. Everywhere. At once."

Farragut reconsidered his position. Good that Rome was without its vast automaton force, but the loss took the killer bots out of his own arsenal now.

"How many Legions are you consigning to my authority?"

A long conspiratorial pause expanded there. Secrets. Rome was accustomed to keeping secrets for millennia. Numa became like gray granite, the patterner Augustus completely inhuman and inanimate. Caesar looked grave.

Caesar answered: "Twelve."

Farragut heard gasps from his com link, his command crew back on *Merrimack*.

Farragut asked, "Where's the rest of them?"

Numa Pompeii came forward with an angry stride, offering something in his fist. Farragut put out an open palm to receive it.

Teeth.

"Sixty-four Legions?" Farragut cried. "How the hell did you lose sixty-four Legions?"

Caesar had to sit down. Explained, "Many were on board carriers when the Hive touched the killer bots' harmonic. Many others perished in the evacuation of Telecore. Thanks to *you,* our first ship evacuated through the Catapult was also our last. You destroyed the Near Cat, and marooned our people in the Deep."

"Load of crap, Caesar. Tote that guilt back where it came from. Your pride killed those people." He handed Caesar his people's teeth. "Who nuked Telecore?"

"The Praetorian Guard. It was necessary. Their last act."

"Would it have killed you to ask for help before it came to that?"

"It does kill me to do so," said Caesar. "Help us."

"Imperial 'us'?"

"All of us. All humanity."

Farragut was about to demand the return of all POWs, including the rest of his crew. A sudden thought quilled his mouth. He asked in dread, "Where are the crew of the *Monitor*?"

A bitter turn of Caesar's lips, too sad to be called a smile. Answered, "They should be safe. *Monitor*'s crew are on a slow prison boat through the Abyss back to Near Space. We were in no hurry to return them, so your people did not go to the Catapult."

Farragut lifted eyes on a prayer. Felt the nearness of death brushing by.

Heard himself saying, "What was *Monitor* doing out here?" A very odd question to be asking his enemy. It just came out. *Monitor*'s mission was so secret his own country's Intelligence agency would not tell him, so he had to ask Caesar.

"Your *Monitor*," said Caesar, "was hunting for Fortress Aeyrie."

"Fortress Aeyrie is not a military target," Farragut blurted.

Made Caesar smile. "They did tell me you were a Boy Scout, Captain Farragut. That is why we offer surrender to you and not to your government." And, profoundly defeated, Caesar asked, "Do you accept our surrender?"

"Just about," said Farragut. "Now rack 'em."

"Sir?"

Farragut picked up a fallen eagle standard from the marble deck. "Make an arch."

That provoked a twitch even from the immobile Augustus. General Numa Pompeii looked about to detonate.

Farragut held out the eagle. "I insist."

Caesar recoiled, aghast. "You *wouldn't*."

"I do."

Caesar Magnus pulled in his quiet dignity, offended. "When one puts his hand under your foot, it is impolite of you to step."

"Caesar, I can almost believe you're sincere. But there

can be no doubt in anyone's mind all the way down to the buck grunt on either side. Down to the kid in the street with a pipe bomb. I have to see it. So does Rome. So does Earth. So no one can say, 'what are they up to?' Rack 'em. Right here, *and* down the Via Triumphalis at the Hill."

He wanted another subjugation on Rome's home planet, Palatine, in their capital city, down their processional way, in front of the Imperial Residence.

Unspoken—heavily implied—was that John Farragut had to see if Caesar could make his soldiers and his world obey. The doubt was too rude to speak, but there it was. If Caesar could not make his remaining soldiers walk under an ancient subjugation, he could not make them honor the surrender.

Caesar closed his eyes. "So be it."

38

PEOPLE ALL OVER THE WORLDS woke each other in middle of their nights to watch, astounded. Images from Fortress Aeyrie. Of Caesar Magnus and the Legion Pompeii walking under the crosswise spear held up by Caesar's own eagles. And images from Palatine, where Roman Legions passed under racked spears on the Capitoline, the same march they had forced upon the armies of many a subject world. Watched in horror, like watching a king put on his own slave shackles.

Not until they saw it did the magnitude of the coming danger hit home.

Invoked their gods.

Merrimack reactivated her res chamber, and immediately received an incoming transmission from Earth, from the Joint Chiefs. Admiral Mishindi, near shouting: "John! Are you seeing this?"

"I'm right *here,* sir."

"This has got to be a hoax! Where's the Praetorian Guard? The Praetorian Guard would never stand for this!"

"No, sir. They would not," said Farragut.

Let the silence speak. The feared and hallowed Praetorian Guard was simply *not.*

"What is Caesar really up to?" Mishindi asked, as if there were a secret to be shared.

"He's surrendering, sir."

"Lord God Almighty."

"Admiral Mishindi, I thought you left the church a long time ago."

"I'm thinking of re-upping. Good *God*!"

There followed an urgent call from Calli Carmel. Not sure where she was calling from. She immediately cried, "John! I only see the *triarii* going under those arches! Where are the crack troops? This has got to be a sham!"

"Speak English, Cal. What's a *triarii*?"

"The reserves. I'm only seeing reserves walk in subjugation."

"That's about all they got, Cal. Look here. This is no reserve unit."

He moved his vid sender to show her Numa Pompeii striding under the racked eagles at Fortress Aeyrie.

Dumbstruck silence sat on the com. Calli Carmel saw her nemesis in utter, humiliating submission. She knew now it was real. Numa Pompeii would never walk under a rack for show. Ever.

Calli might have gloated, but Farragut heard in her silence only real horror.

Merrimack received other signals, newscasts showing people watching the transmissions from Palatine. Showed all of the people, even citizens of Earth, frozen in that universal pose of horror, eyes huge and watery, staring above hands pressed together over mouths.

Did not take long for Congress to throw a primordial fit. John Farragut had passed on the chance to end slavery, take over trading alliances, get a piece of Roman taxes, annex some of those lucrative colonies, investigate Roman bio-research violations. The list was long.

Captain Farragut was summoned before a Congressional committee via the res com.

Farragut shut them down quickly. "This is an expensive call and too late. You don't like the deal, take it up with the pinhead who put this clause in the Navy regs that gave me authority to negotiate it. My enemy, as he says, put his hand under my foot. I stepped on it. But I did not harvest the rest of his body parts, because I need him up and breathing to help me fight. Y'all are really not grasping what happened here."

"What's to say this isn't a trap?" The Senator from Oaxaca there.

"Caesar is going to walk in subjugation for a *trap*? What else do you want said? No, you're right. It's a trap. The moment Caesar put his head under that arch, we inherited his war. Here it is in terms y'all might understand: Fort Eisenhower must be evacuated within six years. That means the Shotgun shuts down in six years. Palatine will be dead in one hundred thirty years. Later that same year, Earth will be eaten alive, which may be just fine for you if you don't have grandchildren. But since we're all feeling human beings here, I suggest you stop dividing up the spoils of the conquered and start fighting the Hive now. Right now. Unless one of you can figure out how to start yesterday. Having said that, y'all will have to excuse me. I have to get back to work."

Gladiator returned the captured equipment, personnel, provisions, dog tags, and teeth to *Merrimack*.

Captain Farragut composed messages to the widows, the moms, the dads, the children. Starting with his XO Sebastian Gray. Hoped like hell the last thing he'd said to Gray was *not* to call him Cal by mistake. Scarcely had time to know him. Knew he'd left behind his wife Narinda with two young boys, Terrance and Justin. A blind springer spaniel named something or other. Knew there was a pocket keettrig nesting in the attic, which Gray had to evict next time he got home. Home was Providence, one of the American colonies. Farragut guessed he ought to arrange for someone to take care of the keettrig for Narinda. Or do it himself if orders took him near Providence. No one had seen Gray buy it, so Farragut couldn't even tell Narinda that her husband had died valiantly.

Oh, yes, he could.

TR Steele had been returned to *Merrimack* in a bag. A med bag. In ragged shape but still alive.

Also returned in a med bag was some idiot, bandaged over his eyes, who kept calling over and over, "Marco! Marco!"

The MPs were beginning to wonder if this weren't a Roman plant, because of the bandaged face, because no one knew his voice, and no one knew who in blazes was Marco.

Till Lieutenant Glenn Hamilton broke out in an astonished sobbing laugh: "Polo!"

No matter what, Patrick Hamilton could make her laugh.

Glenn Hamilton could not follow her husband to the ship's hospital, where he was carried—babbling joyfully "Marco! Marco!" the whole way—until the end of her watch. When she came to his bedside, the bandages over Patrick's face were fresh.

He had taken a dying gorgon in the face. A pair of new eyes were being cultivated for him in a tank next to his cot.

When Glenn slipped her hand into his, Patrick asked, "Have I lost you to Captain Farragut?"

"What do you mean?" Could not believe how lame those words sounded coming out of her mouth.

He gestured blindly at the organ tank next to his cot: "I have eyes!"

Glenn could not speak. Could not think.

"I'm not wrong, am I," Patrick said more than asked.

"You're not right either," said Glenn.

There was a motion of eyebrows lifting under the bandages. *"Meaning?"*

"John Farragut was nice to have around when you were making me feel like—I can't even tell you what it feels like."

"Hull, do you remember what I said when I asked you to marry me?"

Her eyes stung. She remembered exactly. Tried to keep the unsteadiness out of her voice. She recited back to him: "Hull, you could do better, but I wish you wouldn't."

He nodded on his pillow. "And I was lying here thinking, and I thought I was going to offer you your freedom when you got here. But screw that. I'm fighting for you, Glenn Hull." He sat up, put up his dukes. "Let's do it. Point me at your Superman." He jabbed at the air.

"He's not here, Patrick."

"Oh, thank God." He fell back on the cot.

May as well have challenged a bull gurzn. "Glenn, I swear I'll never look at another woman."

"You don't need eyes to see Hot Trixi Allnight."

"Hot Tr—! Who wants *her*?"

"You did!"

Patrick's arm flopped at his side. "I just had to see what all your thugs thought was so special."

Her thugs—what Dr. Patrick Hamilton called the navvies and Marines behind their backs. They were hers because she was an officer. Patrick was just a scientist in
uniform.

"And?" Glenn waited for the verdict on Trixi's specialty.

"I still don't see it. She's no Glenn Hull."

Glenn left Patrick's hospital compartment. Gasped.

John Farragut was waiting in the corridor, leaning back
against the bulk, his arms crossed, as if he'd been there for
some time. Regarded her strangely. Puzzled maybe.

"John?"

He straightened up. Glanced away, brow creased.
Looked back to her. Decided to speak. "Okay, Glenn, here
it is. He's an ass."

She dropped her gaze to the deck grates a thoughtful
moment. At last looked up, looked into his eyes. Nodded
yes.

"But he's *my* ass."

General Pompeii returned the captain's bourbon in person
in preparation to take his leave. The gorgons would be
heading to this location after the recent flurry of res transmissions. It was time for *Gladiator, Merrimack,* and Fortress
Aeyrie to be elsewhere.

Farragut brooded over what Caesar had said earlier regarding *Monitor*—that she had been hunting Fortress
Aeyrie.

No wonder Napoleon Bright had refused to tell him
Monitor's mission.

"What the hell were they going to do when they found
Fortress Aeyrie!" Farragut wondered aloud. "Kidnap the
emperor?"

A bit of Numa's old superciliousness returned. The general gave a disingenuous shrug of his massive shoulders.
"That would be your side's information."

And Farragut understood now Rome's reluctance to ask
the United States for help.

Farragut muttered softly, "God blessed tunnel-visioned
schemers!"

"You blame the snake for having tunnel vision?" said
Numa.

"No, I blame the snake for being a snake. Numa, what was that harmonic you stuck on board my boat to lure the gorgons?"

Numa Pompeii shook his head. He didn't know. "I got it from our snakes."

Farragut checked over the ship's manifest. "I think that's everything."

"Not quite," said Numa. "I have also been ordered to turn over to you a valuable piece of equipment, the emperor's patterner."

The phrasing gave Farragut pause. "His patterner. That's a person, right?"

Numa gave an enigmatic glower. "If you say so."

"Permission to come aboard."

"As if I could stop you."

Farragut collected kisses on either cheek from Jose Maria de Cordillera at the starboard dock along with a bottle of well-aged cognac. "I liberated this from *Gladiator*."

"Good man."

"It is good to see you restored to your ship, young Captain. A bit of a deus ex machina, is it not? As in ancient Greek plays, when all looked lost, a god stepped in and made everything right again."

"Oh, no. Everything is not right, and what's behind this is the furthest thing from God," said Farragut.

"I know that well. And I have a request, young Captain. If your mission is now to destroy this thing, this Hive, I would travel with you. I think I could make myself of use in your lab."

It had the sound of a vendetta. Farragut guessed, "The Romans told you what became of *Sulla*."

Jose Maria's black eyes glistened. He smiled tragically. "They do not know."

"I don't believe it! Where's Numa? I'll beat the answer out of him!"

"They truly do not know. They never found her. *Sulla* was the first victim of the monsters, they think. But she vanished without a trace, so they assume, but they do not know. Hope turns like a thorn in the heart, because this hope is a lie, and I know it."

Farragut made a fist, with nothing to punch. "If only

Rome had asked sooner. This would have been a different ball game. Hell, Jose Maria, you're a learned man, can't you build a time machine? Do this over?"

Rhetorical, but Jose Maria answered anyway. "In theory. If one views our ten-dimensional universe in three dimensions—which is the only way we can view it—picture, then, the universe as an expanding balloon and we all dots on the surface of it. We grow farther and farther apart from each other as the universe expands, but no single one of us can be called the center."

"Where does that take us?"

"Because time and space are a single entity, in theory, to go back in time, you could circle the entire surface of our universe-balloon to bring you back where you began."

"It's a damn big universe."

Jose Maria nodded. "It is. And remember that the balloon is expanding. You would need to travel faster than light to outrun the expansion of our balloon, which, in real time, we cannot do."

"We do it all the time," said Farragut.

"We exceed light speed, that part is true. But not in real time. Mass increases as an object approaches light speed— from a sublight observer's perspective. From *our* perspective, I still measure seventy-eight kilos no matter what speed I travel. At light speed, energy is infinite, time is infinite, neither of which condition is possible in real space-time. We never actually travel at light speed. We go faster or slower, but no one has ever observed us at light speed."

"Which is another way of saying it doesn't happen."

"In effect, yes. Just as when we exceed light speed, we become irrelevant to the universe and, in effect, leave it. We become unobservable from our sublight observer's vantage. Picture us now inside the balloon. We have left the surface of the real space-time universe and are in a sense tunneling from point to point without hitting all the points in between."

"So with a deep enough tunnel we *can* go back in time," said Farragut.

"Alas, that is where reality sets back in. You would need to exceed threshold velocity to dig that kind of tunnel. As you say, it is a damn big universe. And even were you able to break threshold and reach the required velocity, the journey would last several billion years from *your* perspective. You would not arrive intact. From the observers' perspective, of course, none of it would happen at all."

"Jose Maria, you weren't with me at the Myriad. I think we *had* that kind of tunnel. Twelve billion years deep. Maybe, maybe, if I could just have stopped the Arran from going down that hole—"

"We would still be here," a strange voice finished his thought.

Jose Maria de Cordillera and Captain Farragut turned to the speaker.

The emperor's patterner. Not eager to board, he had not asked permission. He waited at the dock between Marine guards.

Augustus was now unplugged from his machines, looking only slightly more human, rigidly tall, but pained, as if their talk struck him as exceedingly tedious and embarrassing.

"Problem?" Farragut prompted, beckoning his Roman "equipment" in past the Marines.

"To speculate on things that are not real and can never be real," said Augustus, "is a waste of energy and time."

Jose Maria smiled benignly. Jose Maria had apparently made acquaintance with the patterner while in Roman company. The patterner's brusque manner disturbed him not at all. "Good heavens, Augustus. Regretting what might have been is an ancient sport. Possibly a Roman invention, though I think Adam and Eve must certainly have played it. Can you say there is nothing you have ever done that you never wish you could have done differently, if only you had the chance?"

"There is," said Augustus, dark and distant. He turned to Farragut. "I'd have pulled the trigger on you at the Myriad."

Confirmed what Farragut already knew. He and Augustus had met before.

Augustus continued, to Jose Maria. "Yes, Dr. Cordillera. I would like to have that one back."

Farragut was afraid he must have looked hurt and personally insulted, because Jose Maria asked for him, "And what would *that* have changed, patterner?"

"In the end, nothing," said Augustus, expressionless. "Which is why this exercise is pointless. Entropy is a basic condition of the universe. The enemy are entropy incarnate. They are inevitable. Done is done. All roads lead here."

"And there you have it, young Captain," said Jose Maria blithely. "There is no going back."

Augustus said, "You won."

"I won," Farragut echoed, no triumph in it.

"The only way out of this is straight ahead," said Jose Maria.

"I can do that."

Not the victory he wanted. But it was the one he had. Straight ahead at full speed was really the only way Farragut knew how to go.

Lieutenant Colonel TR Steele's new fingertips were as broad as the ones he had frozen off in *Gladiator*'s hangar deck, but they were pink, girly soft, with thin, pliant nails.

The new tip of his nose did not bother him so much because he could not see it, and he'd never been much for looking in mirrors.

But those new fingers were right in front of him as he emptied the contents of the late Flight Leader Hazard Sewell's locker into a small box.

These could not be his hands. Didn't look like they'd ever fought beside this guy.

Hazard Sewell had died honorably, horribly, fighting gorgons. Better hands should be handling his stuff.

And Cowboy Carver's locker should not be allowed next to Hazard Sewell's locker.

"Cowboy got himself killed and Alpha's a better squad for it."

Should not have said that. But it was out there now, and Colonel TR Steele could not reel it back in. Left him in the awkward position of having to eat words to a subordinate. The subordinate he had a hopeless crush on.

He talked thick, through a lump in his throat. "Sorry. I know you loved him."

"I didn't," said Kerry Blue. "I never did."

And that sent Steele into giddy orbit, though it was obviously a lie. "Blue, you're crying over his empty locker."

" 'Cause I'm an idiot!" Kerry shouted through tears. "I loved someone I made up. Guy I loved looked like Cowboy, lived like Cowboy. Made me feel like I could fly. But the guy

I loved loved me back just as hard. And I am so damn mad at Cowboy for not being that guy! Cowboy made me feel *this* big when he wasn't making me feel sky high." Marked off the tip of her little finger with her painted thumbnail. "Lying, cheating, married son of a— Hell, if he didn't die here, he'd a died of boredom. Sorry, sir. You didn't need to hear that."

"Not hurting me."

Kerry Blue dragged a khaki sleeve across her angry face. "I am *not* crying. Over *nothing*. Scum. He was scum. I'm not saying I'm glad he's dead. He was one of us. I'm just saying—didn't everybody always say?—that boy's gonna die young. Some things happen 'cause they just gotta happen. There's nothing of mine in here." She slammed Cowboy's locker. "Can I go, sir?"

Steele didn't want her to go. Wanted her to stay here, with her silly pink nails, that slight curl in her soft brown hair. He just liked having her near him. Tough, trashy, girl-soft and Marine-hard Kerry Blue. Talked with her whole body. A great little body. He looked at her mouth and remembered her kiss when he thought he was about to die in that black, cold hangar. Had given him something to live for. He wanted to live.

She was asking to go. And that was probably a desperately good idea.

Steele gave a gruff rasp, "Dismissed, Marine."

Watched her walk out, loose, rangy, rolling.

Keep your eyes above the neck, soldier, an inward rep. *Put it out of your head. Not going to happen. Not in this or any lifetime.*

Some things were never meant to be.